Christy

CATHERINE MARSHALL

AVON BOOKS ◆ NEW YORK

AVON BOOKS, INC.
1350 Avenue of the Americas
New York, New York 10019

Adaptations from the tales "Old Dry Frye," pages 100-105, and "Tall Cornstalk,"
pages 186-196 from *Grandfather Tales* by Richard Chase, published by Houghton
Mifflin Company, used by permission of the publisher. Excerpts from the songs
"Blackjack Davy" and "The Ballad of Montcalm and Wolfe" from *Songs and
Ballads of the Eastern Seaboard* by Frank W. Warner, published by Southern Press,
used by permission of Frank M. Warner. Excerpts from the songs "Earl Brand" and
"The Green Bed" from *English Folk Songs of the Southern Appalachians* by Cecil
Sharp, published by Oxford University Press, used by permission of the publisher.
Excerpts from the song "Under the Yum Yum Tree," used by permission of Harry
Von Tilzer Music Publishing Company. Excerpts from the song "Oh! You Beautiful
Doll," copyright 1911 by Remick Music Corporation, used by permission. Excerpts
from the song "Shady Grove," copyright 1952 by Jean Ritchie & George Pickow,
used by permission of Geordie Music Publishing, Inc. Excerpts from the hymns
"Soon We'll Cross the Border Line"; "Gathering Buds"; "I'm Ready to Go"; "I'll
Sail Away" and "We'll Meet Our Mother" from the collection, *Gospel Joy*, published
by James D. Vaughan Music Publishers, used by permission of Tennessee Music and
Printing Company. Excerpts from the hymn "Be Not Dismayed" from *The
Methodist Hymnal* (1966) used by permission of the Methodist Publishing House.

I wish to thank many friends in East Tennessee whose courtesy in answering questions and whose hospitality and cooperation have been unfailing, especially Miss Mary Ruble and Mrs. Opal Myers; to express my gratitude to Elizabeth Sherrill for valuable editorial suggestions; to Alma Deane MacConomy for help with research; to Dr. William R. Felts of Washington, D.C., for information on medical details; to Eleanor Armstrong for suggestions regarding schoolteaching; to Emma B. Mulrean, my patient and capable secretary; to my family who have borne with *Christy* for nine years, and especially to my husband, Leonard LeSourd, whose support and help have been unflagging.

To Leonora

The Characters

CHRISTY RUDD HUDDLESTON, a nineteen-year-old girl.
   Her father, mother, and brother George.

ALICE HENDERSON, a Quaker mission worker from
   Ardmore, Pennsylvania.

DAVID GRANTLAND, the young minister.

IDA GRANTLAND, the spinster sister of David.

DR. NEIL MACNEILL, the physician of the Cove.

JEB SPENCER, a ballad-singing mountain man.
FAIRLIGHT SPENCER, his wife.
   Their children: John, Zady, Clara, Lulu, and Little
   Guy.

BOB ALLEN, keeper of the mill by Blackberry Creek.
MARY ALLEN, his superstitious wife.
   Their children: Rob, Festus, Creed, Della May,
   Nuda, Little Burl.

AULT ALLEN, Bob's older brother, head of the clan.

JOHN HOLCOMBE, another mountain man.
ELIZABETH HOLCOMBE, his wife.
   Their children: Arrowood, Lizette, John, Sam
   Houston, baby girl.

UNCLE BOGG McHONE, the county squire, humorist of Cutter Gap, teller of tall tales.

TOM McHONE, one of Uncle Bogg's grown sons.

OPAL McHONE, Tom's wife.
Their children: Isaak, Toot, Vincent.

NATHAN O'TEALE, rough highlander.

SWANNIE O'TEALE, his wife.
Their children: Wilmer, half-witted, epileptic son; Smith; Orter Ball; Mountie; George; Thomas; Mary.

OZIAS HOLT, the host of the "working."

REBECCA HOLT, his wife.
Their children: Wraight, Zacharias, Becky, Will, Dicle, Larmie, Jake, Vella.

BIRD'S-EYE TAYLOR, feuder and blockader.

LUNDY TAYLOR, his seventeen-year-old swarthy son.

KYLE COBURN, mountain man.

LETY COBURN, his wife.
Their daughter Bessie, thirteen.

DUGGIN MORRISON, glum mountaineer, and his wife.
Mrs. Morrison's daughter, Ruby Mae, red-haired girl who lives at the mission house.

THE BECK FAMILY, whose cabin is close to the Big Mud Hole.
Their children: Will, Clarabelle, Rorex, Wanda, Ann, Joshua Bean.

AUNT POLLY TEAGUE, ninety-two, oldest woman in the Cove.

LENORE TEAGUE, Aunt Polly's daughter-in-law.

GRANNY BARCLAY, midwife of Cutter Gap.

LIZ ANN ROBERTSON, married at fourteen.

MR. HAZEN SMITH, wealthy Knoxville businessman.

MRS. TOLIVER AND MRS. BROWNING, ladies at the University Club, Knoxville.

GENTRY LONG, United States marshal.

JAVIS MACDONALD, the train conductor.

MRS. TATUM, the boarding-house lady.

BEN PENTLAND, the mailman.

Down in the valley,
   valley so low
Hang your head over,
   hear the wind blow.
Hear the wind blow, love,
   hear the wind blow;
Hang your head over,
   hear the wind blow.

Christy

Prologue

ON THAT NOVEMBER AFTERNOON when I first saw Cutter Gap, the crumbling chimney of Alice Henderson's cabin stood stark against the sky, blackened by the flames that had consumed the house. The encroaching field grass and chickweed and pennyroyal had all but obliterated even the outline of the foundations.

But the old mission house was still there, high on its rise of ground with the mountain towering behind it. Once painted a proud white, the building was gray and sagging, the front porch gone, the screening of the kitchen porch rusted and flapping. There were no other buildings left: the church-schoolhouse had long since been moved to another location; David Grantland's bunkhouse had been demolished.

Nonetheless, I was standing on the spot which I had always longed to see—the site of the adventures recounted so vividly by my parents during all my growing-up years. In a sense, I had lived through those experiences too. Mother stood beside me looking at the house, silent, lost in the thoughts that were pulling her back forty-six years to the last time she had seen the Cove.

The years had brought changes. Two World Wars had reached deep into the mountains to snatch away Cutter Gap men. Those who had returned had brought back some of the world outside: brought-on clothes; canned food; soda pop; autos; battery radios over which blared hillbilly music and soap operas; and latterly, television and consolidated schools. Appalachia's economic problem had never been solved, so, in a variety of ways, the Federal Government had stepped in. On July 11, 1936, President Franklin Roosevelt, by Presidential proclamation, had incorporated the towering scenery of Cutter Gap into the Cherokee National Forest; then on September 2, 1940, the President had personally dedicated 460,000 acres of the North Carolina–Tennessee Appalachians into the Great Smoky Mountains National Park. Most of the families who lived in either the Forest or the Park had—eagerly or reluctantly—sold their small land holdings to the United States Government. By the time I saw the Cove, cabin after cabin stood vacant. Forest rangers and tourists roamed the Gap. The black bear and the white-tailed deer, the raccoon and the bobcat, the red fox and the wild boar were returning to the forests.

But mother was surprised to find that certain things had not changed. Though some of the main routes through the mountains were now well-engineered highways, the way into Cutter Gap was noted on the map as "a poor motor road" and then "a trail," actually almost inaccessible. It was Hugette Lee and his wife Mary who met us in Lyleton and in their old sedan, led us toward the Cove. They and their three boys lived in what had been the old mission house, and they had invited us to be their guests for the night.

The twelve miles from Lyleton to El Pano were a good enough turnpike, but soon after we had left El Pano behind, mother was exclaiming, "Why, imagine this road still not being paved! It's as bad as ever!" She was right. The low-slung modern car in which we were following the Lees was sinking almost to its floorboard in the ruts.

We came to an especially deep and wide rut. "Catherine! The Mud Hole! It's the Old Mud Hole! It's still *here*. It just isn't possible!" Mother sounded as if she mistrusted her own eyes. "Well then, maybe there aren't as many changes as I had thought."

With each mile, the scenery was more rugged, the road more impossible. We drove for an hour at a crawling pace, sometimes with the car's right wheels on the rim of the narrow track.

I was relieved when Mr. Lee led us into the yard of a cabin and motioned for us to stop. He came striding back to us. "Think you'd best leave your car here overnight." His grin was sheepish. "*Yours* would never make it from here on. You'll see what I mean." He held out his hand for my keys. "Let me transfer your bags to my jitney."

Then in the Lees' car we jerked and slithered along the washboard of a trail, sometimes bumping so outrageously that our heads struck the car roof. There were washouts and gulleys, and twice we had to ford a tumbling mountain stream. Mary and mother kept up a lively conversation, for mother was full of questions: "What finally happened to the McHones?" ... "When did Miss Alice's cabin burn?" ... "Did they ever know the cause of the fire?" ... "How many of my pupils from Cutter Gap did Hazen Smith finally send out of the Cove to school?" ... "What year was it that the mission closed?" ... "Where did they move the church-schoolhouse?"

In between mother's questions, Mary volunteered, "I teach fourth grade in the new consolidated school. It's so hard getting in and out of the Cove that I have to get up at four each morning to make it."

Finally, the car bumped over frozen ruts into the edge of the mission yard and stopped. John and Bob and Toe, all towheads, came to greet us (rather grave children, I thought). And mother stood and looked—and looked—trying to see everything at once.

And then she was inside the house, exploring from room to room, I close beside her, as interested in her reactions as in the house itself. Yes, the dining room was still much the same—tan tongue-and-groove walls—only now there was a mail-order stove (providing the only heat in the house) with a pipe through the ceiling. There was still no running water. The old telephone was in its place on the wall in the back hall. "Remember my telling you about our first conversation over it?" mother asked. "Hilarious! That Little Burl..." Yes, I remembered.

She stopped in the parlor doorway, her face aglow. "The Lyon and Healy! Imagine!" The huge concert grand piano still stood there, only now a winter's supply of pumpkins and squash and gourds was piled on top and the ivory was missing from most of the keys.

In the front bedroom upstairs to which Mr. Lee carried our overnight cases, there were fluffy clean curtains at the windows. "How did they know," Mother puzzled, "that this was once my room?"

Since there was some daylight left, she was eager for more reconnoitering. "Catherine, would you walk down the road with me? I want to find out if—well, a lot of things."

As we walked along, I saw that the path by the Branch in front of the mission house was still the same, just as my parents had described it. I sensed excitement rising in mother as the years fell away. She was the nineteen-year-old Christy again, exploring this same road wearing the

17

shoes she had bought at the Bon Marché in Asheville. "Ice-pick toes," David Grantland had teasingly called them. Yes, the O'Teale's tobacco barn to the left of the road was there. Just around the bend would be their cabin.

Presently we were standing at the edge of the yard she knew so well. No one was around. It was like walking into an empty stage setting or into one's own dream. The clumps of old English boxwood in the yard were surrounded by rusty tin cans, rotting tires, pieces of twisted metal, old newspapers. As we walked up the creaking wooden stairs at one end of the porch, I almost caught my heel in a rotting board. The front door was standing ajar, sagging, half off its hinges.

We stood in the doorway giving our eyes time to adjust to the darkness inside. Deserted. Everyone gone. Where had they gone? It was as if the cabin had been evacuated hurriedly, because the floor was awash with a veritable snowstorm of slips of paper. I stooped, picked up one of the slips, looked at it and handed it to mother. It was the receipt of a week's pay from a cotton mill in South Carolina. Curious now, I retrieved other slips and small envelopes. They were all from the same mill, weekly pay envelopes: 250-14-9097 Smith O'Teale ... 279-12-8078 Orter O'Teale ... 246-10-3078 Mountie O'Teale ... *Mountie.* I remembered. The little girl who had giggled, "See my buttons! See my pretty buttons!" The new teacher Christy, my mother, had given her love, had given her life.

Mother shook her head in disbelief at the dates on the envelopes. "They're so many years back," she said. "The children must have left the mountains to work in a mill. And they sent most of their pay home." I watched her turning the slips of paper over and over in her hands as if trying to make them speak to her.

"How could I ever forget," she recalled, "that first evening when I saw the half-witted epileptic boy here? Right there, in that pen in the corner. I lost my supper that first night after I had seen this cabin. It was Miss Alice whose cool hands and warm heart comforted me."

"Miss Alice ..." Mother's expressive blue eyes held a faraway look. "Strange that after all these years, the memory of her is still warm and alive. I suppose because a personality like hers can never die."

18

I thought of Alice Henderson as she had been described to me—tall, blonde, patrician, with that certain sparkle. Her basic beliefs had been as settled and sure as the nineteen-year-old Christy's had been unsure. Yet always there had been Miss Alice's eagerly grasping mind, ready for new adventures of heart or spirit. The Quaker lady had been at the center of all the drama that had been acted out on this gigantic stage, with these mountains—blue and mauve and purple, brooding and unchanging—as the backdrop.

It was at that moment, standing there in the O'Teale cabin thinking of Alice Henderson, that I got my first clear glimpse of the book I had always wanted to write about the mountains, my mountains. For these were the hills of home; I had been born among mountains like these. All my life the wind-swept heights had fascinated me—and challenged me—and steadied me.

As if reading my thoughts, mother said shyly, "The story aches to be told, Catherine. The secrets of the human spirit that Alice Henderson knew, the wisdom that she shared is needed by so many today. And the mountain people, my friends—Fairlight and Opal, Jeb Spencer and Aunt Polly Teague, Ruby Mae and Little Burl, my school-children—I want people to know them as they really were. But Catherine, I'm not the one to put it on paper. You know, sometimes the dreams of the parents must be fulfilled in the children."

And suddenly, I understood how the story should be written—through mother's eyes, as I had seen it all along. Only—from the beginning, my imagination had taken hold of the true incidents and had begun shaping them so that now, after so many years, I myself scarcely knew where truth stopped and fiction began. Therefore, though so much of the story really happened, I would set it down in the form of fiction.

I knew how it would be. Through many a winter's evening before an open fire, through leisurely meals at the round table in the big kitchen at Evergreen Farm, mother would reminisce while I would take notes. I would question her and probe for details: "Now, mother, pretend that Aunt Polly Teague is standing before us now. Tell me what she looked like. David, I need to understand him better. Tell me, why did David act that way?"

As much as she could tell me, I would write. Oh, not the whole story. One book could never hold it all. I would

19

tell the story of the first year only. Eleven months in a young woman's life. But what months ... what a lifetime she had lived in them! How could I get even the events of eleven months onto paper? Already I could see that though I tried to capture truth, truth could never be wholly contained in words. All of us know it: At the same moment the mouth is speaking one thing, the heart is saying another; or events are carrying us in one direction when all the while the real life of the spirit is marching in another.

And so past all those true experiences that mother would relate to me, I would walk softly into the realm of what might have been. The rest would be my imagined story ...

I could not wait to begin. Turning to mother, I asked, "When you first saw this cabin, how long had you been in Cutter Gap?"

"Oh, something like three weeks."

"That big snowstorm you arrived in—was the snow gone by the time you walked down here?"

"No, it wasn't. As a matter of fact, I can never think of my first visit in this cabin without seeing bloodstains on the snow. It was a rabbit. Killed by a hawk."

"But mother, from what you've told me, a dead rabbit is the least of it. You'd been so protected at home! The girl Christy was so young and inexperienced. I've never understood how your parents let you come."

She laughed softly. "A lot of it they never knew. Teaching in a mission school sounded so safe. And Dr. Ferrand was the epitome of propriety. So solid, so reliable. Father was certain he could entrust me to Dr. Ferrand. Father, dear father ..."

One

ONLY MY FATHER saw me to the Asheville station that Sunday morning in 1912. Mother had gotten up early to fix us a hot breakfast. It was one of those moments that would be as sharp and real in my mind years later as it was that January morning: that particular look of love and longing in mother's eyes; the smell of the starch in her crisp white apron; the hissing of the pine resin in the big iron stove; the lake of melted butter in the steaming mound of hominy grits on my plate.

Then father had called from the front room, "Time to start!" And my brother George, hearing the announcement, had stumbled out of bed and down the stairs to the landing, where he had stood leaning sleepily on the banister, tousled hair in his eyes, to tell me good-bye.

"Have to go," father repeated from the doorway. "The engine's running. I had a time cranking the car in this cold."

In the gray light before dawn, the railroad station had a wraithlike look. I saw with a strange leap of heart that the train was going to be pulled by Old Buncombe, a favorite engine on the East Tennessee, Virginia and Georgia Railroad. The engine was painted green with gold trim and lettering and there were big brass ornaments on its headlight. The billows of smoke pouring out of Old Buncombe's smokestack looked blacker than usual against the background of new-fallen snow.

As father carried my bag on down the platform, he was trying to be jovial, teasing me as if I were nine and not nineteen. He still considered me too young to go off alone, especially on a wild adventure like teaching school in a mountain cove of which no member of our family nor anyone in Asheville, as far as he could discover, had ever seen or even heard.

21

I had battled long and hard with him and mother for the chance to do this. All of us Huddlestons have a stubborn streak, no doubt inherited from our Scottish ancestors. How well I knew that it was this quality in father which had earned him so many business successes. And yet this time it was I, not he, who had gotten my way.

But walking along the platform that January morning, the elation I felt at this victory over my parents struggled with other feelings. Father was too heavy now with iron-gray hair. Tenderness for him welled up in me. Impulsively I stuck my right hand into the pocket of his overcoat.

"My hand's cold," I said as if a childish gesture needed an explanation—but he knew. His left hand covered mine in the coat pocket.

"Girlie," he asked suddenly (that was what he always called me at sentimental moments), "do you really think you have enough money to get you through till payday?"

"Plenty, father. Yes—thanks."

"Well, twenty-five dollars a month isn't going to go far." His voice was gruff with emotion.

"Probably for the first time in my life there won't be any temptation to spend money. It will be good for me." I was trying to sound gay. "Right in line with your ideas, father. For all I know there may not be a single store in Cutter Gap."

Then we were mounting the steps to the train. I was to ride the coach, for it was only a six-hour trip. There was that certain smell of coal dust that railroad cars had; grime in every crevice and in the corners of the window ledges; brass spittoons; a potbellied stove in the rear; sacks of grain and produce piled toward the back; a lot of people. I marveled that so many would get up to catch a train at six-thirty in the morning.

Father found me an empty space and I sank down on the scratchy red plush seat, with my suitcase on the floor beside me. The whistle blew shrilly. Father reached out for me; the tweed of his big coat was rough against my face. "Don't forget now—soon as you get there, write us. Want to know you've arrived safely." Trying to be playful, he pinched my cheek—and was gone.

I saw father standing on the platform talking to the old conductor. Once he pointed in my direction, so I knew from long experience what he was saying. "My daughter's in there. Take care of my girl." It was embarrassing: after all, I was too old to want father to do this, too young to be flattered.

Then the conductor was waving his arms and shouting, "All a-boarrd!" He mounted the steps and noisily clicked the guardrail shut. Old Buncombe sputtered and wheezed with the familiar chuff . . . chuff . . . chuff. Our car jerked forward, the one behind slamming into us. The door at the front of the coach swung crazily, but finally the jerking and the bumping smoothed out and the telephone poles were sliding past.

Across the aisle a country woman with a red-faced squalling baby jiggled the child up and down, back and forth, on her ample lap. Then when the crying did not stop, she opened up her shirtwaist to let the infant nurse. The man in front of me was lighting up a pipe filled with home-grown tobacco that stung my throat and made my eyes water.

After Budford, North Carolina, the conductor began moving down the aisle gathering tickets. The old man's blue serge suit was shiny at the elbows and knees. I fervently hoped that he would not mortify me before the other passengers by telling me that he would take good care of me, so I turned pointedly toward the window and pretended to look at the white fields and rising hills. What I actually saw reflected in the window glass was a figure so slender that it should have belonged to a much younger girl. I threw back my shoulders and took a deep breath, trying to fill out my new fawn-colored coatsuit a little better. The blue eyes beneath the piled-up dark hair stared back at me quizzically.

"Ticket, please. You're Christy Huddleston, aren't you?"

I nodded, hoping that if I managed the proper dignified expression he would notice that I was simply another adult passenger. After all, this was not my first train trip, not by any means. The past year and a half at Flora College in Red Springs I had taken the train both ways, a trip of three hours, and once I had taken the sleeper to my aunt's home in Charleston on the coast. But this worldly experience seemed lost on the conductor.

"I'm Javis MacDonald," he went on. "I've known your father a long time." He punched my ticket, handed it back. "So you're bound for El Pano, young lady. Your

23

father said you were going to teach school. In El Pano?"

"No—in a new school—seven miles or so behind El Pano, back in Cutter Gap."

Mr. MacDonald rubbed his chin whiskers reflectively. His eyes took on a wary look. He seemed about to speak, thought better of it, but then finally said impulsively, "That Cutter Gap is right rough country. Only last week followin' a turkey shootin' match, one man got tired of shootin' turkeys and shot another man in the back. Well— probably I oughten to be tellin' you, but you'll be hearin' the likes soon enough."

Then Conductor MacDonald went on gathering tickets, and I was grateful to be left to my own thoughts. I was glad that I had not been forced to explain the reason for my trip. The old man would have thought me sentimental and girlishly impressionable to be basing my whole future on a talk given by a total stranger the past summer.

The scene floated before my eyes ... the church conference grounds at Montreat where the Huddlestons had spent a part of every summer as far back as I could remember. The big semicircular auditorium with its rustic benches. The men and women in their light-colored summer clothes. The ladies in voile or lawn or crepe de Chine, some with long strands of carved ivory beads or jade brooches they had bought at the missionary's shop on the hill. So many palm fans moving, and the cardboard ones that had been stuck in the hymnbook racks with their advertisements of religious publishing houses or HUMP hairpins or pulpit furniture. In the stillness before the service had begun, there had been the pleasant hum of whispering voices and, in between, the gurgle of the mountain stream that sang its way through laurel thickets and ferns to the left of the auditorium.

But then an elderly man with a neatly clipped white goatee and a resonant voice—such a big voice for a small man!—had risen and begun to speak. He explained that he was a medical doctor, and that he was therefore not going to preach a sermon, just tell his own story. He told the facts simply, almost starkly—how during the War Between the States he had ridden horseback through the Cumberland Mountains on his way to join the Confederate Army. Of course there were few inns in that area, so people in the mountain cabins had taken him in. He had been impressed with how poor the people were, yet how intelligent. Years later when he was a successful doctor in Arkansas, he had become desperately ill with scarlet fever. At a crisis point in his illness, he had made a solemn vow that if he lived, he would go back to the Appalachians and help those people. He had sacrificed his fine medical practice to start mission work in Arkansas and Kentucky, and finally in the Great Smokies.

There he had met someone with as much passion as he to help the mountain people: Miss Alice Henderson, a Quaker of Ardmore, Pennsylvania, a new breed of woman, he said, who had braved hardship and danger to serve where she saw need.

My heart beneath my frilled lace jabot beat faster. I would like to know that woman. On her own, he went on to say, Miss Henderson had established three schools: Big Lick Spring, Cataleechie, and the Cutter·Gap school, the latter only a couple of years before.

Dr. Ferrand explained that a year ago Miss Alice Henderson had placed her three schools under the auspices of his American Inland Mission, believing that this unifying of forces would strengthen the work.

"How I wish this vital woman could be here today," the little doctor said, "to stand beside me on this platform so that all of you could catch her enthusiasm. It isn't for want of traveling that she isn't here," he chuckled, "she rides horseback all over the Great Smokies from school to school—rather because she would not leave her work."

Then Dr. Ferrand was painting vivid word pictures of individual "highlanders" as he called them: of Minna Bess who had gotten married at fifteen; of Branner Bill, who had been the feuding terror of Cataleechie Cove until he had heard the gospel story for the first time and had suddenly become a changed man; of Uncle Jason whose sole income was gathering and selling galax leaves at twenty cents a thousand; of Rob Allen who wanted book learning so much that he came to school barefooted through six-foot snows.

I could still hear Dr. Ferrand's voice describing how such deserving people had inspired him to found the American Inland Mission with only one other worker and three hundred and sixty dollars. And then he talked about needing something more important than money: recruits. "Beyond the great mountains, outstretched hands and beseeching voices cry, 'Come over and help us.' These highlanders are your countrymen, your neighbors. Will you

25

hear and help, or will you leave them to their distress and ignorance?" And with that, the little doctor had sat down.

It was a new experience for me to hear someone speak who had a Cause, a mission in which he believed with every tissue and cell of his heart and mind. There in the auditorium I glanced down at my little pointed buttoned white kid shoes with the black patent tops, the ones that I had bought the week before, and I thought about the contrast between my well-shod feet and those of the boy who had gone barefooted in freezing weather. Of course I had always heard about need in places like China and Africa, but I'd had no idea that such awful conditions existed within a day's train ride of Asheville, right in our mountains. Why had not father or mother told me about things like that? Perhaps they did not know either.

As we sang the closing hymn, "Just As I Am," a feeling of exhilaration grew so strong inside me that I could scarcely sing the words.

After the benediction, I made my way slowly down the long inclined aisle. Dr. Ferrand gripped my hand warmly, looked directly into my eyes.

My voice shook a little. "You asked for volunteers," I told him. "You are looking at one."

The little man's goatee had bobbed up and down. "And for what do you volunteer, my child?"

"For the highlanders—I could teach, anywhere you want to use me."

There was a long silence. The man's eyes were penetrating. "Are you sure, child?"

"Quite sure."

So it was done. Then I had gone back up the hill to the Alba Hotel to break the news to father and mother and begin the long task of persuading them. And I had never wavered since—through all their weeks of pleas and arguments. After all, up there in the mountains were boys and girls who ought to have the chance at least of learning to read. I was not the best educated girl in the world, but I could teach children to read. Of course I could.

The screeching of the train lurching to a stop and the conductor's gruff voice broke into my reverie. "We're about four miles from Green Springs, folks. There's a snowdrift on the roadbed. It's flung two outsize rocks with it. I hope it won't delay us long, folks. Train crew comin' now. It oughten to take long to clear the tracks." He pulled a big gold stemwinder out of his pocket, scowled at it, then shut it with a snap.

The potbellied stove at the rear of the coach had been smoking. The acrid smell of the baby's diapers which the woman had been stuffing into a paper poke, had begun to permeate the coach. A breath of fresh air was what I needed. So I got to my feet, buttoned my coat, picked up my little moleskin muff, and walked down the aisle.

Outside I saw that the road crew had already arrived and were putting iron levers under the rocks. The airy snowflakes, as big as goose feathers, were slackening off now. Still I could see nothing but mountains and more mountains, peak piled on peak, shrouded in whiteness. There was a feeling of vastness that went on and on into the infinity of that somber January sky, with wisps of clouds trailing off the tallest peaks, streaking here and there like banners into the gray sky. And below the summits, time—space—substance were swallowed up in tons of billowing white. It was a lonely, formless landscape. I wondered suddenly if I was going to be homesick even before I got to El Pano.

Now the snow was beginning to fall again with the wind rising. It was a strange wind, a whimpering sobbing wind, with pain in it. Yet gales were nothing new to me. Asheville had always been known as a windy city. I had always had to hold onto my hat as I rounded the corner onto Grant Street, sometimes using physical force to push, push against the invisible, yet mighty wall of wind.

But there was something different about this wind. It was not a single note, but many notes playing up and down the scale, harmonizing at one moment, discordant the next, retreating, advancing. It caught at my nerves. And through it all, that sobbing sound. I wanted to shut it out, to flee.

Smoke was now puffing rhythmically out of Old Buncombe's smokestack. The two boulders had been sent crashing down the mountainside. The men on the road crew were standing to one side, preparing to tramp on down the tracks to look for other slides. With the other passengers, I climbed back into the coach. But we were hours late.

As I took my seat, I suddenly realized that I was hungry. It had been a long time since breakfast. I lifted the lid of the little wicker basket mother had given me. There was chicken breast and some thin buttered slices of salt-rising bread. There was an apple, several slices of spice cake, some Nabisco wafers, a small bottle of fresh buttermilk. As I munched on the chicken and bread, memories of home which had already crowded dangerously close came sweeping over me.

I thought of the big old kitchen—the stove with the warming oven above; the sink under the double windows; the tall spice cabinet with its pierced metal doors, some sort of queer design in the piercing. All of my childhood I had delighted in opening the doors of that spice cabinet just to whiff the wonderful fragrances. Why had smells— pleasant and unpleasant—always been so important to me? Sometimes the bad ones were torture, as on this trip. But then the nice ones more than made up for it—like the honeysuckle on the fence behind our house in late May; or in August the grapes hanging in heavy clusters on the trellised arbor-archway leading from the back porch to the coal house; or the fingers of fragrance that reached to every crevice of the house while mother's bread was baking.

I reached in the basket for the buttermilk and a cup. To my surprise, instead of the tin cup that I expected, I brought out a pink lustre one, part of my favorite childhood tea set. I found myself turning the cup over and over in my hands. It was beautiful. Thin, translucent pink. How had it ever survived my awkward child's hands? Perhaps because I had always loved it. Then I realized I was seeing the pink through a blur. So mother had wanted the cup to say something to me. Well, perhaps I was being foolish to leave my wonderful home. Or was I? I only knew that it was an experiment I had to make.

For in spite of the homesickness, I felt elation about being turned loose to make my own way in the world. I had sense enough to keep it strictly to myself, but secretly I was certain that I was about to take the world by storm. Not even father's disapproval of teaching school in a place like Cutter Gap had lessened my enthusiasm. After all, those other men and women down through the centuries who had accomplished things must have had to shrug off other people's opinions too. For no reason at all, those lines from Lord Tennyson that I had memorized for a high school literature course came into my mind . . .

Yet all experience is an arch wherethro'
Gleams that untravell'd world, whose margin fades

For ever and for ever when I move.
How dull it is to pause, to make an end,
To rust unburnish'd, not to shine in use!
As tho' to breathe were life. Life piled on life. . . .

It was queer that I had had to find my clue as to how to get on with that life from a stranger on the Montreat platform rather than from my family or the preacher in our church back home. The family would be there about now in the Huddleston family pew, probably standing to sing the Doxology. No doubt my brother George had asked to sit with some friends of his on the back pew. Father had not yet discovered how often the boys slipped out before the sermon, then reappeared at the end of the service.

The First Presbyterian Church of Asheville with its blue carpets down the aisles, the memorial plaques around the walls, the great pulpit chairs with their tall carved backs. . . . Sunday after Sunday I had sat there as long ago as I could remember. Our preachers had all been good men, nice men, kind men. Of course, I had seldom been able to keep my mind on what they were saying. But I had always thought the trouble lay with me, not with them or their preaching.

It was only at Montreat last summer that I discovered that my attention was not so hard to get after all. Now I guessed that somewhere—out there—there was something exciting about religion which had not come through to me in my church back home. And I sensed that I could have sat in the Huddleston family pew every Sunday until I was an old lady, and it would not have been any different. That was why I had had to leave, explore for myself— "Life piled on life."

And now with each turn of Old Buncombe's wheels, I was being carried closer and closer to that new life. Already we must be crossing from North Carolina into Tennessee.

Suddenly the railroad tracks were running between the walls of a narrow valley. Here in this more protected area was a dazzling winter landscape. Everything was covered with ice, yet this was not the usual ice storm. Apparently fog floating off the higher peaks had covered everything with a gossamer coating of ice so fragile that every lineament of every object stood out from every other

29

object sharply defined, highlighted, underscored—frozen lace.

Then the sun was sinking and every prismatic color was reflecting back from this ice-encased world. The valley had become like Ali Baba's Treasure Cave that I had read about as a child. I found my eyes and throat aching with the beauty that blazed outside the train windows. Jewels seemed to glitter from every bush, every withered blade of grass, every twig: sapphires and turquoise, emeralds and amethysts, rubies, crystals, diamonds.

The glow was dying as the sun dipped behind the hills rimming the valley. The winter twilight was coming now, coming fast. Darkness fell so swiftly in these mountains. The train began to slow down and the engineer blew a long warning whistle. Conductor MacDonald announced that we were coming into El Pano and began lighting all the railroad lanterns on the floor in front of the coach. Old Buncombe's wheels ground to a stop. Hastily I thrust my arms into my coat, buttoned it, picked up my muff and my suitcase, and started down the aisle.

"Let me help you with that, Miss Huddleston." Mr. MacDonald took my suitcase and swung it to the ground beside the train. "Easy, the steps may be slippery. The last one is high. Watch it. You're a mighty pert girl, Miss Huddleston," he said earnestly. "But land sakes—watch yourself out there at Cutter Gap."

"Thank you, Mr. MacDonald," I tried to sound confident. Already my eyes were searching the dusk. There wasn't much to see—just a tiny station building and four or five houses. I had hoped that someone would be coming toward me questioningly. How often during the last weeks I had pictured the scene. . . . "Miss Huddleston?" they would ask. "Are you the new teacher for the mission? We've all been anticipating your arrival. How nice, how very nice—" And they would look me over. And their eyes would say, "We were expecting a young girl, but you're a grown woman." And I would be very warm and very gracious and would extend my hand in greeting, as mother and father did, and they would be more impressed than ever. But no one was approaching at all.

Several men came out of the station and began to unload crates and boxes from the baggage car onto a cart. From time to time they would pause in their work to stare at me. Deliberately I turned my back, my eyes searching the dusk once more. No—no one. Conductor MacDonald was giving me a quizzical look. I didn't want him to see how disappointed I was that there was no welcoming committee for me. Perhaps they were just late in arriving. My eyes searched the road beyond the houses. But as far as I could see, the snow-covered landscape was deserted.

Then there was the "All a-boarrd." The men wheeled the cart of crates and boxes away from the baggage car. Old Buncombe began getting up a head of steam. I watched as the train got underway, at first slowly, then with gathering speed. It was smaller now, the smoke from the engine little white puffs against the somber, snow-filled sky.

I felt fear rising in me—a greater fear than I had ever known. That train was my last link with home. Everything dear and familiar was disappearing there, right there over that horizon with that train. What was I doing standing beside these train tracks in a strange village? I did not know a single human being in this desolate town. What would I do now?

In the still air Old Buncombe's whistle blew—far away. The sound echoed faintly in the valley between the mountains. The fear in my chest clutched at the sound, as if to capture that, if nothing else. Then even the sound was gone, and there was nothing, nothing but emptiness. I stood there wanting to move and yet not able to, staring at the spot on the horizon where the two tracks converged into one.

The men stopped the cart and I felt their eyes on me. They would think it queer my standing there alone. So I swallowed back the lump in my throat, took a firm grip on my suitcase, and blindly, scarcely knowing what I was doing, headed for the little station.

Two

BEHIND the grilled window the ticket agent wearing the green eyeshade did not look up as I approached. I spoke as softly as I could because the group of men lounging around the stove were watching me curiously. "Could you tell me—is there anywhere in El Pano where I could spend the night?"

He did not seem to hear me. "Sir—" I raised my voice. No question about everyone in the station hearing now. "Could you tell me . . ."

"Young woman, you'll have to speak up." The eyes under the green shade were defensive.

After I had almost shouted my question, he finally got it. "Well, let's see now. Maybe Miz Tatum's."

"Where is that?"

"Eh? Oh, close. Nigh. You just—guess it's easier to show you." He ducked out through a door beside the cage. "If it wasn't gettin' dark you could see Miz Tatum's from here."

I followed the man into the stinging cold. He pointed across the tracks. "Can't quite make it out, but it's that big house, second one down. You'll find it."

I nodded.

"Just tell Miz Tatum that Farse sent you. You'll get plenty to eat and a clean bed. Course Miz Tatum can talk the hind legs off a donkey," he chuckled, "but I reckon you can stand that."

I thanked the man, and he disappeared back inside the warm station.

It was not easy to carry my suitcase and hold up my skirts at the same time. Once I slipped, and the snow churned up over my shoe tops, sifting down into my stockings. I pulled the hem of my coatsuit free of the wet clinging mess and struggled on through a ditch and up the other side.

A Victorian frame house loomed out of the darkness. The peak of the roof, trimmed with wooden cutouts, was silhouetted against the dusky sky. The lamplight in several of the windows and smoke pouring from both chimneys were welcome sights.

I set my suitcase on the porch, shook my skirts again, and twirled the bell. The tall big-boned woman who opened the door almost filled the opening.

"Mrs. Tatum?"

"Yes."

"I'm Christy Huddleston from Asheville. The station man—I think he said his name was Farse—told me that you take in roomers and boarders. Could you put me up for the night?"

"Sure could. Don't have no rooms filled right now. C'mon in out of the cold. Bad night, ain't it?"

"Yes. It is." Even as the door shut behind us, I could feel this woman's lively interest, her mind bristling with questions about me. But she was trying hard not to be too forward.

"I'll show you to your room, child. Here, let me take the suitcase. I'm used to carryin' heavy things. You can bring the lamp though. Right on up. That's right. That room just ahead."

It was a plain room with a shiny brass bed. But everything was clean, as the station man had said. "Now, you make yourself to home, and I'll fix you a bit to eat. Tell you what, I'll build up the fire and you can eat by the stove." Mrs. Tatum was already halfway down the stairs. "Come on down when you're ready. . . ." Her voice trailed off and a door slammed in the back of the house.

There was no heat upstairs. Eager to get to that fire in the stove, I changed as quickly as I could, then I picked up the lamp and groped my way down the stairs.

The downstairs hall was dark, but a ribbon of light at the bottom of a door and voices beyond told me where the family was gathered. As I opened the door, I saw a group sitting around a small stove. The walls of the room were tongue-and-groove, painted nondescript tan. A Brussels carpet, scrim curtains, and some house plants in the windows gave the room a certain hominess.

Mrs. Tatum had put on a large calico apron and was clearing the table. "Come on in, child. This here's Mr.

Tatum. Miss Chr—Christy Huddleston. Uncommon name, ain't it? And this is Mandie Lou and Joshu-way . . . and my brother Thomas Grant. And Grandsir McBride. Now you set yourself right down and I'll have your supper in no time a-tall. The rest of us are finished. Know you must be starved." And the big woman picked up a stack of dishes and hurried off toward the kitchen.

The girl named Mandie Lou sat staring unabashedly at me. The man called Thomas Grant was the first to speak. "You come from Asheville-way? Not many women come through here on the train. Where you bound?"

Upset as I was over the recent turn of events, I wanted to be friendly. After all they were being kind to me. "I've come to teach school at the mission. You know—out at Cutter Gap."

Mrs. Tatum was back in the doorway. "Landsakes, child. You a-teachin'? Cutter Gap? Why child," she clucked her tongue and a look that I couldn't quite interpret came into her jet black eyes. "Well, here's your supper. You help yourself. Here's some spareribs and pickled beans. And there's some sourwood honey and some apple butter to put on the biscuit bread. I saved the sourwood honey for something special."

While I ate, the group around the stove slipped silently out of the room one by one. I had a feeling that they were going out to spread the news of my arrival to some of their neighbors.

Mrs. Tatum seemed to be busy in the kitchen, then suddenly she was back in the doorway, wiping her hands on her apron. "Are you gettin' enough to keep body and soul on speakin' terms?"

"Oh, yes—plenty, thanks. It's good too. Anyway my mother had packed me some food for the train trip and I ate it late."

"If I may ask," the voice was hesitant. "How did your mother take it, your comin' to teach in the Cove?"

This was not something I wanted to discuss. "Oh, it was all right with my parents. After all, I'm nineteen."

"Have they seen Cutter Gap?"

"No. No, they haven't." I wondered if all middle-aged people thought alike. Yet, seeing the earnestness in her black eyes, I couldn't be offended.

"Look, I'm not good at fancy talk." She slowly began to scrape the plates and pile them one on top of another. "But I just don't think you know what you're gettin'

34

yourself into. You come from a highfalutin' home"—I opened my mouth to speak, but the voice rushed on— "easy to tell that. Your clothes, pretty fancy do-dads— The way you talk. Oh, I see a lot of folks, and if I do say so myself who shouldn't, I'm a pretty good judge of folks."

"Mrs. Tatum, my home isn't that fancy. I'm not afraid of plain living."

"Mercy sakes alive, you don't know how plain. Me now, I wouldn't want to live back in that Cove. Have you ever had to wash your clothes by beatin' 'em on a battlin' block? Or did you ever have to sleep in a bed with the quilts held down by rocks to keep the wind from blowing the covers off?"

Thinking she was exaggerating, I simply smiled. Yet her fears—not so much what she had said so far, just her attitude about the Cove—had started little shivers up and down my spine.

"I don't want nothin' to happen to you. I'm not speakin' now of your gettin' shot at, though plenty has been shot at. Sometimes real bad things happen—oh, at weddings or play parties or jamborees when the liquor's bein' swigged a little too free. Oh, I know those mountain people all right. They're not naturally bad. And when a body minds his own business, most generally you needn't be afraid. But that's not it . . ."

She could talk the hind legs off a donkey, the station man had said. Was this just so much talk? More to be polite than anything else, I asked, "Well, what then? What is it you're afraid of for me?"

"It's your feelin's. Back in the Cove they don't take much stock in foreigners."

My astonishment must have showed. "I don't understand! I'm an American citizen, born right in these mountains."

"Now don't get riled. By foreigners they don't mean folks from across the waters. Foreigners is folks from out the Cove. And they're proud back there. When they feel that somebody is different from them, they don't like to be beholden, don't like to be monkeyed with. Can't blame them really. It's going to be well-nigh impossible for you to help them. The only person I ever saw that could stick it out is a lady named Miz Henderson. Other teachers has tried and given it up as a bad job."

Eager to change the subject from my probable failure

35

in which everybody but Dr. Ferrand seemed devoutly to believe, I pounced on the name of Miss Henderson. "Oh, would you tell me about her? I've heard only enough to make me curious."

Mrs. Tatum reacted to this opening much as if I had just handed her a birthday gift.

"Oh, she's a character right enough, if I do say so myself who shouldn't. Imagine a high-toned lady like her livin' up there in the mountains by herself! And her a Quaker lady at that. Uses 'thees' and 'thous' sometimes just like in the Good Book. But she don't dress like a Quaker, no little bonnet on her head, nothin' like that. Likes fine wearin'-clothes, dresses like quality folks.

"Howsomever, there's lots of talk about how she ever come to Cutter Gap in the first place. Don't seem like the missionary type, to my way of thinkin'. Some say her fiancy—how do you say that?—went off with another woman and that Miz Henderson come to the mountains runnin' away from her broken heart. Some say her lover got his neck broke in an acci-dent with runaway horses. Course nobody really knows, and me, I just saw wood and say nothin'."

I could scarcely visualize Mrs. Tatum "saying nothing" at any time, but since she was not really telling me what I wanted to know about Miss Henderson, I asked, "How far is Cutter Gap from here?"

"Seven mile, more or less."

"How can I get out there tomorrow?"

The tongue clucked again. "My, you are eager, aren't you? Rarin' to go, jousty." The woman sighed. "Ben Pentland carries the mail to the Cove, but he ain't been out since the snow fell."

"How could I talk to Mr. Pentland?"

"At the General Store most likely, come mornin'."

Then apparently Mrs. Tatum decided to make one last try. "Look, maybe you don't like somebody like me that you never saw afore tonight buttin' in, but my advice to you is to get a good sleep and when the train comes through next, you get yourself right back on it and go back to your own folks. There now, I've said it."

But, I wondered, how could I run away like that before I'd even seen the Cove? "Mrs. Tatum," I explained, "you see, I've given my word about teaching school. A promise is a promise. I'll be careful not to stomp on those proud feelings of the folks back in the Cove." Even as I spoke, the expression on Mrs. Tatum's face told me that she did not really understand. "Thanks a lot for the supper, Mrs. Tatum. And please don't worry about me." I smiled at her. "Is this the lamp you want me to take upstairs?"

As I turned to go up the stairs to my room, she was standing in the dim light of the lower hall staring after me, looking puzzled and distressed.

In the cold bedroom I set the lamp on the marbletop dresser, put my coat around my shoulders, and stood before one of the windows looking out at the village of El Pano. The moonlight was so bright that it had an artificial look, almost like a stage set I had seen at the Opera House back home. The houses were roofed with silver, the railroad tracks a pair of shining ribbons. The town seemed to be set in a saucer with snow-covered mountains on the two sides. I stood there wondering in what direction Cutter Gap lay.

Why hadn't someone from the school met me? Did they really need and want a teacher as much as Dr. Ferrand had said? Could Dr. Ferrand have gotten busy in Arkansas or at one of the other missions and even forgotten to tell them at the mission that I was coming? But I had had a letter from him. No, it couldn't be that.

I could feel the cold air seeping around the edges of the loose-hung window, and my fingers and toes were getting icy. I retreated into the room to the dresser and began taking the hairpins out of my hair, staring at my reflection. Eyes too big for the rest of my face, a little too serious, even a bit frightened, stared back at me. A face too thin, the hollows beneath the cheekbones shadowed by the lamplight. Too angular. For the millionth time, I wished I were beautiful like my friend Eileen back in Asheville.

As the last hairpin was withdrawn, I tossed my head and my long hair came tumbling down around my shoulders. I picked up the hairbrush and began brushing vigorously.

Three

PUSHING OPEN the door of the General Store early the next morning. I was greeted first by smells: coal oil, strong cheese, leather, bacon fat, tobacco. In straight chairs and cowhide rockers a group of men were gathered around a roaring fire in a bumper stove. The whittling and the rocking left off as eyes followed my progress across the creaky floor. At the nearest counter a woman was arranging spools of thread in a cabinet under curving glass. "Excuse me . . ."

"Yes?" The woman straightened up, looking at me curiously.

"I was told that I might find Mr. Pentland, the mailman, here. Is he by any chance—one of those men there?" I inclined my head in the direction of the still silent group around the stove.

The woman's eyes swept the men. "Ben Pentland," she called loudly, "com'here—willya?"

A man looked up from the high boots he was lacing, grunted, and went on methodically crossing and tying the laces. At last he finished, then like a jackknife unfolded to well over six feet of man. As he ambled in our direction, I saw that he was wearing overalls over a gray shirt of some linsey-woolsey material carefully buttoned to the collar, then a frayed and unpressed suit coat on top of everything. But it was his face that was arresting. He had the look I would have expected to find in an English yeoman of Robin Hood's time: a long slim face creased by wind and weather, a patrician nose, thin firm lips, eyes deep-set in their sockets with glints and lights in them, bushy arching eyebrows.

"This here's Ben Pentland, Miss—?"

I stuck out a mittened hand. "Christy Huddleston from Asheville."

"Howdy." He took my hand so firmly that I winced.

"You're the postman, aren't you?"

"Yep." The tall mountaineer was not going to waste any words.

"Could I talk with you a minute? Back there maybe?"

The man looked surprised but followed me towards the back of the store where the hardware and the harnesses and saddles were. Around the stove the hum of conversation began again. "Mr. Pentland, I need help. I've come to teach school in Cutter Gap. I thought someone would meet me at the station yesterday, but nobody did. So I'm trying to find a way to get out to the Cove. Mrs. Tatum—you know, at the boarding house—said you could help me since you carry mail out there."

"Yep, carry the letters regular," he said proudly. "But ain't nobody been in or out the Cove since a couple days. Snow's too deep."

"When are you going next?"

"Startin' now. That's why I was gettin' my boots on. Have to go. Letters are pilin' up something fearful."

"Do you ride?"

He looked astonished at my question. "In fine weather, shorely. But no critter could make it in this snow."

"How far is it, Mr. Pentland?"

"Seven mile to Cutter Gap, good seven mile."

I hesitated, knowing that I'd never walked seven miles at one stretch in my life. But what did it matter? The snow might lie on the ground for a long time and I couldn't sit in El Pano waiting for spring to come. "Could I walk out there with you today?" I asked impetuously.

"Nope, too hard a walk for a city gal-woman."

He sounded so final that I felt desperate. "Mr. Pentland, you don't understand. I'm strong, honestly I am, and the snow may last for weeks."

"Sorry, miss. Ain't no use. It jest wouldn't be fitten for a woman to go along with the U-nited States mail." Abruptly, he took a step backwards, dramatically placing his hand over his heart as if to salute the flag. His voice rang out as he intoned, "'Neither rain—nor snow—nor heat—nor gloom of night—will stay these couriers from the swift completion of their appointed rounds.'"

I stared at him, amazed. I had never heard this slogan before and at first I thought he might be making fun of me. But he was in dead earnest.

"Beautiful, ain't it! Just been told us by the gov-ment in Washington. Now looky here, I figure that if rain nor snow, nor none of those things are meant to stay us couriers, then we shorely can't have no gal-woman stayin' us." And he turned to rejoin his companions in the front of the store.

I ran after him. "Mr. Pentland, *please.* That's a *wonderful* slogan. I promise that I won't interfere with the mail one bit. I won't even slow you down. I'm used to walking. Please? At least consider it?"

The postman's eyes seemed to be taking my measure. "Look, I don't want to disencourage you, but it's for your own good. It's not nacherally easy a-walkin' in the snow—" The eyes deep in their sockets were penetrating. "And what about your go-away satchel?"

So he was weakening—a little. I leaped at the straw he held out. "I've only one small valise, Mr. Pentland, just—oh—that size. The rest of my things are coming by trunk. The valise wouldn't be anything at all to carry. May I, may I come with you?" And I smiled at him, turning on all the feminine charm I could.

"Wal—You stoppin' at Mistress Tatum's?"

"Yes, I am."

"Kin you be ready in a hip and a hurry?"

"Thirty minutes? . . . Ten?"

He nodded—and grinned.

"I'll be ready." And I ran out of the store.

Twenty minutes later a still incredulous Mrs. Tatum was telling me good-bye on her front porch. Impulsively the big woman took my face between her hands, kissed first one cheek, then the other. "That's for your mother. And you let her know that I did my level best to send you home to her. Don't forget though, that I've got good broad shoulders. Just dandy cryin' posts they are, if ever ye need cryin' posts."

She held me off at arm's length looking at me. Under my coat I was wearing the red sweater mother had knitted for me; on my head was a matching turban.

"You're a sight on the eyes," Mrs. Tatum said approvingly. "I'll bet my last sixpence they don't know what they're getting out at that mission. They've never seen the likes of you before."

Mr. Pentland, standing out on the edge of the road, was obviously embarrassed at all this female fuss and eager to get started. I heard him say almost under his breath, "Blatherskite wimmin!" So I cut the good-bye as short as I could. As I turned to go down the steps, Mrs. Tatum thrust a brown paper poke into my hands. "No good walkin' on an empty stummick," she explained a little self-consciously.

"But—how did you get it together so quickly?"

"Now, just a little snack is all, somethin' to keep you and Ben goin'. Away with ye—" Then she waved us down the road, calling after me, "Mind ye watch them slippery log-bridges over the creeks! The Lord bless ye and keep ye, child."

Her kindness was a good omen, I thought. It was remarkable that Mrs. Tatum had not shown any resentment over my refusing her advice. And now here was Mr. Pentland not only letting me go with him, but good-naturedly carrying my valise along with his mail pack. Still, he wanted me to know that he meant business, so he was setting a brisk pace.

For the first half mile or so just the other side of El Pano there was a wide, well-traveled lane which many feet had packed into a hard white roadbed. One side was bordered by a row of giant spruces, black against the snow, their shadows long in the morning light.

For no reason at all the white fields on either side of the narrowing lane reminded me of the top of one of my mother's devil food cakes, thickly covered with white frosting. I remembered my child's-eye view when I had been just tall enough to tiptoe to be eye-level with the cake: that expanse of snowy white icing, glazing over where it was beginning to harden; the little wavy lines in it, so unsullied before any small fingers had sneaked bits off here and there.

Beyond those fields frosted with white, were the foothills, and beyond them, the mountains. A golden glow rimmed the easternmost range, and over the far mountains hung a soft smoky-blue mantle, but in the valley through which we were walking the sky was clear blue.

Could it have been only yesterday that I had stood beside the tracks at the El Pano station and disconsolately watched the train from Asheville disappear over the horizon? Now Mr. Pentland seemed almost to have forgotten me, so that I was having more and more trouble keeping up with his long, loose-jointed strides. Finally he noticed. "Reckon I'd better whittle my walk down a mite," he said.

41

"You'll be nippety-tuck to keep up with me." Then he added generously, "Wimmin's skirts ain't the best for snow. We can jest take hit easy-like."

There was a natural dignity and an innate courtesy about this man that I instinctively liked. His speech was peppered with expressions so quaint that it was like another language: "the sunball" ... "afeard" ... "mought." Twilight, he called "the aidge of dark," and I smiled, remembering his "blatherskite wimmin" for Mrs. Tatum and me. "What's your first mail stop, Mr. Pentland?"

"Beck's mailbox is first. I've got one letter for them." He patted the mail pouch swinging at his side. "I can see it's from Mistress Beck's aunt in Jonesboro. Her littlest settin'-along child's been poorly for some time. Guess she's a-lettin' Mistress Beck know the news. Their mailbox is just the other side of the Big Mud Hole."

"Aren't all mud holes frozen in this kind of weather?" I asked.

"Shorely. Only this ain't just any old mud hole. This is *the* Mud Hole. In the spring it's a sight to be-hold. Wagons sink right up to their axles and mules might just as well be tryin' to hoof it through sorghum."

"Sorghum? What's sorghum?"

"Wal-l-l, molasses."

"Oh, I see. Well then, why don't the roadmen fix the hole?"

"Ain't no roadmen. We have to manpower the roads ourselves. Every vig-rous man is supposed to work three days a year keepin' the roads in repair. But Hell's Banjer! Soon's road-mendin' time comes, most of the men has creeled their backs or their knees or they're hurtin' somewhere. Seems like it's always ill-convenient to work for Tennessee. So the Big Mud Hole gets worser and worser each spring. That's yan—just up there."

We walked in silence for a while. Then came the first mail delivery at Beck's. But I was still full of questions. "Mr. Pentland, how many families live around the Cutter Gap section?"

The mailman thought a moment. "Jedgmatically, I don't know. Maybe 'bout seventy."

"Most of the people farm, don't they? What crops? What do they raise?"

"Raise young'uns mostly," he answered drily, his face never changing expression.

"And do most of these children go to the mission school?"

"Wal-l, hit de-pends. Not all of 'em got religion, and if'n some families go to the school, then there's others just p'int blank won't go near it. But most everyone seems to like the new preacher, David Grantland. He's got good wind in the pulpit and can shore tote a tune."

I wanted to know more about David Grantland. "Has he been at the mission long?"

"Naw—near about three months. He's from somewhere up north—"

"Is he married?"

"No-o-o—" Mr. Pentland looked at me and chuckled.

Abruptly I changed the subject. "Tell me, do you know Miss Alice Henderson?"

"Shorely. Everybody in the Gap knows Miz Henderson."

"What's she like? What does she *look* like?"

The mountaineer shifted my satchel to his other hand, took his time about answering. "Miz Henderson's gettin' up thar—not so young now. But she's a pert 'un—dauncy." He chortled, a soft low chuckle that seemed to come from deep within him. "Tangy as an unripe persimmon, matter of fact. Rides a horse all over the mountains by herself. Sidesaddle, longskirt. Sits like a queen in that saddle. Gallops too, oft as not.

"Right high-stocked with brains. Started two schools and churches before our'n. Keeps busier than a honeybee 'round a rosey-bush—a-teachin', a-preachin', visitin' folks, nursin' the sick, a-comfortin' the dyin'.

"She's a smiley woman. All her wrinkles are smile-wrinkles. Has a heap o' hair, light hair, leetle grey in it now. Wears her hair in braids that she folds round and round her head, like—like a crown."

And I had thought Mr. Pentland a man of few words! Somehow I had had him figured wrong. I had judged this mountain man simple perhaps because of his speech and because he had not had much formal education.

The postman had now reached his second delivery spot. "Mornin'," he called loudly. "Ma-il. U-nited States mail."

As we walked on down the road I saw over my shoulder a woman with a woolen fascinator over her head coming to get the precious letter.

43

"Is that sack full of mail?" I asked him, curious to know how many stops we were going to have.

"Four more letters. Ain't that a wonder!"

"But back at the store you said—" I caught myself, then walked in silence trying to grasp this mountain world where six letters were "piled-up mail"!

At last I returned to the subject I could never stay away from long: the compelling figure of Alice Henderson. "Mrs. Tatum said that Miss Henderson's sort of— different. Do you think so?"

"Aye, she's different. That she is."

I waited expectantly, but apparently he was not going to explain further. "How?" I prodded. "Tell me *how* Miss Henderson is different."

"Talks about God lovin' folks." His answer came slowly. " 'God wants us all happy,' she's always a-sayin'. I could most believe it watching her. She don't put no stock in long-faced persons even when they *think* they've got religion." He laughed softly to himself, remembering something. "Like Christmas—In the mountains we shoot rifle-guns up chimneys and blow up tree stumps to celebrate. Last Christmas Miz Henderson said she had a better idea, so she sent to Philadelfy for a big box of boughten fireworks. Had a play-party for everybody. My, but them fireworks was shorely a sight to be-hold."

An angel of mercy on horseback with a box of firecrackers in her saddlebag. My picture of Miss Henderson was more and more intriguing.

Then the trail began winding upwards and soon became so narrow that we had to walk single file and further conversation was impossible. Because the snow had obliterated the path, I had to walk in Mr. Pentland's tracks. But the mountaineer seemed to know exactly where he was going. For the first hour and a half the walking had not been bad, but we had delivered three letters. But here in this defile it was colder. My eyes were watering, my cheeks stinging. I could no longer feel my toes inside my rubber boots. My skirts, wet almost to my knees, were now half-frozen. The chill air caught in my throat. Even my eyelashes were beaded with wet snow.

Off to the left I heard a strange noise. "Mr. Pentland," I called to him. "What's that sawing noise off there?"

"That ain't sawin'. That's ravens. They can make themselves sound like most anything. Ravens don't pleasure me none. Not a-tall."

44

"Why not?"

"They're mean. Like nothin' better than to pick out the eye of a lamb or a fawn."

"You mean when they find a dead one?"

"Naw. Hits the eye of *livin'* animals they like."

I shivered. The sawing noise had changed to a cackle, then to what sounded like a buzz saw. We walked a long way before we left the sound behind us.

At last we were at the bottom of the hill over which we had been climbing. Here in the valley were different kinds of bird sounds: the gobble of wild turkeys, the drumming of grouse. Holly trees, thick with red berries, stood in a clump in the clearing. From the top of the hill the valley had looked small, but I was discovering that distances in these mountains were deceptive. It took us a long time to cross the bottom land, and as we walked I could hear coming closer and closer the sound of rushing, tumultuous water.

Then we reached the edge of a large creek, and I saw that there was no real bridge across it, only a makeshift affair of two huge uneven logs with an occasional thin board nailed across. The whole contraption swayed precariously six feet or more high in the air above the water. So this was what Mrs. Tatum had meant about slippery logs. I looked down at my boots and at my skirt, the mass of wet cloth clinging to my ankles. If only the logs were not so far above the water, and if only they had put the two logs closer together.

Mr. Pentland said, "I'll go first to see if hits slippery-like. Then you'd better stomp your feet and get warm before you try it." He shifted the mail pouch to the middle of his back, took a firmer grip on my valise, and paused to scrape his feet on the edge of the bridge.

My eyes were on his feet. Halfway across he paused. Below him the water sprayed over the boulders in the middle of the stream where it was not frozen. He called back, "Hit ain't bad. Wait until I get acrost though, so you won't get no sway."

Standing on the bank, I felt sick at my stomach. I never had liked heights. There had been that time on the railroad trestle two hundred feet above the French Broad River when some friends and I were coming back from a picnic. It would not have been so bad except for the wide open spaces between the trestles. And when I had looked down, well—many times since then I had dreamed of it.

And now here was my old nightmare come horribly true.

I heard Mr. Pentland's voice above the roar of the water. "Stomp your feet now. Get 'em warm. Then come on—but first scrape your boots, then hoist your skirts."

Mechanically I did as he was directing me, then took a deep breath and put one foot on the log. It swayed a little and my boot sent a piece of bark flying into the water. I took a few steps, shut my eyes, then opened them again. Another step. Perhaps if I kept looking at Mr. Pentland waiting for me on the other bank—step—or kept my eyes on my valise—step—and did not once look below me— the sound of the water became a roar in my ears. That meant I must be about halfway now.

I heard Mr. Pentland's voice. "You're doin' fine. Keep a-comin'. Not far now."

Again the logs swayed. Each time I came to one of the cross-pieces, I was forced to look at my feet lest I trip over the edge of the board, and then in spite of myself I saw the water too. The logs were swaying, tilting ... I dropped to my knees and began crawling. I hadn't thought it would be this bad! Dizzy ... I felt dizzy. Mr. Pentland was shouting at me. Dimly his voice penetrated, "Only a few more steps. Stand up now. I'll catch you."

Unsteadily I stood up again. The valise, keep my eyes on the valise. . . . Step—getting closer now, only a few more feet.

Then at last I saw Mr. Pentland's grinning face below me. "Guess you ain't crossed the likes of that before." He held out a gnarled hand and almost lifted me off the end of the log.

Yet another hour of steady walking brought us to a second mountain. Once again with the mailman in front, we were climbing upwards on a narrow trail.

Here the path had been sliced out of the side of the mountain at our right. Sometimes the trail jutted sharply to get around an outcropping of rock. At our left, the ledge appeared to drop off into space. Before long it was five hundred feet to the valley floor below; somewhere down there I could hear a cowbell tinkling.

"This here's Lonesome Pine Ridge," Mr. Pentland called to me. "There's another way that's shorter. But that way is so up-tilted, you could stand straight up and bite the ground."

46

I wondered as I panted after him if any piece of land could be more up-tilted than this. There was a sudden gust of wind. The higher we climbed, the stronger the gale that blew from the north. Near the top, the bank to our right was not high enough to give much protection. There were moments when I was sure we were about to be blown over the cliff. Yet the man walking in front gave no indication that he even noticed the buffeting of the wind.

Mr. Pentland must have sensed that I was afraid because he turned his head away from the wind and called back over his shoulder, "Not much farther to the Spencers' now. They live just the other side, near the top of the ridge. Guess we could stop and set a spell by their fire and let you warm yourself. Maybe even have a bite to eat thar."

I yelled back into the teeth of the wind. "I'd like that." Then I braced myself to concentrate on getting one foot in front of the other. I was beginning to understand why the mailman had not wanted to bring me. This morning seemed like days and days ago.

Mr. Pentland looked back at me solicitously. "You must be bodaciously tired out. Buck up. Hit ain't so far. Just a step or two."

But now I knew that this mountain man thought of a step or two as I would think of a city block or two. There seemed to be no end to his vitality. What seemed like half a mile farther on Mr. Pentland commented, "We'll have to get shet of Jeb Spencer's hound-dogs afore goin' into his yard. Jeb's an awful hand to hunt. There 'tis. There's the Spencer place. I don't have no letter for them but we'll stop onyways."

The cabin toward which we were going was made of roughhewn logs chinked with mud, set just on the other side of the backbone of the mountain. In such a crude setting I was surprised to see several clumps of English boxwood almost buried under the snow. In the cleared place inside the split rail fence was an immense black pot, a tall pile of logs for firewood, and some gawky, squawking chickens pecking in the snow. Near the fence was a crude sled. A man wearing overalls and a large black felt hat appeared on the porch and called out, "Howdy." Hounds raced towards us, yapping.

Mr. Pentland called, "Howdy. How you doin'?"

" 'Bout like common."

"Well, call of yer dogs. We ain't a-feelin' to make no dog meat out of ourselves this time a day."

As we got closer I saw that the man had not shaved in a couple of days and his beard was growing out red-blond. His eyes were blue, set deep in their sockets like Mr. Pentland's. In spite of his shabby clothing, there was something debonair about him. Perhaps it was the front of his hat pinned up with a long thorn, and a sprig of balsam—like a feather—stuck jauntily into the hatband. "Git out of the way till you git more sense," he called to the dogs. "Git now. Git!" Immediately the hounds slunk out of sight around the corner of the cabin.

"Jeb Spencer, this here's Miz Huddleston. New teacher from Asheville-way."

"Howdy do, ma'am." There was dignity and restraint about the man's greeting. It was almost courtly.

As he led us through the doorway into semidarkness, it took a moment for my eyes to get accustomed to the gloom. At first I could see nothing but the ruddy glow of firelight. Then I saw that there were several beds piled high with quilts and in the shadows to one side, a tall woman and an assortment of children, all of them towheaded.

The man made no move to take off his hat. He said to the group in the shadows. "C'mon and see the stranger. I don't know as I can handle her name. This here's my woman. And that there's John. And this un's Zady. And that's Clara. And that's Lulu." Then his voice took on more warmth. "And that thar's the Least'un—" and he pointed to a tiny boy.

I wondered if these were going to be some of the children I would teach to read. I smiled at them and held out my hand to Mrs. Spencer. But the woman wasn't quite sure what to do with the proffered hand. She touched my fingers shyly and said to hide her confusion, "Would you like to rest your wrap and set a spell?" She indicated a straight split-bottom chair. Her voice was low-toned and pitched in a musical minor key.

I could scarcely take my eyes off her, for she was beautiful in her plain, artless way. Still a young woman, in her early thirties, I guessed, yet with all these children. . . . She was wearing only a calico dress and was barefooted in this cold.

But the Spencers were looking at me just as closely. All eyes in the room watched as I took off my coat. The children seemed to be fascinated with the red sweater underneath. Mr. Pentland handed the woman the lunch Mrs. Tatum had given us.

While I held my cold hands close to the fire, I had a better chance to look around the cabin. There was only one regular window in the room plus an odd slit of a window high in the wall to the right of the fireplace. There seemed to be two rooms side by side with one fireplace flue to serve both. Judging by the number of beds in the room, I knew that this room was both living and sleeping quarters. The smaller lean-to must be the kitchen, I concluded. A narrow ladder led to a hole in the ceiling, probably a loft.

There was a rough puncheon floor with no rugs. On pegs protruding from the walls hung skirts and garments of various kinds and a worn saddle. A long-barreled rifle was laid across an elk-horn rack. There was only one picture, a picture with a rococo frame of an austere-looking woman, her straight hair parted in the middle. Some flatirons were lined up on the hearth near an ancient cradle. Strings of dried onions and red peppers hung from the rafters, and some gourds.

The children's bright eyes were still watching me. The littlest girl, the one named Lulu, had the high rounded forehead and the fat-cheeked cherub look of a bisque doll. The tiny toddler—the one his father had called "the Least-un"—came up and touched shy fingers to my red sweater. I was just beginning to make friends with the children and to ask them about whether or not they went to school when Mrs. Spencer called us to dinner.

Without ceremony everyone gathered around a plank table set in a corner closest to the kitchen. No mention was made of washing hands or of the bathroom. I took the chair they pulled out for me, then noticed that no such courtesy was being given Mrs. Spencer or the oldest girl. They were standing to one side as if they were not going to join the rest of us at the table. I was about to protest this when suddenly Mr. Spencer began asking the blessing in a loud, sonorous voice: "Thank Thee, Lord, for providin' this bounty. Bless us and bind us. Amen." And out of the corner of one eye I saw a small gray pig come through the open door.

The "Amen" had no sooner been said than the girl Clara spoke up eagerly, "That thar's Belinda, our pet pig—all our'n." And she picked up the pig and put him in her lap.

It was apparent that this was a very typical pig even though he was a pet. I tried not to show surprise or distaste. Probably, I reflected, a smelly pig at the table would be the least I'd have to get accustomed to in these mountains, and mother had always insisted that a lady must be perfectly poised under all circumstances. If only my mother could see—and smell—these circumstances.

Mrs. Tatum's poke dinner had been placed in a tin plate in the middle of the table beside a big black pot of steaming cabbage. For the moment the children were ignoring the pot, fascinated with the strange food in the plate. I hated the idea of parting with all of my lunch since I knew that Mrs. Tatum's food was clean, whereas this. . . . Nevertheless when I asked the little girl across the table if she would like one of my ham sandwiches, all of the children nodded eagerly, and soon my food was gone.

"Can I give you some pot likker?" Mrs. Spencer asked over my shoulder. Then without waiting for an answer, she ladled some onto the wooden plate in front of me. Mr. Spencer and John had already broken out pieces from a huge chunk of cornbread and were using it to sop up the cabbage mixture. The only other thing on the table was a bowl of sauerkraut which looked anything but appetizing.

My eyes kept going back to the barefooted woman who moved so quietly and with such grace to and from the kitchen bringing the family hot corn pone and coffee. Her features were delicate: nose turned up at the end ever so slightly, which gave her a piquant look. Delicately shaped lips. Hair parted in the middle, drawn back into a bun, much like that woman in the rococo frame. But the eyes of the living woman ... what was it about her eyes? Wistful, that was it.

The oldest girl looked like her mother except that she was a bit round-shouldered, as if already she was carrying burdens too heavy for her. She had her mother's low-pitched voice with that melancholy note in it.

I found myself thinking that these were the faces of pioneers. Looking at them I had a curious sensation. It was as if a group of faded tintypes from some family album had come to life before me: all of the women with that austere hairstyle; the faces sensitive but grave, a certain strength and spartan quality to them all.

I had always supposed that faces in old photographs were grave because the subjects had not thought it proper to smile for a picture. Yet here was the same look in these living faces. The look was there even at moments when a certain dry humor was flowing, as when Mr. Spencer commented about a widow-woman down the Cove who thought herself extra pious, " 'Course she ain't much of a hand to housekeep: slut's wool all over the place. When yer mind is that fixated on things above, the dirt's bound to settle below."

Well, certainly it had taken strength and courage to journey hundreds of miles through wilderness such as we had walked that morning. It had taken resoluteness to know that the low whistles of a quail in the woods might not be a quail at all—but the signal for an Indian attack. It would take fortitude to live and try to keep house in a cabin like this one.

Sitting there, I had a strange otherworldly feeling. It was as if, in crossing the mountains with Mr. Pentland, I had crossed into another time, another century, back to the days of the American frontier. Was I still Christy Rudd Huddleston from Asheville, North Carolina—or was this somebody else? It was as if the pages of my history book had opened and by some magic, Daniel Boone might walk into this cabin any moment—or Davy Crockett—or John Sevier. But this was no storybook, this was real. My mind kept trying to grasp it.

Ours was the century of progress, everyone said— electric lights and telephones and steam locomotives and automobiles. Yet in this cabin it was still the eighteenth century. I wondered if all the homes in the Cove were as primitive as this one.

My thoughts were shattered by a man rushing into the cabin. He leaned against the chimney, out of breath. "An accident," he gasped. "It's Bob Allen. Hurt bad!"

Everyone was asking questions at once, trying to get details.

"It was a fallin' tree. Hit him on the head. They're carryin' him here. He was a-comin' to El Pano to fetch on the new teacher. That's when the acci-dent happened."

51

Four

A YOUNG MAN limp and unconscious, his head bloody, was carried into the Spencer cabin on a makeshift stretcher of branches and laid on one of the beds. Mrs. Spencer removed the man's heavy shoes and covered him with a quilt. I stood stunned, the words whirling in my head, "coming to fetch on the new teacher" ... That was me. Because of me this had happened.

"Who is he?" I managed to whisper at last to Mrs. Spencer.

"That be Bob Allen." Her voice was gentle, as if she sensed how I felt. "Ever since it weathered-up to snow, Miz Henderson's been a-pesterin' Bob to favor her by carryin' word to you. I've a mind that it were snowin' too heavy on Sunday for him to journey. Guess he thought the snow had you all gaumed up in El Pano too."

"Whatn'all happened?" I heard Mr. Pentland ask.

The stretcher-bearers appeared to be father and son. The older man answered, "Bob, he'd put out as early as he could. Was cuttin' through the nigh way acrost Pebble Mountain. Solid woods there. High wind come up. In a deadnin', a big tulip-poplar tree got wind-throwed. Fumped him right on the head."

"How'd you find him?"

"Huntin squirrels. Had old hound-dog, Bait-em, swingin' along with us. Bait-em bayed him. Nosed him out. Bob had fell in the bresh. Tree still on him."

Mrs. Spencer asked anxiously, "Doc a-comin'?"

"Aye. Ought to be pretty nigh here."

Within what seemed like minutes, the strangest group of people I had ever seen began crowding into the Spencer cabin—neighbors, I took it, and Mr. Allen's relatives. I was never to fathom how news traveled so fast in those mountains without telephones or any obvious ways of

52

sending messages, but travel the news always did. Some of the first arrivals noticed my presence ... "Howdy do, stranger" ... "Be ye from the level lands?" ... "Proud to know you." But then in the excitement of the Doctor's arrival, I was soon forgotten.

Outside there was the stomping of feet, the whinny of a horse; then the door opened and Dr. Neil MacNeill strode in. He appeared to be a man in his thirties, big-boned, a large frame even for a man. He had a shock of reddish hair, unkempt, looking as if it had not been cut in a long time, tousled and curly. His features were rugged with deeply etched lines. Or was it the shadows cast by the kerosene lamp, throwing into relief every plane of his face, that made it seem so craggy?

The figure lying on the old post-and-spindle bed had not moved. The pale face on the pillow was lighted by a kerosene lamp being held close by Mrs. Spencer while the Doctor made his examination.

Although it was early afternoon, the cabin was so dark inside that the lamplight gave an eerie quality to the room. Giant shadows on the walls moved, danced like monsters ready to spring. I watched the bobbing circle of light on the ceiling cast by the opening at the top of the lamp chimney, my eyes drawn to it with almost hypnotic fascination. Only the hard solid wood of the wall against which I was leaning and the draft of cold air seeping through a crack at my back told me that this was real, that it was all actually happening.

The Doctor had taken off his coat, rolled up his shirt sleeves. I noticed his arms, so muscular, the hair on those arms blond-red.

A voice at my side whispered, "Doc MacNeill's the only doctor in the Cove." It was Mr. Pentland who had made his way through the crowd to my side. I nodded and smiled up at him, wishing that I could let him know how glad I was for one friend in this awful situation. Already, after our trek over the mountain together, Mr. Pentland seemed like an old friend. But I dared not talk because a strained unnatural silence had fallen on the room; all eyes were watching the doctor.

His fingers kept sliding over the man's head on the pillow—feeling, probing. Something about the fingers reminded me of my father's hands, only these were rough and work-worn.

The Doctor would not be hurried. He took the patient's

pulse, then forced his mouth open and looked at the tongue. He checked the pulse again; opened the eyelids and looked intently into the eyes; took the lamp and moved it closer to the still face. Then almost absently, he handed the lamp back to Mrs. Spencer and began checking reflexes of the arms, pulled back the covers to check leg reflexes. Finally when he straightened up, resolution was written on his face.

"Mary Allen, I'm needing to talk to you and to Bob's brothers and sisters. Come closer, please."

There was a rustling among the crowd. So many pushed forward toward the bed that it seemed as if most of the people there must be relatives of Bob Allen's. In the forefront was a distraught woman, and beside her, a man with a heavy black beard. Mr. Pentland had remained at my side. I whispered, "Who's the man, the one in front?"

"That's Ault Allen, Bob's older brother, head of the clan now."

The word "clan" seemed odd. After all, these were our own Appalachians, not the highlands of Scotland. But my attention was on what Dr. MacNeill was saying as he looked straight at the tightly huddled group before him, especially at the woman and bearded man, "Mary—Ault—I'd best speak plain." There was a somber note in his voice. "Bob's bad off—"

The lamplight on the woman Mary's face illuminated a stolid person, accustomed to hardship, but rigid now with fear. "Be it a—mortalizing—wound, Doc?" Her voice had sunk almost to a whisper.

The Doctor's voice was gentle. "Don't know the answer to that, Mary. But Bob's pulse is real slow, breathin' irregular, reflexes bad, one eye doesn't respond to light." His eyes, searching her face, told him that she still did not understand. "That means, Mary, it's getting almost impossible for Bob to breathe."

The woman was using all her strength to keep from sobbing. The effort of swallowing back her tears made the veins in her neck stand out like cords. "Is—Bob—a-hurtin', Doc?"

"No, Mary. He's not, for sure. He's in a coma—like a deep sleep, getting deeper all the time. Listen to me now, you and Ault, listen carefully. Where the tree hit Bob's head, there's some bleeding inside his skull, probably

54

pressing on his brain. If I leave the bleeding there, Bob will die."

He paused, groping for words, and I thought I saw the glisten of tears in the Doctor's eyes. "There's one chance of bringing Bob round though. That's to bore a small hole in the skull to let the bad blood out and try to lift the pressure. Mary, I want to tell you true—I've never tried this operation. I saw this trephine, the burr hole, they call it, done once by an old professor of mine, Starr Gatlin. He told us then that it was a risky operation. You understand what I'm saying? It's chancy either way. Mary, you're Bob's wife. It's up to you to decide. Will you let me try the operation?"

In the stillness, it was now apparent how labored the breathing of the man on the bed was—gasps for air, irregular, painful to hear, rent the silence. Mary Allen rocked soundlessly on her heels, grappling with the stark alternative the Doctor had handed her. Yet no whimper escaped her tight-set lips. Watching her, I felt a great compassion and thought how the grief of the inarticulate cuts so much deeper than the loud wailing of the self-pitying.

"I say 'Naw.' I stand against it," the heavily bearded man exclaimed. "Life and death is in the hands of the Lord. We've no call to tamper with it."

Then Mary spoke. "No, Ault, ye're wrong." Her voice was still low, but there was the resolution of iron and granite in it. "We've no cause to let go so long as there's one livin' breath left in Bob. Try, Doc! Don't mind Ault. We've got six young'uns. Did anything happen to Bob, reckon we couldn't stand it. Try, I want you to try. Will ye try, Doc?"

The Doctor waited, looked at Ault. "Ault . . . ?"

"We-ll, we-ll—" Ault pulled at his beard. Obviously he was torn, though he seemed like a hard type, grim and cold. "Mary, you're his woman," he said at last. "Borin' holes in a man's skull don't make no sense to me. But don't reckon I'm called on to stop ye, if'n that's what ye want. But I don't mind tellin' ye, I don't like meddlin' with the Lord's business." He looked at Dr. MacNeill and shrugged. "Hit's up to you."

The Doctor himself wavered for another moment. I thought I understood the cruel dilemma. There was not much hope for Mr. Allen, with or without the operation. In spite of all the Doctor's attempts to explain the situation to Bob's relatives, if the patient died during the operation Dr. MacNeill knew that some of these people would blame him. And he would have a mountain cabin for an operating theatre, no trained nurses, little light, not even proper surgical instruments. How does a doctor weigh his own limitations of knowledge and skill against a man's only chance to live?

At last the Doctor announced tersely, "We'll go ahead. All of you in this room have heard that I've been given the family's permission for this operation. Jeb Spencer, are you here? And John Holcomb? I need your help."

At this, the crowd surged forward eagerly. Mixed with their desire to help was curiosity about every detail of the operation. They wanted to get close—and still closer—to see. There was that strange fascination that people have with blood and accidents and death, like children shivering deliciously at a horror story.

I knew that Dr. MacNeill had just made a courageous decision. But looking at him with his tousled hair and his rumpled shirtsleeves as he directed the preparations, ordering this, asking for that, I wondered if it was not a foolhardy choice. Certainly there had never been such a setting for a major operation: the wind whistling around a mountain cabin; dirty pots and pans by the hearth; a baby crying in its mother's arms; the smell of chewing tobacco; all these people crowded into one room with the air getting fouler by the minute. It would be germ-laden. Surely the Doctor was going to ask these staring people to leave.

But Dr. MacNeill was saying, "We'll use that kitchen table. Fairlight, will you clear it off and let Lizzie help you scrub it? And Jeb, you have a razor, don't you, and a straight awl and hammer?"

I wondered if the Doctor was going to use the awl and hammer as part of his surgical instruments. Jeb Spencer looked at the Doctor quizzically for a moment, then only nodded and went to fetch the tools.

"Need the razor strop too, Jeb. And Ben Pentland, are you here? Can you help? Need lots of boiling water. Will you and some of the other men get water from the spring? Better start a fire under the wash pot in the yard. And Fairlight, how many pans do you have?"

Slowly Mrs. Spencer answered, "Three big'uns and a small'un. But two are dirty."

"Well, get them all cleaned up and filled with water and

on the fire. And Jeb, you don't have another table, do you?" As the man shook his head, Dr. MacNeill went on, "Then get me a couple of saw horses and two or three boards. That will have to do for an instrument table. And hurry."

At last came the announcement I had been expecting. "The whole kit and caboodle of you'd best leave," the Doctor said gruffly. His eyes swept the room and stopped on me, noticing me for the first time since he had entered the cabin. An expression I could not read clouded his rugged features, an intense light seemed to burn suddenly in his deep-set eyes. He stared at me for a long time without speaking, fingers plucking the unkempt hair on his neck. I felt he was seeing me as the cause of the accident, that he wished none of them in the Cove had ever set eyes on me.

Finally the Doctor turned to the others. "If you close-kin feel called on to stay, then you'll have to stand off there now, clear to that side. And no crying or wailing."

The people had respect for the Doctor, I could see that. Yet after this ultimatum, only a few of them left. I wanted to slip out, but I was on the side of the room farthest from the door, penned in by the crowd.

From the saddlebags on his horse, the Doctor had brought muslin bags containing bandages, sutures, and instruments. Mr. Spencer had found the awl and hammer, and the Doctor had put these tools and all of his instruments into a pot of boiling water. After a time he began laying supplies out on a clean cloth spread on the sawhorse table.

As the Doctor turned his back to tend to the sterilizing, an inquisitive girl with pigtails slipped up and began fingering some of the instruments already laid out on the table. Dr. MacNeill wheeled and caught her. "Confound! You little scamp—" She cringed, covered her face with her arm, as if she thought he was going to strike her. "I ought to tan you right enough, for fooling with those. Now you can just tear off for home—now. And no use blubbering either." And he began sterilizing over again everything the girl had touched.

Though I was impressed by this thoroughness, I couldn't help wondering what good it would do in such an operating theatre. Why try to sterilize instruments when not six feet away stood an anything but sterile audience breathing on the scene? One woman at the front of the group, who wore a kind of rusty-looking black cape, kept rocking on her heels so that the cape swayed back and forth, fanning the air. Several people were coughing. One man sneezed with no handkerchief in evidence.

As some of the men lifted Bob Allen onto the makeshift operating table, I heard a scuffle at the door and turned to see Bob's wife rushing toward the still form with a double-bitted axe in her hands. As I saw her lift the axe over her shoulder and give a mighty heave, I clapped my hands over my mouth to stifle a scream. With a crash the axe bit deep ino the floorboard under the table. Then with shaking hands the woman took a string and tied it around one of her husband's wrists.

I was too stunned to move. To my surprise, Dr. MacNeill took this wild behavior quite calmly. Quietly he said, "All right, Mary. That's fine. That should be helpful. There's not a solitary thing more that you can do for Bob. Will some of you take care of Mary until this is all over?" His voice was kind.

Then the Doctor began vigorously wielding the razor back and forth on the strop, up and down. Carefully he washed his own hands in one of the basins, then began shaving Mr. Allen's head. After all the patient's hair was in the basin, Dr. MacNeill began wiping the shaved head with what was unmistakably ether. The sickly sweet odor hung heavily in the close air. Hastily I slipped through and behind the people and out the door just as the Doctor was ready to make the first incision.

Outside I breathed deeply of the cold air, trying to get the smell of the ether out of my nostrils and shake off the effect of the nightmare scene. The three hounds were no longer baying. The smallest of them came and nibbled my hand. I patted the little dog's head, feeling a kinship with this small black and white animal. Once again there poured through me the feeling of being where I did not belong. Here people still believed in omens and witchcraft. I had been born a century later. I wondered if anything but evil could come of this meeting of two worlds—evil that had already begun.

I came out of my black reverie to see that the ether had driven several other people into the yard including Mrs. Spencer, who was standing only a few feet away. I moved closer to her. "Mrs. Spencer," I began, "did the Doctor call you 'Fairlight'?"

"Aye—"

"That's a lovely name."

She nodded, but seemed preoccupied. Her eyes were focused on the sun setting behind the tall pinnacle opposite. I looked from her face to the peak. Rugged scenery certainly—majestic—but I did not understand her intense concentration on it. Then suddenly, the sun dipped and the shadow of the mountain fell across us, lying like a dark hand across the top of the ridge where we stood. I felt the woman beside me cringe, draw into herself, go rigid. I said to lighten the moment, "The sun sinks in a hurry here, doesn't it?" She had not heard me. "Mrs. Spencer—?"

But the eyes in her lovely face were glazed, turned toward that peak across the valley, seeing not the mountain that had shut out the sun, but some specter I could not glimpse. I stood there ill at ease, not knowing what to say.

In the silence I could hear the sound of shuffling feet as the little knot of people in the yard moved about, trying to keep warm. My hands and feet were numb with the cold; Mrs. Spencer's must be too. I wondered how she could stand there barefoot, so stiff, so unmoving, not speaking. But the fire under the water pot in the yard had long since gone out, not even embers glowing now.

A long time passed, I had no idea how long. Finally a voice spoke from the shadows: my friend, Mr. Pentland. "You must be real tired," he said kindly. "Why don't I take you on out to the mission? It's not far now—"

"But Mr. Allen— How is he? Is he—"

"Still livin' and breathin'," he announced to the group in the yard. "Operation's all done with. Doc MacNeill found the blood clots all right. Says Bob has a fightin' chance now, if the bleedin' in his head don't start up again."

"Oh, I'm glad, so glad." I laughed weakly with relief. Mr. Pentland had my valise in his hand and was already starting. I had had all the walking I wanted for one day, but there was no alternative except to follow him and hope that his "not far" was true this time.

Mostly Mr. Pentland walked in silence, not seeming to want to talk, and I was too tired for conversation. I had not realized what a physical and emotional toll the day had taken until we were within sight of the mission house— a large square frame building set in a big yard with the dark bulk of a mountain rising sheer behind it. Now that we were almost to our destination, I could feel tears of exhaustion just under the surface. I stumbled once just as we reached the gate and Mr. Pentland held me up.

Someone holding a lamp opened the front door. Through a haze of fatigue I saw a tall young man with black hair, warm brown eyes, a wide smile, heard a deep voice. A firm hand welcomed me.

Then an older woman, tall, almost gaunt, with angular features, led me up the stairs. "Now this will be your room. I'm hanging your coat here to dry. Wet as water it is." She seemed to be bustling about a great deal. Or was it just that I was so tired? "Are you hungry?"

"No. Thank you. No, I'm fine." I wished that the jumpy woman would leave.

She hovered about awhile longer. When she finally left me, I fell across the bed too weary even to undress. The last thing I remembered was the sound of a mountain stream somewhere close—flowing—flowing into the night.

Five

I SLEPT LATE the next morning. Sometime during the night I must have awakened enough to creep beneath the covers. My body was stiff and sore from the walk over the mountains. Gingerly I tested out this muscle and that, meanwhile letting my mind roam over the events of the day before. Already the day just past had an illusory quality like a dream. But if a dream, what was I doing in this strange little room?

There was no luxury here: a washstand with a white china pitcher and bowl; an old dresser with a cracked mirror above it; two straight chairs; the plainest kind of white net curtains; two cotton rag rugs on the bare floor.

Curious to know what this Cutter Gap looked like, I slid out of bed and hobbled stiffly over to one of the windows. Nothing had prepared me for what met my eyes. Mountain ranges were folded one behind the other, in the foreground snow-covered; behind that, patches of emerald green showing through; on beyond, deeper green. Then the blues began. On the smoky blue of the far summits fluffy white clouds rested like wisps of cotton. I counted the mountain ranges, eleven of them rising up and up toward the vault of the sky. The Great Smokies . . . now I understood. That peculiar smoky-blue color and the adjective "great"—so right for these towering heights.

As I lifted my eyes to those summits, involuntarily I took a deep breath. The night before, as I had stood outside the Spencer cabin knowing that because of me a man was undergoing a brain operation, probably dying, I had believed that accepting this teaching job had been a dreadful mistake. I wondered about this now, less sure. Had Mr. Allen survived the night? I still did not know. But meanwhile in the face of tragedy and almost because of it, these mountains were whispering to me a different message. I did not realize it then, but from that moment this became *my* view, a source of peace and strength, a stabilizing energy that entered into me to quiet the mind and satisfy the heart.

Just below my window a double plank wall cleared of snow led from the door of the house to the gate. At the edge of the yard was a stand of fir trees. I could see smoke rising from the chimney of a cabin just beyond the firs.

Someone downstairs had heard me and was knocking on my door. It turned out to be the woman who had helped me up the stairs the night before. "I'm Ida Grantland, David's sister," she said. "You were so tired last night— Don't think you quite took in what we were saying."

"I'm sorry. You're right, everything was hazy. Still is, a little."

She was solicitous. "You did sleep well—I hope?"

"Just fine, thank you."

Miss Grantland was a plain woman with sparse graying hair drawn straight back into a meager bun so that her scalp showed through in several places, and with a nose too large for her narrow face. Already I could see that she was a tense person. Restive habits betrayed it: the way she often sucked in her thin lower lip, and restlessly worked her thumbs in and out, back and forth against the other fingers.

"Oh, Miss Grantland, tell me—I've got to know. Mr. Allen, how is he? Is he—?" I couldn't quite say it.

"Alive? Oh, yes. Dr. MacNeill spent the night there. Miss Alice Henderson too. She got back from Big Lick Spring after sundown. Went right to the Spencers soon as she heard about the operation. She's catching a wink of sleep now."

"Then Mr. Allen's out of danger?"

"Not yet, I take it, or the Doctor wouldn't still be there. Now about breakfast—everybody else has eaten. When you get, ah—changed"—and she looked pointedly at the crumpled dress I had slept in—"come on down to the dining room. I'll see you get something."

I wondered who "everybody" was, how many lived in this house.

Miss Grantland went on, "Miss Henderson would like to see you later today." She crossed the room to the window and pointed. "See that smoke? That's her cabin—just there, beyond the spruce trees."

"Oh—yes, I see. She lives by herself?"

"Yes. She said to tell you maybe late this morning." The woman smiled at me as she turned to leave the room, but the smile seemed like an afterthought: it trailed behind Miss Ida and lingered with me as I dressed. It was as if her brain had ordered, "Now smile." So her facial muscles had obediently jerked the lips back showing teeth, but producing a wooden effect with no warmth at all.

The dining room turned out to be an unadorned square room at the back of the house with unplastered tongue-and-groove walls, a round golden oak table in the center. As I ate the abundant breakfast Miss Grantland served me—hot oatmeal followed by buckwheat cakes and maple syrup—she delivered a message: "David's at the Low Gap School. Had to leave early this morning. He said to tell you he was sorry not to be here when you woke up."

"I'm sorry I overslept. Does Mr. Grantland teach at the Low Gap School?"

"Oh no, that school's closed. There were some old desks there; they said we could use them here." She pointed out the window to a still unfinished building about a thousand yards distant. It was a rectangular building with an incomplete belltower. "David can build anything he sets his hand to. He's working on the steeple now." That puppet's smile again. Miss Grantland was trying to be nice but the smile had no real humor in it and so made me feel uncomfortable, patronized.

"Then that will be the church as well as the school?"

"That's right. We haven't the lumber and funds here to put up two buildings when one would do. This will be used for school on weekdays, church on Sundays."

"You've never had a school here before?"

"No. This will be the first term. That's why we need desks. Some of the men promised to help David haul them today. And believe me, he has to grab the help of these mountain men when he can get it."

It seemed that David Grantland slept in bachelor's quarters, a tiny bunkhouse close to the creek, and took his meals at the big house, as did Miss Alice Henderson when she was in Cutter Gap. She did a lot of traveling, Miss Grantland said, between the three schools quite a distance apart.

"David begged me to come and keep house for him. He

63

said he couldn't get along without me," Miss Grantland told me proudly. "Course I know how he likes things fixed and all that. So I told him, yes, I'd come help him out for a while. David says maybe we can find a mountain woman to train as housekeeper. But I have doubts myself that anybody else can cook to suit him." Her thumbs worked nervously as she spoke.

Just then the side door banged and suddenly Mr. Grantland stood in the kitchen doorway. A young girl with a great shock of snarled red hair peered curiously from behind him. In long quick strides, he crossed the room to me, thrusting out his hand. "Miss Huddleston, great that you're here. Oh—sorry. This is Ruby Mae Morrison. Ruby Mae's staying with us for a while."

"Coffee, David?" His sister stood with the coffeepot poised.

"Shouldn't." He glanced at me and smiled. "All right, Ida, maybe five minutes off. Let me wash my hands though."

The long legs strode to the kitchen sink; the booming voice never stopped. "Not much of a welcome yesterday, was it? Snowstorm, injured man. Total confusion." He was back, easing his tall lean frame into the chair beside me. "Say, did you *see* me at all when you arrived?"

"Just barely."

He reached for the sugar. "Thought so. You looked really done in. That was quite a walk you had," he said, and his look held admiration.

Mr. Grantland had black hair, carefully groomed, fine white even teeth, friendly brown eyes set wide apart. They were looking me over carefully, missing—I guessed—not much. And there was something about his nose—it looked a little different. I was to learn later that it had been broken by a baseball.

The girl was still there, eager brown eyes on me. Ruby Mae was a buxom teen-age girl whose abundant red hair looked as if it had not been combed in a long while. I learned later that her stepfather had ordered her out of the cabin in a fit of anger. Since she had had nowhere else to go, the mission had taken her in.

Mr. Grantland's five minutes stretched to ten. Then he left, saying that he and his helpers had another load of school desks and benches to pick up from the abandoned schoolhouse and that he would see me later on, after my visit with Miss Henderson.

Already I could see that though the mission house was a palace compared to the Spencer cabin, it was still primitive. There was no electricity, no telephone, no plumbing. The house was a white frame three-story building with a screened porch on each side. Directly behind it loomed a mountain (I did not know the name of it yet), its base within a few feet of the back door. The house itself had been built on the top of the rising ground at the rear of a very large yard fenced across the front. This, together with the church-schoolhouse, a lattice-covered spring-house, a double outhouse (a very drafty outhouse indeed in this January weather), Mr. Grantland's bunkhouse, and Miss Henderson's cabin, comprised the mission buildings.

AT MY KNOCK, the door of Miss Alice Henderson's cabin swung open and I was looking into her face. My immediate impression was of a woman of slightly above average height with clear, beautifully cut features. She started to greet me, but her sentence stopped midway. As she stared into my face, an odd look leapt into her eyes. For a flick of an instant she stood motionless, her hand still on the doorknob. Almost immediately she realized that she was leaving me standing in the cold. "I'm so sorry—" Whatever it was all about, it had left her flustered. "Forgive me. Do, please come in."

I was as surprised at the room before me as Miss Henderson had been by something about me. There was warmth and color and shine here: firelight gleaming on polished brass and the gray satin of pewter; firelight reflected on the well-scrubbed and waxed puncheon floor; the turkey reds and cobalt blues of what looked to be hand-loomed materials set off by old pine and cherry furniture. A bank of windows all across the back of the room let the outdoors in, with the winter landscape and the towering peaks like a gigantic mural.

So this was Miss Henderson's cabin! I had not realized how homesick I was until I felt relief pouring through me. Then there was some beauty and order in the Cove; it was not all plainness and squalor. Close on this reaction came the thought that only an extraordinary person could have created this room. And that person was standing beside me. I could get to know her.

"Come sit down, child." There was a trace of amusement in the voice. "First, let me hang up your coat. Here, come over by the fire. Down to ten above zero this morning. Does my cabin surprise you?"

"I'm sorry. I didn't mean to stare. After that nightmare scene yesterday, I wasn't sure that I—belonged here. But this is so beautiful that I want to hug it—if you could hug a room. It's like—well, like coming home."

"That's the nicest compliment my cabin's ever had. Here, sit in the red wing chair. One of the few pieces I brought from Ardmore." Miss Henderson sat down opposite me, still a puzzled crease between her eyes as she regarded me.

I noticed that she was wearing a straight blue woolen skirt and an immaculate white linen shirtwaist. To the waist was pinned a handsome brooch-watch with what looked like a family crest at the top, set with rubies and pearls. Mr. Pentland had said, "braided hair wound round and round her head like a crown." He was right. There was something queenlike about her. The hair had once been quite blond, but now was sprinkled with gray. But by far Miss Henderson's most unusual feature was her eyes—fathomless deep gray in which there were traces of fatigue.

"Miss Henderson, how is Mr. Allen?"

"About seven this morning he opened his eyes, spoke to us, asked about his ailing hound-dog. I think he's going to be all right."

I felt a great rush of affection toward Miss Henderson at this news. But then her first question seemed to open a gulf between us. "Now—tell me, Miss Huddleston, why did you come to Cutter Gap?"

I watched one hand smoothing out a crease in her skirt. Surely she must be joking, I thought. But one look at her face told me that she was not. "Naturally, I thought Dr. Ferrand would have told you," I answered. "I came to teach school, of course."

"Dr. Ferrand is a great man," she answered calmly. "Only not too practical sometimes, no judge of the female. He sees in any girl or woman just what he wants to see. You'd be surprised at how little he told me about you. Anyway, what's your version? Why *are* you here?"

I found myself resisting the way the question was put. With a feeling of covering unnecessary ground, I told Miss Henderson about having heard Dr. Ferrand at Montreat present his case for the mountain people, about his pleading not so much for money as for volunteers, for the investment of lives. And about how I had been so moved that I had immediately volunteered.

"Looking back," she asked me, "do you think you were carried away by the emotion of the moment?"

"Somewhat, perhaps." Though I did not understand why, now that I was here and Miss Henderson was probing my motives, I wanted to be honest with her. "Most girls my age can get carried away by an emotional appeal, I suppose."

"And Dr. Ferrand *is* eloquent," Miss Henderson smiled.

A *smiley woman*, Mr. Pentland had called her. *All her lines are smile lines.* "But I've had plenty of time to think it over between Montreat and now," I told her. "Over four months. If I had wanted to back out, I could have."

"Why didn't you? I would be interested in knowing."

"Because Dr. Ferrand made it sound as if you're desperate for teachers. I've had a year and a semester of Junior College, enough to start teaching. Then— I'd like my life to count for something. You know, more than just staying home in Asheville, getting married, having babies."

The gray eyes were measuring me. Did I read cynicism in them? No, not that. But a down-to-earth quality that I was not accustomed to in people in religious work, too much realism for comfort.

A silence more eloquent than any chatter filled the room. It had a quality about it that was new to me, different from the usual embarrassing lapses of conversation in society. The silence was certainly not for lack of something to say, nor from ill-humor or preoccupation. Miss Henderson was a Quaker, I remembered. Was this a Quaker silence?

And in that creative and listening stillness, my mind went back to my life in Asheville. *Teas and receptions and ladies' genteel talk. Church on Sunday mornings. Shopping and dress fittings. Dance-parties and picnics in the summer. A good enough life, only what did it all mean? Where was it leading? There must be more to life than that. Or is there—for a woman?*

What was I born for, after all? I have to know. If I stayed at home going the round of the same parties, I don't think I ever would know. Mother and father didn't understand my eagerness, why I had wanted to come before I'd graduated. But I couldn't wait forever. . . .

Then as if there had been no pause at all, Miss Henderson broke into my thoughts to ask gently, "So it seemed to you that teaching school here was the next step in making your life count?"

"Well, yes. I mean I didn't get any other ideas of anything I could do." *Does she mean to back me into a corner like this? She was the one who sent Mr. Allen to meet me in El Pano. Because of his accident, could she somehow resent me? No. Surely not!* "But it isn't just for me," I added hastily. "It's also for the children I'll be teaching." This sounded lame, not impressive even to me—as if I had wanted to leave home, and since the Cutter Gap job was the only escape route in sight, I had grabbed that.

Miss Henderson made no comment, but I felt certain that the same thought was in her mind. Inside I was squirming under the level gaze from those gray eyes. Yet there was no malice in them, just a calm weighing and measuring and bringing me back, back, and then back again to simple basics. I longed to tell her about that feeling I'd had of some special mission to perform. *But I can't lay my fingers on what the mission is yet. So how can I talk about it? Maybe the feeling comes from reading too much poetry—or just because I'm young. But I don't think so.*

I want my life to be full. I want to laugh—and love. Help others to the limit of my ability too. Those were the hopes that sent me on this wild fling into the mountains, weren't they? Yes, surely that was it. But I said none of this to Alice Henderson.

Then as abruptly as she had embarked on this series of uncomfortable questions. Miss Henderson changed the subject. This was disconcerting too because it was obvious that she had by no means finished with the matter of my motives in coming to Cutter Gap.

"You'll need some facts about your new job," she said brightly. "School opens on Monday next. Perhaps you'd like to know more about the people you'll be working with, the mountain people too. Oh, by the way, they dislike being called 'mountaineers.' Better to say 'mountain people' or 'highlanders.' Also those at the mission call me 'Miss Alice'"—

"With your coming, that gives us an official staff of three—David Grantland, you, and me, with Dr. Ferrand in over-all charge. David was appointed by Dr. Ferrand about four months ago with his special task to oversee

68

building the church-schoolhouse. David just graduated from seminary. He's a Pennsylvanian like me. Dr. Ferrand was traveling in the East and made a speech at his seminary."

"And Mr. Grantland volunteered? Sort of like I did?"

"Well, it was a little different. It seems that the Seminary's Committee on Social Concerns was trying to place graduates or graduate students in various sections of the country to find out where the biggest needs are. A pilot project, they call it. So David agreed to come here."

"I see ..." I felt deflated. A pilot project sounded so much more official, so much more important than my vague yearning to do "something." "How long have *you* been here, Miss Alice?"

"I first came to the Great Smokies nine years ago. Almost ten now. My first school was at Big Lick Springs. That's Sullivan County; the nearest railroad point is Fairview Flats.

"Then two years after that, Cataleechie School got started. Wild scenery there, deep gorges. It's very isolated. John Holcombe was over there on a hunting trip. He happened on the school one day and we met. Later, he and the Spencers joined in pleading with me to come and give their children a better school. Once I'd seen Cutter Gap, I loved it. I felt this was my spot."

"But how did you and Dr. Ferrand get together?"

She laughed gaily. "Oh, he came riding into my life one autumn day, not on a white charger but on a mule. I'll never forget the picture he made: a man of almost seventy, heavy mustache, cropped sideburns, precisely clipped goatee. And his French ancestry showed. Those large black eyes and the hands that never stayed still when he talked.

"An individualist, if ever I saw one. On top of all his medical training, he'd had a full theological course. Several years before, he'd established single-handed what he called the American Inland Mission. His passion was—and still is—to start schools, churches, and orphanages in the remotest sections of the Blue Ridge, the Alleghenies, the Great Smokies, places where no one else will go.

"His visit that autumn came at an opportune time. I'd begun to realize that I couldn't carry on the work of three schools by myself and keep making trips to the outside world for financial support.

"Dr. Ferrand was a gift from heaven to help us with

this work," Miss Alice went on. "So when I asked him, he finally agreed to take us under his wing." She paused and that wonderful smile lighted her face. "Of course, the wing is broad. We don't see much of him. Not nearly as much as we'd like to."

"Then you built your cabin after that?"

"Yes. I had several reasons for putting up this place of my own. I wanted this to be a kind of demonstration cabin to show the people how to use native materials and their old crafts to create beauty."

"What a wonderful idea! You've succeeded too."

"Look, let me show you—" She rose to point out some of the stones in the chimney facing. "See that glistening mica in the rocks? And look, here are imbedded garnets— and rose quartz. Sometimes we even find sapphires."

She spoke knowingly of hewing and notching logs and of riving boards for shingles, of the ways she had adapted the "but-and-ben" of some of the people's Scottish ancestors for the plan of her cabin—that was, one section of the house abutted on another section.

"At only one thing did my mountain helpers balk like stubborn mules," she told me. She gestured toward the bank of windows across the room. The morning sun was streaming in, laying patterns of light across the large oval braided rug. "So many windows were unheard of in these parts, I had to fight for my sunlight and my vista."

She laughed. "I fought all right. You see, I wanted a quiet spot with a particular atmosphere, a sanctuary for me and for other people, where they could talk out some of their problems when they want to.

"And believe me, there's plenty for them to talk out. You see, the religious background of the mountain people is mostly the strict Calvinism of their Scotch-Irish forefathers. It has merits. Breeds steel in folks. Better than a wishy-washy religion that really has no convictions at all. But it's bequeathed to these people a lot of heart scalds. You'll see for yourself. Their Christianity is one of fear, of taboos—you can't do this and you mustn't do that. If you do, you'll go to hell. You know the sort of thing."

"I hate a religion of fears," I said with feeling.

"I do too, and my parents before me. My father was a strict member of the Society of Friends up in Ardmore, Pennsylvania. But he had one favorite saying that sounds anything but strict. I grew up on it." Here Miss Alice's eyes took on a soft remembering look. "He was a tall man, stood so straight, but there were curves of fun around his mouth. 'Before God,' he would often say to me, 'I've just one duty as a father. That is to see that thee has a happy childhood tucked under thy jacket.'"

"I like that. And—did you have a happy childhood?"

"The happiest imaginable. And you see, father was wise. He knew that I couldn't have an earthly father who would provide joy all my days, and then be able to conceive of God as a stern judge wanting to take all my fun from me." Miss Henderson sighed. "One of our tasks here is to show folks a God who wants to give them joy. How they need joy! They have such hard lives ..." Her voice trailed off.

"I'm afraid the hardness is all I've seen so far," I told her.

She nodded understandingly. "At first I couldn't see anything but the dirt and the poverty either. That's what you're really referring to. But then as I rode through the mountains during my first few months here, getting acquainted with the people, flashes of something else began to come through. It was like looking through a peephole in the wall that closes on the past, catching delightful glimpses of earlier ways."

I nodded, fascinated by what she was saying because I, too, had experienced that sensation of walking backward into time, only it had seemed repulsive rather than fascinating. Before this, I had always thought of the American frontier as romantic. Now I was not too sure.

"The glimpses multiplied," she continued, "like that day I came upon a mountain girl playing a dulcimer. Do you know what that is?"

"No, I don't."

"I'll show you one one of these days. It has from two to eight strings—usually three—and is strummed with a goose quill. It must be a crude copy of some very old instrument. Well, anyway in a sweet thin voice this girl sang one English and Scottish ballad after another. Once I began to notice I heard the old ballads everywhere. Strange how music and poetry can preserve the feel of another way of life. Sitting on a cabin porch, I'd see an English manor house with clipped lawns and lords and ladies strolling arm in arm.

"Then my ears began catching seventeenth-century words—a lot of them straight out of Shakespeare and Spenser. When the women talked about Bone-Set as a

71

cough remedy, Mare's milk for whooping cough, or Sweet William for a tonic, through my imaginary peephole I could see a thatched-roof cottage set in an English herb garden. So that's how I began to visualize something beyond the dirt and the poverty. You see, they do have a fine heritage, but they need to be reminded of it over and over."

I remembered Mrs. Tatum saying that Miss Alice was the only person who had been able to help these proud mountain people. Suddenly I saw why they had accepted Miss Alice's help. She had uncovered a legitimate source of their pride—the strengths of a fine heritage—and used it, built on it.

But a doubt crept in. Even the proudest background can become degenerate or lost in a poor environment. What I had seen so far made me think that was exactly what had happened.

"My dear, you're sitting there wondering if through wishful thinking and a good imagination I'm not reading into these people a lineage that actually died several generations ago."

I grinned at her, startled. "Well, yes—I don't know how you knew—" This was my first experience with what I would come to know later as a characteristic of Miss Alice's: A perception of other people so acute that it not only caught reactions but came close to reading minds.

"So your real question is, what solid values are left today out of any good inheritance? Well, just as soon as you begin teaching, you'll find one—sharp minds, good brains—only they haven't had much of a chance.

"There's exceptional awareness too, basically a spiritual quality, I suppose. It could be used to create and appreciate beauty—in things, in lives. Instead, a lot of the sensitivity is used now for smallness; getting their feelings hurt easily, that sort of thing. But put the fine minds and the sensitivity together, and you have gigantic hungers of mind and spirit.

"Then something else they inherited from those ancestors of theirs—those people with their proud self-reliance and intense love of liberty—and that's an iron will. But this will that could result in major achievements is now used mainly to keep feuds alive."

"You mean real shooting feuds?"

"Real shooting and killing feuds." For the first time Miss Alice's face was grim. "We've had a lot of violence.

Probably only two sections of the country are worse—the Cosby, Tennessee area and Breathitt County, Kentucky."

I absorbed this information in silence, thinking how quickly my father would jerk me home if he knew this. "What do you and Mr. Grantland do about feuding?" I asked finally.

"That's another story. The first thing I did was buy a gun and learn to shoot."

"You did! I thought the Quakers—"

"Believe in non-violence. Of course. You're right. I've had my dear ancestors spinning in their graves ever since. Now that I've seen violence close up, I believe in non-violence more than ever. But I had to meet these men on their own ground. So now I'm a better shot than a lot of them, and they all know it and respect it. It's given me a base for talking straight to them that I wouldn't have had otherwise. I tell them, 'I like your fierce pride and your loyalty to your family. That's why I long to keep you from doing anything that will shame your sons and your sons' sons.'"

The room was very quiet. There was only the creak of the snow-laden branches outside and the gurgling of the stream under its ice coating behind the house. The words just spoken had marched proudly out of the Quaker lady's mouth, and now stood straight and tall in the quiet room. Even when the feuding mountain men were not altogether sure what such words meant, the hearing of them must make them feel good, I thought, cleaner somehow, as if they were hearing a bugle call in the clear cold mountain air.

With a shock I realized that two hours had passed. Mr. Grantland had promised to show me the Cove in the immediate vicinity of the mission house and to talk over some teaching plans with me.

As I rose to go, Miss Alice held out her hand to me. "Christy Huddleston, I think thee will do." Something about the warmth in the timbre of her voice as she slipped back into her Quaker speech brought quick tears to my eyes. Did she mean that I was accepted?

73

Six

LOOKING BACK I can see that the young walk unabashedly into many a situation which the more experienced would avoid at all costs. Not that I was cocky or overconfident that first day of school. The truth was that I was trying hard to settle the butterflies in my stomach so that Mr. Grantland would think me an experienced teacher.

He was only seven years older than I, but somehow he seemed a thousand years older in experience and self-assurance. I thought of the Tuesday before when he had sat astride the rafters of the unfinished schoolhouse, driving in roofing nails with powerful blows, shouting down orders from time to time to the men helping him. Later I had watched in admiration his quick orderly decisions as he had supervised the placing of the secondhand benches and battered school desks and the installing of the potbellied stove.

It was no small project, this building of the combination school-church. Mr. Grantland had been struggling all through the autumn to erect the building and to provide a usable road from the mission to the railroad flagstop at Fairview Flats. He had only volunteers for helpers. Sometimes those who had promised to come appeared for work, more often they did not. That was why progress had been so slow. Now that school was opening, the building of the bell-tower could proceed only on Saturdays and school holidays, so it would go more slowly still.

For this first day of school he had put away his working clothes and was dressed in a tweed suit with a white shirt and bow tie. His only concession to the snow was heavy boots laced almost to his knees. The boots were in ludicrous contrast to the dainty heels and pointed toes of my kid and patent leather shoes picking their way along the nicely cleaned boardwalk with David Grantland keeping pace beside me in the deep snow.

"Is this a fashion parade on Fifth Avenue?" His voice was teasing. "Those are silly, silly shoes. Ice-pick toes."

"I know."

"Hold on! Steady!" he exclaimed as I slipped and his arm reached out to support me. I could feel the warmth of his hand even through my coat. I wondered if my hair still looked all right and if he liked the way I wore it.

The yard was swarming with children waiting for the first glimpse of their new teacher. Most were flaxen-haired, skinny, too pale, none dressed warmly enough for January. Some were climbing over the piles of lumber and rocks in the yard, some running in and out of the building, their high-pitched voices ringing in the clear air. What if I could not handle such lively pupils?

"These children are really excited," Mr. Grantland said. "There's John Holcombe. Must have come early to get the fire started. You'd be surprised what a big event the opening of this school is in these people's lives."

Seeing us coming, the children had stopped whatever they were doing to stare at me. As we got closer, I saw with a shock that many of them were barefooted. I knew that some had had to walk several miles in the snow. Suddenly I was painfully self-conscious about my foolish shoes. Their bare feet made me want to tuck my own feet out of sight to hide the tokens of my vanity. What a lot I had to learn!

At that moment a little boy detached himself from the silent starers and came running up to us. He had carrot-red hair with a cowlick and blue, blue eyes. There was a shy eagerness about him. "Teacher, I've come to see you and to swap howdys. I memorized your name. It's shore a funny name. I never heerd a name like it afore."

"Miss Huddleston," Mr. Grantland said solemnly, "this is Little Burl Allen, one of Bob Allen's sons."

So this was one of the children who would have been fatherless if Dr. MacNeill had not operated. All over again I felt grateful for the last good news I had heard about Mr. Allen. I reached down for the little hand. It was cold. "I'm delighted to swap howdys with you, Little Burl." The gentian blue eyes were looking me over carefully, taking in every detail. He was so little—and those icy feet! I longed to pick him up and get him warm.

As Mr. Grantland and I were climbing the steps to the

75

school, I whispered, "At least we could do something about their bare feet. It's shameful. Why hasn't the mission *done* something about it?"

Mr. Grantland stood looking down at me, his brown eyes crinkling at the corners, a smile tugging at his mouth. "I know it's a shock. Was to me too at first. But up in these mountains the youngsters have gone barefooted all their lives—summer or winter. And they're as healthy as pigs."

The school room smelled of varnish and wood smoke and wet wool and cedar pencils and chalk. Already there were puddles of water on the floor from the melted snow the children were tracking in. Most of them filed up to the teacher's desk and stood gazing at me. Many of the girls looked too shy to say anything, but there was whispering among the boys. I overheard snatches . . .

"Got uncommon pretty eyes, ain't she?"

"Ah, ye always git stuck on Teacher."

"No such thing!"

"Full of ginger. Reckon she'll have us a-studyin' fit for a dog?"

"Naw! She's too little to tan any britches."

It was a full fifteen minutes before Mr. Grantland could drag the children away from my desk and get them quiet. He had another problem too: getting some older boys inside who were loitering in the yard. To my surprise, the girls had seated themselves on one side of the room, the boys on the other. I did not know at the time that this was a centuries-old tradition, even followed by the adults in church on Sunday. Mr. Holcombe hung around, ostensibly feeding wood to the fire, not wanting to miss a thing.

I stood beside the battered teacher's desk on its raised dais and surveyed the situation. Several of the pupils seemed to be older than I—including the three boys who had been the last ones to enter the schoolroom. Yet there were some tiny ones, surely not more than five years old. Such an odd assortment of garments they wore—coats several sizes too big, with sleeves turned up. Many of the youngsters looked sleepy, many had faces too old and sober, almost like the faces of tired old men and women. There were several cross-eyed children and some whose eyes were quite bloodshot. I recognized four of the Spencer children and nodded to them—John, Zady, wasn't it? Clare, and Lulu—the ones with whom I had shared Mrs. Tatum's food on my way into the Cove. John was wearing a sweater with carefully button-stitched holes where the elbows had once been.

Now Mr. Grantland was introducing me. He was telling them that my home was in Asheville and that Dr. Ferrand had persuaded me to come to Cutter Gap. As he spoke, I was trying to estimate the number of children in the room. I counted the number of desks in each row—nine; number of rows—eight. Seventy-two, with five desks empty. How preposterous! How could one teacher handle sixty-seven squirming children? How different the reality was from the way it had sounded in front of Miss Alice's fire during our first staff conference with her. At that time, she had asked Mr. Grantland to take over the Bible, arithmetic and mathematics classes; I was to handle the rest. Then Miss Alice had helped me plan a daily schedule. On paper the plan had looked so logical. Now I was not sure.

The introduction over, I moved in front of the desk. "Thank you. I—I'm glad to be here. I know that both you, Mr. Grantland, and you, Mr. Holcombe, have all sorts of things to do, so we won't ask you to stay." I could not bear the thought of these men watching my first fumbling attempt at teaching, so I gave them a bright, confident smile, hoping that they would take the hint.

A titter began at the front of the room and swept backward. What had I said that was so funny?

I saw amusement in Mr. Grantland's eyes. Did that mean I had bungled something already? Suddenly I knew how much I wanted his approval.

He asked softly, "Sure you don't want me to stay?" The look in his eyes suggested that I would be wise to let him. For a moment I wavered, especially when I noticed how closely he had been watching some big boys at the back of the room.

"Lundy Taylor," he commented in a low voice, indicating a boy as swarthy-complexioned and as large as a grown man. I saw that the face above the red pimply neck could have used a shave and looked sullen and insolent, with a vacant expression. "He's never been to school before with Allen children."

I did not know what he meant, but I did know that these big children, even bigger than I, were my problem. Miss Alice had explained that in the mountains where women were still not accepted as equal, it was important that I grapple with the situation by myself and win recog-

77

nition on this first day as "Teacher." That was why she thought it best to stay away. So I tried to put finality into my voice as I said, "Thank you, gentlemen. Thanks so much."

Mr. Grantland was reluctant but without another word, nodded and left. As Mr. Holcombe grabbed his old black felt hat and slowly turned to go, he advised, "Miss, let John thar or my Sam Houston help you stoke the stove." Then he too disappeared.

I took a deep breath. So now we were on our own. All at once the children seemed like giants. I leaned against the edge of the desk for support. A little boy in the front row whispered behind his hand, "She's narvious."

"How can y' tell?" another voice whispered.

"Look at her shakin'."

He was right. My legs were trembling violently. Suddenly I could appreciate Miss Henderson's comment about the school prayer. It seemed that Tennessee law required that each school day begin with a reading of at least ten verses of Scripture and then a prayer. When I had confided to Miss Henderson that I was not sure I could pray before a roomful of children, she had replied crisply, "You'll need all the prayers you can get."

The evening before I had decided that for the Scripture I would read the 24th Psalm. I opened my Bible and in a voice as firm as I could make it, read:

> "The earth is the Lord's, and the fullness thereof;
> the world, and they that dwell therein.
> For he hath founded it upon the seas,
> and established it upon the floods.
> Who shall ascend into the hill of the Lord?
> or who shall stand in his holy place?
> He that hath clean hands, and a pure heart. . . ."

The laughing started again, this time even more openly. I could not understand. Was it the "clean hands" that the pupils thought so funny?

The giggling did not make the prayer any easier, but I held up one hand to try to quiet things down and plunged in: "We thank Thee for those who cared enough to fix up this beautiful new school for us. Help us to appreciate the chance we have here to learn. Be with us as we begin our school. Amen."

"And now we'll have a singing period," I announced. "Let's start off with 'America.' "

"Don't recollect that 'un," a small voice in the front row retorted.

"Don't know 'America'! You're teasing me! You know, the one that goes—" Though I was still a little trembly, I cleared my throat and began

"My coun-try 'tis of thee,
Sweet land of lib-er-ty,
Of thee I sing—"

Several of the children were shaking their heads. "No ma'am, we're not throwin' off on you" . . . "No, Teacher, jest never learnt hit."

It scarcely seemed possible that any American school-child anywhere would not know "America," but I decided that this was no time to make an issue of it. "Well then, 'America the Beautiful' That's a good one."

Once again heads wagged. "Vow and declare, Teacher, never heerd tell of it" . . . "Guess, Teacher, you'd better rassle up a song we can handle."

"Then you tell me the songs you do know," I said in desperation.

A small forest of hands shot into the air. Since I did not yet know names, I had to point to call on each child. "All right, your song?"

" 'When the Roll Is Called up Yonder,' " an older girl answered.

"A boy now. What's yours?"

" 'Froggie Went A-Courtin' "—from a little fellow.

"And your song?" I pointed to a larger boy.

" 'Oh, for a Faith That Will Not Shrink,' " he said proudly.

I thought this was rapidly turning into the most incongruous list I'd ever heard. Fingers were wiggling violently to my left. "Yes?"

" 'Marching Through Georgia.' Could we commence with that 'un?"

"We'll see. All right, one more?"

" 'Sourwood Mountain.' "

"Yes, yes," a chorus went up. "Let's settle on that." "Yes, Teacher, that 'un first. That's the sweepingest song."

Someone in the room went "Fa-sol-la" to give the pitch and they were off, the singing quite out of my hands:

"I've got a gal in the Sourwood Moun-tain
She's so good and kind,
She's broke the heart of many a poor fellow,
But she's never broke this-un of mine."

Brown feet tapped softly, fingers drummed on desks, heads wagged to the rhythm. Some of the boys and girls even sang parts. I could see that these mountain children had music in them. They sang more unself-consciously than they talked, and with more emotion, charm and skill than I had ever heard in impromptu singing:

"I've got a gal in the Buffalo Hollow,
Hey-tank-toddle all the day,
Oh, she won't come and I won't follow,
And a hey-tank-toddle all the day."

The children smiled at me, first shyly and then broadly, and I found myself smiling back at them and getting caught up in the fun of the mountain song.

After all the songs had been sung, innumerable verses of each one, I was thinking reluctantly that my next task was to get an attendance roll on paper, the children's names and some information about how much schooling they had had. Last year some of the children had gone to the Low Gap School (the one from which Mr. Grantland had gotten the desks) but there the school year had been only four months, and no attendance roll or grade books had been kept to hand over to the new school. Apparently this was because the teacher had been almost as ignorant as the pupils. There were many stories about teachers in these mountains, like some of whom Miss Alice had told me: one man who had stubbornly refused to believe or to teach that the earth was round; another who had used just one sentence written on the blackboard—"Where will you spend eternity?"—to teach both reading and spelling; a woman who had taught that the stars and the stripes on the American flag were God's pledge that the earth would never be destroyed by another flood.

I beckoned to Ruby Mae and she came obediently up to the desk. "Could you and two other girls help me take a roll?"

"Well'm, guess so. What's 'take a roll'?"

"Write down the pupils' names, ages, addresses—so on. I'll tell you what to do. Ruby Mae, who's that tall brunette girl there? In the second row, third from the front? Brown eyes?"

"Oh, you mean with the dark hair? That thar's Lizette Holcombe."

"She'll do fine. Now one more. The blonde girl? Red bow in her hair?"

"That's my best friend, Bessie Coburn."

"Well, would you get them up here? This is a special job, an important one."

Ruby Mae was puffed with pride already as she went back to enlist the two girls. "We want to write down the full name of each pupil," I explained, handing each of them a ruled tablet and a pencil. "Age ... beneath that, parents' names ... grade the child attended at the Low Gap School ... home address."

The one named Bessie shook her head. "I vow and declare, Teacher—that home address now—much obleeged if you'll tell us what ye're a-meanin' by that 'home address'?"

"Where they live. For reports and notices and so on," I explained patiently. "We have to know that."

"Jest can't mortally—" Ruby Mae looked as puzzled as the others.

"Tell you what. Let's each take a row. You watch me with the first name and then you'll understand perfectly."

All of the pupils in my row were boys. The first one looked to be about a second-grader, flaxen-haired, with eyes that looked at me directly as he spoke and the firmest mouth I had ever seen on a youngster. My notebook was ready. "Now—your name?"

"Front name or back name?"

"Well—er—both."

"Front name be Sam Houston."

Long pause.

"A fine name," I prodded. "A Tennessee hero. He picked up where Davy Crockett left off, didn't he? Was Sam Houston an ancestor of yours?"

"No'm, no blood kin."

"Well now, your—what did you call it—back name?"

"Holcombe."

"Oh, yes. Of course, now I remember. That was your

father who helped us this morning. Now, what's his full name?"

"He be John Swanson Holcombe."

"And your mother's name?"

"She's just Mama."

"But she has a name. What's her name?"

"Wimmin folks call her 'Lizzie.'"

"But her *real* name?" I persisted.

The small brow wrinkled. "Let me study on hit now. Oh, shorely. Now I know. Elizabeth Teague Holcombe," he intoned triumphantly.

I glanced over at my helpers standing at the head of their rows watching me. Their faces wore a quizzical expression that seemed to say. "Uh-huh, you see, not quite as easy as you thought."

But Sam Houston Holcombe and I pushed resolutely on into the wilderness of facts. He was nine years old. He had never before been to school. There were five other children in the family. His "Paw and Mama were all-fired tickled pink 'bout this scholl a-startin'."

"Last question, Sam—"

"Generally go by Sam Houston, Teacher."

"Of *course*. I beg your pardon— And now your address? Tell me where you live."

"Wal—" That puzzled look on the small face again. "First ye cross Cutter Branch. Then ye cut acrost Lonesome Pine Ridge and down. Through the Gap's the best way. At the third fork in the trail, ye scoot under the fence and head for Pigeonroost Hollow. Then ye spy our cabin and pull into our place, 'bout two mile or so from the Spencers."

Acutely conscious of the three girls watching me, I scribbled something that made no sense even to me except that the Spencers seemed to be the nearest neighbors to the Holcombes. Obviously I was going to have to devise some new system in a hurry for addresses in Cutter Gap.

I nodded to my three helpers and they started down their rows as I went on with mine. My second boy had pathetically crossed eyes. "Your name?"

"Orter."

"Full name, Orter?"

"Name's Orter Ball O'Teale."

"Age?"

"Eleven year old a-goin' on twelve."

His address turned out to be easier because his family lived just down the road from the mission house.

Although this was turning out to be a somewhat unconventional roll, it was valuable to me because the children volunteered all sorts of information on the side. John Spencer, fifteen, had a battered plane geometry book on his desk.

"Teacher, I worked these figgers—"

"You mean you've done the problems?"

"Yes'm."

"All of them? All the way through the book?"

"Yes'm, mighty near. Could you get me a harder book?"

"I'll surely try. May have to send to Asheville for it."

"I'll thank you kindly for that."

"John, have you always been so good at math?"

"Yes'm. Plumb crazy about workin' figgers. Not a solitary thing I like better."

"Well, that's *great*," I said looking at him with new interest.

"Don't aim to take no big-head 'bout it with the other young'uns though," he added quickly.

That brought me to a boy who said that his name was Zacharias Jehoshaphat Holt—to snickers all around him. The boy immediately behind him said softly, "Plumb crazy. Ain't yer name a-tall."

"This isn't the time for fooling," I said. "We're trying to get the roll down. Now tell me your real name."

"Zacharias Jehoshaphat—" With that his right ear jerked violently.

Now the children laughed uproariously, some of them doubled over—all but the boy who had spoken up. He kept a straight face as he volunteered, "Teacher, that's not his name. He be a-packin' lies. You can tell. Jest look at his ear."

Sure enough, Zacharias' ear jerked again. "Certainly, I see his ear," I said. "But what's that got to do with not telling the truth?"

"Oh ma'am! All them Holts when they tell a whopper, their ears twitch—"

I ignored this and turned again to the boy in front. "Tell me your name," I tried again.

"Zacharias—" He snickered—and swallowed. "Jehoshaphat—"

Once again, the ear wiggled. But now I saw it—a string

over the ear. Slightly unnerved, I reached over to remove the cord. But the boy in back jerked it away from me and stuffed the string in his desk. Incensed, I marched to the desk and reached in, only to have my fingers meet a mass of wriggling fur. As I squealed and stepped backwards, a small animal as frightened as I clambered onto the desk screeching in protest. A ring-tailed raccoon sat there looking at me from behind his funny mask of a face, one end of the cord held fast in his mouth. Then he took one paw (so like a small hand) and delicately extracted the string from his teeth and began trilling and scolding at me, as if he were the teacher and I the naughty pupil.

Naturally my schoolroom was by this time a bedlam, the girls giggling, the boys holding their middles and laughing so hard that one of them got the hiccoughs. But the boy on whose desk the coon sat held a straight face. He seemed a reincarnation of what Tom Sawyer should have looked like: overalls ... bare feet ... tousled hair ... lots of freckles ... two front teeth missing. It was his too-straight face that tipped me off. He had masterminded the whole thing, I suspected.

"Now—let's begin all over," I said to the boy in front. I was trying hard to be patient, but who ever heard of this much trouble just getting a few names on paper!

"Creed thar put me up to it," the small thumb jerked toward the Tom Sawyer character behind him. "Said if'n I'd do hit, he'd let me sleep his coon for one night." Meanwhile the boy in back was whistling softly.

"I see." I could wait no longer for identification of the whistler. "What's your name? Creed *what?*"

"Creed Josiah Allen," he smirked.

"This is your raccoon, Creed?"

"Yes'm. Pet coon, 'Scalawag.' "

"Might be a good name for you too. You're a scalawag. Now stop whistling and—"

"Jest whistlin' a catch—"

"Never mind that. *Cut it out,*" I said severely, "and we'll talk about you and the matter of a pet in school in a minute." Then I returned to the boy in front.

"Name?" I asked for the fourth time.

"Front name be Zacharias. Fer a fact, Teacher. Ye can jest call me Zach. That 'Jehoshaphat' now. That was made up. Back name be Holt. Six of us Holts in school."

I learned that Rebecca and Ozias Holt had eight children, four of them boys. The oldest, Wraight, was seventeen. He had been one of the pupils Mr. Grantland had been watching, the one with the cunning look. The Holt cabin was somewhere southeast of the mission on the slopes of Runyon Rowe Mountain. The directions for getting there took an entire paragraph.

That brought me back to Creed whose eyes glittered with—was it intelligence or mischief? Perhaps both. Quickly I decided that I'd better try to make friends this first morning. "How old is Scalawag, Creed?"

"Got him from a kit last summer."

"What's a kit?"

"Like a nest. Where other young'uns are. He's most grown now. Sleeps with me." Then seeing the expression on my face, he added defensively, "Oh, he be clean. Coons wash every natural blessed thing afore they eat hit."

"I've heard that."

"Coons are the main best pets in the world," he confided. "If ye'd like one fer yerself, Teacher, come spring, maybe we'uns could spy out a kit and git one for ye."

"Uh—thanks, Creed. Thanks so much. It's very nice of you. Well, tell you what, let me think about that offer. Now—about Scalawag and school—"

"Oh, Scalawag won't cause no trouble. Cross my heart and hope to die."

What could I say without caving in this friendship before it got started? Suddenly I had an inspiration. "It's like this, Creed," I lowered my voice. "This is just between you and me. Promise you won't tell."

"Cross my heart." His face was rapt.

"Scalawag is such a 'specially fine coon—I can see that already—you know, so good-looking and such a little comic actor, that the children will want to watch him instead of doing their lessons."

"Land, no, Teacher." Creed's look said that this conversation was not going the way he had hoped and that he was ready to do battle for his pet. "We'll study on, study on, better'n ever."

I leaned even closer. "Let's make a pact. You leave Scalawag home after this, then I'll let you bring him to the last social, the big recitation just before school closes. We'll fix it so that Scalawag will be part of the entertainment."

"Honest, Teacher!" His face was shining. "That be a sealed bargain, fair and square. Land o' livin'! Why then pretty nigh everybody in the Cove'll see Scalawag. Put it thar, Teacher!" He stuck out a grubby hand.

So, feeling rather proud of the way I'd handled that little crisis, I went on down the row: Joshua Ben Beck ... and one more O'Teale: Smith, age fifteen, and then two empty seats. The last note I had made for each boy was what school supplies and books he had. Only there was pathetically little to put down, no notebooks, little paper of any kind.

Obviously the matter of books and supplies was urgent, yet the parents of these pupils could contribute almost nothing. I was going to have to make an immediate survey of the schoolbooks available. The day before, David Grantland had carried over to the school all textbooks that the mission owned. There were so few it was scarcely believable! And these were tattered, with pages missing and torn, most with no covers.

Among the boys in my row, I had seen on desks one worn copy of *Red Riding Hood*, one Fowler's *Arithmetic*, a *Jack and the Beanstalk*, and a Smith's *Primary Grammar*. I thought of my father's library at home—books floor-to-ceiling on three sides of the room, many of them bound in calf, embossed and tooled in gold. How odd life is, I could not help thinking. Why are things so disproportionate? Why do some people have so much and others so little?

AS THE MORNING went on, I had a growing uneasiness about the big swarthy boy in the back row. Ruby Mae had put his name down as Lundy Taylor and his father as Bird's-Eye Taylor. Perhaps Mr. Grantland's covert watching of several of these boys had alarmed me unnecessarily, but I noticed that the Taylor boy was uncooperative, never joined in the singing, never took part in anything. Resentment of some sort smoldered in him. Already, he seemed to dislike me. I forced myself not to keep looking at him.

On the other hand, there were those children who were particularly bright and appealing—like Vella, the little sister of Zacharias (ear-twitching) Holt. The tiny girl with auburn pigtails was only five, straight brows over mahogany-colored eyes looked at me with a direct level gaze. Her nose was shaped into a little bump at the tip; below that, a pale rosebud of a mouth with almost no lower lip.

All morning long she stared at me with those so-brown eyes; ever so often she would yawn, the eyes big and round and never wavering during the yawn.

Then there was Little Burl. Twice during the morning he slipped up to my desk to reach out admiring grimy fingers and touch the embroidery on my shirtwaist. "Teacher, hit's a wondery sight to be-hold." On his second trip he entreated, "Teacher, when will ye set up and sup with us? Our house is over furrenist the crik, over the ridge and down. Ye can cut through the nigh way."

"Of course I'll come. Little Burl, how is your father?"

"Oh, Paw's head be mendin' fine now. Doc MacNeill shore fixed it good. If'n ye'll come and sup, I'll ask my Mama to make ye a Scripture cake." The blue, blue eyes were pleading.

"I'm so glad about your father. And I will come soon. That's a promise."

All morning I was conscious of the constant roar of the fire in the stove. Much too hot close to it, with the rest of the room always uncomfortably cold. There were the dripping noses, no handkerchiefs at all; the shining eager faces during the spelling bee; the lilt of the voices. What was it, I wondered, that gave the voices that musical quality, that rhythm? "Teacher, ever-who seen such pretty wearin'-clothes as yours!" ... "If happen you pass" ... "I wonder me if" ... "Tuesday, 'twas a week ago" ... "Teacher, be ye sorry at our meanness?" ... Where, I asked myself, do I begin to correct English? How can I unravel bad grammar from picturesque traditional idiom that it would be a shame to change ... "I hope, Teacher, it won't discomfit you bad" ... "Teacher, the day long you're makin' this a thronged day."

Next in that "thronged day" came noon recess, which the children called "the dinner spell." Even before they opened their dinner pails, some of the children organized a singing game. Their voices were high and sweet in the crisp cold air:

"Here come five dukes, a-rovin', a-rovin', a-rovin'
   Here come five dukes a-rovin', with a heigh a-ransomtee. . . .

We're quite as good as you sires, one of us, sires, one of us sires,

Pray will you have one of us sires, with a heigh a-
ransomtee. . . ."

The song sounded so British. "Dukes" and "sires" in these
isolated mountains!

After I had eaten the basket dinner that Miss Ida had
prepared for me, I stood in the doorway watching the
children. I was aware of a kaleidoscope of impressions:
the oak-split baskets or lard buckets with large soda biscuits, sometimes with a slice of pork between, more often
with sugar heavily sprinkled on the bread; cold roasted
sweet potatoes which the children peeled and ate like
bananas; corn bread, big hunks of it; an occasional apple.
Very few children had milk. Those who did not, went back
and forth to the cedar water bucket in the back of the room,
everyone drinking from the same gourd. I made a mental
note that I was going to have to put a stop to that. The
communal gourd would be a good way to start epidemics.
What we needed was a supply of those new paper cups just
on the market called "Health Kups." I had seen some of
them in Asheville. But if they were too expensive, perhaps I
could teach the children to make folding cups out of glossy
paper.

I left my post at the door and began a list on a scrap of
paper on my desk:

Solve matter of communal bucket. Health Kups?

Books: Write father. Are there books from our library which the children could use? Give him list of
possibilities such as:
>   *Treasure Island*
>   *The Scottish Chiefs*
>   *Little Women*
>   *Hans Brinker and the Silver Skates*
>   *Huckleberry Finn*
>   *A Tale of Two Cities*

Write our minister's wife in Asheville. Perhaps ladies'
societies would help us buy textbooks.

Write report to Dr. Ferrand of first day's school and
desperate need of books.

Think through need of warm clothes, especially shoes

for the children. Would church at home help there too?

Handkerchiefs? Perhaps a pile of clean rags each morning on my desk.

Saw suggestion of tobacco juice stains on outside of new building. Could any of the boys be chewing? Track this one down.

Problem: How to go about grading the school?

Problem: Is sex segregation good or bad? Think through.

And that other matter—the constant tittering and the giggling. I had not been able to stop it all day and it bothered me. Was it that the children were so excited over this first day of school and the new building with its shining windows of real glass and their new teacher who had been "brought on" and Creed's pet raccoon? Perhaps. Even so, the laughter in the wrong places at moments which were meant to be serious was making me increasingly self-conscious. What was I doing wrong?

The background hum of the high-pitched voices outside was shattered by a screech of pain and then violent crying. I ran out to find tiny Vella Holt crumpled up on the ground, sobbing, with the other children gathering in a circle around her.

"Has a pump knot on her head," a voice volunteered as I took the child in my arms.

The little girl did have a large bump. It was going to be a nasty bruise. What was worse, the blow had been dangerously close to the side of her temple.

"What happened?" I asked.

No one answered. I looked up. The circle of faces looked too grave for children's faces, too noncommittal. "Someone has to tell me," I persisted. "Did Vella fall down?"

"No'm," a girl's voice said softly. "She got hit."

"How? With what?"

Someone thrust a homemade ball into my hands. It was so much heavier than I expected that I almost dropped it. The ball appeared to be made of strips of old cloth wound round and round and then bound with thread. But when I pushed a thumb through the cloth, I found a rock at the center. "Vella got hit with this? No wonder she has a bump on her head! Who threw this?"

Again, the silence. Then out of the corner of my eye I caught a movement. I turned my head to see Lundy Taylor and Smith O'Teale slinking into the empty school-house.

"Did Lundy or Smith throw this?" The children answered not a word but their eyes told me the truth. I felt chilled and frightened. Could either boy have done such a thing on purpose? As we comforted Vella and put cloths wrung out of fresh snow on her "pump knot," my mind struggled with the problem. I decided that it might be better to make the boys stay after school and ask Mr. Grantland to help me get to the bottom of the mischief, rather than talk to them before all the other pupils.

From then on, the day did not go too well. For one thing, already I had used up all my lesson plans for the day and I was running out of ideas. Surely one of the chief differences between the veteran teacher and the recruit must be that the experienced can never find enough time, whereas the ingénue struggles to fill the hours, looks forward to dismissal time as a reprieve. I told myself that the real problem was no books; textbooks would make all the difference. Of course they would. How could *anyone* teach without books? Only twelve-thirty. It had to be later than that. Perhaps I was not cut out to be a teacher after all. I was grateful that Mr. Grantland would be helping me in the afternoon.

What subjects had we not touched on today? Penmanship. Happy thought! I was proud of my handwriting. It was a nice script, I had always flattered myself. I would enjoy putting some sentences on the blackboard to be copied for penmanship.

About halfway across the floor, I almost stepped on several marbles. Automatically, I stopped to pick them up. But at that moment a child hurled himself toward me almost in a flying tackle. "Teacher, don't touch them." It was Little Burl hanging onto my arm, shrieking at me.

I was startled at his ferocity. "Why not? I can't leave them on the floor, someone will step on them and go scooting."

The little boy looked at me, his face flushed and contorted, his cowlick jerking. "Teacher, them thar marbles are hot, they'll burn ye."

"Hot?" I still didn't understand.

Some of the pupils looked embarrassed. Obviously there was something Little Burl did not know how to explain. In the back of the room the laughter started again. It seemed to be led by Wraight Holt and a boy named Rorex Beck, but I also heard Lundy babbling in idiotic fashion, "He! He! Hot marbles!"

Finally it was John Spencer who spoke up. "Teacher, I'd thank ye to let *me* pick up the marbles for you. Little Burl was afeared you'd burn your fingers. He's right, them marbles are red hot."

"How did they get so hot?"

"They was put in the stove, ma'am."

"You—did you—?"

"No ma'am, not me. Guess it was just foolery."

Calmly John took a rag from his pocket, gingerly picked up the marbles one by one and then left them on the rag on my desk.

This whole episode struck me as a low-down prank, ingenious—but mean, almost as bad as the one on the playground. "Look, a prank's a prank," I heard myself saying to the roomful of children. "But this wasn't funny. There are tiny children in this room. What if some of them stepped on red hot marbles with bare feet? They'd have gotten badly burned. You see, glass holds heat—"

"It sure does!" a self-assured masculine voice said from the doorway. "And your Teacher's right," Mr. Grantland was speaking as he strode toward my desk. For me, his presence filled the room. Suddenly I realized how drained I was; the marble trick had been one too many.

"And this isn't the kind of prank we're going to put up with here." He was by my side protectingly. "Recess time for you, Teacher," he said quietly and I looked at him gratefully.

As I turned to go, I heard him say, "Girls and boys, I have here a letter from Dr. Ferrand for the opening of school. I thought you'd like to hear it."

Seven

I HAD BEEN teaching school for almost a month. It seemed so much longer. Was it only four weeks ago that I had followed Mr. Pentland up that mountain trail into this new life? Why, my life in Asheville seemed so far away that it could have been months or years. After the first couple of weeks in Cutter Gap when I knew my way around some, I had thought that everything would get easier. How wrong I was! Instead, my troubles were multiplying faster then the freckles on Ruby Mae's face.

For one thing, neither Lundy Taylor nor Smith O'Teale had admitted throwing the ball-rock at little Vella. Not even David Grantland had been able to penetrate Lundy's wall of surliness, and Smith—frightened of something—would not talk at all.

Nor was I making any progress with what I had supposed would be acomplished by the first or second week: dividing the school into proper grades. In order to handle so many children, I needed to seat the pupils of each grade together—regardless of sex. Yet over and over I was told, "No'm, I can't sit by no boy. This ain't a courtin' school. My Paw'll take me out if'n ye make it a courtin' school." None of the children would budge from this attitude.

They were equally immovable on their insistence on Latin, Latin, and more Latin when what they really needed were the most elementary of subjects. It seemed that from the Old Country had come the conviction that any boy or girl without Latin "didn't have no l'arnin' a-tall."

"Don't hanker for fancy doings and foolishness in the school," parents told me, "but don't you let my young'uns go till they can read Latin real good." Or "Don't mean to be onery, but my mind's sot and I'm that long-headed 'bout Latin."

They were too—long-headed stubborn Scots with a sprinkling of equally flinty Irish and German. In taking this job I had supposed that a year and a half of Junior College on top of High School would enable me to teach ordinary subjects in a one-room country schoolhouse. But I had not counted on having to teach Latin and I was terrified at the prospect.

Then there were various behavior problems—like the tobacco chewer who was depositing amber spittle on the freshly painted outside walls of the schoolhouse. And some crude obscene drawings had appeared on the walls of the privies. Increasingly, evidence pointed to three boys as our chief troublemakers: Lundy Taylor, Wraight Holt and Smith O'Teale, with Rorex Beck sometimes joining in the mischief.

Then there were children who were not alert because they were not eating properly, were actually hungry, I suspected. And there were several with eye problems. I would see them shielding their bloodshot eyes from the light; on sunshiny days they would sometimes slip beneath their desks to get into a shadow.

Nor could I ever have anticipated the pigs—what the children called "hawgs." In the Cove most hogs were not penned, so they wandered at will, fattening themselves on "mast"—beechnuts, acorns, and chestnuts. Some of them had taken to sleeping under the schoolhouse floor, grunting with what must surely be the most repulsive sound in the world, scratching their backs on the foundation posts. The pig noises did not help a bit with the effort to teach seventy-two classes in six hours: that was, for three days of the week, six subjects in all twelve grades; for the other two days when Bible was added, eighty-four classes. Of course it was impossible!

After any such day I desperately needed some time to myself to take my mind off pigs and Latin and get back some perspective. But in the mission house privacy was as hard to come by as four-leaf clovers in a patch of dandelions—chiefly because Ruby Mae Morrison was always appearing at my bedroom door. In Ruby Mae I had an unsought protégée. She stared at me, questioned me, talked ceaselessly while she wonderingly fingered my possessions. Or if I fled from my room to escape her, she would trail me around the house and grounds like a devoted collie dog.

Since Ruby Mae wanted to be with me that much, I

93

tried enlisting her help in running errands, like spying out for me when Miss Ida would be out of the kitchen. Then I would rush down to wash my clothes. Otherwise, Miss Ida would stand there as I worked, gazing at me steadily with pursed lips, rubbing her thumbs against her fingers, disapproval shrieking from her cold silence. I could never seem to do anything to please her.

Of course Miss Ida was just Miss Ida, often irascible, as I knew now, a stickler of a housekeeper and always clutching of her brother David. Mr. Grantland did not take his sister too seriously, and neither should I, he told me. In fact, David Grantland was a support to me in all of these troublesome matters—in school and out—because his light approach helped me ward off self-pity and hang onto my sense of humor.

It was he who had explained to me that first day of school when I had been so bothered by the children's giggling every time I opened my mouth, "Don't worry. It's nothing. Your way of speaking, the way you use the English language sounds just as queer funny-queer, that is, to the pupils as their way of speaking sounds odd to you. You'll get used to one another." He had been right. Within the week the snickering was tapering off.

And he was soon telling me, "Look Christy, enough of this 'Mr. Grantland.' Makes me feel like your father."

I blushed ridiculously. "You don't seem a bit like my father—"

"Then make it 'David.'"

"But not before the children."

"No, not before them, but everywhere else—"

So it was agreed.

As I got to know David better, I found that he was a tease with a tongueful of banter on any subject—even those I took most seriously. Like that Tuesday night at the supper table when, having added the last name to the school roll that day, I admitted my discouragement. "Just imagine it! A grand total of sixty-seven pupils in one room! That's just too many, especially when they're in all twelve grades."

"Well, my offer still stands," David told me as he helped himself to more corn pudding and reached for another hot biscuit.

"Which was—?"

"Which was to take over the Bible classes on top of all the mathematics classes."

"Does that include Bible memory work?"

"Yes—and I'll even go you one better," he added impulsively. "If you like, I'll take one or more of your advanced Latin classes. And there you have a magnificent offer."

Before I could answer, Miss Alice put in, "It really is a good offer, Christy, with all David has to do."

"That's right!" David continued. "And if you think you have it bad, look at me! I must call on a minimum of sixty families each month. Dr. Ferrand's orders. Build schoolhouse-churches, barns, springhouses, roads. Write sermons and preach, organize Sunday schools. Set up parties and hay rides and stir-offs and get good wholesome fun going for the young folks. Shall I go on?"

"No need. I'm impressed," I told him. And I really was. He and Miss Alice were each doing the work of several people. But then I asked, "Where's the barn you built?"

"Afraid you'd ask about that." He leaned close to me, a wide smile lighting his features. "No barn. Just thought I'd try tossing that in for effect. Now—do you want my help—or don't you?"

"As my students would say, 'I do! And thank you kindly.'"

But even with David's help and his jocular attitude, whenever I could be by myself of a night after Ruby Mae had gone to bed, I felt that I had to face the sober facts: the school was too much for as inexperienced a teacher as I was. All the doubts I had had that day of Bob Allen's accident, and again when Miss Alice had questioned me about my motives in coming to Cutter Gap, returned in full force. It was not that I was superstitious about Mr. Allen's accident. He was recovering nicely. But perhaps, I reasoned, the accident had nonetheless been one of many signposts trying to tell me that I had made a mistake, pointing me back to my world where I belonged.

ONE AFTERNOON after an especially exhausting day in school, I thought that a walk would clear my head. So I slipped out the side door of the mission house, for once evading Ruby Mae. The air was cold, still with the tangy crispness of winter. Gratefully I drew deep draughts of it into my lungs. The snow which had covered all of East Tennessee on January 2nd had still not melted here in the mountains.

Snow never lasted so long in Asheville, and by the second day it was always dirty from soot and traffic. I never knew that snow could be so beautiful until I saw it miles away from a city. Such sparkling pristine pure white!

But just ahead of me down the road there were some dark blobs scattered over several yards, marring the whiteness. As I got closer, I saw that the blobs were torn fur—some black, some reddish-brown with— Oh, no! Some poor little rabbit had been caught by another animal and literally torn to bits. On the crust of the snow there were blood stains and bits of torn fur clinging to bloody viscera. I did not want to see any more, so I skirted the spot and walked on rapidly down the road.

I wished that my mind were a slate so that with one swipe I could wipe off what I had just seen. Instead, a train of kindred memories came rushing in. Like that time when I had seen a tomcat streaking across our lawn in Asheville with a baby squirrel in his mouth, the squirrel crying in pathetic, high-pitched squeals of animal terror. I had dashed after the tomcat but he had been too quick for me. Sadly, I had turned back towards the house, the baby animal's protest at death reverberating in my ears. *Why did nature have such a vicious, tooth-and-claw aspect?* Or that time when I had been playing hide-and-seek with playmates and had stepped on the body of a dead bird in the boxwood serpentine of the yard next door. Right now, so many years later, the nerves up my back crawled at the thought. I remember that I had refused to look while mother had slipped off my shoe and cleaned it. And after that, I had never wanted to wear that pair of shoes again.

I jerked my mind back. *I'll think of other things.* I was passing the O'Teale's tobacco barn, so their cabin must be somewhere near. There were four of the O'Teale children in my school and since I was in no mood to pay a call, I knew I'd better turn around and start back. But it was too late. Suddenly, I was at the edge of their yard and Mrs. O'Teale had seen me. She put her hand to her mouth and hallooed. There was no escaping now.

The O'Teale cabin was like all the others I had seen, except more unkempt. In the yard, the trampled-down snow was littered with trash—rags and papers and junk, with pigs and chickens wandering at will. There was the usual big black pot turned on its side, rusting. No effort had been made to stack the firewood; the logs lay in wild disarray where they had been tossed. But in the midst of the squalor were the usual clumps of old English boxwood, snow-capped, incongruous in this setting.

I paused at the edge of the yard as I saw that the debris was worse than it had looked from a distance. There was filth, human filth along with the animal. The chickens were pecking at it; the pigs were walking through it, rolling in it, grunting. I lifted my skirts, and with my eyes on the ground for each step ahead, picked my way across the yard. *Isn't there an outhouse in the back yard? Aren't they teaching the children anything?* I found myself wishing fervently that I had started my walk from the mission house in the opposite direction.

Mrs. O'Teale (whose first name, Swannie, did not seem to suit her at all) was delighted to see me, obviously flattered by what she thought a deliberate visit from the new teacher. She was a tall slender woman with stringy, dirty-looking blonde hair. She was wearing a faded calico shirtwaist and an ill-fitting skirt with an apron on top of it. Her shoulders sagged, as if for a long time they had been carrying too heavy a load. Her eyes were dull and tired and sad, beaten by life. In the next few moments I saw why.

"Come in and set," she said warmly as we went inside. As soon as my eyes adjusted to the dim light, I was puzzled to see a penned-off area across the opposite corner of the room, looking as if they kept some pet animal there. Then the back door slammed, and a boy in his teens, big and hulking, shuffled into the room and stood staring at me with watery, vacant eyes. He wore no pants, only a tattered sweater that came over his thighs, almost to his knees. I could tell that he had nothing on under the sweater. His dark hair was long and matted, though it looked as if it had been whacked off by someone months before; his face was smudged with dirt. Saliva drooled from the corners of his mouth and trickled through the grime on his chin.

Since he was still staring at me, I said weakly, "Ah—hello."

He made no answer, just stood there. Empty desolation looked out of his eyes. And the stench, the terrible stench ... How could two women "visit" in a situation like this?

"That thar's Wilmer, my first-born," Mrs. O'Teale said as matter-of-factly as if she saw nothing wrong.

The boy pointed to a tin plate of cold corn bread on the table. "Unh—Um-humh. Ah-h-mm. Oo—anh."

"Hongry, Wilmer? Wal, don't squawk." She thrust the plate into his hands.

He crammed a fistful of corn bread into his mouth. I could not look. Should I ignore the boy and talk about the other O'Teale children in my school? Or should I pretend that there was nothing wrong with this boy? (I had heard at the mission that he had been born half-witted and was also subject to frequent epileptic fits.) But would it not be better to admit the reality and be sympathetic? His mother decided for me.

"Wal now, that should keep Wilmer from starvin'—And how are my young'uns doin'? In the school, I mean?"

"It's probably a little too soon to tell," I hedged. "It takes a while, you know, for pupils to get accustomed to a new teacher."

"Aye. Some teachers from the level lands has had theirselves a time. Recollect one that didn't stay no time a-tall. Left sayin' she weren't gonna put up with boy-persons a-carryin' knives to her school, flashin' them at her."

There was a loud clatter and I jumped. Wilmer had finished the corn bread and dropped the tin plate. He pointed to it, rolling across the floor, and bared his teeth in a caricature of a grin. "He! He—Mm—oo! Unh, he!" Saliva poured down his chin.

I was revolted and then ashamed of my revulsion. I looked away, only to have the boy shuffle into my line of vision as he crossed the room to a pile of glistening rocks and pieces of metal and glass inside the pen.

Mrs. O'Teale's eyes followed mine. " 'Course sometimes Wilmer takes a notion to run off a piece. Don't know himself where he be. Then we'uns have a time findin' him. Don't want him to git ahold of a rifle-gun or fall off-n the moun-tain—er nothin'. So when he takes fits like that, we fence him in."

Animal grunts came from the corner in the gathering darkness as Wilmer sat on the floor playing with his rocks.

I decided to risk one question. "Has he always been like this, Mrs. O'Teale?"

"Yes'm. Since he was birthed, that is. But he's a good boy. Never gives me no trouble."

There was a long silence. I could not sort out my feelings and swallowed back a nauseous lump in my throat. *What ultimate tragedy, to have brought a son like this into the world!* But Mrs. O'Teale gave no indication that she felt any tragedy. Compassion for her and for her boy rose in me. Yet I dared not express it for there was the strange feeling that if I did, she would look at me blankly and wonder why I felt sorry or embarrassed for her. Perhaps, I thought wildly, since she must live with this, she was better off with the insensibility.

The room was dark now and there seemed nothing more to say. "I must be going," I said as I rose. "And we haven't talked much about Smith and Orter and Mountie and—" Suddenly I was aware again of the dreadful odor from the corner and my mind went blank. I couldn't remember the names of the other two O'Teales. "By the way, where *are* all the children?"

"Went a-visitin' to my sister's. They'll be a-comin' back most onytime now. Here—let me light the lamp so's ye can see where ye're goin'. Real neighborly of you to come and say howdy to us."

"I want to help however I can," I told her as I went down the steps. "Next time I'll be able to tell you more about the schoolwork." But if only I had real answers to give this O'Teale family.

The minute I was out of sight of the cabin, I lifted my skirts and ran wildly down the road, making a wide detour of the dead rabbit. At the mission house, I dashed up the stairs directly to my bedroom. There I changed all my clothes, brushed my long hair by a wide open window so that the clean mountain air could pour through it. Then I washed my face, first in warm water, then in cold, scrubbed my hands over and over and over. Like Lady Macbeth, I thought ruefully ... But I could not scrub my memory, nor rub out what I had seen.

Miss Ida's piercing voice came up the stairwell, "Miss Huddleston—supper's on." And a few minutes later she was serving us salmon croquettes and hash-browned potatoes. There was nothing wrong with Miss Ida's cooking. Any other time I would be enjoying this food, but tonight my stomach was churning.

Now Miss Ida was bringing in a bowl of cooked apples. I swallowed, took a deep breath in an effort to get my unruly stomach under control. *Mind over matter. Any thought will do. David's sister is not a pretty one. She knows that. Maybe that's why she's so cranky and hangs on to David so hard.*

At that instant, Miss Ida passed the apples over my shoulder and the steam from the bowl wafted close to my nose. Through a haze I saw Miss Alice looking at me questioningly. I swallowed again. It was no use. I managed to blurt out, "Excuse me——" as I fled toward the yard.

Moments later I felt Miss Alice's firm cool hands, one hand on my forehead, the other on the back of my head. "Go ahead, Christy. Get rid of everything. Thee will feel better now."

"I— haven't been so sick since . . ."

"No, don't try to talk."

The strong hands supported my head. Finally it was over. Miss Alice asked, "Just one question, where were you this afternoon?"

"O'Teales." Even to me, my voice sounded weak and far away.

"Oh—I see. No wonder. That's the worst place of all."

Later on that evening Miss Alice came to my bedroom. I was propped up in bed working on lessons, but my mind was not really on what I was doing. So many questions and thoughts were tumbling over themselves inside me. There was the need to spill them out to someone. Miss Alice must have known that.

She had no sooner sat down on the edge of the bed than I started. "Father was right," I blurted out. "Even the old train conductor and Mrs. Tatum were right. I wasn't willing to listen, that's all. I don't belong here. I'm going back home. Miss Alice, I'm sorry about the children and all." Then I started crying. "It's no use, just no use."

Miss Alice let me sob, talk, rave on and on, patted me now and then. She made no protest when I told her that I was going to leave, offered no arguments why I should go or stay, asked no questions, never even said anything about my finishing out the school year. In the end, her silence was more eloquent than any words.

At last I lifted my head, tossed my tousled hair out of my wet eyes to look at the serene woman sitting so erectly on the edge of my bed. Suddenly I needed to know what

100

she was thinking. The gray eyes looked back calmly, unblinkingly for long minutes. Depths of quietness, wells of thoughts seemed to lie behind those eyes. Still she said nothing.

"Am I wrong to feel this way?" I asked, suddenly unsure of myself.

"Any sensitive person would feel exactly as thee feels." The voice was crisp, matter-of-fact.

That odd habit of hers of lapsing into her Quaker "thee" at tender moments. Yet she wasn't a bit consistent about it.

"Maybe it's just as well this happened," she went on. "Now is as good a time as any to decide whether you'll go home or not—provided you make your decision on a true basis."

"What do you mean—a true basis?"

"The way life really is."

"Not much of life can be as bad as what I saw this afternoon." My words had rebellion in them, I knew they did.

"You'd be surprised. Every bit of life, every single one of us has a dark side," she retorted "When you decided to leave home and take this teaching job, you were venturing out of your particular ivory tower. I know. I was reared in an ivory tower too. Then we get our first good look at the way life really is, and a lot of us want to run back to shelter in a hurry."

"You? Did you ever want to run back?"

Her reply was a chuckle so soft that it was almost a sigh. "I? Yes, certainly. I'm a classic example. At age sixteen I had, shall we say, a difficult experience, so difficult that after that I didn't ever again want to see any dirt—or blood—or disease—or cruelty—or whoring—or death. Ever since God has been gently, steadily, prying the little girl's hand off the little girl's eyes."

"How? How did He pry your hands?"

"Through circumstances. Through plunging me over and over into situations where I had to look . . . had to see reality."

"Bad circumstances? Really bad?"

"Really bad."

There was no mistaking the quiet emphasis of the words. My eyes searched Miss Alice's face in an effort to read everything there. "But how could it have been *that* bad?" I probed. "I can't see that you've been scarred by any of it—or coarsened."

A variety of thoughts were mirrored in her smile, a slow smile with sadness in it. "Yes, really bad," she repeated thoughtfully. "Like the crippled nine-year-old girl who was beaten over and over by her mother's lover, day after day, then finally brutally raped by the same man. The child died the next day."

I hoped she would not give any more details. My horror must have shown. But Miss Alice took no notice.

"Or there was the day I walked into a cabin over on Hog Back Mountain and discovered a woman strung up from the rafters—swinging—dead. Her imbecile husband was there gaping at the body. He was the murderer. When I asked him why he had done it, his only explanation was, 'A woman what can't stand hangin' a few hours ain't no woman a-tall.' Then there was—"

"Please," I interrupted desperately. "I don't want to hear any more."

Miss Alice looked at me curiously. "You're sensitive, Christy. So am I. You want to know why seeing stark evil hasn't made me rough or bitter?" She seemed to be seeing into her past. Then she took a deep breath, plunged on. "Remember, I said it was God who was prying the little girl's hands off her eyes. As if He were saying, 'I can't use ivory-tower followers. They're plaster of paris, they crumble and fall apart in life's press. So you've got to see life the way it really is before you can do anything about evil. *You* cannot vanquish it. *I* can. But in My world the battle against evil has to be a joint endeavor. You and Me. I, God, in you, can have the victory every time.' After that, He was always right there beside me, looking at the dreadful sights with compassion and love and heartbreak. His caring and His love were too real for bitterness to grow in me."

"Then if God was standing right there, looking and caring, why didn't He stop things like that?" The bitter question clawed at my throat. "A Supreme Being with real power and real love wouldn't stand by and watch a little girl raped and a woman hanged. How *could* He?"

"He would have to, if He'd given us men and women a genuine freedom of choice." Miss Alice's voice was gentle. "I think it's like this ... The Creator made the world a cooperative enterprise. In order for it to be that way,

102

God had to give us the privilege of going His way or of refusing to go His way."

"But how? How do we go His way?"

"He's specific about that." She ticked the points off on her fingers: " 'Love ye your enemies' . . . 'Do good' . . . 'Be ye therefore merciful' . . . 'Judge not' . . . 'Forgive' . . . And best of all, 'Give, and it shall be given unto you; good measure, pressed down, and shaken together, and running over shall men give into your bosom.' A great promise to claim!"

"What do you mean by 'claim'?"

The Quaker lady was silent for a moment. I had the impression that she was not so much thinking as listening. Then she said, "You've heard of 'staking a claim' in the old frontier days?"

"Yes."

"There was lots of rich land available back then. But in order to get any for himself, each man had to move out and claim what he wanted. If he didn't make that move, then for him nothing happened.

"This isn't a perfect analogy, but perhaps it will help to explain . . . God has all kinds of riches for all of us. Not just spiritual riches either. His promises in the Bible are His way of telling us what's available. But this plenty doesn't become ours until we drive in our stake on a particular promise and thus indicate that we accept that gift. That, Christy, is 'claiming.' "

"This is all new to me," I told her. "I like it."

A wonderful smile lighted her face. Then quickly she was grave again. "But we were talking a while ago about running back to our ivory tower. You see, Christy, evil is real—and powerful. It has to be fought, not explained away, not fled. And God is against evil all the way. So each of us has to decide where *we* stand, how we're going to live *our* lives. We can try to persuade ourselves that evil doesn't exist; live for ourselves and wink at evil. We can say that it isn't so bad after all, maybe even try to call it fun by clothing it in silks and velvets. We can compromise with it, keep quiet about it and say it's none of our business. Or we can work on God's side, listen for His orders on strategy against the evil, no matter how horrible it is, and know that He can transform it."

The words poured over me. Desperately I wanted to understand. I knew that we were on the track of one of those big question marks at the heart of the universe. "But the little girl—?" I asked softly.

"The answer isn't easy. I doubt that with the limitations of our humanness we can ever fully understand. But in that particular case, I think the little girl was raped because the person appointed to reach her in time to prevent the murder refused to hear—or to obey. I happen to know that a certain man for two days disregarded a strong inner impulse to go to her. Finally he did go, but it was too late. So God's clear order went unheeded. And evil had its day. The result of our disobedience can be that simple, that terrible."

I sat, trying to take this in, thinking it over for a long moment . . . The words rang in my mind: *That simple . . . that terrible. But that doesn't explain Wilmer . . . not even the little rabbit that never had a chance.*

"Christy, you have questions on your mind. I'm glad you do. Perceptive people like you wound more easily than others. But if we're going to work on God's side, we have to decide to open our hearts to the griefs and pain all around us. It's not an easy decision. A dangerous one too. And a tiny narrow door to enter into a whole new world.

"But in that world a great experience waits for us: meeting the One who's entered there before us. He suffers more than any of us could because His is the deepest emotion and the highest perception.

"Not, mind you, that He approves of suffering or wills it. Quite the opposite. And He doesn't just leave us and Himself in the anguish. At the point where His ultimate in love meets His total capacity to absorb and feel all our agony, there the miracle happens and the exterior situation changes. I've *seen* that miracle."

Looking at my puzzled expression, Miss Alice said quietly, "Probably I'm not making sense to you, Christy. But I'm sure you've realized that love has mending power. All of us have watched it work in small situations. Well, what I'm talking about is a vast multiplication of that power."

"I'm not sure I do understand. But I want to," I told her.

She nodded, smiling at me with her eyes, saying nothing more, falling into one of her Quaker silences.

She can be so eloquent, then so quiet—but always poised. She's a beautiful woman, not just the way she looks either. There's a deeper kind of beauty in her too:

the beauty of a near perfect relaxation. An aura of peace. A knowledge of being at home in the universe. A sense of belonging. It seems effortless but now I know that it was not: sometime in the past she came to terms with life. How? It must have been painful. She just said so. But that was a long time ago, and now——that inner relaxation that sometimes even borders on gaiety. She can laugh at herself. Often does.

But around and behind my thoughts, still before me in the silence stood the big question: Was I going home? Or wasn't I? I knew that Miss Alice had not been trying to philosophize; she had been talking directly to the point at issue.

"So what does all this have to do with my going home or not?" I dared to ask her.

"Everything to do with it. Who are you, Christy?"

"I wish I knew."

"But you can know. You're important, terribly important. Each of us is. You're unique. So is David. And Miss Ida. And Dr. MacNeill. No one else in all the world can fill David's place, or mine, or yours. If you don't do the work that's been given you to do, that work may never be done."

She rose to go. "It's late and you're tired. But here's the question for you to sleep on: were you supposed to come here, Christy? Or were you just running away from home?"

And she was gone.

Eight

I AWOKE to a sunshiny morning feeling so good that at first I had trouble remembering what I had been so gloomy about the night before. Oh, yes—the O'Teale cabin and my feelings of inadequacy as a teacher. But nothing could be *that* bad, I thought, as I stood before the front window savoring my view, feeling the warmth of the sun through the glass. The tops of the far peaks were still mushroomed in clouds, but the sun in the valley would soon melt the snow and we would see the ground again. Spring could not be far away.

I had driven with my parents and my brother George, first in our carriage and then in our Dodge touring car, up into the mountains around Asheville every spring for as far back as I could remember. Spring ... That first pale fresh green suddenly lacing the mountainsides. Then the blur of the redbud, delicately Oriental in the arrangement of its branches like strokes from the brush of some Japanese artist. And the pure white of the dogwood climaxed by the flame of the azaleas. I longed to see that procession of bloom again.

Then I realized there was something else I wanted more than to see spring in the mountains—to be with Miss Alice. I could learn so much from her. Where else could I find a teacher like her?

What she had said last night about running back to the ivory tower had not only stuck to me like a burr, but it still pricked. I did not want my prime consideration to be thinking of myself, protecting myself. Nor did I want to be a quitter.

Odd ... It suddenly struck me that this train of thought—springtime, learning from Miss Alice—did not belong to someone who was leaving immediately for Asheville. And that was how I knew that somehow, some

106

way in the night behind me, I had decided. *Somehow this Cove was my Cove. The children were my children. Little as I had to give, I had to give it here. It was as Miss Alice had said last night, we have to decide to give—even in hard spots where there's lots of evil.* Well, I had decided. I rested my forehead on the cold wood of the window sill. "Dear God," I said inside myself, "when I came here, maybe I was partly running off from home for fun and freedom and adventure. But I have a notion that You had something else in mind in letting me come. Anyway if You can use me here in this Cove, well, here I am."

That morning I entered the schoolroom eagerly. In an effort to understand "my" children better, two weeks before I had decided to assign the older ones a theme. They were to write on "What I Want to Do When I Grow Up."

The themes turned out to be even more revealing than I had imagined. Clara Spencer wrote:

" ... When I grow up, I want to have a lot of shoes like Catskins did in the mountain story; two, three pairs even. And I want a fine house with enough pans to cook in and a rug on the floor to sink my toes in."

Rob Allen had different dreams:

" ... Sometimes I get to feeling lonesome. I want to tell my thoughts, my good thoughts on the inside, to somebody without being laughed at. It would pleasure me to know the right way to put things like that on paper for other people too. I don't want to keep mill when I grow up, just read books instead. ..."

Ruby Mae wrote that she wanted to smell nice and have lots of pretty shirtwaists like Teacher.

Smith O'Teale wanted "to go far away from home across the mountains to the level lands and get me a fine job with plenty to eat."

There was only one theme that sounded a false note, Wraight Holt's. Unsuspecting, I picked up his theme from my desk one morning and began reading:

"I thought at your question about growing up. I

107

disgust being a slickfaced boy and want to be a masterest man-person now. I wud be proud for a woman grown something like you are to claim me for her feller because when I set eyes on yer hair and yer pretty clothes that fit you so neat I cannot think a solitary thing about my book learning. It wud tickle me right smart to carry you for a walk anytime now."

Hastily, I thrust it to one side under some other papers. But color had flooded into my face as I realized the gist of what Wraight had written, and instantly the three boys at the back of the room were smirking.

Wraight's theme did serve a purpose, however, because it raised to my conscious mind a problem which I now realized had been nagging me at a deep level: why were these boys in school?

By now I realized that everyone in the Cove was surprised to see Lundy Taylor in our school so long as any of the Allen children were attending. This was my first real-life glimpse of the family feuding that even Miss Alice had acknowledged.

When I asked David, he explained, "A long way back, Allens and Taylors got shooting at one another. I'm not sure anybody much remembers now what the fighting was about. I can't figure it out—this is the first time Bird's-Eye's ever let Lundy come near the school. Makes people uneasy. Maybe it's just that Miss Alice's teaching about forgiveness is finally making a dent in the Cove's hate-traditions."

I would like to have thought that was the explanation. Instead, there was the reluctant conviction that something else was afoot.

Meanwhile, the themes were dramatizing for me the poverty of the Cove. Most of the boys and girls could not see beyond the next corn crop. One pair of shoes would be wealth indeed. Most had only the vaguest idea of the world beyond the mountains.

Naturally the mission reflected this poverty. Everywhere I turned during those weeks I saw the lack of articles we needed. One day after finishing the compositions, I deliberately took a walk through the mission house, notebook and pencil in hand. In my mind were the irksome home situations of a few of my students. Some had to walk long

108

distances to school. There were occasions when the deep snows or the ravaging sleet storms made it impossible for them to get to school. Already I was finding that spotty attendance and interrupted work were slowing down the entire group. So there had always been the thought of taking in a few boarders for the worst winter months. That was why Miss Alice had designed such a large house. The barnlike room on the third floor could be used as a sort of dormitory. But before we could make even a beginning with the boarding school, we needed all sorts of supplies, even money for food for boarders.

So I began my list. There were no shades at any window; no rugs. All the mattresses were makeshift and dreadful. The linen closet was almost empty: sheets, towels, blankets were needed. Miss Ida's kitchen cupboard lacked even basic cleaning supplies.

Then my thoughts went to the yard. The mission did not own a horse for us to ride. There was only Old Theo, a mule with a crippled hip. Miss Alice had her own horse Goldie, but since her regular routine kept her in Cutter Gap only every third week, Goldie was of little use to the rest of us. David and I had talked about the fact that buying a horse could not be postponed much longer. Yet a good horse cost about a hundred dollars and Dr. Ferrand struggled for every penny he sent us.

That night as I sat in my room looking at this long list of things we needed before we could take even a few boarders, wondering where it was all going to come from, I remembered the words that Miss Alice had quoted from the Bible the night before. Something about "pressed down and running over." There was a picture in my mind of golden wheat being heaped up and up.

Suddenly it seemed important to find that verse—but where in the Bible was it? I got out my Sunday-school-graduation Bible, rather guilty to find it near the bottom of my trunk, and began turning the unfamiliar pages. I was glad Miss Alice was not there to see how long it took me to find that passage. Finally I stumbled on it. "Give, and it shall be given unto you; good measure, pressed down, and shaken together, and running over, shall men give into your bosom. For with the same measure ye mete withal it shall be measured to you again."

I chuckled to myself at those heaped-up words piled on top of one another like the golden wheat: *Good measure*

. . . pressed down . . . shaken together . . . running over.
An exuberant promise, if ever I had seen one! Abundance
sure enough.

My thoughts carried over into my own kind of prayer
. . . "Lord, Miss Alice said that 'if we give, it shall be
given unto us.' Well, she is giving, Lord. And so are Dr.
Ferrand and David. And even I'm trying to give, though I
don't yet see what I have that You can use. I don't have
the faith that Miss Alice has, Lord, in You, in this Book,
in anything. Can You help me with my faith (I hope it
isn't wrong to ask this) by giving unto us—as it says here,
good measure? Maybe by giving unto us a horse or—or
anything else on the list . . .?"

THREE DAYS LATER Mr. Pentland brought me a letter
postmarked Plainfield, New Jersey. The heavy cream-
colored envelope had been addressed with a distinctive
feminine handwriting, very large capital letters slanting
sharply to the right.

As I opened it, a check dropped into my lap. It was for
one hundred and six dollars, made out to me. Wonderingly, I read:

Dear Miss Huddleston:
 I hope that you will forgive a stranger writing to
you. Let me explain that I have just returned from
Asheville where I was visiting my sister, Anne (Mrs.
Dellafield) Boggs. At a tea which she gave in my
honor, I met your mother. In my presence, some of the
ladies were inquiring about you, and your mother
told—most charmingly—about the contents of some of
your recent letters, your fascinating pupils, their needs
and so on.
 On the journey home, I could not get this off my
mind. Then in the pile of mail waiting for me at home
there was an unexpected, larger-than-usual dividend
check from some stock of mine.
 My husband (who is the head of a linen import firm)
and I are trying the experiment this year of tithing all
our gross income and giving it, as we feel led, to
churches and charities. The enclosed check represents
the ten percent on my dividend check. My heart tells
me that it belongs to your work. Since I could not for

the life of me remember the exact name of the mission, I have made the check out to you. I send it with real joy.

Yours most sincerely,
Lucy Mae Furnam
(Mrs. Charles Furnam)

The horse! It was for the horse! Of *course*. "David—Da-vid! Where are you?" I went running through the house waving the check in the air.

"Here I am. Here in the kitchen."

"David, look! Just look . . . Isn't it *great!*"

"What's great?" He was lifting the lids of Miss Ida's pans steaming and bubbling on the stove, sniffing them one by one. "Stop waving that piece of paper in my eyes." He took the check, read the amount, and whistled. "Say, not bad. Who's Mrs. Furnam?"

"I don't know her! She was visiting in Asheville and heard about the mission at a tea. This is her tithe on some unexpected money—David, remember you said that a good horse would cost about a hundred dollars. This is it—for the horse."

"But if Mrs. Furnam meant it for the mission, Miss Alice will think she should send it to Dr. Ferrand."

"Oh, *no*—she couldn't!"

"She sure could."

"Not when she hears what's behind it, she wouldn't."

"What do you mean, 'what's behind it'?"

I was shy about telling him. "Well, David, it's that—you see, Miss Alice believes that the things that are promised in the Bible are there for us to claim. So—I tried it. I found a special promise and I asked God to send us some of the things we need around here—like a horse—some of the other things we need too. So David, this is it. Don't you see? This is *it!*"

"Christy, you surprise me. Really you do." His voice was gentle. "Do you honestly think this Mrs.—whatever her name is—Furnam sent this check as the direct result of your thoughts or 'suggestions' or prayers one night in your bedroom? Probably she would have sent the check anyway. A coincidence. Perfectly natural thing for her to do. Nice though. Hope we *can* use it for a horse."

But when I told Miss Alice the story, she agreed at once to our using Mrs. Furnam's check for a horse.

111

"Then you don't think the check was just a coincidence?" I asked her.

"No. I think you reached out for faith in the best way you knew. I think it's the intent of the heart that matters. And I think you got your answer."

"But David seemed to think I was silly—"

"Perhaps you misread David."

"I don't think so."

"Anyway, what goes on at a deep level inside you, Christy, is *not* silly, whatever else it may be."

"Oh, Miss Alice!" I hugged her.

To help in purchasing a horse, David took along John Holcombe, a man known in the Cove as a sharp trader and a good judge of horseflesh. At Overbrook Farm near Lyleton, they found "Prince," a black stallion with a distinctive white star on his head, a long silky mane and a flowing tail. Mr. Holcombe came back saying, "Blamed if he ain't the finest brute-beast ye ever flung yer leg over." And David, having picked up the horse-dealer's jargon, talked knowingly about Prince having "good depth of chest, well-muscled withers and slender, strong legs." He and Mr. Holcombe bid the horse in for ninety-five dollars and paid thirteen dollars and ninety-eight cents for a saddle and bridle.

"Roughly three dollars more than Mrs. Furnam's check," David reported to me. "If we were going by the gospel according to Christy, Prince plus his saddle should have cost exactly one hundred and six dollars, not one penny more, not one penny less. Some angel got his figures garbled. Anyway, I made up the small difference out of my pocket."

But David's teasing could not deflate me. "Give and it shall be given unto you!" From being weak, my faith now knew no bounds. Mother had been sending me her copy of the *Ladies' Home Journal* each month as she finished with it, partly, I suspected, as her way of reminding me that life along gracious and comfortable lines was still going on in the world. One night as I browsed through the latest issue, looking at some of the advertisements, an idea struck me. What about asking these advertisers to contribute not money, but some of their *products* to our mission? Could I draft the kind of letter that would present the mission's case dramatically—yet briefly enough—for a business firm? In the same notebook in which I had made the list of needs, I turned to a fresh sheet . . .

"Esteemed Sir: . . ." Pompous. I crossed that out. "Dear Sir:" Better. I plunged into the letter. "Let me introduce myself as Christy Huddleston from Asheville, North Carolina. A few months ago I accepted a job teaching a mission school in the Great Smoky Mountains. Quickly I discovered great destitution back here . . ." No, it wouldn't do. It was all wrong to begin the letter with *me*. I tore out the page and crumpled it up.

If *I* were the executive of a mattress company or a window-shade company and received a letter from some unknown girl, would I read it? After many tries, I evolved what I hoped was an acceptable letter, a sort of master one which could be altered to suit each company:

Dear Sir:

You are a busy man and do not know me, so I shall come to the point at once. This is to ask if you will share with us in our mountain mission work by making a donation of some of your fine Ostermoor mattresses to help furnish our mission house?

This is the story: This mission was established five and a half years ago in a remote and poor region of the Southern Appalachians in the Great Smoky Mountains, seven miles from the nearest railroad. This is an interdenominational work, now under the American Inland Mission, with Dr. Mercer O. Ferrand of Blytheville, Arkansas, at the head. We have a big mission house, a small chapel which doubles for weekday school and Sunday services both. I volunteered to come here from my home in Asheville, North Carolina, to teach in the school. There are sixty-seven pupils, all ages, quite a handful for a new teacher like me.

There are some awfully bright pupils but we have only a few books and practically no supplies. Many of the children walk a long way, even four and five miles to school, some—believe it or not—barefoot even in the coldest winter weather.

This work is supported entirely from free-will offerings. Funds are scarce. The highest salary paid to anyone on the mission staff is twenty-five dollars a month.

Yet out of this situation, love and hope and help are being given to the mountain folks. I thought perhaps you might like to be a part of this work. For our staff

113

and for the boys and girls we hope to take in as boarders, a good night's rest on one of your great Ostermoor mattresses could help a lot!

I shall be happy to supply references, any further information, or to answer any questions you may have. Let me thank you ahead of time for any help you may be able to give us.

Yours most sincerely,
Christy Rudd Huddleston

Over the next few days, exhilarated by the success with the horse, I got carried away with the letter writing and sat up nights working on it. After I had covered firms that manufactured basic items like shades, mattresses, and soap, I thought how nice it would be to have some communication with the outside world. So I included the Bell Telephone Company, asking them to donate wires and equipment for a telephone. Then my mind went to those long winter evenings. How pleasant it would be to have a piano so that we could gather around it and sing! So I wrote to the Lyon and Healy Company.

The promise said "heaped up." I hoped that I was not overdoing it.

Nine

RUBY MAE was sitting sideways on a straight chair in my bedroom while I tried to comb out her shoulder-length tangled red hair. "Sorry if I'm pulling. How long has it been since you combed this hair, Ruby Mae? Or shouldn't I ask?"

"Factually, I lost my tuckin' comb," she answered sadly. "Disremember when. Onliest tuckin' comb ever I had too."

"There are some bad tangles."

"Yes'm, but my head ain't tetchy. I'll try not to holler when you hit them mouse-nests. Ohoo—weee!"

"Sorry."

"Don't matter. What d'ye aim to do when ye git hit all combed out?"

"How about nice long braids? Like Miss Henderson's?"

"Be tickled to death with braids. But ye'll have t'learn me how."

"Braiding's easy. I'll teach you."

And braiding hair is not the only thing I'll have to teach you, I was thinking as I held the hair firmly in my left hand and eased the comb gently with my right, trying to unravel the snarls. Ruby Mae's sole idea of cleanliness was to wash her face and hands a few times a week—never a full bath—with the result that it was not pleasant to be near her. I had dodged and fled and resisted until now I realized that there was no escape. One of Miss Alice's Quaker sayings was apropos: "Such-and-such a person is meant to be my bundle." Well, I might not like it, but Ruby Mae was clearly my bundle, no getting around it.

That being so, there was nothing for it but to get on with teaching her what I could about cleanliness and basic

115

grooming. After the hair, I was going to suggest a bath in the portable tin tub and then make her a gift of a can of scented talcum powder.

But even more disturbing than her slovenliness was Ruby Mae's chattering. It was an unthinking kind of talking. like tying the reins of a horse to the whip socket and letting him run off in whatever direction took his fancy. I had been almost at the point of making cotton plugs for my ears when another of Miss Alice's teachings came to my rescue.

"My father always told us," she had said one night at the supper table when David was complaining about the slow progress of his belfry, "that if we will let God, He can use even our disappointments, even our annoyances to bring us a blessing. There's a practical way to start the process too: by thanking Him for whatever happens, no matter how disagreeable it seems."

Though she had been speaking directly to David's exasperation with the mountain men whose promised help rarely materialized, I had begun to wonder if it could not apply equally well to my feelings about Ruby Mae. But how could I ever bring myself to be thankful for her prattle?

Well, I decided to try it. I sat down and, feeling foolish, made myself say, "I thank You that Ruby Mae talks so much." To my astonishment, even before the first day's experiment was over, I was beginning to hear what Ruby Mae was really saying. Suddenly, I did feel thankful, for here—so close that I had nearly missed it—was a priceless opportunity to get inside the mountain mind.

Thus to Ruby Mae, the mission house was a mansion and Miss Alice Henderson incredibly wealthy. "She come over here from Cataleechie. Independent rich, she was. Paid cash-money for this land. Built her cabin. Went right on, built this here house—so tall, like one house a-top another house same as a stack cake, without no by-your-leave from nobody.

"Took a heap of paint too, pails and pails of hit," the girl went on with wonder in her voice, "to make the big house as white as a sarvice bush in the springtime. Swear to Josh-way, if she didn't put a heap o' windows in her cabin too, shiny glass windows to let the sun through."

Even more wonderful in Ruby Mae's judgment had been the fact that Miss Alice had had two deep wells dug, one for the mission and one for her own cabin before the

116

foundations had been laid. Pumps had been connected to the wells and stood beside the sinks in the two kitchens for "water piped right into the house," obviously an unheard-of convenience in the Cove.

It was delightful to see Miss Alice through Ruby Mae's eyes. She had insisted on unprecedented things like having the spring in the yard covered. She kept telling the mountain people that they could get sick from dirty water, might even get the dread typhoid. The little house over the spring was a pretty one, lattice-work painted white like the big house.

It seemed that Alice Henderson had started a Sunday school, then a few months after that a worship service. At first it had caused consternation that a woman would "take up church" and speak in public.

"First off, folks was so scandalized they couldn't see straight," Ruby Mae reminisced. "Old men used t' snort, I can hear them yit, 'Ain't nary bitty sense in it.' Said, 'Wimmin and keepin' house belong together like sap and bark. Nothin' a-tall outside the house and yard be fittin' for wimmin.'

"Miz Henderson had gumption, didn't pay them no mind. In no time a-tall some folks was argufyin' with the snortin' ones, sayin' 'No sech thing. The string of her talk is good. I confidence the way she jest rares back and faces us down. She don't have the weavin' ways of most man-preachers. Just talks quiet, like a woman, says things I memorize during the week, can think on while I'm a-doin' up my work or plowin' or haulin' my corn to mill.'"

It was apparent that Miss Alice had carefully explained to the Cove people that in the Society of Friends the women had always taken an equal role with men, a new idea in the mountains. Yet the truth was that the highlanders had never heard anyone, man or woman, talk like this one. Behind and underneath Ruby Mae's gossipy words was the lasting impression made on her by the Quaker lady's emphasis on two favorite subjects—the love of God and the immediacy of His guidance for anyone willing to receive it. Miss Alice kept insisting that God wants all of us to be happy. To the mountain people this was at first suspect because their religion equated happiness with what they called "the pleasures of the world." They reasoned that those who were enjoying themselves must certainly be sinning.

But to Miss Alice it was lack of joy that was the heresy.

Though Ruby Mae's summation of all this was halting and confused and incredibly picturesque, the gist of it got through to me. By delving deep into Scripture, by telling story after story out of real-life experience, Alice Henderson was constantly painting a picture of a God who longs to guide His creatures into goodness, kindness, caring, justice, unselfishness. Irresistibly, her listeners were drawn back again and again to hear more. They came as thirsty people; they had been thirsty for a long time.

Quietly, Miss Alice was demonstrating this God of love and beauty too—in small ways and in large. For a few, the concept that life did not have to be all starkness and misery was slowly taking root. Tentatively, timidly—constantly encouraged by Miss Alice—some of the women were at last reaching out for light and beauty and joy.

FROM UPSTAIRS I heard an incessant banging on the front door, then Ruby Mae's heavy footsteps. "Law me! I'm a comin'. Don't pound hit down!" There was the sound of a muffled male voice and then the girl loudly summoning me.

As I reached the head of the stairs, Ruby Mae called up, "This here's Kyle Coburn—you know, Bessie's Paw."

"Howdy, ma'am," the man said. "I'm on my way to mill. Stopped to tell ye about our neighbor-baby. The McHones' baby—she quit breathin' last night. Opal's carryin' on right bad. This was the only gal-baby followin' a passel of three boys. She says, would ye come, Miss Christy? Miss Henderson's over Big Lick Spring way. Opal says if she's got to give up this least'un, would ye come and fix up the baby real pretty?"

Me, fix up a dead baby? But I had never even seen anyone who had died, let alone prepared a body for burial. "I'm so sorry about the baby," I stammered. "Of course I'll come. Isaak told me at school that his new baby sister wasn't well. What was wrong?"

"They thought it was liver-growed. Weren't even no time to call Doc MacNeill."

I was about to ask what "liver-growed" was, then quickly decided I'd better wait and ask David or Miss Alice. "Mr. Coburn, do you think Mrs. McHone has a baby dress?"

"Don't reckon they had nothin' for this baby."

"Then I'll try to find something here. Oh—and I'm not sure I remember how to get to their cabin.

"Well, you know the crik right out here—Cutter Branch?"

I nodded.

"When the crik branches, ye take the right fork for a mile, then cut acrost Coldsprings Moun-tain, then hit's the second right hand holler nigh onto Turkey Trot Crik."

To my relief, Ruby Mae came to the rescue. "I know where 'tis. I'll show you the way."

As I searched for a baby dress in the mission's used-clothing box, I kept wishing for Miss Alice—or David. Where was he? Out calling? I was not the one for this assignment. Yet how could I refuse to go? Finally I found a baby dress that would do, and in my room some ribbons that had decorated going-away gifts from friends in Asheville. These I put in a basket with a cake of soap, some clean rags, some safety pins and a needle and spool of thread.

It was two o'clock in the afternoon by the time Ruby Mae and I started. She knew the route all right, but to me it seemed a long way. At last we reached the edge of a clearing at the foot of Big Butt Knob beyond Coldsprings Branch. The setting of this cabin was different from any other I had seen because it stood in the horseshoe bend of a wide creek. The effect was of a peninsula surrounded by the stream on three sides, with woodland and the rising mountain in the back. Several immense old trees, their bare branches stark in the winter sky, grew near the cabin.

"That's it there. That's the McHones'." Ruby Mae put her hand to her mouth. "Hallo—it's us—Ruby Mae and Teacher!"

Almost immediately the spare figure of a woman appeared on the porch of the rickety cabin. She was a young woman with abundant brown hair. She had tried to part it on the side, but it was so carelessly pinned up that strands of hair staggled down her neck. Brown eyes looked out from a white face, so drawn that it made her look ill. She was wearing a skirt and an old sweater buttoned over her stomach and men's shoes.

The house was built in two sections several feet off the ground, as on stilts, with a crude dog trot between. As with all of the mountain homes, no paint had ever been used and the building had weathered to a silvery-gray.

Part of the porch appeared to be held up by bean poles so that we walked across a floor listing to one side.

Mrs. McHone received us warmly and seemed eager to talk. "The baby cried something awful all night and we thought it was liver-growed."

"Mrs. McHone, I never heard of that. What's liver-grown?"

"Lots of newborned babies has it. You take the baby by the left heel and the rght hand and make them tetch. Then you take the left hand and the right heel, and if'n they won't tetch then you know hit's liver-growed."

"What do you do then?"

"You got to force the hand and heel to tetch. When I pulled, the baby hollered and went as limp and white as a new-washed rag doll. Never could do nothin' with her after that. Give her tea all night long, but nothin' holped. Jest afore the sunball come up, we heerd the death tick in the wall. Jest quit breathin' then, she did."

The woman had started crying quietly, wiping her eyes with the edge of her apron. She led us inside the house and pointed to the little waxen body lying in the middle of a large bed, a white cloth over the tiny face.

The horror of this sickened me. The baby must have had cruel internal injuries. Yet Opal McHone had wanted this baby daughter. She was not a callous, indifferent mother but had acted out of love, love mired by her ignorance and by the superstition handed down to her.

At that moment, for the first time in my life, I knew grief. I had had childish disappointments, yes. Hurt pride, often. A sense of loss, sometimes. But compared to what I was feeling now, these had been superficial emotions because they were so self-centered. On my tongue now was the first bitter taste of a grief not my own. My heart was mirroring back from the world's pain just one episode from all the endless woes and infamies caused by the not-knowing and the not-caring. Opal McHone had not known what she did. And I had to understand and to forgive her on that basis, otherwise I could be no comfort to her at all.

With relief, I turned for a moment to the three McHone boys who had been standing in the background watching. Toot and Vincent were still tiny; Isaak, the oldest, was twelve. He had his mother's dark eyes, unusual with such white-blond hair. I wondered why I found Isaak so appealing. Perhaps it was the trace of small-boy plumpness left in his cheeks, and the dark, brooding eyes that looked out on the world with a certain quizzical expression. He was wearing his usual raggedy patched overalls over a shirt equally threadbare and heavy work shoes that looked several sizes too large. The brown eyes were watching my every move as he saw his teacher in a new role.

The father, Tom McHone, diffidently came forward and shook my hand. Then the older man, Uncle Bogg, said, "Howdy-do, Miss. Mighty proud that ye drapped in." He smiled at me with his mouth shut to hide his almost toothless state. I had heard of this man. Everybody in the Cove called him "Uncle Bogg" and laughed whenever they spoke of him. He was shiny-bald on the top of his head, but what hair remained was long and curled jauntily, like fluff, over his ears, giving him a puckish look. A Roman nose, deep creases across his forehead and around his eyes, and several days' growth of stubble on his chin completed an amazing picture.

"Let me holp ye if I can," he offered. "I can git ye some water."

He meant for the washing before the laying out, so there was no avoiding getting on with it.

While he went for the water, I saw that five beds were crowded into this main room of the cabin. There was also a quilting frame set up near the fireplace with a quilt stretched on it.

"Aye, here 'tis," Uncle Bogg set a pail of water on the floor by me. "Calculate that'll be enough. Ye mought need this too." It was a copper basin.

Mrs. McHone sat on the edge of the bed and watched while Ruby Mae and I washed the ivory body. The baby's eyelids were transparently thin with the fine lines of blue veins still showing. The little rosebud mouth was open slightly with the lower lip drooping. It was the droop that wrenched me.

"It was to be, I reckon," she said. "Hit was the Lord's will. We'uns just has to bow to it. The Lord giveth and the Lord taketh away. Blessed be . . ."

I thought I would scream if she finished the sentence. I bit my lips to keep from saying what I was thinking. It had to be said sometime—but not now, not right now. Someday this mother must understand that God's will had been this beautifully formed baby girl with a fuzz of blond curls on her shapely head. As I took one of the tiny hands

121

in mine to wash it—the dimpled fingers that should have been warm and clinging to my fingers—I wanted to lash out against something, somebody. Dr. MacNeill—why wasn't he teaching mothers how to take care of their babies? Surely his call of duty went beyond peddling pills and crude operations. Now there would be another tiny grave in the mountain cemetery. Even Miss Alice, as long as she had been in this Cove, why hasn't *she* found a way to teach these people better?

Of course, I knew perfectly well that I was too new to stand in judgment of either the Doctor or Miss Alice. My father had always scolded me for my snap judgments and sweeping condemnations. But what a world of teaching needed to be done back in these mountains! That alone could use a full-time worker.

Though I understood Miss Alice's efforts to underscore the fine heritage of these people and to build on that, I could also see just by looking around me how we tend to over-romanticize history. Life in those other centuries had not been all knights-and-ladies stuff. There was nothing romantic about cottages where eight or ten people slept in one room with no privacy; where there were no bathrooms, not even outside privies—even if the cottage did happen to have picturesque thatch on the roof. There was nothing glamorous in any century about no running water in which to bathe or about fleas on human beings; or about the blackgum twigs with which some of the women right now, in 1912, dipped snuff and then rubbed their teeth and gums. So many of the people had terrible-looking teeth or no teeth at all. And the eye trouble that was so prevalent. I had learned that it was trachoma and that it was a dangerous infection which, if unchecked, resulted in blindness.

All at once a heavy shadow blotted out the cabin door. I looked up to see three men standing there. "We've come to see the fancy layin' out." The voice was thick. All of the men were unsteady on their feet; it was obvious that they were drunk. Trying to ignore them, I turned back to my task.

"Come on in, if'n ye must," Uncle Bogg said, "but don't none of ye bother Miz Christy." He made no effort to introduce the men.

"Now ain't that purty! Ribbons—aah—law!" The tallest of the three was leaning over the foot of the oak bed. The smell of home-brewed liquor was overpowering. The face with the bloodshot eyes and the heavy black beard was distastefully close. I recognized this man: he was Ault Allen, Bob Allen's brother, the one who had not wanted Dr. MacNeill to operate.

I moved away as far as possible to the head of the bed and sat down to sew ribbon rosettes on the little dress. One of the men was staring at me, then I saw him wink at his friends.

The room was growing dark but no one seemed to think of lighting lamps. When finally I had the dress on the baby, Mrs. McHone came and picked up the little body, cradling it in her arms. "It even has ribbons. No baby in the Cove has ever had ribbons afore. It's plumb purty, as pleasant as the flowers." Her rough fingers caressed the sheer cotton fabric. "My baby's so purty. Oh, Miz Christy, I'm obleeged to you!"

"I'm glad I could help—a little." I groped for something comforting to say, but I was out of my depth and knew it. "Maybe—maybe you'll have another baby girl sometime."

The man lolling on the foot of the bed laughed uproariously. "That oughten to be hard. Breedin's easy for Tom. He's as healthy as a coot."

Uncle Bogg came forward, anger in his voice. "You can jest shut up. Not never one more word out'n you. Devil take ye! You're drunk, jest plain drunk and this ain't no time for talk like that."

"It's late," I said. "If there's nothing else Ruby Mae and I can do . . ."

"I'll git the lantern lit and see ye to the aidge of the woods," Uncle Bogg said.

"Thanks so much, but you don't have to do that."

The old man appeared not to have heard me. He was watching the drunken men as one by one they slipped out the door. Then with deliberation he lifted a lantern off a nail in the wall, lighted it, took a rifle from its rack beside the fireplace, and started out, beckoning us to follow. At the edge of the clearing, Uncle Bogg paused, lifted his hand up to caution us not to speak and then stood, listening intently. I heard nothing unusual, but after a time, he said with sudden vehemence, "I'm a-goin' with you to the Mission."

"But that's too much," I protested. "Ruby Mae knows the way and it's a long walk to the Mission and back."

"No use argufyin'—long walk don't matter. I'm a-goin'.

C'mon." And the old man set off walking briskly and silently between Ruby Mae and me.

I knew that it was useless to protest. Soon we saw that he was taking a different way back to the Mission. The path led through great pillared tulip trees, the bare branches ghostly in the deepening twilight. Dry leaves and twigs crunched underfoot. All around us was the chatter of the little boomers, the red squirrels, and at a distance, the drumming of ruffed grouse.

Uncle Bogg kept throwing the lantern light first to one side of the path, then to the other. His eyes were searching the woods, though it was impossible to see more than a few feet. There was a tenseness in him that had quickly communicated itself to Ruby Mae and me.

Suddenly a twig snapped loudly in the woods to our left and all of us jumped. The old man stopped, set the lantern down on the ground, his gun instantly in position, his right hand on the trigger. But our straining ears heard only the creaking of the branches and the eerie cry of a hoot owl. "Thought I heerd a varmint," he explained after a long time.

The explanation was not convincing. Wild animals would not make him that jittery. Few wolves or wild boars must be left in these mountains and certainly no mountain man would be afraid of a bear. Hunting was the sport they liked best.

Ruby Mae's face looked chalky white in the dim light. "Thought I seen a shadder movin'—there!" she whispered, pointing into the woods, sidling closer to Uncle Bogg.

Once again the old man raised the lantern and peered. "Lots of shadders," he answered briefly. "C'mon, let's go."

He quickened his pace so that Ruby Mae and I had trouble keeping up with him. I noticed that he kept his right hand on his gun. No, he was not watching for animals.

I was relieved when Uncle Bogg suddenly broke the silence. "Miss Christy, onybody told you yit about the tall cornstalk in our barnyard?"

"Tall cornstalk? No."

"Wal, it happened like this— Our family was all out on the porch 'bout the crack of dawn one mornin' shellin' a turn of seed corn for plantin' when Opal called us to come git breakfast."

While I was puzzled at his sudden talkativeness, I was

124

delighted to sense a tall tale coming. "When I went to breakfast. I drapped the ear of corn I was shellin' off'n the porch. After we'd et, I saw that the ear of corn had fell into the pig trough. Water in the trough had done swelled up one of the grains on that corn cob to 'bout as big as a small apple. Wal, I shelled the rest of it off, but put that big one in my pocket.

"Went on down to the field to plant the seed corn. Directly felt somethin' bumpin' my leg. Swear-r-r, if that grain of corn hadn't swelled big as a ball. Took it out, set it at the aidge of the field, went on plantin'.

"Got all the corn in by the aidge of dark. Went to look at that grain of corn—wouldn't you know—hit had swelled so, looked big as a pumpkin. Must have weighed nigh on thirty pound."

The story was rolling out exuberantly now. Uncle Bogg was still walking fast, as alert as ever, and as he talked he kept holding the lantern up and peering into the woods. I realized now that he was deliberately trying to divert us.

"Wal, I called Tom and Isaak and we dug a good-size hole, rolled that grain of corn in. Shoveled the dirt over, stomped it down, turned to go, when a-whammity-bang, heard somethin' behind us. Jerked round, and that stalk of corn had shot out'n the ground and was already ten foot or so in the air.

"Wal, that evenin' Jeb Spencer come over, said one of his cows had got out. Asked had we seen her. Told him we hadn't.

"When Jeb started to leave, I asked him, 'Jeb, did you ride over?' Said he had. 'Where'd you tie your mare?'

" 'To a big saplin' there in your cornfield.'

"Had a good idey what that saplin' was. Boys and me went down with Jeb to the field where we'd been plantin' and I says to him, 'Is that where you tied the mare, Jeb?'

" 'Yep, that's the place all right.'

"We looked, but there warn't no sign of any horse. Jeb had thought that cornstalk was a poplar tree or somethin'. Told Isaak to run for the lantern and my old rifle. Flashed the lantern up that stalk and Lord help my time-a-day, thar was the mare 'bout sixty foot off'n the ground a-hangin' by the bridle. So Isaak held the light and I shot the bridle rein in two, and when the horse fell, Jeb got on and rode off back home."

The story was having the effect Uncle Bogg wanted.

Ruby Mae was chuckling. "That's the most plumb durn foolishness I ever heard."

"No such thing."

"Ungle Bogg," she giggled, "everybody knows you like a good story and don't mind handlin' the truth a little careless-like to git one."

"Why, you needn't be so gosh-derned skeptical. What I'm tellin' you is facts as pure as Scripture. Why, in less than two weeks time that cornstalk was as tall as a big oak tree. It sprouted a purty big ear for every blade, most of 'em 'bout a hundred foot from the ground. Slowed up a little when the rest of the corn tasseled out and commenced silkin'. You couldn't see the corn on that stalk by then, not even with a spyglass.

"Come cuttin' time we had to ask all our neighbor folks to holp. Took me and Tom and Jeb Spencer and all the men we could git together most all day hackin' at that cornstalk. 'Bout sundown it started a-fallin'. We watched it fall awhile, but it got plumb fit dark before it had fell all the way. Heard it hit the ground about midnight. Made a purty big racket. Woke us up, as a matter of fact. Knowed it must have fell over a big scope of land.

"'Bout day-bust, we walked up into the pasture field to see which-a-way it had fell. It lay acrost the crik, over Jeb's place, by some thick woods northside of the road. And still we couldn't see the end of it. We rode over Coldsprings Branch and all the way acrost Pebble Mountain, and—don't you know—directly t'other side of the mountain we met a string of people who had come from miles around to see that thar cornstalk. Some excite-ment, runnin' hither and yon. Matter of fact, that cornstalk was lyin' yander acrost the Tennessey-North Carolina line and the state police were gatherin'. Hit was a fearsome sight to behold. Course, we acted like we'd never seed that cornstalk before in our born lives, jest wheeled and run, come back home like streaks of greased lightnin'."

The moon had risen and we were coming out of the woods. Somehow the darkness no longer seemed threatening; moonlight was bathing everything in a soft amiable light. I looked back and realized that we were almost home. Uncle Bogg had so beguiled us with his tall tale that he had brought us all that long way through the woods without our knowing it.

"Mission house jest around the bend now," the old man said blithely. "Be glad to see it myself."

As we reached the edge of the mission yard, we saw David leaning on the fence. He came striding forward to meet us. "Am I glad to see you! Where have you been? Uncle Bogg, thanks for walking the girls home."

The old man set the lantern on the ground and let go a stream of tobacco juice. "You're not half as glad as I am t' see you. Opal's baby died last night. She asked Miz Christy to come and holp lay out the young'un. While she was doin' that, some neighbor-men come in. They'd had too much likker. I heerd them . . ."

"Hold the story a minute, Uncle Bogg." David turned to us, "Girls, Ida has waited supper for you. Guess you'd better go on in and eat it."

We told Uncle Bogg good-bye and as we turned toward the house, I heard David say, "You know a Cutter Gap man—drunk or sober—wouldn't harm a woman."

But what Uncle Bogg answered we could not hear.

Ten

THE WAY sometimes led through the woods, sometimes along the edge of cliffs tilted precipitously over ravines. I was glad to be riding the mission mule rather than the new horse Prince. Theo might be ancient and disreputable-looking and have one bad hip, but at least he was sure-footed on the mountain trails. An hour ago when we had set out for the Lufty Branch church (where David held an outpost Sunday school twice a month) he had insisted that I ride Prince, but I had demurred. The stallion was too spirited for me. All of us in the mission house had teased David about selecting a horse so fiery that only he could ride him, but he consistently ignored our comments. There he was now on a dangerously narrow ledge, controlling the beautiful black animal with a softly spoken sentence and a touch of the hand.

We were coming now to the deepest part of the woods. David and Prince were already out of sight among the tall trees. Here where the virgin timber grew, the path was wider. Tulip trees, giant beeches, and red spruce lifted massive limbs overhead to form an arching roof like a cathedral. Theo's slow jogging—nothing could ever persuade Theo to go faster—would turn one into either a philosopher or a dullard.

All around me the trees stood sentinel over a solitude that stretched backward into time. It awed me to realize that these proud trees had been here for centuries before any human eye had seen their grandeur. Later the trees had stood vigil over the Indians—Cherokee land. After that had come the first white settlers streaming down from Pennsylvania on the Wilderness Road, most of them walking, a few riding, with their worldly possessions on pack horses—an axe, a gun, a frying pan, some gunpowder, a little salt, and some starter-dough. As they struggled along the Indian trails or followed the river-routes to make their way in a new land, they had looked upon the same trees I was seeing now.

Silence enfolded me. Here in the deep forest even the animals' hooves were muted, for underneath was a carpet of pine needles inches thick. Suddenly my mule stumbled over a root in the path and I reached out to pat his neck reassuringly. Immediately David called back over his shoulder, "You all right?"

"Yes, fine. Theo's just dragging his feet."

David reined in Prince and waited for me to catch up. "We'd better stay together." He looked at me and grinned.

I knew that I was a funny sight, riding sidesaddle using a man's tack. My long black woolen riding skirt was draped over the mule's belly, almost dragging the ground. "I'm self-conscious enough as it is," I pleaded. "So don't laugh at me, please."

"You should be riding Prince," he retorted. "Change your mind?"

"No. I'll stay this way. I'm no horsewoman. You know that."

"You could be. It's no harder than walking seven miles in the snow." There was approval in his voice.

We rode awhile longer in silence. When David spoke again his tone was serious. "Christy, don't take any more trips away from the mission without me."

I stared at him, astonished at the change in his mood.

"Why, David? What's the matter?"

He stared down at the reins he was holding, as though trying to make up his mind whether to speak or not. "I don't know," he said at last. "But when Uncle Bogg walked you and Ruby Mae home the other night, it wasn't those three men from the cabin he was afraid of."

"Then—then what was it?"

"Some other men followed you through those woods, Christy. Men Uncle Bogg had never seen before."

Apparently my face did not register sufficient surprise because he said it again more slowly. "Uncle Bogg didn't know them, Christy. And Uncle Bogg knows every man, woman and puppy-dog between here and the North Carolina line."

"They were strangers, then?"

"Not only strangers, but strangers from a long way away. And, Christy, until we find out who they are and what they're doing here, I want you to stay close to the mission."

"But—what would bring anyone into Cutter Gap who didn't belong here? What would strangers want here?"

"That's what I don't know," David said, and again I heard the grim edge to his voice. "And that's what I intend to find out."

Ahead we could hear the sound of rushing water. But not until Prince and Theo had rounded the bend did we see Big Spoon Creek plunging down the mountain across our path. It was still frozen near the edges but in the center of the creek the water swirled and eddied, whipping itself into frothy bubbles as it plunged over rocks and floating branches.

David halted on the bank, his eyes appraising the situation.

"Water's higher than I've ever seen it. If Prince and Theo refuse to ford it, they won't be seeing us today at any Sunday school." He looked at me quizzically, obviously trying to throw off the uneasy mood that had gripped us both. "I'll go first and hope that Prince will set an example for old Theo. Wish me luck—"

The stallion stepped confidently into the water. A few feet from shore Prince paused to drink. "Recognizes good drinking water when he sees it," David flung over his shoulder. "Know what I've discovered about horses in these mountains? They're choosy. Let garbage or any such thing be dumped into a creek and they won't touch a drop." When finally Prince had gotten all he wanted, he plunged on into midstream, carefully avoiding the biggest boulders.

As soon as I saw horse and rider splashing up the opposite bank, I urged my mule into the creek. Everything went well until we were almost in the middle, then suddenly I felt icy water on my legs. "David," I shrieked, "he's falling."

"Stay on his back! Hang on. Encourage him, he'll make it."

The mule struggled but could not get his footing. I was leaning forward clutching Theo's neck to keep from sliding off his back. I tried encouragement. "Take your time, old boy. There—now. Try again. Oh David, it's his bad hip. I'm too heavy for him. His bad leg slides right out."

David was shaking his head. "It's too deep to wade, Christy. You're too gentle with that old mule. Hit him with the bridle. Hit him harder."

Finally even David saw that it was no use. He groaned, "What a mess. Jump off and I'll help you."

"No, don't! You'll ruin your suit," I called. "Stay there, I'm coming." The water was almost to my waist with my wet skirts tugging me downstream. I wanted to shed the heavy woolen one, but instead tried to drape it over one arm as I struggled toward shore.

David pulled me up on the bank. My teeth were chattering. He began rubbing my hands between his. "We've got to do something for you in a hurry. Doc MacNeill's cabin is somewhere near. If I can find it, I'll take you there."

I nodded mutely as I tried to wring the water out of my skirt. By now the mule had gotten to his feet and was across the creek. As David grabbed his bridle he said, "You can't walk in those sopping shoes either. You ride the horse, Christy, and I'll lead poor old limping Theo and stay close to you. It can't be far."

We didn't say much as we went up the narrow trail. Our eyes were searching the horizon. Finally we saw a cabin, silvery gray etched against the shadows of Green Ridge. Smoke trailed from the chimney.

"That's it. Doc's place," David said with relief. He put his hand to his mouth and shouted. In a moment the door opened and a man's stocky figure appeared.

"Who is it?" a voice called.

David answered, and the Doctor came striding down the hill toward us. He was wearing brown corduroys and a plaid hunting shirt, open at the neck. I got the same impression of overflowing vitality that I'd had in the Spencers' cabin, only I couldn't help thinking that this man seemed more in character in hunting clothes than with surgical instruments in his hands. What was it about him that made him more like a farmer or a woodsman than a physician?

"Anything wrong?"

"Nothing serious. Christy got soaked in the creek. Could we dry her out by your fire?"

The Doctor turned his full attention to me—and again that curious look came into his eyes that I had noticed at the Spencer cabin before the operation. "Delighted," he said briefly. "Come on up."

At the top of the hill near the cabin door, I tried to dismount, only to find that my legs were numb with cold. David almost had to pry me off the stallion. "Oh, my shoes are so stiff," I groaned.

"Hang onto my arm. Only a few steps more."

Once inside the door, I saw that this was strictly a man's place. There was the smell of tobacco, stuffed deer heads on the walls, antlers, a bearskin rug on the hearth, and a great many framed pictures, mostly men.

"Miss Huddleston, sit down here." The Doctor pulled out a three-legged stool for me. He stood there scrutinizing me. Then suddenly he said, "Those clothes mustn't dry on you. Let me see what I can find for you to wear."

I was only too willing. "My skirt's wool. It's going to take a while to dry."

The Doctor strode into an adjoining room and in a minute returned with some clothes over his arm. "Here, try these."

I took them. One was a faded flannel shirt. Then I held up a pair of man's pants in front of me.

Dr. MacNeill stood gazing down at me, his hazel eyes sweeping me up and down. "You can't wear those," he concluded. "They come up to your armpits."

"She could turn up the pant legs," David suggested.

"But how would I hold them *up*? Two of me could get inside."

"Well, then, let's see what else we can do." He paused a moment, then abruptly turned toward a closed door that I had not noticed before, to the right of the main living portion of the cabin. Surprisingly, the Doctor took a key out of his pocket to unlock the door. I glanced over at David questioningly, but his eyes were fixed on the door which Dr. MacNeill had entered and then carefully closed behind him. He looked as puzzled as I.

The minutes dragged by. I sank down on the little stool close to the fire. When our host still did not return, I found myself looking around the room. On a tilt-top table beside me sat a canister of tobacco with a man's pipe lying beside it. The pipe was so distinctive-looking! Gingerly, I picked it up to look more closely at the wide silver band on the stem. There were words engraved in an antique script on the silver, but they made no sense to me . . . *Tha mo chas air ceann mo naimhdean.* Puzzled, I laid the pipe back in its place.

Just beyond the table on the hearth sat a luster jug with cattails and dried flowers, now dust-covered. On the other side of the fireplace was something not quite in character with the rest of the furnishings—a low chair, certainly not a man's chair judging from its dainty spindled back. Then my thoughts were pulled away by a gradual awareness of a clock ticking loudly on the mantel. Looking closely I could read the inscription: "London—1743." I wondered where the Doctor had gotten the clock.

"Think you could get into this?" Dr. MacNeill had walked into the room so softly that neither of us had heard him. Looking over his shoulder, I saw that the door behind him had been closed again. He was holding up a flower-sprigged dress; other garments were over his arm.

"Oh, yes! They look just my size!" With difficulty I restrained my curiosity.

"Better slip out of those wet shoes too. Here's a pair of my carpet slippers."

I followed him to the room he indicated and he left me there, shutting the door after me. It was his bedroom. There was a pine four-poster bed with an unbleached homespun spread hastily pulled up over the voluminous featherbed, and a cherry chest of drawers. An open cupboard with medical books piled in it, a small wooden chest, and one hooked rug completed the furnishings of the room.

I spread the garments on the bed. The dainty underclothes were of fine lawn trimmed with handmade lace and narrow ribbon. When I stepped out of the wet riding skirt into the bloomers (though slightly old-fashioned) they fit as though they had been made for me. As I picked up the dress, a fragrance—woodruff, I thought it was—came from its folds. I had caught a whiff of that somewhere else recently, but I couldn't place it. The dress was of barred muslin, a summer costume, but I could stay close to the fire.

My return to the living room interrupted the flow of masculine voices. Both men looked up inquiringly. "These are perfect!" I was holding my wet clothes at arm's length. "Could I dry these by the fire?"

"Sure." Dr. MacNeill took the garments. "David tells me that you have to be at Lufty Branch crossroads by three." The Doctor looked at the clock on the mantel. "It's two-thirty now."

David sat there considering, then made a decision. "That heavy wool won't dry in fifteen minutes, Christy. And you can't go out in this weather in a cotton dress. You stay here and I'll go and make excuses for you. They'll understand. By the time I get back, your skirt will be dry."

I agreed reluctantly. "Sorry I messed things up, David."

"Never mind. Doesn't really matter. Thanks, Doc, for your help." And David turned to go.

Alone with Dr. MacNeill, I felt immediately ill at ease. Until I had seen David's broad back disappearing out the door, I had not realized what a difference his presence made or how much I had been relying on him to shield me from the strangeness of the Doctor and his cabin.

For there were contradictions in this man and his surroundings. All kinds of questions forced themselves to the surface. Why the locked door in a community where most of the people scarcely bothered to shut their front doors, much less lock them? To whom had these clothes belonged? From where were these evidences of education and refinement—like the pieces of fine old furniture, the framed inscribed photographs, and the pipe lying on the table with the wide engraved silver band on its stem?

Dr. MacNeill seemed of the mountains, yet strangely not of them. He would have had to get his medical education somewhere else. But then, once he had seen and known the world outside the Cove, why had he come back to practice medicine here and then let things go on as before—like that liver-grown superstition that had killed the McHone baby?

"You're a silent one, especially for a female." The deep voice broke into my thoughts. "I'm going to fix you a hot grog."

"Please don't bother. I'm thawed now."

"Not afraid of a little mountain dew, are you?"

My answer must have sounded defensive. "Not afraid. I just don't like the taste."

"Then call it medicine, insurance against any side effects of your swim in the creek."

It was useless to protest; Dr. MacNeill had a dominating way about him. As he took an old pewter jug from the shelf, wiped it, went about mixing the grog and placing it close to the fire, I studied his face.

134

In profile it was a rugged face, as if the features had been chiseled out of rough stone and the final smoothing and polishing never quite completed. Yet that was not quite right either, for when finally he turned to look at me, I saw that the hazel eyes were intuitive, perceptive; their corners were crisscrossed with smile lines. And he had a sensitive mouth, as if the sculptor had given special attention to that. All in all, it was a strong, unmistakably masculine face. Yet his curly, sandy-reddish hair—apparently always too long and unruly—gave him a boyish look. The hair curled a bit at the back of his head and over the tips of his ears. And that restless habit I had noticed the day of the operation, of running his fingers through the back ends, squeezing them—he could not keep his fingers still.

"Drink that." There was a peremptory note in his voice. He thrust the pewter mug at me.

Dutifully I raised the mug to my lips but did not drink the bitter stuff. "Dr. MacNeill, I'm confused about something."

He stopped and turned around to look at me, smile lines pulling at his mouth. "What do you mean?"

Now that I had taken the plunge, I was embarrassed. "Oh, lots of things." I wondered in what order to ask my questions. But then I blurted out, "Like babies dying."

"Are you referring to the McHone infant?"

I nodded. "I helped prepare the baby."

"I know you did. And you think I was remiss in my duty? Not a real doctor to my people. Is that it?"

I looked him full in the face. "Yes, I admit it. I did have that thought."

Suddenly the Doctor became preoccupied with filling his pipe. Carefully he tamped in the tobacco. His hands looked just as they had that afternoon of the operation—stained and roughened by work. His deliberation was maddening.

"You've got a lot to learn about the mountain people," he said finally. "I've known Opal McHone all my life. She had a granny who came from Aberdeenshire originally, then lived in Ulster awhile—true Scotch-Irish. The old lady was revered in the Cove as an herbalist. Some of her knowledge was sound enough, some of it nonsense—like the liver-grown ailment. But granny's word is still gospel. The Scotch-Irish are stubborn, you know."

"You mean Mrs. McHone won't listen to you?"

"Not when my word crosses granny's." He paused, then went on tersely. "I can guess your next question. You're curious about the dress." There was an almost imperceptible change in the expression on his face, a softening of the lines. "It belonged to my wife. She died three years ago in childbirth. Typhoid complications."

"Oh, I'm sorry." I found myself wanting to ask about the locked door and whether or not that had been her room. But the Doctor's manner told me that the subject was closed for now.

"As for me," he went on, "I was born in this cabin. So were my parents and my grandparents. So you see—I'm a hillbilly."

"You don't talk like one."

He puffed on his pipe, again took his time before answering. "I lapse into mountain talk easily enough when I'm with the natives, like an Irishman whose brogue gets thicker by the minute when he's with another Irishman. However, I've had some schooling outside—college, then medical school."

"If you don't mind my asking—where?"

He did not answer immediately. He put two more logs on the fire, felt my skirt and turned it over. Then he said slowly, as if reining in his impatience with my questions, "When I was sixteen, a group of New York physicians and surgeons hired a special train and came down to the Smokies on a vacation hunting trip. They used an uncle of mine as a guide. I went along to help carry their camping gear. For some reason they took a liking to me, found out that I had ambitions to be a doctor. So—they made college and medical school possible for me. I went to Jefferson Medical College, then got my bedside training at Jefferson Hospital and the Will's Eye Hospital."

"Are those the pictures of some of the doctors?"

"Yes, great men, long-time friends. I owe them everything."

I rose to have a closer look at the pictures. The Doctor came and stood just behind me.

"That's James Healy, orthopedic surgery . . . McDougall, abdominal surgery . . . Kinnigan, a great professor of ophthalmology . . . William S. Paget. . . ." I felt his breath on my neck. Abruptly, I walked over to the pictures on the other wall. "And these?"

"That's Starr Gatlin—dead now. He was the brain surgeon who did the only trephine I ever witnessed."

"Trephine?"

"You know, the same surgery I performed on Bob Allen. Tricky operation. Matter of fact, that particular surgical procedure hasn't often been tried in our time."

"In our time?"

"Yes. What I mean is old-timers say the trephine burrhole was used fairly often by pioneer doctors for those who survived Indian sealpings."

"I didn't know anybody survived Indian scalpings."

"Oh, a few. Naturally not when the whole top of the skull was hacked off."

I winced. "But I still don't see how the operation would help."

"For anybody who lived through the scalping, the problem was how to get the skull covered again. So the frontier doctors used to bore a series of holes into the dura mater with a straight awl until they drew blood to the surface. That caused the scalp to grow again—in time."

Sometimes I wished that my imagination was not so vivid. "They did all that with no ether?"

"Wasn't any ether. Anyone who lived through an Indian raid and being scalped was strong enough to stand a little more."

I had had enough of scalping. "Going back to the day of the operation, there were two things I never understood. Somebody said Mr. Allen was hit by a *girdled* tree . . ."

"Oh, that—a tree hacked with a deep series of gashes all round the trunk. The tree eventually rotted and died. In the process of rotting, those trees are always dangerous because they're so easily wind-thrown. Girdling was the lazy frontier way of clearing land. Terrible waste of good lumber. But then the early settlers thought the timber supply limitless." He paused. "But you said *two* questions?"

"Yes, Mary Allen—when she hove that axe into the floor, what was that about?"

He smiled. "Mountain superstition. Axe is supposed to keep a person from hemorrhaging. Maybe you don't remember, but Mary tied a string around Bob's wrist too. That's to keep disease away."

137

The Doctor was tapping the tobacco out of his pipe on the edge of the fireplace. Then he picked up a reed from the luster jug, ran it through his pipe stem and blew on it. "But let's get back to the medical situation here in the Cove," he said. "Or—am I boring you?"

"No. I want to hear about it."

"Well then, as for the question in your mind about why I'm not reforming things around here, if I didn't care about these people, I'd sure be practicing medicine somewhere else."

"You mean it's a hard place to practice?"

He looked at me tolerantly. "I could soliloquize on that one for so long you'd be yawning. I'll limit myself to one fact: Last year I was out on calls one hundred and seventy-four different nights."

I found it hard to believe. "You mean you keep records about every night call?"

He shrugged, turned in his usual unhurried way to put another log on the fire. Then he stood on the hearth, a faraway look in his hazel eyes, absently squeezing his hair in his fingertips. I wondered why he didn't get his hair cut more often. Obviously he didn't care about his personal appearance. "I'm practicing here in Cutter Gap," he resumed, "because of a particular afternoon I spent with Starr Gatlin. It was a rainy May afternoon. How could I ever forget? At that time I had three offers to consider for a beginning practice. Two were flattering offers. I was confused, torn about where my duty lay, how to make such an important decision. So—I went to see Dr. Gatlin. He was a wise old man. Just sat there smoking, let me do the talking.

"By the time dusk was falling, I had talked myself out. And I knew what I had to do. The call of the mountains and my own people was too strong to deny. I knew how desperately they needed a doctor back in these hills and coves. Personal ambition didn't matter really. I've never regretted that decision, simply because I wouldn't have been happy anywhere else. One of these days some of the men I interned with will probably be as famous as Gatlin, McDougall, and the rest. I follow their careers with a lot of interest, rejoice in their successes, keep closely in touch with them." With a sweep of his eyes he indicated the pictures. "As a matter of fact, they're the ones whose gifts of money and drugs make it possible for me to practice in the Cove."

"It's a sacrifice you've made, though," I said softly. "But since you *did* come back here, I don't quite see—I mean—"

"You don't see that I've accomplished much. You've been at the mission how long, Miss Huddleston?"

"A little over two months."

"You're young. Impulsive too. When you feel something, you feel strongly, don't you? I can tell. And you've made some sweeping judgments in those two months, haven't you?"

I could feel my cheeks getting hot. Why did he have to put it like that? "I suppose I have made some judgments. But some things are obvious enough," I added stubbornly. "Like cabins and yards so dirty and so smelly that I lost my supper after one visit."

Suddenly the Doctor threw back his head and laughed. It was a deep rumbling laugh that rippled over his entire body.

At the moment my sense of humor was missing. "Dr. MacNeill, a queasy stomach may seem funny to you. You've been trained to stand anything. But the sights and sounds that made me lose my supper aren't funny. They really aren't."

"Forgive me. But if you could have seen your own face! When your nose wrinkled up, I could just see some of the sights you were remembering." He was still chuckling. "I know it's bad—but these people can't be changed all at once. They have their own timing. The pace is slower back in these hills than outside. Let me tell you something Uncle Bogg said only last week. He was talking to me about the Great Northern Lumber Company trying to buy up land—a man was up here last fall looking around. 'All the trouble them outlanders are makin' for us tryin' to git our land, that ain't so bad by itself,' Uncle Bogg said. 'But hits comin' right on top of the War Between the States that seems more'n we can stand.' "

In spite of my annoyance, I couldn't help laughing, and the tension between us relaxed.

Yet, I was thinking, how odd that for the highlanders time moves that slowly. Ever since I've been in the Cove, for me it has been just the opposite. Is it because this seems such a new world and I'm having so many new experiences so fast? Like the way time telescoped for me when father took our family on that four-day holiday to

New York City. We made every minute count and packed so much living into a brief time that when it was over, I could scarcely believe we had been in New York only four days.

Again, the Doctor pulled me away from my thoughts by a change of mood. "Resistance to change isn't all. We've worse problems than dirt and smells back here. How much do you know about the murders back in these mountains?"

"Not much. Several people have hinted at it, that's all."

"You don't know the Taylor-Allen story?"

I shook my head.

"In my father's time, the spring of '79 it was, Otis Allen was murdered by MacKinley Taylor. It was a land boundary dispute. Involved Coldsprings, one of the best springs in these mountains. I won't go into details, they're too involved. But since then nine men have been killed, three since I've been practicing. Oh, we've got things patched up enough—mostly Miss Henderson's doing—so that Allen and Taylor children are both going to your school. You have no idea what an achievement *that* is. Just for example, there's a couple other side Raven Mountain who haven't spoken to one another in twenty-six years."

"You mean, they're divorced?"

"No! That's my point. They've lived together in the same cabin all that time. Lived together as man and wife and have had seven children. The mother will say to one of the children, 'Liz, tell yer Paw for me . . .' Then the father will send his reply back by Liz. They think it's a virtue, a mark of strong character, to carry a grudge to the grave." He looked at me and laughed. "Your eyes are very expressive, Miss Huddleston. They tell me you don't believe me."

"Well, I—"

"It's true though. And that's why rooting out the grudges and the hates that lead to killings is even more pressing than sanitation."

"Are these what you'd call feuds?"

"In a way. But this area isn't a feuding district like some other sections."

"But still, Dr. MacNeill, you're a doctor. Stopping killings isn't your job. That's the law's job."

"Sure. But out of nine murders and several woundings, nobody's been convicted."

"How did they get off?"

"Lots of angles to it. In these mountains, family loyalty comes before everything else—including the law. It's Jacobite Scotland and Tudor England all over again. In the eyes of the mountaineers, the courts are always unfair, slanted toward one side or the other. So when the state can't insure real justice, they think that private war, ambush, assassination, murder—are justified."

"But that's ridiculous about the courts being unfair. This is twentieth-century America, not Tudor England."

"It isn't as silly as you think, not when families plot for years to get one of their clan elected a judge, sheriff or county squire. If the case comes before a jury, the jurors put family loyalty ahead of everything else too. So do all the witnesses."

I sat there trying to take in a lot of new ideas at once.

"But then there's another reason why murderers get off around here," the Doctor went on. "The El Pano district, the Old Twelfth, has a county squire who's ruled this county for eighteen years and there hasn't been a sentence for murder in all that time. There are ways and ways of seeing that nobody ever gets convicted."

"Who's the squire?"

"Uncle Bogg McHone."

"You can't be serious!" I was shocked and made no effort to hide it. "He seems like a harmless, likable old man."

"I know. And he has his own brand of chivalry. And I like him too. Yet I'm serious, quite serious."

"But Dr. MacNeill, you said everybody in the Cove takes sides. Why wouldn't the squire want anybody who's guilty on the other side from his family and friends to be brought to justice?"

"Because he subscribes wholeheartedly to the view that our family quarrels are our own business, to be resolved in our own way outside the courts. If he didn't feel that way, he'd never have gotten elected—and then re-elected seventeen times."

"I never heard anything so tangled."

"Yet I haven't told you a fraction of all the ins and outs." The Doctor walked over to look out the front window. "I think we began this conversation when you challenged me in a pert, feminine way about my lack of reforming zeal about sanitation and superstitions. If you'd really like to see some reform, stopping the hate and feuding and killing is a fertile field for your mission."

There was a note of something close to contempt in his voice. He had said "your mission" as if it was far removed from his sphere of activity.

"I take it that 'thou shalt not kill' is authorization enough," he went on. "Besides, I agree with you that it would sure be pleasant to spend some time teaching mothers how to take care of babies instead of probing for bullets in lungs, suturing slashed abdomens, operating on eyes half gouged out."

While he heated some coffee in an old white enamelware coffeepot and we drank it, the Doctor talked on about some of the families in the Cove, telling me story after story, some of them gruesome, many of them funny. When we heard a light rap on the door and David walked in, I was startled that so much time had passed.

After I had dressed again in my own clothes and as we were leaving Dr. MacNeill's cabin, David said, "Theo will mind me better, so I'll ride him and you take Prince."

"But—"

"No buts. You'll be safe enough if you ride astride. No, not a word, I insist. Safety before modesty."

"But David, I've *got* to say it, this isn't a split skirt—"

"Doesn't matter. Anyway, I already know what a woman's leg looks like."

Actually I did feel more sure of myself not riding sidesaddle. We got back across Big Spoon Creek without any problems and onto the trail for home.

Along the edge of the ridge, the path was wide enough that David and I could ride side by side. I was letting David do most of the talking; my thoughts were still on what Dr. MacNeill had told me. How could the Cutter Gap that the Doctor had pictured be the same place that Dr. Ferrand had talked about that day from the platform in Montreat? What did Miss Alice think about all of these murders? And how much of all this did David know? He had seemed so friendly with Uncle Bogg. Did he know about the old man's obstructing justice? Finally I broke into my own thoughts to ask David.

"I know enough," was his answer. "I haven't said much because I didn't want to scare you. For your comfort, those who mind their own business and don't take sides are usually safe enough. But the Doc is right about the mission's responsibility. My mind's been wrestling with this. I may have to rip open the subject from the pulpit soon."

"But that won't exactly be minding your own business. That could be—well—"

"Dangerous? Sure. I know."

"David, about Dr. MacNeill . . . I was glad of the chance to know him better this afternoon. But after all his explanations, I still don't see how he can go in and out of these cabins year after year and leave them in as bad shape as always. He's a strange one. I don't think I like him."

"That's not fair, Christy. You women judge too quickly. Don't be fooled about the Doc because he doesn't wear a white shirt and a collar and tie. I've spent some evenings with him, talking. Good talk, too. His ancestors were as distinguished a family as ever came out of Scotland—the MacNeills of the Island of Barra. Their ancestral castle is still there. Pry the story out of the Doctor some time—or get Alice Henderson to tell you."

Eleven

FOUR of Miss Ida's hot buckwheat cakes, six—David was enjoying his breakfast. I poured him a second cup of coffee.

"When you have something important to say to a man," my mother had always advised, "never say it to a hungry one. Wait until he's had a good meal." Well then, now should be the moment.

"David," I plunged in, "I've gotten notice of some shipments at Lyleton and El Pano—for the mission, I mean." I tried to sound casual.

"What kind of shipments?" His black eyebrows lifted. Already he was wary.

This was hard. For days now I had been trying to think of a way to soften the news, but I couldn't figure out any way at all to make the shipment of a concert grand piano and a Harvester wagon sound—well, usual. "Oh, just a few things." I looked away from him, traced the pattern in the tablecloth with the tip of one finger. "A wagon and uh—a grand piano."

"A *what*?"

"No need to get upset, David."

"Now let's begin all over." He pushed his chair back from the table, crossed his legs and looked at me. "Will you get that pleading look out of those big eyes of yours? Now whatinthunder is this about?"

"Sort of a long story. I got the idea of writing to some businessmen, a nice letter, really nice, telling them about the mission and giving them a chance to help by donating products rather than money."

" 'Giving them a chance,' she says. That's turning things around."

"But," I protested, "how could I know that so many of them would respond? I never expected the Lyon and

144

Healy Company to come through. And if they did, I was thinking of an upright, not a grand piano. Let alone a *concert* grand."

David grimaced, put his head in his hands, laughed shakily, and then started probing and prodding and pulling the truth out of me bit by bit. "How many letters have you written, Christy?"

"Thirty-eight."

"How many replies have you gotten so far?"

"Ah, let me think—twenty-one."

"And are *all* of these firms donating something?"

"All but one. One flat refusal."

"I see. What kind of stuff are they sending other than wagon beds and concert grand pianos?"

"Oh, mattresses, soap, paints, windowshades, soup."

Poor David got his answers soon enough. For the next few weeks, hauling freight out from El Pano took most of his time. Three bedsteads arrived, then some towels and sheets. David had to borrow a team of oxen to get the wagon sent by the International Harvester Company out to the Cove. Yet the wagon proved to be invaluable. It arrived in the mission yard piled high with cartons and boxes.

Soon Miss Ida was complaining loudly that she could not get around the kitchen because of the cases of soup, evaporated milk, baked beans, and cocoa that had piled up. "We have enough Pincine baking powder and Plymouth Rock gelatin and Wizard furniture polish to last the rest of our lives. Miss Huddleston has been most efficient. Too bad while she was about it, she didn't ask for a warehouse to store the stuff. David," she fumed, "you've got to find somewhere else to dump all this paraphernalia."

But the back porch was already heaped high with the cartons of pins, insulators, and the wire from the telephone company. A lot of wire was needed for seven miles. Besides, David would pay no attention to what he called under his breath his sister's "picayune complaints." He escaped the tension in the house by staying busy each day hauling out more freight.

Then the piano arrived, the largest and most elaborate concert grand made by Lyon and Healy. It took two pairs of oxen hitched to the new wagon to pull it. David and three of the mountain men spent two days of hard work getting the huge instrument over the rutted roads across

145

the mountains. But the piano was given a place of honor in the big, almost empty living room and was to prove a delight to all of us.

At supper the day the piano arrived, Miss Ida commented waspishly, "Christy Huddleston, you're sure going to get the beggar's reward when you get to heaven."

David laughed but I noticed that Miss Alice did not. "As a matter of fact, Christy," she said seriously, "Dr. Ferrand doesn't like begging."

Miss Ida pursed her lips primly as if to say, "I told you so!"

"Now's the time to explain the Doctor's philosophy of money and fund-raising," Miss Alice went on, not noticing her at all. "David, you should know this too. He loathes even the term 'raising money.' Whenever he makes a talk about the work—and believe me, that's usually several times a week—he won't even let anyone take a collection afterwards. The point is, Dr. Ferrand won't accept any money unless he knows the individual has had inner direction to give it. He feels that money dunned out of people won't be blessed for the work anyway."

These were new ideas to me but I respected them. In fact, in the light of such a philosophy of giving, now I thought I saw what was wrong with the never-ending pleas for funds from charitable organizations and pulpits: most of the time these solicitors were trying to pry money out of people by riding roughshod over their individual right of choice.

But Miss Alice continued, "I believe each person has something special he's meant to do. That being the case, surely we have no right to foist 'causes'—even our favorite ones—only present them. Dr. Ferrand believes—and I agree—that only one motive is good enough to warrant giving: because the self, without pressure, freely chooses to make the gift."

As we left the table, Miss Alice took my arm and led me to the far corner of the living room. "Christy, as much as we need these supplies, I'm forced to say this to you. All those letters you wrote could place the mission in a bad light. And Dr. Ferrand *does* have the right to be consulted about policy and procedure. So do the rest of us on the staff. I honestly don't think this going ahead on your own was even good teamwork."

I nodded, gulped back several explanations, but I knew she was right. I *did* sometimes pull away and go running off on my own. David's attitude about the telephone underscored her point on teamwork. If he was expected to string the wires and install the telephones, he felt that I might at least have talked it over with him before writing the Bell Company. On my side, I had just thought that if David could build a schoolhouse-church, he would have no problem installing one or two little telephones.

"It has to be connected up, you know. Two ends, something to carry the voice." There was mild irritation and a trace of sarcasm in David's voice. "The wire has to be strung across Pebble Mountain, then across Coldsprings Mountain—that's even higher—over Allen's Branch, across the French Broad River. How do I get the wire across a river? Tell me that."

Woefully, I acknowledged that I hadn't the least idea. I had been too eager, astonishingly impulsive and thoughtless. After my rebuke from Miss Alice I was abject about it. But that did not stop the boxes and barrels from continuing to arrive.

Evening after evening we pulled down the new shades and unpacked some of the plunder. At least "plunder" was the way Ruby Mae thought of it; she was certain that Christmas had come to stay.

One evening it was several boxes of secondhand books and clothing from my Asheville church. Miss Alice was there because she was more tolerant of this type of contribution—probably, I thought, because she was accustomed to missionary barrels. Ruby Mae was sitting cross-legged on the floor, her brown eyes dancing with excitement. Miss Ida was close to an oil lamp, darning her brother's socks.

At my insistence, David unpacked the books first, and eagerly we scanned the titles. On the whole, they were fine; most could be used at the school. What a relief to have some books!

Then David got the lid pried off the first barrel and began pulling out the secondhand clothes. He held up a party dress of stiff gray silk, heavily beaded.

"Oh-h! It's beau-ti-ful." Ruby Mae reached out eager fingers for it. She held the dress in front of her and began dancing around the room, her long red hair flying.

"Perfect for hoeing—or carrying water from the spring," was David's dry retort. "Look what we have next—" and he pulled out a pink corset with many stays

147

and long strings. We women chose to ignore that, but David, teasingly, draped it prominently over the edge of the barrel. Next came a swallowtail coat and several voluminous nightshirts and then a series of ladies' hats. One was black velvet shaped like a gigantic boat, heavy with once-white aigrette feathers. Another was a soiled pink, layer upon layer of ribbon, the whole swathed in yards of mauve veiling.

"Now this one is re-ally packed. You should see the tissue around it. Must be valuable." And David twirled on his finger a natural straw wreathed in red roses, wired so that a cluster of the roses towered high above the hat.

I was feeling increasingly let down. Apparently in my letters to my Asheville friends I had not gone into enough detail about the kind of clothes to send; I had thought they understood that the mountain folk had no need for such dress-up clothes.

David raised his head out of the barrel and looked at me. "Hey, Christy, come on now, don't take it so seriously. Here, model this millinery," and he shoved the hat down on my hair.

The brim was over my eyes and I could feel the tower of roses vibrating in the air. It was a relief to laugh and soon all of us—including Miss Alice—were caught up in the hilarity. Each item out of the barrels was more ludicrous than the last: a muff, half-eaten by moths; a ruffled nightcap; a pillow-top which had been a souvenir of Niagara Falls; ladies' chemises, and men's vests, a lot of them.

I had pushed the hat with the roses back on my head, but each time I moved, the tower of roses fluttered and swayed. "Whatever can we do with these?" I asked counting the vests, all eleven of them.

"After all, men's stomachs do have to be kept warm," Miss Alice said. "I'll predict these will be known locally as 'wes'coats' or maybe 'vestees.'"

Miss Ida snorted. "Four quilt pieces from the front of each vest, that's all they're good for."

The third barrel was better. It seemed full of children's shoes. At last I'd be able to get some of those bare feet in my classroom shod. But mixed in with the sensible ones were a few ladies' shoes with high heels and very pointed toes, some of them satin.

Before we parted for the night, we decided that it would not do to give away the clothes. "There's a strong mountain code," Miss Alice explained. "No mountain person wants to be beholden." Here she looked directly at me, hoping to drive her point home. "Any mountain man has contempt for anyone who won't let him earn his own way."

This posed a dilemma. Finally David had an idea. "Why not sell the clothes—priced very low, of course?" His thought was that we could set up store in his little house down by the creek one afternoon a week. We could charge something like seventy-five cents for a good suit or dress; twenty-five cents for a blouse; five cents for a vest; fifty cents for a pair of shoes. And since even small amounts of cash were so short in the Cove, we could take produce in exchange when it was necessary.

Ruby Mae was given permission to set the mountain grapevine in motion with the news of the store. It caused immediate excitement. To our astonishment, the first items to be bought with the tiny hoardings of cash or surplus food were the ones we had thought most useless. Every woman wanted a fancy city dress, every man a vest to wear on top of faded and patched overalls. Within a week after the store was opened, Bob Allen was wearing a swallowtailed coat as he tended mill, and high-heel satin shoes had been filled with sand or pebbles from creek banks and were being used as door stops in many a mountain cabin.

Every Saturday for the next three months we kept store and on the whole it was a great success. The only problem was that soon the mission was drowning in sorghum and sauerkraut, the two items which had rapidly become the principal media of exchange. There were nights when David waited until everyone was in bed and then stealthily got rid of gallons of sauerkraut by burying it in the back yard.

Twelve

EVERY MONDAY MORNING of each successive week handed me problems in schoolteaching for which no Teacher's Training Course could ever have prepared me. First of all, strangely enough, were the smells. What was I to do about the body odors of children who were disinclined to take any baths during the cold months; who, if they owned any underwear, usually had it sewn on for the winter?

Whenever my pupils and I could stand the cold, we would conduct school with as many windows up as possible. That helped. But on some days the wintry blasts sweeping down from the mountains would whistle through the Cove, shaking the frame building as if it had been a rat in the teeth of some giant terrier, quivering the timbers, shivering us, making it impossible to open the windows.

Of a morning while I was dressing, I came to recognize these bad days by the truculent whistling of the wind: we would have to huddle close to the stove that day. So I would prepare by carrying up my sleeve a handkerchief heavily saturated with perfume. Then when one of my more difficult pupils had to be near me to recite, I could always pull the handkerchief out and dab at my nose. I hoped that none of the children guessed my strategy.

Over and over I rued that too-sensitive nose of mine. Many an evening in my bedroom as I was preparing next day's lessons, some incident would rise to haunt me: how I had backed away from Larmie Holt when I should have hovered close to check his work. There had been that certain look in the child's eyes, puzzled, a little hurt. Larmie had not understood. How could he!

Then I would chew my pencil and walk the floor pondering my dilemma. I wondered how others trapped in

150

similar situations had managed. All those foreign missionaries, hundreds of them, must have had it far worse than I. Yet I had never heard any returned missionary speak of grappling with poor sanitation and uncleanliness. Perhaps they considered it too delicate a subject to discuss. And then—in desperation—I would feel like crying out, "Oh God, it might be funny, but it isn't, really it isn't. Ple-ease—change my nose, or help me get the children cleaned up in a hurry."

This led directly to the idea of including a hygiene or health lesson in each day's curriculum. I sent to Asheville for several hygiene textbooks. These gave me lots of material.

One day we would talk about the skin, how the body got rid of waste through the pores and the necessity of washing perspiration and sloughed-off cells off the skin. But then we had to get down to practical points about *how* to bathe, since most of my pupils had only a granite tub or pan to use in front of the open fire, and even that was not easy with a large family in a one or two-room cabin.

Another day the lesson would be about pure drinking water, the dangers of typhoid and hookworm, and how to keep a spring clean. It was then I discovered how often the children would go to the bathroom in a mountain stream and I realized that I had to forget prudishness and speak candidly.

In addition, as I saw how closely the children watched "Teacher," how much they wanted to be like me and in how many ways they were copying me, I tried to be more meticulous about grooming than I had ever been, wearing freshly starched and ironed shirtwaists, always keeping my hair clean and shining. I hoped that some of this effort would rub off on my pupils—and it did. Soon Lizette Holcombe, Bessie Coburn, Ruby Mae and Clara Spencer were asking me if they could take a bath or wash and iron clothes in the mission house. Since Miss Ida did not take too kindly to this, my room had to be the scene for most of this activity. And when the girls would comment wistfully, "Teacher, you smell so good," I furthered my crusade by keeping a can of violet-scented talc on hand just for them.

Then as time went on, I made an amazing discovery: the odors ("funks" as my children said, using a sturdy Shakespearean word) were no longer so much of a problem for me. It was not that my hygiene lessons had yet made that much difference, nor that I had grown accustomed to the smells because in other situations my crazy nose bothered me as much as always. It was rather that as I came to know the children and to think of them as persons rather than names in my grade book, I forgot my reactions and began to love them. I suppose the principle was that the higher affection will always expel the lower whenever we give the higher affection sway. For me, it was letting love for the mountain children come in the front door while my preoccupation with bad smells crept out the rathole.

A problem of a different sort was the plight of those pupils who were far behind their age group in everything. It was not fair that a big boy like Lundy Taylor should have to recite in the primer class with the six-year-olds just because he had never before been in school.

But I felt equally sorry about a child like Mountie O'Teale whose real problem was the O'Teale family home. The picture of the epileptic boy in his pen in the corner would rise before me. When Mountie tried to speak, she showed a serious speech defect—halted gruntings and croaking like an animal—more like a three or four-year-old than a ten-year-old.

Also Mountie wore hand-me-down clothes and her hair was rarely combed. And the little girl never smiled or laughed or showed any emotion whatever. She seemed so dead inside that I could not be sure there was any possibility of helping her.

Then one afternoon I caught Creed Allen and her own brother Smith teasing her. On the playground they bent a sycamore sapling into a bow, lured her by, then released the branch to hit her in the face. It hurt, and when she started crying, they chanted in unison . . .

> Mush-mouthed Millie,
> Can't even speak,
> Jabber jabber jaybird
> Marbles in the beak.

"Look at her blubber, bawlin' her eyes out. Dare you t' blab to Teacher," I heard them stage-whisper to taunt her. "Only Teacher couldn't understand you if'n you did blab. Cotton-mouth!"

Since I was trying not to interfere too often on the

playground, I waited to see what would happen. No, Mountie did not tell on the boys, but I looked at her and saw misery staring out of her eyes. So she was able to feel, feel deeply. Suddenly, I glimpsed real intelligence buried behind the wall she had put up to ward off more hurt. There was just a chance that Mountie might turn out to be the white lamb of the O'Teale family. But what to do for her? How to begin?

It may be that my wondering and pondering, and the fact that now I really wanted to help Mountie, constituted a sort of prayer. Prayer—that is, the kind that asks for idea-help with some particular problem life hands you—was still new to me.

However that may be, later on that day, as I was standing before my front bedroom window letting my eyes drink in "my view," the clear thought came to me: Watch for an opportunity to do something special for Mountie O'Teale, something that will please her.

The chance came the next day. For the first time, I noticed that the shabby coat the little girl always wore to school had no buttons. So during recess I dashed over to the mission house, selected some large buttons from Miss Ida's button-box along with needle and thread. As I ate my lunch, I sewed on the buttons, then carefully hung Mountie's coat back on the peg at the back of the room where I had found it.

After school was dismissed, while I was straightening my desk, suddenly I heard a giggle at the back of the room. I looked up and saw that it was Mountie.

"Mountie, what's funny?"

She came bouncing up to my desk, pointing to the buttons, stood there, gleeful and excited. "Look at my buttons! Look at my buttons!"

"Mountie, what did you say?"

"Teacher, look! Look at my buttons! See my pretty buttons!"

I could scarcely believe what I was hearing. In spite of the chortling, the giggles up and down the scale, the child was speaking plainly for the first time. It was like watching something open up inside her. I felt triumphant for her and left school so excited that I wanted to tell everyone about it.

That night as I pondered this breakthrough, the thought came that Mountie's speech defect just might have an emotional base. Perhaps what she needed most of all was to be sure that she was a real person, that someone loved her for herself. For two days I wondered how best to demonstrate that to her. Finally I decided to give her a gift—that bright red scarf which my mother had knitted for me. This had to be presented privately after school the next day so that the other girls would not be envious. The scarf was meant to tell Mountie that she was a very special person to me. It conveyed the message all right. This time she not only delightedly laughed but hugged and hugged me, did an impromptu dance up and down the schoolroom, waving the scarf. Then we practiced over and over, "See my buttons" ... "I like the scarf" ... "Pretty scarf" ... "Oh, pretty red scarf." And the child's heart and mind opened up some more.

With every bit of encouragement Mountie received, each time I could tell her that she was doing better, she would try even harder. Teacher cared about *her*. Teacher loved *her*. Did she not have the buttons and the scarf to prove it?

Now that the little girl's mind was released, it could function. Mountie O'Teale's reading ability grew astonishingly fast. Later on that year, I gave all of my pupils reading tests. I could scarcely believe my own grades when the results showed that through the twelve-year-old group, Mountie had come out highest of all.

Of course, the speech defect was by no means over— the emotional blocks went too deep—but astonishing progress was being made. And this little girl was teaching me such a lot about what an adventure schoolteaching is, and more, that what these children needed most was love instead of lives governed by fear and hate. The adults, hanging onto hatred in the name of virtue, were reaping a bitter harvest in their children.

Part of the harvest was a morbid preoccupation with the negatives of life; sickness, death and dying. For example, one day in the middle of the arithmetic lesson Creed Allen began to cry. I stopped the lesson to look at him inquiringly.

"My dog Bud-boy's dead." Tears were making two clean channels through the grime on his face. "Teacher, where's Bud-boy now?"

I cast around for what to say. Probably if I assured Creed that animals are immortal, I was going to be on shaky ground. But one thought did come to me.

"I'm sorry, Creed." I patted his shoulder. "When a boy

and a dog have tramped the mountains together, it's hard for them to be parted."

He nodded—and gulped.

"Creed, did you ever wonder how it is that good hounds have such wonderful noses? How they can track a possum or a fox or a bear for miles and miles just by the scent? And when a hunting dog has found his quarry, what makes him stand still, pointing? Or a dog like Bud-boy stand, baying his hound-music? Scientists call it 'instinct.' But what's instinct? Must be that God had put a bit of His wisdom, a little of Himself inside every living creature."

Creed lifted his head and looked hard at me, his eyes still glittering with tears. Hastily he brushed the tears away with one fist. "Uh—got something in my eye. Ain't cryin' water though."

But now he was intent on what I was saying. "Well, Creed, if God cared enough to think up hound-dogs in the first place—with their pleading eyes and their floppy ears and their built-in sense of smell and their devotion to their masters—don't you think you could trust Him to take care of one hound-dog like Bud-boy?"

Still his eyes searched mine while he chewed on my idea. Finally, his tear-streaked face crinkled into a half-grin. "Why, Teacher, I reckon so, Teacher. Why shorely, Teacher." And the tears stopped.

But a week later the crying about the dog started all over again. I was puzzled. "Creed, you told us last week that your dog had died. Is this the same dog?"

"Yes-s," his voice rose to a wail, "but Bud-boy didn't go to hea-ea-ven."

I made my voice soft and gentle, trying to soothe him. "Creed, why do you say that Bud-boy didn't go to heaven?"

"Be-cause when I put my dog in the bury-hole, I buried him with the tail stickin' up out'n the ground, so I'd know if you was a-foolin' me. And the tail's still there. So Teacher, ye told me wrong and Bud-boy *didn't* go to hea-ven-en—" and he plopped his head into his arms on the desk, shoulders shaking with sobs.

School was no sooner out that afternoon than I sent an urgent message by Ruby Mae to be delivered orally and secretly either to Mary or Bob Allen: "*Please* see to it that after you're certain Creed is asleep tonight, Bud-boy is properly buried—tail and all."

I soon saw, however, that Creed's obsession with death

155

was typical of most of the children. This came out in their play.

"Let's play funeral" was a favorite game at recess. To me, it seemed bizarre and mawkish play. All that saved it was the spontaneous creativity of the children and the fact that, unerringly, they caught the incongruities and absurdities of their elders.

One child would be elected to be "dead" and would lay himself out on the ground, eyes closed, hands dutifully crossed across his chest. Another would be chosen to be the "preacher," all the rest, "mourners." I remember one day when Sam Houston Holcombe was the "corpse" and Creed Allen, always the clown of the group, was elected "preacher." Creed, already at ten an accomplished mimic, was turning in an outstanding performance. I stood watching, half-hidden in the shadow of the doorway.

Creed (bellowing in stentorian tones): "You-all had better stop your meanness and I'll tell you for why. Praise the Lord! If you'uns don't stop being so derned ornery, you ain't never goin' to git to see Brother Holcombe on them streets paved with rubies and such-like, to give him the time of day, 'cause you'uns are goin' to be laid out on the coolin' board and then roasted in hellfire."

The "congregation" shivered with delight, as if they were hearing a deliciously scary ghost story. The corpse opened one eye to see how his mourners were taking this blast; he sighed contentedly at their palpitations; wriggled right leg where a fly was tickling; adjusted grubby hands more comfortably across chest.

Creed then grasped his right ear with his right hand and spat. Only there wasn't enough to make the stream impressive. So preacher paused, working his mouth vigorously, trying to collect more spit. Another pucker and heave. Ah! Better!

Sermon now resumed: "Friends and neighbors, we air lookin' on Brother Holcombe's face for the last time." (Impressive pause.) "Praise the Lord! We ain't never goin' see him again in this life." (Another pause.) "Praise the Lord!"

Small preacher was now really getting warmed up. He remembered something he must have heard at the last real funeral. Hefty spit first, more pulling of ear: "You air enjoyin' life now, folks. Me, I used to git pleasured and enjoy life too. But now that I've got religion, I don't enjoy

156

life no more." At this point I retreated behind the door lest I betray my presence by laughing aloud.

"And now let us all sing our departed brother's favorite song:

> 'I'm as free a little bird as I can be,
> I'll build a nest in a weeping willow tree. . . .'

All together now!" Creed waved his arms in wide sweeps to lead the singing.

And then later: "Now all of you'uns gather round and see how nateral Brother Holcombe looks."

Now it was the "mourners'" chance for action, mostly the girls. Much screeching, groaning and moaning followed; they pantomimed throwing themselves sobbing on the coffin and talking to the dead person. "Ah, Lordy, he be a sweet bouquet in heaven," someone shouted.

Suddenly from somewhere in the middle of the huddle the corpse's booming voice was heard, "Stop it, yer ticklin' me. Ground's too hard anyway. Lemme go. I ain't no sweet bouquet in heaven yit. I'm a-gettin' out of here."

After I had been teaching for a while, I began to realize how hungry my pupils were for love expressed in physical contact. They were forever reaching for me, touching me, squeezing me—like Little Burl, on my first day of teaching, coming up again and again to my desk to crowd his little body close to mine and trace the embroidery on my shirtwaist with a stubby forefinger.

I noticed too how all but the older boys acted with David, either in or out of the classroom: often clutching his arm and making excuses to walk along beside him.

At first I had not realized the significance of this yearning for touch, even as I had not known how far into childhood the need for physical contact is carried. But then I stumbled on the link between the need for touch and a child's ability to learn. Three of my beginners, Jake and Larmie Holt and Mary O'Teale were having a great deal of trouble learning to read. When I would take them one by one on my lap and give them a lesson, they learned twice as fast. Loving them up seemed to remove blocks, just as it had with Mountie.

Naturally with sixty-seven pupils in all grades to teach, it was hard to find time for such individual attention. Nor did it seem right to give most of my time to the dull, slow children rather than to the bright ones. Part of this I solved by appointing Junior Teachers to help me. These were my oldest and best pupils like Bob Allen, John Spencer, Lizette and John Holcombe. They in turn profited from the experience of teaching the younger ones. In no time at all, being appointed a Junior Teacher became the most coveted honor in school. So much so that I had to design a special badge for these children to wear: a piece of heavy cloth cut in the shape of a shield, each one trimmed differently with bits of fancy braids or beading or shiny buttons or sequins off the dresses in the mission barrels.

Recess provided me with another way of trying to appease this hunger for touch with several children at once. Whenever I would go out on the playground, my littlest ones would swarm to me, each wanting to hold onto a finger. Gradually the "Finger Game" evolved. Ten children could play, five on each side of me, each holding onto one finger. But in order not to get tangled in one another's legs, fall down and break one of Teacher's fingers in the process, we had to march close together with me at the center of the flying wedge, each child with one hand on the child in front, in a lock-step with perfect rhythm and coordination. If one of the ten got out of step, then all of us fell in a heap. But whether we marched perfectly or whether we tumbled, always there would be gales of laughter. Miss Ida, hearing us, must surely have thought we had lost our senses.

The Finger Game proved to be perfect for teaching a first lesson in working together in order to live together happily. I was at that time still too new to the Cove to realize how desperately the lesson was needed by the parents of the children along with them. For cooperation beyond the immediate family unit came hard to the highlanders. It was at that point that they showed rather more of their highland Scottish heritage than the typical American frontier pattern. For I had always supposed that in frontier days a high degree of neighborliness and cooperation had been necessary for survival: the "Workings" for building cabins or barns, or for clearing land or harvesting crops; the drawing together into stockades for protection and to resist Indian attacks; the relay system in pushing westward.

But in the mountains, though there were still a few Workings, many factors, including the terrain itself, the isolated coves and the difficulty of travel (a surprising number of these people lived and died without going more than a few miles from home) bred a self-contained individualism. Set down on its own hollow, each household had to depend on itself—and did. The Cove people were suspicious about joining any group effort or organization. Sometimes I wondered if they yet considered themselves to have joined the United States of America.

I could get impatient with this attitude, as David often did too: "Let Tennessee man-power its own roads. Hit disconfits me t'work" . . . "Naw, let preachin' take up fer the rest, I hain't comin'. Don't want nobody to think I treat my religion too familiar-like."

Trying to get work done for the school or the mission was often like trying to move mountains by shoving against the mountain with one's shoulder. As I struggled to like, much less love some of the worst of these individualists who wanted no part of accepting anyone's ideas or leadership, I comforted myself with the thought that, "Oh well, it's certainly my privilege not to like everyone."

It was Little Burl, of all people, who helped me to understand that rather it was my privilege to *try* to like everyone, at least to make an effort to see the good in each individual.

One morning we had interrupted our spelling lesson to watch the birds at our school feeding station. At my suggestion Mr. Spencer had built this for us and placed it atop a pole close to one of the schoolroom windows. As spring approached, a greater and greater variety of birds were appearing. My pupils were fascinated. This morning we had seen several juncos and some titmice. Now a pair of cardinals, the male with the most brilliant red feathers I had ever seen on a bird, were stuffing themselves on the crumbs and sunflower seeds.

Looking at that glorious red plumage, I exclaimed, "Isn't it great how many different kinds of birds there are, each one so special! God must have cared about them or He wouldn't have made them so beautiful."

Then I couldn't help adding, "He loves everything He's made—every bird, every animal, every flower, every man and woman, every single one of you, loves *you* extra specially."

As the children reluctantly turned from the birds back to preparation for the week's cross-spelling bee, I noticed two men crossing the schoolyard heading toward the back of the building. Shortly they were retracing their steps in the direction of the road, striding—not sauntering as most of the mountain men did. As they passed the school windows the second time, I saw their faces and felt sure that they were strangers. I tucked the incident into my mind to tell David, then turned my attention back to the spelling bee.

Little Burl was not working on spelling at all, but sitting at his desk staring up at the ceiling, his cowlick standing straight up, his funny little face puckered into a look of intense concentration. Something I had said had made an impression on him; I hoped he would let me in on his secret thought.

I had reached down to get fresh papers out of my desk drawer when I felt arms around my neck hugging me fiercely. It was Little Burl. He put his bare feet on top of my larger ones, locked his two hands behind my neck, stretched his head up to look me full in the eyes. "Teacher, Teacher, hain't it true, Teacher, that if God loves ever'body, then we'uns got to love ever'body too?"

I looked at the six-year-old in astonishment. "Yes, Little Burl, it *is* true." Forever and forever and forever.

So once I shut down my privilege of disliking anyone I chose and holding myself aloof if I could manage it, greater understanding, growing compassion came to me, more love for the children and as time passed, for the older people too. And suddenly I woke to the fact that smells in the schoolroom no longer seemed a problem.

Thirteen

MY NEW LIFE was a stretching process all the way. I had always thought of myself as shy, not naturally a leader, and Miss Alice saw this tendency to draw into myself and would have none of it. But Miss Alice was not one to dissipate energy in theorizing. Rather she was that rare combination: an idealist who could deal in specifics. So her first dictum designed to force me out of my reserve was her insistence that I visit the family of each of my school children in their homes.

Since I was already overwhelmed with schoolwork, at first the visiting looked like an impossible task. Still, I knew that Miss Alice was right to ask this of me. Knowing the children at school could never substitute for seeing their settings for myself, and more and more I was realizing what a far step it was from the Huddleston family home on Montford Avenue in Asheville to these mountain cabins.

But then I wondered how I could make these calls more than a perfunctory gesture on the part of the new teacher. For there was a wall of reserve around the mountain people not easy to penetrate; friendships were not made quickly in these parts.

I had yet to see any glad-handing or backslapping or the making of small talk for the stranger in Cutter Gap. How often already I had struggled with this situation: the atmosphere of cool unhurried courtesy as the highlander held his hands quietly at his sides while his eyes, with a glint of curiosity and humor, appraised me, the "outlander." He was forming no hasty judgments, but neither was any least effort being made to impress me. If the mountain man or woman had nothing to say he considered worth saying, then he said—nothing. Sometimes I would squirm uncomfortably at this and strain to fill the silence

161

with talk because I sensed that the highlander's silence was more than shyness: there was too much composure along with the diffidence. I kept wondering how long it would take the Cutter Gap folk to stop thinking of me as a foreigner. Perhaps years and years. Not until I got married and had reared children and grandchildren. I wondered if there was anything I could do to be accepted?

Plunge in, I supposed. So I decided to make my first call on Ruby Mae's parents. Her relationship with them was not of the best. Perhaps I could be an intermediary.

The Morrison cabin on the other side of Coldsprings Mountain looked no different from most except that the cornfield back of the house was tilted at about a forty degree angle. It strained my imagination to picture a man pushing a bull-tongue plow up that hillside. An old man and a much younger woman were sitting idly on the porch.

"Hello," I began, more heartily than I felt. "I'm Christy Huddleston, the new teacher at the mission."

The old man had his feet on the railing, his long white beard sunk on his chest. "Howdy." The feet did not move. The woman said nothing, sat staring at me.

I was still standing on the top step. The old man must be Ruby Mae's grandfather, I decided. "Is Mr. Morrison at home?"

There was no answer. My words might as well have been dropped into a bottomless hole. Finally they struck bottom. "I'm Duggin Morrison."

"You are Ruby Mae's stepfather?"

"Aye."

"I'm glad to meet you, Mr. Morrison. Ruby Mae is—I've gotten to know your daughter well."

The old man's eyes were on the scenery. He lifted his feet off the railing, leaned forward and let go a stream of tobacco juice. Fortunately, the spittle missed the long white beard. "Settin' chair over yan," he volunteered, relaxing back into his own.

I picked up the chair and set it beside the woman. She was barefooted and had coarse features with hard lines in her face. Her eyes were like steel balls, so calculating that I could not tell their color. "You're Mrs. Morrison?"

"Yep."

These people are taciturn and I'm shy. So what are we going to do, sit here in a row staring straight ahead?

When two walls meet head-on, something has to give.
I suppose I'm the one to make the supreme effort.

"Mr. Morrison ..." my voice sounded too loud in my own ears, so I cleared my throat and began again more softly, "Your daughter is unhappy because you asked her to leave home. She'd like to let bygones be bygones."

"Which?"

"She wants you to forgive her, let her come home."

"She's stiff-necked. Needs to be took down a peg."

"But I think you'll find Ruby Mae different now," I said eagerly. "Won't you talk to her?"

He appeared not to have heard me. "Wouldn't mind her Maw here, so I locked her in the smokehouse. Ornery young'un."

"Well," I said lamely, "it would be nice if you and Ruby Mae could get back together."

No reply. I tried another direction. "Mrs. Morrison, have you seen our new school building?"

"Naw."

"I hope you'll look in on us sometime."

"Wel-l—"

"How about you, Mr. Morrison? Come see us at the mission house. We'd be so happy to have you."

"The which? Oh, I don't go round no church-houses. That thar's fer the wimmin."

I thought about that for a moment, then plunged ahead recklessly. "Mr. Morrison, every church I've been in has been run by men. The church doesn't mean anything in a community unless the men are a part of it. We have a wonderful man named David Grantland in our mission. I think you'd like to meet him."

"Don't take no stock in a brought-on city fellow comin' here, a-tellin' us how to live."

Heated words leapt to my tongue. I managed to stop them just in time. It was no use. These people were suspicious of me. I could not say anything right. As a caller, I was a catastrophe!

I rose, but still they did not move from their chairs. "It was nice to meet you. Well, good-bye." And I got away from there as quickly as I could.

Of course, the visiting was easier when David went with me. Most of the folks knew him by now and responded to his liking for people generally and his easy way with them.

David offered to go along on my first official visit to the

Spencer cabin since he was afraid I would never find it on the back side of Lonesome Pine Ridge—and he was probably right.

There was such a warm touch of spring in the air this last week of March that I suggested to David that we walk instead of ride. The evergreens were tipped with vivid green and the willows overhanging the streams were a whisper of green lace. Here and there in the fields of the valley, spicewood bushes waved yellow plumes. It was spring and I felt light and carefree. Nor did I fear being tongue-tied with the Spencers as I had with the Morrisons.

As we reached the top of the ridge, I realized that I would never have recognized this as the same cabin into which Mr. Pentland and I had crept for shelter from the howling wind and the stinging cold during my first trek from El Pano to Cutter Gap. In the charm of this sunlit cabin, it was hard to recapture the eerie quality of that day of Bob Allen's brain operation.

For there was charm here. It was in the site which must have been chosen carefully by someone a long time ago. I felt almost on top of the world. I was standing now on one of those peaks to which I lifted my eyes every morning and every evening from my bedroom window. Here with the silent gaze of the mountains upon us, trivialities and pettiness and meanness faded and dropped out of sight. All around us were the rich odors of sunbaked earth and pine and spruce and balsam. A clean cool quality of the woods and of the mountainsides where spring was burgeoning had crept indoors. Entering the cabin was like sticking one's nose into one of those souvenir pillows filled with balsam needles or cedar chips they made for the tourists back home in Asheville.

Fairlight Spencer had arranged galax leaves in two old pewter bowls, the leaves mostly bronze and winey-red from the winter, here and there new green; and in a chipped cup she had put trillium and violets.

"The very first," she told us, and unself-consciously reached out slender fingers to caress the flowers. "The least'uns of the springtime."

The grace of the gesture and the long tapering fingers (even though they were red and rough with chipped and broken nails) caught my attention. I stood there thinking that these should be the hands of a lady handling an ivory fan or smoothing her skirts of velvet or satin. They were the hands of an aristocrat, and here they were on a mountain woman, buried at the back of beyond.

Nor could I see in this woman any trace of that shrinking Fairlight, rigid with fear, who had stood beside me watching the sun sink behind the far peaks while the operation went on inside the cabin. Today she was eager to show me everything, including an unusual quilt stretched on a quilting frame near the hearth. So while David was talking with fifteen-year-old John, teasing him, rumpling his hair, I was examining the quilt. It was not the commonplace hit-and-miss patchwork, but a moon-and-star motif. When I asked Mrs. Spencer about it, she pointed to a small window set high in the wall to the right of the fireplace. "See that lookout? I get a heap of joy from that. When I'm lonesome-like, it pearts me up to look up there and see the sun-ball or the moon and stars. So thrice one night I drawed me an idea—three picture-pretties of the new moon and a star."

I looked at her in astonishment. "Mrs. Spencer, you mean you drew a picture of the new moon at three different positions and then copied that onto your quilt?"

She nodded. "Weren't much work. Seems right nice to have the starry heavens on my counterpin."

"Mama aims t'make *me* a counterpin after a spell." It was Clara's voice. She and Zady had just come into the room carrying heaping plates of gingerbread. David grabbed a piece as it went past and the girls giggled, delighted at his eagerness.

"Say! This is good. Tastes different. What's in it?" he asked.

"Made out'n sorghum and wheaten flour," Zady explained.

Then John brought in a cedar pail filled with roasted chestnuts. And when their father appeared with an antique-looking musical instrument under his arm, I knew this was to be a real party which the Spencers had been planning for days. There would be no sitting and staring silently and answering in monosyllables here!

Mr. Spencer's "Howdy-do, Ma'am" to me was so courtly that it could have been a bow to one's sovereign or the opening of a performance on a stage. "Howdy, preacher." He shook David's hand vigorously. "How's the steeple-makin' and the road-buildin'?"

"Coming along, Jeb. Much too slow to suit me though! And now I've got to knock off on the steeple for a while to string telephone wire. Say, Jeb, how about giving me a hand with the wire-stringing?"

"Aye. Been thinkin' I mought lend you a hand-up with something. Truth is, I'd kinder like to speak into that newfangled contraption myself."

This was my first chance really to know Jeb Spencer— blond, debonair. Lively too, as I realized from the moment he began plying the goose quill back and forth across the strings of—a dulcimer. Yes, that was it! One of those old-time dulcimers Miss Alice had described to me.

> "Oh, as I went down to Derby Town
> All on a summer's day,
> It's there I saw the finest ram
> That was ever fed on hay. . . .
>
> Oh, the wool upon this ram's back
> It drug to the ground,
> And I hauled it to the market
> And it weighed ten thousand pounds. . . ."

Something about Mr. Spencer's exuberance must have made the girls feel that their father was "of a real song-ballad-singing mind," as they would have expressed it, because they were squealing with delight. John would have no part of girlish giggling, but I noticed that his eyes were glowing as he coiled his big frame and settled down beside his father.

This dulcimer had four strings. Shaped differently from a guitar, with a slender waist and heart-shaped holes, the tone was clear, flutelike with a plaintive quality. It would never take the place of the fiddle for foot-tapping rhythms, but already I could see that it was the perfect accompaniment for the half-singing, half-talking ballads.

> "O rise you up, ye sev'n breth-e-rens,
> And bring your sister down;
> It nev-er shall be said that a Stu-art's son
> Had taken her out of town.
> He mounted her on a milk-white steed,
> He rode a dap-ple gray.

He swung a bu-gle horn about his neck
And so went blowing away. . . ."

As the story of Earl Brand went on for eight verses,
twelve, sixteen, it was like a door opening for me. I was
ushered into a new land with an assortment of new images
and ideas crowding in. I realized that in these cabins
where there were few if any books, the tales handed down
by word of mouth through ballads and tall tales must have
been the only substitute for story books. I'd only to look
at the eager faces of the Spencer children fastened on their
father to see how hungry they were for stories.

As for the music— I thought of how hard my parents
had tried to give me some appreciation for good music.
Yet somehow I could not deprecate the homespun min-
strelsy I was hearing now. I sat there thinking about how
all real music has to be born in the human spirit. Well,
these ballads surely had been. There was something child-
like and basic about them, an absence of sham or pretense. And something else even behind that—some rare
race knowledge. Listening to them was like looking into
the exposed hearts of folks everywhere, of all of us with
our common heritage on both sides of the Atlantic.

Jeb Spencer was enjoying himself, relishing the enthusiastic reaction of his audience as he watched the witchery
of the old tales reach out and capture David and me along
with his family. Effortlessly the ballads recreated the atmosphere of other centuries for us—snow white steeds
and dapple grays; bugle horns and broad swords; fair
maidens at casement windows listening for the beat of a
horse's hooves on the wild moor; castles and porters and
the peel towers of the border country between England
and Scotland. Now to these had been added the buffalo
hollows and the Indians of the American frontier; horses
and buggies; bed quilts and rocking chairs; cornbread and
biscuits; raccoons and possums and mules—and always
there seemed to be plenty of blood flowing and of men
being hanged. But then the ballads were honest about that
too, for life in seventeenth- and eighteenth-century Britain
and on the American frontier later on must always have
had its gory side.

Suddenly David injected a new note, "Now I'll match
you with one of the latest hit tunes. Wish I'd brought my
ukulele. I'll sing it once, Jeb, then you can pick it up:

'You tell her, I s-s-s-stutter—' "

"Oh, a *foolery* song," Clara enthused. And soon the children were tapping and pretending to stutter the words along with David. He went on from that one to "Swingin' Down the Lane" and then to one of his favorites:

"Under the Yum Yum tree,
That's the yummiest place to be. ..."

Then the impromptu concert ended with Jeb singing a song that was going to haunt me forever:

"Down in the valley,
    valley so low
Hang your head over,
    hear the wind blow.
Hear the wind blow, love,
    hear the wind blow;
Hang your head over,
    hear the wind blow. ..."

How is it that sometimes a melody and a lyric will wing their way into mind and heart to lodge there like a homing bird? Here in these astringent lines someone had captured what I had felt so deeply, especially about the plight of the mountain women. There was something about Fairlight Spencer that brought my feelings about them into focus.

As David and I were leaving, Mrs. Spencer sought me out, timidly tugging at my sleeve. "Miz Christy, could I speak with you?" She pulled me away from the others to the far corner of the room.

"Look-a-here—you've never handled a school afore. That's a heap of young'uns for one gal-woman. Is there anything I can do to help, like clean up the school yan? I'm a good hand to work. Or wash some of your go-to-meetin' clothes? It's my turn to favor you now."

The words were spoken with a gentle dignity, as if a parting gift were being bestowed on me, as was indeed the case. Here was a mountain woman with a husband and five children to care for, living in such poverty that if she had any shoes, she was saving them to be worn outside the house, yet thinking of *me*. Even as I started to answer, I realized something else ... there was more to this gracious offer than met the eye. Fairlight Spencer was not just volunteering to do some washing and ironing for me; she was also holding out to me the gift of her friendship. Among the mountain people, this was the most cherished gift of all. It was a breakthrough of those walls of reserve that had so far seemed impenetrable.

"Mrs. Spencer, that's the nicest offer anyone has made me since I left home. You're right. Sixty-seven children are a handful and I do need help." I paused, groping for words that had no condescension in them. "I'll accept your wonderful offer, if you'll let me be your friend. You see, Mrs. Spencer, I'm a long way from home. Sometimes I get lonesome for another woman to talk to. And maybe there'll be something I can do for you too."

The face that in repose could look so spartan and pioneer was now wreathed in smiles. "Aye, you can holp, Miz Christy." Suddenly she was shy again, her voice sinking almost to a whisper. "I cain't read nor write. Would— you learn me how? I'd like that!"

The eagerness in her voice added such pathos that at that moment I wanted to teach this woman to read more than I'd ever wanted to do anything before. "I'd love doing that, Mrs. Spencer. Could you come down to the mission house, maybe Saturday?"

"For shore and sartin, I'll be there," she said joyously. "Oh, and would you—handle my front name, 'Fairlight'?"

On the way back to the mission I was so gratified by the success of the afternoon that it was all I could do to keep from skipping along.

David sensed my light-heartedness and began to whistle a tune. Spotting a pink flower ahead I forgot my resolution about acting more grown-up with David and ran over to pluck it. There was an aromatic scent. Impulsively, I thrust it under David's nose.

"What's that smell like, David?"

He shook his head, "I can't tell."

I studied him for a moment. He seemed a little preoccupied and I didn't want him to think I was a giddy little flirt. I threw the wild geranium to one side and walked on beside him quietly.

"Why so solemn?" David finally asked.

"I get annoyed at myself sometimes—especially when I act like a little girl."

"But I like you that way."

"What way?"

"Little girl-like. You seem so natural and uncomplicated."

"You talk as if I were your little sister."

David stopped and looked at me sternly. "That's a lot of nonsense. You have more maturity than a lot of older girls I know."

"Do you know a lot of girls, David?"

"A few."

"Have you been in love with any of them?"

David considered the question for a moment in silence. "I'm not sure. There was one who was rather special for a while. But she would never have been interested in this kind of life."

"What was she like?"

"Dark-haired, quite good-looking, rather reserved—and I'm afraid her family had too much money."

"David, do men like girls to be, well, reserved and a little shy?" When David looked at me quizzically, I rushed on to clarify, "What I'm trying to get at, David, is that we're all taught to be modest and not too talkative and not too forward and all that sort of thing. Sometimes I feel like a hypocrite and . . . and sometimes just plain stupid when I try to act demure."

"Well then, be yourself."

"All right, I will, but there will be some people who won't understand and who will think I'm being too aggressive. Why, I even got into trouble with Miss Alice just with my letter writing! You see, David, there are so many things I see and feel and want to *do* something about— and then when I rush ahead, I suddenly feel like I'm being a fool."

"But there's a difference between the kind of ideas you get and the way some aggressive women I know want to run other people's lives."

"One thing is sure, David. The women around here will never be like that."

"How do you mean?"

"Well, it's almost as though they aren't people. I mean the hard life they have, so much work, and the way the men here sort of use them and then dismiss them."

David let his hand fall on my shoulder for a moment while he stopped to consider this blast. "Christy, you're full of fire, aren't you? Why, I can see you marching down the street as one of those suffragettes with a

170

sign saying 'Women Have Rights.' But I wouldn't try it in the Cove—at least not for a while."

He let his hand slide off my shoulder—I thought, almost reluctantly. I felt secure and yes, exhilarated walking beside him.

Fourteen

ON SATURDAY MORNING Fairlight arrived at the mission before we had finished breakfast. She was wearing a freshly laundered blue-checked gingham dress with a wide white collar and this time, shoes. Since David was going to be stringing telephone wire rather than working on the bell-tower, I took Fairlight over to the empty schoolhouse where we started our lesson on two desks pulled side by side before an open window.

I had a box of materials ready and Fairlight was all eagerness to see what was in the box. From magazines I had cut out some pictures of landscapes to use for background scenery; some figures of men, women and children pasted onto cardboard bases so that they could be stood upright (as I used to do with my paper dolls when I was a very little girl); a copy of the alphabet printed in large clear letters from my first grade class; a Bible, a fresh ruled pad and some pencils.

Since teaching an adult to read was a new experience for me, I was not sure how to begin. It would not do, I felt, to down-grade the dignity of a human being like Fairlight Spencer by using the primer books for six- and seven-year-olds: "The rat ran from the cat." "Here the boy sat." Then too I believed that Fairlight would learn more readily than the children, and I wanted to give her even in this first lesson the concept of words as ideas. And since I knew from having seen some of her quilt patterns and flower arrangements that she was a creative person, surely she would learn fastest if I could find an imaginative way to teach her. My problem was how to achieve this.

I picked up the Bible. "There are lots and lots of words in this book."

"How soon will I be able to read it, Miz Christy?"

"In no time! And I'll tell you why. Every single word in this book and all the words together use only twenty-six English letters—these here. So after you've learned just twenty-six and know how to put the letters together to form different words, then you can read. Easy!"

Her eyes shone. "I'd like that the best in the world." Already she was concentrating on that alphabet. After we had read it aloud twice, she became so intent on learning it that she almost forgot I was there. So I sat back watching her, feeling instinctively that I should let her set the pace, even do most of the talking—if she would. At last she sighed and looked at me. "Think I've got it ... A-B-C-D—" on she went making only one mistake.

Next we propped up a backdrop picture of a landscape drenched in sunlight. "Now, Fairlight, you pick out one of the paper people from this pile." So she selected a dapper-looking man and stood him up before the landscape.

We learned MAN and my eager pupil practiced saying it and forming the letters. Soon we went on to TREE, LIGHT, SUN, GRASS, SKY ... It was at that point that Fairlight stumbled onto her own kind of phonetics—the relation between the way the word looked and how it sounded. She was as thrilled as if she had found a jewel in the dust. She rolled the word "sky" over and over her tongue, spelled it again and again. This went on until we had our first ten words.

Then I opened the Bible to the first chapter of Genesis. "Now, Fairlight, look at this. The words on this page are just ideas marching. Like this one, 'And God said, Let there be light—'

"L-I-G-H-T! There it is! I *see* it." Her slender forefinger was on the word. "Oh, I love the light! Don't you? I hate the darkness."

Let there be light ... I sat there thinking that I had never seen light dawn so quickly for anyone as for this woman. *What an alive mind she had!* She scarcely needed instruction, only a chance to let the light come.

Teaching Fairlight Spencer was going to be pure delight. Up to this point in her life, she had been like some outcast child staring through the iron railings of the tall fence around the great estate of knowledge, longing to romp with the other children on the clipped lawns inside, but always excluded. She saw learning to read and write the English language as the key to unlock those gates. For the first time that Saturday morning the hinges moved, the gates began to swing open. The Elysian fields of knowledge and of identification with other human beings would soon be hers where she could roam and explore and even cavort.

On another Saturday morning, I was invited to Miss Alice Henderson's for the Sewing Circle which met on the only two weekends a month that she was in Cutter Gap. But the women enjoyed the meetings so much, Miss Alice told me, that they wanted to gather every week. Would I take charge of the Circle in her absence? This first time she wanted me to watch and listen as preparation for that.

As I headed down the hill I noticed how the gently sloping roof of Miss Alice's home seemed to tie the building to the ground. Sunshine and snow, rain and the heavy mountain mists had already weathered the unpainted shingles and the logs. Native shrubs hugged the walls closely, so that the cabin though only five years old, looked as if it had always stood on its patch of earth—solid, immovable, at one with the hills and the sky.

How unmistakably her cabin bore the flavor of Miss Alice's personality! In both the woman and her home there was an effortless beauty, never a straining for effect, a harmony that seemed to come from having one's roots down in the place where the roots were meant to be.

There was something else I had noticed too: an initial acceptance of herself as she was and so of other people with their foibles. And so she did as little scolding or criticizing of others for their foolish behavior or their sins as anyone I had ever known. It was not that she was willing to compromise with wrongdoing or poverty or ignorance, just that she was a long step ahead of wasting emotional energy on fretting. And she never put pressure on the rest of us to accept her opinions. The secret of her calm seemed to be that she was not trying to prove anything. She was—that was all. And her stance toward life seemed to say: God is—and that is enough.

But why was it enough? That was what I had to find out. Even supposing one had proof of the existence of God, how could the fact of God suffice when all around us were conditions crying to be righted? How could Miss Alice be so sure that He had the world in His hand?

After only three months in the Cove, here I was already

fretting and stewing and pawing the ground in my reforming zeal—at least inside myself. Not Alice Henderson! There had been times recently when I had found her Quaker calmness maddening. Always my thinking came to this point—and stopped. Beyond that my understanding ceased. Miss Alice knew something I did not know. That was why I watched for every chance to be with her, to observe her in action, one reason I had agreed so readily to these Saturday mornings with the women.

I quickened my pace toward the cabin; I should be there ahead of the others to help greet them. But as I stepped from under the fir trees, I saw that an old woman had reached the yard ahead of me. The old lady made quite a picture with her black skirt over a Balmoral petticoat as she stepped up to the door, holding herself with unself-conscious dignity.

Miss Alice heard us and opened the door. "Aunt Polly Teague and Christy, have you two met? No, I thought not. Do come in."

At closer range, the one called Aunt Polly looked as if she had stepped out of a Rembrandt portrait. Above the black skirt, a faded calico shirtwaist was buttoned high on her neck. Cornflower blue eyes were sunk deep in a parchment skin, crisscrossed with a network of fine wrinkles. Because the face was shrunken, the ears looked too large for the head.

"Aunt Polly, how have you been?" Miss Alice asked solicitously.

"Tole'able, tole'able. Can't complain. Old bones be cold bones, guess."

Miss Alice turned to me. "Aunt Polly has a rare distinction. She's the oldest woman in the Cove. Ninety-two. Isn't that right, Aunt Polly?"

"Ninety-two, ninety-three, I cain't be bothered!" The cornflower blue eyes snapped and crackled. "When my eighteenth young'un was birthed on my fiftieth name day, jest took a notion to drapp all such out'n my head. Birthdates are jest a botheration."

I looked at her in astonishment. Eighteen children! A baby when she was fifty! And she was apparently far from done with the business of life.

But now the rest of the group was arriving. Finally there were twelve, including Fairlight, who had already had her reading lesson with me that morning and Ruby Mae, who refused to be left out of anything and who had been looking forward to the Sewing Circle as a great social event. She had persuaded Lizette Holcombe to come with her and Clara Spencer. I was glad to see other mothers of my schoolchildren too—Opal McHone (still pale and wan from childbirth) and Mary Allen and Lenore Teague. Then there were two others whom I had not met before—Granny Barclay, who was said to be the last "Granny" woman of the Cove—official midwife—but whose continual squinting showed something now seriously wrong with her eyes. Then there was a young girl, Liz Ann Robertson. Liz looked fourteen—certainly not more than fifteen—but was already married and obviously in a family way.

It was a group with such extremes of age that I was curious to see what Miss Alice would do. She began by serving sassafras tea and big chunky sugar cookies, using delicate Limoges china. All over again I noticed Fairlight's hands as she handled the beautiful china cup, putting it carefully to her lips, and I had the curious feeling that they were the hands of a great lady, that the red, work-worn skin was only a disguise which would drop away when some evil enchantment broke. When the tea was gone, she lifted the cup out of its saucer and nestled it between both hands. "Feels good," she said wonderingly, "like silk to the skin."

She must have been speaking for all of the women because they acted as if they were sipping liquid ambrosia straight from Mount Olympus out of those cups. Politely they tried to restrain themselves on the cookies, but soon there was not a cookie left.

"I see that most of you have brought quilts to piece," their hostess observed. "While you sew, Miss Christy and I could take turns reading to you from the Bible."

"Now that would be purely a delight," Aunt Polly agreed.

"Then after the readin'," Granny Barclay broke in, "would ye pray a little for the folks that has miseries and poorly young'uns and such-like?"

"Of course we will."

"My eyes are worse than ordinary. Don't see good no more. But Doc's a-studyin' on it."

Clara Spencer asked cautiously, "Granny, you be seein' a lot of Doc. Is it true what pretty nigh everybody says, that thar's a room at his place that he keeps locked up and won't let nobody see?"

Miss Alice picked up some teacups and the empty cookie plate to take to the kitchen.

"Aye, lassie, for a fact." Granny smacked her lips as if over secret knowledge.

"Thar's scattered talk," Liz Ann's voice lowered confidentially, "that yon's the room where Mistress MacNeill died. So Doc won't take no nonsense 'bout a single thing bein' tampered with."

This was the kind of talk that Ruby Mae like best. Her eyes glittered. "I heerd more'n that ... Doc knowed how to preserve his wife's mortal remains and he wouldn't have no funeralizing a-tall. Still keeps her in that room."

On her way into the room Miss Alice had heard the last sentence. I could see that she was eager to turn off such wild talk. "Lizette, didn't I hear that your mother had a new baby?"

"Long time back, that was. Four month now. Ailin'. Sure cries a heap."

"Was the young'un a gal-baby?" Aunt Polly asked.

"Yes, it was a gal." The girl paused a moment, her face immobile. "And it's a gal yit."

I choked back a laugh. I still could not tell when these people were joking. Did Lizette mean to be funny?

Clara, sitting on a stool in the corner, said, "I know somebody who's sick—Bessie Coburn hurt her leg t'other evening when the sled turned over on her. Doc MacNeill says the leg's not broke though."

It made me feel like an insider to know that they were not referring to a snow sled but to the drag-sleds pulled by a mule or a horse, used because of the almost perpendicular slopes.

"You'd best pray for Liz Ann too," Ruby Mae added. "She wouldn't tell you herself, but her time's well-nigh here."

While the women worked on their quilt pieces and Miss Alice cleared away the rest of the dishes, I started to read at the place she pointed out. I was still self-conscious about reading aloud to grown-ups from the Bible because I was afraid of the pronunciation of all those strange Oriental names. The passages selected were marked by numbered slips of paper stuck between the pages. It was just as well, since I would not have known whether Jude was in the Old Testament or the New, or whether I Kings came before or after Isaiah.

But I had not covered more than a few verses before I

177

realized that the women were listening not to me but to the stories Miss Alice had chosen. Somehow their absorption made me forget myself so that I too was caught up in the words: "A certain man had two sons. . . ." It was the familiar parable of the Prodigal Son. "And he arose, and came to his father. But when he was yet a great way off, his father saw him, and had compassion, and ran, and fell on his neck, and kissed him. . . . Let us eat and be merry: for this my son was dead, and is alive again; he was lost and is found. . . ."

In this tranquil room the ancient words had life in them. Suddenly I realized that the language of Scripture did not sound strange to these women because the King James translators had been closer to the Cove speech than was present-day English. Every day I heard "Aye" and "verily" and "at cock-crow" and "thrice" and "brutish" and "noisome" and "hireling."

When I paused at the end of the parable, there was only the faint hissing of the apple logs on the fire and the echo of Miss Alice's soft footsteps in the kitchen. The concentration of the group was so intense that it was almost palpable.

Then Miss Alice came back into the room and settled herself in the red wing chair and took the Bible. It was soon apparent that she had selected the passages with one thought in mind: she wanted these women to hear for themselves the assurance and reassurance in the Scriptures of the love of God for them. She made few comments, just let the passages speak their own message.

Whether from the Old Testament or the New, one by one the verses were laying a perfectly fitting mosaic—a picture of God as a Father who loves us more than any earthly father could; who knows our needs before we ask Him, but who still wants us to come and ask confidently as any rightful son or daughter should. It was the unforgettable picture which Jesus had etched in such earthy words of His Father going after a single lost and bruised lamb; of God, the Father, running down the road to receive any child who has been in a far country and who at last wants to come home.

I sat there entranced as I watched Miss Alice. I had noticed that in her presence often I would have big thoughts, ideas that went so far beyond my usual ones that they astonished me. It was not so much what Miss Alice said that sparked the thoughts, rather what she was.

Even now on the perimeter of my mind, new ideas hovered and darted, some of them just eluding me. Miss Alice seemed to think that once the poverty-stricken highlanders gripped the fact of God's love for them—even for them—then in time they would have everything else they needed. But how was that? Would their really believing in a loving and adequate God end fear, for example? Or poverty? What would it do to educational needs? Or how would it affect their belief in superstitious magic?

But now Miss Alice closed the Bible and was bringing this part of the morning to a close with the prayer that the group had requested. Her words were informal and direct, clothed in no liturgy at all. In the simplest kind of way they were directed at God's adequacy to meet human problems. After all, the needs of these women were real—as solid as the earth on which they walked and the garden dirt in which they dug, as substantial as the mountains that towered over them; as near as pain and disease and childbirth. In their simplicity, they knew about the need for daily bread. So once again, a towering thought came to me. True prayer then, can be rooted only in the recognition of genuine need.

"Aaa-*men*," Granny Barclay pronounced resoundingly. "I fancy that. Miz Henderson, your talk would put heart in a hollow log. Ye make the Almighty seem—come-at-able."

"Aye, makes my soul happy," Aunt Polly agreed. "Not like most preacher-persons always hollerin' about the hellfires. Been hearin' them talk that-a-way ever since I was a slip of a girl. They'd start out slow, but as soon as they'd git limbered up and goin' good, they'd take to poundin' and poundin' their fists on the pul-pits, sweat rollin' off'n their faces . . . wipin' and wipin', till Lord holp my time of day, seemed like they'd crept a leetle too close to them fires theirselves."

The blue eyes blazed in the wrinkled face as the voice went on, "All my born days them preacher-men made me think I was backslidin' down the slippery path to hell. But when I hit my seventieth name day and still couldn't feel no singein' from them fires, I calculated that from thar on in, I'd jest disremember about all them devils, pearten up, and let the fires roar on without me."

Granny Barclay shook her finger at the old woman. "Pollyanne Dillingham Teague, ye have a sassy tongue in your head."

179

"Fiddlesticks! Better than bein' a say-nothin' person."

Tactfully Miss Alice changed the subject. "Granny, I want to show Miss Christy your quilt. It's a nice pattern. What do you call it?"

"Hearts and Gizzards. Here 'tis."

I moved for a closer look. "Is it an old pattern?"

"Aye. Mostly the patterns was handed down."

"It's beautiful!"

"But weavin' is a heap purtier than quiltin'." Fairlight Spencer spoke with feeling. "Sometimes I hanker after it, a-sittin' on the weavin' bench, watchin' the blossoms come out and smile at you from the kiverlid."

Her words seemed to make all of the older women nostalgic. Weaving was apparently almost a lost art in the Cove.

"You know, store-bought clothes don't wear a-tall," Aunt Polly offered more quietly, now that she was off theology and onto more domestic matters. "Thar's something about a-settin' and trompin' the treadles—nothing can fret a-body then. Granny, ain't I seen a footpower loom in your yard?"

"Aye, ain't nobody used it in years. Nobody exceptin' the chickens, that is. They like it for roostin'. I memorize how I used to make up ballads to the hum of the shuttle and the thud of the loom beatin' up the web. It was purely a pleasure, that it was."

Miss Alice had been listening carefully. "How hard would it be to start weaving again? Do any of you remember how?"

Aunt Polly answered promptly. "Shorely! Granny Barclay and I know. We made our weddin' kivers together."

"And in my loft," Fairlight Spencer said eagerly, "I've got a heap of drafts that come from Scotland. Belonged to my mama, and her mama before her."

"What are drafts?"

"Patterns for weavin' the de-signs. Come from the other side of the water. Pieces of paper, rolled up, tied with black thread. Look kind of like music. Tell you how to make Queen Anne's De-light, Trailin' Vine, Young Man's Fancy, Whig Rose, Road-in-the-wilderness."

"You know, some of my friends in Pennsylvania and Miss Christy's in Asheville would leap at the chance to buy handwoven things. I'm sure they would. What would you think about doing some weaving to sell?"

"If you mean for cash-money," Mrs. McHone answered, "that would sorely be welcome."

The group was immediately enthusiastic. "Think ye," Granny Barclay asked, squinting and wiping her eyes, "that we could use the new wagon that Miz Christy holped us git, t' tote my loom? Could you holp us find som-wheres to set it up, Miz Henderson?"

"Certainly I could."

"What about the dyeing?" Clara asked.

"Ain't hard." Granny sounded a little smug. "Walnut and butternut hulls for browns and blacks. Pokeberries made lavender. Hic'kry bark makes the lastingest yeller ever ye seed. Madder's for red and pink, and—"

"But blue's best of all," Aunt Polly interrupted her. "Howsomever, we'd have t' put off till August to set the blue pot. Indigo don't bloom till then. My mamma had a blue pot that's in our barn yit."

"Don't you use any brought-on dyes?" Ruby Mae asked. She and Liz Ann and Clara seemed to know as little about these old-time skills as I did.

Aunt Polly rolled up her quilt scraps and rose to her feet. "Don't fancy boughten colors for wearin'-clothes. Fade right away. Wal, got to take my foot in hand and git along home."

As the meeting broke up, the women were still chattering, full of plans for the future.

I stayed to help Miss Alice wash up the Limoges china and put it carefully back into place in the corner cupboard. While we were washing dishes, I questioned, "By the way, what's wrong with Granny Barclay's eyes?"

"I'm afraid it's trachoma. The eyes get irritated and bloodshot from granulations on the lids. A lot of itching and burning and discharge. Eventually, the eyeballs harden, you know, and the sight gets progressively worse."

"It seems as if there's a lot of eye trouble around here. I never saw so many crossed eyes before."

"You're right. The crossed eyes are probably from too much intermarrying. The trachoma is something else again. A real scourge. There's a surprising amount of it—along with hookworm and typhoid and consumption. Dr. MacNeill helped persuade the Public Health Service to make a survey of parts of the Appalachians to see for themselves how much trachoma there was. That's how we have the temporary eye hospital in Lyleton. Many a Saturday Neil takes a wagonload of patients in there."

"Oh! That reminds me—I've been wanting to ask you something about Dr. MacNeill ... David hinted at a story about the Doctor's ancestors. Said something about a castle and for me to ask you sometime ..."

She smiled at me, amused at my undisguised inquisitiveness. "Why not ask Neil?"

"I don't know him that well."

She rinsed out her dishcloth, carefully hung it over the side of the sink, dried her hands, and took off her big apron. "It's a good story all right. And you don't really understand the mountain people until you've heard it. You want it now? Can you spare another fifteen or twenty minutes?"

"Of course!"

"Well then, let's see—where shall I begin?" She was talking as we made our way back to the fire. I relaxed, curled up on the rug near the hearth. The red chair set off Miss Alice's light hair, and there was a faraway look in her eyes. As the story unfolded, it carried us both out of the quiet, firelit room in Cutter Gap, Tennessee, back ... back across space, through time to the summer of 1745 in Scotland ...

"It seems that Neil MacNeill, ancestor of the Doctor, born in oh, something like 1720, lived in a castle on the Island of Barra in the Outer Hebrides of Scotland. The nearest town, I'm told, was a tiny port called Campbeltown. That year of 1745 this Neil had been visiting cousins and friends in New York and Philadelphia, then had gone on to Wilmington, North Carolina, and Cape Fear. He was over here to feel out a business venture. He and a friend named Baliol of the Island of Jura had gotten the idea of forming some sort of land-holding syndicate in the New World.

"But while they were away, hard times fell on the Highlands: That summer Prince Charles Edward, great-great-grandson of Mary, Queen of Scots, had determined to try to win back the throne of England and Scotland for the Stuarts. He'd hired a French frigate and landed on the Island of Eriskay. To the highlanders, he was the "Bonnie Prince": twenty-four, tall, handsome, curly hair almost gold at the ends, large brown eyes. It was said that he

182

could charm anyone out of all conscience.

"There are numbers of songs about him sung by the mountain people to this day. I heard little Sam Houston singing one of them in a thin piping voice just last week when I returned some candle molds to his mother:

'Come o'er the stream, Charlie,
　Dear Charlie, brave Charlie,
Come o'er the stream, Charlie,
　And dine with McLean.
And though you be weary
　We'll make your heart cheery,
And welcome our Charlie,
　And his royal train.'

"But 'dear Charlie's, brave Charlie's' coup had failed. The promised French help never came. Many of the clans never did rise to the support of Charles Edward, and the highlanders were defeated by the English in the bloody massacre of Culloden Moor in April, 1746.

"Well, when Neil MacNeill returned to Scotland in November of 1746, somehow he still had not heard about the disaster at Culloden, nor did he know the situation he was heading into in the Highlands. Communication was slow in those days.

"Details of that homecoming have been handed down in the Doctor's family: How Neil strode over the ancient bridge across the moat to his beloved castle Kisimul, pausing to look back at the tossing sea and the wild headlands that he loved. Every detail of his ancestral home was just as he had remembered it. There were the desolate peat bogs where the peewit cried, the wine-red hills beyond. There were the Hebridean "black houses" of his people, thatched roofs weighed down with stones. There was the odor of burning peat and the smell of the inescapable fish industry. And inside the damp stone castle, there was still the deep glow of polished walnut and mahogany, the ancestral portraits on the walls. But there was a change—ordinarily there would have been a lamb roasting on a spit on the gigantic fireplace. There was none; food was very scarce.

"It was then the Neil learned the hard facts. After Culloden his father had been taken prisoner along with some thirty-five hundred other Highland men. No one knew what had happened to him, though they did know

183

that seven hundred odd had died from their confinement in filthy, overcrowded prisons, and that another one hundred and twenty had been hanged in London.

"The English government, thinking that clan loyalties were the basis of all the trouble, had passed the Disarming Act which, among other things, prohibited the wearing of any tartan garment. The Duke of Cumberland's men, under order, were roaming the countryside, burning homesteads and grain, driving away cattle. Their aim was to destroy the economy—and they succeeded. So few men were left to provide for their families that many women and children were actually starving.

"Prince Charles Edward, with the help of many including Flora MacDonald—still a heroine among these North Carolina and Tennessee folk—had escaped back to France. A reward of thirty thousand pounds in English gold had been placed on his head. That much gold would have set up a poverty-stricken Highland community for the rest of its days. And many of the people might, understandably, have felt resentment at the Prince who had led them into such sorrow and trouble. Yet not a Highlander could be found who would touch a penny of the reward.

"But there had been even worse news for Neil. It was the last bitter dreg to learn that a great price had been put on his grandfather's head, since he was Roderick, the thirty-ninth Chief of the Clan MacNeill. The frail old man had had to flee the castle to live in a cave somewhere in the mountains. In fact, all of Argyllshire was full of clansmen hiding out, hunted like wild deer by Royalist troops, a price on every head. But the people were intensely loyal; they would not betray kinsfolk.

"Neil watched his Granny Jean, failing already before the tragedy, now all but out of her mind haunting the upper windows of the castle, her old eyes searching, searching—hoping, hoping.

"Naturally, the business venture which MacNeill and Baliol had evolved was out of Neil's head at once, of no consequence compared to the suffering around him. He had friends in London and legal contacts, so he went there to see if he could get any relief or alleviation for the Highlanders. Neil did not succeed, but there in London his solicitor, William Dick, pointed out to him the one legal loophole left: because he had been out of the country during all of the Rebellion, his portion of the family

184

fortune could not be touched by the English Government.

"So after much thought, Neil decided to buy a ship and offer to transport to North Carolina as many of his countrymen as wanted to emigrate.

"Thus in the spring of 1747 there was jubilation on the docks of Campbeltown as four hundred and eighty Scottish men and women sailed in Neil's ship *The Curlew* for America and a new life. Now they would be able to wear all the tartan they pleased, to speak their native Gaelic, to make a living without having it wrested from them, to sing as they worked, yes, rousing Jacobite songs if they wanted to. The townspeople went wild on the docks that morning: *The Curlew* meant for them freedom—freedom to breathe, freedom to be! And Neil MacNeill of Barra watched with tears streaming down his cheeks.

"He did not himself sail with that first group. There were still business details to be concluded since he intended to shuttle *The Curlew* back and forth so long as his funds lasted.

"Word had been received from other fugitives that Neil's grandfather had died as a result of the months of exposure and hardship. Now Neil's mother took Granny Jean's place at the upper windows of the castle, her eyes searching the sweeping uplands and the misty glens, listening to the bleating of the few sheep left and the cries of the seabirds, hoping, always hoping to see a familiar figure striding across the moor. But the weeks and the months went by and Neil's father did not come. They never learned what his fate had been.

"At last Neil put his estate in the hands of a solicitor and appointed trustees. (His family had always been canny business men.) He provided for Granny Jean and for his mother, who refused to leave so long as there was any hope left that her husband was alive, and for their retainers and the upkeep of the Castle Kisimul. The rest of the profits from the rents and the mercantile business which he had inherited, would be used to bring immigrants to America.

"With him, at the second sailing of *The Curlew*, Neil brought some mementoes of the hoary old castle. Perhaps you've seen them, Christy, in his namesake's cabin—a cherry chest of drawers, a low chair with a spindled back, an English mantel clock, that pipe of his with the silver band inscribed in Gaelic, some smaller things.

"Up to that time Neil had been a bachelor, too preoc-

185

cupied to think of romance. On the long voyage to North Carolina, he met Flora Riddell and fell in love with her. They were married at Wilmington soon after they landed.

"In all, *The Curlew* made four round trips. Neil was personally responsible for bringing some eighteen hundred Scottish folk to the New World. At first they settled in the established farming communities near the coast. But the newcomers from Scotland with their strange dress and speech, their violent convictions and prejudices and reckless sincerities, seemed savage to the townspeople. And in no time at all, the exiles were homesick for the sight of a mountain, longed to find a spot which they could call theirs for their 'ain folk.'

"So in 1750 Neil led them across the narrow hazardous passes, fording rivers, penetrating into the virgin forest of what was then Washington County, North Carolina, later to become Tennessee. Some of the grannies, like Aunt Polly Teague and Granny Barclay, have told me that when at last their forebears lifted their eyes to the smoky blue of these mountains, the peaks lost in ragged cloud edges—for all the world like Ben Nevis or the Coolins—when once again they saw valleys thick with morning mist, so reminiscent of their Scottish bogs, when they listened to the music of the tumbling mountain streams—they wept. They had come home again.

"Never would they forget their ballads, their highland stories of the occult, their Gaelic superstitions. Always their men would be fighters, quick to take offense, slow to forgive. To their children and to their children's children they would hand down their love of race, their personal loyalties, their stubbornnesses, their distrust of governments, their servility to no man. These are their strengths and their weaknesses, their glory—and sometimes, Christy, their damnation."

Miss Alice had finished. We sat silent for a long time watching the flickering firclight, lost in the spell of the story. At last I thanked her and slipped out, eager to be alone with my thoughts. No wonder Dr. MacNeill had said, "These are my people. I love them."

It was not until later that I began to wonder how Miss Alice had been able to tell it like that. Not as though she were telling someone else's story at all. As though somehow, sometime she had lived so completely into the MacNeill family that she had made it her own.

Fifteen

MANY of the mountain schools were in session only about twelve weeks of the year—six weeks in the summer after spring planting and six weeks in the winter after harvest-time. The Low Gap School had managed four months. Though we hoped to do even better, there was still the necessity of planning around crop times since then the children were needed at home. The parents were insistent because the highlanders had firm traditions about planting times: beans must always be planted on Good Friday. (No one could tell me why.) Corn should be put in when the oak leaves were as large as a squirrel's ear; late · corn and cabbage on the Fourth of July. Since the holiday could not encompass everything, we announced a six-week Spring Planting Holiday to begin on March 29.

For me it was a welcome recess because it gave me time for calling in the homes and for Fairlight's reading lessons. And now Opal McHone, hearing about the lessons, pleaded that she too wanted to learn to read.

Perhaps it was teaching Fairlight and watching the other women at the Sewing Circle that brought into focus some of my dreams for the Cove. When adults were hungry to learn to read, who could deny them that? Or when Fairlight's spirit was so athirst for beauty that she kept arranging flowers in the one chipped crockery cup she owned, then she was ready to have some beauty added to her life.

Yet if we were eventually to have more adult classes in reading and in household arts and crafts (as Miss Alice had all but promised the Sewing Circle), then we were going to need either another schoolteacher or a helper for these new projects. Then too, I had that long list of supplies we would need if we were to take in boarders. All of it added up to money and Dr. Ferrand's work was

187

already stretched financially over seventeen missions scattered over Kentucky, Tennessee, North Carolina and Arkansas. Was there some new way to obtain funds? My thoughts began darting from one idea to another.

The week before school let out for the Holiday, I had been trying to select an exciting action story from the Bible one evening for my Scripture reading the next day. Going through into the book of *Esther*, I ran head-on into superlative drama. I had not read before about this King Ahasuerus, an Eastern potentate so absolute and cold-blooded that unless one was ordered into his presence, he ventured into the inner court only at the risk of his neck. For such a stumbler, if the king held out his golden scepter, well and good. In that case, you could tell his excellent Majesty why you were there. But if the king ignored you—say, happened to be too deep in his cups or too engrossed in conversation or just too lazy that day to hold out the scepter—then you were dragged off and hanged.

Young and beauteous Queen Esther decided one day that she had to risk this dangerous game of Russian roulette, for she had a pressing request to make and the king had not noticed her for a month. In preparation for her uninvited trek into the inner court, the queen asked her kinsfolk to fast and to pray for her for three days; she also fasted and prayed herself.

But this extraordinary woman did not stop there. She was as aware of outer values as of inner ones. She knew that as a man the king would not be attracted by a wan and spiritual look. So Queen Esther turned her woman's mind toward an overall strategy which included what to wear, and which of all the perfumes of Arabia would pique His Majesty's nose best and how to use her rouge-pot and her kohl to best advantage.

The result must have been good because when she walked across the pavement of the Shushan palace with its colorful squares of red and blue, black and white marble, through the hangings of fine linen, the king was so charmed by her beauty and so impressed by her courage that he not only held out his scepter but added impetuously, "What is thy request? It shall be given thee to the half of my kingdom."

The queen's reply was coy: merely an invitation for King Ahasuerus and his prime minister, Haman, to attend a banquet which she had prepared.

188

Naturally the king was puzzled as to why she would risk her life for a mere invitation; she could have sent *that* by any little slave girl. He guessed correctly that the queen had still not stated her real mission.

But even at the banquet (which must have been a dizzying success in entertainment), the king did not ferret out what was on Queen Esther's mind. She persuaded him and Haman to come to yet another party the next day.

Now King Ahasuerus was piqued as well as intrigued. That night he was unable to sleep. And then at the right moment on the following day, the queen revealed her secret and made her request. She was a Jewess. (The king had not known that.) Her plea was for the life of all of her people—those Jews scattered throughout Persia and Media who had recently been condemned to death by a royal decree suggested to the king by Haman. The terrible day was now approaching—the thirteenth day of the twelfth month—when every Jewish man and woman, even children and babes in arms were to be slain. And King Ahasuerus, by this time thoroughly warmed and mellowed by the companionship of this beautiful woman, immediately granted her plea. Then it was Haman who lost his life.

I thrilled to hear how this woman had dedicated her beauty, her femininity, and her intelligence to a great cause. It was also a perfect example of my mother's spirited teaching about the importance of a good appearance for those in religious work. Mother had always insisted that disorder and dowdiness did not glorify God or help His cause one bit.

So well had mother gotten her point across that as soon as I volunteered to teach at Dr. Ferrand's school, I had made the secret vow, "So help me, I am *not* going to look like one of those caricatures of a missionary."

Sitting there at the writing table, at that moment, the idea was born. What Cutter Gap lacked was someone to dramatize its need to people outside. I could do that. I knew that I could! But where to begin? Knoxville was the nearest largest city with people of real financial means.

And why think small? Who was the wealthiest man in Knoxville? That was easy. Hazen L. Smith, of course. His firm supplied retail grocery stores all over East Tennessee. I knew about him because he was a good friend of my father's. Still I decided not to use that as an entrée. I wanted to test out a growing conviction that if one had an idea or a dream that was right in the sense of being honest and unselfish and of help to other people—and had an all-out desire to make this dream come true—then a way could always be found. So I wrote a letter to Mr. Hazen Smith telling him simply that I was a schoolteacher in a mission school in Cutter Gap and requesting an interview—nothing more. I received back a brief reply setting up the interview for April 16.

But this time—thoroughly chastened by Miss Alice's criticism of my letters to the businessmen—I cautiously discussed my plan of the Knoxville venture with her. She gave me her permission, only warned me to go slowly and to stay well within Dr. Ferrand's philosophy of fundraising: no pressure on anyone for a donation.

As I planned my trip, I saw that there was no way to escape its being something of a production. Since the best train for the city left El Pano at 8:05 in the morning, I would have to spend the previous night at Mrs. Tatum's boarding house as well as stay with her on the return trip.

And the remembrance of my walk into the Cove in the deep snow was still too vivid for me to want to walk the seven miles out. So I inquired of my friend Mr. Pentland. "It ain't to be thought of, your walkin'," was his reply. "Tell you what I'll do, I'll drive my lumber-waggen and team out Tuesday week next and you can ride to El Pano with me. Only I'm gonna have t' git the waggen mended first. It was damified right bad Friday, 'twas a week ago, when it slid into the ditch where a chunk of road had clean washed out."

He was as good as his word. On that Tuesday I could hear the wagon rattling down the road long before it came in sight and Mr. Pentland's soft "Whoa, boys," and then his booming "Howdy, Preacher"—floated up from the front yard. I was all ready and ran down to meet him.

"Whee-ee!" was his greeting. "Them's mighty fancy clothes. Why, she's a sight t' make a man stand at gaze, ain't she, Preacher?"

David did not answer. He stood there looking at me with an expression I could not quite read—not disapproving, yet not his usual jocular self either. He seemed to be annoyed because I had not confided in him. But I had not felt that I should; after all, this trip might be just a waste of time.

"David, I'm really not trying to be mysterious. It's an idea I have—maybe silly, but something I've got to try."

"I understand perfectly." The tone was a little too dry. "You have another idea about improving the mission. That's what bothers me."

He turned to Mr. Pentland. "Better keep an eye on her, Ben. Once these women start getting ideas, nothing is ever the same again, is it?"

"Well now—wimmin! Aggervatin' contrivances, I always say!"

A little self-consciously I moved toward the wagon, and David swung my little going-away satchel into the wagon bed and helped me up on the seat beside Mr. Pentland. He lingered, obviously not satisfied with the conversation The teasing look was back in his eyes.

"If anything goes wrong," he said, "the mission will stand loyally behind you—but do be careful." And he waved us off as Mr. Pentland clucked at the horses and the wagon went lurching down the road.

There were no springs in this vehicle, so the wheels creaked and jolted, the wagon box jumping into the air at our backs as we rattled over rocks in the corrugated roadbed. Whatever screws and bolts and nuts were holding the wagon together would surely soon be loosened and flying through the air!

"Devil's washboard," Mr. Pentland muttered as we skittered into an especially large hole and swerved out the other side. "Them's gizzard-shakin', teeth-rattlin' holes! Fair to wear out a person's patience."

When finally we came to a better stretch, Mr. Pentland commented, "You're a traipsin' gal for sure. If I mought ask, what are you a-figurin' to do in Knoxville?"

I hesitated. "Well, there's a businessman I want to call on. I thought maybe I could get some help for the school."

"What kind of holp?"

"Money, I guess. We need so many things."

"Well, law! Why are ye tryin' to keep *that* a secret from the preacher?"

"Oh, I suppose because he makes fun of me sometimes. Anyway, if I shouldn't get what I'm going for, then the less I've said, the less embarrassing it will be."

" '*Course* you'll get it! You've got gumption and you've got a pert and nimble spirit. Well then! That'll git the wherewithal onytime."

In the wagon we were having to take a more circuitous route, one that followed the streambeds with the rise of the nearest mountains to our right. Sometimes we would be jolting along in open countryside where it was pleasantly sunny, then our way would swing in close to the base of a mountain and lo, the sun would vanish, blotted out by the mountain. Then we were in stygian gloom, a shivery place without light or life, and I would marvel that such a few paces back, it had seemed such a benign landscape.

In my mind these eerie spots came to be connected with the ravens that Mr. Pentland had told me about on my first day with him—those monstrous ravens with their wide wingspread and their savage bills; with feathers so black that they could look iridescent-purple—those swooping, craven ravens who liked to prey on weak or sickly creatures, and whose best delicacy was the eyes of live baby animals. Surely I must be an odd one, I told myself, to let the gloom cast by mountain shadows affect me. Naturally I mentioned this to no one. But then I thought of the fun and adventure of seeing Mrs. Tatum again and of being on my way to the big city, and I noticed the shadows no more.

I got off the train in Knoxville, made my way to the nearest intersection and stood there bewildered at the traffic. Trams and carriages and electric town cars and touring cars were rushing to and fro. The people were walking so fast, all of them in such a hurry! And everyone was so dressed up, the men in dark suits with vests, tipping their hats to the ladies as they passed; some wearing shiny shoes and spats and carrying canes; the ladies sweeping along the board sidewalks, their heads held so proudly. And such elaborate coiffures, with almost all the women wearing hats and gloves. Beautiful hats. Big elaborate hats . . .

I looked down at my black broadcloth suit and with the palms of my hands tried to smooth the wrinkles out of my skirt. It was the best-looking garment I had taken with me to the Cove, fine material and well-tailored lines, but even with my shirtwaist with the frilled jabot, it looked so plain beside all the finery passing in front of me. I felt like a country girl, dowdy and out of place; somehow I had to get in step with civilization again.

I boarded a tram car and asked the conductor to let me off in the main business section. There I walked until I found a hairdresser's. When I emerged, my long hair had been brushed and brushed and elaborately arranged in curls on top of my head, caught up at the nape of the neck in a figure eight. I emerged marveling what civilization could do for a girl's morale.

And now I knew that what my suit needed was a dramatic hat to set it off, so I sought out millinery shops. It was at the second one that I found what I sought—a beautiful black hat, the brim faced with white velvet, with swooping ostrich plumes. There was nothing mousy about this millinery. I would have to hold myself erect, carry my head high—not walk, but sweep into Mr. Hazen L. Smith's office to bring this hat off. But it was exactly right for the black suit and the new coiffure.

However, I was flabbergasted when I looked at the price tag: twenty-five dollars. My entire salary for one month! I thought of Dr. Ferrand's plea of how much even one dollar could help with the mission work. For a moment I wavered so much that my Queen Esther plan was almost lost forever. But then came the counterthought of the spiritual law that we have to give in order to receive. Businessmen like my father often spoke of it as the law that you have to spend money in order to make money. And I had a notion that drama has to be well done, never cheap, or it is best not tried at all. So I told the shoplady impetuously, "I'll take it!" and walked out wearing the hat.

From the moment the hat rested on my curls, there was no problem about feeling queenly. That hat was magic! Its first test came after I had reached the Smith building and was on my way to the president's office. At the reception-ist's request, I found myself following a young man with a celluloid collar and a pimply neck down an immense room filled with rows upon rows of stenographer's desks.

As I swept down the long aisle formed by the desks, I was thinking of Queen Esther and her unfaltering walk across that vast marble pavement. For her, there must have been a moment when the king on his golden throne looked so far away that she might as well have been seeing him through the wrong end of a telescope.

But then my thoughts were pulled sharply back to the present. As we passed, heads were lifting, eyes were turning from papers to stare. Hands lifted from clicking typewriters. The change in the atmosphere of the room was so noticeable that red started creeping up the young man's neck above the celluloid collar. But I couldn't share my guide's embarrassment at the stir we were creating because my female instinct told me that these were looks of admiration.

I was shown into a large carpeted office where a heavy-set man beginning to gray at the temples, sat behind an enormous desk. He stood as I entered—and all but whistled.

"You, a missionary! I don't believe it. Won't you sit down? Here . . ."

As he pulled up a deep upholstered red leather chair for me, I could feel his eyes sweeping me up and down in amazement. Back in his chair, warm kindly eyes continued to study me from behind gold-rimmed spectacles. "Why didn't someone think of sending out missionaries like you before!"

I thanked him, trying hard not to show any of the feelings of embarrassment that his frank admiration had stirred. Masculine interest and attention were always fun. Already the clothes had done their part. But now was a decisive moment. I had to see to it that the interest shifted from me to the cause. My part now was to forget myself and concentrate on the story I had come to tell.

For days I had been planning my presentation to Mr. Smith as carefully as any lawyer draws up his brief or any novelist outlines his plot. The problem was how to capsule the situation in the Cove for a busy man, who was coming at the subject with almost no background. I set myself a twin aim—to capture Mr. Smith's imagination and to give him the kind of facts and specifics any businessman wou!d want.

In thinking about this, I realized that too many well-meaning solicitors present only one side—the need. Certainly need can be made appealing, especially to the sentimental. But more realistically, the poor, the improvident, and the lazy will always be with us. Therefore the sketching in of the potential seemed to me to be as important as portraying the need. A man with Mr. Hazen L. Smith's rapier-sharp mind would want to know what would be the return on any money invested.

Still there was Miss Alice's admonition, so I had to put this in such a way that I would not be begging, but offering Mr. Smith the privilege of sharing in the adventure of turning human potential into productivity for Tennessee and for the nation.

Already, even in describing the crude living conditions of the Cove set down in such unbelievable beauty, I knew that I had Mr. Smith interested. When I told him about my astonishment at finding such an authentic Anglo-Saxon heritage (with a little German thrown in) preserved almost intact from eighteenth-century Europe, he broke in only occasionally to ask a question or to clarify a point. From there, I went on to talk enthusiastically about the fine minds and budding talents of some of my pupils.

"There's a girl named Bessie Coburn," I told him, "not quite thirteen, who's worked her way through a second-year Latin book by herself. Mr. Smith, the funny part of this is that it's given Bessie real status in the Cove."

"Status? Latin?"

"I know it's crazy, but the mountaineers don't think you're really educated if you can't read Latin. Another carry-over from old-time Britain, I guess.

"Then there are some mathematical geniuses," I went on. "A boy named John Spencer is soon going to be beyond the point where any of us at the mission can teach him, he's ready for calculus. And a girl, Lizette Holcombe, can add any figures in her head fast—no matter how complicated we make them—as fast as we can read them out to her.

"And there are amazing memories. You should hear some of those children reel off long lists of dates and specifics. A few minutes' study of the page of a book and it's stamped on their minds.

"Then I've one boy, Rob Allen, who has a real gift for writing. Rob can put details on paper so that you can see and hear and smell them. And he has a feel for the rhythms and the cadences of the language."

My audience of one had been following me so intently that I was becoming more exuberant by the minute. "Children like that are so great. Who knows what they can do or where they'll end up?"

"Did I understand you to say," Mr. Smith asked, "that you're trying to handle sixty-seven children all by yourself in one room?"

"That's right. But, Mr. Smith, don't feel sorry for me. Lots of one-room country schools have more than that. Odd thing too—I'd always thought that lumping all grades together in one room would slow everybody down. It works the other way. The children finish their own work, then listen to the recitations of the older ones. They retain a surprising amount. Gives them a sense of direction too."

"They're *that* eager about schoolwork?"

"Yes, that eager. In fact, it's been a shock comparing them with my friends and me back in Asheville. We took school for granted, certainly didn't consider it any great privilege."

"Yes—I know. Mrs. Smith and I have a fourteen-year-old son." A frown creased his forehead. "I know just what you mean."

"Well, in the mountains it's different. Those youngsters think lessons are a treat. And competition! I've never seen anything like it. Their enthusiasm terrifies me sometimes. How am I ever going to keep ahead of them?"

"I can't imagine how you do."

"But the point is, Mr. Smith, children as bright and eager as those simply have to have the chance for more education. It would be a crime for some of them not to go on to college. If necessary, I'll plead their cause right up to the President of the United States."

The eyes behind the glasses smiled. "I think the President would like your vehemence on behalf of higher education."

"For girls too? What's the right thing for positively brilliant girls like Lizette Holcombe and Bessie? Is it enough that they end up just having babies, cooking cornpone, and churning?"

"You're a feminist already, Miss Huddleston?"

His voice was teasing, but remembering that David had hurled this at me too, I answered seriously, "No, Mr. Smith, I don't think so. Not really. Because there's always the danger that the extreme feminist will end up quite unfulfilled as a girl."

He looked at me in astonishment. His eyes widened, and he almost whistled again as he'd done when I'd first entered his office.

"You have to admit," I said more timidly now, "that up to now you men have been inclined to play down and pooh-pooh a fine mind just because it happens to be in a woman's body."

Conflicting thoughts were apparently flitting across the masculine features before me. I had the feeling that with this latest idea, Mr. Smith was doing his best to take me seriously, but wasn't quite making it. "We men bow our

196

heads in deep contrition," he said, half mockingly. "I could make another comment—but I won't."

He turned and stared out the window, drumming a pencil softly on the side of the chair. While he thought, I did not break the silence. Oddly, the lull in the conversation was not uncomfortable. In less than an hour I had opened my mind and heart to this man to such a degree that already he seemed like an old friend.

Just as suddenly, he stopped and looked straight at me. "You're an unusual girl, you know. Am I the first person you've come to for help for the school?"

"The very first."

"Why? Why me?"

For a moment I hesitated, then took the plunge. "You're a businessman. I think you'd like honesty. So all right, I'll be honest. I've been to church all my life but it never meant much really. Just routine, you know. But recently I've learned something exciting about it. It's that a Christian has no business being satisfied with mediocrity. He's supposed to reach for the stars. Why not? He's not on his own any more. He has God's help now.

"So educating boys and girls takes money. Lots of money. And who has money? Who's the most successful businessman in East Tennessee? Mr. Hazen L. Smith, of course. I was told to reach for the stars. So I walked in on you."

Sitting there looking across at me, Mr. Smith laughed delightedly. It was almost a chortle. "That's refreshing candor all right, even if it is a trifle materialistic. So I'm supposed to be old Money-bags himself, eh?"

His use of the word "materialistic" made me remember Dr. Ferrand and his philosophy of giving. Had I overstepped myself again? "It isn't as materialistic as it sounds, Mr. Smith," I added, talking too fast. I could feel the color creeping up into my face. "Honestly, I don't want you to give a single dollar to this work unless you really feel that you should. Probably you have certain funds earmarked for charity. If your conscience has laid other causes on you, then I'll respect a loud resounding 'No' from you for my cause. And I really mean that."

"I believe you *do* mean it." He looked at me thoughtfully. "All right—so now for my reaction. I like what you've told me, Miss Huddleston, and I like your way of telling it. I'm flattered that you came to me first, even though"—and a teasing note crept into his voice—"you did think of me as old Money-bags. I'll help all right. I want to, very much. That is my decision—with no pressure from you. But I've felt selfish sitting here listening to a story that deserves a bigger audience. If I can arrange it, would you come back to Knoxville and speak to the University Club? Maybe to a church group too?"

This was something I had not expected. "Mr. Smith, I've never done any speaking of *that* kind."

"Never mind that. You're a natural. You've asked a favor. Now I'm asking one. How about it?"

Impulsively I rose and held out my hand to him. "Mr. Smith, if you think I can speak to audiences like that—well, I'll do my best."

As Mr. Smith moved forward to open the door for me, he paused, his hand on the doorknob. "I've decided to make that comment after all. Let me put it in this framework. After my initial reaction to you, you could have flirted with me a bit. A lot of girls would have. You didn't. Sometime in the future I suppose I could try to take some sort of advantage of your friendship. I won't. So we understand each other perfectly. But here's something for you to remember some dark day when schoolteaching seems like a thankless task . . . Here's one man who thinks you have the most beautiful eyes God ever put in a woman's face."

Sixteen

UPON MY RETURN from Knoxville, there were letters from mother and father awaiting me, urging me to use the coming holiday for a visit home. Surely, father wrote, I was ready for some relief from missionary work by now. And mother held out a ball at the new Battery Park Hotel, a spate of receptions, luncheons, teas and clothes-shopping to lure me, even mentioned two families with attractive sons my age who had recently moved to Asheville.

I puzzled over what good reason I could give my parents for not going, since I guessed that the truth would not please them: I was beginning to enjoy my new life too much to want to leave again right now.

Of course compared to Asheville's social whirl, recreation in Cutter Gap was limited, but we found many ways of having fun. For instance, of an evening after supper, we in the mission house could not often resist the shiny new piano in the big parlor. Miss Ida was a reasonably good pianist while I was a limping one who read music only tolerably well.

David had brought with him to the mountains a ukulele which he would produce at the slightest provocation—to the delight of the children and young folks. They were familiar with fiddles, dulcimers and banjos, but the ukulele was as strange and fascinating an instrument as the piano. By the time I got to the Cove, David already had a reputation as a "song-followin' man." With his sense of rhythm, his rafter-raising baritone, and his nimble fingers, David had a ready-made way into the hearts of the people, for music was the universal language of the highlanders. They sang as readily as they talked. There was a song or a ballad for all occasions: to lighten housework, for hunting or hoeing corn or driving the cows home or churning or piecing a quilt or rocking the baby. And if the right ditty did not come readily to mind, then one was promptly improvised.

I noticed that more and more David just "happened" to have his ukulele along when he went calling in the homes. As soon as he would bring it out, he told me, barriers would go down. The young children would creep up to him and ask shyly for a "gettin'-goin' tune" or a "foolery one." The older people would plead for some of the familiar old gospel hymns which they loved ... "Twilight A-stealin'" ... "What a Friend We Have in Jesus" ... "Just As I Am" ... "Wondrous Love." Everyone would join in, voices mingling, heads keeping time. "Prettiest durn music ever heerd" was the invariable pronouncement. "His fingers goin' like a blue streak on that thar ukalale could tear down the house and put hit in the loft."

"I don't need to *say* much of anything," David remarked to me. "The hymns say it for me, probably minister to folks better than I could anyway."

One evening soon after I got back from Knoxville, some of the older boys from school—Arrowhead Holcombe, Wraight Holt, and Will Beck—heard us singing and stopped in. "Be tickled to death," Wraight requested of David, "if ye'd take a runago at one of them whittleding songs."

"Aye," chimed in Ruby Mae, "dizzifyin' music, that's what we want."

So David started in on

> "Oh, you beautiful doll,
> You great big beautiful doll. . . ."

as I tried to pick it out on the piano. Soon the boys were patting and clapping, then tapping and wheeling and clogging while they sang.

"Look at them rambunctious boys a-flaxin' east and west," Ruby Mae exulted. "Feel gaily as bucks, don't they! Makin' so much ruckus, now the preacher's got t' put on his shouty voice."

After that, with apples roasting in the fire and corn popping, we had a party. By the next morning word "got norated around" of the fun to be had at the mission house. Soon we had to limit the open houses to two a week to leave us time for our homework and the necessary grading of papers. Then too, no matter whom we invited, Wraight and some of the other boys would try to crash the party Finally David called an after-school planning session for all the boys to work out a plan fair to all.

But when we were by ourselves for a few minutes' recreation after supper—as on this evening—our impromptu concerts were more sedate. So far we were limited by owning only a hymnbook and one songbook, *All America Sings,* but David had sent a big order to New York for some more books and a stack of popular sheet music.

I was trying to carry the melody of "Danny Boy" but was missing a lot of notes, and several times lost my place while David kept right on twanging and singing away Every few bars, we hit a screeching discord. Ruby Mae dramatically clapped her hands to her ears "Gee-oh! Ol-oo-whee-ee-ee law! Scrapes my eardrums."

"It would scrape anybody's," Miss Ida put in from the doorway, sucking in her lower lip and looking at us as if she were a bird about to pounce. Sometimes her hands reminded me of a bird's claws. "Do you call that music?"

David shrugged. "Would you like to play for us, Ida?"

"Certainly not! I would not deprive Miss Huddleston of the chance to practice. However—" she advanced to the center of the room where she stood balancing a letter on the palm of her hand as she looked piercingly at me "Here's a letter that came earlier today."

"And saved for this moment. And interruption a relief to all," David observed drily, as I slid off the piano stool to take the letter.

"Oh, it's from Mr. Smith!" I tore the envelope open eagerly . . .

Knoxville, Tenn.
April 24, 1912

Dear Miss Huddleston:
Your visit to my office on Tuesday last has given me a great deal to think about. I know good salesmanship. You could scarcely realize what a quality selling job you did. However, I want to give considerable thought to what my part should be in your work, keep in touch with you, and go slowly.

For the moment, enclosed, please find a cheque for two hundred ($200.00) to be used as a start towards your boarding school and adult education program. There will be more from time to time.

Then I have shipped you two boxes of new textbooks, all on the High School level, and some maps.

Eventually, I would like to look forward to helping individual (carefully selected) worthy students—yes, a few girls too!—towards college, with job placement for the boys. More about that later.

Finally, the arrangements for your talk before the University Club are pending. At that time, you might like to call on other outstanding businessmen whom I can hand-pick for you.

Your visit afforded me real pleasure. By the way, are you related to the John L. Huddleston family of Asheville? I've known John Huddleston for many years. Mrs. Smith looks forward to meeting you and joins me in best of good wishes.

Sincerely yours,
Hazen L. Smith

Underneath his signature, he had crudely sketched in a tiny money bag with coins spilling out of it.

David was watching me. "Her eyes are bright. Her cheeks are glowing. Must be good news. Want to share? Or is it a secret?"

I tossed the letter at him. "Of course I'll share. It's great news." I couldn't help humming and doing a little waltz around his chair as I waved the check in the air . . .

"Whirl and twirl,
    Tiddley-um—
This ole girl
    Feels frolicsome. . . ."

I had forgotten that Miss Ida was still standing there.

David finished the letter, looked up at me and laughed. "You are a daffy girl. May I have this dance?" He put one hand lightly on my waist, grasped my hand and we went whirling and twirling around the chairs, faster and faster.

We heard a snort as Miss Ida strode out of the room, her heavy footsteps echoing down the hall and up the stairs. I knew that I would hear from her later about this.

202

It came the next day when she sought me out to ask, "Christy, where is David? I need him to put up a clothes line."

"Don't have the least idea, Miss Ida. Haven't seen him."

"Do tell!" she clucked irritably. "You're always seeing him. See more of him than I do. You girls are all alike when it comes to David. All got notions about him. That was quite apparent last night."

I was annoyed and choked back a retort. But on second thought, I knew that I should not let this one pass. "Miss Ida, I don't like what you said and it isn't true. If I had nothing on my mind but getting a husband, do you think I would have picked Cutter Gap, Tennessee? Believe me, there are lots of eligible men in Asheville, lots more than here."

"Really! Now do tell!" And she dropped the conversation as if it had been one of those hot marbles in my schoolroom.

DURING THESE DAYS of freedom from school, we had time for more calling. Aunt Polly Teague was high on our list, but before we could get there, she sent for David and me. After ninety-three years, Dr. MacNeill told us, her tired heart was failing.

The old lady's doll house of a cabin was set on a V-shaped plot of earth between the dirt road and a stream, with a waterfall close by the side of the house. Some twenty years before, after she was a widow, Aunt Polly had settled her eldest son, Dale, and his family into the big family homestead where she and her husband, Freeman, had reared eighteen children. Then she had prevailed on her boys to build her the tiny house where she could be independent.

David's knock was rewarded by a hearty "Come on in! Howdy-do, come in and set." The front room was almost filled with an old cherry post-and-spindle bed, but Aunt Polly was not in the bed; she was sitting in a chair like a queen on a throne, only this queen was wearing an outing flannel nightgown with a shawl around her shoulders, a black stocking cap on her head pulled down almost to her eyes. The bright blue eyes in the wrinkled face lighted with pleasure as we walked in.

She lifted gnarled hands to grasp both of David's. "Praise the Lord! You come in time."

"Why, of course," David's resonant voice filled the room. "We came just as soon as Dr. MacNeill told us."

"Set down, both of you. Pull up that settin' chair thar for Miz Christy. Law, I've been that fearful you wouldn't git here in time."

"Why Aunt Polly, you're indestructible. Dr. MacNeill tells me you've fooled the doctors so many times before."

"Not this time. This is my time to go. Won't be top-side of earth long. Feel it in my innards. So I'm needin' you mighty bad, Preacher. Been longin' to speak with you. Need comfortin' to my heart."

She turned her blazing blue eyes on me. "And Miz Christy, I asked for you because I hankered to see yer fresh young face once more and that white neck of your'n holdin' yer head up so proud-like. For us old folks, it be a treat to rest our eyes on you sprightly young things."

Before I could say anything, David was remonstrating, "Come on now, Aunt Polly, you're not about to die."

"Son, you won't do a dyin' old lady any good with that rattletrap talk. You're not a-foolin' yerself and you're not a-foolin' me. Now I've got this all thought out. First off, Preacher, I want you to read out'n the Good Book. Read me them certain-sure words about the life to come. There 'tis." She pointed to a big, worn family Bible on the table.

David picked up the Bible and began leafing through it while Aunt Polly waited expectantly. As he turned page after page, then flipped them over again, she thought to help him. "Find that spot where it says 'bout many mansions."

"Oh yes—the gospel of John, I believe." His eyes scanned the pages. "Yes, here it is." There was relief in David's voice:

"Let not your heart be troubled. . . .
In my Father's house there are many mansions: If it were not so, I would have told you. I go to prepare a place for you.
And if I go and prepare a place for you, I will come again, and receive you unto myself; that where I am, there ye may be also."

"Aye. That's good. But don't be stoppin' there. I be a-thirstin' for the Word. Read on, son. Read on."

David's fingers began riffling pages again. He looked at me appealingly and I cleared my throat, casting about in my mind for something to say during the awkward pause. "Aunt Polly, I was thinking, you've had a long life. Why, you were in midlife while Abraham Lincoln was President."

"Aye, lassie. I've been lasty-like."

But this was no time for small talk, and she turned again expectantly to David. His eyes were still scanning pages. The wrinkled face broke into a gentle smile. "Preacher, you're not exactly lick-splittin' through the Book, are ye?"

"Here, this is what I was hunting for:

"And this is the promise that he hath promised us, even eternal life."

"Now that's wondrous good. But why don't you find a spot where you can read straight through? Don't mean to be cranky or to put you out none, but ye're a-skitterin' all over that Book."

"All right, Aunt Polly," David answered cheerfully. With that, he settled back in his chair to read the long passage from Nicodemus' midnight talk with Jesus, ending with those timeless words:

"And as Moses lifted up the serpent in the wilderness, even so, must the Son of man be lifted up:
That whosoever believeth in Him should not perish, but have eternal life. . . ."

Aunt Polly had her eyes shut, nodding her head. "Aye, satisfies my soul." She opened her eyes and addressed herself to David. "Now, I want to ask you a question straight out. What's gonna happen when my heart gives out beatin'? Is my speerit gonna see Him right off?"

David closed the Book. "I guess lots of people have wanted to know that, Aunt Polly. We used to discuss things like that at seminary."

Please, David, don't! Not now. Not that way.

"Preacher, I ain't needin' to know what you gabbled about when you had time on yer hands. Tell me whatn'all you *know* for a fact."

"Well, Aunt Polly, after all, we can't experience death while we're still living, so how can we know—the way you

205

mean it? Even Scripture seems a little confusing. Of course, you realize too that the Jews themselves did not believe in immortality until far along in their history."

My heart was sinking into my shoe-tops. *David, David ... This isn't the time.*

Aunt Polly was silent with her face so expressionless that David looked at her curiously and cleared his throat. "Some think that at physical death we go into a state of unconsciousness, but then are raised up on the last day when this old earth will end in some kind of catastrophic upheaval. Scientists—"

Aunt Polly held up one hand to interrupt him, her eyes snapping fire. "Ye mean that some folks think that when we die, our speerit don't know nothing and gits kept in a sort of icehouse, all froze up stiff for hundreds or thousands of years till the trump sounds at the last day, and then we git unfroze?"

David smiled. "Well, that's putting it picturesquely. But yes, something like that."

"Preacher, is that what you're believin'?"

"Aunt Polly, these are points I haven't quite settled with myself."

"Wal, son, it's past time you was thrashin' a few things out with yer Creator. Shorely, you can't disremember about Jesus tellin' that rascal of a thief a-dyin' on the cross beside Him, *'This day* thou shalt be with me in paradise.' Does that sound like ony icehouse?"

"I really don't think—well, you see, time in Scripture is not always the same as—"

"Fiddlesticks! those men were in *pain.* They was a-dyin'! Weren't no time a-tall for foolin'-around talk. Think ye 'this day' and 'thou shalt be with me' means onything but just what it says?"

David looked hurt and embarrassed. "I'm sorry, Aunt Polly. It's just that I try to be intellectually honest."

She placed a blue-veined hand with its swollen knuckles over his hand and spoke as if to one of her grandchildren. "Poor man-person! You've most fractured yer head tryin' to be wise-witted, ain't ye?"

She sighed—and shut her eyes. Indeed, they were closed so long that I was beginning to think she had fallen asleep when suddenly, she began to speak again. Her eyes were still closed, but her voice had changed: it was soft, almost caressing, with a smile in it. "Ever-who heerd tell of sech! Me, unthoughtedly fotchin' on a boy preacher-parson who's hardly seen thirty summers yit, tongue-larrupin' him with questions that abody could scarce answer in a lifetime. Didn't have no call to heave my load onto his young shoulders. Got a little gimp left myself, guess."

The thin eyelids fluttered open. "I'm a-thinkin' I'll tell you a true tale. Be ye listenin'?"

David and I both nodded, not knowing what to expect.

"Nigh onto sixty years ago 'twas, Freeman and I was still young and spry. I was always childing, always with a baby to my breast. We housekept whar Dale and his brood is now. Owned a big scope of land and as the babies came on, Freeman had to keep addin' on to our cabin. 'Twas pretty, with a big black walnut tree crowdin' it and honeysuckle a-creepin' all acrost the porch. The crik and the road was like a necklace round it and the everlastin' hills closed us in warm and cozy, like in the holler of a cup.

"The work, like the hills, was everlastin'. There was the garden and the chickens to tend; the milkin' and the churnin'; the bread to bake and the grub to cook to feed twenty hongry mouths regular; water to tote from the crik; always the babies to mind. I'd commence long afore the crack of dawn and still be at it by firelight after all the young'uns and even Freeman was abed.

"Wal, finally my heart give out. It would take spells of beatin' so hard like it would fly out'n my breast. Went to the nighest doctor. Said I should bed it to rest. If'n I didn't, I would die sure, least to hear him tell it.

"But sakes alive! There wasn't a natural blessed thing I could do about restin', not with a house full of little shavers stacked right up to the loft. So when the queer spells would come on and I was real bad off, I'd go out and querl right up on the grass under the walnut tree, jest lie thar quiet-like, a-drinkin' in the strength of the earth till the spell passed, then go back to my job of work again. And I didn't die like the Doc had said.

"But something worse was ailin' my heart, only Doc didn't know about *that:* it was starvin' to death. The Cove didn't have no church-house then and that was long afore Miz Henderson come. Onct in a long while a preacher-person would come ridin' through, but not often enough to do us no good.

"That longin' inside me burned and ached and cried for something, I didn't rightly know what. Then one day—

207

seems like 'twas only a week ago—I was goin' acrost the foot log bridge, along that path windin' through the thickets and the blackberry brambles. And at one certain spot on that path—I could show you where—why, He met me. Somethin' happened to me there. It was simple-like, but clear as mornin' light. I says to Him, 'Lord,' I says, 'I don't rightly know whether I'm gonna live or die, but it don't make no differ. From here on, my life belongs to You.'

"And it did too, for a fact. From that day I could feel His love a-feedin' my starvin', thirstin' soul. And the more I tried givin' His love away to my young'uns and my man and the neighbor-folks, the more love He gave back to me. Reminded me of openin' up a spring: first, a muddy trickle. Then a leetle stream, gettin' stronger and clearer with every day that passed.

"Wal, then one spring when the moun-tains was greenin' and the grass in the pasture was half-a-grab-high, Freeman had a huntin' acci-dent and went on afore me. And no sooner had he gone from his body than there he was in the room with us'uns. Not that I could see him, but I shorely could feel him. Jest himself, laughin' easy-like, tellin' us as clear as ever a body could that everything was all right, not to worry a mite. It was then I knowed for sure that death ain't nothing to be afeerd of. Thar was other times too—but I've spoke enough for now."

The look she gave us with those blazing blue eyes was a benediction. "I've been livin' with my Lord for over sixty year now. It's been nippety-tuck to git through this life a-tall, but I'd never of made it without Him. So son, don't worry yer head no more 'bout us bein' put to sleep in some old speerit icehouse. The minute I take my leave of this wore-out flesh, that second He'll be a-waitin' for me. Rest yer soul on that, son, like this old lady does.

"And now I aim to give you and Miz Christy my blessin'." She reached up to lay one hand on David and one on me. "May the Lord bless and keep you both—till we meet over there in the glory of His amazin' love. And I'm that beholden to you for bringin' yer brightness to take away some of an old lady's lonesomeness. Thank ye, lassie."

I reached down to hug Aunt Polly, but I could not speak. The cheek I pressed against hers was moist with tears.

Seventeen

I WAS SEEING more and more of Fairlight Spencer. Our friendship was a natural outgrowth of my teaching her.

What the record time is for learning to read, I do not know, but the prize probably belongs to Fairlight. Three long sessions accomplished it. She "practiced" all the time, read everything imaginable—the old newspapers pasted on the walls of the Spencer cabin, the pieces of a tattered dictionary, the family Bible, even the labels on jars and bottles. Within a few weeks, so far as reading was concerned, she had caught up with most of the pupils in my school and was borrowing books two or three at a time.

I wondered if Fairlight's family might not suffer; after all, they could not *eat* books. I need not have feared. The young Spencers' stomachs were too healthy and clamorous to stand for any neglect.

But Fairlight did invent ingenious ways to do her housework and read at the same time: a book propped on the window sill while she was washing dishes; a book open on a chair at her side while she was churning or spinning or shelling shucky beans or stringing green beans.

In the beginning I had thought of teaching her to read as just another do-good project. (I admit it, to my shame.) But Fairlight soon changed that with the debt in her favor. Her return to me was—all unknowing—such priceless insights into her heart and spirit that in a few short weeks I had begun to love this mountain woman.

For example, she taught me something important about the use of time and how to enjoy life. With a husband and five children to cook, clean, wash, even make clothes for, and with no modern conveniences at all, not even piped-in water, Fairlight might have felt burdened and sorry for herself—but she did not. Often she found time to pause in her dishwashing to let her eyes and her spirit drink in the beauty of a sunset. She would interrupt her work to call the children and revel with them in the grandeur of thunderheads - piling up over the mountain peaks, heat lightning flashing behind the clouds like fireworks. "It lifts the heart," she would say, and that was explanation enough for any interruption.

There was always time for a story in front of the fire with the children snuggled against her; always leisure for the family to gather on the porch "to sing the moon up."

Fairlight told me how on the first fine spring day, she considered it only right and proper to drop her housework: "The house, it's already been a-settin' here for a hundred years. It'll be right here tomorrow. It's today I must be livin' "—and make her way to one particular spot she knew. There she would kneel and with her long slender fingers brush aside the dead, sodden leaves and gaze wonderingly on the first blossoms of the trailing arbutus. Knowing her as I did, I could picture her fairly crooning over the flowers.

She and I agreed that never had we known such delight at an end to winter, perhaps because it had been a drab one. Yet I was discovering that spring did not come suddenly in the mountains but on tiptoe, stealthily, with retreats and skirmishes, what Fairlight called "sarvice winter" and sometimes "redbud winter." Still, the mountainsides were burgeoning at last and I was eager to explore them. Since Fairlight knew just where to take me, she and I were often in the woods, sometimes just the two of us, sometimes like a pair of female Pied Pipers with the Spencer children and some of my other pupils trailing along. They would race ahead of us swinging on the limbs of trees or on wild grape vines, "plumb crazy," as Fairlight would say, "cuttin' shines. Never did see such a doo-raw." Obviously my pupils considered all of Teacher's excursions "jollifications."

The children would wade the creeks (every stream swollen and tumultuous this time of year), screaming with glee when their feet dipped into the icy water. Or they would select smooth pebbles and skip them across the water, what they called "skeeting the rocks." Often they would line up and make a game of seeing who could cross from one bank to the other by hopping stone to stone on one foot. But then rocks would "rockle," bare feet would slip. Dunkings! At first I worried about wet clothes in cold spring winds until I finally learned to take it in stride. These children had been dunked before!

We were out so often that I began to question Fairlight about whether our proposed lessons or walks would interfere with her work. I can only remember twice when there were household tasks which she could not interrupt lest something be spoilt. Her reply was more likely to be, "It's a fair day. Shorely we'uns can pass the time with one another." Then more shyly, "Never have been with you enough, Miz Christy, to see my satisfaction yet."

The highlanders were often accused of being lazy and shiftless. As I got to know them better, my conclusion was: relaxed, yes; shiftless, a few of them; greedy, scarcely ever. Fairlight's "It's today I must be livin'" summed up their philosophy well—a philosophy that aggressive people would spurn.

Yet which is right? Human life is short. Each of us has a limited number of years. So are we going to go through those so-few years with little time for our family and friends, and unseeing eyes for the beauties around us, concentrating on accumulating money and things when we have to leave them all behind anyway? I began to wonder if the mountain values were not more civilized than civilization's. At least I found the absence of greed and pushiness as refreshing as a long cool drink of sparkling mountain spring water.

Now I realized why these mountain people were shy with strangers. They had never learned the citified arts of hiding feelings or of smiling when the heart was cold. Friendship was dangerous to them because they had built up no protection against it. Once they let you in it must be into the deep places of the heart as Fairlight had with me. Though I had known her only four months, already I was far closer to her than members of my own family or girl friends whom I had always known.

She was teaching me about true friendship too. Through Fairlight's eyes I came to know a quality of friendship which bore little resemblance to the casualness of our relationships back home. The mountain type of friendship was a tie of substance between people with a sort of gallant fealty about it. It had to do with a time in the past when there was no more final bond than a man's pledged word; when every connection of blood and family was firm and strong, forged in the past, stretching into the future.

And so this kind of friendship was for life—yes, and for eternity too. One would never deceive or defraud a friend, nor allow him to be in need so long as you had one coin, one garment, or one meal to share with him. His sorrow was your sorrow; his joy, your cause for rejoicing too.

Through all of this I began to understand—at least a little—about the feuds. Whenever a member of one's family or a friend was considered to have been betrayed, the betrayal sunk lower and bit deeper than it would have with those whose relationships are more shallow. Such a betrayal was a difficult matter for the highlander to swallow. To forgive and to forget it seemed to him to cut across the integrity of life itself. All of this Fairlight was teaching me—and much, much more.

I was thinking about all this as I started for the spot at the base of Pebble Mountain where Fairlight and I had agreed to meet today. Her husband and some of the other men were helping David complete the stringing of the telephone wire. We wanted to see the men at work. The telephone was a big event. It would be the Cove's first real link with civilization, and we could scarcely wait to hear that telephone start ringing in the mission house.

The school grounds and the road running past the mission were still quagmires of mud. I paused for an instant at the end of the board walk, but could see no dry spots, so there was nothing for it but to plunge into the sea of mud. With every footfall there was a scrunch and then a sucking sound.

I thought back to Mr. Pentland's cryptic comments about spring mud in general and the Big Mud Hole in particular during our walk together through the snow. Now I could appreciate what he had meant. Once frozen ground had thawed through April rains, there was mud everywhere in our big front yard, tracked into the mission house. Even pernickety Miss Ida had almost given up scrubbing floors after us.

In the valley the blossoms of the "sarvice" tree were fading now. But as I began climbing Pebble Mountain, I was delighted to find the trees still in full bloom, clouds of creamy-white blossoms, incredibly beautiful set against the dark green background of the firs and spruces.

For a few minutes the trail was in the open, then it passed again through forest cover. All at once I came upon an astonishing performance—a ruffed grouse doing his courting dance before his lady-love. I half-hid myself

212

behind a tree, scarcely daring to breathe lest I interrupt this fascinating sight. As the male strutted, his tail feathers were spread and held erect, his neck feathers ruffled, his body swollen. At intervals he would wag his head to the ground giving the effect of a courtly bow. I wondered how often Fairlight Spencer had seen this dance.

She was waiting for me now sitting on a fallen log at the edge of a clearing. I could tell by the childishly eager look on her face that she had something to show me.

"Pyxie lichen." She pointed to an unusual-looking moss that covered the rotting balsam log. "Jest a-settin' here I spied nine kinds. That thar's reindeer moss. That's beard lichen."

All of this was new to me. Some of the mosses were so delicate as to be elfin. Week by week I was finding that Fairlight knew so much about the woods: where to find fields of bluets and crowfoot violets and maidenhair ferns and jack-in-the-pulpits; the spots for "Monkey-jugs," as she called them (really wild ginger); trillium—as gorgeous a wildflower as I had ever seen; and "sang"—the gingseng so wanted in the Orient that they are willing to pay big prices for the roots.

She also had favorite spots for all the herbs she needed for her family doctoring: mullen, out of which she made cough syrup; crabapple bark for asthma and sneezing; wild ginger for diarrhea; witch-hazel bark from which she made a salve for burns and skin sores; gingseng and sassafras mixed together for a tea.

When Fairlight had finished showing me the mosses and the lichens, she pointed in the direction of the hill behind us, "Men-persons jest over there—yan." But I had already been hearing their voices.

"Bin workin' since sun-up," she commented as she rose and tried to smooth her wrinkled cotton skirt. "They'll most likely be chiseled down by now, I reckon."

"Yes, they're just pigs for work today."

Fairlight looked me in astonishment. "Why Miz Christy, that's not the way to call it. You jest don't know pigs a-tall. Why pigs *never* work."

We were both laughing as we scrambled through the bushes to find David and some men lifting a tall pole into a hole; another group was following the same procedure several hundred feet on up the slope. David waved to us; he had on his oldest work clothes and looked almost as dirty and sweaty as the rest. Yet there was no question as to who was directing the operation. His voice was as loud and booming as always; listening to him, I wondered if he realized how abrupt and overbearing his orders sounded.

"Eas-sy, Jeb. Two more feet. To the left, Jeb, more to the left. Now—let her drop!" With a thump the pole hit the bottom of the hole, and while two men held the pole steady, the rest shoveled in the dirt and tamped it in around.

I was puzzled to notice one man half-slumped behind a tree trunk off to one side, absently whittling on a piece of wood with a jackknife. I recognized him as Ozias Holt, the father of eight children in my school including Wraight and Vella. David had apparently not yet noticed that Mr. Holt was taking it easy on the job. What had begun as a volunteer project had now turned into a paid one.

At first David had thought that he and two or three other men would have no trouble stringing the telephone wire. He had soon learned differently. The first bad news had been to find that the insulators and pins could not be fastened to live trees. The mere thought of having to cut tall straight trees, skin and smooth them, lug them where there were no roads, plant them up and down mountains, meanwhile hacking off branches of any living trees that might swing against the wire, was staggering. And I had started all this by one innocent little letter to the telephone company!

David had, first of all, studied a map to plot the route for the wire. He found that the closest point where we could tap into an existing line was at Centerport, not quite three miles across country from the mission, four and a half miles east of Lyleton.

For the portion of the route which cut across any land owned by mountain men, there was no problem about getting permission to cut the necessary trees for poles. But one strip which had to be crossed belonged to the Scottish Timber and Land Company. They had given David permission to string the wire across their land, but were adamant about any timber-cutting, so the poles for that section had to be hauled. They would have to be brought partway in the Harvester wagon, carried on shoulders the rest of the distance. Worse, close to Centerport the wire was going to have to be taken across the French Broad River by boat before being tapped into the line on the other bank. Fortunately at that place, the river was only about three hundred feet wide.

So much work was involved that David finally decided to give out the word that he would pay his helpers twenty cents an hour. David was taking part of this money for wages from his own pocket; the mission helped a little. Eleven men had volunteered, but David soon found he never knew when any given man would show up for work. I had to admit that the same relaxed attitude toward life which I so admired in Fairlight did make for some working problems. A case in point was Mr. Holt loitering behind the tree, unnoticed.

"Men, we've got to get at least six more poles in the ground before dark," David was announcing.

"Announcing" was the right word too. You would have thought that David was talking to a congregation of two thousand. The Cove folks were always saying that their new preacher had "good wind." Well, probably the residents of Centerport were hearing this pronouncement.

At that moment Mr. Holt slid from a sitting position to stretch himself full length on the ground, hands under his head staring up at the clouds. The movement caught David's eye. Amazement in every movement, he strode over to where the man was stretched out. "And just what ails you, Ozias?"

The big mountaineer did not stir. "Why, Rev'end, hit's jest not generated in me to work right now. I'm bodaciously tired out."

"Tired out! Well, now isn't that too bad! You're being paid for this job, Ozias. The rest of us are tired too. You don't see us quitting." A thought struck David and his voice rose higher. "Come to think of it, Ozias, you haven't done much work all day long."

As if in answer, Mr. Holt raised himself on one elbow and let go a stream of tobacco juice aimed at the nearest tree trunk.

David stood there shaking with fury. "Ozias Holt, I'll be blasted if I'm going to pay you one red cent for loafing around here all day. Start working—or quit."

Mr. Holt still would not look at David. He answered nothing, spat again. Finally very slowly, he rose and stretched and yawned, turned, and slouched off through the woods.

David watched him go, making no comment. Obviously he was still seething inside. Embarrassed, the rest of the men turned back to their tasks—mostly in silence now, and a somewhat thoughtful and chastened David picked up where he had left off.

Fairlight crept close to me. "It puzzles me a little grain," she said in a low voice. "Some folks are an everlastin' despair. Lordamercy, that Ozias now. Always has been tough as a laurel burl. Tetchious too. Shorely wearin' his gredges outside his shirt this day." She sighed. "Never did like upscuddles myself. Sorter wears the bright off the day." Her voice sank to a whisper. "But I don't like preacher-parson tanglin' with Ozias Holt. He's a mean'un. Don't want nothin' t'happen."

Eighteen

THE DAY AFTER the big shipment of books and maps arrived, David and I spent all of the evening into the small hours unpacking everything and putting up the maps. Then I could scarcely wait to get through the opening exercises and the singing period the first morning so that I could announce, "Now I have a big surprise for you!" And I began pulling down the large colorful maps from their shiny roller-cases fastened to the wall, then holding up one by one some of the new textbooks from the piles on my desk for all the children to see. It was easy to make a story for my pupils out of my trip to Knoxville, with Mr. Smith as the hero-benefactor.

They were entranced with the beauty of the maps and their gay colors. Immediately we found Tennessee on the map of the United States and stuck in a pin with a red paper flag at the approximate location of Cutter Gap. At last I had some tools to help me convey some notion of the world beyond this isolated Cove. At last, we could get on with geography and even history.

I was the only person in the classroom who had ever before seen books so fresh and clean, with all their covers still there, with not a page missing, with no tears and fingermarks. I made a speech about taking care of the books. "Books are like friends. We must treat them like friends. Let's have clean hands before we handle them. Turn the pages carefully. Never, never bend the covers of the books backwards."

Already John Spencer had located the calculus book and was turning the pages joyfully, looking as if he had been handed a gift of the moon.

On the whole, Mr. Smith had centered on textbooks for the High School level, partly because he had guessed correctly that this was our greatest need, partly because he was a man whose inclination, I already knew, was to help the more advanced and superior students. So we had algebra and geometry books, Latin texts for four years and especially fine literature books. I noticed that Rob Allen and Isaak McHone were fascinated with the latter.

Later on that day I read from one of our new copies of *English Romantic Poets*, Samuel Taylor Coleridge's "Kubla Khan," thinking that my pupils—even those too young to understand the meaning—would enjoy the rhythm and harmonious sound of the words.

I had no sooner finished reading than Isaak raised his hand to ask, "Kin I learn it by heart, Teacher? All of it?" And before school let out that day he proceeded to do just that, memorizing every beautiful line of the poem. Exuberantly, he left school that afternoon rolling the rhythms over his tongue, marching out the door reciting to the other children:

> "In Xanadu did Kubla Khan
> A stately pleasure-dome decree;
> Where Alph, the sacred river, ran
> Through caverns measureless to man
> Down to a sunless sea. . . ."

I could hear his voice going down the road proclaiming to the mountains, exulting to the heavens . . .

> "A damsel with a dulcimer
> In a vision once I saw:
> It was an Abyssinian maid,
> And on her dulcimer she play'd
> Singing of Mount Abora.
> Could I revive within me
> Her symphony and song,
> To such a deep delight 'twould win me,
> That with music loud and long,
> I would build that dome in air.
> And all who heard should see them there,
> And all should cry, Beware! Beware!
> His flashing eyes, his floating hair!
> For he on honey-dew hath fed,
> And drunk the milk of Paradise."

On Friday morning I started for the schoolhouse early

to make some extra preparations for the end-of-the-week spelling bee. I wanted to find some especially hard and tricky words because the eight best spellers on each of our two teams were to compete that afternoon for "head marks." As I crossed the yard, I noticed some papers on the ground. I quickened my steps. Even from a distance I could see that the schoolhouse door was standing ajar.

Fearing I did not know what, I pushed the door open—and drew in my breath sharply. The room was wrecked. Books littered the floor around my desk. I ran toward the front of the room for a better look. Books had been thrown wildly and were lying where they had fallen, some on their faces with bent covers, some face up with their pages fluttering in the breeze from the open doorway, looking as if several pairs of feet had tramped through them and over them, not once but again and again. Pages had been ripped out, some slashed and then wadded up. Our books! Our beautiful new books! Hot anger rose in me. I stooped and picked up one of them lying by my toe. It was a Cicero book with pages torn out, only pieces left, the spine broken. I stood there looking at the mutilated book in my hands through a blur of tears. *What is the point of this? I don't understand. I just don't understand. Are some people mad at the mission? Mad at the school? Why? Why would they be?*

For no reason at all I thought of little Vella Holt and that mean prank on the first day of school—the rock camouflaged to look like an innocent rag and string ball. This assault on our books was of the same order: there was viciousness in our midst.

But I was not finished with nasty surprises. I looked up and—oh, no! Two of our new maps had been drawn down out of their cases and then slashed with something sharp— like a boy's Barlow knife. Weak-kneed, I sank into the nearest seat and sat staring at the rampage of destruction spread out before me. The faces of different children, all sorts of thoughts went chasing through my mind. But I had to tell David about this. I went to get him.

There were some sad faces in school that day but a great many more enigmatic ones. Most of the children were withdrawn, subdued, suddenly remote, unwilling to say much of anything. We spent much of the morning putting torn books and maps back together as best we could, matching pieces, mending and pasting those that could be mended. I hoped that all this effort would at least impress on everyone the seriousness of such malicious destructiveness.

After mending books we went on to preparation for the spelling bee. I started to put a long list of words on the board for the contestants to study when I realized how chilly the room was. We were having another spell of "dogwood winter" with clouded skies and a cold wind, so I went over to poke up the fire. But I had no sooner opened the iron grating and thrust the poker in than a series of explosions like a gun going off spit sparks and flame into my face and onto my hair and dress. With an involuntary cry I backed away, slapping at the sparks.

Ruby Mae, who was sitting in the nearest seat, rushed to me, frantically raking burning pieces of something out of my hair. When we had finally gotten all the tiny conflagrations stamped out, I saw that there were several scorched places and burned holes in my dress, and the way one place on my neck was stinging, I knew that it must be burned. Ruby Mae examined it. "Hit's burned right enough, Teacher. It's a-raisin' a water-bubble already."

I stood there with flushed face and disheveled hair looking at my schoolroom, so flustered that for a moment I could not trust myself to speak. Finally with a shaking voice I asked, "What was it that exploded?"

There was a long silence. Some of the children would not look at me. Finally Joshua Bean Beck spoke up, "Hit be buckeyes, ma'am. Buckeyes in the ashes. They git hot and then pop and fly all t'pieces when the air hits 'em."

I was opening my mouth for the next obvious question but Joshua Bean was ahead of me. "No ma'am, Teacher. I wouldn't do that to ye. Not me, Teacher."

Then who? Who? ... Haven't I gotten through to these youngsters at all? Mrs. Tatum's voice came back to me as through a tunnel, "Goin' to be well nigh impossible for you to help them. Only person that could stick it out was Miss Henderson. Other teachers has had to give it up as a bad job." *A bad job ... Was this the beginning of the end for me too?*

Then I heard a torrent of words pouring out of my own mouth, "I bragged about you in my letters to Mr. Smith, talked you up, told him you were different from boys and girls in other schools. Told him how proud I was of you—that there never had been students so eager for a school, so wanting to learn, so longing for books in order to learn.

"So what do I tell Mr. Smith now? That I was mistaken in believing in you?" I bit my lip, choked back the words. In an effort to get control of myself I whirled to the blackboard to get on with the writing of the spelling words which the buckeye trick had interrupted. *You're going too far. You're angry and don't know what you're saying. Only a few are to blame.* There were tears in the eyes of some of the children. *Don't lump them all together. That's not fair. That's not the way to handle it.*

But I had written only a few words when a steady noise at the back of the room penetrated my tortured thoughts. I whirled just in time to see Lundy stalking down the aisle, poking a stick into Mountie O'Teale's back, loudly "He-heeing" as he went.

It was deliberate defiance. The sneer on his face and the shifty look in his eyes made me suspect that he was the one responsible for the buckeyes. Yet of course I could not be sure. "Lundy," I said with an immense effort to speak calmly. "Stop talking and get back to your seat. Do you know anything about this?"

The huge boy stood there gawking at me, the stick in his hand, his mouth slack, his eyes empty. Then fire leapt to his eyes. "No gal-woman's goin' tell me what to do," he snarled. "I'll stop when I'm good and ready."

Momentarily I was startled, then fury took over. The storm inside gave me a courage I would not ordinarily have had. I walked rapidly down the aisle toward the sneering face. The fact that the boy towered at least a head above me mattered not at all now.

"You'll stop when I tell you to," I said, almost shrieking, "and I'm telling you—right—now." Then I reached up and grabbed his shock of hair with all the strength I had, dragged him down and shook him as I shoved him into the nearest seat.

The yank of the hair had taken Lundy by surprise. His watery blue eyes blinked back tears. But then the next moment he was standing up, his fist doubled as if to fight me back. Most of the children were on their feet now. I could feel John Spencer close to me trying to force his body between Lundy and me.

"Lundy—stay—right—there—in your seat!" A stern masculine voice spoke from the doorway. It was David who had arrived for the mathematics lessons. "One more

221

word out of you, and I'm the one you'll fight," he added.

The boy slunk down immediately. Then I could feel David's eyes riveted to my face. Now that the immediate crisis was over, suddenly I was shaking all over.

The next instant David was by my side propelling me to the front of the room. "Sit down," he whispered. "I'll take over for awhile now. We'll settle with Lundy later."

At supper that evening the topic of book-slashing was carefully avoided since it was obvious that I was still tense and upset. But I knew that I had to talk about it, so as we were leaving the table I asked Miss Alice if I could go with her for a chat.

"Of course," she answered. "Why don't you ask David to come too?"

When we were settled in front of her fireplace, I began. "I don't know how much David has told you—"

"Only the bare facts."

"Then I'll begin at the beginning, if I may." And I described it all, beginning with the mud on the steps, through my losing my temper so completely after the buckeye trick.

"Well, don't condemn yourself for that," David protested. "Who wouldn't have lost their temper? I certainly would! Miss Alice, I wish you could have seen that scene. Priceless! Christy, so fragile looking, wading into that hulk of a boy. I'm proud of you, Christy. And believe me, I intend to stay clear of that strong right arm of yours!"

I laughed a bit shakily. "Thanks, David, but let's talk about the real problem. Who would make a special trip to the schoolhouse for the deliberate purpose of tearing up new books? And why?"

Miss Alice's gray eyes beneath the shining blonde braids were thoughtful. "Perhaps because to a certain type of person back here, anything new and strange poses a personal threat."

"I don't understand how new books pose any threat."

"New schoolhouse ... new books ... new starry-eyed teacher with a head full of plans for the future who's constantly talking about them. I don't know—I'm only guessing. But for some, that may add up to a threat to the only way of life they've ever known."

"Then is it wrong to have so many new ideas?"

222

"Of course not!" David said quickly. "Stop condemning yourself. I like you when you're fired up."

Miss Alice only smiled.

"But how can we find out who tore up the books?" I persisted. "And I did lose my temper today. So how can I get order and discipline back in my classroom now?"

"You already have it back," David answered. "You saw how good everyone was the rest of the day. Even Lundy was docile."

"Not docile. Surly."

"Well, manageable at least. It won't happen again. But if there ever should be any more episodes, then I'm for asking Lundy Taylor to leave school. I'm not sure he has the brains for school anyway."

"But David, I wouldn't like to expel anyone. That really would be failure."

All at once I realized that Miss Alice was saying nothing at all. I recognized one of her quiet moments; that was when she had her best thoughts. "I'd like your comments," I prodded.

"All right, Christy. You've mentioned your anger. I disagree with you, David, that Christy should be applauded for what she did. Christy's own deepest instinct tells her that the anger didn't finally solve anything. Perhaps it would help, Christy, if you recognized *why* you got so furious. Do you know?"

"Well, I guess because— No, I really don't know. What do you mean 'Why'?"

"I believe it was because the new books were the product of your latest brain child, thoughtfully conceived, brought to birth with flair and success. Those books are a tangible token of a triumph of self—therefore dear to your heart. True, you undertook the trip to Knoxville to help other people, but self went, self wore a ravishing hat, self sold her cause to an interesting wealthy man. Therefore, when the books were slashed, it was as if *you* yourself were slashed."

David was looking at Miss Alice in amazement—as if he wanted to argue with her. But her words had hit home. In my heart I knew she was right. Yet that only made me feel more despairing. I wondered again if I really belonged here. I had thought that love was the answer for Mountie O'Teale, for all my classroom. Perhaps love had not solved anything after all.

"Don't look so woebegone," Miss Alice smiled at me.

"No need to be discouraged. Christy," she continued, "have you ever watched a baby learning to walk? He totters, arms stretched out to balance himself. He wobbles—and falls, perhaps bumps his nose. Then he puts the palms of his little hands flat on the floor, hikes his rear end up, looks around to see if anybody is watching him. If nobody is, usually he doesn't bother to cry, just precariously balances himself—and tries again."

I smiled at the picture.

"Well, the baby can teach us. What you've undertaken here in Cutter Gap in your schoolroom isn't a state of perfection to be arrived at all of a sudden. It's a *walk*, and a walk isn't static but ever-changing. We Friends say that all discouragement is from an evil source and can only end in more evil. Wallowing in self-condemnation or feeling sorry for yourself is worse than falling on your face in the first place. So—thee fell into a temper! So thee is human. Thank God for thy humanness."

Nineteen

THAT WEEK Lundy Taylor did not come back to school. By the second week gossip began to reach me that Lundy's father had taken my jerking his son by the hair as an affront to the Taylor clan and was busy plotting revenge for the new "brought-on" teacher. Though I did not believe this, still the object of discipline was not to alienate pupils from the school. So as one day followed another and Lundy did not appear, I knew that I was going to have to wade into this misunderstanding—and I dreaded it.

But my mind was temporarily pulled off the Lundy problem by the completion of our telephone installation. The telephone exchange at Lyleton had notified David that the first call to check our number would come through at about four o'clock on a Wednesday afternoon.

The word quickly circulated and by three o'clock on the appointed day quite a group had gathered. The first to arrive were Fairlight and Jeb Spencer with all their family but Little Guy and Clara, who had stayed home to take care of him. Then John Holcombe sauntered in, trying to be casual: "Jest drapped by." Bob Allen appeared with Festus and Little Burl and Isaak McHone. As usual Ruby Mae was hovering around, staying close to David, with Miss Ida and Miss Alice in the background.

To the mountain people the idea of a tiny wire carrying a voice seemed incredible. Most of them did not really believe it would happen, but just in case it did, they wanted to be on hand. The telephone itself had been positioned on the wall in the back hall just outside the dining room door. The group sat tensely in the parlor, speaking almost in whispers so they would be certain to hear the bell.

"Hit's such a far piece for a body's voice to reach," Mr.

225

Holcombe murmured. "Good thing you've got wind, Preacher, 'cause you're goin' to have to beller mighty loud to be heard yander in Lyleton."

David shook his head. "But you don't have to shout if the connection's good."

"What's a 'connection'?" asked John Spencer.

So David set about trying to explain the technical aspects of the telephone system being set up in towns and cities throughout the country. Soon his audience was shaking their heads in disbelief. "Swear-r-r! It's a wonder and a revelation!" . . . "All that wire atwixt home and home and acrost mountains and rivers, a-runnin' from town to town must cost a right smart passel of cash-money."

As the time crept toward four, Ruby Mae asked, "What'll ye talk about, Preacher?"

David looked amused. "Haven't the least idea. Depends on what they ask me."

Suddenly the bell started ringing, vibrating and clanging. David jumped up and dashed to the back hall. At first the group sat there as though paralyzed, then everyone was crowding around David, who had picked up the receiver, put it to his ear and was leaning forward close to the mouthpiece. "Hello . . . Hello . . ."

"What does it say?" . . . "Can you hear anything?" Those in front were pressing against David, some in awe, some in perplexity, some of the rest of us in a sudden spirit of gaiety. Poor David was hard pressed to hear anything.

"Quiet!" he bellowed frantically waving one hand at us. Then he turned again to the mouthpiece. "Hello . . . Hello . . . Hello."

With all eyes on David there was silence. Then someone hissed, "Y'see! That thar contraption don't work."

David was getting red in the face from being hemmed in so closely, with everyone straining against him to catch any possible sound. The children were jumping up and down. Miss Alice, standing at the back, was obviously enjoying the scene; Miss Ida looked as if she wanted to bang the children's heads together to make them be quiet. Ruby Mae was wearing a look close to rapture.

"Yes, this is the Mission house," David was shouting into the phone. Now the excitement was intense. "Yes, I can hear you. Seems to be all right. To whom am I speaking, by the way? No, didn't get that. No. Just a minute—"

David put the palm of one hand over the mouthpiece and turned around, looking helplessly, imploringly at us. But it was no use. The group was too excited. Little Burl was yanking on David, nearly pulling his pants down in his eagerness to know what was going on. Finally David grinned at him, lifted him up, took the receiver and put it against Little Burl's ear. "Would you say a sentence to my little friend here?" he said into the phone. The boy's face was a study: bewilderment, confusion, joy, awe.

After a moment David took the receiver from Little Burl and held it out for everyone to listen. Five heads promptly bumped together. By then I was laughing so hard that I had to retreat hastily into the parlor. Apparently David must have rescued the receiver because I heard him say, "Thanks so much. Yes, checks out fine. You'll be hearing from us often. Good-bye."

For a moment there was silence. Then everyone began talking at once.

"Lordamercy, it works!" Ruby Mae exclaimed.

"Miz Christy," Fairlight came rushing at me, "weren't ye plumb mesmerized!"

I was not allowed to forget Lundy Taylor for long. By the time I got to breakfast the next morning, I found that David and Miss Alice had already eaten and left. As usual my redheaded shadow, Ruby Mae, was waiting for me and now that the excitement of the telephone was over, she started in at once on her next favorite subject: the fate awaiting me at the hands of Lundy's father. "Teacher, ye're in for trouble with the Bird's-Eye. More trouble than ever ye saw in all your born days."

It was a beautiful sunshiny day, much too nice to talk about problems. "What kind of trouble?" I asked unconcernedly.

Ruby Mae hugged herself with both arms and shivered, "Don't know what kind. But he's the awfulest man. Don't take nothin' off nobody."

"But I've never even seen Mr. Taylor."

"Ye seen his son right enough, the way ye yanked Lundy's hair most right out'n his head."

"Lundy deserved it. Probably if we only knew, his father is relieved that somebody could finally discipline Lundy."

Ruby Mae looked at me as if I were a freak. "Y'mean ye ain't scart?"

"No, I'm not scared."

"But Teacher, his hair or his son's hair, don't make a particle of difference to Bird's-Eye. Talk is that he's sore as a skinned owl at you and is planning his re-venge."

"And my talk is that I think you're getting a big whizz-bang out of exaggerating the whole thing."

Ruby Mae was nonplused at my frankness. Then she said slowly, "But ye see, Teacher, what happened in school ain't lost a bitty-bit in the tellin'."

"I'm sure it hasn't. That's the trouble. And you be careful that *you don't*—"

"No'm, I won't. But I'm afeered Mr. Taylor has heerd that ye did things that ye didn't do."

"Oh, I'm beginning to see."

"Yes'm. And he has his head set to believe what ain't true."

"Then that decided it. I'm going to have to go see him and tell him what *is* true."

Real consternation now constricted Ruby Mae's freckled face. "Oh, no'm, you mustn't do that! Not on yer life, ye mustn't. Teacher, you couldn't stand that man off. He be fractious. He's been known to spill mortal gorm. And them as he don't want t'kill, he may take a notion to rock."

"Rock? You mean he throws stones at them?"

"Yes'm, and if the rock jest happens t'hit a mortal spot, then hit be the rock's fault."

Her face showed that she did not think this funny. "Ruby Mae, you're a chatterbox for sure. You talk and talk and I haven't the least idea what to take seriously."

She grinned at me. "It's true, Teacher. My mouth don't open jest for feedin' baby birds. But pleas'm, don't ever go to nobody's cabin round here without stoppin' at the edge of the yard and hollerin'. Ye should take *that* serious."

"That a custom in the Cove?"

"Well'm, not a custom exactly. It's jest that if'n ye don't holler, ye mought git shot at."

Already I had heard so much of Ruby Mae's constant jingle-jangle that I paid little attention to it. Still, there was that exaggerated clan loyalty in the Cove. That could make Mr. Taylor take Lundy's chastisement personally.

Later on that day I asked David about it. He did not answer at once. "Bird's-Eye's an ignorant man," he said at last. "A troublemaker. But Christy, my advice is, don't worry about it. These mountain men don't harm a woman. And get that Ruby Mae to keep her jabbering mouth shut."

I could forget the jabber, but if I was going to keep my promise to give school my all, then I could not forget the Lundy matter. Apparently there was no way to resolve it except by seeking out Mr. Taylor.

Surely David was right. Mr. Taylor was not going to shoot at me. But just to make sure, I thought that I'd best go by myself. A lone woman and he would not dare—but since I knew that neither Miss Alice nor David would ever agree to my going alone, I decided to slip off without telling anyone.

The Bird's-Eye Taylor cabin was the most isolated and freakishly placed one I had seen so far. It had been built between twin shelves of rock planes forming the top of a small mountain and it looked more like a fortress than a home. So steep was the final ascent that I tethered Theo to a tree two hundred feet or so below the cabin to climb the rest of the way on foot. But I paused first to "Hallo" as Ruby Mae had advised.

There was no porch to this cabin perched like an eagle's nest on the rocks. From where I stood, it looked as if one stepped out the front door into space.

No sooner was the call out of my mouth than the doorway was filled with a man's figure, shotgun in hand. It was too quick; he had been watching me all the way up the mountain.

"I want to talk to you, Mr. Taylor," I called. "May I come up?"

"Come up then," but it was said grudgingly.

The path was steep, hard-packed, and slippery. As I came closer I saw that there was a level spot something over a yard wide in front of the door. Bird's-Eye Taylor was not as large a man as I had imagined. Of a different build from his son, he was not quite medium height and slight, though slim and erect. He was dressed in a dirty plaid flannel shirt above a pair of shabby trousers held up by galluses; he was wearing high shoes—muddy—fastened only half way up and gaping at the top. Since where I was standing was on a level with his feet, I noticed that he had on one blue sock and one brown.

"I'm Christy Huddleston, the new teacher, Mr. Taylor." I tried to sound as if there was nothing unusual about this visit.

"What d'ye want with us?" The tone was churlish. The eyes looking into mine were watery blue, hard eyes. A slit of a mouth was set in the grizzled face which had not known a razor in days. He was wearing a felt hat with the brim turned down all around, holes in the top held together with a large safety pin.

"Just wanted to meet you, Mr. Taylor. And talk to you about Lundy. We've been missing him at school. We wondered why."

"Ye know why."

"May I come in?"

"Ain't no place fer a woman. Jest Lundy and me here."

"I know. I understand. But I'd like to talk to you."

He seemed surprised at my persistence in the face of his deliberate coldness, but finally moved to one side. "Come in and set then." For the first time I saw Lundy standing behind his father.

The interior of the building was tiny and seemed more like a cave than a cabin. There was a fieldstone chimney at the back with black pots on cranes, no cook-stove in sight. I had the impression that somewhere in the walls there might be an entrance to a cave under the rock ledges. The room was furnished with only bare essentials and had not been cleaned for a long time.

With one foot, Mr. Taylor lazily pushed a straight chair across the floor in my direction, then sat down on another beside the one table. The tabletop was so warped and bowed that any plates placed on it would slide downhill toward the center.

"Hello Lundy." I tried to put as much warmth as possible into my voice. The hulk of a boy so much larger than his father had still not moved from Mr. Taylor's side. "When are you coming back to school?"

"Dunno—"

The slits of eyes were ogling me so that I felt as if he were undressing me. For the first time I was afraid and realized how foolish I had been to place myself in such a defenseless position. What was worse, no one at the mission knew where I was.

"Mought as well tell ye," Mr. Taylor said, "don't confidence wimmin teachers none."

How was I to answer *that*? I started in lamely, "Mr. Taylor, I know you must want Lundy to have some schooling so he can get on in life. I'm not the best teacher

230

in the world. But I think I can teach Lundy something."

He ignored my speech, rubbing his hand over his stub-bled chin. "Want t' whop my young'uns my own self. Don't want no gal-woman a-doin' it."

"Mr. Taylor, I didn't whip Lundy."

"Didn't hide him?"

"No, I didn't. Lundy is bigger than I am. How do you think I could whip him?"

Lundy was sidling toward the door. His father's hand shot out to whack at him but the boy ducked. "Consarned fool. Ye lied t'me."

"Ah, Pap, I jest—"

"I'm a-goin' ketch a-hold of ye and smoke yer britches till the fire catches."

But Lundy was already out the door.

"Don't be too hard on him, Mr. Taylor. Lundy was testing me out, that's all. I have had a little trouble with him, talking and wandering around the room, changing seats and playing mean tricks on younger pupils. Finally I had to talk sternly to him. And I *did* jerk him by the hair."

For the first time there was something close to a thaw on Bird's-Eye Taylor's face. He did not seem to think yanking Lundy's hair such a bad idea.

"Lundy will be all right. I hope you'll send him back."

"Oh, law! Dunno if schoolin's any use to Lundy. He may be twitter-witted. His Maw was."

Cautiously I asked, "How do you mean, Mr. Taylor?"

"His Maw was fitified and addlepated. Acrost the line in North Carolina that was. Pulled out from thar. That's why I'm a-raisin' Lundy."

"I see. Well then, seems to me you need help. That's what the mission's here for—to help."

"Ye can't squeeze milk out'n a flint rock."

"No, but don't give up on Lundy. He can learn."

"Maybe. Maybe not. Look-a-here, churches and their goings-on ain't fer us. Always been a sinner myself. Ain't never been a hypo-crite though. Never lied to the Lord. Ain't no sech can enter the king-dom of heaven. Course I know that ain't the edzact words."

"But I'm a sinner too. Everybody is. As I understand it, that's what church is all about—to save sinners."

"Don't want savin'. Always been a sinner. Always will be. I disgust churches."

231

There seemed little point in pursuing this. "Mr. Taylor, I'd better be going. You'll send Lundy back to school then?"

"I'll study on it."

"And drop by the mission house yourself sometime. We'd like to be friends."

He did not respond to that, but then said slowly, "I ain't got no rocks to throw at nobody."

What a queer comment, I thought. Then I remembered what Ruby Mae had said about Bird's-Eye Taylor "rocking" both animals and humans at times.

"Well, good-bye——" I called over my shoulder, and I hurried down the slope as quickly as I dared. I had the feeling that somewhere near Lundy was spying on me from behind a bush or a tree-trunk, but I did not wait to find out.

More than a week went by. Then one day at school I looked up from my desk and there, to my astonishment, stood Lundy looking at me. "Could I clean the blackboard for ye, Teacher?"

He seemed like a new Lundy, not so sullen or obstructive, only now there was a new problem: It was plain that his attitude toward me had changed. He looked at me differently; he came up to my desk as often as he dared; he hung around after dismissal time, talking and ogling.

Lundy was obviously more hostile than ever to David, however, and greeted him each day with scowls and muttering. David, on his side, still did not trust Lundy. He thought that there was little material in this boy to work with and that my optimism about the change in Lundy's attitude was premature: I had not made as much progress with him as I believed.

On the following Friday I was at my desk during noon recess, working out some assignments for Rob Allen and Bessie Coburn; the children were happily playing hide-and-go-seek outside. Suddenly above the usual playground noises, there were shouts followed by angry voices. I dropped my pen and rushed out to see what was happening.

The children were out of sight around the corner but the voices came through, "I'll crunch you, you little b——"

"Dirty bully!"

"Shut your mouth, I'll knock your block—"

"Oh, shinny on yer tintype!"

"Weasel—"

A tight circle of children hid the identity of the fighters.

"Hit's Teacher! Better *stop* it—"

"Stand back, you-all. Let her through."

As the children made a path for me, I saw Festus Allen and Lundy Taylor fighting. Festus, only eleven, was using his feet as well as flailing with his fists, but he was getting the worse of it. Already blood was streaming from his nose.

"Quit that. This instant!" I thrust myself between the two boys and only barely missed getting a fist in my face. Festus was shaking mad. "No Taylor's gonna lay out my brother and git by with it."

Then I saw! It was Little Burl, white and limp, stretched out on the ground. I bent over him. He was unconscious.

Frantically, I ordered, "Someone run quick, anyone! Dip a rag in cold water and bring it to me." My hands felt the little boy's heart. Beating, thank God! I could see no cuts or bruises on his face. Then I lifted his shirt. There it was, a round red mark on his stomach. No skin broken, but it was going to be a bad bruise.

One of the girls thrust the wet cloth into my hand. I took Little Burl half into my arms, putting his head a little lower than his body, then gently put the cloth to his forehead. "Burl! Little Burl, can you hear me? It's Teacher. You're going to be all right. Burl! Burl—"

Behind my back I could hear someone snuffling. Festus, I thought. Rob Allen had been kept home to tend mill today or this might not have happened.

It seemed a long time before Little Burl's eyelids fluttered open. "Hurts, Teacher," he moaned. "My stummick hurts."

"I know. Just lie still. I'll hold you." As I sat there on the ground, I looked up at the circle of faces over me, but Lundy's was not among them. "One of you go to Lundy," I told them. "Don't let him leave. Tell him I want to see him." *But should I try to handle this alone? Perhaps David—*

"Lizette, Ruby Mae, can you tell me how this happened?"

Ruby Mae looked frightened. Lizette answered, "Dunno, ma'am. Some of the little 'uns was playin' hide-go-seek. Next thing I knew, Lundy was takin' out after Burl like a streak of greased lightnin'. Took a runago at Burl, kicked him flat. When Festus saw that, he took a fit, got fightin'-mad, started punchin'."

Ruby Mae crept close to me and lowered her voice. "I'm a-dyin' sure, Teacher, wasn't exactly like that. I was standin' behind one of them gopher trees thar. Little Burl was a-scroungin' around under the schoolhouse someway. Lundy seed him under thar. Give a panther-shriek, took out after Burl, started kickin' him."

The situation was beginning to be clear now. "Ruby Mae," I asked her, "would you go to the house and ask Mr. Grantland to come here? It's early for his classes, but tell him I need him."

Finally Little Burl seemed to be feeling better and thought that he could walk, though he said his stomach still hurt. I helped him to his feet and we walked slowly to the schoolhouse. I was relieved to find Lundy Taylor in the classroom by himself off in a corner. "Lundy, get in your seat and stay there. I'll be back in a minute." Then I put two of my junior teachers in temporary charge of the room.

Outside I met Ruby Mae and David coming up the hill.

"Thanks, Ruby Mae. Don't know what I'd do without you. My best helper." I patted her on the back. "Now will you do me another big favor? Go back inside and help keep order until I can get in there."

"What's happened now?" David asked, as Ruby Mae's back retreated.

I told him briefly about the fight, ending with, "But David, why would Lundy kick such a little child?"

"I can't answer that one. Lundy's big—and sometimes brutal. But even Lundy would need a powerful reason to kick a little boy unconscious."

"But why would Lundy get that angry over Burl accidentally finding a hole under the floor?"

David made no attempt to answer my question. "Christy, I think you'd better let me handle this. I'm going to have to do some quizzing."

I was relieved. "That's fine with me, David. You don't know how fine."

He was already off to see Lundy.

Twenty

ALL AFTERNOON I waited for some report from David on what he had learned during his conversation with Lundy Taylor. David was nowhere to be seen. Finally, toward dusk I decided to investigate under the schoolhouse for myself. As I reached the edge of the playground, a pig walking oddly, almost on the slant, came from under the building and crossed near me. I had no great knowledge of pigs, but I had never seen one look like that.

Something else was odd too. I stood at the foot of the schoolhouse steps, trying to think what could be giving me such an uneasy feeling. I tried the door. It was locked, with everything apparently in order. Then I realized . . . What was missing was the usual background noises of the hogs rooting and scratching and snuffling under the building. And there was a strong smell, not of pigs. Suddenly I was panicky about what I might be about to find. *I'd best go get David,* I thought. *Wherever he's been, perhaps he'll be back for supper by now.* So I picked up my skirts and walked rapidly, almost running, toward the big house.

David met me on the porch. "What's the hurry, Christy?"

"I think something's wrong. At the schoolhouse, I mean. Will you have a look, David?"

I trailed his long strides across the yard and up the hill. Borne toward us on the evening breeze was that same strong odor. Then as we turned the corner at the back of the building, I almost stumbled over a broken jug. Nearby were several hogs stretched out asleep—too sound asleep. They did not stir as we approached; they were breathing heavily and rhythmically.

David stopped and stared at the pigs, walked around them, even poked first one and then another with his foot,

235

but they responded not at all, just snored on. "Queer. I don't get it." Then he walked on a few paces and stooped to look under the floor. "It's almost too dark to see anything. I'll have to go in under there."

Already he was crouched over, making his way under the building. I could hear his fingers groping, then some boards being moved, then he whistled loudly. "Holy thunder! Christy, you should see this. This is *something*!"

"What, David?"

"Somebody's fixed a place under the floor like a little storage room. There are a lot of jugs in here. Moonshine whiskey. Christy, can you take them from me? I'll hand them out one at a time."

The jug he thrust into my hands was full—and heavy. I set it on the ground and reached for another, and another, and another. Finally David came out, rubbing the dust off his hands. He stood staring at the collection of jugs, a puzzled crease between his brows. "So this was what Lundy didn't want Burl to find! But Christy, this can't be all Lundy Taylor's doing. That little room was well planned. No boy could have done the carpentry work either. Adults are involved. Blockaders, that's who!"

"But what did Lundy say when you talked to him?"

"I never got the chance. He slipped out. I spent the afternoon searching for him."

"David, is this meant to be a joke?"

"Certainly not! How could it be?"

"Well, I mean under the church is a crazy place to store moonshine. And there isn't space for many jugs either. You should see Bird's-Eye's cabin. I think he's built it against a cave where he could store a hundred jugs."

He looked at me thoughtfully. "If you're right, Christy," the words came out slowly, "then the blockaders are trying to make me look like an ass. Well, could be! I suppose they think that the church-schoolhouse I built is my pride and joy. So they'll store their moonshine practically under the altar. Sap-heads! What I wouldn't give for the chance to knock their heads together! I could too, if they'd lay down their blasted shotguns and fight like men. Well, I'll show them!" David was speaking from between clenched teeth.

He grabbed a jug, uncorked it, sniffed it with an expression of distaste, turned it upside down and the amber liquid gurgled and spattered as it poured onto the ground. I backed away.

236

He uncorked another jug and swung it upside down. He was shouting now. "I'd like to heave this infernal stuff right in the face of some people I know! Pickle their brains in it!"

I had never seen David so angry. His hands were trembling and even in the murky light, I could tell that his face was flushed, while the little dip where he had broken his nose was dead white. The yard was beginning to smell like a brewery. "David, will this smell go away before church Sunday?"

"I don't know and I don't care. If the building smells like a distillery, then maybe that will alert some sleepers to what's going on around here. But you and I should act as if we don't notice a thing."

"You mean we smell moonshine and pretend it's roses?"

David was silent a moment, breathing hard. "All right, Christy, bring me back to earth. I shouldn't lose my temper that way." He went on uncorking jugs and pouring. "Tell you. what I'm going to do. I'll put the empty jugs back in their hiding place but leave this big hole. Then tomorrow and Monday we'll watch for reactions. We're bound to get some clues."

"David, those pigs still haven't moved. Do you suppose —? No, that *couldn't* be."

"Oh yes, it could. Remember I told you that horses like Prince won't drink a drop of water with mash in it. Well, pigs like nothing better. Only this time they got more than they bargained for. Those hogs are drunk!"

"Drunk pigs! That one we saw walking across the yard wobbling from side to side. How funny!"

He managed a wry smile. "The pigs are funny," he said, "but the situation isn't."

Sunday passed without our gaining any new information about the cache of blockade liquor. The men and boys who ordinarily spent as much time wandering and lounging in the yard as they did in the church service, confined themselves that day to the front yard.

Then that evening as we were leaving the dining room after supper, David tapped me lightly on the shoulder. "I need to talk to you. Not inside the house though. How about a walk?"

Outside it was a clear night with a brilliant canopy of

stars. Silently David took my arm and steered me across the yard toward the wide trail that paralleled Cutter Branch and led on down the narrow valley. On our right the dark bulk of Pebble Mountain loomed over us; to our left the branch gurgled and sang as always.

David was sunk in his own thoughts, so I waited for him to break the silence. "I've talked to Lundy," he began.

"Where did you find him?"

"I rode up toward Bird's-Eye's place. Lundy was hunting squirrels in the woods. This time he couldn't escape."

"So—?"

"He was defensive. Sullen. Wouldn't say much. It took some doing but finally I pried out a little. Two other boys are in on it: Wraight Holt and Smith O'Teale."

"Smith! But Smith's only fourteen."

"I know."

"But you thought that storage room was their fathers' doing. You mean these boys are really involved, David?"

"Afraid so. Only Lundy wouldn't give me details."

Neither of us spoke for a moment. I was thinking of the O'Teale boy, undersized for his age, with his big black eyes that always seemed to be pleading for something.

"When Lundy finally refused to say another word, I got angry again. I admit it. What I really wanted to do was to punch Lundy Taylor right in the nose."

"Did you?"

"No. What stopped me was that I was too mad. So I warned Lundy that he and his two friends might have to leave school. Told him that their punishment would have to be decided by their parents and the entire mission staff."

David paused for breath. "At the mention of parents, Lundy started smirking. It was a dead giveaway about his dad. So that told me I'd been right all along. Adults are managing that setup under the building. Anyway, that sickly smirk was more than I could take. Lundy took one look at my face and lit out for home like a coon with a hound in pursuit."

"But David, I still don't understand the point of the liquor being hidden there in the first place."

"I think I do. The pieces are beginning to fit. You remember Uncle Bogg saying that he was pretty sure the men who followed the three of you through the woods that night were not Cutter Gap men? Well, I'm afraid we've got a little blockading business going on right under our noses with schoolboys as the go-betweens."

David let go my arm. I stood looking at him, trying to grasp what he was saying. The moonlight put deep hollows in his cheeks, gave him a look of gauntness. "David, are you suggesting that someone has a moonshine whiskey business going? That strangers are coming into the Cove to get it and that Lundy Taylor and the others are front men?"

"Something like that."

"But it still seems like too small an operation for that. What evidence do you have for all of this?"

"Not much, I realize. It's mostly guesswork. You see, right now there's considerably stricter law enforcement for blockade-runners in North Carolina than in Tennessee. They've got a county sheriff over there now who's cutting down barrels and furnaces right and left. So now good whiskey is in more demand here in Tennessee than it's been in a long time. What's more, I've made it easier to get the stuff to the state line by building and improving the road from the flagstop as far as the mission."

"But I just can't believe that they'd dare count on a spot under our school building as their steady supply depot."

"They'd dare anything. That might be stupid or it could be positively brilliant. Like deliberately hiding something in the most obvious place possible, so you miss it."

"But it isn't quite like that."

"Well anyway, I wanted to tell you this much."

My thoughts swung back to my schoolroom. "David, what will I do with Lundy now? I mean, if he comes back to school and we don't have all this settled, how will I treat him?"

"Treat him normally. Only I don't think he'll be back right away. But beyond that, we're going to have to talk this out with Miss Alice as soon as possible. And I'm going to have to find out which men are behind these boys, maybe go after the still."

Suddenly I was afraid for David. As if sensing this, he reached for my hand. "Do you have to go after the moonshiners yourself, David? That's dangerous. You know it is. Those men won't stand meddlers."

"I know. But I can't get the federal marshals on the

case without more evidence. As for meddling—believe me, the blockaders are asking for it. These mountain men can guzzle all the corn liquor they please, but when they start involving our school children—"

As we walked back to the mission house, David and I were both preoccupied with our thoughts. I was remembering that I had seen strangers several times during the last few weeks, and at the time, had wondered about it. By now I knew the Cove folk, at least by sight. And tourists did not ordinarily make their way so far back into the mountains; those who took the trouble to journey to Cutter Gap had a reason. But my thoughts were so jumbled by all that David had told me that I could not, at the moment, recall the exact incidents involving the strangers.

It was not until the next night that one of the scenes came back to me. About two weeks before, I had been hanging out some wash after dark (since that was almost the only time of day I dared invade Miss Ida's kitchen to do my personal laundry), and I had seen three strange men on horseback riding along the edge of the mission property. They had come out of the woods to the west behind the schoolhouse, had loitered out of sight behind the building for a time, and then had galloped off down the road northward toward the flagstop. Most local people had mules, not horses, and I had never before seen those horses or those men. And few people in these parts galloped—with the exception of Miss Alice. I had tucked the incident away in my mind to tell David, but then had not thought of it again. Now—with all that had happened—he should know about it.

Miss Alice and David had each gone off to their cabins. Miss Ida was reading by the big oil lamp in the parlor. To avoid her I went outside on the porch. Should I tell David tonight? Suddenly I found myself walking down toward his bunkhouse. It was not that I had any intention of inviting myself inside. It was a nice night; perhaps he might be outside too.

Halfway down the walk I looked across the road and noticed that lamps were lit inside the bunkhouse with all the shades drawn tight. Unusual! David did not ordinarily close things up so completely.

As I got closer I thought I saw a movement in the bushes close to the little building. I stood still to listen.

There it was again, a branch moving; yet there was no wind this night.

Not having any idea what was going on, I ducked behind a thicket of laurel bushes and held my breath, listening. Not a sound except the gurgle of the stream and the low hum of voices inside the bunkhouse. Someone was with David.

Holding my body very still, cautiously I parted two branches and peered through. Clouds were scudding across the moon casting murky shadows. The foliage was inky, blurred before my eyes. Then a shadow moved and a pebble rolled down the incline to the road. I stared at the place where I had seen the movement, but still I could see nothing: the darkness was impenetrable.

Then momentarily, the clouds parted and moonlight bathed the foliage in soft light. Whoever was hiding there had on dark clothes. I could almost see his face—Lundy! It was Lundy Taylor skulking in the bushes.

At that instant the bunkhouse door opened and Bob Allen stepped out on the stone step, with David silhouetted in the doorway. Certainly they did not suspect anyone of spying on them, they were still talking earnestly. Though I was glad that I had seen Lundy, I did not relish being discovered hiding like a fugitive, so I drew back even further into the shadows and gave up trying to peer out. After a time I heard Mr. Allen's footsteps going brisky down the road. Then I waited for awhile and looked out again. The pale moonlight caught Lundy's retreating form moving across the road and through the field beyond the schoolhouse.

This was not the time to talk to David about the three mysterious men. Perhaps it was not important. I would confess my hide-go-seek game to David tomorrow. Slowly I walked up the hill to the big house.

Ruby Mae and I were almost finished with our breakfast the next morning when David strode in looking weary and grizzled, his riding clothes and boots muddy. Ruby Mae, never reticent, asked in surprise, "Where have you been so early, Preacher?"

"Prince and I were having an early morning ride, that's all." He looked at me and grinned. "You know, mountains in the spring . . . good way to get exercise. Ida, got any hot coffee out there?"

Ruby Mae was not satisfied with the explanation. She prodded and hinted but David parried her every query. Finally she finished breakfast and left while I lingered over my coffee.

"David, I've a confession to make."

"Sounds interesting."

"Last evening while I was out for a little stroll, I saw someone hiding in the bushes near your bunkhouse. It turned out to be Lundy Taylor."

David looked startled. "Did Lundy see you?"

"I don't think so. That's my confession—I hid too."

"Well, more important, did he see Bob Allen?"

"Yes, I'm sure he did. Saw him leaving."

"Then thank God I didn't find anything this morning, or Bob Allen would be a dead man."

LUNDY did not come back to school that Tuesday. When he was still absent on Wednesday and Thursday, David seemed relieved. I guessed that he was going to use the lull to go scouting for the still, though he told me nothing. Actually it was not until the following Tuesday during our regular weekly conference with Miss Alice that I learned what was happening. There over after-dinner coffee in her cabin David and I discussed the week gone by and planned for the week ahead. Miss Alice had the knack of making these Tuesday evenings a refreshing oasis in the midst of our otherwise hectic lives.

I often marveled that the interior peace of the woman was reflected so faithfully in her surroundings. Even the selection and arrangements of her possessions gave an aura of uncluttered calm. In addition, there was a directness in her approach to all of life—including the art of housekeeping—that never failed to fascinate me.

Miss Alice was a woman to whom color, symmetry of line and contrast of texture were important. She flouted the accepted custom of covering her table tops with doilies or small scarves; the sheen and patina of the lovely old wood were all the decoration needed. In a pewter bowl she could arrange with artistry a few well-polished apples and some nuts, or a piece of quartz picked up somewhere in the mountains along with some unusual leaves and berries.

I reveled in all of this. Though David, manlike, noticed

none of these details, he nevertheless responded to the atmosphere they created.

On this particular Tuesday night, he sank gratefully into the easy chair, stretched his long legs and sniffed appreciatively the fragrant aroma of brewing coffee. Both Miss Alice and I were immediately aware that he had important news to discuss.

"We've found the still," he began abruptly.

Miss Alice's hand, pouring a cup of coffee, paused in mid-air. "Who? What men?"

"I don't know."

We looked at him quizzically, not comprehending.

"You see, the men weren't there. The still had just been moved. But maybe I'd better begin at the beginning."

In silence Miss Alice finished pouring the coffee as we listened intently. "Yesterday afternoon Prince and I started in the direction of Big Lick Gap. You know how good the water of Coldsprings Branch is, as good as its name. Well, we got to the Branch and Prince stopped and stretched his long neck down to drink. Then he began acting strangely—sniffed the water, snorted and backed away. Wouldn't drink a drop.

"Right away I knew something was wrong. So I dismounted and scooped up some water in my hands. You couldn't miss the smell of mash. That told me. I knew there had to be a still—maybe the one we were hunting for, somewhere upstream. I started to follow the stream to its source and found the path along the Branch trampled. Also—and this was odd—small branches had been broken at more or less regular intervals and left dangling all along the path. Then I saw a piece of copper tubing lying in the leaves.

"Well, right about then I decided it was too risky to go further. It was time to bring the United States marshals in on it. I didn't dare use our new telephone—too public—so I rode to the telephone exchange in Lyleton and from there phoned the federal office in Knoxville."

David paused, sipped his coffee, then went on. "The marshal who answered seemed grateful for the tip and eager to move on it. Within an hour they had two of their men on the train to El Pano. I was to meet them in that grove of trees behind the general store. They told me where to pick up two horses which I was to bring with me for the agents. Apparently they have connections all over for such details.

243

"By the time the marshals got to El Pano. It was a little past midnight and so far as I could see, the streets were deserted. There was a bright moon out so we pushed on immediately to Coldspring Branch, but when we got to the place where I'd turned back before, one of the marshals said he thought I'd better not go on with them. Said that if they surprised the blockaders, bullets might fly. So I watched them light their hooded lanterns, wished them luck, and Prince and I rode on home."

"Then how did you find out what happened?" I asked.

"Because one of the marshals, Gentry Long his name is, telephoned me today. Told me they had gone a mile or so upstream when the path ended abruptly at a rocky ledge. There, hanging from a branch at the edge of the woods, they had found a dummy stuffed with straw, swinging in the breeze like a man strung up. The usual warning message for revenue men. The marshals had wriggled on through the underbrush finally worked their way to a clearing. But then they had been disappointed. There was nothing there but some pieces of copper tubing and a pile of devitalized lye. Somebody had warned the blockade-runners so they'd cleared out just in time. The ground was actually still warm.

"Officer Long said it had been a large still, probably with a production of twenty to thirty gallons of whiskey a day."

"So they want you to keep looking?" Miss Alice asked. "They think the still will be set up somewhere else?"

"Oh, sure. Men around here don't scare easily."

"Weren't you tempted to go along with the agents?" I asked curiously. "I think I would have been."

"Not really. No point in my getting involved. Well anyway, that still leaves us not knowing which men are in this. Frustrating, isn't it?"

Miss Alice nodded, saying nothing. Obviously she was thinking hard, her mind roaming over the Cove, cabin by cabin. This man? That one?

I voiced the question with which she was plainly wrestling. "David, who could have warned the moonshiners? Who could possibly have seen you?"

"I've no idea. The mountaineers have had a century of experience with this sort of thing. All 'revs' are their mortal enemies. Anything goes, even bushwhacking. To

244

the last person, they'll stick together against the agents."

"David, what's bushwhacking?"

My innocence seemed to amuse him. "Bushwhacking, Christy, is their term for a murderous attack from ambush. But relax! They made their getaway, they're not going to harm me."

Miss Alice broke in. "David, I want to change the subject a bit. I would have an opportunity with thee—"

"A *what?*"

She laughed at his bewildered look. "A Quaker expression, David. In the community of Friends they speak often of 'opportunities.' By an 'opportunity' they mean a strong inner urging to speak their mind about something that's burdening them."

"Oh? Something about me is burdening you?"

"Yes, your run-in with Ozias Holt. Fairlight Spencer told me about it."

"Well, I hope Fairlight told it straight. Anything I said to Ozias, he deserved. If he wasn't going to work, I wasn't going to pay him."

Miss Alice's voice was mild. "I'm not passing any judgment on the rightness or wrongness of any part of it. All I want to point out is that there's now a breach between Ozias and you, so it's up to you to take the first step towards righting it."

"Why me? He's the one who was wrong."

"David, I've been back here in the Cove a little longer than you. One of the worst evils around here is nursing grudges, sometimes for years. Retaliating evil for evil is considered a virtue, the mark of strong character. Here with this Ozias situation, you've got a ready-made chance to demonstrate a better way: the strength of forgiveness."

"I fail to see how my forgiving Ozias for being a lazy bum would demonstrate anything to him and the other men except weakness."

"David, no Christian ever has a right to sever any relationship with anybody out of anger or pique, or even injustice, no matter how much he disapproves of someone's actions. It's our place to demonstrate reconciliation—not judgment or revenge or retaliation. That's God's business, not ours." Her voice grew softer. "Beware the chasms in thy life, David. Sooner or later thee will fall down in the chasm thyself."

She paused. "David, I bring this up now simply because

with the blockading problem unsolved, this is no time for misunderstandings around here."

"What do you think I should do?"

"I suggest that you make a point of talking to Ozias. Extend the hand of friendship. At least try it. After all, David, when the lines of communication are cut so that two people can't even talk, what have you gained then? All you've done is sever what may have been God's only route into a man's heart."

"Well, I guess you're right," said David slowly. He rose to end the conversation. "I'll walk you to the big house, Christy, if you're ready to leave too."

David had little to say as we went up the hill.

Twenty-one

FROM THE PARLOR I could hear the loud banging on the side door (only highlanders pounded like that!) and then a man's voice talking to David. "Here to give ye and Miz Christy an in-vite to the Workin', come Satur-day." Whoever it was sounded halting and ill-at-ease. "Aim to clear Deer Moun-tain back of our place."

"Ah—thanks, Ozias." David was not comfortable either. "Appreciate that. Nice of you to ask us. What time do you want us?"

"Onytime suits you."

"Well, we'll sure be there." The voice was a little too hearty. "Thanks again."

David looked puzzled as he walked slowly through the parlor door. "Did you hear that? Ozias Holt."

"Yes, I heard."

"I don't get it. Not a bit like these people."

"How do you mean?"

"I mean I haven't done a thing about following Miss Alice's advice on contacting Ozias. And when mountain men are mad at you, they'd never invite you 'to break bread with them.' They just don't forgive and forget that easily. Wonder what's up?"

"No need to be suspicious, David. Mr. Holt seemed friendly enough. Whatever else, the highlanders aren't devious. They wouldn't know *how* to put on an act."

"Maybe. Maybe not. But I think Ozias intends this Working to be a challenge to me. Some of these men still aren't ready to accept me as a man."

"Why not? They watched you build the church-schoolhouse and dynamite for a road and string telephone wire."

"Yes, but in their minds, there's always a catch. For the road there were sticks of dynamite to help: it wasn't all

247

muscle. About the school building, I've heard them say it 'weren't real buildin', 'cause sawed boards and fancy do-dads were used.' What they want to know is, can I handle my end of a crosscut saw? Can I keep up with the rest of them swinging an axe? How good a shot am I? Can I use my fists, if I have to?"

I laughed at David's seriousness. He looked like a youth about to face his first examination. "So can you do all those things?" I teased.

"I doubt it." Finally his brown eyes lit up and a smile crinkled his face. "Have no trophies to show for bare-knuckle fighting. That and target practice just weren't entrance requirements for seminary."

"That's because the seminary didn't know about Cutter Gap, Tennessee." More seriously I asked, "Do we have to go? To the Working, I mean?"

"I'll say we do! Especially now with this moonshine mess. If I didn't, I might as well catch the first train back to New York. Nope, this one I'll have to see through to the end."

Since I had already attended one "Working," I knew that this mountain custom was a carry-over from pioneer times when there were few workmen to be hired, even if the frontiersmen had had any cash with which to hire labor. A man's only chance to get his land cleared, a roof over his family's head, or a barn built was to ask for the help of his neighbors. "Many hands make light work" had been a favorite pioneer axiom. So all the way from the Appalachians to Abraham Lincoln's Illinois and on into the great west, an acre of land could be cleared or a cabin or a barn "raised" in a day.

The custom was to combine hard work and play, make a holiday of it, with the women providing plenty of food. All the men took pride in their ability to handle the broadaxe. A fine "scriber" who could hew logs to precision was a man to be admired. Some could split and notch up to two hundred logs a day. I had watched some of them at work. It was beautiful to see the walnut and other straight-grained timber split like mellons beneath their axes. I loved the ring of the axes in the still air of a winter's day, the rhythm with which they swung the axes, the fragrance of the newly cleft wood.

Saturday saw us resolutely heading for the Holt cabin, David with his tools over his shoulder. By reputation the Holts' was one of the cruder places and there would be no way to avoid eating the noon meal inside. By the time we got there, most of the people had already gathered.

Deer Mountain, which rose directly behind the Holts, still had dense undergrowth. Some of the men guests were already toiling side by side up the slope, each having been given a vertical strip to clear. I saw that the hillside was a tangle of huckleberry bushes, poison hemlocks, scrub oaks, rhododendrons, small pines, and tough little locusts to be grubbed out.

Mr. Holt dropped his mattock and came toward us. "Howdy, Miz Christy. Mornin', Preacher." His attitude was not exactly gracious; there was a trace of gloating in it.

This was my first good look at Ozias Holt. Always I found it difficult to guess the age of the mountain people, but Mr. Holt was no youngster: there was gray in his beard, which was short around his chin, bushy at the sides of his face. He had a prominent nose and large ears. He was wearing overalls over a gray shirt and the inevitable dirty and torn felt hat. With a crusty forefinger he pointed to the strip they had saved for David.

David appeared not to notice that Mr. Holt was the only man who had really spoken to us. Several of the others had looked up briefly, then had gone on working silently—among them Bird's-Eye Taylor. He stood staring at us, looking through me, giving no indication that he had ever before seen me. I could not believe that the rest were really that preoccupied with their axes and their mattocks. Their silence created an ominous atmosphere.

But David only grinned at me as he took off his jacket, rolled up the sleeves of his shirt, and prepared to go to work. I wished that I could stay in the open air and watch the men, but Rebecca Holt had already seen me from the cabin door and was beckoning me in.

When I walked through the door, as always it was my nose that registered the first impression. By now I could even sort out some of the specific odors—cornpone and bacon grease, half-cured animal pelts, wood smoke, snuff—and always, somewhere in the background, the smells of chickens and pigs and unwashed clothes and perspiration and urine.

The women welcomed me. Some of the Sewing Circle group were there: Liz Ann with her month-old baby in her lap; Granny Barclay, Lenore Teague, Opal McHone, Fairlight Spencer, and some others. Most of them were wearing cotton dresses faded from much washing. Fairlight came forward to greet me eagerly.

The room was already so crowded that I wondered how any space was going to be found for the men. Rebecca Holt had set up a table of pipe boards across trestles for the noon meal. The five beds that this "settin' room" ordinarily held had been pushed back against the wall.

Two of the Holts' eight children would not leave their mother's skirts. Both of these had dirty faces and running noses. I had to look the other way. Despite all my experience at school, I still could not get accustomed to the no-handkerchief custom.

Then I spied four dirty faces grinning down at me from the hole in the ceiling at the top of the ladder leading into the loft. The common term "loft boys" was so apt! Apparently the older children had found the best spot from which to see and hear everything, lying on their stomachs peering down on the room.

At first the talk was general. Yet inside the cabin, as outside, there was something different today. For one thing, I found myself missing Aunt Polly Teague. At any moment, I kept expecting to see her balmoral petticoats come sweeping through the door.

Aunt Polly's premonition had been right: the week after David and I visited her, she had died of congestive heart failure. As Dr. MacNeill had walked in three hours before the end, he had found her lying in bed singing a beautiful melody in a loud, clear voice. Yet everyone in the Cove knew that the old lady had never been able to carry a tune.

"Hit's heavenly music," she had told him. "Was give to me."

And the look of heavenly music had still been on her face when Lenore had found her four hours later.

But Aunt Polly's absence was not the only difference today: there was something else, a restraint unusual for the women. Since the cabins were far apart and there was so little social life, female tongues usually wagged unceasingly in an effort to catch up on all the news. So why the reticence today?

I decided to test it out. "I'm sorry Mary Allen isn't here. I wanted to ask her about Little Burl. He hasn't been at school lately. Got hit in the stomach, you know. Has anybody heard how he is?"

Silence hung heavily around me. Fairlight's face

250

clouded over. Her eyes grew wary with pleading in them as she looked at me. "I heard that Burl can't eat much. Reckon he'll make out though."

What does the pleading look mean? That I should not talk about the Allens? On which side are the Allens in the moonshining situation anyway? David said that this was one issue on which everyone in the Cove hung together. Yet here's Little Burl already an indirect victim. Are the Allens torn about it as a result?

By the time the men had been called to the midday meal the tension in the room was unmistakable. If only I knew the right way to rip open the subject bothering everyone. *How much better it would be if only these people would air their questions, doubts, and fears instead of suppressing them.*

It was the mountain custom for the men to eat first and for the women to serve them, then the women ate at what was called "second table." As soon as the men were gathered and seated, Mr. Holt asked David to say the grace, "Preacher-parson, will ye wait on the table for us?"

David stood up. His deep voice filled the room. "For the bounty of this table, for the hands that prepared this food, for this home, for friends to help us, Lord, we give Thee our thanks. Amen."

He looked beaten. His broad shoulders were sagging, his shirt wet with perspiration. After all, he was not used to grubbing out mountainsides! As he reached for a piece of corn bread, I saw that the insides of his hands were like raw meat.

After the blessing David said little, perhaps because he was so tired. He seemed preoccupied with little interest in the food before him.

Then a large bowl of applesauce was passed. David helped himself to a generous portion as if relieved that here was one dish without grease. But he must have found the applesauce tart, for after his first taste he asked, "Mrs. Holt, could I have some sugar for the applesauce, please."

"Sure, Rev'rend. Long sweetnin' or short?"

I knew that "long sweetnin" was molasses or wild honey—the honey often scooped out of a tree trunk with grimy hands. "Short sweetnin' " meant brown sugar. There was little or no white sugar in the mountains. David settled for the short sweetening.

"Have to git it for you," Mrs. Holt chortled. With that, she moved some dishes aside, hoisted her skirts and stepped up on the plank table, her legs up to her thighs in plain view of all the men. She reached for something overhead in the rafters. Dirt sifted down onto the heads, the table, and the food. No one seemed to notice.

Finally Mrs. Holt clambered down, triumphantly clasping an old shoe box. She lifted off the lid, dipped into it with her fingers, and vigorously shook a generous portion of brown sugar on the mound of applesauce on David's plate.

David gulped, thanked his hostess, then determinedly dipped into the applesauce.

Usually Workings were also jollifications. The custom was for the women to bring their quilt pieces or keep their hands busy with stringing dried shucky beans. One or two of the men would bring fiddles or dulcimers. At intervals during the day or when the work was finished, there would be fiddling and ballad-singing. Uncle Bogg's jokes and tall tales were always a part of every Cutter Gap get-together.

But today there was little fun. Though the women were quietly chattering among themselves as they waited on the table, the men had little to say. Their silence was becoming strained and ludicrous when Uncle Bogg took it upon himself to try to liven things up. "Just listen to them wimmin cacklin' like hens," he began. "Just t'other day I asked a woman-person to show me her tongue. Wanted to see if it was wore down. She couldn't stop cacklin' long enough even to show it to me."

Since this seemed to be directed at Rebecca Holt, she lashed back as if on cue. "Con-found ye, you ugly old coot. Got no time to fool with ye. I'll feather into ye and sweep ye out of here like you was slut's wool."

The laughter rippling over the room had relief in it. Encouraged, Uncle Bogg went on as if he were composing an essay on women's tongues. "Oh, la! We cain't handily blame Becky, men. You could take all the brains she's got and put them in a goose quill and blow 'em in a bedbug's eye.

"Tell you somethin'. Tongue-tied wimmin are ve-ry scarce and ve-ry valuable. If ever you find one, men, hang onto her. All wimmin's tongues be good for onyway is for spreadin' secrets. And secrets are like measles: they take easy and they spread easy."

Now Uncle Bogg had his audience in hand. The mountain folk liked his brand of humor. It was astringent enough to suit them, always picturesque, often crude. And their guffaws were all the reward the old squire required. It was generally known in the Cove that the old man could forgive anything more readily than not responding to his jokes.

He looked over at David. The tense lines in David's face had still not relaxed. He was smiling with his eyes but he was off somewhere lost in his own thoughts.

Uncle Bogg's blue eyes flashed as they fastened on David. "Some men," he said pointedly, "are so fun-proof you couldn't fire a joke into them with a double-barreled gun. What ails you, Preacher? You on the down-go today? Aaa-law!"

"Uncle Bogg," Mr. Holt said, "I've got it in mind that you mought tell us that tale about the preacher named Dry Guy."

Something inside me turned icy. David must know as well as I did that Dry Guy was a story about a preacher of whom all the mountain people wanted to be rid. They ended up by killing the preacher.

A sly smile spread over the old squire's face. When he opened his mouth, his near-toothless state together with the fuzz of hair over his ears gave him an infantile look. "Why, Ozias, that's a good idea. Waal, let's see now. Onct in this-here Cove there was this old preacher-person named Dry Guy. Weren't good for much 'ceptin' takin' up collections in all the sarvices and eatin' all the fried chicken he could git.

"Now some differ as to what'n'all happened. Thar be them that say a chicken bone got stuck in the preacher's throat and he choked to death and went out that way. Then there be others that say that after most all the chickens in the Cove had got their necks wrung for the preacher's dinners, weren't nothin' for it but to git shut of him. Thar be ways.

"Waal, there was a-goin' be a baptizin' down by the crik one day, so two of the men sat old Dry Guy's dead body on the crik bank, propped him up to look natural-like, elbows on his legs, head on his hands.

"Along come a bad boy. 'Howdy, Preacher,' he says.

"Guy jest sat thar, a-starin' and a-meditatin.' Must be havin' lofty thoughts for sure, the bad boy was a-thinkin'. 'I say, howdy, Rev'rend Guy.'

"Didn't answer nothin'.

" 'If'n ye don't give me the time of day, I'm a-goin' knock your elbow right out. Howdy, I say.'

"Answered not a word.

"Lickety-split, that bad boy swiped at old Dry Guy. Preacher fell over, tumbled down the bank into the crik water and sank.

"Now I've done it, the boy thought. Done drowned the preacher. I'll hang for that, sure.

"Come time for the baptizin', folks from all over gathered on the crik bank waitin' for the preacher. Didn't come and didn't come. Folks got to askin', 'Where in thunder is Rev'rend Guy?' That bad boy was a-sittin' thar on one of the benches in the back, hearin' all the talk. Got tickled, couldn't stop gigglin' for the life of him. Meetin' finally broke. Folks went home.

"When everybody had gone, bad boy fished Dry Guy out of the crik and put him in a gunny sack. Dragged it down the road a piece, wonderin' what in tarnation to do with it. Comin' the other way was a couple thieves, had stole two hogs and had them sacked and on their shoulders. Saw the boy a-comin'. Dropped the sacks and run. Hid in the bresh.

"Bad boy, he hadn't seen the thieves a-tall. Set Dry Guy down to see what was in them sacks in the road. Delighted to find a porker. Picked up a sack with a pig and went a-whistlin' down the road, leavin' Dry Guy thar.

"Thieves come out directly, picked up the two sacks, went on home. Hung the sacks on hooks in the smokehouse.

"Next mornin' old woman wanted her some side meat for breakfast. Went to the smokehouse, cut the sack, let out a bloodcurdlin' scream. Thar was the preacher, sacked and a-hangin' on the meat hook.

I wanted to scream like the old woman, "Stop it! Oh, stop it! This is cruel—cruel." Ordinarily the tall tale was funny enough as Uncle Bogg told it, but with David so obviously in mind as the butt of the joke, today the story had a macabre quality. Most of the women were staring at the wall or at their hands in their laps. Fairlight's face was flushed. David looked drained of color. He was doing his best to appear nonchalant but was not quite making it. But the story went relentlessly on . . .

"So they had to git Dry Guy off'n their hands someway. Found a wild horse and roped him, tied Dry Guy to him, turned that horse loose. All the men-folks tore around shootin' rifles into the air, shoutin'. Scared that horse most to death. Horse took off with Rev'rend Guy a-bouncin' first to one side, then t'others, a-headin' straight for the North Carolina line. Ain't been seen since. Must be a-tearin' yit."

The men were laughing, the women were silent.

"Aaw-law! C'mon, men, on your feet!" Uncle Bogg concluded. "Back to grubbin'."

In the midst of the joshing and hilarity, all the men left except Jeb Spencer and David. I guess that Jeb did not know what to say or to do, but that he wanted somehow to help David.

Finally David got to his feet, his shoulders sagging. I tried to catch his eye but could not. Slowly, he turned to go, Jeb close behind him.

I felt the need of doing something with my hands—quick—so I started clearing the dishes off the table. But my mind was in the yard, wondering what was going to happen next.

Later that afternoon I left the quilt-piecing inside the cabin to see how the outside work was progressing. Several of the men had already finished their strips but David still had almost half of his to clear. In a situation like this, especially with a newcomer, I would have thought that those who finished first would lend a hand to the others. No one was making any such gesture to David. Yet I sensed that even if they had offered to help, though David would have been grateful, he would have refused. For gradually, over the last weeks, we had come to recognize the mountain code: no man's leadership was accepted on someone else's say-so.

The fact that the American Inland Mission or any other group sent in a man tagged "leader" impressed the highlanders not at all. For them there was but one criterion of leadership: recognized ability and superiority. And for a man this had to include the hands and the brawn as well as the book learning or the glib tongue. It had become increasingly obvious to David that the mountain men would listen to what he had to say from the pulpit only if first he proved himself to them as a man among men. And this would have been all right except that the proving had to be by their standards, not those anywhere else in the world.

255

I brought David a dipper of cool water, and as he drank thirstily, I was concerned to see that the palm of his right hand was now bloody. His left was almost as bad. When I asked about bandaging it, he shook his head grimly. "Thanks, no. I'd better try to finish this way." He smiled at my solicitude. "You can doctor me this evening." Then he picked up his mattock again.

About an hour later, we women heard sounds of a disturbance in the yard. I rushed to the back door, dimly aware of Fairlight just behind me. I thought that I recognized one voice—Bird's-Eye's. David was almost at the top of his strip, Bird's-Eye shouting up at him. His voice was slurred and thick.

"Aint been treated so fine today, have ye?" he taunted. "That's what we think of folks that pester with other folks' business." He spat contemptuously on the ground. "You'uns and your religion." He spat again. "Religion ain't got nothing to do with blockadin' or feudin' or gredges or bushwhackin' no way. Religion is for women-persons and white-faced weaklin's and liver-growed babies. You keep your religion inside the cupboard in the church-house where it belongs or I'll give ye this—"

As he raised his rifle to his shoulder, I clapped my hand over my mouth to stifle the scream that rose in me. Three rapid shots spattered into the ground at David's feet; the fourth whistled within inches of his head. Then Bird's-Eye stood there, brazen and churlish, with his hand cocked tantalizingly over the trigger which would release the fifth cartridge.

David had not jumped—as I had—at the four shots. The situation in the yard was inflammable. I could feel my heart beating wildly. What if David started talking and said all the wrong things, and then some of the men ganged up on him? Jeb Spencer and Tom McHone and several others looked embarrassed, but most of them wore hard faces—immobile, registering nothing. Not a man moved. David was pale but he was looking Bird's-Eye straight in the face, his brown eyes unblinking.

"Oh, you're a good enough hand to work. But Preacher, you mind your own play-pretties and we'll mind our'n. That is, less'n you want to see your great-great-grandmammy real soon." And once again Bird's-Eye made as if to raise the gun to his shoulder.

There was a ripple of ribald laughter. Then every eye was on the tall young man on the hillside. Behind me the cabin door was full, the other women peering anxiously over my shoulders. Only Granny Barclay had elbowed her way into the yard and stood with her hands on her hips, as if for two cents, she would leap into the fray and start fighting Bird's-Eye herself.

Still David stood unmoving. *Will the mountain men consider their preacher a coward not to avenge the insult by fighting? Is a sound thrashing the only reply Bird's-Eye is capable of understanding? But he's been drinking—and anyway, he has a gun.*

David's face was ashen, but an icy calm seemed to have taken possession of him. Under his level, unwavering gaze some of the bravado left the mountaineer. Slowly Bird's-Eye lowered the rifle and began shuffling his feet in the dust. The quietness in the yard was so intense that a cow mooing on a distant mountainside sounded like a bugle call.

From the beginning to end, David still had not spoken a word. Slowly his eyes traveled to the circle of men, as if trying to see how many friends he had among them. The silence seemed interminable. At last he spoke one sentence, "If any of you would like to hear my answer, come to church tomorrow."

Then David stooped, picked up his mattock, turned his back, and attacked the last of the bushes on his strip.

Twenty-two

ON SUNDAY MORNINGS the schoolroom was usually a comfortable half to three-quarters full of worshippers; today it was crowded. By now everyone in Cutter Gap knew about the incident between Bird's-Eye Taylor and David at the Holt Working. Curiosity was rampant as to what the preacher's answer would be to the challenge Bird's-Eye had flung him.

The church service was at eleven o'clock. I had gotten there early and had found a place toward the back near the wall so that I could be as inconspicuous as possible. I sat there picking nervously at my nails, not realizing how tense I was until the base of a nail began bleeding.

As I had washed David's raw hands in disinfectant and bandaged them the night before, he had been thoughtful, not talkative, as if the isolation thrust upon him at the Working had been complete—even from me. His eyes had a "No trespassing" look, as though he wanted to be left alone to think things out for himself.

Once during the night, a noise had wakened me and I had gotten out of bed to look out the front window. It was David, still up and walking back and forth near his bunkhouse in the moonlight. He looked like a man in deep thought—and deeper turmoil. At breakfast, though he had seemed weary, there had been a determined set to his jaw. Too determined. That was why I was afraid now.

What, I wondered, was the missing ingredient for communication with these people? This morning I was seeing them in the scene before me with fresh eyes. No effort was made to move my school desks each Sunday for the church service since the mission owned only five benches. Two of these "pews" had been placed at the side of the room to the left of the pulpit, the rest of them at the back. Already the adults had filled up the benches, leaving

258

the low uncomfortable school desks for the children and young folks.

The front of the room was a mass of wriggling children, shuffling feet, and rustling Sunday-school papers. A couple of hound-dogs circled round and round the bucket of drinking water with its big dipper sitting on a stool. It was fortunate, I thought, that the bucket was just out of reach of the thirsty hounds; surely someone would run them out before the service began. All over the room were the bobbing heads of babies in arms. Now and again one of them would cry and the mother would unbutton her shirtwaist, pull out a breast, and let the baby nurse right there. Already I had grown accustomed to it.

But what I had not adjusted to—nor had David, he had told me—was the undignified, noisy type of worship service that the Cutter Gap folk wanted. In seminary David had been taught certain liturgical forms for church services. And even I, having never been near a seminary, had always known a degree of majesty in worship, the rich tapestry of words from Scripture and creeds and prayers mellow with age, pregnant with meaning, bequeathed from generation to generation. Snatches of those sonorous clauses hovered round my mind now: "That our hearts may be unfeignedly thankful. . . ." "Gloria in excelsis Deo. . . ." "For ye shall go out with joy and be led forth with peace. . . ." "Cantate Domino canticum novum. Alleluia alleluia. . . !"

And I could never hear words like that without visualizing a procession of monks in their drab robes—their faces half-hidden by their cowls—followed by the priests in their gorgeous vestments, slowly making their way along the shadowed arches of the nave of some medieval church. And above their heads would be the sunlight stabbing through jewel-like windows, each piece of stained glass put into place by the loving hands of artisans

> to give light to them that sit in darkness, and in the shadow of death: to guide our feet into the way of peace. . . .

I could see this caravan of worship winding down across continents and over centuries. I liked to think that I was somewhere in the procession, following in their train, using some of the same words that they had used . . .

Honor and majesty are before him;
strength and beauty are in his sanctuary. . . .

But how could one worship and adore without at least a semblance of dignity? That was why I could sympathize with David in his desire to teach these mountain folk a little more about worship.

But so far the people had resisted any changes at all, and on the whole, Miss Alice sided with them. I remembered one of our afternoon sessions with her when David had quoted lines from some of the hymns that irked him most:

I'm ready to go, I'll sail away. . . .

or

He has taken a beautiful bud
Out of our garden of love. . . .
Full blooming flowers alone will not do,
Some must be young and ungrown. . . .

And he had put his head in his hands and groaned, "Why can't I teach them some of the great music of the church?"

Miss Alice had laughed at him. "David, dear boy, haven't you watched the people's faces while they're singing? Their foottapping hymns are one of the few joys of their lives. Why tamper with that? They're praising God in their own way. Well—let them!"

So they were praising God in their own way right now because the first hymn was in full swing, and I do mean swing. And this was no medieval cathedral, but a raw wood church in Cutter Gap, Tennessee, with babies crying and children wriggling, and men standing just outside the church door dressed in overalls and spitting streams of tobacco juice.

There was a hypnotic quality in the wearisome repetition:

Hits the old ship of Zion, as she comes,
Hits the old ship of Zion, the old ship of Zion,
Hits the old ship of Zion, as she comes.
She'll be loaded with bright angels, when she comes,
She'll be loaded with bright angels. . . .

The people sang lustily, tapping their toes, exactly as my school children did when they were singing ballads.

When it was time for the sermon, I found myself looking at the preacher with fresh eyes too. What did the people see? A tall young man who insisted on dressing in proper ministerial garb. For though David had so far given in on the choice of the hymns and the type of worship service, he would not be pressured about his own appearance in the pulpit. Dressed as he was now, he could have stepped into the pulpit of any city church—striped pants, a Prince Albert, a white shirt, a dark tie, his shoes shined, his black hair carefully combed.

I had noticed that when David was conducting a service or preaching, an innate dignity took over, so much so that he became rather a different personality in the pulpit from the everyday David. He even spoke differently.

In fact, the first few times I had heard David preach, I had realized that in the pulpit he did not yet know how to speak the language of the Cove people. Since he was fresh from classes in theology, he was overly fond of words like "polemic," "exegesis," "syntax," "Christological, "Apocrypha" and that one that capped them all—"anthropomorphism." Obviously, his congregations understood little of this.

Their reaction to not comprehending was the opposite of what I would have supposed: the Cutter Gap folk were enthusiastic about their new preacher's sermonizing. His four and five-syllable words and his "highfalutin' talk" had them convinced that they had snared the most educated preacher in those parts. The men had slapped David on the back so often and the women had complimented him so regularly that David had assumed that his ministry in the Cove was off to a great start—that is, until yesterday at the Holt working.

It was a sobered earnest David who stepped to one side of the little pulpit that had been placed on the platform where my teacher's desk was during the week, and began: "I had planned to preach today on Mark 6:30–46, the story of the Feeding of the Five Thousand. But certain things have happened in the Cove in the last few days which must now be brought into the open. So folks, I'm not going to preach a sermon at all this morning. I'm just going to talk to you out of my heart." And he thrust his notes to one side.

The children stopped shuffling their feet. There was

silence in the room. The people were leaning forward, all attention. The men in the yard had crowded up to the door to listen.

"There are those among us who think that Christianity is just for Sundays and has nothing to do with the rest of the week; that religion should be kept within the walls of the church, that it has no bearing on life outside. They think that the preacher should stand up here on Sundays and give out a string of fancy, high-sounding talk. And if some of you don't understand everything the minister has said, so much the better, you think. Well, this morning I want you to understand what I'm saying, so I'm going to talk in the simplest possible way.

"Some of you also feel that after the preacher has finished his Sunday service, he should shut his eyes to everything going on outside the church. 'Mind your own business' I have been told.

"But friends, the church's business is my business. In deciding to become a minister, that's the business I agreed to take on.

"Take on what? What is the church? Not just a building, certainly, because many a church in the first century had no building. People met in a room in someone's home—or anywhere. We could hold church out under that tree there and in God's eyes it would be just as real.

"Well then, is the church its minister? Not at all! Once again most of those first churches had no minister either as we understand the term. They had to rely on one another for their teaching and preaching—or on visiting evangelists and teachers—or on letters written by Paul and Peter and others. That's why we have Paul's epistles, for example, and the Letter to the church at Corinth, at Phillipi and so on. So the church is not the preacher.

"The church is a fellowship of people, you and me and folks like us who want Christ to be their Head or Leader.

"And where would He lead us? How does He want His church to act? Do you remember the story about Jesus standing in the outer court of the temple in Jerusalem, knotting cords together to form a whip to drive the moneychangers out of the temple, His muscles rippling beneath the bronzed skin, His eyes blazing with fury? Do you think that all those moneychangers, whose tables were overturned with the coins spilling everywhere took that without fighting back? They wouldn't have been human if they had. But Christ dealt with them, Man to man.

"Once again, taking a look at the gospels, Jesus dealt in a special way with those who tried to justify their wrongs, who pretended to be good on the Sabbath and then did anything they liked the rest of the week. He had a way of looking them in the eyes, piercing through their double talk, penetrating their real motives. Then with utter fearlessness, He would tell them what He thought of the rottenness that He sometimes found there. Some of those men—as important in their community as our squires or sheriffs or judges here—He called 'ye serpents, ye generation of vipers . . . hypocrites . . . blind guides . . . ravening wolves . . . whited sepulchres . . . doers of iniquity.'

"Men, those are fighting words any time, any place. They are also the words of a Man who has left behind any fear for Himself.

"Now in the last twenty-four hours I've done a lot of thinking about what Jesus' attitude would be about us here in Cutter Gap right now in 1912. What's *His* opinion of leaving religion shut up in the church on Sunday, about preachers who close their eyes to what goes on outside the church? And I am reminded that it was those very Sabbath-religionists whom He called 'hypocrites . . . vipers . . . whited sepulchres.'

"He called them names like that because during the week they were cheating poor widows. They were involved in quarrels and lawsuits. They looked on women with lust. In their minds were evil thoughts, seductive picturings that led to fornication. They were hanging on to hate and resentments that led to killings and murders—even of good men, of prophets and apostles.

"The reason that Jesus drove the moneychangers out of the temple court was that they were greedy men who loved money, but who didn't care one whit about the people. They short-changed their customers. They cheated. They even thought it was clever to cheat. And that dishonored God, the Father of our Lord Jesus Christ."

I was caught up in what David was saying. Something had been added to him this morning. He was always earnest in the pulpit; but this was more than earnestness. For me, his words had wings.

"So I believe that this Jesus would say to us this morning," and here David stepped back behind the pulpit again and leaned far over it, his eyes sweeping his congregation, as if to talk personally to each of us, " 'either you

263

do right on Monday and Tuesday and Friday, or you needn't come crying to me on Sunday.' 'Take heed,' He warned, 'that thy whole body be full of light ... having no part dark.'

"You see, Jesus had watched how men who do evil always liked to work in the dark. 'Everyone that doeth evil,' He explained, 'hateth the light lest his deeds should be reproved. But he that doeth truth cometh to the light.'

"He talked about the light of the body being the eye. And He said, 'If therefore thine eye be single, thy whole body shall be full of light.'

"The man of the single eye is the one who is as straight on Wednesday as on Sunday; the man who doesn't have to work in darkness, who isn't afraid of everyone knowing what he is doing.

"And Jesus went on to say, 'No man can serve two masters.' In other words, you can't serve Christ on Sunday, and then on Monday nights serve evil. That just is not possible.

"Men and women, in this Cove there are those who are working at night—in the darkness—and they are serving evil."

I felt my throat constrict, suddenly go dry. I dared not look at anyone. The front of the room was still quiet, the children as if mesmerized. But at the back among the men near me, I could sense the beginning of restlessness— whispering, muttering. Prickles ran up and down my spine. David was hitting too hard.

"The white lightning being brewed here is the devil's own brew. You know and I know that it inflames men, that it leads to lust and quarrels and fights and killings. And now even schoolboys are being used to help sell this blockade liquor. That too is evil's own work. There are other abominations too. I can't talk about them all this morning but, folks, speak about them I will straight out from time to time from this pulpit.

"Because folks, the Christian religion is not a *thing* —like a piece of paper—that we can tuck away in the cubbyhole of a rolltop desk and then put the lid down and lock it. Christianity is a *life* and contains the germ of life in itself. If you were to confine life in a coffin and nail the lid on, the life would die. Even so, Christianity dies just as surely every time we confine it.

"So Christ meant for life inside the church on Sunday and life outside the church on every day to be of one piece. That was why He declared unrelenting, unending warfare against the sin and evil in our world. And believe me that includes the evil in Cutter Gap. All these wrongs must be brought into the light of day. Even as Jesus pitted the strength of His manhood against the moneychangers, so now in June, 1912, He pits all His strength against the deviltries in our Cove.

"Don't make the mistake, men and women, of underestimating Him. Our God cannot lose; He will not lose the fight against evil in this Cove or anywhere in our world."

He paused. His face was flushed, his eyes glowing, "How many of you want to be on His side? Do you?" He was pointing his finger. "And you? How about you?"

I was caught up in the intensity of David's emotion. Then just as he was saying, "Let us pray," someone tapped me on the shoulder. I jumped, turned around. It was Dr. MacNeill who had somehow pressed through the tightly packed group at the door.

"Can you come with me?" he whispered. There was urgency in his voice.

Dr. MacNeill said nothing more until we were well out of earshot of the group at the church door. "I hated to barge in on you at church," he began, "but I've an emergency on my hands."

I looked at him questioningly, my thoughts still partly back in the church.

"It's Little Burl. A torn abdominal muscle with a localized abscess. I'm going to have to operate right away. Will you help, Christy?"

This jerked me into the present in a hurry. Little Burl! And I was no good at this sort of thing. I made a gigantic effort to focus my thinking. "Dr. MacNeill, I'd do anything to help Little Burl. But you ought to know—I had to dash for air during his father's operation. And I wasn't in the front row either. I'm willing to help—but suppose I fold up on you?"

"You won't. You're the type who never folds while the crisis is going on, only afterwards."

"How could you know that?"

"I can tell. You have stamina and determination."

I wanted to believe him, but doubt must have shown on my face.

"I wouldn't ask you to help, only there's no one else. Alice Henderson is at Big Lick. Mary Allen is too emotional, too ignorant anyhow. Bob will have all he can do just to keep his wife out of my way."

As we walked on down the hill, I asked, "Where is Little Burl now?"

"At home. Can you ride that horse over there in the pasture?"

"Prince? I'm still not comfortable with him. But I'll try."

As the Doctor bounded off toward the pasture, I picked up my skirts and ran for the house. I was going to have to tell someone where I was going with Prince or leave a note for David.

A few minutes later the churchgoers were beginning to stream out of the door as the Doctor and I rode side by side out of the mission yard. Our destination was about two miles away on Blackberry Creek where Bob Allen had set up the only water-powered mill in the Cove.

The six children in the lively Allen family were each delightful in his or her own way. I had never seen so much individuality in one family: Among them, Rob, at fourteen, was already a blossoming writer; Creed was the snaggle-toothed clown with the gift of mimic; Della May was a dainty fairylike little girl; and, of course, Little Burl who had captured me from that moment when he had come racing down the hill "to swap howdys." I could see him now with his jerking cowlick of red hair, the pug nose peppered with freckles, the blue, blue eyes, in the puckish face.

Dr. MacNeill was riding ahead leading the way. Prince was behaving well today. He seemed to sense that this was no pleasure trip but some special errand, and was making it easy for me. Maybe David was right about how smart this horse was. I patted Prince's neck in approval.

The Doctor flung over his shoulder, "What happened to Little Burl at school? Was he in a fight?"

"Not exactly. He discovered something the big boys had hidden. Lundy Taylor tackled Burl and kicked him in the stomach. First there was a red mark on his stomach and then it turned black and blue. But that was days ago."

"I know."

I waited for some further statement, but none came. The Doctor's silence was ominous. Immediately my over-keen imagination was painting the picture of a gaping

266

incision in a little boy's abdomen. Miss Alice had often had to help Dr. MacNeill with his operations. How had she reacted at first to having to be an anesthetist and an operating room nurse? Had her stomach ever rebelled at the sight of blood? Had she ever had to dash for air?

Yet what more could I say? The Doctor simply did not understand my problem. I had already given him quite a discourse on my stomach during that first Sunday afternoon's visit to his cabin and he had only laughed at me. No, I was caught in circumstances which neither Dr. MacNeill nor I could help. So—where was I? Panic rose in me. I fought it back, tried to swallow it, only to find the fear like a dark wave of emotion washing over me.

Then the unexpected happened. Another series of thoughts—quite apart from the fear ones—swirled upwards as though out of some deep cavern from the depths of a sea of churning memories and ideas. The new ideas surfaced into my conscious mind with peculiar clarity. And whereas the panic had been so chaotic these were orderly thoughts, presented to me with slow deliberation ...

It was not a case of Miss Alice adjusting. You know that. You have watched her listening and waiting. Get your attention off the problem—yes, even off your stomach—and look at Me. I am greater than any problem. Light follows light. You are about to discover this for yourself.

Then my own mind took over again. Had I prayed? No, not consciously. Then how odd that I no longer felt alone in my difficulty. And this intimate understanding of all that had been troubling me, with humor thrown in. The humor was the last thing I would have expected.

But whatever this was that I was experiencing seemed to require some kind of response from me. That was not hard. Gratitude bubbled up. I found myself saying "Thank You" in every way I could think to say it. The problem, so heavy before—where had it gone? My body felt light, almost weightless. It was only with the greatest effort of will that I reined in my buoyancy. The pace Dr. MacNeill was setting seemed intolerably slow now.

After all, it was June in the mountains, beautiful June. The rhododendron was in full bloom with great heads of fluffy blossoms trailing down the hillsides; higher up, compact masses of the flowers in every conceivable shade of rose set against the purply-blue of the background peaks. I wondered if any painter had ever caught—or ever could—

these colors on canvas! Spring! Why should anybody ride sedately in the spring?

I looked at the back of the Doctor's head jogging up and down, up and down, up and down. The last words I had spoken aloud must have been my explanation about the blow that had caused Little Burl's hemorrhaging. How much time had passed since then? A minute? Five? Ten? I had not the least idea. Here we were, two people riding within a few feet of one another, with Dr. MacNeill oblivious of what had been happening to me. Yet this interior experience was as real as those red hairs on the back of the Doctor's neck. The Doctor needed a haircut.

Once we reached the Allens, everything happened quickly. Little Burl's face showed his joy that Teacher had come to be with him. "You'll stay right with me? Hit won't hurt?"

"Of course not. I'll hold your hand." He looked so tiny in that big bed with the raccoon "Scalawag" curled up beside him. (Creed had generously lent his pet racoon as his contribution to the occasion.)

Then there was Mrs. Allen, more distraught now than she had been at the time of her husband's head operation. "Something awful wrong in Burl's belly," she kept moaning over and over as Dr. MacNeill completed preparations for the operation.

There was the sickly sweet smell of the ether as it dripped into the cone I was holding. "I'm going to tell you a story now, Burl. It's about the wicked Hoptoad and the Little Yellow Dragon. Now this was a beautiful little Yellow Dragon and he lived right down there by the edge of your own Blackberry Creek. He was very happy because he loved that gurgling water. Only one thing was wrong, the poor little dragon couldn't speak . . ."

The light from the kerosene lamp laid a shadow across the small face, such a white face, so still now. For a moment there was only the sound of the boiling and bubbling of the water in the washpot on the open fire and the Doctor's swift movements.

But not for long. Dr. MacNeill had been right about Mrs. Allen. Somewhere behind us, she began wailing, "He won't never wake up. I know he won't never wake up. I knew we was a-goin' to have a grave dug before the year was out. That diggin' tool somebody left inside the house

268

the week afore last—" Finally in desperation, the Doctor ordered her taken out of the room.

Since the kerosene lamps and the firelight were such inadequate light for operating, we left the cabin door open. But then chickens wandered in. One rooster got close to the kitchen table doubling as an operating table, flapping his wings, about to hop up on the table. So Rob was delegated to get the rooster out and then to stand guard at the door to shoo away all chickens.

At the moment of the first incision, I reached out for help. Even as I was shrinking from the sight of the blood, the gift of a beautiful objectivity was given me. With it came that strange welling up of joy and gratitude I had felt before, this time appreciation for the skill of the hands moving so deftly, the hands that were going to save a child's life.

Then about halfway through the operation, Mary Allen, hovering outside the door, must have thought that the operation was taking too long and become terrified. Thrusting her husband aside, she came running back into the room, moaning and sobbing, close to hysteria. Running after her, Bob caught her just as she was about to fling herself on top of Little Burl. Though Bob forced his wife outside again, there was no way to stop her loud intermittent wailing.

Then as I watched Dr. MacNeill expose the pocket of pus in the wound, almost a cupful, once again I found myself hanging onto that strong Presence for myself and for the small still form on the table.

Finally there was the Doctor's "Almost finished now. You see how much infection there is." Then he noticed that I was not looking at the wound but at Little Burl's face. "Don't worry. His heartbeat's strong. And you're doing *great*—"

But when the operation was over, Dr. MacNeill would not relax. "He's still in some danger," he confided to me. "I'm leaving a drain in to take care of residual pus and blood clots. Burl's had fever for several days and complained that his side hurt. There was such localized tenderness that he didn't want anyone to touch it. His mother did all the wrong things—gave him an emetic and Apple Brandy."

After what seemed like a long time, the child began to come out of the ether and the blue eyes struggled open. Finally there was a weak grin at seeing me still there. "I came for another piece of that Scripture cake, Burl. And we didn't finish the story of the Yellow Dragon."

The little boy floated in and out of consciousness, clinging all the time to my fingers. "Can't risk any heaving or straining of the abdominal walls from nausea," Dr. MacNeill said softly. "That's one reason we've got to watch him every minute."

But then, finally, Little Burl had fallen back into a deep natural sleep. "He'll be all right now for a while. Let's take a break. I'll ask Bob to sit by his bed."

We were both glad to stand in the yard and breathe deeply of the good air. "Christy, I need to talk to you about something," the Doctor said unexpectedly. "Let's go down to the mill where we can have privacy." He led the way down the path to Bob's one-room mill, built tall about Blackberry Creek among the alder bushes and the willows. It was a picturesque place—with its water wheel almost as tall as the building and the dam and the millrace with the water turbulent, almost thunderous from the spring rains, racing down the flume.

Dr. MacNeill opened the creaking door and stood aside for me to enter. Inside, the last rays of the sun were filtering down through a deposit of the grainy corndust lying heavily on the windowpanes, hanging in the air.

"Was it blockade whiskey Little Burl found hidden?" The question was so abrupt that I knew Dr. MacNeill was struggling with something. He did not even suggest that we find seats.

"Little Burl found the hiding place. Later, David poured out the whiskey."

"I thought so." He sighed and leaned against the grain sacks piled against the wall. "Well, then, I understand why David is on such a rampage against liquor. I heard only the last few sentences of his sermon, just enough to gather that he really declared war on moonshining this morning."

Something about the Doctor's inflection struck me peculiar. "Well, why on earth wouldn't you understand? Especially after the operation you've just done? After all—"

The Doctor held up a restraining hand, his mouth half-smiling at me, but something more serious in his eyes. There was the same impression I had gotten that afternoon in his cabin: he was amused at my intensity and vehemence; he would deal with me patiently as with a child. And there in the old mill I reacted with exactly the same annoyance I had felt the other time.

"No, let me talk first," he interposed. "There's an awful lot that you and David need to know before you judge. But there's something I have to tell you, Christy. You've got to hear this from me before you learn it from someone else. I was the one who warned the blockaders that David was on his way to the federal marshals."

My lips formed the word, "You?"—but no sound came.

"Sorry if I've shocked you. And no, Christy, I have not lost my mind. Really I haven't. I had good reason for informing. Naturally I'll talk to you and David about it whenever you want to talk."

Talk! I wanted to talk right then. "Dr. MacNeill, I don't understand. I don't understand anything about this." My words were lashed with disillusionment, even anger.

At that moment the door flew open. It was Festus. "Burl's wakin' up. Papa said for you to come, Doc."

After that, there was no time for further conversation. Dr. MacNeill decided that he should stay at the Allens' all night, and Mr. Allen courteously rode with me back to the mission house.

Twenty-three

DR. MacNEILL looked the picture of composure lounging there on David's couch-bed, smoking that pipe of his with the wide silver band on the stem. Certainly, I was thinking, he did not seem like a man with anything sinister on his conscience. I had been given the only comfortable seat in the bunkhouse, an old leather-covered Morris chair. Yet I was far from feeling easy, any more than I had at any time during the three days since the Doctor had told me that he was the informer.

I had tried to withhold judgment until we could hear the Doctor's side of the story, but I could not help remembering his words to me that Sunday afternoon when I had dried off by his fire—with that telltale note of contempt in his voice—"If you'd really like to see some reform for *your* mission . . ." It was beginning to look as if he did not want to see any reform.

"In tipping off the stilling men"—here Dr. MacNeill looked down at David who was sitting on the floor, his back against the wall—"I was simply choosing the lesser of two evils. The choice was, let this particular still go a little longer—or risk more feuding and killing."

"Just a minute," David parried. "I don't follow that. In my book, letting the moonshining go on leads to killings."

"Didn't Bob Allen come to your bunkhouse one night to tip you off about the still?"

"No, he didn't. I mean, yes, he came to my bunkhouse. But all Bob did was offer to help me find the still. Bob didn't know where it was."

"I see." The Doctor leaned back, sucked at the stem of his pipe. "All right, I'm glad to get that straight. The fact remains that the stillers thought Bob tipped you off. So if you or the Revs had found the site and Bird's-Eye and his cohorts had been taken by the law—"

"So Bird's-Eye is one of the culprits?"

"Sure."

"Who are the others?"

"Hold it. I'm coming to that in a minute."

David leaned back and the Doctor continued. "Even if you got Bird's-Eye behind bars, there'd be plenty of others left on the Taylor side of this fight. Regardless of what information Bob Allen gave or didn't give, he'd still be the number one target. You see, it's the Taylors and the Allens who've had the basic quarrel all along. And I figured that with two accidents and two major operations in their family recently, the Allens have had enough trouble for awhile."

I shivered and looked at David. His face was a study of conflicting thoughts and emotions. I did not understand all these family loyalties and quarrels and I wondered if David did. I had the same impression of hopeless tangle that Dr. MacNeill had given me when he had first ripped open the subject that afternoon in his cabin.

"There are some other factors," the Doctor went on. "One is Bob Allen's brother, Ault. How well do either of you know him?"

"I've seen him a couple of times," I answered.

"He's not the man Bob is," David added. "Drinks too much, for one thing."

"And let's add that when Ault's had anything to drink, he has the quickest trigger-finger in the Cove. Ault considers himself the head of the clan too, and that gives him an additional excuse. So if the still had been found and the shooting had started—well—let's just say that we're sitting on a powder keg. It only takes one match."

"Let's get back to the main issue, Doctor. I don't see how your line of action—or rather inaction—will solve the matter of twenty to thirty gallons of liquor a day pouring into the Cove, a lot of it peddled by our schoolboys."

"Stalling isn't going to solve anything, I grant you that, except that it gives us a little time. The solution has to come from strategy worked out between us. Believe me, basically I'm on your side."

David took a deep breath, sat up straighter, as if some of the pressure was off his chest. But before he could make any comment, the Doctor hastened on. "But I would like to go on record as saying that I think you're

273

off on the wrong foot, David. The type of sermon you preached Sunday isn't right strategy either."

"Why do you say that?"

"Because it won't accomplish what you hoped."

"I didn't see you there, Doc. Were you?"

"No, I wasn't there."

"Then how can you judge the sermon?"

"So far I've heard three detailed versions of it. But I'm really not concerned with the sermon itself. The sermon may have been great. What I am concerned with is the people's reaction to it."

"Well—?"

"That isn't great and you may as well know it now."

David looked a little nonplused. "That may be. I wasn't preaching it to get a high popularity rating. But by precisely whose reactions are you judging, Doctor? That might make a difference, you know."

"That's my point. Even those who are fondest of you think the kind of blast you let loose Sunday hurts more than it helps."

"Why? Because they're afraid too?"

"No, that's not why. I'm no theologian, so I can't analyze it for you. All I know is, when you accuse people, a wall goes up. Then the last thing they're interested in is changing their view or their actions. All they do then is crouch behind the wall to defend themselves."

I thought of Miss Alice and wished that she had been there to hear David's sermon; her opinion would have been more unbiased than anyone's.

"But I haven't finished about the still. There's another fact you must have, David. The second blockader is Tom McHone."

My thoughts raced. Opal McHone's husband. Uncle Bogg's own son. "Does Opal know that?" I asked.

"She suspects, I think, but she doesn't want to face it. Up to now Tom has stayed very clear of all stilling."

"Then why now?" David's voice was sharp.

"Because since the baby's birth, Opal's had anemia. It's serious, bordering on pernicious anemia. She needs expensive medicine, good food. As their doctor, Tom will let me supply the medicine, but as for money for 'brought-on' food 'I'm obleeged to ye, Doc, but I don't choose' is his final word.

"You've never seen pride until you've met the fierce passion for personal independence in these folks. Believe me, it didn't just happen that the first Declaration of Independence came out of the Appalachians' Mecklenburg County more than a year before the 4th of July one we celebrate."

The Doctor ran his hand through his hair, so curly at the top and on the ends. "So—Tom's in a box. I know what he's up against. Back in these mountains there's only one real source of money and that's the sale of good whiskey to outlanders. Tom loves Opal and he'd like to keep her above ground. Can you blame him? I'm sorry, folks, but I just couldn't see a man like that turned in."

There was silence while we assimilated this latest news. Finally David said, "I respect your friendship with the McHones and your compassion, Doctor, but I think your conclusion's wrong. Selling blockade whiskey isn't the only way of getting food and medicine. Why didn't Tom come to us for help?"

"Too proud. That's not the way of these folks. They want to solve their problems themselves. Besides, how much cash do you have at the mission? They know what your salaries are."

"What about Miss Alice?" I asked.

"Alice Henderson understands the independent spirit of these people. She's never given them handouts. Not a person would ask her to. No, the problem goes deeper—and farther back."

Dr. MacNeill had gotten to his feet, was pacing up and down the little room. David still sat on the floor, his knees drawn up in front of him. His brown eyes were wary now and skeptical as they followed the Doctor back and forth across the creaking floor.

"Yes, farther back. In fact, do either of you realize how far back? 1912 is faced with precisely the dilemma of 1794."

David looked impatient and opened his mouth to interrupt.

"No David, hear me out on this," Dr. MacNeill growled at him. "It's important. Ever hear of the Whiskey Rebellion?"

"Yes—vaguely—in some history course or other—"

"I bring it up because if Tom McHone was of a mind to, he could stage his own whiskey rebellion for the same reason as the frontiersmen did. Nothing's changed—except that the government has steadily raised the excise tax on whiskey."

"I'm afraid I don't remember my history too well," I said apologetically. "Would you mind—?"

"History lesson aside, Doc, what does that have to do with the present problem?

"It has to do with the solution to the present problem. I don't think we can work out a real solution until you have all the facts. I'll make it brief.

"In the old days there weren't any roads into these mountains, just trails. As you've both seen, the roads aren't much better yet. The mountain farms never have produced much and there was no way to get what they did produce to market. The most a pack horse could carry was about eight bushels of grain, corn, or rye. Believe me, that wouldn't buy much sugar, salt, gunpowder or calico.

"But if you made the eight bushels of grain into liquor in a little homemade still on your own land, the same horse or mule could carry sixteen gallons of liquor—which doubled or trebled the money on your grain. The mountain men simply couldn't figure out any other way to get even a subsistence income.

"The seaboard farmers have always had a big advantage over the highlanders. During the American Revolution they got rich from scarcity and high prices. But then the treasury of the new nation was broke, so Hamilton, then Secretary of the Treasury, pushed through a stiff excise tax on liquor (over the sharp protests of Jefferson, Gallatin, and others) to replenish the coffers. The Colonies had never had that tax before, and of all forms of taxation, the excise has always been most loathed by the English, the Scottish, and the Irish.

"Anyway, to the highlanders it seemed grossly unfair: the seaboard farmers could go right on taking their grain to market without one cent of tax, while in effect, the new excise levied a heavy tax on the mountain men's grain. So they rose to protest, and that's what the history books call the Whiskey Rebellion.

"These Cove people don't see anything criminal about a little homemade brew. Try and understand their point of view. The know-how has been handed down for centuries. During all that time, whiskey has been used as their most common drug to doctor everything from colds to snake bite to heart trouble. They figure that it's their grain that goes into the whiskey. They grew it. They got together a few pieces of copper tubing and some other odds and ends and put together a little contraption on their land. To them that's no more morally wrong than their wives making wild strawberry preserves in their kitchens or soap from lye drippings in their yards.

"But that aside, the point I want to make is, the problem of cash income for the necessities in the mountains never has been solved. Tom McHone's predicament just dramatizes it all over again."

The Doctor's words stopped abruptly. He sat down again on the bed, calmly took out his tobacco pouch, and began filling his pipe.

It was David who finally broke the silence. "All right, Doctor"—he sounded a bit rueful—"you've made valid points. I can't agree that moonshining sidesteps all moral issues—because of its results. You should know. Three days ago you operated on one of the results. However—so we've got one good guy and one bad guy in a trap together. That makes separating the lamb and the wolf a little tricky. By the way, most operating stills need at least three men. Who's the third?"

"Nathan O'Teale."

"I might have guessed. So your long-range proposal is that we pick up where the Founding Fathers left off in 1794 and solve a problem they couldn't solve: cash for the mountains other than moonshine. And what's your immediate proposal?"

"I don't know."

"Come now!" David sounded sarcastic. "You thwarted justice last week. You must have some alternative plan."

The Doctor gave David an enigmatic look. "I'm not God. I just live here—and want to help."

I wanted to help Opal McHone too. I had not forgotten the quiet promise I had made to myself at the time of her baby's death that somehow, sometime I would try to give her a vision larger than her ignorance and superstition. And now that time had come, for Opal had a new burden to carry: her Tom was in trouble. He had gone over to blockade-running for her.

While David and the Doctor thought and struggled with themselves and with each other as to the way out of the moonshining situation, I was finding that my own idealism about what was really right for the Cove quailed before the knowledge that George Washington and Thomas Jefferson had not found an answer to the mountain men's poverty either. But meanwhile I could at least offer compassion and understanding to Opal.

She was a shy woman with almost no education and little self-confidence. It was sometimes painful to watch her struggle to express even a simple idea; I could not see in her the fine mind or the sharp sensitivities of a Fairlight Spencer.

Yet for all that, she was appealing. Whenever I saw her, she would sidle up to me, reaching out to me mutely—like an animal with sad eyes pleading for attention and affection.

So at the first opportunity I went to see her. She received me warmly, even eagerly. Looking at her in her old loose-fitting clothes with strands of her lank hair around her face, it seemed to me that Opal's wistful eyes, her lacerated heart, and her mute longings were more evident than ever.

She did not confide about the stilling to me (I had not expected that she would) but she knew about it all right. The mountain women had an intuition about such things. However, she did let drop the fact that Dr. MacNeill had been to their cabin for a long talk with Tom. We talked amblingly, in leisurely fashion, about when to begin the reading lessons I had promised her, and then about the Maternity Clinic which I hoped the Doctor would help us start soon. There the mountain mothers could be taught proper care for their babies. In imagining this I was able to give Opal an altogether new point of view about baby care. And the more I talked, the more my enthusiasm for the project grew. I made up my mind that the minute the men's minds were free of the blockading problem, I was going to press hard for the clinic.

By now I knew how much more Opal needed than the knowledge of how to care for babies. There were her fears and superstitions (many of them like the liver-grown idea, laid upon her by Granny McHone, now dead). All were tangled up with crude and irrational ideas about God. How could a novice like me set about correcting Opal's theology? I did not have Miss Alice's knowledge of the Bible, nor her perceptions distilled out of her lifetime of experience. Still, I had to try.

"You know, Opal," I suggested hesitantly, "have you ever thought that the only ugly things in this Cove are man's fault, while the beautiful things are God's work? Look at those mountains." We were sitting on her front steps and her eyes followed mine to the far horizon where the blue peaks melted into the skyline. Always I had to take a deep breath when I looked, really looked at the amplitude of beauty all around us. Only now in the late afternoon with twilight coming on, it was a delicate beauty, not so spectacular as usual. The sky overhead was an inverted bowl with a pale blue lining; over the far mountains, rose faded to peach, with tiny gray clouds looking as if they had been given their marching orders to tramp as majestically across a twilight sky as small clouds can.

"Living in the middle of beauty like this," I said, "we've no call to have puny ideas about God. Why do you suppose His world is so fancy-fine, so full of wonderment," I asked, reaching for some of Opal's own expressions, "if He doesn't want everything to be good and perfect and right and healthy? But we can spoil His good work. When we mess things up, then we shouldn't blame Him and try to make ourselves feel better by contending that it's what He wanted." Even as I was speaking, I was thinking how glad I was that neither David nor Miss Alice could hear my fumbling words.

Still, Opal's eyes had grown more soft and luminous as I talked, so some part of this was getting through to her.

But then, my inner thoughts ran, how does someone like Opal, caught in the predicament she is, find God's way out? Suddenly I was looking down into a great gulf fixed between my pat religious theories and the real-life problems of folks like Opal and Tom, and before the yawning abyss I was mute.

Sure, I believe the theory, believe it deeply. My heart as well as my brain tells me that it is so. But how do we go about applying to this situation the fact that God lives, that he wants His world—including Opal and Tom and this Cove—to be right? "We have to cooperate with Him," *I've just finished saying to Opal. But where do we start cooperating? What are we to do now?*

I could never have guessed that it was Opal herself who would point the way.

Twenty-four

SITTING at the table-desk in my bedroom on Wednesday evening, I saw lights moving across the yard and heard men's low voices. Then a few minutes later, there was a knock on my bedroom door. It was Ruby Mae. "Teacher, thar's a ruckus in the yard. Prince is a-carryin' on something fearful."

"How? What's he doing?"

"A-snortin' and a-pawin'—"

"Well, anything wrong with Prince, you'd better call Mr. Grantland."

"Yes'm, but would you be willin' to come and see first?"

So I went with her. Even as we reached the back hall, I found that she was right: Prince was banging the sides of his stall and snorting. I picked up a lamp from the hall table as we went through into the yard.

"That horse sounds plumb miserable," Ruby Mae commented.

We found the stable door standing ajar; that was unusual because of an evening David was always careful to close and latch it. The familiar odors of hay and manure and leather rose to meet us as the door creaked open on its hinges. I held the lamp aloft and the soft light fell across David's saddle, only it was not hanging on its peg but was lying on the floor. I stooped to look more closely. The saddle had been slashed over and over in long vertical gashes, the girths ripped out and flung on the floor beside it.

Alarmed, I ran forward holding the lamp even higher to get a look at Prince—and in my shock almost let the lamp drop from my hand.

Ruby Mae shrieked, "Oh! Lordamercy!"

Prince was pawing and kicking the sides of his stall in

280

riotous protest. His beautiful flowing tail and his mane and forelocks had been sheared off and were lying in the hay at his feet. I thrust the lamp into Ruby Mae's hands and began a hasty examination of his flanks, running my hands over his high shoulders, searching for any cuts or wounds. So far as I could tell, there were none—only the shearing. Prince looked denuded, pathetic—and he knew it. He nickered and nuzzled me with his soft moist nose, then put his head on my shoulder as if pleading for consolation.

"Oh Lordy, I could bust out cryin'," Ruby Mae said.

I was already; tears were standing in my eyes. Prince had been as beautiful as his name, a proud animal. Now he was a caricature of a horse.

"Hit's the meanest job of work I ever seed. Now who would do a thing like that?"

"How I wish I knew! But Ruby Mae, we've got to— Will you go get Mr. Grantland? Only I'm not sure I can bear to look at his face when he sees this. I'll stay with Prince."

She ran out, but could not have gotten far, when she began shrieking, "Holp! Holp! Teacher—Mr. Grantland— Quick! Somebody, come quick!"

I dashed to the barn door. In front of the schoolhouse, flames were leaping into the night. I picked up my skirts and ran toward the fire. David had heard too, and he and I reached the spot almost at the same instant. It was the wooden pulpit from the church, carried into the yard, ablaze.

"Can't save the pulpit now," David snapped. "No use. But we've got to keep flying embers from leaping to the church roof. Buckets—we need buckets and everybody's help. Get Ida—"

"There's one pail in the springhouse," I offered, even as I sprinted in that direction. "I'll fill that one."

Ruby Mae and David bolted for the house calling for Miss Ida. Soon we got a bucket brigade going. Fortunately, there was about twenty feet between the fiery pulpit and our new building, and with the fifth pail of water, the fire began to sizzle and die. After that, the four of us stood there in the moonlight staring at the charred pulpit— four wet, confounded people—Miss Ida looking ludicrous in her white nightgown and wrapper with streaks of dirt and soot across the front, and the ruffled nightcap on her head askew over one ear.

Now I had to say it. "David, this isn't all. There's more." My heart was in my throat. "It's Prince."

"He's not—not dead?"

"No, thank God. Not that. But it's bad. His hair, it's all been cut off. It's awful!"

David was already running toward the stable.

The next day David made no effort to keep the events of the night before from the school children—or from anyone. The result was that poor Prince was on exhibition most of the day. The children stood in clusters staring at the horse, growing more indignant by the hour, their comments flying.

"He was so purty with that long mane a-sweepin' back in the wind."

"And with his tail a-flyin' . . ."

"And now he looks plumb onnatural, like a mule."

"Pet him. He can't holp it."

"No, but can't holp hit don't mend it."

"Look at them flies a-pesterin' him. Now Prince don't have nothin' to flick 'em off with."

"It's that pitiful."

"Reckon we could take turns a-fannin' the flies off'n him?"

"Somebody was full of pizen-meanness for sure. Wish I could knock-fight the livin' daylights out'n them that done it."

The youngsters of the Cove had always been fond of David. Now they rallied around him ready to do battle for him and his horse. Perhaps it was the swelling tide of support among the school children that gave David the idea. At any rate, he announced his plan in school one afternoon.

"All of you know the dreadful thing that was done to Prince. And because you feel as badly about it as I do, I'm wondering if you'd be willing to help me?"

Hands eagerly went up all over the room. "Shore, Preacher."

"Tell us what ye want, Preacher. We'd do most ony-thing."

"There seem to be some folks in Cutter Gap who hate the church—and me—and even Prince—and who want to run us out and close down the church and the school. Well, that would be wrong. Anyway we don't scare that easily, and we're going to fight right back. But not with fists or guns. We're going to fight in a different way.

"Now, this is my plan. I've saved the hair from Prince's mane and tail. If you'll help me make that hair into a great many watch fobs, then we'll tell a lot of people—not just in the Cove, but outside too—what happened to Prince. And we'll sell the watch fobs to buy a new saddle and a new pulpit and to help the church. Maybe buy some hymnbooks."

The children were enthusiastic. David set up sawhorse tables in the stable yard, and early and late, the boys and girls came and went, working on the watch fobs. Mr. Holcombe, who knew how to shoe horses and was also a tinsmith of sorts, made us several hundred tiny tin necks and rings which we used to grasp the horsehair and hold it neatly at the top of each little fob. David made a long list of individuals and of organizations and I agreed to help him write the letters. In each letter we told the story briefly and asked for any amount that the recipient wished to send in return for the unusual watch-fob memento.

The response exceeded anything we could have anticipated. In the end, something over three hundred and fifty dollars flowed in. This was enough to replace the pulpit and Prince's saddle, buy new hymnbooks, and even purchase a second horse for the mission, a chestnut mare, Buttons.

Prince's return from his unwitting sacrificial contribution to the mission work was that he became the most petted and beloved animal in the Cove.

WE HAD FINISHED breakfast and I had gone out on the back porch to shake the crumbs out of the tablecloth for Miss Ida when I saw the strange tableau approaching. Two mounted men rode silently toward the misson yard. A third in line had a gun pointed at the two in front. The one bringing up the rear had dismounted and was walking beside some sort of burden on his horse—no, it was a man's body slumped, almost doubled over in the saddle. As they got closer I recognized the two leading the procession—Bird's-Eye Taylor and Nathan O'Teale. Their hands were manacled to the saddlebows. Then there must have been a raid, a successful raid. Then—where was Tom McHone? Oh no! Let it not be!

By this time the group had seen me. "We've a wounded

man here." The voice carried clearly across the yard. "Can you help?"

But I was already running toward the voice, thinking as I ran. "Wounded," he had said. So if that crumpled figure on the saddle was Tom, at least he was not dead. I stared at Nathan and Bird's-Eye and I ran past but they were looking the other way.

"Miss, I'm Gentry Long, United States marshal." He was tall and lean with piercing blue eyes. One hand was laid protectingly on the body of the man in the saddle. I noticed that the other officer was keeping his full attention on guarding Nathan and Bird's-Eye.

"Didn't want to take this man clear to Lyleton," Officer Long explained. "He's lost too much blood. If we leave him here, can you get a doctor?"

"Surely. Of course." The wounded one was Tom all right. He looked dreadful, his face white and still, his shirt bloodstained. No flicker of consciousness.

The officer's eyes were on my face. "Now don't worry, Miss. He may not be so bad. Mountain men can stand an awful lot." David appeared then and immediately took charge. He helped the marshal carry Tom into the house to a pallet of quilts which Miss Ida had hastily thrown down on the parlor floor.

It was now within thirty minutes of time for school to open. Already some of my pupils were swarming over the hillside. Naturally they were going to stand and gawk. How embarrassing for Nathan and Bird's-Eye to have all these children, including their own, see them not only under arrest but handcuffed. Once my pupils saw this drama, there would be little schoolwork done this day.

Though I wanted so much to help with Tom and to be there when Opal arrived—already Ruby Mae had started a message on its way to Opal—I knew that my role was to get school under way as quickly as possible. The children were going to ask questions; it was just as well that I had no information about what had happened.

As I ran upstairs to get my schoolbooks I saw that David and the marshal were having a whispered consultation in the back hall. But David could not have learned much because as I came down the stairs three minutes later, the officer was already on his way out the front door.

I paused momentarily. "How bad is it, David?"

"If you mean Tom, he's lost a lot of blood. We've sent

for Dr. MacNeill. Doc's had lots of practice with gunshot wounds."

"What happened?"

"Don't know. Mr. Long says he's not free to talk yet." David's eyes focused on my armload of books. He shook himself as if coming out of a reverie. "Have a good day, Christy." Something like tenderness crept into his voice. "For a few hours forget all this—and concentrate on Luly Spencer's grammar and Mountie O'Teale's diction and Bessie Coburn memorizing a Shakespeare sonnet or something. And before the morning's over, I want to hear a lusty, gusty rendition of 'Oh, For a Faith That Will Not Shrink' come billowing down the hill. Mine's shrinking rapidly." His brown eyes were smiling at me but behind them was a puzzled, hurt look.

Tom had been wounded, Dr. MacNeill told us, with a thirty-two-caliber Smith and Wesson Special. The bullet had penetrated his left shoulder, coursed downward to lodge in his lower back. Of course the Doctor had to operate to probe for the bullet. Miss Alice had just returned to the Cove from Big Lick Spring and she offered to assist him. I was relieved because I had had enough of operations and blood and ether for a while. The Doctor impressed us all with a combination of surgical skill and intuitive knowledge; he located the bullet so quickly that the operation was mercifully short.

That afternoon after school I passed the door of the bedroom to which Tom had been moved. The door was open with the Doctor sitting by the bed. Thinking that I would inquire about Tom, I tiptoed in, but so softly that Dr. MacNeill did not hear me. He was sitting there studying Tom with a look of intense concentration mingled with something else—I read it as surprised shock that it was Tom McHone lying there before him. But the moment Dr. MacNeill became aware of my presence, the odd look left his face as if wiped off, and quite deliberately, he shifted into another mood.

"How is he?" I whispered.

"Sleeping now. Barring complications, he should make it. A couple of days and we'll know for sure."

"Thanks to you, he'll make it. Is Opal here?"

"Down with Miss Ida getting a cup of coffee. Opal's taking it great."

As indeed she was. So far, everyone had been amazed

at Opal's calmness and this never wavered in subsequent days. Apparently she had expected something like this and now that it had happened, she appeared relieved that the crisis was over, the still found and broken up. Though technically Tom was under arrest (and that could mean a prison sentence) not even that seemed to bother Opal. She was like a woman consoled: her man was alive; she need worry no more about her Tom "followin' stillin'." Somehow they would find the answer to the problem with which they had begun—the need for cash.

For some reason not clear to me, Dr. MacNeill seemed more disturbed than Opal. Though he was in and out of the mission house often, dressing Tom's wounds and attending him, there was an air of holding himself aloof, a silent drawing apart from all of us, even from Miss Alice. But if Miss Alice noticed this, she gave no hint.

By the fourth day I was beginning to wonder why no officer had dropped by to check on Tom since he was under arrest. I had heard that most federal agents considered all mountain men slippery characters indeed and guarded them with particular zeal. They were certainly giving Tom relaxed treatment, even though he was wounded.

As I was puzzling about this I remembered what Dr. MacNeill had said about Tom being shot with a Smith and Wesson. A picture sprang to my mind of the two men on horseback riding into the mission yard with the agent walking behind, his gun trained on them. I knew little about guns. Yet in my mental picture there was the clean impression that the agent had been holding a Winchester, not a Smith and Wesson. Then a thought washed over me like a revelation: the possibility that Tom had not been shot by a revenue agent at all.

About that time, Ruby Mae—our inveterate scandalmonger—got me off in a corner. "Things is shorely catawampus in this-here neck of the woods," she began in her doomsday voice.

"How do you mean?"

"Wal, I heered," she began, her eyes shining as she savored her juicy morsel of news, "that Tom didn't tote fair with the others. Don't know what the fraction was between them, but they say—"

" 'They say . . .' Ruby Mae, who is they?"

"Folks all over, guess."

"Well, go on."

"They say thar was trickery some-where, that Tom—turncoated."

"You mean that Tom decided to pull out of the blockade-running?"

"Well'm, more than that. Leastways, talk is that he informed on Nathan and Bird's-Eye."

"I see." And in the Cove, my thoughts went on, that would be considered about the worst thing any man could do.

"Yes'm. They're faultin' him all right. Can't handily blame them, can ye?"

"But Ruby Mae, we don't know that the talk is true. Let's give Tom a chance. Please don't stoke up this gossip-fire by more talk. You shouldn't mention this to another person."

Later on that day I had taken a pile of torn-up sheets for bandages to Tom's room. As I started back down the stairs, I heard the Doctor's voice, "How much do I know about what?"

"About how the still was taken and how Tom was shot? You're hiding something."

It was David and Dr. MacNeill in the parlor. Their voices were so loud that I couldn't help hearing. I paused, uncertain what to do.

"Are you accusing me?"

"Of sitting on information, yes. I'm accusing you of that."

"And since when is there a law against a man tending his own fences?"

David's voice was harsh with impatience. "Seems to me I remember some high-sounding talk about our working together. So—when do we start?"

"When do you start minding your own business?"

David's voice was rising. "Liquor stored on church property is sure my business. A man wounded in a raid and carried into the mission house is definitely my business. The business was dumped on my doorstep."

Not wanting to eavesdrop, I started to slip back to the kitchen. But the parlor door was open and as I went past, I saw David standing in the center of the parlor, taller than the Doctor, slim, with his carefully groomed black hair and the color in his face making his brown eyes seem even darker. *Odd, how at stressful moments like this when color creeps to David's face, that spot where his nose was broken stays so white.* And the Doctor, stockier of build with broad, muscular shoulders, sandy-red hair—tousled as always—hazel eyes flashing as he lashed out at David, "You're meddling in stuff you know nothing about. Lay off! For God's sake, man, lay *off!*"

Blindly, never seeing me at all, he strode down the hall and went out, slamming the front door.

That afternoon our new telephone rang. It was the jailer at Lyleton wanting to speak to David. Nathan and Bird's-Eye Taylor had escaped from the Lyleton jail.

Twenty-five

TOM'S WOUND was healing and he was getting restless. He made it clear that no mountain man "puts much stock in doctor-medicine or bedding it for long." But still he would not talk about the raid.

So long as Tom was with us, we thought him relatively safe. But if the gossip had it right and Tom had been wounded by Bird's-Eye or Nathan, then they had been shooting to kill. In that case, there would be a second attempt and they would not miss the next time.

This was still speculation, however, and David felt that facts were necessary for intelligent action. Therefore, he decided to go to Knoxville to talk with the federal agents. Surely they would respect him for his part in the first raid and tell him all they legitimately could. At the least, perhaps he could find out how Bird's-Eye and Nathan had escaped from jail and whether or not Tom was going to have to stand trial.

I felt desperate for Tom, though I tried to hide this from him and Opal. What chance did he have against one of Bird's-Eye's ilk? In such heavily wooded terrain as surrounded us, shooting in the back from ambush presented no problem. It was the taking of retribution into one's own hands, the localized justice of the American frontier all over again: the self-composed posse, the court under the maple tree, ending all too often in the hangman's noose and a body swinging from a limb of the nearest maple or oak. Only these mountains never had ceased being the frontier, and here—because of the predominantly Scottish background—the "court" was confined to the family or clan, so that there was not even the check of a more objective viewpoint from the men of other families.

It was a system whose weaknesses led to baneful results. Most of the highlanders seemed to think the government was something separate from them "out thar somewhars." From their basic lack of respect for law and government officials had come the concept that if a citizen did not agree with a law, then he need not obey it. They thought of such lawlessness as "freedom." Yet something was wrong because out of that kind of freedom could come no stable society—only, it seemed to me, more lawlessness, violence, and eventually, anarchy.

With this philosophy undergirding him, a man like Bird's-Eye Taylor knew that if he murdered Tom, he could justify his action in the eyes of the community: the pattern had been drawn too many times in the past. Or, I wondered, was there the least chance that Cutter Gap finally knew Bird's-Eye for what he was and in this instance, could reverse their centuries-old point of view?

Thus my thinking brought me back full circle to the Doctor. Was it possible that he had advised Tom to try to pull out of the blockade-running and that Tom's attempt to do so had somehow miscarried? Was that what Dr. MacNeill was hiding?

I watched for Dr. MacNeill's next visit. It came late that afternoon soon after David had left for Knoxville. I caught up with him in the mission yard as he was leaving after checking on Tom.

"I need to talk to you—and privately," I said, a bit out of breath.

He looked at me in surprise, his sandy-red eyebrows raised. "Well, Miss Huddleston. A pleasant day to you—and I'm just fine, thank you."

I smiled apologetically. "Sorry. I suppose I did sound a little abrupt." How was it, I wondered, that the Doctor always managed to put me on the defensive? And now he was smiling at me with that other look that I could not quite fathom.

"A private conversation with you would be a pleasure anytime." He sounded almost courtly. "How about your schoolroom?"

I nodded. "That would be fine."

"Then just let me tether my horse again." I watched silently as he carefully looped the reins around the fence post. In silence we walked to the empty school, neither of us making any effort at small talk. One of the things I had noticed about the Doctor was that conversational gaps bothered him no more than they did Miss Alice.

Inside the school I sat down at my desk, but Dr. MacNeill was walking around the room looking at the children's work on the walls. I was eager to get into the subject of the raid and Tom and Bird's-Eye immediately but he was in no hurry to begin.

"You're doing a good job with these children, Christy," he said.

Again I was disarmed, the heated words trembling on my tongue suddenly cooled. "Thank you. They're wonderful children. Only they have so many needs and most of the time I feel so helpless."

"The children like you too. I know. Word gets around."

He was trying to beguile me with compliments—and it was working. I sighed and tried to remember how I had planned to start this conversation. "You baffle me, Dr. MacNeill."

"Do you really mean that?" he asked quickly.

"I mean about your role in this stilling business."

He pulled up a chair and took his pipe and tobacco pouch out of his pocket. "Can adults smoke in here after school?" he asked quietly.

I nodded and watched his relaxed, methodical movements as he filled the pipe and tamped the tobacco in with his thumb. He was taking his time about lighting it. On a sudden impulse, I asked, "That pipe, Dr. MacNeill, it's unusual. Would you mind telling me what those words are in the silver? What language is it?"

With his head down, still holding the match to the tobacco, he looked up at me quizzically from under sandy-red eyebrows. "Um-m—" He took the pipe out of his mouth and grinned at me. "It's Gaelic. I suppose it would seem odd to you ... *Tha mo chas air ceann mo naimhdean.*"

It had looked like gibberish, but out of the Doctor's mouth it sounded musical.

"Literally translated, it means, 'My foot is on the head of my enemies'—a favorite saying of one of the MacNeills."

"It sounds warlike."

"The highland Scots were not exactly drawing-room dandies. And they could wield a claymore, and they weren't noted for their forgiveness. But you, Christy, didn't get me in here to talk about my pipe. What's on your mind?"

"Several things." I took a deep breath to get time to

think. "Remember the day you and David and I had that talk in David's bunkhouse?"

"Sure."

"Well, we agreed to cooperate with one another. Yet David and I feel that you're keeping facts from us. You seem unwilling to tell all you know. Somebody tipped off the Revs on the second location of the still. Was it you?"

"No."

"Do you know who helped them?"

"Christy, how do you know the agents didn't find the still on their own? They're clever men."

"Because I hear that they scarcely ever take a still in these wild mountains without a tip. And because when the first raid was unsuccessful, they asked David if he would continue to help them. They told him that they had no leads at all."

"I see."

"So somebody must have informed. Was it Tom?"

"Why do you say that?"

"That's the gossip going around."

The Doctor paused to relight his pipe. "Do you believe all the gossip you hear, Christy?"

"No, but I think the fact that Tom was shot in the back is significant."

Dr. MacNeill thought about that for a moment. "I could give you five different situations where Tom could have caught a bullet in the back in a normal gun battle between the Revs and the blockaders."

This was getting nowhere, so I started on a different approach. "But on the night before the second raid, you went to the McHones' and had a long talk with Tom, didn't you?"

"I go to the McHones' regularly," he replied mildly. "And I talk with everyone in the family."

"But you were there the night before Tom was shot?"

"True."

"Well, I just can't believe that Tom would have turncoated unless somebody nudged him in that direction. You, perhaps?"

"Is that what you and David think?"

"I admit that David isn't as convinced as I am."

"And why are you so sure?"

"Because when you came to the mission after Tom was brought in wounded, I watched your face. Dr. MacNeill, you did a mighty poor job of hiding your surprise that it was Tom."

The Doctor threw back his head and laughed. "Upon my word, females do have good imaginations."

"That was not imagination. You expected to find Nathan or Bird's Eye wounded, but not Tom. Isn't that right?"

"Christy, Christy—come now! The expression on my face was surprise all right, mixed with concern. I haven't yet learned to take the shooting of my friends with professional nonchalance. No, I haven't!"

Either he is a good actor, I found myself thinking, or else I have this man wrong. I knew I was outmatched but I pressed on anyway. "Then tell me why you've been so quiet recently. You've come in and out of the mission house with scarcely a word to anyone. Ordinarily, you'd have plenty of normal comments to make, I know you would. And then you blew off at David."

"I'm sorry about that. David means well, but he's too impulsive so he makes moves that don't go down well with the mountain people." The pipe still was not drawing to satisfy him. He relit it once more. "As for my silence—yes, sure, I've been preoccupied. This stilling business is bad. I want it straightened out as much as you do."

"Dr. MacNeill, I have a feeling you think me officious to ask all these questions. But there's one other reason why I'm asking them. You should know. Opal suggested it."

"Opal asked you to question me?"

"That's right. When I asked her if she knew why Tom got shot, she said 'Ask the Doctor.' Then she clomped her lips shut and wouldn't say another word."

The Doctor shook his head in dismay. "I'll never understand the workings of a woman's mind. It picks up all manner of fact and fiction and indiscriminately stitches the pieces together like a crazy quilt. Now you really are jumping to conclusions, Christy, without any facts at all."

"Maybe. Only here *are* facts: Tom was shot by someone. Bird's-Eye and Nathan are out of jail running around loose in these mountains. If one of them shot Tom, now they're free to try it again. So if you really care about Tom and Opal, you'll stop holding back any information that would help us protect Tom."

He met my gaze unflinchingly. "Christy, I cared about Opal and Tom McHone long before you met them, while you were still in pinafores. I know a lot more about the Cove than you and David do. I suggest that both of you stick to your mission work."

Totally nonplused now, I looked at Dr. McNeill long and hard trying to see through that stolid mask. No flicker of embarrassment or discomfiture showed through. He was actually enjoying sparring with me. But he's too cool, too dispassionate, I concluded. I was more certain than ever that he knew things he was not telling. Meanwhile, he sat there smoking, not saying another word, while wraiths of smoke drifted past my head. But something in his tone when he had referred to the mission nettled me.

"I'm curious about one more thing, Dr. MacNeill. You don't believe in what we're doing at the mission, do you?"

He turned the palms of his hands outward in an expressive gesture. "Don't believe in? What do you mean by an expression like that? Can you be more definite?"

"What I mean is," I explained, "you've carefully detached yourself from any real involvement with the church or the mission work. Your attitude comes through clearly as 'the church, that's for other people—not for me.' You don't think religion has anything to offer you, do you? And you don't have one tiny speck of vision about all the great work the mission could be heading into, if we got some solid help. Do you?" I was gathering steam as I went and the Doctor seemed surprised at my vehemence. He was looking at me with a new kind of interest.

"That's quite a bundle of charges and questions," he said thoughtfully. "I'm willing to try to answer them. But first, tell me what *your* vision is, Christy. I'd like to know that."

Since his tone held no teasing or facetiousness, I answered with equal seriousness, "That's not hard. I'm full of ideas and dreams. To begin with, for the school we need two more teachers right away, more space, the beginning of a school library.

"Then during the winter months, quite a few pupils simply can't make it to school through the snow. We now have the money in hand for the start of a small boarding school setup. We're going to put it in that big loft of a room on the third floor of the mission house.

"Then there are grown-ups who'd give anything to learn to read and write. I've taught Fairlight Spencer and now I'm beginning with Opal McHone. But there are lots more. That means some adult classes.

"The women need housekeeping help too. These rustic mountain cabins could be made beautiful—like Miss Alice's. She's shown the way. I'm brimful of ideas about that. For example, the ancestors of these women had real knowledge of herbery in their English and Scottish gardens. We could start herb gardens again, then that could be used as a spark toward teaching them good cooking. You know, something better than their greasy food and their sauerkraut. Weaving, quilting, canning, preserving; cabinetmaking for the men—all that's in their background. This could lead to trade schools of some sort."

I knew that my enthusiasm was carrying me away, but this was the first chance to tell anybody about the ideas that had been bubbling up like fizz water. "Then there's the clinic—we've got to get started on that right away. That involves you, of course. There we can give the school children their inoculations, centralize your work so you don't have to spend so much of your time on the road. Maybe some of the trachoma operations could be done here, so you don't have to cart whole groups of people to Lyleton so many Saturdays. We could set up classes for mothers to teach them how to take care of their babies.

"Then there's music and recreation—the ballads, the tall tales, the old dances. There what I see is—"

The Doctor was staring at me with such a mixture of interest and delight that suddenly, I became self-conscious. "I guess I'm getting a little off the track—"

"No, I think those are all great ideas for the mission. And I like your enthusiasm. But from what I hear from Alice Henderson and David, this isn't their total definition of Christianity in action."

"No, of course not," I said, uncertain of my ground now. "Of course, there's belief. Action wouldn't be any good without believing in something or Someone."

"And the purpose of the mission is to get people believing in all these Christian doctrines?" the Doctor asked.

"Well, yes. I suppose so."

"But what if the people don't want to believe these things? Does this mean that they can't send their children to the school or get help in beautifying their homes?"

"No. The mission doesn't force people to believe anything. You know Miss Alice better than that."

"Then why don't you just concentrate on the school and

the good works and forget all about the religious doctrines that just confuse the people anyway?"

I knew there was a good answer for that question, but I could not think of it at the moment. So I tried the Doctor's tactics: I evaded an answer by asking him a question. "Dr. MacNeill, what do *you* believe in?"

"You're stuck on that vague phrase, aren't you? Are you asking me what my philosophy of life is?"

"Well, yes. What is it?"

"I believe in God, in the sense that I'm willing to admit some starter-force for the universe. And I believe that love is the most creative force in the world. Trouble is, I've seen so many diseased bodies, so much suffering, pain, hatred, death and dying. Alice Henderson is always talking about a loving God who's concerned about people as individuals. I can't quite go along with that, else He wouldn't let our world be so awash in trouble and suffering. I suppose the truth must lie somewhere in between believing in nothing and the elaborate case the Christians have built up." He waved his pipe airily. "But this is much too serious a discussion for a girl like you."

I chose to ignore that. "You said 'the case that the Christians have built up' as if you aren't one of us. Is that right? You don't consider yourself a Christian, Dr. MacNeill?"

"No-o—come to think of it, I don't suppose I do. It never seemed important one way or the other."

"But what if it turns out to be the most important thing there is?"

"How? Why? Why is it important to you, Christy?"

"Well, if— That is—" desperately I tried to sort out my thoughts. If only I could express what I felt. Here was a great chance to win this scientific mind to real belief. That could be important, because Dr. MacNeill was so looked up to in the community with so many chances to help people.

"Miss Alice is just so great," I began, the words tumbling over one another. "She's the greatest person I've ever known. I wish you could have heard her the other day teaching a Bible class at the church. It was really good. She was telling about how the church has been the custodian of this precious truth for over two thousand years, but about how lots of people don't get this truth because it's hidden—you know, hidden like a treasure in a field or leaven in a lump of dough, with meanings that you

296

can take several ways, such as in parables and all, and about how once we begin to understand all this, it just makes our lives over, that's all. And Miss Alice went on to say that——"

The Doctor rose to his feet and stretched his big frame. "Christy," his voice was gentle, "I did not ask you what Alice Henderson believes or for a résumé of her latest talk to her Bible class. I wanted to know why Christianity is important to *you*, what *you* believe——" He went to the stove, opened the door, and tamped out his pipe. "What's your working philosophy of life?"

Since he was emptying his pipe, then he must be getting ready to leave and I still had not said anything impressive. My philosophy? What was my philosophy? How could I think under pressure like this? He was standing there looking at me, waiting for my answer.

"Well—I believe that God made us with a free choice. We can choose for Him or against Him, decide to go His way—or—or not——"

"And what does that mean? For instance, how will that affect a situation like Tom's, one way or the other?"

"It affects it, I suppose, because evil is very real and very powerful and some of us have been living in an ivory tower and——"

"You're quoting again, I don't know from whom—probably Alice Henderson again. Let's stop mouthing platitudes. The original question was, why is Christianity important to you?"

I was messing this up and I did not know how to retrieve it. I could have cried with disappointment at my ineptness. But why did this man have to be so cruel, so everlastingly superior? He had won this round, no question about it. The whole thing. Every bit of it. He knew how to turn every word I said to his advantage.

My frustration suddenly boiled over. "All right, *be* sarcastic about what Miss Alice believes, *make* fun of what all of us believe. You learned better in medical school, I suppose. Religion is for frustrated people or not-quite-normal people. Spiritual solutions to any of the problems around here aren't real solutions, you think. You're a realist, a red-haired, broad-shouldered, barrel-chested realist, so nothing religion has to offer can hold a candle to hard cash and a loaded shotgun and a box of pills—or some of your medicine in a bottle. That is what you think, isn't it? Isn't it——?" I was furious at him and I

297

didn't care a bit. Hot tears stung my eyes. To keep him from seeing, I jumped to my feet and turned my back on him.

"Let it pour out, Christy. I don't blame you. But this is the real you talking now, not some character you're trying to be. You have fire in you, and I like fire in a woman."

His coolness nettled me more than ever. I whirled to face him. He was giving me that same measured look—and I wanted to slap his face or pound my fists on his chest because he made me feel like a ten-year-old child, and I hated that feeling—and I hated him. I wanted—I wanted—I didn't have the least idea what I wanted. I turned and fled.

Twenty-six

IT WAS that old dream of mine about being forced to walk the open railroad trestle suspended high over swirling water. In my dream, the pit of my stomach was contracting in fear. I was balancing myself, struggling foot by foot across the trestle, when I heard a voice calling me. An unknown hand was shaking me by the shoulder. The dream-fear exploded into consuming terror. Desperately, I fought to ward off the rough hands. But in the struggle I was losing my balance. I was toppling headfirst into the swirling water.

"Miz Christy—please. Please wake up. Miz Christy, we need you. Some men are on the porch. They're a-tryin' to break in."

The last words snapped the sequence of the dream and I plummeted back into consciousness. Words reverberated, "Men trying to break in—" It was Ruby Mae's voice, Ruby Mae's hand shaking me, Ruby Mae standing there, quiet frenzy in her voice and manner.

Thoroughly awakened now, I sat up in bed. "Ruby Mae, how do you know someone's trying to break in?"

"I heered them foolin' outside the house. Woke me up. I'm skeered. What'll we do?"

"But you're certain they're trying to get inside the house?"

"I'm shore. They've been a-tryin' doors."

"Then let's wake up Tom. He's well enough to help now."

"No use. Gone. He's lit a rag for home."

So that was it. I had called a goodnight to Tom before going to bed. He must have crept home sometime after that. Well, we had been expecting it. But if only he had waited just one more night—until David got back from Knoxville.

Suddenly a thought struck me. "Ruby Mae, one door must be open, the one Tom left by."

"Fixed that. Crawled to the back door and shot the bolt acrost just afore the men got thar."

"Good girl!" I grabbed my wrapper, swung my feet to the floor. In the upstairs hall we found Miss Ida standing like a frozen statue at the head of the stairs. In the inky blackness I could just barely make out the contours of her white face with the braids of hair hanging dark against her nightgown. She whispered, "Are they after Tom, I wonder? Or could they be those strange men we've been seeing around here?" She did not wait for an answer, but padded softly down the stairs for a closer look.

As Ruby Mae and I stood there listening, I was thinking about Miss Ida's questions. If that was Bird's-Eye and his friends outside, then no doubt they would think Tom still inside. In that case, they would probably challenge us to send him out to them. And how could we ever persuade them through the locked door that Tom was no longer here? Then too, if they had been drinking, as would be likely, how could we hope to handle them once we opened the door? Most of our Cutter Gap men were courteous and manageable except when they'd been pouring mountain dew down their throats, though of course a man like Bird's-Eye was unpredictable at any time.

But if these were the North Carolina men David thought were somehow connected with the still in our Cove, then what? Miss Alice had told how men trying to escape indictment in North Carolina often crossed the border to hide out on the Tennessee side, and we were only fifteen miles from the state line. Whether moonshiners or not, often these escapees were desperate men, sometimes murderers wanted by both the police and the revenue agents. And here we were, three women alone. On any ordinary night with David sleeping in his bachelor quarters bunkhouse, we felt safe enough. He was only a few hundred feet away. A raised window, a woman's voice in the night, and he would hear and come instantly. But David was still away. And while we had the telephone, the closest contact point by phone was El Pano or Lyleton.

We heard steps on the porch—soft, furtive. Muffled whispering. Obviously there were several men out there. Yet they sounded too quiet for drunk men. As always, night sounds seemed thunderous; each time we moved the floor boards creaked beneath our feet.

As I peered into the lower hall, my eyes caught the faintest glimmer of brass; the knob of the front door was being turned quietly in someone's hand. I thought of how loosely all the doors were hung and of the flimsy locks and catches. Almost any tool could pry off those hinges, any strong shoulder crashing against that door would bring it down. And I had heard of men shooting hinges off a door. Could they really do that? And of course, they could break window-glass.

Suddenly the prowlers cut loose. A bawdy voice rang out, "Hey, open up. We'uns aim to git in thar." This was followed by raucous laughter and pounding on the door with what sounded like the butt of a gun.

Now that all pretense of stealth was gone, we leapt into action. Miss Ida stood at the foot of the stairs snorting, "I don't care who they are, maybe they will break the door down. But come on, let's make it hard for them."

As of one mind, Ruby Mae and I bounded down the stairs and began dragging a bookcase toward the front door. Soon we had added chairs and the piano bench which we heaped against the door to barricade it. Then we started in on the back door. The dining room table with chairs piled atop it made an even better barrier there. By now we no longer cared about how much noise we were making in moving all this.

Having assembled almost every moveable piece of furniture in front of the doors, we paused to listen again. The men had left the porch and were standing at the side of the house, apparently arguing among themselves. Ruby Mae and I crept to one of the windows to listen.

"Ye're a keerless woodscolt and I'm a-gonna crack yer bones," we heard . . . "Not till hell freezes over" . . . "Shet yer dirty mouth" . . . then the sound of scuffling feet and a hoarse cry.

Miss Ida was tugging at us. "We're wasting time. They're just having their own type of consultation before trying again. Come on, let's scout to see what we can use for weapons in case they do break down one of the doors or come in through a window."

It turned out to be a pathetic assortment: two pokers, a fireplace shovel, some planks which David had put aside for another bookcase. From the kitchen, Miss Ida brought three cast iron frying pans to add to the pile. "One good

301

whack on the head with one of these," she said, waving it. I could feel the swish of air and dimly see her moving form. I ducked out of the way of the lunging figure in the voluminous nightgown thrashing the frying pan about in that ferocious stance. I could imagine the fire in her eyes, ugly as she could be—even though she was David's sister. Her funny pantomime released some of the tension I had been reining in, and nervously I laughed aloud.

The men outside must have heard. "Thar's our doney gal," a voice called out. "Cuttin' up capers, plumb feisty. How 'bout some sweetheartin'?"

We heard them pounding around to the front porch again. My laugh had been a mistake.

"We're goin' whiffle right through the door to git our doneygal. We're caigy—"

Now I really was frightened. I felt Miss Ida's hand cover mine. "Don't answer, Christy. Not a word from you. Let me try to find out who they really are."

She went to the door, Ruby Mae and I close behind her. "Who are you? And what do you want?" she called out in a loud, clear voice through the door. "I'm Ida Grantland, David's sister."

"It's the old 'un, poppin' her teeth," we heard one man say.

"We just drapped by," another voice picked up. "Ah, maw, don't be nervish now. We're not likkered up."

"You are too liquored up," Miss Ida retorted. "And I want you to leave here right now." She was trying to put authority into her voice.

"Ah now, maw, don't be tetchious." Then with a sudden shift of mood, "Ye needn't shurl up yer nose at us. We belong in thar. No wimmin-folks are a-goin' tell us what to do. We come for Tom McHone."

I grabbed at Miss Ida's arm. "Don't answer yet," I whispered desperately. "Let's get back away from the door. There's something I've got to tell you."

She went with me to the back hall, and I put my mouth close to her ear. "Miss Ida, don't tell them that Tom has gone. If we let them know that, they'll head right for his cabin to kill him."

"But if we don't tell them," she whispered back, "then they'll get mad and break in. And you know the vile notions your laugh gave them. But I don't recognize Bird's-Eye's voice out there. Must be men he's rounded up, heavens knows where. They may be capable of anything."

"But if we tell them, they'll murder Tom in bed."

"Christy, come morning, they'll find out that Tom's back home anyway. I've got to think of you and Ruby Mae. We can't risk those men breaking in."

"Well, at least let's try stalling a little longer," I pleaded. "Promise me you'll wait as long as you can. Maybe somebody will come riding by. Or maybe they'll just get tired and leave."

"I'll try," Miss Ida agreed, "but you keep out of this. Not one word from you." She was more concerned about Ruby Mae and me than about herself, and at that moment I was more fond of her than I had ever been.

"What's goin' on in thar?" came through the door. Then guffaws. "Air ye chiseled down? Give us a glimpse of ye."

Miss Ida went close to the pile of furniture at the door to try a new argument. "Miss Henderson is going to hear this racket and be up here any minute now. I advise you men not to be foolish. You'd better leave quietly before you get in real trouble."

Actually I knew that Miss Alice's bedroom was on the far side of the cabin from the mission house, and that there was little likelihood that she would hear unless the men got really raucous.

"We'uns not scairt of her. Folks say she'd jump out'n the way of a worm ruther'n step on it."

Then came a lull. Plainly we could hear the gurgling of liquid in a jug as it passed from hand to hand. The picture began to come clear; Bird's-Eye must be hiding out somewhere and had sent men to abduct or kill Tom. But as usual liquor was sabotaging their mission. This accounted for their erratic behavior. If they really wanted to break in, all they needed to do was to smash the glass in a window. It would have been so easy. I now saw a glimmer of hope: hold out, let that corn liquor pouring down their throats take full effect. Then they just might forget about Tom, forget everything.

The minutes dragged on with the banter outside getting more ribald all the time. "Open up and we'll have a real playparty, a real hullaballoo. Mought even give ye a swig of our bumblings."

"Naw, maw, we ain't a-gonna lay off! We're in no swivvit, can outwait ye onytime. It's the laughin' gaily one we want."

"No hardness atween us," a deeper voice picked up. "We don't aim to hurt ye none, jest enjoy ye. Come on now, we'll even let Tom agg hit up too."

"Hell we will." The voices were getting thicker all the time. "I done told ye, it's the blossom-eyed laughin' one for me. Come on, let's go on in thar."

Then all at once, fortune was with us. It began raining—hard, a real gully-washer. "Hey, lay off, turn off that Noah rain. Ye ain't a-gonna outsharp us with nothin' like that." There followed strings of profanity so raw that I had never before heard most of the four-letter words.

Lightning stabbed the sky. Thunder growled, reverberating from peak to peak across the narrow valley. Out of the northeast a strong wind sprang up, driving the rain in horizontal sheets against the windowpanes, flooding the porch. By now the men would be drenched and yes, their spirits had been dampened too because their guffaws were drifting away. Ruby Mae, crouching under one of the front windows listening, finally announced, "Oh hallelujah, glory be, they've gone. They've left fer good, I do believe they have. Can't hear nothin' a-tall now except the rain."

Desperately weary from all the tension, I lighted one of the lamps to look at a clock. It was four-thirty in the morning. Without another word, too tired even to make any comments about our moments of terror or to move any of the furniture back into place, we listened awhile longer, then hearing nothing more, crept upstairs and crawled into our beds.

Tomorrow I knew that except for those barricaded doors to remind us, the events of this night would seem like part of the nightmare with which I had begun the night.

David arrived back late the next afternoon, not in good spirits. The trip to Knoxville had been less successful than he had hoped. Not only had Bird's-Eye escaped jail, but all the other prisoners too. This emptying of the Lyleton jail—even of the especially strong cage in the center of the jail-room in which the most dangerous prisoners were confined—had been so dramatic and cheeky that scathing criticism had been heaped on the officers. Consequently, David had found the law officers glum and uncommunicative, harried by lampooning. Their attitude was that the less they heard from anybody in Cutter Gap for a while, the better they would like it.

After finding the jailer and the Lyleton police so morose, David had sought out the Federal agent, Gentry Long. Mr. Long had been taciturn too. He had talked to David kindly enough; thanked him for all the trouble he had gone to on the first raid; put on a show of assurance about arresting Bird's-Eye and Nathan again before many days. But when David had tried to get the details of the raid in which Tom had been shot, Mr. Long had dodged with, "Oh, that! That's past history, old hat. One of the principles they pound into us agents is never to look back—always to concentrate on the present and the immediate future."

Nor had Marshal Long given David a clear answer about whether Tom would be tried. "Don't worry about it, Mr. Grantland. No problem there. We know where McHone is, have our eyes on him." He had laughed (David called it a mirthless laugh). "After all, the county squire can't very well lose his own son for long."

So that was that, leaving us where we had started with most of our questions unanswered. For the first time I could sympathize a bit with the mountaineer's attitude toward the law. It looked as if we could expect little help from Lyleton or Knoxville and were completely on our own. I could see now why sometimes in desperation the mountain men had gotten together their own posses, deciding that unofficial action was better than no action.

Then when David heard about the wild incident of the night before, he was furious. On the spot, he decreed that we women would never again be left unarmed and that we were going to learn to shoot. Target practice, he announced crisply, would begin the following afternoon in the front yard of the mission where all who passed by could see.

After dinner David went off to the corner of the front porch to read a book he had bought in Knoxville. I hesitated, but then decided to approach the thing directly.

"David," I asked, "could I talk to you for a moment?"

"Why sure, Christy." He laid the book aside. It looked like a novel.

"I always seem to be full of questions but I don't know how else to get answers." I paused, trying to decide how to begin. "I did talk to Dr. Mac-Neill yesterday while you were gone. It was a rather unsatisfactory experience."

David looked startled, so I rushed on to stop the direction of his thoughts. "No, nothing he did, only the things he said."

"So he did reveal something about the raid?"

"No, nothing."

"You mean that? Literally nothing?"

"Not one single fact."

"That seems scarcely possible. Well then, what did you talk about?"

"David, either he doesn't know anything about the raid or else he's the best actor I've ever seen. But it isn't the moonshining I want to talk about right now. It's this other thing. It's—well . . ."

"Go on, I'm listening."

"You asked what the Doctor and I talked about. It's— David, I was a bit surprised to find that the Doctor is practically an atheist. That put me off, but not too much. But when the Doctor questioned me about my beliefs, I—I just talked around in circles and didn't even make sense. It was humiliating."

"But why should you feel that you have to explain your faith to him? The Doctor is odd in some ways. I'm afraid he was just trying to get your goat."

"Perhaps so, but there is no reason why I couldn't give him straight answers to his questions. What good will I be as a school teacher if I don't know where I stand as a Christian? David, when you tell people why you are a Christian, what do you say?"

Momentarily he looked startled. Then he began smoothly, "Christy, if I answered that question fully, we'd be here all night—and I'm done in."

"Well, don't try to go into detail, just the essence."

David looked reflective. "Well, I can tell you one thing, I'm no hell-and-damnation preacher. I believe the ways of God are written into the law of nature and therefore there's a scientific explanation for everything."

"Are you talking about the Bible, David?"

"Well, yes—and no.

"I don't believe that every word in the Bible is true like some fundamentalists do," David continued. "At seminary most of us felt that the seemingly weird and mysterious happenings in the Bible have perfectly natural explanations—if we but knew."

"What about Jesus raising Lazarus from the dead?" I asked. "Bethany was only a little village and everybody would have known Lazarus. You couldn't hide an event like that."

"That's a tough one, I'll admit," David said thoughtfully. "But you have to realize that these stories were passed to us through many people and many generations and many translations of the Bible. Lazarus may only have been in a coma. There could be any number of explanations."

"David, then you don't—well—really believe in Jesus' miracles?"

"Christy, you're getting into deep theological water which, I'm afraid, will only confuse you more. Let me say this. I don't believe it matters so much what you believe as how you live. Jesus was concerned with ending injustices, with people's health, how they lived, whether they forgave one another—all that. Dogma isn't important. It's the results in the community that count. As for the Bible it's an amazing book, the greatest book of wisdom we have."

"But David," I interrupted. "my minister in Asheville was always saying that the Bible is more than that; that it's the inspired Word of God and that our only chance for admission into the kingdom of heaven on earth or in the next life is to believe that Jesus is who He claimed to be. He used to say things like that over and over. Yet I can see now that I never knew what he meant, not really."

"Christy, you have to face facts. There are almost as many different beliefs as there are Christians. And I'm afraid that doesn't help those outside the church any either."

"So you're telling me that I have to make my own decisions about what to believe and not to believe?"

"That's what it generally comes to."

"But that makes Christianity sound like—like vegetable soup—full of most anything and everything."

David laughed. "I wish you could have been in some of our discussions at seminary. You would have made a big hit."

David was moving off the subject and I felt unsatisfied. "One more question and then I'll quit, David. Why are you here, now, at this mission?"

"Because I was assigned here for a job that needed to be done. But just the same, I—"

The screen door banged. It was Miss Ida coming toward us, marching like a sergeant major. She had been listening, I was sure she had. Even in the dim light, I could see the fingers of her right hand rubbing back and forth across her thumbnail with that gesture she used when she was especially irritated. "David, you've had a hard two days," she said sharply, then looked at me. "If David took time to give a course in theology to one girl at a time, he'd never get anything done. Besides, I never realized you were so interested in theology, Miss Huddleston."

"Yes, I really am."

"Oh, I'm sure! That's what all the girls say."

David laughed at her. "Come off it, Ida. But it is late. I'll knock it off and turn in."

He seemed relieved at the interruption.

Twenty-seven

THE NEXT AFTERNOON, as soon as my last pupil had gone for the day I started for Miss Alice's cabin. She was at home and showed no surprise when she opened the door and saw me standing there.

I had scarcely gotten inside before I found myself saying with no preliminaries, "I have to talk to you. Two days ago in talking with Dr. MacNeill, I discovered something about myself. It's that I really don't know what I believe about my religion. I guess I never thought it through before. I made a stupid hash of answering some simple questions Dr. MacNeill put to me. It was embarrassing."

The half-smile around Miss Alice's lips and her gray eyes looking into mine conveyed the message, "Go on. I'm listening." Out of her quietness a thought flowed to me: was I more embarrassed because of the bad impression I had made on the Doctor or because I was confused about my belief?

I blurted out, "Miss Alice, I'm here because something on the inside of me seemed to point an imperious finger in your direction and command, 'Go!'"

A smile tugged at her mouth. "Christy, child, whatever that is on the inside of thee, it certainly has rare dramatic talent. It should go on tour immediately to play *Hamlet* or *Macbeth*. But thee was speaking of a conversation with the Doctor about religion."

"Yes, I'll say this about Dr. MacNeill: his questions were clear all right. Maybe his medical training helps him to think clearly. But suddenly I got to remembering all the vague preaching I've heard and the foggy Sunday-school teaching and the fuzzy religion in general. Why does it have to be that way?"

"But what were those clear questions of Neil's?"

309

"He accused me of parroting other people—you especially, I may as well tell you. He wanted to know what I believe about God. I think he put it, 'What's your working philosophy of life? Why is this Christianity important to you?' He wanted to know what difference it makes to me."

"And your answer left you dissatisfied?"

"Worse than that. I didn't have answers. That's a horrid discovery to make."

"That's a great discovery to make." The gray eyes were sparkling now.

"I don't understand."

"So many people never pause long enough to make up their minds about basic issues of life and death. It's quite possible to go through your whole life, making the mechanical motions of living, adopting as your own sets of ideas you've picked up some place or other, and die—never having come to any conclusion for yourself as to what life is all about. But you, Christy, are facing these issues early. That's good."

"But Miss Alice, how do I fathom what life is all about? Here are all these great philosophers across the centuries with better minds than I have, and one religion says this and another religion says that. Maybe one religion *is* as good as another. Who knows? Maybe there isn't any final truth. How can a person like me be sure?"

"Somebody very wise anticipated your question. All thoughtful men ask the same question sooner or later. So He left us a way so that we can be sure. It's as specific as a doctor's prescription or as an algebraic equation. Here, I'll write it down for you."

There was a little desk in the corner. Miss Alice went over to it, sat down, opened one of the desk's cubbyholes, took out a piece of notepaper, and began to write. As I stood watching her, a faint fragrance—something like dried sweet clover, only a bit more aromatic—wafted toward me. It stirred some memory but at the moment I could not recapture it.

Then Miss Alice blotted the paper, folded it, and handed it to me. "Whenever you've taken a written prescription from your doctor," she said, "the first step after that is yours. You move on this," she indicated the folded paper she had given me, "and then God will move. I'll guarantee it. And as for religion being vague—well, it isn't. It's been the delight of my life to find God far more

310

common-sense and practical than any human I know. The only time I ever find my dealings with God less than clear-cut is when I'm not being honest with Him. The fuzziness is always on my side, not His."

I stared at her, fascinated at the certainty with which she spoke. The piece of paper lay warm in my hand. I wanted to look at it but Miss Alice had not quite finished. "More people than not think religion dull. Some religions are dull. But believe me, Christianity isn't. It's the most fascinating, delightful thing I know. You're standing poised on the threshold of great adventure, Christy. Go on now, you're dying to see what I wrote," she said airily. "Go—and take that first step." Gaily she waved me off.

So I left her and started walking in the opposite direction from the mission house, still restraining myself from reading what was written on the slip of paper. But I did lift it to my nose. *Yes, that same fragrance clung to the paper*. Then I remembered. *The clothes, a woman's clothes that Dr. MacNeill had loaned me to wear that afternoon Old Theo had dumped me in the creek. Woodruff—that was it. But not many women in the Cove could possibly use such a sachet*. I thrust the paper in my pocket.

The dirt trail I was following was well known to me. For the first part of the way it rose in a gradual ascent, skirting the outside margin of Coldsprings Mountain. Black-eyed Susans were thick along the path. Then I came to a certain giant tulip poplar tree where I left the trail and plunged into the woods. Here it was crunchy underfoot, mossy in spots, and cool—a world in itself. A few hundred yards on, I parted the rhododendron and laurel thicket and slipped into the sanctuary of my little woodland room. This was a site that I had happened upon about two weeks earlier at the height of the trouble with Lundy and the schoolboys and the moonshining worry when I had felt the need of solitude to escape confusion and to think. Immediately this had become my secret retreat.

Outcroppings of flat rock surrounded by moss had kept the forest undergrowth from impinging on the enclosure. Water tumbling down from the heights above formed a miniature waterfall over one of the boulders, the clear cold water being caught in a hollowed-out place in the rock floor. Ferns overhung the tiny pool. When I parted the laurel and rhododendron branches that formed the

311

walls of my woodland room, there before me was a panoramic view of the valleys of Pigeonroost Hollow and Cutter Gap running together to form the Cove, and the mountains of Lonesome Pine Ridge to the west of El Pano.

But at the moment, I was wasting no time on the scenery; I had waited long enough. The jaunty handwriting with its exaggerated curving capitals read:

If any man will do his (the Father's) will, he shall know of the doctrine, whether it be of God, or whether I speak of myself.

I read the words over two, three times trying to comprehend. I felt let down. Why did the Bible always disappoint me this way? Other people seemed to get meaning out of it: Miss Alice certainly did. Why couldn't I? What had I expected while I had been standing there watching Miss Alice write? Some magic, obviously. Then I tried to recall her exact words. "Go and take the first step," she had said. Something about the next move then being up to God. But what first step?

I looked at the paper again, stared at it a long time. "Any man" . . . Well, that could be me. "If Christy will do the Father's will—" What was His will for me, Christy? I had thought I had been doing God's will when I had marched up to the front of the Montreat auditorium and told Dr. Ferrand that I was volunteering to come to this forsaken place. What more? What now? I set my mind to reason it out. The words seemed to say that obedience was important and since this must have been Christ speaking, then He was telling us that some sort of knowledge or insight about Him and His "doctrine"—what he taught—the ability to know whether it really was true or not, would follow on the heels of obedience.

A kaleidoscope of impressions and faces danced through my mind. David . . . with his jet-black hair, his intense brown eyes, his manliness, his booming voice, the impatience of his fervor about what he thought right. Dr. MacNeill . . . the way annoyance toward him would build in me time and again. I would not think about him. Little Burl, with the freckles marching across his face . . . always reaching out for love. He might have slipped away from us. Perhaps it had been the little boy's capacity to receive love that had helped to save him. Lundy . . . big, brutal, with his pimply face and his small ugly eyes, but somehow one of God's creatures too, who had to be dealt with some way. Fairlight Spencer ... a princess in homespun, I had come to think of her. Her name was so right. Spenser's "faery queen," to the manner born, her mind athirst to learn, her hands reaching out for beauty. Tom McHone ... I could see again his crumpled bloodstained body slumped over in that saddle. Opal ...

Opal! The swinging thoughts stood still, like the gyrating needle of a delicate instrument finally coming to rest to point steadily. *Go to Opal. Talk to Opal. Opal is the key.* But talk to Opal about what, I asked back? She holds the key to what? To the tangled mess of relationships in the Cove at the moment? Surely not! Opal and Tom were themselves caught in the thick of the mess. But the gyrating needle did not move again. There it pointed quietly, with a take-it-or-leave-it, obey-it-or-not, it-was-up-to-me quality, however fantastic or silly I might think all this.

I rose from the rock where I had been sitting, wondering how long I had been there. Quite a time apparently because my legs were numb. I parted the laurel branches to look. There was the Cove, the troubled Cove with its poverty and its smells, with so many problems, as if it embraced within the borders of one small kingdom a sampling of the hungers and lacerations of the whole world. The light breeze of the earlier afternoon was gone now; not a rustle stirred the leaves around me. A brooding quietness lay like a presence over the mountainside and the valley.

The sun was low in the sky, the light mauve. If I hurried, there would be time to get to Opal's before dark. Yes, I would go, though I had not the least idea what I would say or do when I got there.

Twenty-eight

AS MY FEET sped over the familiar woodland path that Ruby Mae and I had taken that day the McHone baby had died, there must have been the same crouching shadows, the same rustlings as before—but I took no notice. My thoughts were with Opal wondering why this strange summons to be with her.

At the edge of the girdled trees marking the boundary of the McHone land, I remembered to call out loudly and clearly—but there was no response, none at all; that was not a bit like Opal. As I got halfway across the front yard a group of men stepped from the woods at my right. I stopped short, my heart thumping. The man in the center was Bird's-Eye Taylor. I saw now that there were four in all; they stood there rigidly with their hands on their rifles, looking at me. I had been all but running; now I stopped as suddenly as though some giant hand had thrust itself in my path.

No one spoke. Four pairs of eyes stared at me, waiting for me to make the first move. For me, Bird's-Eye stood out from the others—dirty overalls held up by galluses, old felt hat with holes in the crown, brim turned down all around, several days' growth of stubble on his chin, mouth narrowed to a grim slit, eyes like steel—a look of frozen immobility. I realized that I had never before looked into faces as hard as these, made spartan not through discipline but through hate.

Finally Bird's-Eye spat into the dirt at his feet in that same gesture of contempt he had used toward David the day of the Working. "Come traipsin' to do some more pesterin' with other folks' business?" His mouth snarled like an animal's.

Still I did not move; I did not dare. I wondered how

314

long he had been hiding out here, wanted by the sheriffs of three counties. At last I found my voice. "I've come to see Opal, that's all."

"Yon," Bird's-Eye jerked his head in the direction of the cabin, though he never once took his eyes off me. "Go on in, but don't try no dodge with me. I'm right spang nervish this evenin', leetle keerless-like with this here hog-rifle."

Slowly I moved forward across the bare, hard-packed earth. The men did not shift direction until I reached the creaky porch. Then as if on cue, they turned to face me, rifles ready. It might have been funny—except that it was not. What did they think *I* could do?

I saw that the heavy wooden shutters had been closed across every window with even the bars in place, making the cabin look like a place besieged. Before I could knock or call again, the front door swung slowly open. As I walked across the threshold Opal rushed at me from the darkness; I felt her before I could see her. She clutched at my dress as if to satisfy herself that it was really I. "Oh, Miz Christy—I kept wishin' and hopin'——" Her voice was soft, almost stifled behind pent-up emotion. "I needed you—so much." She seized my wrists and sank to her knees, clasping my arms. "How could you know that I wanted you?"

"I didn't know you needed me. I didn't have any idea what was happening." I reached down to pull her to her feet. "Opal, you may as well know the truth. I'm here because—well—God told me to come."

Immediately the words were out, they sounded so pat. What I had just said, I meant literally. But would Opal take it as just so much theological jargon?

Instead, she asked wonderingly, "He did! Comin' here this evenin' weren't your idea?"

"No, it wasn't my idea. I started for your place just about the time Miss Ida always puts supper on the table at the mission house. I wouldn't ever have thought of coming this time of day."

"But how'd He tell you?"

"By a thought that wouldn't leave, like an order on the inside. 'Go to Opal—Opal needs you—Now—' over and over."

Slowly my eyes were adjusting to the shuttered gloom, and I could see that Opal's face registered in turn wonderment, then acceptance, then joy. "Then God knows about

Tom and me and Bird's-Eye." A note of awe crept in. "He cares—about us."

She was looking at a new and startling concept. But I still had no realization of what it was going to mean to Opal to have this proof that God cared about her.

Somewhere in the room a child whimpered. In the minutes since I'd walked in, the children had been so quiet that we had not been aware of them. They were sitting on the floor in a corner huddled together with Isaak—the twelve-year-old—in front as a sort of shield for Toot and Vincent. I realized that this must be a terror-filled situation for them. Isaak would understand that the men outside were waiting for his father to creep home after he'd gotten tired of hiding out in the mountains, but the smaller ones would not know what it was all about—the dark shuttered cabin, the tension, the fear-filled atmosphere.

Opal sank into a rocker, held out her arms to her children, and the two younger boys came scrambling. Still her mind would not be diverted from the fact I had just given her. She was stretching toward a new dimension. As she cuddled Vincent and absently stroked Toot's head, she reasoned, "Look-a-here! If God knows what's goin' on here and if He would tell you to come that-a-way, don't you reckon He'd talk to me too? D'you reckon?"

"Yes, Opal. Absolutely. Else He wouldn't have told me to come here."

"Then let's ask Him to tell us what to do next," Opal urged. "Will you ask him?"

I might have known! Having started this direct-approach business, someone like Opal was going to see it through to the end. I sat down on the cricket stool by the hearth, realizing that I had never prayed aloud in my life except for the school prayers. But as I remembered those hate-hardened faces outside, I knew this was no time for coy reticence. "God," I plunged in, "this is all new to Opal and me. We've trouble on our hands, and we don't have the least idea of the way out for Tom and Opal. We just can't believe that You would have told me to come here, if You didn't have some sort of plan. Would You please tell us what to do next, and what to do about Bird's-Eye? And—" sudden self-consciousness all but smothered my words, "thank You very much."

Opal said nothing. Gently she slid Vincent off her lap, rose, and began stirring the cabbage and side meat cooking in a black pot over the fire. Finally when she had

316

finished stirring and tasting, she turned away from the fire, wiping her steaming face with her apron.

"I'm recollectin' what Granny told me 'bout how Bird's-Eye was raised," she observed. "His daddy didn't treat him good. He was a hateful-like man, had a gredge against the world. Used to smoke that young'un's britches for the least thing, whupped him not only for badness, but just to be whupping. When he was a real teensy boy, his daddy learned him to cotch birds in a trap, bust their legs, make a play-game of rockin' them till they querled over dead. His daddy taught him to be such a good aim that he would drive a rifle-ball plump through the eye of a bird as far as he could see it. That's how he come by his name 'Bird's-Eye'.

"But the young'un couldn't stomach all that hatefulness, so when Bird's-Eye was fourteen he lit out from home. Peeled the bark off'n a hick'ry log, scooched down with the bark over his head in the bresh at the edge of the yard. Watched while his daddy hunted for him and his mother cried. Weren't a bit of use, never did find him.

Opal got up, took another look at the black pot, then continued her reminiscing. "Then Bird's-Eye put out for the thick wilderness. For goin'-on seven years, let his grievin' mother think a varmit had got him. Traveled on, traveled on, never slept the same spot any two nights. He was a sharp one. Begged and roamed from one settlement to another, worked a leetle, done fairly well.

"Then sudden-like, Bird's-Eye showed up at his old home one evenin'. It had set in t'rain that evenin', thunderin' and light'nin', awful racket. Bird's-Eye's mother heard an uncommon sound—hallooin', knockin' on the door. There stood her son. 'Course his mother didn't know him right off. But Lordamercy, when he told her who he was, her jaw was hangin', her eyes popped, she most died dead on the spot. But then she welcomed him in and he stayed. T'was good Bird's-Eye come back then 'cause his Maw died a short time after from milk sickness and his Paw was kilt the next year when his horse throwed him in a thunderstorm.

"And now I'm re-callin' something else. Bird's-Eye was bad stuck on me for awhile. One reason he's as mad as time at Tom is because Tom courted me away from him. 'Course that really weren't no job of work for Tom; in no time a-tall I thought right smart of him.

"Only time I ever seed Bird's-Eye nice was one spring

317

afternoon whilst he was still courtin' me. Bird's-Eye and I had gone traipsin', struck out through the woods, pretty far piece. Without meanin' to, jumped a deer and Bird's-Eye shot it with his rifle-gun. When we got to it, saw that it was a doe and in the breshes was its fawn—spotted, wobbling on tall thin legs, bright leetle eyes. Bird's-Eye picked up a rock, swung at it, busted one of its legs, commenced to swing again, that time at its head.

"I was already riled that we'uns had killed a doe, but when Bird's-Eye fixed to kill that baby that-a-way, I got fightin' mad. I fumped him on the head, scratched and pounded him. At first he laughed at me, thought I was a puny girl carryin' on. But then when I kept on standin' him off and he saw that I was rea-lly aggravated, he drapped the rock and looked at me considerable.

"Told him that while I was thar he wasn't a-goin' rock any more animals that couldn't fight back. Saw he couldn't do no good with me actin' like that. Guess Bird's-Eye never had nothin' to do with animals but to kill 'em—ceptin' for hound-dogs, that is."

"Well, then Bird's-Eye he looked at that leetle cryin' fawn like he was seein' it for the first go-round. Seemed like he took pitysake on it then. Studied a little, opened his knife, cut a saplin', took the baby onto his lap, splinted that pore leetle broke leg.

"He was as gentle as a gal could want. Real handy with the docterin'. His face was a study too as he looked into the eyes of the leetle thing, like somethin' new was bein' borned inside him. Seemed like it weren't Bird's-Eye a-tall—leastways not the Bird's-Eye I knowed—but some other man. A body could have confidenced that Bird's-Eye—if'n he had stayed that way." Opal's eyes were soft and warm, remembering.

"It must have been like seeing through a peephole in his armor," I remarked, "seeing the man as he was meant to be."

"Aye, that's it. Miz Christy, you said that God talked to you with an idea that wouldn't go by. Wal now, here's *my* idea—that I'm to mosey out to the yard thar and keep a-thinkin' and a-seein' Bird's-Eye like he was whilst he was docterin' that baby fawn. Talk to him, see what'n'all happens after that."

Turning this over quickly in my mind, I knew that Opal was already way out ahead of me in perception—and in courage. "But what are you going to say when you get out there?"

She shook her head. "Seems if I keep a-seein' that peephole in the armor like you said, I'll know what to say to the hole."

"Shouldn't I go with you, Opal?"

She hesitated, considering. "You'd best stay with the young'uns. But I'd like it, if you would stand in the door."

She secured the bun at the back of her head with hairpins, blew her nose, took off her apron. One of her rare smiles broke over her face. "God told you to come. He told you to come—right here—to this here cabin," she repeated, as if fingering the thought lovingly, like counting the beads of a rosary. Then she hugged me—and was gone.

I stood in the doorway with Vincent and Toot hanging onto my skirts, Isaak standing to one side, trying hard to act manly.

As the men saw Opal leave the porch, they stepped into the clearing from their hiding place in the edge of the woods.

Opal had a fine line to walk, it seemed to me. Taking the fact that Bird's-Eye had once considered himself her sweetheart, she would have to avoid letting him think that she was turning her back on Tom now. There was far too much of what the Cove folk called "step-husband" business going on anyway—another man stepping in when the husband stepped out. In fact, most of the killings in these mountains were over either women or land. It would not be easy for Opal to remind Bird's-Eye about the episode of the baby fawn without his misinterpreting it.

"You'uns must be hongry," we heard Opal say. Her voice was disarming; I could hear a smile in it. "Thar's some cabbage and side meat cookin' in thar—and hot corn pone."

Then the tone changed. " 'Course you're sorry fellows and I don't confidence any last one of you. And if I wasn't a woman, I'd feather into you and knock-fight every last'un of you into the next dist-rict. But then on the other side, I never did like nobody t'have gnawin' stommicks—even torn-down scoundrels. So I could tote some of the vittles out to you. Or if you'd druther, you kin come inside."

It was a strange invitation, so unprecedented that the

men were obviously at a loss how to react. With the men silent before her, Opal now tried more strategy, pure female. "Bird's-Eye, if you'd like to leave yer kinsmen guardin', Miz Christy and I can bring vittles out to them. It would be more fittin' for you—bein' the head of the clan n'all, to eat inside, comfortable-like."

In the darkness I could not see Bird's-Eye's face to get his reaction to this appeal to his status. Still there was no reply. The men would be thinking that Opal was trying to trick them. But working for her was their real hunger.

"Eatin' yer vittles won't change nothin'," Bird's-Eye finally said, his voice sullen. "Don't know as we'uns ought t'—"

Opal immediately picked up the fact that he had not turned her down altogether. "Looky-here, Bird's-Eye, I'm no lack-wit. And I'm sure you're atter Tom yit. But you cain't eat gredges and hate won't fill up your stommicks, and my hot corn pone and huckleberry pre-serves will. Sweet milk too and sweet 'tater pie. Some folks are plumb foolish 'bout my 'tater pie."

The men with Bird's-Eye made no comment, but somehow I knew that Opal had won her point; they were all but smacking their lips already.

"Waal, I reckon—" Bird's-Eye hesitated a long moment. "Con-found it, woman. Probably I'm a con-sarned idiot." He was following Opal toward the porch.

I backed away from the door and the children retreated again to the farthest corner of the room. Bird's-Eye paused on the porch and to my surprise, removed the cartridges from his gun. He nodded briefly to me but did not take off his rusty hat. Carefully he placed the cartridges on the mantle-shelf, stood the gun at the side of the fireplace in sight of us all. This was the first time that I had seen this part of the mountain code acted out, though I had heard about it: One who breaks bread in a mountain cabin would not dare violate the hospitality tendered him by fighting or killing while "eatin' another's salt," nor can the host betray this rule. So Opal's move was inspired in that she had won a brief truce in the feud.

Also, she knew that she could not have talked to Bird's-Eye about the old days in front of his kinsmen. On Bird's-Eye's side, he felt that his situation was covered by his men on guard in the yard. So now in these moments of relaxed neutrality, Opal would have her chance to talk to that hole in the armor.

I carried out tin plates heaping with food to the men outside. They fell on the food ravenously, and when I got back inside, I found Bird's-Eye eating just as eagerly, though silently and obviously ill at ease.

"How 'bout some sass?" Opal asked him. "And thar's a heap more side meat."

"I'm near 'bout foundered now," the man said between mouthfuls. "Waal, some sass, maybe. Right tasty," was his grudging compliment.

So Opal ladled some applesauce onto his plate, then an immense piece of pie. With every bite, Bird's-Eye was feeling more mellow. "Hah! That pie hits whar ye can hold it!"

In the strategy Opal was trying was her faith that this strange man's heart could be changed. Looking at him sitting there with hat on eating Opal's home cooking, it strained my imagination to believe that any such change was possible.

In the time-honored way of women, as soon as her guest's stomach was full, Opal began. "Reckon ye're a-wonderin' why I asked you in. It's jest that onct we'uns got along real good. And I memorize how you favored me. Thar was that fawn with the leg you busted, and you splinted hit up for me. Remember? Did you know that I had that thar fawn for a pet till he was full-growed? Aye—so I got to thinkin' 'bout all that whilst you was thar in the yard, and I sez to myself, 'It's my turn to favor Bird's-Eye now.'"

For Opal this was a considerable speech. Standing well out of the way in the shadows, I had been watching Bird's-Eye's face. The hard mouth-lines had relaxed a little.

"Aye—I knowed 'bout the fawn bein' a pet. Looky-here, what'n ever happened to it?"

"When he was growed he went boundin off to the woods one day. Never saw him again. Always kinda hoped no hunter got him." Opal went closer to Bird's-Eye, took his empty plate. "Looky-here, Bird's-Eye, whilst you was fixin' that fawn's leg, you was a real man. You know that? It's plumb foolish for you not to let more folks in the Cove see a heap more of *that* Bird's-Eye. They have the wrong idea 'bout you."

The man looked at her in genuine astonishment. "That must be woman tease-talk. Are you a-joshin' me? Fixin' animals' legs ain't no man's work."

"Fixin' onything is man's work," came Opal's firm answer. "Tearin' down or killin', that thar's easy. Any addle-pated fool kin pull the trigger of a rifle-gun or fling a rock. It's *fixin'* that's hard, takes a heap more doin'."

Listening to this, I could see again the baby girl's tiny body lying in the middle of the big bed. How amazing that this homespun mending philosophy and the awful liver-grown superstition could be part of the same woman.

"And I knowed," Opal went on, intent on what she was saying, "whiles you was a-fixin' that baby fawn's leg that ye was a good fixer, Bird's-Eye. Lordamercy, you are so good that if ye'd a mind to, you could fix up this whole Cove. 'Course ye'd have to stop killin'. But Bird's-Eye, you was meant to be a real man, a fixer, a clan leader. I reckon I've knowed that for a long time."

The man sat silent, I hoped transfixed by a new idea. Yet if Opal's words had hit target, Bird's-Eye's pride was not going to let him show it. He sat there cracking his knuckles nervously. "Waal, Opal, you jest mought have some good notions thar."

He rose to his feet, reached for his cartridges and his gun. "Tell you what I'll do," he said carefully, "what's fittin' fer one is fittin' fer all. We'uns will lay off here for a spell. Got more pressin' business onyways fer now down to Allen's grist mill. Got some corn to be ground," he laughed mirthlessly. "But don't expect nothin'. We'uns will be back di-rectly."

And he walked out the door.

Twenty-nine

I STAYED THE NIGHT with Opal, sharing Toot's bed. I
was uneasy and slept fitfully, knowing that they would be
alarmed about me at the mission. We dared not send
Isaak to tell them where I was lest Bird's-Eye or one of
his men be watching and misconstrue the message being
sent.

Toot and I slept on a muslin tick filled with straw and
corn shucks; whenever either of us moved or turned over,
the rustling was like dry leaves crunching underfoot in the
autumn.

It must have been about two in the morning when we
heard soft tappings at the door. It was Tom and Uncle
Bogg. The old man, being familiar with his son's favorite
hunting stands, had been able to find Tom's hiding place.
We dared not light a lamp lest some of Bird's-Eye's
vigilantes be watching. By a window where the pale
moonlight filtered through cracks in the shutters, we huddled for a whispered consultation.

The men already knew about Bird's-Eye and some of
his men picketing the McHone cabin. Wherever Tom's
hideaway had been—and they did not reveal this—he and
Uncle Bogg had seen every move in and out of the cabin.

It was obvious that the hours of crouching in the woods
like a hunted animal had debilitated Tom more than his
father. Perhaps it was because Tom was still not altogether recovered from his wound and because, after all, he
was the fugitive. In the murky light his eyes were sunk
deep in their sockets. Haunted eyes, they were. The shifting shadows drew his cheekbones sharply as with a black
crayon with furrows of pain and tension around his
mouth.

Opal's solicitude was wrenching to watch. She kept
thrusting food at her husband for which he had no appe-

tite, hovering over him, plucking at his sleeve, even offering to go to the spring to fetch him a drink of the clear ice-cold water which he had often declared the best water in the world. Tom scarcely saw or heard her; no creature comfort could reach or assuage the hurt in those pain-filled eyes.

All of us knew that if Tom could have fought Bird's-Eye alone, he would gladly have done so. But how could he contend with a group in collusion, all determined to kill him, many of them even now lying wait for him in ambush? His only other alternative was to hide out for a while, and unless Tom crossed the state line or went far from home (both of which ideas he rejected), that left only the jail or the mission house as sanctuaries. We agreed that Tom's best course was to leave immediately and try to reach the mission before sunup.

But he lingered long enough to look down into the face of each sleeping child as if to imprint the images on his mind. Opal trailed him to the door.

Clumsily, Tom put one hand on his wife's shoulder. "Don't be a-frettin' yerself, Opal. Leastways, hit's bound to be settled soon, one way or t'other."

He patted her and slipped out.

The next morning I had breakfast with the McHone children and Uncle Bogg. All of us ate mechanically, our thoughts centered on Tom, wondering how he had fared. For once Uncle Bogg was cracking no jokes, asking no riddles, telling no tall tales. As county squire he was caught in a web of circumstances. I could see his mind skipping hither and yon, searching for those loopholes and duplicities by which he himself had always before escaped and by which he had finagled freedom for other people as well. But this was his son now, his family caught at the center of the web. In the morning light his face was grizzled and dirty, his mouth as grim as Tom's had been in the night.

The children and I made it back through the woods in plenty of time for the opening of school. As we came in sight of the mission house, we knew that something was wrong. People were milling around the yard, standing in little clusters staring at the house, talking softly. My immediate impulse was to protect the three children from any bad news, so I tried to send them off to the school-room. But they refused to leave my side until they found out whether this commotion had anything to do with their father.

Fortunately, it was David who saw me first and came loping across the yard toward us. He looked haggard. "Christy! Where on earth were you last night? I spent half the night searching for you. Thank God, you're safe!" But then his eyes told me.

"Tom?" My lips formed the word soundlessly.

"Almost time for school," David said, his voice too loud and hearty. "Isaak, why don't you go on ahead?"

Isaak stood his ground, looking at David scornfully. "Preacher, you ain't foolin' us none. Have they got my Paw? Is my Paw—?"

I had never seen such an agony of compassion on David's face. He stood looking at the little boy, taking his measure. Finally he said, "All right, Isaak, you're a man. I can see that. But Toot and Vincent here—"

"They ain't no babies. They've got *me*." He stood very straight, bracing himself, hastily throwing up his fortifications against David's message.

"We found your father in the woods, there," David pointed, "not more than three hundred yards from the house. He almost—made it. Shot in the back—just once."

None of us spoke, yet our question filled the air.

"Yes," David's voice was soft, "Tom—is—gone."

I sank to the ground, heedless of my skirts in the dirt, and drew Toot and Vincent toward me to cuddle them. Then I reached out for Isaak too but it was David who got to him first. He put one arm protectingly across the boy's shoulders. "It's rough, Isaak. You're the man of the family now. Mustn't think about ourselves right now. Your mother, how are we going to tell her?"

Opal. I wanted to thrust the thought of Opal from me. Opal with her new-found hope, her dreams of reforming Bird's-Eye. Now this.

"I want to see my Paw, Rev'end."

"Isaak, that isn't a good idea," David answered firmly. "No use of putting yourself through that."

"He's my Paw, Preacher." All at once there was an old man's face on a twelve-year-old boy's body. "Take me to my Paw now, Preacher."

Without another word, David turned and led Isaak toward the mission house.

I sat staring after them, vaguely conscious of Vincent huddled against me, and of Toot, his face buried in my lap, his fat little bottom sticking up in the air. My longing was to run after Isaak, somehow to stand between him and the moment toward which he was walking so steadily.

There was no callousness in this boy now, only sensitivity and hope. I remembered his response to the beauty of "Kubla Khan." He was so impressionable! Oh, shield him some way, I wanted to cry out to that heaven to which he had declaimed. Don't let this look at his dead father's face send the bitter desire for revenge hurtling on down to yet another generation.

If I were with Isaak now, I would not know what to say to him. Oh, let David know! Let him speak words loving enough to release the grief, strong enough to stop the hatred.

FOR ME the rest of the day was a blur. At school I went through the mechanical motions of teaching. Afterward, I could not even remember what subjects we had covered nor what I had said. Then there were the explanations to Miss Ida and Miss Alice about my experiences at the McHone cabin.

That night I had trouble falling asleep. I kept seeing Isaak's face . . . and Tom's . . . and Opal's. I awoke resolved to ride over to the McHones with David when he went to make plans for the funeral.

That was agreeable to David, so we started soon after breakfast riding Prince and Buttons. Our way led us past the cemetery on the brow of Persimmon Hill. In the distance there were two moving figures who seemed to be shoveling dirt. "David," I asked, "who's that up there?"

David reined in Prince and stared in the direction I was pointing. "Can't tell from here but they're digging a grave."

"But they look like *boys*."

"Christy, you stay here and I'll have a look." Prince wheeled and started up the hill in long easy lopes.

But I could not stay there. I rode slowly, skirting the perimeter of the cemetery, carefully avoiding the graves, not wanting to see what I feared we would see.

But there ·they were, Isaak and his best friend, Rob Allen, one working with a pickaxe, the other with a shovel beside a small mound of dirt, the beginning of an open grave. Already David had dismounted and was talking with the boys.

As I rode up, I saw that Isaak's face was white, his eyes

326

stricken. "He woke me up at the crack of dawn," he was saying, the words beginning slowly, then tumbling out. "Mama tried to stop him. Preacher, I was frightened of him, so stern and quiet, he was. Lips pulled tight, breathin' heavy-like. Collared me and brought me here. Took the shovel, heaved it in the dirt. Says 'Dig here.'"

I felt my stomach contract with anger and revulsion. The same emotions were struggling on David's face.

"Isaak, this is man's work. Didn't your grandfather offer to help?"

"No sir, Preacher. Jest left me here, then put out down the road."

Rob explained, "I was moseyin' by on my way fishin'. So I thought t'help Isaak dig."

David persisted, "But didn't your grandfather make any explanation before he left?"

"Told me facts was facts. Said they'd killed my Paw, and I mought as well—his mind was so honery-fixed. Weren't no use to talk back. But Preacher, I don't even know how deep to dig hit——" His voice trailed off.

David reached out his hand. "Isaak, give me that spade."

The boy handed it over, hastily brushing away a tear with his sleeve. David put one arm around his shoulders. At not quite thirteen we could not treat Isaak as if he were a small boy. But out of what perversion or coldness of heart, I wondered, would a youngster be asked to dig his father's grave? Surely the old squire had a will like a steel trap.

Eagerly the boy turned his back on the gravesite to grasp Prince's reins. Isaak began stroking his neck, burying his face in the horse's shoulder, talking softly to him as if grateful for the comfort of any living thing. Prince stood without moving, his brown eyes liquid, nickering now and again. He seemed to understand Isaak's need to fondle him.

I dismounted and Isaak tethered both horses close by. After a while the boy came and sat down on the grass close beside me. My mind struggled with what to say to him. "Isaak, you know sometimes when people hurt on the inside, they say or do things they don't understand themselves, things they're sorry for afterwards. Maybe it's that way with your grandfather."

His forlorn eyes gazed at me but he did not respond to that.

I went on lamely, "It's just that—well, it's better to try to understand so that more hurt won't grow inside you."

David's shovel scraped at the earth rhythmically as the pile grew beside the hole. I knew that David had never dug a grave before any more than Isaak had. From the convulsive energy with which he was wielding the spade, he must be working off on that clay-soil some of his anger against Uncle Bogg.

It was taking a long time. Finally David worked out a system: he took the pick and loosened the hard clay, then Rob would shovel it out.

Isaak sat with his knees almost touching his chin, chewing on a blade of grass. We were silent now; there seemed nothing more to say. In the stillness the sound of every clod of earth falling onto the heaping mound, every sharp metallic sound of metal striking rock, tore at us.

At last David straightened up, threw the pick down, mopped his face with a large clean handkerchief. "That should do it. Isaak, why don't you ride home on Prince with me? You can tell your grandfather that it's all finished. And thanks, Rob, for your help."

"Don't differ none. I'll git along fishin'."

"Yeah, Rob. Obleeged to ye."

But when we reached the McHones, Uncle Bogg was not there. Opal explained, "It's the hate spillin' over, and him wantin' to hand the spitefulness on to Isaak. He told Isaak to say out loud with every shovelful of dirt, 'They killed my Paw.'"

Often the men killed in a feud were buried furtively, sometimes because the one faction did not want their enemies to know whether or not a particular victim had been killed or merely wounded. But Opal in the tender beginnings of her new-found faith refused anything secretive: she wanted "a real funeralizing" for her Tom with all the Cove invited.

David, on his side, was immediately wary of what Opal meant by "a real funeralizing" since he knew only too well what sentimental orgies the mountain funerals usually were. He had told me how helpless he felt before the highlanders' attitude toward death. The idea was that if we really loved the dead, then we would show it for all the world to see. Therefore a proper funeral should last at least three hours, during which time the wilder and more prolonged the demonstration of grief, the greater the proof of love.

On these occasions the mountain parsons were expected to use a lot of "wind" to give a good performance, a minimum of an hour of preaching, usually with much exhorting of sinners to frighten them into the kingdom. Sometimes there would be several preachers, each one discoursing until exhausted, he fell by the wayside, at which time the next preacher would proceed. Often there would be no preacher around at the time of death, so the service would be held months or even years later, becoming a cumulative memorial for all who had died meantime. In that case, the services might go on for several days becoming also a sort of camp-meeting revival. Sometimes by then the widower would have remarried, so his second wife would attend the funeral of the first wife, weeping and wailing as copiously as the other mourners.

At the very least, such lamentations provided no comfort for the bereaved family and Opal and her children were in desperate need of consolation and help. Also there was good reason to suspect that the emotional orgies around the coffins helped to feed the fires of hate always smoldering under the feuds and now—with Tom's murder —blazing again.

David had described with what mounting uneasiness he had watched the whipped-up mania of grief as it played from person to person, tears here and jerkings there, moaning and flailing of the arms, the heated feelings mounting, darting—like summer lightning playing from one mountain range to another. There seemed altogether too close a connection between this and the anger, the hate, the passion for revenge that could whip through a community, inflaming people to shocking group action which they never would have thought of by themselves or stooped to as individuals.

So David tried persuading Opal to make the funeral for Tom a different kind of service, quiet, victorious, comforting. But Opal had her own ideas. "Preacher, ye jest can't stop folks from mournin' their loved ones. I've got it all figgered. I want you to hold the meetin'. But, Preacher, I'm a-longin' to hear Miz Henderson preach the Word. That way it's bound to be a first-rate funeralizing."

"Fine, Opal. That's a great idea." He seemed relieved that Miss Alice would share the responsibility.

Most of the Cove people were at the funeral, packed into the cabin, spilling out the doors onto the hard-packed earth of the front yard. They had worn the best and the darkest clothes they had. As usual, it was an odd assortment of mismatched trousers and coats, overalls, calico dresses, ancient watered silks, and faded shirtwaists. They were sitting on cane-bottomed chairs and makeshift benches, some of the women fanning themselves, sniffing, dabbing at their eyes with handkerchiefs.

According to custom Tom's coffin was open, placed in the middle of the McHone cabin. Opal had covered the outside of the raw yellow poplar coffin with black calico, the inside with white muslin. With infinite care she had tried to make it fancy by fringing the edge with scissors. A little American flag and a badge reading, "God Is Our Trust and Confidence" had been pinned on one lapel of Tom's "best" suit in which he had been dressed. Opal had tucked one of her aprons in at his feet.

It was the apron that hurt me most. I looked at that faded apron, and suddenly it became a symbol of the heartbreak of women in a man's world where fighting and violence and vendettas and wars must always go on—and on—and on. For what? For a man's compulsive inner pride, driven or ordered by what he calls "honor" or "integrity," his own or his family's or his nation's, with the result that in every century and in every country women are stripped of those whom they most love. Then there is nothing left except to bow the head and to handle the grief and the emptiness as best they can. And—tuck an apron in at the feet.

The solemn-eyed children were gathered close around the coffin. Toot and Vincent and Isaak had been given front-row seats. All of the Allen children were there except Little Burl, who was still recuperating. Tiny five-year-old Vella Holt was sitting on the floor, her mahogany-colored eyes under their level brows looking as solemn as ever. There were the five Spencers, even fat-cheeked Lulu and Little Guy. I wondered why the highlanders insisted on exposing children to death in this way.

Uncle Bogg was pathetic to see. The heart seemed to be taken out of the old man. He had so far refused to talk to any of us about Tom's death, and this withdrawing into himself was a bad sign.

I was sitting to one side on Opal's cricket stool, the jut of a rough-hewn log built into the wall poking me in the back. There was not even enough elbow room to maneuver myself away from the jut.

I wondered what even Miss Alice could say to sustain Opal in a situation like this. My thoughts roamed back over the road my own meager faith had traveled so far, as if counting my resources, searching for any coin of the realm—real, not counterfeit, that would ring true—that I might use to cheer Opal.

By now I knew that my religion, inherited intact from my family, had been mostly rote. Little about it had penetrated to where I, Christy, really lived. Back home church services had all but anesthetized me; I had become wonderously adept at dialing my mind to "off" for every word that the minister said and all that went on in church services, and to "on" for whatever was more interesting to ponder.

Already my brush with the raw life of the mountains had blown away much fog. Either this Christianity was true—or it was not. That day in the Montreat auditorium Dr. Ferrand had inspired me to gamble a year or so of my life to find the answer. And that move had led me to Alice Henderson, to whom the inner world of the spirit—man's and God's—was more real than the bread she ate.

And now Miss Alice's reaction to my talks about religion with Dr. MacNeill and David (as I had reported them to her) was challenging me further. The Doctor and David were trying to be realists, but Alice Henderson was the first person I had ever known with a meld of idealism along with hard-headed realism. So she not only encouraged me to think, she demanded it. "Can you really suppose that you were given that incredibly wonderful instrument—the brain—and weren't meant to *use* it?

"Go on, Christy," she had said to me, "ask questions, never be afraid of truth. Ask questions of yourself and of me. Go back to David and to Neil and ask them more questions. Yes, and your schoolchildren too. You'd be surprised how much children can teach us ossified adults, if we'd only stoop to listen. And ask God. Ask Him ultimate questions—about the why of things: about your place in the world, about life—and death. Ask, Christy, ask. Seek. You'll find. The promise is sure."

So—I was asking now, sitting here in the McHone cabin staring at Tom's body in his raw wooden coffin. Perhaps I looked calm on the outside, but inwardly my thoughts were rebellious, tinged with bitter grief and skep-

331

ticism. *The facts of life are so brutal and the hearts of men so easily bruised. It seems all wrong, all out of proportion.*

At least my thoughts were honest ones. On one thing I was determined: I was not going to hide behind any false piety. *God—if You really are there, and this isn't all a hoax—why did You let this happen? You could have prevented this, that is, if You have any power at all. Then why didn't You? Only another three hundred yards and Tom would have made it inside the house. Why? Why? You're supposed to be a God of love. That was the message Opal picked up from me—and believed—and moved on. This doesn't look like love to me. Opal and Tom were trying so hard to do the right thing. Why didn't You reward that?*

Once I caught Miss Alice's eye. She was sitting on the other side of the room with some of the older children around her. Today she was dressed all in white, an immaculate white mull dress, simple and beautiful. Her blonde braids (such a wealth of hair for a woman her age!) looked more than ever like a coronet. Her face was composed, so much so that her expression betrayed no hint of how she was taking all this. We would only know when it came time for her to speak.

The singing was beginning now. The hymns chosen by the family did not help my rebellious mood a bit: "Come and Lie with Me in the Old Church Yard" and then one that began:

> He is gone, our precious darling,
> They have laid him in the tomb. . . .
>
> We're sad and we're lone since you've gone away,
> In our humble home we'll miss you each day;
> But still we rejoice with glory unknown,
> To know you await at heaven's bright throne.

Finally the singing was finished. David spoke briefly and then acknowledged Miss Alice. She came forward, smiling at the children, and they moved over to make a place so that she could stand at the foot of the coffin. She looked at Opal, her gray eyes tender, and then at each of the McHone children in turn, her gaze lingering longest on Isaak. The room was hushed, waiting for her to begin. When she did, it was the story of the raising of Lazarus, the account of Jesus' friendship with Martha and Mary and their brother.

Forever and forever these people loved a story, so she had their attention immediately. She told about how Jesus had gotten hot and dusty and weary like the rest of us; how He was sometimes lonely, lonely enough to reach out for human friendship, so He had favorite friends and a spot He loved best—a particular home in the village of Bethany.

"When the Master had walked too many dusty miles and slept outdoors too often; when crowds had jostled Him and the sick and the ailing had tugged at Him until He was all but pulled apart; when He was too weary and tired to go on, then He knew that there would always be a welcome awaiting Him at this home in Bethany where Lazarus lived with his two sisters, Mary and Martha. There would be a quiet patio with its arbor of thick green leaves—and long shadows—and a breeze. There would be quietness—and His favorite dishes that Martha liked to cook. And after they had eaten, the four friends would sit around talking. It would be good talk, but it was always Mary who enjoyed it most.

"And so the two sisters and their brother came to love this Friend like no one they had ever known. The souls of four people were knit together. Somehow they knew that theirs was a friendship for life, yes—and for eternity too.

"But then one day when Jesus was several days' journey from Bethany, a runner came with the news that Lazarus was dangerously ill. Martha and Mary had sent for their Friend. Their need was urgent. Would He come immediately?

"But the Scriptures say that Jesus did not rush to Lazarus' bedside. He 'tarried.' So the runners went back to the sisters who were keeping the deathwatch, the women by then almost out of their minds with worry and grief. Day followed day. No Jesus. Their Friend did not come.

"The hours of the night came on. Their brother did not recognize them now. His breathing grew shallower, his pulse feeble. Once his eyelids flickered open. Then he was gone. Dead . . . Their brother was dead. Why had their Friend failed them? It was hard not to be bitter as they looked down at the quiet form.

"So now there was nothing to do except to prepare for burial this one whom they had loved so much. The body was wound round and round with linen bandages, layers of spices in between. They laid Lazarus in the family tomb, a cave made in the side of a hill, with a huge stone rolled up to the entrance.

"And then four days later, finally—when it seemed too late—Jesus came. The two sisters ran down the road to meet Him, first Martha, then Mary. In turn, each spoke words which carried a rebuke, 'Lord, if You had been here, my brother would not have died.'

"But Jesus did not accept the rebuke. For it had not been laziness that had kept Him from coming four days earlier—or because He had important business to attend to—or because He did not care.

"Gently He spoke to Martha one of the greatest promises ever to fall from His lips, 'I am the resurrection, and the life: he that believeth in me, though he were dead, yet shall he live: And whosoever liveth and believeth in me, shall never die.'

"Yes, He cared, because now as He looked at Mary, in the eyes of this strong Man tears formed and glistened and trickled down His cheeks. And Mary—kneeling at His feet, looking up at Him—saw the tears. Her friends who had followed her down the road, saw too. 'Behold how he loved him!' they said with wonderment. 'See—how He cared.'

"And He cares still. He cares about Tom. He cares about how unnecessary Tom's death was. He cares about Opal and Uncle Bogg and Vincent and Toot and Isaak. He knows and He cares. And if our spiritual eyes were opened, we would know that He is weeping just at this moment with us too, now—in this cabin in Cutter Gap— just as He did with Mary and Martha and their friends in Bethany long ago."

Now Opal was crying softly, her face hidden in her lap.

But Alice Henderson went on. "But friends, the Master didn't stop there. That would be great—to care that much. That's as far as you and I can go in our present state of understanding. When the Master had spoken to Martha about seeing the glory of God, he had meant that literally. So now He went on to fulfill that promise. Immediately Christ ordered, 'Take me to where you have laid him.'

"And Martha, always so practical, objected, 'But Lord, if you have in mind what I think you have in mind, it's impossible. You don't understand. You're being like all other prophets, impossibly visionary. My brother has already been dead four days. This is a hot country. Already his body has begun to decay.'

"But Jesus only looked at her in compassion. 'Martha, trust me. Didn't I tell you before that if you would only believe, you would see the glory of God?'

"So He marched to the door of the cave and asked that the stone be rolled away. He prayed. And then loudly, boldly, He commanded, 'Lazarus, come forth.'

"Try to imagine it. Suppose that I were able now to command Tom to rise up out of his coffin and to be reunited with his family. What kind of rejoicing do you think would be here in this Cove today? Wouldn't we all go wild with joy?

"So Mary and Martha, close beside Him, breathing hard in their excitement, watched wide-eyed. Yes, there was a stirring inside the tomb. Yes, they could hear sounds. The two sisters rushed closer to the mouth of the cave. It couldn't be true. But it was true. Their brother was struggling to stand upright.

"They dashed in, delirious with joy, at their heels their friends and neighbors. In the air around them was still the fetid air of the cave, the odor of decay. Feverishly, their hands all thumbs, they unwound the grave clothes, alternately laughing and weeping, weeping now for joy. Then they supported Lazarus, weak from lack of food, out of the cave where he stood blinking in wonderment at the sunlight.

"Then a mighty shout went up from the townsfolk— hallelujahs ... hosannas ... yells ... songs ... impromptu dances. And Martha, again the practical one, raced to the house to bring food to her brother.

"Jesus was no longer crying now. He too was rejoicing with His friends, laughing. 'Said I not unto thee that if thou wouldst believe, thou wouldst see the glory of God? You see, Mary? Understand now, Martha? My friendship is vindicated, isn't it? I didn't fail you. You have seen the glory of God this day. I shall never fail you, not ever, I promise you that.'

"Not then, not now. No, He doesn't fail His friends, 'Ye are my friends,' He said. He would be friends with *us* just as He was with Mary and Martha and Lazarus. He would stop in our homes too and tarry with us. Ah, but there was a condition: 'That ye do whatsoever I command thee ...' And this is His command, 'that ye love one another.'

335

If we had loved one another, as He loves us, Tom McHone would be alive today.

"So I want you to carry two thoughts away from this service: First, the Master cares. He suffers with us. He weeps when we weep. He aches when we ache. He cares.

"Second, we can have His friendship only if we are willing to let go our resentments and our bitterness and our hating and our feuding and our name-calling and our shooting and *love one another*. Tom McHone will not have died in vain, if finally we can drop the quarrels based on false pride, the petty differences that bring us sorrow and are not worthy of our Master.

"You see, my friends, bitterness is like a weed with a strong root growing in us, like the Spanish needles that harass us here. If we allow that root to get started, soon it will take over the heart and contaminate us, mind and spirit and body.

"But that does not have to happen. We can trust our Friend. He will root out the bitterness and fill up the hole where the root came out with His love—if we will let Him. 'I will never leave thee, nor forsake thee,' He promised. It is a sure promise.

"Let us talk to Him now in prayer."

It was easy to see that Miss Alice's words had had an effect on the people. There was soft weeping—but nothing else.

A square of white cambric, cut in a curious design as if with a first-grader's scissors, was now laid over Tom's face for the trip to the cemetery. Then the lid of the coffin was nailed on lightly. Usually the coffins were pulled on a sled or slung onto poles carried over the shoulders of several men, but we had loaned the new harvester wagon for today. All of us walked behind the wagon in a solemn procession.

How fervently I wished that I did not have to witness the interment. But there was no way to escape it. If I slipped out of the procession, I would be certain to be missed.

Finally we came in sight of the cemetery. None of the graves had headstones back in the Cove, for there was not the money here for that. There were only piles of stones at the head of the graves, sometimes with a tin can holding wildflowers stuck in the rocks. There were so many tiny graves of babies and young children. And the hole, the hideous hole with its freshly turned earth. Mountain superstition said that all graves had to be dug due east and west, with the face of the dead to the east. I did not know why, unless it was some sort of symbolism that the dead should face the rising of the sun.

The coffin was carefully lifted off the wagon and set by the grave. Then came a sound that I shall remember as long as I live—the screeching of the long nails as they were drawn out of the poplar wood.

The lid was lifted off, the cambric square removed so that the family could have a last look at Tom's face. One of his hands had slipped during the trip to the cemetery and had to be placed back on his chest. To me, the most awful custom of all was that each member of the family, even every child, was supposed to come forward in turn and kiss the lips of the dead person. Toot had to be lifted up to reach his father's face, I could not look at that, so I turned the other way and concentrated on the top of a magnificent hemlock on the hill opposite.

Suddenly, behind me, someone started a dirge in a loud wailing voice. Soft moans began. Soon they became screams. A cousin of Opal's keeled over in a faint, then another woman, one whom I did not know. What puzzled me about this performance was that the emotion could not be make-believe. I marveled that these highlanders, so reticent on other occasions, could exhibit so much emotion now.

Opal threw herself on the coffin. "Tom, Tom, darlin'. I can't let them put you in that ground. Tom—Tom, speak to me—Tom, I can't let you go. Tom, this can't be all!"

David stepped forward to pull Opal off and to support her. Speaking so loudly that he was shouting, he tried to drown out the dirge,

"I am the Resurrection and the Life.
He that believeth in Me, though he were dead yet shall he live. . . .
In My Father's house are many mansions. I go to prepare a place for you. If it were *not* so, I would have told you. . . ."

The dirge and the shouting were now a rising crescendo so that we could scarcely hear David's voice, though it had such resonance that usually it carried above any sound.

David signaled with his free hand. There was the sound of the coffin lid being nailed on, securely this time, then a soft thud as a group of men gently lowered it into the earth. Then the clods of earth falling, falling. Opal turned the other way, sobbing. She would not look. Another brief prayer—and then it was over.

In my heart I knew that I should go back to the McHone cabin and share Toot's corn-shuck bed for one more night. It was this night when Opal was going to need me most. But I was a coward. Still sounding in my ears was the screech of those nails being drawn out of the poplar wood. I slipped away, fled back to my room at the mission house.

Thirty

TOM'S MURDER cast gloom over the Cove. Immediately, incendiary feelings quieted down and there was a lull in all blockading. Perhaps Miss Alice's words at the funeral had had some effect; perhaps the highlanders were frightened at the results of their own passions.

Bird's-Eye and Nathan were still at large and had not, so far as we knew, returned to their homes. Lundy had crept back to school but would not speak of his father. Day by day, the boy looked more and more unkempt and wild-eyed.

Uncle Bogg McHone and David were both plunged into a deep trough of discouragement—oddly, more than Opal. She was still riding the crest of a wave of combined numbness and victory that I confess I did not understand at all. But for Uncle Bogg there was no victory. In his peculiar way, he had loved Tom above all his family. Now the old man would have to care for his ailing daughter-in-law and be responsible for Tom's children. With the killings striking into his immediate family for the first time, suddenly the county squire was seeing them in a new light. This might be one good result from Tom's death: The shoe was on the squire's foot now and the shoe pinched; the toothache was in the squire's mouth and he did not find the pain to his liking.

David's discouragement was of a different order. There was a sense in which he felt responsible for Tom's death. Perhaps, he lashed himself, if he had not pressed so relentlessly against the moonshining, Tom might still be alive.

Miss Alice was so concerned about David that she postponed her regular monthly trip to Cataleechie to stay close at hand. I watched her use conversations at mealtimes and every opening she saw to try to get through to

David. "You know, David, we're out to win people, not war with them."

A favorite Quaker word often on her lips was "reconciliation"—reconciliation between man and God, between man and man. Her view was that we at the mission had laid on us an infinitely larger task than finding and hacking up stills: that was, creating an atmosphere in which men's hearts could be changed so that they would want a better way of life than "followin' stillin'" represented. "Clean up a pigsty," she commented one evening, "and if the creatures in it still have pig-minds and pig-desires, soon it will be the same old pigsty again. Preach the gospel, David, teach it, preach to the hearts of men. That's your business. Then the fruits, including the reforms in other areas, will follow *as fruits*. But it's no good tying apples onto a tree. Soon they'll be rotting apples."

David did not agree with this. "You weren't at the Holt Working to hear, Miss Alice, but that's exactly what Bird's-Eye hurled at me: 'Preacher, keep your religion inside a cupboard in the church house. Don't you dare take it beyond the church door.' You say, 'Preach and teach.' Sure. Fine. I have been. I intend to. But what's wrong with preaching the gospel and cleaning up the pigsty at the same time? Why should I put on blinkers to walk by the pigsty? Besides, I don't agree that if I preach and do nothing else, men's hearts are automatically going to be changed and then they're automatically going to want to do the right thing. No, ma'am! Not by a long shot!"

Miss Alice smiled at his vehemence, then patiently, quietly reasoned out her concept from yet another angle. "David, I hate blockade-running and murders as much as you do. It hurts to think that because back in February, Tom McHone decided to try blockading for some quick cash, Opal will never again hear his footfall crossing the yard or mounting the steps. And the McHone children— how could either of us ever forget their stricken faces? So, David, your aim and mine are the same. The only question is, what's the surest and quickest way of arriving at that same end?"

"But Miss Alice," David countered, "isn't this 'religion-in-the-cupboard philosophy' the very reason that good church members could carry on the slave trade, operate sweat shops and underwrite child labor, reap a golden harvest from shameful slum dwellings they own themselves? They shut their eyes to the evils around them.

340

You're virtually asking me to shut my eyes to the blockading. The ministry has had enough of winking and blinking. So help me, I will not be a part of it!"

"The question at issue, David, is how to get rid of the evil in men. Attacking corruption in the environment won't do it. That's like cutting weeds in a field. In a fortnight the weeds will be grown again. And attacking the men themselves won't work either. Whatever separates men from love can't be of God."

Though David was stubborn, at last humbly, he asked the question Miss Alice must have been wanting him to ask, "Well then, how can we deal with evil?"

"By demonstrating to people a way that's more powerful than evil. And that's good news! Let's get on with living and teaching and preaching that good news with all the verve and enthusiasm we have."

"Then," David said, "if that's the technique, why aren't people changed more drastically by today's preaching?"

"Could be because we don't often have the courage to give the good news to people straight. Most of us are still talking religious theory that we haven't begun living, and talking in wornout clichés at that. A watered-down message is as futile as applying rose water to a cancer. When your heart is ablaze with the love of God, when you love other people—especially the rip-snorting sinners—so much that you dare to tell them about Jesus with no apologies, then never fear, there will be results. One of two things will happen. Either there'll be persecutions, or the fire will leap from your heart to catch and blaze in the depths of other men's beings. I've watched the process over and over. And then when the blaze starts, the reforms will follow as surely as the flower follows the bud, or the fruit comes after the blossom on the tree."

"It's too slow a way."

"No, David, it isn't too slow a way. The other is no way at all."

Actually, though David was not ready to admit it to Miss Alice, her thoughts had made an impression on him. He and I talked about the two ideas that were eating at us both: "Love God, love people! If the love of Jesus is ablaze in your heart, if you love even the old reprobate sinners enough ..." David and I agreed that we did not yet have that kind of love. Nor could we manufacture love in ourselves.

The second enigma followed the first. David suspected

that he did not yet know *how* to preach or what to preach so that people's hearts would be ignited and changed. I wondered how many preachers did know? And in that case, what could they do except fall back on building programs, creating more church organizations, appointing more committees, calling more meetings, plunging into (what was that new term?) "social service work"—all of the busy-busy church activities for which Miss Alice had a delightful tag: "digging worms instead of fishing."

TWO NIGHTS after that David asked me, "Anywhere you and I could talk?"

"If you mean without an audience," I answered, "outdoors is the only place I can think of."

Outside it was foggy with not many stars to be seen. Even the mountains were blotted out by the swirling mists. David began abruptly. "Christy, I've been thinking—you know, I'm not a bit sure that I belong in the ministry."

"David! How can you say that! You're just discouraged, that's all."

"No, this isn't just a mood, Christy. Remember you asked me why I came to Cutter Gap? Well, that started me thinking. Why am I in the ministry at all?"

"David, you've been through so much lately. This just isn't the right time to think of things like that. It's bound to be colored by all that's happened."

"No, that isn't it. You see, entering seminary wasn't entirely my choice. It was too much my mother's and sisters' decision. Mother's always been determined that one of her three sons would be a preacher. My two older brothers went into business. That left me. So from the time I was a little boy, it was assumed that I would be a preacher. I let myself be stampeded, that's all. That's not a good enough reason."

Somehow I was not too surprised at this news that his mother and sisters had pressured his choices, but I could not say that. "Well, no, of course it isn't a good enough reason." I was groping my way. "But David, sometimes—just occasionally—a mother's choice might be the one a son would make if left to himself."

"Maybe. One chance in a million. So you're on their side too."

"Of course not! I'm not taking anybody's side."

David had been holding the fingers of my right hand as

342

we walked along. He said nothing for a moment, only his fingers tightened on my hand. "But I do want you to take somebody's side—mine," he said.

"But David, you yourself don't know which side you're on. You've just said so. So all I can do is try to help you find answers—and wait."

"It's come to me recently, Christy, how much I need you. I'm going to need you always. Do you know that? In the ministry, out of the ministry, no matter what I'll be doing, I'll need you. I'm asking you to marry me, Christy. And this isn't any sudden impulse idea either."

I stood in the road staring at him, not knowing what to say, too astonished to say anything.

In the silence, he leaned over and kissed me lightly, gently. But then he pulled me to him and kissed me harder full on the mouth.

"It's all right, Christy. Speech isn't necessary between you and me. Anyway, I don't want you to give me an answer tonight because it might be 'No.' "

I was awake into the small hours of the morning, excited and yet puzzled about David's proposal. How often I had dreamed of that tender moment in my future! In my mind it had always been in a romantic setting like a rose garden or a summerhouse, and I would be dressed in white, perhaps with a flower in my hair. And the man would be dashing and so tender, and he would speak beautiful words. There would be nothing prosaic about his proposal. What was it Miss Alice had said to me the other day? "Christy, thee is inclined to think of the poetry side of things, not the prose side." Lying there, remembering my daydream pictures, I smiled to think how well Miss Alice understood me.

David's proposal had been so different from the imagined one. As we had walked back to the mission house, I had expected him to kiss me good-night, but he had not. He had only given me an intense look followed by the usual, "Have a good sleep, Christy." Then from the other side of the screen door I had stood in the darkened hall watching his broad back disappear over the hill in the swirling mist. What was there in this man that I could not yet understand?

There was something tentative and indefinite in his approach to life. He had asked me to marry him and yet, it had been a strange half-commitment of himself. It

343

reminded me of David's attitude about the moonshining. He had preached that thundering sermon against it, yet there had been a certain lack of follow-through in actions.

Yet David was seven years older than I, old enough to begin to know what he wanted out of life. But he did not seem to know. He had come to the Cove at the suggestion of his seminary. Tonight he had told me that he had entered the ministry because his mother and sisters had expected it. So naturally, he was puzzled about where he belonged. Was that the reason he could not commit himself fully to anything?

"Christy, be on my side," he had said. But he had no side—yet. Perhaps part of the feeling of destiny that had driven me to the Cove was not only for myself but to help David too. Was my future bound up with David's? That was what I had to find out.

Thirty-one

THOUGH Fairlight Spencer's formal reading lessons were finished, I was still seeing her once or twice a week. Miss Alice encouraged this, though she and I both guessed that some of the women in the Cove might be jealous of my singling out Fairlight.

At first Fairlight had difficulty believing that I enjoyed her for herself and not because I thought it my duty to help her or from some other motive.

She admired me extravagantly, beyond any deserving. And if I—the girl from "yan"—cared about her enough to single her out to spend long hours with her, well then, perhaps that secret person on the inside, who from shyness and deprivation had kept herself so covertly hidden all these years, was a woman worth knowing. This gave Fairlight the courage gradually to let her true self out of prison.

Having tasted freedom, she was certain that the world of knowledge and beauty was hers for the taking. And because she gave me full credit for laying the world at her feet, she could not find enough ways to express her gratitude. Sometimes it would be a bunch of wild flowers on my desk at school. A homemade basket lined with galax leaves and filled with wild berries or fresh eggs might be left at the mission door for me. On occasion it would be a jar of wild blackberry jelly or a honeycomb or a poem she had laboriously copied out. Once I unfolded a scrap of paper to find written on it:

I love you for what you are making of me.
I love you for what I am when I am with you.

On another day she left me a tiny basket lined with moss containing portions of three robin's egg shells. I got the message: Fairlight wanted me to share her enjoyment of that delicate robin's-egg blue color against the green.

Now she was able to identify with her children in their schoolwork. She cajoled Zady or Clara or John into reading their lessons aloud while she was cooking or sewing or sweeping the floor. Though the children teased her about this and sometimes mildly protested, they humored her because, secretly, they were proud that their mother had learned so quickly.

Since school would soon be dismissed for the long summer-autumn holiday, I was tapering off lesson assignments. This gave more time for Fairlight and me to take a few hours off to explore the woods and mountains. She did not hesitate to leave her children during daylight hours. They were surprisingly self-sufficient, accustomed to roaming and playing by themselves, and the older girls could be trusted to take care of the "Least'un."

Fairlight would cut three fresh whistles from the willow trees along the creek, leave one with Lulu, the eight-year-old, one with the youngest, and one with whichever older child had been elected "keeper" for the day. "Here y'are, Clara. One for you, Lulu—stop your bawlin'. I'm afixin' one for you too."

At that point Lulu would already have the whistle to her mouth, tooting shrilly. "Purtiest whistle you ever made, Maw."

"Mainly so. Now Clara, when you cain't spy Lulu or the Least'un, I'm countin' on you to blow the whistle hard and go after 'em in a hip and a hurry. Hear me?"

"Yes. Shorely, Maw. Where ye started, Maw? You goin' fishin' today?"

"No, jest a traipsin' trip. But Miz Christy and I mought go a-berryin'."

And so we would be off with our picnic food packed in one of Fairlight's homemade honeysuckle baskets.

I might never have discovered who I really was or have gotten answers to the relentless questions that had driven me to the Cove without those quiet hours spent with Fairlight in the mountains. I do not know why it is that an intimate contact with wild life and a personal observation of nature helps so much in this self-discovery. But that it is so, I have seen in other people's lives as well as my own. Not that my hometown Asheville was such a large city. Perhaps it is just that even a small city provides artificial distractions which separate us from the roots of our life; even a few bricks and a little macadam are a shield between us and the wisdom that nature has to give.

But there was no macadam in the world of Cutter Gap. And there was Fairlight who had so much to teach me: where the delicate pink lady's-slippers grew; where the best huckleberry balds were for berries for her juicy pies; that when the jay-birds were "a-hollerin' and raisin' a scrapin'-fuss, it was a-clabberin' up for bad weather", how to make a superior fishing line out of plaited horse hair—one that would not tangle when caught in branches overhanging the stream; and some spots for brook trout so good that we never failed to bring fish back home.

I reveled in all this. Each time the two of us went out, it became a game with me to find a picnic spot more delightful than the last one. My favorites were always beside one of those clear mountain streams. We would hear the music of the tumbling water in the distance and make our way toward it over a woodland carpet of pine needles inches thick, or down the incline of a narrow, ill-defined path winding between huckleberry bushes, skirting the boulders. If there happened to be a weeping willow overhanging the water, then for me this was a spot out of a dream.

Most of these were shallow streams, but always with the water rushing and rollicking, so clear that every pebble on the bottom was magnified. Baby trout playing tag in and out of the rocks could be seen as plainly as if they were swimming under glass. The sun sifting through moving branches overhead would splinter the light into diamonds on the water, tossing them back into my eyes with such magic that I would want to shout and dance just for the joy of living—and usually did. Fairlight understood. She always understood.

Then like a couple of children we would toss off our shoes to wade, tying our skirts around our waists with a belt or a string, and go squealing into that achingly cold water. Tired and dusty feet would cool off in a hurry; in minutes we would be blue to the ankles. We would dry our toes luxuriously on moss or in a bed of ferns and proceed to the selection of that perfect flat rock for our picnic table. If watercress and mint, sometimes even wild strawberries or raspberries, happened to be growing nearby these could always be worked into our menu. The delicate cress washed clean would be added to our sand-

347

wiches. The strawberries or raspberries mounded on large clean galax leaves would be our dessert.

If we found a spring nearby, Fairlight taught me to pick a few sprigs of mint, wash it, chew it thoroughly; then when my taste buds had been refreshed by the mint, take a drink of the spring water. Most mountain water was superb but this mint appetizer surely made it the longest, coolest, most delicious drink of water in the world! I often thought that it should have been served in a silver goblet.

The noon meal over, sometimes we would doze off lying on the moss or the fragrant pine needles, or just lie there looking up at the sky through the trees. Neither of us felt uneasy about not talking.

These days, more often than not, I would lie there thinking about David. Over and over I had relived those moments that night when he had first kissed me. Since then there had been little chance for conversation between us. Wistfully, I wondered if men were always taciturn in romantic situations. In the love stories that I had read the hero always poured out his heart to the maiden and won her with eloquence and passion. Secretly I had hoped that the man of my dreams would approach me like that. Well, romance in books and in real life was obviously not the same.

So far David had acted more like the boys at home than the men in the stories: quick to demonstrate feelings and slow to commit anything to words. I remembered how my friends and I in high school and junior college had puzzled about this masculine trait.

We girls wanted to talk, wanted to know what the boy was thinking too. We felt cheated when males suddenly became uncommunicative just because they were feeling romantic, as if the effort to kiss you took all their concentration.

David was falling in love with me, I could tell. He reached for my hand whenever we were alone—which was not very often. Recent developments had put all of us under abnormal pressure, so there were but fleeting moments for a whispered conversation. After kissing me, I knew David would look for ways to take more walks.

If only he would tell me more about himself! He liked to joke and tease, but he was so reluctant to discuss serious matters. I enjoyed the light banter, but love needed more than that to grow and flourish.

348

As I lay there on the pine needles, a fluffy white cloud bank floated into view. The top of it looked almost like a man's head. Why was I thinking about men so much these days?

Then I became aware of the forest sounds: the rustling of the tree tops swaying in a gentle breeze; the tinkle of a cowbell somewhere in the distance; the antiphonal trilling melodies of the tiny brown winter wrens; the nesting purple martins making a queer gravelly noise deep in their throats; and always, always the background music of the water.

I turned over and lay on my stomach and looked at Fairlight. She was not sleeping, but she was so silent. I had learned by now that stillness was a part of these mountain people. I lay there studying Fairlight's face in repose. She looked tranquil enough. Little did I realize at the time what depths there were underneath the tranquility, or that it was not altogether a reposeful peace, nor in what particular way Fairlight needed my help, though she did not know how to reveal all this.

Increasingly I glimpsed facets of this woman for which I had no adequate explanation. How is it that sometimes out of some slag-heap of an environment there emerges a boy or girl who demonstrates almost aristocratic refinement? From my junior college literature course I remembered that one such had been immortalized by William Wordsworth when as a young man of thirty-three on a walking tour into Scotland with his sister Dorothy and Coleridge, he had spied a peasant princess:

> Sweet Highland Girl, a very shower
> Of beauty is thy earthly dower! . . .
> Thou wearest upon thy forehead clear
> The freedom of a Mountaineer: . . .
> And seemliness complete, that sways
> Thy courtesies, about thee plays; . . .
> That gives thy gestures grace and life! . . .

"The freedom of a Mountaineer . . ." Fairlight was teaching me. But even in those pleasant valleys, I hungered for the heights. Upwards, upwards my eyes would rove to the necklace of deep blue-green near the top of each summit. I wondered why the mountains were clothed with successive bands of varying shades of green, not clearly outlined, but serrated and undulating, with one shade of green licking in long narrow tongues into the next shade. And was that black-green belt a tall forest of spruce-firs? And what would it be like to walk those emerald aisles? I had to know.

The first time I expressed this to Fairlight, she protested even as she made ready to humor me, "But Miz Christy, that knob, it's a fern'ist piece, more'n four good looks and a right smart walk." But we struck out anyway across country seeking the base of the mountain, through scrub woods—she-holly and he-holly, sweet-gum, redbud, and persimmon trees.

From there, I was surprised that the trail wound upwards so slowly, conservatively following the contour of the land. Would it not have been more like real mountain-climbing to go straight up over the face of the mountain? That showed how ignorant I was. For we still had several thousand feet to climb, and even on this easy contour path, pebbles were sliding out from under our feet, and I found myself reaching for the edge of an outcropping rock or for a rhododendron or laurel bush to hang onto.

Here there were some buckeyes and black locust trees, some second-stand tulip trees, magnolias, and pines—what Fairlight called "spruce-pines." Blackberry bushes and thorns and briers slashed at our faces as we stumbled over roots in the path. And though I was in better physical condition than ever in my life, the calves of my legs were soon aching.

At that point, Fairlight said, "Time to lay off and rest yerself." Much of the mountain still towered over us; we had achieved little more than its shank. Then why all this effort? For what? For my pride, I guess it was, at least that first time. I was not going to let any mountain defeat me.

Even on that first climb I discovered the truth of the race knowledge about a "second wind." When I thought that my panting lungs and my aching legs were finished for that day, suddenly I was handed new strength. It was like turning in my old self and being handed a fresh self. Or like boring through unproductive rock and striking suddenly a freshet of water. I had read about this second wind in the case of athletes, especially runners, but to experience it for myself was a wondrous thing.

So, revived, we plunged on through the belt of hardwood trees—the sugar maples and beeches, yellow birches, lindens, and horse chestnuts. From there we made the final push into the blue-green cathedral that we had seen from a distance, the fragrant groves of balsam and red cedar. It was a sylvan, fairy place as entrancing as I had pictured it. Cloud mist drifted overhead. Only an occasional shaft of light struck through the tall trees. Underfoot there was a clean carpet of bracken with delicate lichens and mosses everywhere. At any moment I expected to see a troupe of elves holding a conclave.

Then suddenly, we left the fairy wood behind to cross a tiny sub-alpine meadow. From far away, this had looked smooth and pale green; but now, we could see, it was not smooth at all, but full of tangled growth, hard to get through, with Queen Anne's Lace and a red flower that I did not know among the bushes.

And then—at last—the top, and that feeling of achievement at having the world at one's feet. I lay flat on my stomach, inching as close as I dared to the edge of the rock shelf, letting my eyes drink in the thundering wave upon wave of verdant green and smoky blue spread out below. The primordial splendor would tolerate no pettiness; majesty and power spoke their own language.

Fairlight was somewhere behind me, sitting hugging her knees, silent, not wanting to interrupt my thoughts.

I might have felt unimportant pitted against the awesome might of the mountains. I did not. Rather, on that mountain top I found something important that I had never known before: an awareness of a vital connection between me and the Authority behind all this beauty.

I remembered my conversation with Dr. MacNeill that afternoon in my schoolroom. He had said that he believed in some "starter-force" but that he could not credit a loving God with concern for individuals. But the "starter-force" behind the magnificence displayed before my wondering eyes had an authority behind it that could be no abstraction, for it had immediacy—known and felt. Now I knew how to answer the Doctor's question. Call this what you might—"starter-force," "God," "Father"—it was personal all right. It thrust deep into me. It pulled. And it insisted that life was precious—all of life—Fairlight and I, and every bird and every squirrel and every tree reaching through its forest cover for the light. It cried that all effort was worthwhile; that doubt and fear and discouragement were a desecration of beauty, that hope was always right. It insisted that small achievement was not

351

enough; that hopes and dreams must be large enough to stand up beside those soaring summits and not once bow their heads in shame.

I KNEW that the lessons learned on the mountain-top had to be lived out in the valley. One day as Fairlight and I were on our way home an idea came to me. On our rambles Fairlight was forever pointing out to me an amazing variety of edible wild plants—fruits, nuts, and berries. My idea had to do with experimenting with these wild products for more nutritious and imaginative cooking. Fairlight obviously had a longing for better homemaking skills. She already had an herb garden but she used the herbs more for doctoring than for cooking.

Not that I knew enough about cooking or any kindred subject to teach it. My mother would have hooted at the idea! But until the mission got that other full-time worker to set up a program of adult education, perhaps Fairlight and I could make a start in her kitchen and thus interest some of the other women.

My friend was immediately enthusiastic about the idea, and our first product "that didn't cost no cash-money" turned out to be no farther away than the Spencer backyard—honey from Jeb Spencer's bee-gums. There were thirty or so of the bee-gums, some of them set back under the cherry and plum trees, but most out in the sunlight near the tall double yellow hollyhocks along the rustic fence.

The bee-gums were queer-looking objects, simply constructed out of two sections of hollow basswood logs set on end with a flat board over the top. Basswood was used because it did not crack under weathering like other woods.

Many of the mountain cabins had one or two gums in the yard for honey for the family's use, but only Jeb had so many. Rather by accident he had discovered some years previously that sourwood honey was not only "choice eatin'" to the mountain man, but also prized by epicures all over the world. Connoisseurs of honey ranked it with the rare wild thyme honey of Greece or the heather honey of Scotland. Like those other rare honeys, there was never enough supply for the demand so they were willing to pay dearly for it. Jeb had been clever enough to see in sourwood honey a source of income for his family, so each year he had added a few more gums.

It was in this month, July, that the sourwood tree bloomed, holding up proud candelabra of cream-colored blossoms, delicately fragrant. I learned that bees too have connoisseur tastes. So long as there is a sourwood in bloom, they will scarcely notice anything else—leaving strictly alone the locust and doghobble blossoms around which they ordinarily would have been swarming—and work tirelessly until their gums are filled with this finest of honeys. By the end of July, Jeb could usually market two hundred pounds of sourwood honey which he carried out of the Cove in huge lard cans.

All of us enjoyed watching Jeb gather the honey. His first preparation was always a hot soapy bath and clean clothes. "Bees are the cleanest critters there is," Jeb explained to me. "They'll sting you to kingdom-come if'n ye be sweaty and dirty. A man can learn a heap from bees, learn from 'em all his life long."

Once dressed in clean clothes, Jeb covered his face with a meal sieve sewed to his hat, his hands with homemade gauntlet gloves. Each pants leg was tied by a string around his ankles.

The "smoker" was an old bellows in which Jeb put rags which he set on fire. Thus he would smoke the bees into the bottom of the hive and take the honey from the top combs.

Fairlight and I experimented with the honey Jeb left to us until we could use it for her two favorite desserts— stack cake and sweet-potato pie—without any of the sugar which had to be bought with cash. Soon the Spencer children were also smacking their lips over baked acorn squash, the centers filled with honey and spices.

As we went further afield, Fairlight would tell me about the edible plants. Then I would set my imagination to work as to how they might be used in dishes already known and loved—or in new ones. The woods gradually yielded secrets: that the young shoots of bellwort in May and June were as good as asparagus; that if the fronds of ferns were gathered before the leaves had uncurled or before there was any down, and were boiled gently in salted water, they were as tasty as any garden vegetable; that juniper berries—holding in themselves an essence of the aroma of the woods—could give spectacular flavor to meats; that crabapple yielded a different and refreshing cider; that the sour fruit of mountain ash or sumac berries made a summer drink; that hazelnut cake was an oh, so wonderful dessert.

It was Fairlight who, inspired by all that we were doing, worked out an improvement on cooking the possum that Jeb and John were forever bringing home: she stuffed the possum with chestnuts. And then she thought up a cream of chestnut soup made with a pinch of thyme in it, so delightful that it could have graced the finest Paris restaurant. We found that lentils should always be cooked with a bit of marjoram, and that both wild mushrooms and young green sorrel made savory soups.

To green salads (important because the mountain diet was short on fresh greens) the woods lent delightful taste surprises: watercress and American brooklime, English smartweed, saxifrage lettuce, and slender pigweed—what Fairlight called "Keerless."

The Spencer children, like all children, were at first wary of new dishes. Perhaps it was my delight in some of their favorite foods that helped them to begin thinking of food as an adventure. It was at the Spencers' that I did my first churning in Fairlight's old wooden dash churn, and cultivated a taste for clabber sprinkled with sugar.

There was no need to cultivate a taste for gritted bread made from freshly grated corn; it was love at first meeting. And what could equal the fun of picking wild gooseberries, blackberries, and huckleberries, making them into ambrosial jams and jellies, and watching the glass jars fill up kitchen shelves? But what I liked best of all was also the simplest: homemade bread broken into pieces in a glass, covered with cold milk, and eaten with a spoon.

Making apple butter in the big black pot in the yard over a hickory-fed fire was a family project. The bubbling and popping mixture fragrant with the goodness of red apples combined with sugar and spices, had literally to be stirred all day, for apple butter burns quickly. So we would take turns at the long wooden paddle while Jeb brought out his dulcimer and the rest of us sang ballads:

As I went a-walkin' to breathe the pleasant air,
Rolly-trudum, trudum, trudum-rolly-day,
As I went out to breathe the pleasant air,
I saw a lady talkin' to her daughter fair,

Rolly-trudum, trudum, trudum-rolly-day. . . .

Oh, if you was to marry, who would be your man,
Rolly-trudum, trudum, trudum-rolly-day,
Oh, if you was to marry, who would be your man?
"I love a handsome farmer and his name is—Sam,"
Rolly-trudum, trudum, trudum-rolly-day. . . .

The stirring did not seem like work at all so long as we were singing, "Rolly-trudum, trudum-rolly-day—"

But Fairlight and I did not stop with canning and cooking. We also made window curtains out of flour sacks, the first curtains that the Spencers had ever had. Soon there were flour-sack curtains at many windows in the Cove, for all the women were watching our activities.

One afternoon Fairlight had been up to the loft to fetch onions and dried apples. She came down bringing under one arm an old book. "The Compt book," she said, thrusting it at me.

"The what?"

"Compt book. Have a look."

I took the book curiously, having never heard the word "compt" before. It was a very old book covered with rawhide, sewn together with thread with hinges of rawhide thongs. The paper was rough, the entire book written in longhand, the brown ink faded, in some places faded out. On the first page was the notation "1702" and then "Alexander Malcombe Morrison, at Achinhoar, Argyllshire."

I was immediately engrossed in the pages covered with a meticulous spidery script. It took me a while to figure out that the book was a sort of estate journal, a Scottish laird's records of day-by-day business transactions—how much "Silver rent" he had collected; the buying of "five tydie Cows with three Stirks"; the selling of "Seven pecks meall"; etc., etc.

The first ten pages or so had actually been written in Latin. Then abruptly, that had been dropped for English, only English with antique spelling.

Immediately I was aching with curiosity. "Fairlight, where did you get this book?"

"When I married Jeb, my mama give it to me. Said I mought as well take it along with the coverlids and the three silver spoons."

"This was in your family then?"

355

"Shorely so. My name was Morrison."

"And Alexander, who wrote the Compt book, was an ancestor of yours?"

"Rightly so—"

But it was soon obvious that Fairlight knew little more of the family history, so I borrowed the book and pored over it eagerly to see what I could discover. The entries had begun in 1702 and had ended in 1747 with three blank pages left. Judging from the rents collected, the laird had owned large acreage and also some ships. He had had four daughters and two sons, for whom he recorded payment to a tutor, a retired cleric. He was prosperous enough to buy "fyne shurts and cravats" a dozen or so at a time. There were several references to His Grace, the Duke of Argyll, who had apparently been an adjacent landowner and with whom Alexander had had frequent business dealings.

The laird must have kept the Compt book in his saddlebags and have made entries in it as he rode over his land. Apparently he did not trust his memory and, besides, he had been a methodical business man who recorded every penny—whether in "Scots money" or Sterling.

One page was headed:

Rentall Crop and Martimas 1703 years

Reed from Gilbert McShenoig full and compleat payment for Crop and Martimas—29:04:04

Or on over in the book . . .

Apryll third Day, 1711–Then counted and delivered of sheep and muttons to Donald Dugald my heard Fourscore and two wt ane Ram grof yr is eight yt has lambs and 4 to lamb. In all—86.

And as I flipped over to the next to the last entry made, I was startled to see the name "Neil MacNeill."

March 1747–Bought from Neil MacNeill of Barra ane Kow at Seventeen mrks qch and ane bull qch. he is to deliver me att whit-Sunday next.

Of course I wondered about the sudden cessation of the entries in 1747. Was that the date on which Fairlight's ancestor had sailed for the New World? And why? Obviously he had had a good life in Scotland, for the Compt book spoke of wine and mutton and seed, and "blanketting musline," "linene napkins," even "ane pair pumps for the maid." Was Alexander one of those whose lands had been confiscated by the English after Culloden?

I sat a long while holding the open book, reading ... picturing in my mind ... wondering.

Fairlight and I had been fishing and were on our way home through the edge of the Holcombes' land. The way was steeply downhill, and we were approaching a huge boulder to one side of the path. Suddenly my eyes caught movement and I realized that a man's shoulders were sliding along the far side of the boulder.

Fairlight saw it too and grabbed my arm. "Looky, I spy—" But she was never able to finish the sentence. The figure was standing directly in our path. It was Bird's-Eye Taylor. Involuntarily I drew back.

"Don't aim to do ye no harm." He looked the same as always—the inevitable gun in his hands, the dirty felt hat pulled down over his eyes—except that he had let his black beard grow. He was holding out a piece of folded grubby paper. "I'd be beholden, if'n ye'd give this here to Opal." Forcibly he shoved the paper into my hands. "And thank ye kindly." And he disappeared around the boulder.

When Fairlight and I had recovered from our surprise, we agreed that we should tell no one except Opal of this episode: it would not help matters for people to know that Bird's-Eye was back in the Cove. Then I left Fairlight and struck out with the note for the McHone cabin.

An hour later when I handed the note to Opal, her first reaction was pleased surprise that anyone would write a letter to her. "First letter ever I had," she said wonderingly. "I be that glad, Miz Christy, that ye thoughted me to start readin' afore this." And she went off into a corner to try to decipher the note for herself.

For several minutes, I talked to Toot and Vincent, now and again glancing over at Opal. Letter by letter, she was laboriously trying to spell out the words. Finally she gave it up and came back to me. "Can't rightly make hit all out," she sighed. "Reckon, Miz Christy, ye'd best read hit aloud to me." So I took it and read

Opal—it was not me that kilt Tom. When I can cum back safe I will tell it to you how it was. A friend writ this for me.

X BT

I looked at Opal. Her eyes were filled with tears.

Thirty-two

THAT MORNING I awoke with the dawn. For a moment I let myself luxuriate in half-drowsiness, enjoying the air, so deliciously fresh and cool, pouring in through the open windows. Then I remembered, there was something special about this day. Oh yes, the last day of school, the closing exercises towards which we had been working so long.

My mind went back to that snowy January morning when the schoolchildren and I had first met, back to that moment when they had stood in tight little clusters staring at me. So much had happened to them and to me in those seven months—prickings and problems, disappointments and triumphs. I hoped that the program today would be a showcase for some of the victories. If only my mischievous boys would behave for this one day. And if only stage fright did not blank out memory work at critical moments.

We were attempting a great deal, going far beyond the customary closing exercises: a few recitations, perhaps a cross-spelling bee, with the teacher providing a treat such as twenty-five cents worth of hoarhound drops or peppermint sticks. In the light of recent events in Cutter Gap, Miss Alice, David and I had felt that we needed to use this last day of school to try to pull the Cove people closer together. Thus every pupil was to have some part in the program and all parents had been invited.

Two prizes were to be given: one for the pupil with the highest marks in all subjects; the other for the child who had memorized and could recite correctly the greatest number of verses of Scripture. There would be refreshments for all—blackberry shrub and cakes and cookies. All of my children had been roaming the mountains gathering the blackberries, and Miss Ida, Ruby Mae,

Bessie Coburn, Fairlight Spencer and her daughter Clara had been baking for several days.

After breakfast, I went on over to the schoolroom early to be certain that everything was in order. To my consternation, some of the parents and children were already arriving. There was the Beck family and all of the Allens, including Little Burl who was well and bouncy again, and Creed with his pet raccoon sitting on his shoulder. Creed had never lost sight of the pact I had made with him that first day of school.

"Miz Christy, this school is a sight to behold," Lenore Beck enthused. "My eyes are just a-stickin' out for lookin'."

"I holped sweep the floor, Maw," Joshua Bean Beck bragged.

But his brother Andrew was not to be outdone. "Yes, but Maw, I'm the one that fetched some of them Turk's-cap lilies."

It was true that the schoolroom had never been so clean and garnished. My pupils and I had even washed the windows and then had decorated the room with rhododendron leaves, fronds of cinnamon ferns and the wild lilies and branches of red elderberry bushes picked high in the mountains. In between the leaves and ferns, I had tacked up the best work of the term: the nicest drawings and maps; the themes with the highest grades; some extraordinary Latin translations and arithmetic papers.

"Since we're going to have such a big crowd," I said to the two fathers, "would you men raise the windows for me?"

"Glad to accommodate ye," Will Beck answered. Even as he spoke, Lundy Taylor sauntered in and came directly to me. "Fotched ye a present, Teacher." He handed me a tin pail of huckleberries. There was a smirk on his face as he leaned close. "Picked them myself—for you."

There was no mistaking it, the smell of liquor on Lundy's breath. "Thanks, Lundy," I said automatically. "Maybe we can have a huckleberry pie or—something." I wondered what I should do. If I told David, there might be a scene, and I could not bear the thought of anything spoiling this day. I decided not to say anything and hope that Lundy would not tangle with anyone or make a fool of himself. I had been nervous enough about how my pupils would perform; now with this complication, the butterflies in my stomach reminded me of that first day of school. But Lundy went to his usual seat and sat down docilely.

Within twenty minutes the room was crowded to the doors with parents standing along the walls, many of them wearing their missionary-barrel clothes. Miss Alice was there, and even Miss Ida had decided to come. She was dressed in her best black taffeta buttoned high on her neck, sitting in a chair which David had carried over for her.

David opened the program with a greeting to everyone: "Mothers and fathers, boys and girls—this is a big day for our school. We're proud of what we've accomplished, and you can be proud of your children. After the exercises are over, during the refreshment period, we hope that you will wander around and look carefully at the samples of the work posted on the walls. And now, first on our program is a welcome from Mountie O'Teale."

The Mountie who came forward to stand in front of the room was a different child from the defeated Mountie of seven months ago. She was dressed in a clean starched gingham dress, her hair neatly combed, her eyes sparkling with excitement. She spoke slowly. "Fathers and mothers— we are glad you—have come today. We hope—you like— our program. We hope—that you have—a good time." Not a single lisp. Not a stutter! It was a proud moment for Mountie and for me. The little girl looked at me triumphantly, adoration in her eyes. I knew that she could scarcely restrain herself from running and throwing herself into my arms. I smiled back, forming the word "Good!" with my lips.

Then all the children rose and filed to the front of the room to sing a favorite song, "Smiles," followed by "America" (which I had finally taught them), and then the ballad they loved best, "Sourwood Mountain."

After that, all went back to their seats except nine especially chosen first, second, and third graders. These children stood in a row and each brought forward, from behind his back, a large sheet of paper with one letter printed on it. All of the letters together spelled, "OUR SCHOOL." Beginning at the first O, they recited in turn:

Vella Holt: O stands for oblige. We're much obliged for yer comin today.

Joshua Bean: U stands for united—all together.

Mary O'Teale: R stands for reading, one of the subjects we like best.

Lulu Spencer: S stands for studying. That's what we do here.

Little Burl: C stands for cheerful. We are.

Sam Houston: H stands for helping.

Jake Holt: O stands for others. Helping others.

Della May: O stands for obey too.

Toot McHone: L stands for learning. For laughter too.

Then they said in unison, "Much obliged for comin' to *our school.*"

The audience applauded enthusiastically, and the children, very proud of themselves, sat down.

Then I called on them one by one for the poem or oration or whatever bit of performance they had chosen. They enjoyed "speak pieces" as they called them, and it had seemed best to allow them latitude in their selections. But as one followed another, I began to think that perhaps I had given too little supervision because there was wild variety. "Excelsior" was top choice, with three pupils reciting it. The drama of Longfellow's poem fascinated them—the runner through the Alpine villages, found later at daybreak by the monks of Saint Bernard, half-buried in the snow, "still grasping in his hand of ice" that banner "Excelsior." The audience clapped loudly each time.

Dick Holt had memorized Stevenson's

> Dark brown is the river
> Golden is the sand . . .

from *A Child's Garden of Verses*. Bessie Coburn, who currently had a love affair with Shakespeare's sonnets, recited:

> "When, in disgrace with fortune and men's eyes,
> I all alone beweep my outcast state,
> And trouble deaf heaven with my bootless cries,
> And look upon myself and curse my fate. . . ."

But then Larmie Holt, not quite nine, stood up and intoned solemnly:

> "Ashes to ashes
> Dust to dust,
> We've all said something,
> I reckon I must—"

and sat down. To my surprise, the people applauded, but did not laugh. I never would understand what they considered funny.

"And Smith O'Teale is next," I announced.

Smith started in bravely on "O Captain! My Captain!" But when he got to "Rise up—for you the flag is flung—" he had lost the next line. "Flag is flung . . . is flung . . ." he repeated desperately. "For you . . . The ah, flag is ah—uh—" Red streaks were creeping up his neck. He stared at his feet, cleared his throat. "Hit's clean gone out'n my head. Blame it all! Made a bobble of that'un," he said ruefully. The sympathetic parents clapped anyway.

"Now we have Lundy Taylor," I said, my eyes on the list in my hand. There was no response and I realized that the room was too quiet. Instantly alerted, I looked up to see Lundy slumped back in his seat, his eyes closed and his face flushed, his head thrown back, his mouth open, breathing heavily. A titter began at the back of the room near him and swept forward.

In a way, I was relieved; perhaps it would be better this way. I would not try to waken him. But David, not knowing the reason for my hesitation, walked quietly back to Lundy's desk and tapped the boy on the shoulder. He stirred, but then slid out of the seat onto the floor and lay in a crumpled heap, still snoring. Instantly David understood. The titters became guffaws as David signaled me to go on to the next child.

"And next on our program we have Creed Allen." I spoke with more animation than I was feeling at the moment. Necks craned and there was much oohing and aahing as Creed marched to the front with the raccoon riding cockily on one shoulder. I knew that this was not the actual coon that had so frightened me that first day of school. By April that one had been full-grown and so restless that Creed had taken pity on him and decided to keep him captive no longer. The boy liked to think that the raccoon with him now was one of Scalawag's babies, so he called him Scalawag II. Already, the pet animal was large and plump.

There were exclamations from all over the room: "Now ain't that a sight in the world!" . . . "Vow and declare! Never saw nothin' like that! Not since John Sevier shamed the Redcoats!"

From the expressions on the faces of the men particularly, it was obvious that they thought of coons only as animals for killing. From frontier days coonskin caps had been popular and often as I went around the Cove I had seen coon pelts tacked up on barn doors and cabin walls.

From his pocket Creed extracted a rock shining with bits of mica and hid it in his thatch of hair. "Wal, now Scalawag, I double-dare ye to fetch it."

The little coon slid around his master's head to the other shoulder and stood there staring ahead with mischievous beady eyes behind the black markings around them, so like a highwayman's mask. Without turning his head toward Creed, still looking to the front, one paw reached up and began nonchalantly feeling around in the hair. At last he located the rock, and after transferring it to the other paw with its finger-like claws, he turned the rock over and over examining it, smelling it, while he trilled delightedly at the gaping audience. The children laughed and cheered.

"Raccoons like anything shiny," Creed declaimed solemnly. "Now this time I'll try to outsharp him. See this piece of tin, Scalawag?" The coon stretched out an eager paw for it. "No, not yit. Turn around, Scalawag. Zacharias, come up here, will'ya, and keep him a-lookin' the other way."

Zacharias bounded up, delighted to be a part of the show, and while he distracted the raccoon, Creed buried the tin carefully under a tall stack of papers on my desk. "Now Scalawag, ye can start searchin'. Rassel up the tin."

The little animal seemed to understand that this was a game. He scurried over to the desk, trundling from one side to the other, methodically lifting papers and looking under each one. The children were rooting for him. "Don'tcha like him?" "He's a ring-tailed roarer." "Wisht he was mine." Finally, Scalawag found the piece of glittering metal and stood on the desk fondling it, almost bowing to his audience.

"Now I'll tell ye about coons," Creed said, as if beginning a naturalist's lecture. There were snorts from some of the men; they thought they knew everything about coons. "Good fer victuals, that's what," said a voice in the back of the room.

Creed was undaunted. "There were five babies in Scalawag's kit. He's not grown yit, about twenty-seven inches long now. Coons are awful good hands to climb trees and to swim. They eat frogs, turtles, berries, crayfish. Corn too, and they wash everything before they eat it. Some eat chickens, but *not* Scalawag," he added defensively. "This here is the second coon I've had as my main best pet, and I know now that it's pleasured me a heap more to watch what'n' all they do than jest kill them. When I'm a man grown, I'd live happily if'n I could—"

His voice was drowned in yiping and growling and furious barking as two hounds streaked toward the front of the room, rushing the coon. Children began shrieking. Scalawag leaped from the top of the desk to Creed's head, hanging onto his hair, screaming frantically as the dogs reached Creed and began leaping and clawing at his legs. The children were out of their seats now, in turn, flinging themselves on the dogs. "Grab a-hold of them dogs!" "Not *that* way—Scat, you hound! Scrunch him."

Creed's voice could be heard above the tumult, "Quit that tryin' to shinny up me. I ain't no tree."

The noise was so great that I could not make my voice heard. I recognized the dogs as Jeb Spencer's. Now Jeb came running forward to take charge. "Jasper, settle thar! Such a franzy. Big Ed, I'll lay my hand to you. Down, dog!" He hit the dog with his open palm and Big Ed whined and backed away. Obviously, the dogs were confused; heretofore, their rushing a coon had always pleased their master. They had smelled coon, so they had gone after coon! But now Jeb was herding them away. "Numskull hound-dogs. They bark big," he said apologetically to the room at large, "but they bite small."

It was not exactly the windup of his performance that Creed had planned. But the other children had enjoyed it. "Tarnel good fight, wasn't hit?" Zacharias spoke for all of them.

In spite of lapses and botches and absurdities, our program was turning into a success. The people were in such a holiday mood that they took each misadventure as part of the entertainment to add to the fun.

About the middle of the morning, Miss Alice Henderson rose to bestow the first of the awards. "Friends," she said, "during this school term we've had three students with top grades—Rob Allen, Lizette Holcombe, and John Spencer. Their averages were so close that it was difficult to choose between them. The highest average, however, is 96.7%. It is my privilege to present this prize for outstanding grades to—Lizette Holcombe."

The cheering and clapping and whistling was deafening as the tall dark-haired girl came to the front of the room. I could tell that Lizette was so excited that she was close to tears. Miss Alice's voice was warm as she handed the girl a package, "Lizette, I congratulate you."

"Thank you, ma'am."

"Why don't you open it here so that everyone can know what it is?"

But Lizette's hands were trembling so that she could not get the cord untied.

"Here, let me help." Miss Alice reached for the package. "There now."

"Oh-h! How beautiful!"

"Friends, this is a copy of *The Complete Shakespeare*, the poems and the plays. Yours to enjoy, Lizette. You've earned it."

Lizette went back to her seat hugging the book. I saw Bessie Coburn's eyes fastened on that wonderful copy of Shakespeare with envy and longing.

But the action was not over for the day. Since religion was David's subject, he had been in charge of the Scripture memorization. He too had allowed the children their own selections. There were some nice ones: Zady Spencer recited the Twenty-fourth Psalm; Rob Allen, a portion of the eighth chapter of Romans; Charles Holcombe, the One Hundred First Psalm; Little Burl, the familiar and beloved "For God so loved the world. . . ."

But then Festus Allen stood up and began reeling off in a singsong voice one of the "begat" passages:

"These are the generation of Shem: Shem was an hundred years old, and begat Ar-phax-ad two years after the flood. . . ."

David opened his mouth to protest, but then reached frantically for a Bible off my desk and began flipping pages, hunting for the spot in Genesis.

"And Ar-phax-ad lived five and thirty years and begat Salah. . . .

"And Salah lived thirty years and *begat* Eber. . . ."

The incredulous look on David's face as he checked up on Festus line by line was very funny. How could any child recite correctly a genealogy with all those difficult names? But the monotonous voice went on and on, emphasizing only one word, that all-important *begat* . . .

"And Nahor lived nine and twenty years, and *begat* Terah. . . .

"And Terah lived seventy years, and *begat* Abram, Nahor, and Haran. . . ."

Festus went barreling on right to the end of the chapter. David looked sheepish. He had offered the prize for the most verses and he had not stipulated what kind of verses. The reaction of the highlanders was enthusiastic approval. I could not understand why, unless memorizing an intricate genealogy was as impressive to them as declining a Latin word. So Miss Alice, making little effort to conceal her amusement, gravely bestowed a beautiful new Bible upon Festus of the red hair and the impudent grin.

During refreshments when I was at last relaxing, thinking that the program was happily behind me, there came a further surprise. Miss Alice asked for quiet. "Christy Huddleston, I want thee. Up here by me—please."

Puzzled, I went to her.

"Friends, last January someone who had never taught school before came to us. In her heart was a dream, the dream of helping boys and girls because she cared what happened to them. Already we have seen the beginning of the fulfillment of some of her dreams. Folks, we've had the longest school term ever seen in Cutter Gap so far and it's been a great term. So much of it we owe to David Grantland who built this church-schoolhouse, and to Christy Huddleston, whose presence has made it vital and living and full of fun. Christy, this is for thee."

I had not expected this and emotion rose in me, stinging my eyes. I took the package and opened it. It was a deer, whittled and carved out of a single piece of wood, smoothed and polished, grace in motion somehow captured in wood.

"John Spencer's work," Miss Alice told me softly. "He wanted it to be from all of us. He worked on it for three months."

In a few days I was to leave for Asheville for a vacation with my family. Gradually, during the days since David had asked me to marry him, I had realized that I could not, for some mysterious reason that would not come clear to me, rush into a formal engagement. Perhaps I needed to be away from David to get more perspective. The situation might look different to me in Asheville. So I told him that I needed more time to think about it. But we agreed that we would exchange letters.

To my surprise, David made no protest at my postponing a decision.

Thirty-three

THE DAY before I was to leave to spend the month-long harvesting holiday at home, Miss Alice sent for me. No reason or explanation was given. It was mid-afternoon when I got to her cabin. She had tea ready and poured me a cup, but it was clear at once that she was not of a tea-party mind. She sat looking at me as I sipped the scalding tea, those gray eyes of hers as guileless as ever. Scrutinizing her face over the rim of my teacup, I thought, *The eyes really do mirror the soul, don't they?*

"I knew thee would come, Christy." Her voice was soft.

"You mean today?"

"No, to the Cove. I didn't know how or when—or what thee would look like. Or from what kind of background. But I was expecting thee. Does that sound whimsical?"

"Perhaps. A little—but I like it."

"Looking forward to thy coming, I've been storing up spiritual treasures for thee for some time now. Whenever I've had a real breakthrough in working with the highlanders, I've thought 'I must remember to tell *her* that.'

"Or whenever a new insight would come to me, almost always I would jot it down and tuck it away in a particular cubbyhole in my desk, thinking even as I wrote, 'This is for *her.*'

"Or there have been those rare instances when I have been able to take a new step forward in total obedience, so that some of the fog of my self-will that veils His face has rolled away. Then when new understanding of what He is really like has come to me, I've thought, 'What joy it will be to share this with *her*. Oh, let me not forget a single bit of it.'"

I felt overwhelmed, suddenly very small and very humble. "Miss Alice, I—well, how can I deserve all that?"

"Deserve! Child, none of us deserves anything. We couldn't, no matter how hard we tried."

But then, as on that day of my first talk with Miss Alice Henderson, abruptly her mood shifted. "Anyway Christy, for some time now I've been wanting to talk to you, woman to woman. You're so eager to taste life, all of it, to the full."

Her eyes sought mine in a level straight gaze. "Remember when you reported to me your discussion with the Doctor about what he believed?"

"Yes."

"How you kept quoting me to him that day? And how he reacted against your parroting my thoughts?"

"I remember."

"That and other instances have told me that you've been seeing me through a rosy glow. Basically, you're a realistic girl, so perhaps I'm one of the few persons on earth still on something of a pedestal for you. Christy, that won't do. We humans weren't meant to sprout wings on this earth."

I said nothing because I did not quite understand where this conversation was leading.

"You mustn't leave the Cove, Christy, with any such notions about me. As you go home and consider your second school term here, it cannot be with any illusions."

Still, I did not understand. Though the gray eyes were still looking at me as unwaveringly as ever, a smile tugged now at the corners of Miss Alice's mouth. But there was no trace of teasing in the smile, rather something that seemed out of place, a gentle pity for me. "So now, Christy, I'm going to tell thee a true story. That's why I asked thee to come here today." Her voice trailed off and I could sense her mind going backward into the past.

"No little girl ever loved her father more than I," she mused. "I used to sit on his lap by the hour. One of my earliest recollections is of our family in the comfortable parlor of our home, father sitting at the end of the sofa, mother close beside him, I on his lap with one arm about his neck, the other children leaning against his knees or perched on the arm of the sofa.

"Touch is important to children. You've discovered that in your school. I know that I drew a sort of nourishment from this physical contact. I can remember the feel of leaning back against father's black broadcloth cutaway coat. In his Quaker garb he may sometimes have looked austere to others, but never to me. He had twinkly eyes, curves of fun around his mouth. He called me 'Purtie.'

"I would go with him on errands for the family business—we manufactured stoves, heating and cooking stoves —and I was always proud to sit beside him in the buggy. We talked about everything, often quite grown-up conversations. When father had to go inside a store for a business conference, I'd wait for him in the buggy, keeping our horse Mollie company, not a bit impatient, content with the thought that father had trusted me enough to take me with him on such important excursions.

"I adored my mother too and my two sisters and my brother—but in a different way. My mother was gentle and lovely and made a delightful home for us. But it was always my father with whom I had that special bond.

"In those days parents were reluctant to talk to their girls about sex. Perhaps father talked to my brother. I don't know. But mother scarcely mentioned the subject at all. I learned about conception and birth when our cat had kittens. I knew where babies came from, but that was about all I knew. This silence was a mistake, of course; in the case of our family, a tragedy.

"You wouldn't believe how ignorant I was. We Friends were forbidden to visit art galleries or even look at a statue. Headily, just once I defied this and stumbled into the Academy of Fine Arts in Philadelphia. There before me was a cast (imported from the Louvre) of Michelangelo's "The Bound Captive." I'd never seen a nude man before and I found myself blushing crimson, so I raced back onto the sidewalk, my heart beating wildly.

"When I was just turned thirteen, a 'ministering Friend,' as we called those itinerant preachers, a Quaker from England, first visited us. To us children, English Friends seemed like visitants from some angelic sphere. To be noticed or spoken to by one of these personages was heaven come down to earth. Thus when this particular man made much of me, I was ecstatic. His mannerisms, many of his ways were so like my father's. He had traveled in the South Seas, had engrossing adventure stories to tell. While novels or fiction stories were not allowed to us, true stories were. So he would spin these stories out endlessly, and while I was too old to sit on his lap, I would sit on a stool near his knee. Sometimes he would reach out and stroke my hair.

"At that age I was still very much the little girl, still

climbing trees, sliding down hills, making hundreds of mud-muddly pies. So my parents saw nothing odd about these story hours. They looked on, amused, half-listening to the wild tales, proud of the compliments that the visiting Friend paid to their children.

"This man came back the next year and the next. He and I were by this time fast friends and he had my complete confidence. By now I was a big girl. We still had our long talks, but now when my parents were not around, he began to tell me of a new and delightful discovery he'd made. It had to do with the Spirit of God and of how this was a sort of divine electricity which could flow at its highest voltage through touch, through laying the hands on the body of another. He opened the Bible to passage after passage to show me how Jesus had laid His hands on people to heal and to minister. And he told me of the new insights which could come to one, even of physical healings and thrills from the rediscovery of this ancient truth.

"I believed all this because I trusted the man. And there was just enough truth mixed in with his false interpretations and motives to make it all seem valid to an eagerly questing young girl. Then too I was a dreamer. I wanted to be a good and noble woman to make myself worthy of some glorious destiny that would bless the world."

I wanted to put my fingers in my ears to stop the story before it went any further. There was a weight on my chest; I felt as if I were choking. "Miss Alice, if you're going to say what I think you're going to say—please, do I have to hear it? I'd rather not."

Her voice was gentler than ever. "Yes, you know the end of the story, Christy. But thee must hear me out. Christy, I'm sorry! Bear up. When I'm finished, thee will understand why I had to tell it."

Relentlessly, she picked up where she had left off. "The only thing not understandable now is the carefulness and patience of the seduction. Usually passion wants to grab and to yank. Perhaps for this man vestiges of his Quaker virtue remained in the midst of his despoiling. Also I believe that he had a number of such situations under way in different stages so that he was content to bide his time for me.

"That year when I was fifteen there was a certain amount of experimentation, what he called 'the laying on of hands.' Some of it I thought odd all right, questioned it in my own mind. But the man was so much older than I. And we children had been taught to think of these 'traveling Friends' as such divinely chosen oracles of the mind of God that almost every word they spoke was supposed to be inspired.

"And yes, I felt the thrill because I was a perfectly normal girl. But because I was so ignorant of sex, I interpreted the thrill in exactly the high-flown spiritual way that the man meant for me to interpret it.

"So the groundwork was all laid and eagerly I looked forward to the man's visit that spring that I was sixteen. Because this Friend had been in our home so many times, my parents trusted him implicitly. The usual careful chaperonage didn't even occur to them. Word had not yet reached Pennsylvania that the man's teaching and ministry had just been sharply discredited in England.

"One afternoon when my parents had gone into the country to visit a sick aunt, the man and I were alone. He had made even greater discoveries than last year, he told me. There was a way to have wave upon wave of spiritual blessing which one felt as a physical thrill through one's body. But he would have to show me. Was I game?

"His hands moved to my breasts, my thighs. I should remove some of my clothes in order to feel the thrill best. The words that he whispered to me as his hands moved over my body were blasphemy.

"Mercifully, I'll draw the curtain there—but you need to know that much, Christy. Except—except to say that when he was finished, I was weeping violently, crumpled up at his feet, no longer a virgin. I had never felt anything like this before. I was mesmerized. Yes, there was wave upon wave of physical sensation, but suddenly, with his body on top of mine, I had known that this was wrong, was of evil all the way. I had been duped. So I began fighting the man, pummeling him with my fists, trying to kick him off me. But it was too late."

My eyes were fastened on Miss Alice's face. I moistened my lips and tasted salt there. I had not known that I was crying, crying for the girl who had been, crying for the loss of a girl's idealism, crying because life is like that. Crying, Oh God, God, God—why does it have to be?

Miss Alice did not appear to notice my tears. She was lost in remembrance.

"I should have told my parents that night. But the same silly Victorian reticences that had sealed their lips to sex instruction, sealed mine. I didn't know how to tell them. I hadn't the least idea what words to use, how to begin.

"So I took a bath and changed my clothes and dashed cold water on my eyelids until the tear stains were gone. That night at the dinner-table I was silent, the visiting Friend very talkative. I remember that he declaimed long and eloquently about the dangers of being led by 'law' instead of by the indwelling Light, and my parents listened, fascinated. He left the next day for England.

"By the next month I guessed that I was 'with child.' There are no words in the English language or in any language to describe the agony of those weeks. I kept my news to myself, though looking back now I honestly don't know how a young girl could stand that much pressure with no one in whom to confide.

"It was frightful morning sickness that finally brought the story out. In the end, I told all of it to my father and mother.

"Sorrow descended on our home, such sorrow as we had never known, even through death. Father ran the gamut of emotions. He was a gentle man. I had not known that he was capable of such anger. He spent great sums of money with secret agents in the British Isles trying to track down the man. But it was no use. The Friend had returned to his South Seas, had disappeared somewhere into the wilds of New Zealand.

"The next question was what to do? My parents wanted me to go away to have the baby, then find someone to adopt it. I was willing to go away for a time to save them and myself the embarrassment of the months of being heavy with child. But in my eyes, it didn't seem right to give away my baby. Nothing could change what had happened, no fairy-tale imaginings, no dodging, no amount of running away. My life, I felt, was set now in a certain pattern. Probably I would never marry, not because I was warped on the subject of sex forever, but because I was not at all sure that the kind of man I wanted to marry would want me now. So why run at all? Why not do the direct and honest thing, bear the consequence of my own act and rear the child I was bearing?

"My parents agonized with me in this decision, but in the end they agreed. I did go away to Burlington, New Jersey, to stay with Grandmother Seebohn until the baby was born, a girl, a beautiful child. Then I came home to Ardmore.

"Having decided on this course of honest transparency, father summoned the head of our Quaker Meeting to our home. She was Sarah Lindsay, a tiny slight woman, but a great spirit. In our parlor that evening she sat primly, her shawl around her shoulders, her placid face framed by her thin muslin cap, and listened gravely while father as the head of the household, related the sequence of events. Then he told Sarah of my decision to rear the daughter myself.

"That evening father virtually placed in Sarah's frail hands our family's standing in the community—which was considerable—as well as my future. When he had finished, there was one of those long Quaker silences. Even now I can see Sarah's tiny hands resting, palms up, relaxed on her lap, as if ready to receive anything heaven might care to give. There was no hurry. We all knew that Sarah was praying—and listening.

"Finally she spoke directly to me. 'Thee has made the right choice. Now thee will know as few humans ever know it, the love of thy God. Betimes it will mold thee into a great spirit. And that love will come to thee too from every soul in our Meeting. Our Meeting will be to thee as thy larger family. And thy daughter, this little girl, shall be loved as no child has ever been loved before.'

"At that I started weeping, and couldn't stop. Sarah's words had begun the melting of something hard and rebellious and bitter in me. I had indeed made the right choice because in rejecting secrecy I had also rejected the road to cynicism.

"Sarah's prophesy came true. We never knew exactly how she chose to tell our Meeting, perhaps the Elders and the Overseers first, perhaps then in tiny groups. But there never was any gossip or any finger-pointing. Once when one woman tried a little holier-than-thou attitude, she was stringently disciplined by Sarah, who had her own methods, and that was that.

"The true greatness of the Society of Friends—for all its human weakness—was manifest in a situation like that. They rallied round me. They were the ones who protected me from any gossip-mongers of the larger Ardmore community, though I never quite knew how.

"Through them I learned that true forgiveness includes total acceptance. And out of acceptance wounds are healed and happiness is possible again.

"Nevertheless, my experience had two far-reaching

effects on our Quaker community. One was, they concluded that in believing that the inner Light would teach each individual all he needed to know, they had neglected sex instruction as well as religious instruction for the young. They had even neglected the revelations which God had given other men as put down in Scripture. So courageously this branch of the Friends began revolutionary instruction for the young. That, in turn, led inevitably to the first Friends schools. Those fine secondary schools have multiplied and are thriving throughout Pennsylvania.

"The second long-range result was a new look at the place of emotion and feeling in religion. As our Meeting quietly pondered this, they realized that in their emphasis on the inner Light, the typical Friend had come to judge the state of his relationship with God entirely by what he found within himself. Obviously that made for an up-and-down religious experience, dependent upon how much sleep one had had the night before; or if a teen-ager, whether one's glands were cutting up capers; or if older, whether damp weather was making one's arthritis hurt.

"Such morbid introspection," Miss Alice added crisply, "was nonsense. Either God exists—or He does not. If He does, either an individual has a relationship with Him—or that relationship has been severed. Indigestion or arthritis can't change the bottom fact that *God is* or the unfailingness of a single one of His promises.

"So our Meeting decided that henceforth there must always be 'checks' to present-day revelation: after sharing such insights with a group, several persons bringing their common sense and their intelligence to bear must then agree on a course of action. And although emotions of love for one another were fine and admirable, there must also always be integrity of motive—honesty, purity, unselfishness.

"But to get back to me. After that, I lived at home and taught school. Happiness flowed into our home again. Of course for me there was a scar—but nothing more, except perhaps the distillation of a realism and a wisdom that was not possible for me before, and a great overflowing compassion for anyone who has been hurt by life.

"Finally, before his death, I let my father have his way and legally adopt my daughter. So in his old age, it was Purtie's daughter who sat on his lap and made the rounds with him on his errands for the stove business.

"She grew up to be a tall beautiful woman with large

expressive blue eyes—like yours, Christy. And except that your hair is darker, you look enough like my daughter to be her twin."

I thought back to my first morning in Cutter Gap, to that moment when Miss Alice had opened her front door and had been visibly startled at seeing me.

"Did your daughter marry and have a family?" I asked her.

"No children, but a husband."

"And where do they live now?"

"She died three years ago." Miss Alice paused. For the first time, she seemed to be making an effort to keep her voice matter-of-fact.

"Thee must know, Christy. My daughter Margaret See-bohn Henderson—became Dr. MacNeill's wife."

Thirty-four

FOR THE first few days at home I sank into a state of pampered bliss, sleeping late, stuffing myself on mother's cooking, seeing my friends. Then gradually there came the realization that while Asheville had not changed much, I had. In comparison with the flavorsome personalities of Cutter Gap, many city folk now seemed almost colorless to me and city life unexciting. Even so, there was the value of perspective in having put some distance between me and the Cove.

For that reason, I was glad that my last talk with Miss Alice had come just before I had left for home. In the simple recital of her poignant story she had jolted me. Slowly during the weeks at home, by a process which I did not understand, seeds buried in the tale itself were germinating and producing fruit after their kind—new awareness, accretive insights. The first was that Alice Henderson, in trying to step down from any pedestal on which I had unwittingly placed her, had succeeded paradoxically in making herself seem greater than ever. It was the difference between a plaster-of-paris saint and a flesh-and-blood woman who had been through the fires and had emerged, not unscathed, but a stronger woman with a deeper compassion.

Also, I saw for the first time that we have to accept people the way they are and not be shocked about anything. In my idealism, that had been hard for me. I had not understood Miss Alice's acceptance of the mountain people, nor Dr. MacNeill's, and had often been frustrated, sometimes even infuriated by their unwillingness to push harder for changes.

In the light of Miss Alice's story, I understood that the reason we have to accept other people is simply because God receives us just the way we are. Yes, all of us to the last person—even to Bird's-Eye Taylor and to Lundy. It was ironic that someone like Opal McHone had understood that better than I.

I had never thought it should be that way. Had I been doing it, I would have arranged gradations of acceptability according to how bad or how good we were—or how hard we have tried. But Miss Alice had helped me to see that the Power who broods over our aching world has quite a different idea: He persists in receiving us and loving us all even when we reject Him and refuse to have anything to do with Him, even when we strut our little intellects and insist that He does not exist.

Throughout my months in the Cove, there had been Alice Henderson's gentle, unfailing teaching about the validity and the "presentness" of the inner Light, and her insistence that I not take her word for this but actively experiment with it, as on that day of Little Burl's operation. Perhaps the most important single secret she had taught me so far was the *how* of looking to this inner Reality for the help I needed:

First, I had to recognize evil for what it was. That meant honesty—which could be costly in day-by-day dealings with people. It took vigilance too.

Second, I had to declare war on that specific evil—whether it was disease or mental illness or a child who was on the wrong path or snarled human relationships or my own impatience or temper or resentment or just that I violently hated some duty which I knew perfectly well I had to perform.

Third—and here was the heart of the secret that I was struggling to grasp—I had to step aside and ask Someone else to do the fighting for me. And every time I thought of my particular battle—usually many times a day—I had to step consciously out of the way again and give gratitude to Him for the battle He was waging on my behalf right then. Sometimes it took days, sometimes longer, for evil was rarely flimsy but the outcome was sure; sure because He was and is the Lord of life. And sure, because evil is at the last always a coward that slinks away when finally challenged and faced down.

Eventually the results of the victory would be there for anyone to see, whether in a healthy body or a restored mind; or a boy or girl whose values—all awry—were back in place; or a ruptured relationship healed; or, perhaps, just in the miracle of finding joy in what had once been a hateful task.

It was wonderful to have the time during my vacation to try to assimilate discernments like these.

David, too, was taking a vacation, a short two-week one. His letters came regularly, not exactly love letters, but warm and teasing, jocular, with tidbits of news about this person and that. And I discovered that my heart was back in the Cove with Fairlight and Little Burl and Opal and Isaak and Mountie and many another. And sometimes I caught myself thinking about that young wife of Dr. MacNeill's who had looked something like me. I wanted to know more about her, what sort of person she had been.

At the beginning of my third week at home, David forwarded to me a letter postmarked Knoxville. It was from Mr. Hazen L. Smith.

Dear Miss Huddleston:
    You will soon receive an invitation from Mrs. Lawrence Toliver, Jr., President of the University Club, about talking to the women. I hope that you will choose one of the two dates Mrs. Toliver suggests and come, preferably to their first meeting of the season.
    Also when you do come back to Knoxville, Mrs. Hazen and I would like to have you stay with us overnight. I have a list of businessmen for you to contact with the hope of their donating additional supplies. Who ever told you that the mountain work is wholly your opportunity!
    I remain, your faithful servant,

                                        Hazen L. Smith

P.S. May I add my word to that of my husband? My dear, we do so want you for our house guest. May we expect you?

                                        Mary Smith

In a few days the letter from Mrs. Toliver arrived. After some correspondence, we agreed on September tenth for my talk. This woud be at the end of my holiday on my way back to Cutter Gap.

Of course, once again mother and father tried to get me to drop schoolteaching and return to college. During several evenings in father's library, I listened to all their arguments, feeling that in theory they were right. Of course I should finish college. But after hearing in detail my feelings about the future of the Cutter Gap work and talking all around the subject my parents agreed, in the end, that if I did not return to the Cove that September I would be leaving an unfinished task. And my father had always said that a true Huddleston tried hard to finish what he had begun! So, to my relief, they gave me their blessing on another term of schoolteaching.

The fall session would not begin, however, until after "fodder pulling" (when the blades of corn were stripped and tied together into bundles to dry for "roughness" or food for cattle and horses during the winter) and most of the harvesting were over around the first of November.

And so, at the end of my wonderful vacation at home, I took the train to Knoxville.

I WAS SEATED at one end of a large, ornately furnished room crowded with well-dressed ladies. The woman who was introducing me was short and stout, and her introduction was turning out to be as elaborate as her clothes, all flounces and ruffles. She was wearing a green watered silk dress with gathered tiers all the way up the skirt; a ruffled collar edged with Venetian lace; a concoction of feathers and froth on her head with a filmy green veil over her face. Around her throat was a black velvet band secured with an amethyst pin. "... dear and delightful girl gave up a comfortable home ..." I watched, fascinated, as the amethyst pin bobbed up and down with every word she spoke; any minute it was going to catch in the green veiling under her chin.

"... left fond parents and a dear brother, parted from her loving friends and her host of beaux, to go into the destitute mountain regions ..."

You would have thought that I had gone to Africa. I squirmed uncomfortably on my velvet chair at being made out the self-sacrificing heroine. I was thankful that I had heeded mother and bought a new outfit. The dark red charmeuse dress and hat were gay, not a bit like what a suffering martyr should be wearing.

My hands were tightly clasped together in my lap to control their trembling. Suddenly I realized that I was moistening my lips over and over. I tried taking a series of slow deep breaths, hoping that this would get my fright under enough control so that the ladies would not notice.

With effort I brought my mind back to what the lady was saying. "Our own dear Hazen Smith whom you all know, always so swift to hear the cry of the orphan, the lament of the widow, opened his warm heart one day last spring to . . ."

Mechanically, I began rehearsing to myself the first sentences of my speech, "Ladies of the University Club: I was greatly honored by Mrs. Toliver's invitation to speak to you today about . . ." But how could I say anything that would make women like these see and understand the mountains, my mountains? These women, kind and warm-hearted though they were, had never seen anything like the Cove. I felt all but suffocated with the luxury of this room. So many Oriental rugs; the blue velvet portieres and sweeping draperies with their heavy brass cornices; the huge overstuffed chairs with their crocheted tidies; every lampshade with its petticoat of fringe; the Sèvres figurines on the mantelpiece; the stuffed birds and wax flowers under glass domes.

". . . will not detain you longer with any poor words of mine. I know you are as eager as I am to hear what this charming young lady has to say to us. It is my very great privilege to present to you our very first speaker of the year for the University Club, *Miss Christy Huddleston*. My dear, right over here. Stand right here, so that everyone can see and hear you. There now. Just tell us *all* that's on your heart."

She patted my arm and left me standing, trembling in the middle of the floor. If only, I thought, I might have had a table nearby for support. "Ladies of the University Club . . ." The voice, strained and far away, did not sound like mine. "Thank you for inviting me to be with you today." Desperately I cast around for the next sentence, but my mind had suddenly gone blank with the faces in the room a blur.

Thoughts flew by me like telephone poles flashing by a train window. Clickety-clack, clickety-clack . . . "Ladies of the University Club . . ." Clickety-clack, flash, flash, clickety-clack ... "Thank you for ..." But then finally (how much time had gone by?) I roped in one telephone pole, snared one idea: Mr. Smith, that was it! "Mr. Smith thought that you might be interested in hearing something of what I told him of my experiences in the mountains." Better. "I suppose my story begins on the day when I first heard about the needs of the mountain boys and girls." Gradually my fear receded as thoughts rose to take its place.

I told them about Dr. Ferrand's speech and how it had inspired me to teach school; about how it had felt to walk behind Mr. Pentland into a different world, to walk backwards into time where people spoke English sprinkled with Anglo-Saxon and Gaelic words. A peppery speech with that "bow and arrow twang" that Henry Thoreau had liked so much, and that made the English the rest of us used seem tame and stale. And about how in this strange country they still sang ballads and told haunt stories out of the seventeenth and eighteenth centuries.

I tried to describe the fierce pride of the people; their self-reliance and love of liberty; the rebellion against taxation and all governmental restrictions or even "benefits"; how out of centuries of tyranny they had learned the lesson well that for every benefit, a freedom must always be surrendered.

"But I surely don't want to make life back in the mountains sound romantic. Mrs. Toliver was right to use the word 'destitute.' There's nothing picturesque about homes without toilets, indoors or out. There's nothing glamorous about a tired woman pushing a bull-tongue plow up a steep hillside, trying 'to skelp the weeds out'; or about soap made out of hickory ashes and hog meat leavings; or about children who came to school barefooted in the snow or with "dew-pizen" sores in summer—yes, it really is true!—or it was until women like you sent them shoes. And it's hard to get sentimental about a child who needs a bath so badly that the only way I can stand to be near him is to put perfume on a handkerchief up my sleeve and keep the sleeve as close to my nose as possible.

"So please don't think that I'm heroic. I've had just as much trouble adjusting to all of this as any of you would have. In fact, at first I almost gave up and went back home. It was a struggle to see underneath the rags and smells, the human beings—some with fine minds, some

383

with great spirits, lovable, proud, sensitive—and begin to care about them, really care.

"It's like—well, like garden vegetables. If you threw out your turnips because they came out of the ground with dirt clinging to them, you'd never discover the goodness there." And then I tried to make the ladies *see* Fairlight and Opal and Little Burl and Aunt Polly Teague and Mountie and that crazy little clown, Creed.

"They're people and they need a chance and you and I have it in our power to give them that chance." Then I sketched in some of the specific needs of the school and the mission, and sat down.

There was silence in the room for a moment, then the beginning of conversation, like bees humming. Mrs. Toliver rose and fluttered her hands at the ladies for silence. "I know everyone in this room will agree with me that we are speechless—absolutely speechless—with admiration for this brave and courageous young woman. Our sex is supposed to be the weaker vessel, and yet when we reflect . . ."

Mrs. Toliver's speechlessness lasted for some time. But at last, seeing hands raised around the room, she asked me if I would answer questions from the floor.

"I'll try," I said.

As the questions began coming, I found that I had underestimated my audience. A motherly looking woman sitting near the front window asked, "Why is the school so poverty-stricken, with so few books and all? Why doesn't the church support the work better?"

"Ma'am, this mission is not under any one church. It's interdenominational work. Anyway," I added gently, "I guess the church is you and me and folks like us."

Another voice spoke up. "Miss Huddleston, are there many adults who are illiterate?"

"Yes, quite a lot. I've seen the 1910 figures from the United States Census Bureau somewhere. Something like sixteen percent of those over ten years old in the mountain regions of Tennessee can't write. That's against a little over three percent for the national average."

"What are the plans for handling that? I mean, you've talked about school for children, but what's going to be done about the grown people?"

I took a deep breath and plunged in. "There aren't any plans really. So far I've taught one woman to read and write, Fairlight Spencer, and I'm beginning on others now. But can you imagine a big boy of seventeen or twenty who desperately wants to learn to read, coming to school and being put in with the seven- and eight-year-olds? Most of them just won't brave it and I can't blame them. Yet that's the way it is now."

A lady sitting near the marble fireplace raised her hand and Mrs. Toliver acknowledged her. "Yes, Mrs. Browning. By all means."

The woman who stood up was dark and petite, tastefully dressed in sapphire-blue duvetine. "Miss Huddleston, all the while you were talking I could not help recalling the trip Mr. Browning and I made recently to Scandinavia. Have you heard about the Folk Schools of Denmark?"

"No, I haven't."

"I hadn't either until this trip. Then our host in Denmark took us to see the Folk School in Askov and now I'm full of admiration for them."

I nodded, wondering what connection the schools in Denmark had with the subject at hand.

"It's hard to describe in a few words," the lady in blue went on, "but the Folk Schools are for older young people, seventeen and over. The boys go four months after the crops are in, November through February; the girls, three months during the summer. There are no entrance requirements except the desire to learn; no examinations, no grades, no degrees. They don't use many books, but mostly rely on the spoken word through lectures and then discussions. It's called 'Training for Life' and the idea is not to educate the student *away* from the land, so that all the bright students want to rush off to live in cities, but rather to send each pupil back to his own community a better person, quickened, more productive."

Suddenly in the words this stranger was speaking, I caught a glimpse of something alive and exciting. Almost breathlessly I asked, "And, this idea—has it worked?"

"That's what's so startling. It really has!"

"Ladies . . ." Mrs. Toliver interrupted. "I've just had a signal from the back of the room from our refreshment chairlady. The luncheon is ready, so we'll have to bring this fascinating discussion to a close. Once again our heartfelt thanks, Miss Huddleston. Ladies, a big hand!" Amid the clapping of gloved hands, the meeting was adjourned.

A little later, carrying chicken salad and hot beaten

biscuits on a hand-painted plate, I made my way across the room to Mrs. Browning. She seemed to have realized that I would be coming and had managed to keep a chair next to hers empty by placing her handbag on it. "Mrs. Browning, I thought I was the only one who got all excited over ideas."

She laughed gaily. "Then we have something in common. No, I'm noted for it. Ask my poor suffering husband as with gusto I drag him from book to book, from art gallery to museum, from country to country."

"You didn't say so, but you must think the Folk School idea could be adapted for our Southern mountains—or you wouldn't have brought up the subject."

"I know it!" Mrs. Browning answered. "It's the answer, I feel. You asked if all those big ideas worked? Just wait till you hear. . . ."

Then for half an hour Mrs. Browning raved about Denmark, how in 1864 the nation had forfeited some of her best farmland as the result of a war lost to Germany and Austraia. And how a poet-pastor-teacher named Frederick Grundtvig had conceived an inspired idea how to wrest victory out of defeat through a new type of education—the Folk School concept.

In time, the results were maximum productivity from Denmark's tiny farms; Danish shipping growing and growing; ninety percent of all her farmers becoming members of a farm cooperative. So Denmark became a proud, successful little nation. And Mrs. Browning insisted that almost everyone gave the Folk Schools much of the credit.

I had been so drawn into Mrs. Browning's enthusiasm that I had not noticed Mrs. Toliver approaching until she stood at my elbow. "I'm so sorry to interrupt, my dear, but I have to run. Do visit us again. I'm sure the Club will do something for your school. You'll be hearing from us. You were an inspiration, *sim*ply an inspiration." And she was gone in a flutter of green ruffles.

The group was breaking up and I saw that Mrs. Smith was waiting to take me home with her. There was so much I still wanted to ask Mrs. Browning, especially about those ideas of Grundtvig's. Before we parted, we exchanged addresses and Mrs. Browning promised to send me a book. "That will tell you what you want to know," she said, "better than I ever could."

386

Most of the next day was spent walking from store to store, going down the list of the businessmen Mr. Smith had given me. Everywhere I was received with such openness and promised so much that by the time I boarded the train for El Pano, I was fairly bursting with admiration for Mr. Smith. What had he said to those men that had given me such open sesame? One hundred pounds of flour from one merchant. Two hundred pounds of sugar and three cases of pork and beans from another; three cases of canned milk, a case of Log Cabin syrup; Peter Henderson seeds and some tools from a hardware merchant; Ivory soap, Crisco, and Jello in quantity. And best of all, folding cots and bedding, even blankets, warm blankets! Each donor would send his gift by prepaid express. Mr. Smith must have suggested that too. So now that I knew our boarding school was as good as a fact, I was dizzy with elation.

How different this arrival at El Pano from the one eight months before. Even before the train ground slowly to a stop I spied David standing waiting on the platform, anxiously searching the train windows for my face. Then there was his firm hand under my elbow guiding me down the high train steps, collecting my bags, carrying them to the Harvester wagon. He put both hands around my waist, hugged me and then boosted me into the wagon.

"David! People will see."

"See that I'm glad to have you back? Well, let 'em. Cutter Gap's been a dull place without you." His eyes held mine.

"David, wait till you see all the stuff that's coming. Those people were so nice. And generous. If you thought you were hauling Express before, this time you'll really moan."

David took the wagon reins with his right hand and reached for my hand with his free one. "How did your speech go?"

"I was scared at first, but after I got going it was all right, I think. Wealthy ladies mostly, but nice. They seemed really interested. And David, with all that stuff coming, now we can get the boarding school going right away. Isn't that great!"

David nodded. He laced his fingers through mine and kept watching my face. "I missed you," he finally said.

He really had. I could tell. His hand was warm around mine. "It's nice to be missed," I said softly.

David moved closer and not knowing what else to do, I began chattering again. There was so much to tell. About the two nights at the Smiths' elegant home. Their friendliness, their hospitality.

"Oh, yes, David," I said above the rumble of the wagon wheels; already we had left El Pano behind. "I met a wonderful woman at the speech affair. A really wonderful woman. She had just gotten back from Denmark. Well, after I finished my speech, she told me a lot about some schools over there. They call them Folk Schools. They sound really exciting. I think they have some ideas we can use."

"Sounds great," said David. But he seemed to be only half listening. Suddenly just beyond the Big Mud Hole, he began pulling on the reins lightly and steered the wagon off the road into a little grove of trees at a watering place.

"Why are we stopping?" I asked, though the thudding in my ears told me.

David secured both reins, turned to me with a half-smile. "Because Prince and Buttons can use a drink and I can talk better this way."

"But—but aren't they expecting us at the mission?"

"Sooner or later." He took my hand again and moved still closer. His breath was on my hair. As David's mouth found mine, I thought, *I wonder how many other girls he's kissed.* But I brushed the thought aside, for I liked his arm around me, the way he cradled my head on his shoulder. Somehow I was surprised that my mind would be so aware of details. Shouldn't I be feeling more and thinking less?

David was chuckling. "Now this is the kind of conversation I like best."

He kissed me again. I touched his cheek lightly with the tip of one finger. "David, I think we should get back to the mission, really."

"Not yet. We need to talk."

"About what, David?"

"You and me, of course. About the question I asked you last July."

I knew what he meant. In my heart I was ready to say, "Yes, David, I will marry you." In fact, I opened my mouth to say it. But then something deep inside me held back the words, and I heard myself saying, "I care a lot for you, David. But I need a little time to be sure about marriage. You understand, don't you?"

388

Only for an instant did David lose his bouncy mood. He would play the role of the impatient suitor, he said, if that was the way I wanted it, but it was only a matter of time. The rest of the way to the mission I was the silent one while he did all the talking. He told about the last four weeks and about his vacation and about how often he had thought of me. He was full of plans for the future.

I sat there in a warm glow saying scarcely another word. But I was thinking that this school term was going to be quite different from the last one.

Thirty-five

IT FELT GOOD to be back among my friends in the
Cove and they were all here today. But standing there,
wedged in between Rebecca Holt and Granny Barclay in
the crowd on the Morrisons' porch, I was wishing that I
felt easier about Ruby Mae's decision, made while I was
in Asheville to marry Will Beck. She was still not quite
fifteen, Will only sixteen. From the plateau of my almost
twenty years, it seemed to me that these child marriages
were no good, that the girls caught in them never had a
chance. They were worn out with having babies and
drudgery by their middle twenties; usually they were
grandmothers by their early thirties. And since they were
rushing at the pretense of being grown up when they were
scarcely out of childhood, they could bring so little to
marriage. As Granny Barclay had once commented,
"Green apples don't have much flavor."

Then too, all of us at the mission had hoped that Ruby
Mae would get more schooling. Since my first visit with
her parents, we had succeeded in bringing about a reconciliation between the girl and her stepfather. But that had
turned out to be a mixed blessing because about a month
before school was out, Ruby Mae had gone back home to
live. There during the summer she had had more freedom
for Will's courting. All too easily she had fallen back into
mountain patterns where it was the accepted custom for a
girl to get married when she should still be skipping
around climbing trees and catching lightning bugs and
pumping high in a homemade swing and playing elves and
fairies in a cool glen.

I looked at her now standing in the yard, the center of
attention of a knot of admiring relatives and friends and
gawking children. Granny Barclay's eyes followed mine.

"Looks like a woman grown this day. Pretty as a hummin'bird round a rosy bush."

Age looking at youth admiringly, I thought. While Ruby Mae's buxom figure was scarcely like a hummingbird's, it was true that her red hair was shining like a flame in the sunshine and her face was aglow. Gone were the heavy pigtails down her back; for the first time, her hair was piled on top of her head, woman-fashion. Her white muslin wedding dress was a poor makeshift affair, bearing the unmistakable look of having been made by the "loved ones at home"—as in fact it had. I had offered Ruby Mae one of my nicest shirtwaists, thinking that we could make a white skirt to go with it. But when she had tried on the waist, it had come nowhere near buttoning, so she and her mother had made her dress out of yard goods from the country store.

Today her constant chattering was punctuated with giggling. As Granny Barclay (who was good for a steady stream of priceless comments) put it, "That gal could talk water uphill." As for the people milling around, she clucked her tongue. "Hit's so crowded now you couldn't cuss a cat 'thout gettin' fur in yer mouth."

It was true; it seemed as if the entire Cove was here. Even Opal McHone, whom I really had not expected to come. Even Dr. MacNeill, whom I had not seen since before Tom's death. There he was, laughing and joking with Uncle Bogg. Rows of mules, horses, a few lumber wagons were hitched to the rail fence. The cabin, the porch, and the yard were teeming with people. In our Cove, weddings and funerals were prime social events; no one stayed away if he could avoid it. Besides, the bride's infare (as it was called in the Cove) was to be held immediately following this ceremony. Word had circulated that Miss Alice, anxious to give Ruby Mae some support since she could not persuade her to call off or postpone the marriage, was helping the Morrisons supply the food. So who wanted to miss "good vittles"?

David was standing against a post at the edge of the porch with Isaak McHone beside him. His father's murder had drawn Isaak and David together. The boy was still seeking David out, staying as close to him as possible; we saw him often at the mission house. At Isaak's request, David had been letting him help with various carpentry projects, and he was teaching Isaak to play the ukulele.

391

They had taken some trips into the mountains together, David riding Prince, Isaak on Buttons.

I was too far away to hear what the two were saying, but I was interested in the camaraderie between them. From time to time David would lay an arm protectively across the boy's shoulders. Once Isaak must have said something that amused David vastly, because he threw back his head and laughed, his deep bass rumbling out as he playfully rumpled Isaak's hair.

But I knew that underneath the banter, David was not happy about today. He felt that somehow we had failed Ruby Mae. After all, she had lived at the mission for months, and it seemed as if we had had so little influence on her.

All eyes were on Uncle Bogg now as he made his way to the center of the yard, flourishing the quart bottle of whiskey, a big white bow tied to the neck of the bottle. The look of distaste on David's face was only mildly disguised. For this particular wedding, he had tried to turn off the horse race custom with the "Black Betty" bottle as the prize, using as his argument the youthfulness of the bride and groom. But neither Ruby Mae nor her parents nor Will could see his point. "Who ever heerd of a wedding without Black Betty? No celebration a-tall 'thout a little dram!"

Humor is sometimes a matter of viewpoint, I suppose. Waiting now for the riders for Black Betty, the crowd thought this hilarious fun. But I could not help thinking of eight men lying dead because of moonshine—one way or another—the latest, the son of the old man out there right now holding the festive bottle high. Even after this interlude, the thought that Tom McHone was dead was a stabbing thought. *Dead.* It still seemed unreal.

And that was why David had a valid point about the "Black Betty." Everyone in Cutter Gap knew that it was on occasions like this that the potent whiskey unlocked old grudges. Tempers usually flared, knives and guns might be whipped out. Fights and eye-gougings, knifings and shooting—celebrations all too often ended in tragedy.

So if they were going to insist on mountain dew as usual, David had almost refused to perform the ceremony. But there was not another preacher within many miles, and he could scarcely see the couple start out without benefit of clergy.

There was loud chatter and much squealing as the

crowd backed away from the old squire to leave plenty of space for the racing horsemen, then quietness as everyone listened for the hoof beats and the shouts of the racers. At last we heard them. From the gleeful shouts, I knew that the bridegroom's friends who had been elected to run for the bottle were riding dangerously, whipping and spurring their horses, streaking over boulders and gulleys and streams, jumping fences, headlong and heedless.

"They're a-comin'," yelled Uncle Bogg as the horses' hooves pounded closer and closer. "And they're not moseyin'. Yippee, Ya, Ya! Makin' a noise like the whole Cher'kee nation full of corn juice."

The crowd surged forward to see, then fell back for safety as Uncle Bogg held the bottle high. Soon we could see that it was Arrowood Holcombe out in front, Wraight Holt several hundred yards behind. Arrowood's horse sailed over the fence, and with a swoop and a holler, horse and rider were into the yard, Arrowood's hand stuck out to grab the bottle, the horse rearing and pawing as he reined him in. Now the crowd surged forward engulfing the winner. From where I was standing on the porch I watched Arrowood uncork the bottle and offer it first to the girl-bride. Ruby Mae tilted her head back to drink, then red of face, coughing and sputtering, handed it back. Now Arrowood was taking his dram, and from his hands the bottle would start the rounds of the bridegroom and his friends. Looking at the poor horses, their sides still heaving, their flanks glistening with sweat—all done in—it seemed that it was the horses that could have used the drinks.

David made no move until the last drop of Black Betty was gone. Then before any other bottles or jugs could be brought out, his booming voice rang out from the top step. "Ruby Mae—Will—big moment's come. Make way for the bride and bridegroom, folks."

The ceremony was to take place inside the cabin. David stood with his back to the fireplace. Something in his bearing must have seemed a rebuke to the attitude of many in the crowd, for the conversation ceased and one by one the men began removing their hats. And then the ancient and beautiful words rang out: "Dearly beloved, we are gathered together here in the sight of God and in the presence of these witnesses, to join this man and this woman in holy matrimony, which is an honorable estate—" I knew that David was doing his best to throw a cloak of love and caring over the unseemly situation in its shabby setting. The meaning he was pouring into his words had an immediate effect on the bride: her voice was quavery as she spoke her vows.

"Look ye," Granny Barclay whispered to me. "Her eyes be a-puddlin' already." I noticed tears in the groom's eyes too.

As I stood there thinking of the life this girl-bride was assuming, more than ever the plight of the mountain women was dramatized for me. Typically, the couple would pile a brokendown bedstead, a few quilts, some split-bottom "settin' chairs," a minimum of kitchen utensils on a lumber wagon, hitch a cow to the tailboard, and be off to make their way in the world. In these mountains even that many possessions were considered "a heap of house plunder." Yet the women accomplished so much with so little.

In fact, I had never known such courageous and hard-working women as many of these. Literally and symbolically, they never let the fires go out on their hearths. I wondered how city wives back in Asheville would react to having to spin wool or flax into yarn or thread, then weave the cloth, then make all the family's clothing. They not only did all the washing and ironing (without tap water too) but even made the soap. They baked all the bread and cakes, milked the cows and churned the butter, or there would not be any butter. I thought of the advice I had overheard a granny giving a younger woman after church one Sunday. "You'll jest have to do like the rest of us wimmin and stand what the good Lord sees fit to put on us. He'll not overload ye, honey."

Well, the good Lord was blamed for a lot of things. And "overload" was too mild a word for what these women suffered—often while their men were spending whole days roaming the wood with their favorite hounds, hunting. Or else the womenfolk stood by helplessly in misery and heartbreak over the feuding.

David's voice went on, "So you are pledging each other in the language of Ruth and Naomi, 'Whither thou goest, I will go: where thou lodgest, I will lodge: thy people shall be my people, and thy God, my God; where thou diest, I will die, and there will I be buried: the Lord do so to me and more also, if aught but death part thee and me.' "

Then came the exchange of the vows themselves, only there was no ring for Ruby Mae. David's deep voice rang out, "Whom God hath joined, let no man put asunder. By the authority committed unto me as a minister of the church of Christ, I declare that Ruby Mae and William are now husband and wife. Let us pray."

After that, Ruby Mae laid her head on the bridegroom's shoulder and let her tears flow. Once she raised her head to choke out, "Hit was so beautiful, Rev'rend Grantland. Didn't know as I could stand it."

The Cove people scarcely knew what to make of this ceremony. All around me I heard comments: "Best talkinest preacher-parson I ever saw. Lifts my heart" ... "Lordamercy, that couple should stick better'n mollasses. They was shorely j'ined in that sarvice."

Suddenly Opal was standing beside me. Her eyes were red. "Guess I shouldn't have come. Whole way through, right from the start my eyes were shammily with tears. I kept rememberin' ..."

I pressed her hand. "I know, Opal. But this fall you must see more of your friends. Being here is better than staying home by yourself."

Now the room was clearing around us since all the guests knew that the feast came next. Boards over sawhorses formed long tables. They were soon groaning under wild roast turkeys, deer meat, fried ham and sausage, all sorts of vegetables, pies, and cakes.

It was later on while we were eating that Dr. MacNeill made his way across the room to me. He was munching on a wedge of sweet-potato pie. "Still mad at me, Christy?"

I looked at him in astonishment. "Why, hello, Dr. MacNeill. Of course not! Why should I be mad at you?"

"For today I haven't the least idea. Seems like the last time we were together you ran out on me." He took another bite of the pie. "Could I get you some pie or cake or something?"

"Thanks, no. I've finished."

My mind was not on food. *Why, he must be referring to that conversation in my schoolroom. Here he is picking it up as if it had happened last week. Perhaps time does all but stand still back in these mountains. But our talk was so long ago. To me, it seems like years ago. And since then so much has happened. Tom's murder. Miss Alice's revelation. My trip home. The speech in Knoxville.* Then with a start, I realized that I had not seen Dr. MacNeill since back in July.

"That day in your school," Dr. MacNeill went on, "you know, you actually thought I knew something that would save Tom. Do you still think that, Christy? I'd hate to have you blaming me for Tom's death."

Such a frontal approach caught me unprepared. I cast around for a quick way to change the subject. "Maybe this isn't the best place to talk about it. Too many people to overhear, don't you think? Opal, for instance."

"True."

"And not exactly wedding festivity talk."

"Point made. Another time then." He rumpled the back of his hair with his restless fingers in that characteristic gesture of his. Banter came into his voice, "Are you prepared for the ceremonies?"

"I thought we'd had the ceremony."

"That's right, you've never attended one of our mountain weddings before, have you?" He waved a hand in the direction of the fireplace where David had stood. "That now, David's part, that was pure preliminary. Real ceremony's coming up—if the scalawag boys can catch the bride and groom to shivaree them. Riding the rail's another name for it. Then there's belling the bride. And putting the bride to bed."

The last topic seemed like a good one to avoid, so I pounced on the first, "I've heard of riding the rail but I never quite saw the point. It always seemed like children playing horse."

Dr. MacNeill's eyes crinkled. "Christy, you amaze me. Grown girl leaves home to be on her own." He shook his head at me. "All right, Papa will explain. Bit more to it than children playing horse. Practical joke stuff, sure. Pretty crude. Let me think how I can put this so's not to offend you. No riding the rail side-saddle for the bride allowed. Strictly astride."

The Doctor was enjoying the look on my face, making no effort to hide his raillery. Well, he was more right than he knew. For no reason at all, at that moment I thought of my mother and how little sex information she had given me. How could she, mother, who could scarcely even bring herself to say the word "sex"? On these rare occasions when she could not sidestep it, she had a way of

396

half-swallowing the word so that it came out sounding like "sect."

Over the Doctor's shoulder I saw that Jeb Spencer had set the fiddle against his chest and was tuning up. Wraight Holt had joined him with a banjo. With twangy chords sliding into a fast jog and Jeb's bow singing across the strings the music started. As in the past Uncle Bogg was in the middle of things ready to call the figures. I marveled that from all appearances the old man had recovered so quickly from his son's murder. Or, I wondered, was this just another example of Uncle Bogg's callousness?

"Scrooch them settin' chairs against the walls, boys. Gonna need a heap of room." The old squire was clapping his hands. "Gyarner 'em in, folks. In—a—cir-cle. The Tenn'see Wag-on Wheel. Here—we—go!"

The tune was the familiar "Skip to My Lou." The music snaked across the floor, swirled around my ankles, set my toes to tapping. Dr. MacNeill saw. "Come on, Christy. Into the circle we go."

"Cir-cle *left!*" ... Cir-cle *right!* ... Swing your partner ... *Now* ..." The Doctor was surprisingly nimble. I had never done much square dancing, so did not know all the intricate figures. But by whispered instruction and skillful leading, he was steering me with scarcely a step missed by either of us. The rhythm beat and surged around us. The man must have learned this dance in his cradle!

"*La*-dies back ... Gents to the cen-ter ..."

Close up, some of these men were a little pungent. Out behind the cabin or somewhere the jugs were being tilted.

"With a Right Hand Wheel ... And back the other way ... With a Left Hand Wheel! ... Pick up your partner!"

The Doctor's strong arms lifted me off the floor as easily as if I had been a child. Whirl and twirl ... bend and swing ... round and round. The music was so delicious. It ached behind my eyes and pulled and titillated.

"Swing your part-ner!"

I was spun through the air, blood racing with the music, aware of the Doctor's face close to mine, sometimes half-smiling, sometimes laughing, drawing me to him. "Right—left, Right—left ... Right—left, Right—"

"And now, once a-gain, swing your part-ner— Prom-e-nade!"

We were making an arch with our raised arms and the couples were coming through. "Bend low! Through the tun-nel. Follow the leader— Now for the Bas-ket ... All to the center! ... Ladies stay in and the gents come back!"

This one was really ingenious. Soon I saw how "the basket" was made. Women in the inner circle joined hands raised; men in the outer circle ducking under. We were joining arms at waist level to circle the basket. As complicated and delightful as an old quilt pattern, I was thinking. The American frontier had its dangers and its hard work but it also had a rare talent for making its own fun.

"*Off* the floor . . ." And the Tennessee Wagon Wheel ended.

I half collapsed against the wall. "*You* aren't—breathless—a bit—" I chided Dr. MacNeill.

"Used to it. Anyway that was only a middlin' fast tune."

More music . . . Jeb had itchy fingers for his fiddle bow today. But no one was dancing this one, so I took it to be an in-between tune. In a rich baritone the Doctor started singing the words:

> Cheeks as red as a bloomin' rose,
> Eyes of the deepest brown,
> You are the darlin' of my heart,
> Stay till the gun goes down.

All around us, voices picked up the song. Such an enigmatic look on the Doctor's face! What did that look mean?

> Shady Grove, my little love,
> Shady Grove, my dear,
> Shady Grove, my little love,
> I'm goin' to leave you here.

Only a song, but why did he keep his eyes on my face? "I'm thirsty," I said abruptly—and turned toward the one sawhorse table left pushed against the wall. There were pitchers of spring water and what looked like several kinds of fruit juice. I poured a little of one and gingerly tasted it. Raspberry juice, I thought. It was refreshing. So I poured a full glass.

As I drank, I spied David across the room talking to Miss Alice. I had not seen much of her today because she had been so busy in the kitchen. As I stood there sipping the fragrant juice, I was thinking what a difficult position David was in even with the dancing. Most of the shouting mountain parsons forbade dancing, in fact preached that dancing feet might be on the slippery road to hell-fires. This was not David's viewpoint naturally, since he had enjoyed dancing back home. It was not Dr. Ferrand's either, I had heard, and since the little doctor had left behind all denominational shelters, the Cutter Gap people felt more freedom about dancing and other customs. On the other hand, they were still not willing to give their preacher the liberties they enjoyed. "Ain't fitten. Not proper for a preacher-parson." So David, not wanting to flaunt this, was not joining in. Perhaps, I was thinking, I should go and keep David company.

But Jeb, that natural-born fiddler, was tuning up again. Jeb must like fiddling better than he liked eating, and that was saying a lot. The fiddle whined and cried and sang.

"We're a-goin' 'Step Charlie,' folks," Uncle Bogg called, dancing a pigeon-wing all by himself in the middle of the floor.

> Charlie's neat and Charlie's sweet,
> And Charlie he's a dan-dy—

"Circle up, folks ... Circle up ... Wimmin on the right."

Dr. MacNeill was instantly at my side, expertly propelling me to the center of the floor.

> Over the river to feed my sheep
> And over the river, Charlie,
> Over the river to feed my sheep
> And to measure up my barley.

"La-dies *in!*"

The Doctor sang as he swung me:

> My pretty little pink, I once did think
> I never could do without you. ...

"Gents in! ... Grab, boys! Grab!"

This was fun! I was feeling better and better, warm and tingly. My feet had wings.

Overhead strange noises cut into my thoughts, girlish giggling, laughs and squeals. I had not noticed anyone leaving but now I saw that the circle of dancers was noticeably smaller.

As if in answer to my unspoken question Dr. MacNeill jerked one thumb to point at the ceiling. "I told you. Ceremony's beginning. Putting the bride to bed.

"All to the cen-ter. Just *go!*"

> Charlie's neat, and Charlie's sweet
> And Charlie he's a dan-dy—

Scrape, scrape, scrape over our heads. More giggling and shrieking. Step ... step ... right and left ... right and left.

"You mean really putting the bride to bed—now—with all of us still here?" I asked.

"Sure—now."

The girls were trouping down from the loft—without Ruby Mae—and the men made a dive for Will Beck. There was a lot of scuffling, several chairs turned over, while the music went right on. "Git him. Pound him. Sure's the world, we'll fix him proper."

"I'm batchin' it, fellers," Will yelled from where he had been flattened on the floor and was lying now between the legs of one of his friends. "Didn't I tell ye? Con-found you— Un-unh!"

Will never had a chance. Held roughly by the scruff of his neck, jerked and pummeled, he was already on his way to the loft, tightly wedged in the group of boys. The whole picture was absurd.

And then somehow, what was happening to Will and the wedding night scene in the loft receded into the distance. I was caught up in the gleeful harmony beating at my temples, singing in my blood, pulling at my nerves, tinglingly delightful. The Doctor danced as naturally as a bird flies or a fish swims. By now I knew that I didn't even have to think; I could just give myself to his arm around me with assurance. The guiding arm was so sure and firm, the rhythm such a part of my body now that I could almost forget about my feet.

It ended too soon. My partner spun me around with a final flourish. As I let my head fall back in a moment of joyous rapture, I met the Doctor's eyes. They glistened with approval—and something else. When I pulled my head back up, his lips brushed my forehead. For a moment his arm stayed firmly behind my back with my body pressed tightly against him.

Then he loosened his arm around me and the room spun slightly. Was it the music and the twirling which made me feel this way? A panicky thought chased through my mind. What was happening to me? I was dizzy!

Dr. MacNeill was pulling out a chair for me, then he sat down backwards on one near me, propping his arms on the back of the chair, Fortunately, at that moment, there were new and bawdy noises overhead. The partitions of the cabin were so thin. Cornshuck mattresses were self-advertisers. Inwardly I was wincing and the Doctor knew it.

"Actually, Christy, you ought to consider something," he said, never one to lead into a subject delicately. "The mountain attitude towards sex may be more nearly right than society's attitude—in the warmed-over Victorian tradition. It sure is more realistic. It's the way things are. Way they were meant to be too. Here in the mountains, folks see sex for pleasure and for procreation. They're right. Leave out either one, and you're in trouble."

Well, I was thinking, *so maybe there is still a lot of prudery about sex even in the younger set back in Asheville—especially among the girls. But why a lecture on sex to me?* I was having trouble meeting the Doctor's level gaze.

With relief I saw David approaching. "Excuse me, Doctor, for interrupting. I'm leaving," David said to me. "Didn't want to go without letting you know, Christy. May I take you home?"

Suddenly I knew that I very much wanted to go with David. I tried not to sound as eager as I felt. "Yes, thanks. I *am* ready to go."

Late that night a strong wind arose. This happened often in Cutter Gap, something about the way the mountains cupped the valley so that they created a sort of wind tunnel. I lay in bed listening to the wind wailing around the eaves of the house. And then it increased in tempo and became a wild wind, as if it had blown many a mile from behind the mountains—and beyond.

And I thought it sounded like women, a chorus of women crying, sometimes moaning, sometimes chanting in a high-pitched lament. And in the wistfulness of their sweet sad song, I could hear the words

> Down in the valley,
>   valley so low
> Hang your head over,
>   hear the wind blow;
> Hear the wind blow, love,
>   hear the wind blow;
> Hang your head over,
>   hear the wind blow.

Thirty-six

IT BEGAN AS THE golden autumn. Long summer days had melted into shorter autumn days with heavy rains in their wake. Then suddenly, all the stored-up beauty of summer blazed forth in an avalanche of color that tore at the eyballs and dazzled the senses.

This must be love, I thought. My eyes must be open to beauty because I was in love with David. I was young and he was young and wasn't this what the poets sang about? So I went through my days wanting to sing and to dance. The trees in their shouting colors were just for us! Only in the mountains had I seen such hues: the dark red of the sourwoods; the brown and bright orange of the red oaks; the luminous gold of the hickories; the crimson of the sumac and the scarlet oaks—always with the purple-blue Smokies for a backdrop, like the stain of ripe Concord grapes.

Even the nights were lighter and the stars brighter than I had ever seen them. Surely the Little Bear was laughing and the Dipper dripping wine, and all for me, for me—for us, for us.

And of a morning there would be mists rising from the valley floor. Then day after day the sun would break through to dissolve the frost, to chase away the vapors, and to shine on those golden leaves.

David and I walked and rode horseback through woodland avenues of gold and bronze and copper. Sometimes we would rein in our horses to stare, bedazzled by a single tree, looking, with the sun shining full on it, as if a fire had been lighted at its heart. And David would lean far over in his saddle to plant a kiss on my lips to seal the moment. Or to tease him, I would go galloping off down one of those woodland avenues with him in full pursuit.

Once I had let David kiss me, a barrier had gone down;

403

each kiss was easier and more natural than the last. So every time we were alone, David would reach out for me.

David was adept at romance and almost too sure of himself, I sometimes thought—and then wondered at myself for thinking it. But surely he was assuming much in our relationship. I still found myself holding back from giving him a final answer, and this did not seem logical even to me. I tried to go back in my mind to exactly what he had said, gesture by gesture, sentence by sentence, on that July night when, in the midst of his sorrow and discouragement after Tom McHone's murder, he had asked me to marry him. His actions now, his kisses, told me that he considered us engaged, a sort of mutual, unspoken agreement. What bothered me most was that though David acted as if he loved me, he never really used the words. If David did not love me enough to say so spontaneously, yes, even to shout it to the world, then could this really be love? If not . . . and then would come a suffocating sensation in my diaphragm, as if I needed air that my lungs could not suck in fast enough. What was wrong?

But then he would appear, gay and vital; and in his presence my doubts would vanish like those morning mists being chased out of our valley by the rising sun. For I enjoyed David's warm lips on mine. I liked being in his arms. Surely, I could not have all that physical feeling for him and not be in love. I must be wrong to be insisting, in my heart, on his saying certain words. Perhaps his actions *were* all that was necessary. Time would work this out; of course it would.

And there were other causes for joy that golden autumn. All the hard work of the previous year was at last reaping rewards. I now had all the textbooks and supplies I needed for my school.

And we were readying space in the mission house for the boarders. We planned to start slowly with three boys and four girls. The girls would sleep on cots set side by side across the back of the second floor room in the mission house; the boys in the third floor attic room. In the evening, the big living room would be the study hall.

The boarders were being chosen for a variety of reasons: Mountie O'Teale, since my experience with her had given every reason to believe that the child would blossom away from her terrible home environment; Isaak McHone because, with his father gone, he so needed to be near

404

David that Opal and Uncle Bogg had agreed. Then Becky and Dicle Holt lived so far away and the long walk was harder for them than for the Holt boys; Wanda Ann Beck, ten, had bad eyes (trachoma, Dr. MacNeill said) and needed to be closer for his care. Also it looked as if we might have to take in Lundy Taylor. If his father was returning home at all (as we suspected), it was too sporadically to do Lundy any good. Then Arrowood Holcombe wanted desperately to be with us, and though David was having trouble persuading Mr. Holcombe to give up Arrowood's help at home, it looked as if we might win our way on that too.

And almost best of all, there was the book on Folk Schools that Mrs. Browning—true to her promise—had sent me. For the first time I saw where we could go with the Cutter Gap school—or at least where *I* thought we ought to go. It was exhilarating to see a goal ahead and start driving towards it. Previously I had had many ideas about the school—a clinic and adult education and the rest—but there had been too many holes in the fabric of my dreams: problems which city and town schools did not have and for which I could find no solutions. But now Grundtvig and Christen Kold, as I came to know them through the book, were reweaving the fabric so that it was whole and complete: I had been full only of questions; they had answers.

Like that big question I had wondered about during my first meeting of the Sewing Circle at Miss Alice's: How would believing in the love of God solve problems like illiteracy and poverty for the highlanders? Now I saw the connection between Miss Alice's certainty about the inner guiding Light and Grundtvig's ideas. God did have a master plan for the Cove and Grundtvig was saying that we could find that plan by looking deep into the human spirit, our own and the children's and their parents'.

It was a startling experience to have this book, printed in London, come into my hands at precisely the right moment. Half-formulated ideas, in a blaze of recognition of their own kind, rushed out to meet the luminous thoughts on the printed page. I all but chained *Among the Danes* around my neck; carried it around with me until it was thumbed and worn; talked about it at the table until the others must have dreaded mealtimes.

"You see," I explained one evening at dinner, "Bishop Grundtvig believed that childhood shouldn't ever be

405

thought of just as a prelude to becoming an adult. Childhood ought to be enjoyed for itself. Too much brain work forced on children kills something in their spirit. Let them run and play and make treehouses and catch lightning bugs and lie in a field staring at the clouds floating by. Provide them a wholesome environment, and then let their spirits go free, free, free."

Miss Alice smiled appreciatively. "My Quaker father would have agreed with that."

"As far as *I* have observed," Miss Ida remarked primly, "children need no encouragement to play."

"Grundtvig saw each stage in growing up as needing a special kind of education," I continued. "He said, 'Life is growth, and everything must come in the order of nature.' "

David was not really listening, but Miss Alice had a question. "What about those hard teen years?"

"A lot of physical activity during adolescence. Deprive young people of that and you get trouble every time. Lessons, sure. But also a taste of several kinds of work, things they may choose as a vocation later. Much work with the hands for both boys and girls. The learning of respect for manual work, never something to be looked down on as somehow inferior to mental work. Then lots of athletics. Wear them out with folk dances, things like that."

At least I had Miss Alice with me, so I went on. "Grundtvig saw youth—seventeen, eighteen on—as the time of awakening. And he was strong on the point that awakening and enlivening always have to come before enlightenment. Otherwise, cramming facts down the gullet is mostly lost motion."

"So that means," Miss Alice picked it up, "that Grundtvig would begin with serious education about the time pupils are leaving school for good in most countries."

"That's right. He would get serious then because they're finally ready. By then they *want* answers as to what life is all about. Their heads and their hands are full of question marks. So that's why he thought they shouldn't be met with more questions: there are no examinations in his schools. Rather the purpose of school is to help youth find answers."

"And this man Grundtvig had all the answers, I suppose, to what life is all about?" David said, finally entering the conversation.

"No, he didn't claim that. But he was full of ideas. He used a fascinating method to find answers. It's really what Socrates did, the spoken word, the dialogue. Grundtvig and Kold both thought of the spoken word as lots more important than books.

"Even the printed words they did use were really just the spoken words committed to paper. I mean like folk tales, Nordic and Grecian mythology, folk songs—all those things."

Miss Ida was rather pointedly clearing the table for dessert, so I jumped up to help her. David was still not taking what I was saying seriously. "Wonder what deep significance this Bishop would find in some of Uncle Bogg's tall tales?"

I started to poke him with a fork I was carrying, but caught Miss Ida's look and hastily went on gathering up dishes. "As a matter of fact, he'd find more significance than you think. He didn't think that Nordic mythology, for instance, could be dismissed as pagan superstition, but that it was a living expression of the human spirit, therefore creative, and should be paid attention to!"

Miss Alice's smile twinkled at me, but David said, "Christy, how can you get so worked up over the ideas of some foreign churchman?"

"Because they're fascinating. And because that's just the way I am."

"Am what?" It was Dr. MacNeill standing in the dining room doorway. None of us had heard him coming in.

"Come in, Doctor." David seemed glad of the interruption. "Set sail with us. We're afloat on a sea of ideas."

The Doctor picked up a straight chair from its place against the wall and set it down between David and Miss Alice. "Ideas about what?"

"Oh, a school. Sweden or somewhere."

"David! Not Sweden! Denmark. I *knew* you weren't listening." I carried my stack of plates into the kitchen.

"Sweden? Denmark? Both quite a ways from Cutter Gap. Why schools in Denmark?"

From the kitchen I could hear Miss Alice explaining to the Doctor some of the ideas we had been discussing. Only filtered through the quiet and order of her mind they seemed not only logical, but eminently feasible.

I was halfway to the table with a deep-dish apple pie when I heard the Doctor say, "Sure, I've heard about Danish Folk Schools."

"You have! Where?" I asked wonderingly.

"From a visiting professor in Medical School, specialist in eye surgery. A Dane who got his start at a Folk School."

"What did he say about them?"

"Let's see. He had a lot to say. Jensen, his name was. Son of a peasant farmer. Said deciding to go to that school one October changed his life."

With effort I controlled the rising excitement inside me and made myself ask slowly, "How? How did it change his life?"

The Doctor smiled at my eagerness. "He credited the personality of the teacher with that. Can't think of the teacher's name. Said his teacher gave him a great love for Denmark and her people." A remembering look came into the Doctor's eyes. "Come to think of it, Jensen was the happiest man I ever knew. I remember him whistling, striding around the campus, always whistling."

"That's right! Grundtvig had that joy too. But not always. Up to the age of forty-one he'd been a serious, gloomy sort of perfectionist and a serious critic of his country. But then he had a deep religious experience and he realized that he had to build people up, to love them. And it was then he got all those great ideas about the part education would play in a national awakening."

"But we mustn't just talk about it," I plunged on. "I think we should do something about it right here in the Cove. For example, why couldn't David start a school for the men in the mornings? Use the parlor here. That way we'd get the older boys in my school away from the little children, and you could add to them any of the other men who want to come."

David smiled at me in a patronizing way. "It just wouldn't work, Christy."

Dr. MacNeill held up a restraining hand. "Wait a moment before we judge. Christy, what would David do with the men? What kind of classes?"

"Not the same as for children. Even if a man can't read or write, treat him as an adult, an equal. Begin small, maybe with only three or four men in a class."

David was leaning back in his chair tilted precariously on its two back legs, twirling his watch chain in his fingers. "So a group of mountain men have just ambled into the parlor across the hall, rusty black felt hats in hand, to go to school. What do I do then?"

"There are several things you might do," I retorted, stung by his tone. "It might be smart to begin with a merry story, for example."

" 'Merry story!' That must be straight out of that wonderful book of yours!"

"It *is* a wonderful book!" I flung back. "So you begin with a funny story that takes them into history. Like an episode from John Sevier's life, something like that. Before they know it, you're into a history lesson, not for memorizing facts or dates or anything like that, but for the excitement of it, the fascination of it. What real men and women did. How they succeeded. What their failures were. How these mountains were settled. Some of the men would have stories of their own to contribute too about their own ancestors."

Miss Alice was looking at me out of those pools of quietness that were her gray eyes. "Then——?"

"Then you'd have to sell the men on real reasons for learning to read and write and for mathematics. Like figuring out land acreage, and what a cord of wood is, so they can handle money and keep a record on paper. They'd be proud of learning those things.

"And literature. Begin where they are, with Jeb Spencer's ballads and Uncle Bogg's tall tales. And then introduce them to some rollicking poetry and some stories from other countries.

"Oh, and David, it would be so easy for you to teach woodworking! Their fathers made handcrafted furniture. They could copy some of the wonderful old pieces in the cabins. And it would take arithmetic to figure out the lumber you need, wouldn't it? Let the men sell the furniture and keep books. That's writing and arithmetic, isn't it?"

David spoke patiently, as to a child. "Nice ideas in theory, Christy. But you're forgetting how these men are. They'd come for two or three mornings—and then quit. As for learning community responsibility, forget it. They're not capable of it."

"Then why are you here, if you think we're that hopeless?" the Doctor asked.

" 'We'?"

"I'm a mountain man."

"You're different."

"But you were lumping all mountain men together. If I'm any exception, it's because of several men who felt as

Christy does—they saw possibilities in some of us. Maybe you should know—even today it wouldn't be possible for me to practice medicine in Cutter Gap if my friends and some of their wealthy patients didn't help. The Cove people can't pay a doctor. So what does that mean? That they go without medical care? You see, those men dreamed a dream for all of us back here, so they gave me the chance to help fulfill it."

"Well—yes. That's fine. But Christy's ignoring the contrast between most of the mountain men and the Scandinavians. Scandinavians are energetic. These men were born lazy and raised tired."

"They weren't born lazy. It's just that they grew up with nothing to look forward to."

David pushed his chair away from the table and rose to his feet with a look on his face that he meant to be good-humored. "Look Christy, I'm not against your ideas about building up the school here in the Cove. In four or five years—who knows? But right now we have one small schoolhouse that has to double as a church and has just sprung a leak in the new roof. And I've got to get out there and fix it. So—if you'll excuse me . . ."

No one said anything for a moment after David left. The autumn, the golden autumn. What had happened to the shine of it?

I felt deflated suddenly, and tired.

Thirty-seven

NOW THAT MANY shared experiences with folks like Miss Alice and Fairlight and Opal, Little Burl and Mountie and Isaak had laid foundations of mutual caring and trust, these relationships—even with the children—were striking deeper levels. More and more often my school-children were opening up to me these hidden areas.

One Thursday afternoon Zady Spencer came by the mission excited about a "hant tale" that her father had brought home from the man-talk at Bob Allen's mill. "Teacher, Granny Barclay *seen* Old Marthy. Old Marthy's a witch, ugly as a coot. No hair hardly. Monstrous red eyes—" The little girl's black eyes in her thin face were aglitter with an unhealthy excitement. "Ye dasn't not believe hit. Lots of folks has seen Old Marthy! Keeps a-creepin' from house to house, hidin' things from folks. One time throwed ashes into Mistress Allen's churn, spoiled all of it." Zady was shivering, her breath coming in little palpitating gasps.

I knew that Granny Barclay was reputed to have "second sight"—a belief in seeing into the future which the Scottish and Irish immigrants had brought with them to the New World. Some of it may have been authentic. But the superstitions still being handed down to children like Zady were incredible.

I thought about how often—after my pupils had come to know and to trust me—they had come to school bright-eyed and excited over ghost stories replete with vivid details: jealous witches forcing someone in the Cove to eat "witch balls" (pine needles wrapped round and round with human hair); the devil forcing a group one by one to kiss his buttocks as a pledge of allegiance; or the devil driving a cart black as ink drawn by black oxen down the mountainside.

I put one arm around Zady. "And what did your father and mother say about the story of Old Martha?"

"Mama jest got a funny look to her eyes. Said she'd heerd a pack of dogs a-howlin' in the night. Said that was a bad sign."

I sighed, remembering Fairlight's long silences, knowing well that same look Zady had seen in her mother's eyes. Yes, there was trouble there, somewhere in the depths of Fairlight's spirit, and I must find the way to reach it. Again I pulled my thoughts back to the little girl leaning against my arm. "Zady," I asked gently, "are you afraid of the dark?"

"Oh, yes'm! It's scary to have to leave the firelight and walk into the shadders to bed. Most nights I put the kivers over my head. Gives me prickles to peer at the dark. Always scared for fear I'll see a ghost."

"I know. I used to be like that when I was a little girl."

"You was!"

"Yes, I was. Sometimes I'd long to run and climb in bed between mother and father. But then I'd be too ashamed to let them know that I was scared because I was too big a girl for that. So I'd lie there in my own bed shivering and shaking."

Zady was looking at me with interest. "How'd ye git over hit?"

"One day they sang a certain hymn at Sunday school. Seemed as if it was just for me. I'll sing the refrain for you:

> God will take care of you
> Through every day, o'er all the way,
> He will take care of you,
> He will take care of you——"

"That's nice."

"So whenever I was scared of the dark, I'd sing those four lines over and over to myself. And you know what, Zady? After a while the love of God was more real to me than any old ghost. And then all the ghosts went away, and ever since the dark has seemed friendly and cozy."

Zady hugged me and planted a wet kiss on my cheek. "Sing hit again, Teacher, and then I won't disremember hit."

So I did—and the little girl skipped out the door,

humming. After she had gone, I sat there pondering the fine line between faith and superstition; between that realistic facing up to life that Miss Alice was always urging on me and a handing over of faith to the power of negativism and evil.

Like that sixteen-year-old girl in Miss Alice's school in Cataleechie. The girl had been dying of tuberculosis and her one request of Alice Henderson was not for help to get well, but that she would make her a shroud so that she could see it and try it on before she died. Indignantly, Miss Alice had refused, suggesting to the girl that instead, she would do better to center her thinking on health.

But death had had more dramatic appeal. The girl had finally persuaded her father to measure her and build her a pine coffin. Then she had had herself photographed lying in the coffin "so that I can see how fancy-fine I'll look." The girl had died eight months later.

How could one so young actually prefer death to life! Yet the sixteen-year-old's fatalism was common in the mountains.

Some of this pessimism seemed to have its source in nature itself. In the highlander's experience, nature was more stern than benevolent. From the depleted soil of the rock-strewn hillsides the mountain people wrested their meager harvests. There was no kindliness, only travail and misery in the howling winds whipping down from snow-capped peaks, whistling through the chinks of cabins, penetrating scanty clothes to the bone marrow. Man, little man, stood defenseless and insignificant, forgotten and forlorn against the mighty mountains.

God—where was God? Somewhere out beyond that vast sweep of nature. His lightnings flashed. His thunderbolts were hurled. They reverberated from peak to peak, zigzagging across the skies, splitting the trunks of great trees from branch-tip to root-top, at times striking dead a man caught in the elemental fury.

And so for them the issues of life and death were joined. Nor did God stay His hand—not for storms or pestilence or the disease that carried so many to early graves. Not for the hatred that rived hearts before it riddled bodies. Not even for the poverty that ground men and women and children into the dust of not caring.

So this God must be Jehovah-Yahveh, the God of Mount Sinai, from whom Moses had hidden his face in terror. He was the God of the Old Testament, whose prophet Elisha could curse naughty children in the name of the Lord and count it proper revenge when she-bears came out of the wood to rend the babes. And men hacked their enemies to death shouting the name of the Lord. The winds blew and the seas raged—and men fled this Being lest He wrest from them the scanty security they had. How could little man hope to comprehend such a Being? So man's only chance was to ally himself to Him through such obedience as he could manage, to "stand what has to be stood," to slough his way through day by day—and desperately hope that in the end this terrible Jehovah would bring the faithful ones to glory in a better life than this one.

That was the highlander's faith. It was a belief to make the heart quake, not to comfort it. Shadows, stygian shadows of the mountains had cast their pall even on faith.

As with Zady in her fear of the dark, so with her mother. After I had known the Spencers for several months. I came to see a connection with these fears and the location of their cabin. Anyone seeing the Spencer land for the first time would have supposed that the cabin at the top of Lonesome Ridge would always be in full daylight. Instead, the land wore the sharpest contrasts of light and shadow of any place I had seen in that area. At different times of day the higher peak opposite shut out the sun, plunging portions of the Ridge into blackness.

Since that afternoon of Bob Allen's brain operation when I had first watched the sun dipping behind the sheer rise of the Pinnacles opposite, how often Fairlight and I had seen that shadow creep across the face of the ridge. It was like an immense hand raised between the sun and the one who watched. From between the fingers of the giant's hand a few streaks of light filtered through the trees, but in between, eerie ebony dusk lay across the land.

Once I had asked Jeb why his ancestors had not built in a more protected and accessible spot. He had not known. Grandsir Spencer could have told me, but he had died in the spring two years before.

Perhaps the answer was that Jeb's great-great-great-grandmother, just over from the misty highlands of Scotland, had been the first Spencer to watch that giant's hand come between her and the sun. She must have seen that shadow creeping up the side of their ridge day after day. So she had directed her menfolk, "Build as high up as possible—there on the backbone of our land near the sun."

But not even the top bald of the ridge had been high enough to escape the gloaming. And I wondered if that ancestress of Jeb's had been as depressed by the daily shrouding of the sun as Fairlight often was, as almost anyone would be.

In fact, it was uncanny how faithfully Fairlight reflected in her nature the variations of light and shade of the mountains around her. For she could be as gay as a careless child. Then abruptly her mood would change, and I would see behind her frightened eyes the cimmerian shadows of a complex nature. While it pleased me that my company mostly drew out the gay side, I was more and more troubled that at this deepest level, I did not seem to be helping at all. Gradually I had learned how deep these inarticulate emotions ran, how surging they were.

I was thinking about all this one afternoon when Fairlight and I were sitting on her front porch shelling shucky beans. She was not very talkative, though she had commented that "Jeb's had a right good turn with the bees. He muscled out'n the Cove two hundred thirty-five pounds of honey. The best ever, for a fact."

"That's wonderful, Fairlight!"

"Course if we was makin' tracks for fortunes, we could make some more bee gums."

"Of course!"

"No, it ain't to be thought of."

"Why not?"

"Don't need no more of this world's goods. Some folks gits plumb mesmerized when paper money is shook afore their eyes."

"But Fairlight, you still need so many things, basic things. There's not the slightest danger of your getting greedy."

There was no answer. I looked at Fairlight and realized that she had not heard my last sentence. It was late in the afternoon now with the sun dipping. She was staring at the Pinnacle opposite with a look on her face that I had seen so often, a look that frightened me.

"Christy," her musical voice was low, confidential; still

she did not turn her head to look at me, "See that other mounting? Sometimes I think it's witched. Most every day it puts me in mind of the shadder o'death." Her pan of beans slipped off her lap. She slid to her knees, reached for my arm, clinging to it, her mouth set in a grim line. "What is to be, will be. Nothing can stop it. It has to come to us all some time, I reckon. But Christy, I git the trembles when I think about bein' put in a box and a-lyin' out thar somewhere covered over with dirt." Her voice had sunk to a whisper as if she was revealing too much.

I started to say, "Fairlight, how silly! You're not going to die—" but the words withered on my tongue. That would be too glib a reply. Not true either. All of us *do* have to die sometime. But I was still too young to have thought much about death. And death wasn't real to me, whereas it was for Fairlight. In her short lifetime she had seen so many die, two of her and Jeb's children—a newborn baby girl, Ceclie, and Jeter, a little boy of three, a score of friends and relatives. And back here in the mountains people were forced to look starkly into the face of the black-hooded figure. There was no way to soften or to dodge any least malevolent detail. No undertakers; nothing but a pine box or a half a bee-gum log—which the family must prepare; a hole in the red clay—which the family, sometimes boys as young as Isaak McHone, must dig. No camouflage or self-deception was possible. For one as impressionable as Fairlight this had left permanent scars.

Knowing this, there struggled in my mind some thought about the danger of getting our gaze riveted on that dirt as the only reality, about how necessary it is to raise our eyes to see something beyond the pine box and the clay. What about all the promises that Christ made us about immortality, I wanted to ask. I knew that to Him the sensitive spirit of the woman beside me would be cherished. I had watched that spirit waken, start to leave resignation behind and begin the struggle to cast off limitations. "Let there be light," she had learned in her first reading lesson. Fairlight's spirit was not going to be snuffed out like a gutted candle and plunged into darkness, not for a moment could I have believed that.

Fairlight seemed to expect no reply, no consolation in words; she simply needed to feel me close to her. With a shock I understood that I could not speak to her fears as easily as I had to Zady's. In her thinking at least, it was too late for discussion or argument against the deep emotions that tortured her. Her battle with the mountain had become a personal battle; this was now her life pitted against the shadow. And even as I watched, the sun dipped behind the peak and the heinous gloom slanted across her upturned face.

Thirty-eight

HOW CAN I ever forget that day in early October when Fairlight Spencer sent Zady to tell me that she needed me. Would I please come as soon as possible? No clue was offered as to what the need was. Only Zady's dark brooding eyes and thin face screwed up with worry underscored the urgency.

Nor would the child leave my side until she had seen me saddling Buttons. Then her mission accomplished, without another word she bounded off toward home, streaking across the mission yard, leaping from rock to rock across the creek, running like a brown-legged deer diagonally up across the face of the mountain.

I followed by the more tedious trail, giving Buttons the rein up the low foothills. But as we reached the first heavily wooded spur from which the path rose steeply, my mare was forced to a slow walk. The rhododendron leaves were still straight and shiny, like summer leaves, not beginning to curl as they usually did in the fall. At moments the silence of the woods was so intense that the patter of acorns falling from the oak trees onto the dry leaves sounded like gentle rain.

Though Buttons and I had made this trip often, the mare had never been sure-footed on the heights and she was always skittish about the final ascent to the Spencer cabin. As I rode over the crest of the last rise, I saw that all of the children—except John and Zady—were in the yard watching for me, their faces solemn.

"What a nice welcoming committee," I greeted them. But there was no gaiety in their response.

Clara came to help me dismount. "Been waitin' for you." She spoke softly, taking the reins from my hands. "I'll hitch the post to Buttons."

Such a funny way to say it! "Where's your mother?" I asked.

"Mama's inside." The tall girl's face was expressionless. She would not look me in the eyes. "She's abed."

I hurried on into the cabin. From the open door, brilliant autumn sunlight spilled across the floor. But the cabin, usually noisy with activity—children's voices and laughter, kitchen sounds, Jeb's music—was so quiet it seemed deserted. Then I saw her, Fairlight, lying on the bed, the outlines of her body defined by the quilt tucked in around her.

Her face was flushed with a heavy look about it that changed her features. Her eyes were open but bloodshot and dull, her head moving restlessly from side to side on the pillow. I felt her forehead. Hot! Incredibly hot!

"Christy—" One hand crept across the quilt toward me. "You've come."

"Of course, I've come, Fairlight. Why didn't you send for me sooner?"

"My side hurts—here—so bad."

Her breathing was heavy with such wheezing that I thought she might have pneumonia. *But it was so early in the autumn. We haven't even had any cold weather.*

The children had trailed me into the house and were standing at the foot of the bed, watching me carefully. Their mother held her right hand up in front of her face. "It's bigged. All swelled up. Why is it so big?"

I looked at the hand. Perfectly normal except that the skin was so dry that it was pulled taut. Fairlight's lips, cracked from the fever, were twitching in a strange way.

"Clara, how long has your mother been like this?"

"Mama was ailin', right bad off all last week," the girl answered. "Complained of a-hurtin' in the head. Yesterday had the trembles. Shook all over like an aspen tree in the wind. But she wouldn't take to her bed."

"Where's your father?"

"Took the hound-dogs, went ba-ar huntin'—over Laurel Top somewheres."

"How long has he been gone?"

The girl thought a moment. "I'm not certain-sure. Left at day-bust, 'twas three days ago, reckon."

"Christy—" the voice from the bed sounded desperate. Fairlight raised her head off the pillow to look at me, but I had the feeling that her eyes were not focusing. The pupils looked dilated. "Christy, tell them to take the chairs off'n

419

me. All that house plunder they're a-pilin' on me. The chairs—all them chairs. Tell them— They're a-smashin' me. Tell them—" She began coughing, a deep racking cough, painful to hear.

I pressed her hand reassuringly. "Fairlight, there's no furniture on you, no chairs."

"Off'n me, off'n me. Tell them—*Christy*—"

"Fairlight, I'm here now. Right here. I won't let anybody pile anything on you."

My heart was thumping and my legs trembling. *I must not let the children see my alarm.* I forced myself to speak slowly to try to keep panic out of my voice. "Clara, hasn't anybody sent for Dr. MacNeill?"

"Mama didn't reckon to need no doctor-medicine."

"How about John? Is he around? Could I send him for the Doctor?"

"Papa carried him ba-ar huntin' too."

At that moment Zady appeared in the doorway, breathless and panting from the long climb from the mission.

What was I to do? For the girls it was too long a journey to Doctor MacNeill's cabin and he might not be there anyway.

"Clara," I said, "we've got to have help. Would you run over to Holcombes' and get one of the men to go fetch the Doctor?"

Already Clara was at the door. "Say they can use Buttons if necessary. And tell them to try the mill first. Usually one of the men there knows where the Doctor is. Oh, and Clara—" The girl stood in the doorway looking at me with large solemn eyes. "Tell them that your mother is really sick. This is an emergency." She turned and in a moment had disappeared over the brow of the hill.

The rest of the children were standing without moving, looking at me gravely. *What shall I do now?* Fear was a lump in my throat. Fear was a weight on my chest. A fog in my brain. I could not think. *But I have to think. I have to do something.* Blindly, I struck out. "Zady, I need your help."

"Yes'm?"

"Would you bring me a pailful of cold water from the spring?"

The girl was as eager to get into action as I was. "Yes, ma'am."

"And Lulu, do you think you could find me some rags? Any rags will do."

Lulu ran off and was soon back, thrusting at me some of her mother's best quilt pieces. Fairlight would not want me to use these, but this was no time to be choosy.

Then Zady was setting the brimming bucket on the floor by me. I dropped the cotton scraps in the water and wrung out two of them for cold compresses for Fairlight's forehead and wrists. Somehow, we had to bring down her fever. But it was impossible to keep the compresses on her wrists; she kept waving her hands in the air, grasping at something invisible. Or she would pluck at the quilt over her, her lips moving all the while.

I dared not put cold compresses on her chest, for if this was pneumonia, that might be the wrong treatment. I pulled a chair close to the bed and kept changing the cloth on her forehead every few minutes, but she was so hot that in no time at all the compress would be warm from body heat.

Zady stood close to me, watching. Once she said hesitantly, "Teacher, Mama kept a-wakin' us up, talkin' last night. Couldn't make no sense out'n some of it."

Then Clara came rushing back in to report breathlessly, "Mr. Holcombe's gone to fotch the Doc. Said he was certain-sure to search him out somewhars. Mistress Holcombe's not thar. Gone to kinfolks over the far holler. Her cousin, onct-removed, belongs to birth a baby soon."

"Thank you, Clara. Let's hope Doctor MacNeill gets here soon." I wrung out another rag and gently sponged the rest of Fairlight's face. It was then that I saw through her open lips some brown fuzz on her teeth and her tongue. I stared, trying to understand what this could be. *I thought feverish tongues got white, not brown.* The muttering went on. Most of it was not intelligible.

Then Fairlight reached for my hand and clung to it, looking directly at me, the fog lifting from her mind, love and longing in her eyes. "Christy, my time's come. I know it. But Christy, I don't want to die. Don't want to leave my young'uns." She half-raised herself in bed, her grasp on my hand like a vise. "Why do I have to die? Holp me. Christy, will you holp me?"

"Fairlight, you're not going to die. Sure, you're sick, plenty sick. But Doctor MacNeill is on his way to you right now. He'll know exactly what to do. Try to rest now. And please don't worry. Everything's going to be all right. I know it is." Desperately, I was trying to put conviction into my voice.

But she appeared not to have heard me. Slow tears coursed down her cheeks. "It's no use. I've knowed this for days. Hold my hand, Christy. Stay with me. Please don't leave me. Jeb—I don't want to leave Jeb—or the least'un. Baby Guy needs me. Why do I have to leave? I'm not old enough to die."

"Fairlight, *don't talk that way*. It's wrong for you to talk that way! The Doctor will be here any minute."

"Can't you holp me, Christy? A body shouldn't have to die when she don't want—to—die." She faded back into the delirium. Her eyes were open, but now there was no recognition in them.

The room was electric with tension. Lulu was crying softly. Zady was standing rigid, the back of one hand pressed to her mouth, her eyes pools of despair. Fairlight had flung off the compresses, so I picked them up from the bed, wrung one out again and put it on her forehead. My own face was wet with perspiration. I dipped my hand in the chilly water and rubbed it over my eyelids and cheeks, grateful for the cooling touch.

Then the lines of Fairlight's face softened and into her voice came the lilt of a young girl's gaiety. "Race ye to the branch yonder ... What ye got to do that's so blessed important? See that sycamore a-hangin' out over the water? Bet I can skin-the-cat afore you."

Fascinated at the change in their mother's tone, the children gathered closer, the three youngest thinking that she was telling them a story, "Oh-h-h," she shrieked, "fell in. Scared me fitified. Water's cold, so-o-o cold." And the children laughed delightedly.

Her comments were so graphic that we could see the fun ... One moment she was picking wild strawberries in Pleasant Valley. Then she and her sister were making necklaces of scarlet haws and crowns of oak leaves ... They were running to climb a persimmon tree laden with heavy yellow fruit. "Not hardly a leaf left on this-here tree. So many persimmons. I'll throw one down to you, ye little wildcat ... Ugh! I bit one that wasn't ripe." Her lips, cracked and flaked from the fever, puckered as she relived the moment.

Or Grandsir and Granny Spencer were alive, and all the family were rollicking through a molasses stir-off. "Prettiest yellow foam ye ever did see. No, Web, don't! That green foam'll give ye a stummick ache, sure. Aye,

422

right smart patch we had this year. Oh, I can taste this 'lasses now on hot crusty corn pone."

Then it was night before the fire and Granny was telling stories. The voice from the bed was hoarse now, racked by the cough and the compulsion to talk and talk. From her parched lips came the verse that she must have known as far back as she could remember, part of the story Granny was telling, it seemed:

> "Three drops of blood I've shed for thee!
> Three little babies I've born for thee!
> Whitebear Whittington, turn to me. . . ."

I sat there weak from emotion, wondering which was the more frightening—the imploring "Why? Why? Why?" of the more lucid moments, or the mind's wide wanderings. Then Little Guy crept close to me and crawled onto my lap. I found myself cuddling him close, stroking his short, sturdy legs, cradling his grimy little fingers in mine.

At last the voice from the bed fell silent. Fairlight was slipping into a sleep or a coma, I could not tell which. Once again, her features changed. She was a girl no longer. The tired lines came back. The color was slowly ebbing from her cheeks.

The children were around my chair now, watching first their mother, then me, not understanding, not knowing what to expect. Over and over, Clara went to the door or to the edge of the yard, her eyes searching for the approaching figure of Dr. MacNeill.

Fairlight was peaceful now, her face quiet, her hands still, though her breathing sounded shallow. Perhaps the cold compresses had helped. She had worn herself out talking; a good sleep would help. I smoothed her covers and then sank back into the chair, Guy still sprawled across me. The little fellow was asleep.

Suddenly, there was such a violent movement of the bedclothes that I jumped, almost dumping Little Guy off my lap. Fairlight screamed, "Oh, *no!*" hysteria in her voice. "The shadder! The shadder's a-comin' for me!"

The strength of her voice startled me. Then I realized that she was throwing off her covers. Frantically, I set Guy on the floor and reached for her. But she was already out of bed, several steps across the floor. "Christy, holp me ... Hide me! The shadder's after me. Holp me git away."

Even as she sank dizzily to her knees, I saw that she was right: the shadow's time of day had come. Though the late afternoon sun was still streaming through the open door, lighting the room and illuminating Fairlight's distorted face, even as I reached her and she flung herself at me, grasping me around the legs, the slanting shadows were crawling across the floor toward us. How had she *known*, lying there in bed with her eyes closed?

"Christy!" It was a wild shriek now, terrible to hear. "The shadder o' death—push hit away. Hide me! Oh, holp me—!" Her head was upraised, her eyes only for that peak across the way, her arms before her face as if to ward off a blow.

I was on my knees beside her, trying to take her in my arms—but her body was rigid. I began crooning to her, not knowing what I was saying, all my love pouring into torrents of words: "Though I walk through the valley of the shadow of death, I will fear no evil, for Thou art with me ... For Thou art with me ... For He is with us, Fairlight. Oh, Fairlight, do you hear me? I will fear *no evil*—for He *is* with us—" Sitting there on the floor, I hugged her, stroked her face with my hands.

Suddenly the rigidity went out of her and she relaxed in my arms. Still holding her tightly, I looked up. The giant's hand was upraised now, the light in the cabin all but extinguished. And as I glanced down again at the beloved face in my lap, quiet now, the blackness of the shadow fell directly across her face.

Her features were too composed. "Oh, no! Oh, dear God, no!" I stared in disbelief. It could not be. But it was. There was no breath. Her eyes were still staring, but no breath escaped her sagging jaws.

My cry had told the children. Clara rushed to her mother, felt her breast in a knowledge beyond her years, then straightened up, tears flowing down her cheeks. Zady threw herself on Fairlight, sobbing inconsolably, then collapsed into a heap on the floor. Lulu crawled up and began hugging her mother's feet. I was too stunned to think—or to move—or to know what to do next.

I don't know how long the children and I sat there in a tightly huddled group on the floor. Still, I could not believe it. This was crazy superstition. It could not be

424

true. Things like this did not happen. I was dreaming. Any moment now I would wake up and find this a bad dream.

I did not hear Dr. MacNeill enter the cabin. Gently, he took me by the arm, got me to my feet. He spoke, but I did not hear what he said. Then he and Mr. Holcombe picked up Fairlight and carried her to the bed.

At last when Dr. MacNeill had finished examining her, slowly, almost tenderly, he pulled the quilt over the beautiful face. His eyes sought mine. "She's had it for a good ten days. When it's not caught and the patient keeps going, death can come in the second week."

" 'It'? Pneumonia?"

He hesitated, as if reluctant to answer me. "Typhoid, Christy. It's typhoid."

Thirty-nine

A BLESSED NUMBNESS carried me through Fairlight's funeral. Shock? Some special dispensation from above? No matter. Like an anesthetic, it served its purpose, enabled me to get through the days, to speak words of comfort to the Spencer children who clung to me now in place of their mother. Mr. Spencer was obviously relieved when I suggested that I take Guy, Lulu, and Zady down to the mission for a time. Between Miss Ida and me, we could at least take care of the littlest Spencers.

But their questions—how could we answer these: "Where is my mother now?" ... "What is she doing?" ... "When will I see her again?" And Little Guy, over and over in his high-pitched tremolo, "I want my mama. I want my mama—" I could only gather him in my arms and let him cling to me. Many a night he cried himself to sleep.

Often during these days I would hear my own voice as from a distance reassuring Lulu or Zady, mouthing platitudes to Jeb Spencer or to John or Clara, dispensing comfort as a doctor dispenses pills. But for me there was an air of unreality about it all. I was still treading air, walking a foot above the earth.

It must have been about the eighth day after the funeral that the world came back into focus, the soles of my feet again touched the soil of the commonplace. Then I knew how sorely I had been wounded by Fairlight's death. This was no ache but a wild, searing pain boring into my vitals, piercing every thought.

I doubt that my torment was altruistic. Probably most grief contains a large measure of self-reference; mine no exception. Clawing questions gave me no peace. What if I? ... Why hadn't I? ... If only I ... If only I had not failed my friend. Fairlight's superstitious terror of the shadow, for instance. How great a part had this abnormal

426

fear played in her death? Could fear actually have paralyzed her body's defenses against the typhoid? And with the hours upon hours that Fairlight and I had spent together through the spring and summer, why had I not found a way to help her see that the shadow cast by a mountain had no power over her of any kind?

Beyond that, however, my resentment was directed at God Almighty Himself. I wondered why Fairlight had been taken by typhoid rather than someone not quite bright or someone old and crippled, whose children were grown and whose life was almost over anyway? Why were the good and the beautiful so ruthlessly plucked?

Then the scene at the graveside festered in my mind: that pathetic cemetery against the background of the titan peaks, as though to mock life's fragility: the stem of the flower broken, and no man can mend it; the soaring bird felled so suddenly that the tiny body is warm in death, the unfinished song still in his throat; the invisible germ that cuts us down; the heartbeat stilled so easily.

In my ears still rang the plaintive melodies of the hymns echoing back from the wall of mountains, wafted on the whimpering wind:

> Soon we'll cross the border line,
> To that land of love divine. . . .

And they had sung "We Have Mothers up in Heaven," but it was on earth that the little Spencers needed a mother.

Snatches of the comments I had heard at the funeral hovered around my mind like those darting black ravens Mr. Pentland had told me about . . . "I knowed her time had come. Dreamt about her a-gallopin' into the day-down on a black yearling horse" . . . "'Tis the fairest flowers wilt the soonest. Too good for this world, she was—" . . .

Too good to stand gazing in delight at the plum trees in riotous bloom? Too good to tell hilarious stories to Little Guy? Too good to pull taffy with her girls? Or to sing the beautiful old ballads while she churned? No, it made no sense to me. Justice was justice. And fair was fair. Apparently we could count on no justice in this life; heaven's ways are surely not our ways. In my rebellion I was not certain that I wanted any part of such a heaven—that is, if there is any life after this one, for doubts now gnawed like rats at the fabric of my faith.

Dr. MacNeill too was coming by the mission more often than before, watching me closely, for I was now a prime suspect to come down with the disease. But what happened to my body was not my chief concern now. I could live to be an old lady, but if I never knew final truth about life and death and God, what good would life be? With a mind often far off the work at hand, I would sometimes jump guiltily when spoken to, or else not hear at all.

Each night sleep came only with exhaustion. And even then I tossed—hot and restless—pursued by dreams that had a nightmarish quality. Often I would awaken with a throbbing head and aching legs. After one such night, feeling I could not live another day if I did not get answers to the questions that tormented me, I turned for help to David. I found him at the side of the house putting new screening on the porch door. "David," I plunged in, "what happens at death? I mean, can Fairlight still see Jeb and her children and us?"

He stopped pounding in the brads and straightened up to look at me, almost blankly at first. My questions kept coming, spilling over themselves. "David, I have to know that life goes on, that this isn't the end for Fairlight. How are ministers so sure there's a heaven? What proof do you have? And don't give me book answer like you tried to do with Aunt Polly. I mean, what do you believe yourself?"

David looked down at the hammer in his hand, turning it over as though he had never seen such an object before. "I believe it's a tremendously big subject. But I believe in immortality."

"Why do you believe in it? I mean, how can you be sure that when we die, we don't just die—and that's it?"

"Because man's a part of the natural order, and dying each winter and being resurrected each spring is part of the rhythm, the normal ebb and flow of life. Surely, if it happens to mere flowers and trees, it happens to us."

David turned back to stretch taut another edge of the screening. "Sure, David. I know about spring, and everything. I know I'm supposed to believe. But what do you do when suddenly you find you can't believe?"

"Believing is never easy, Christy. And right now you're tired and upset." He put down his tack hammer and drew me into his arms, cradling my head against his chest. "The way you feel now, words aren't going to help you. That's not what you need."

He tilted my head back and kissed first one eyelid and then the other and then my mouth. "Foolish girl ... Do you think you can solve all the philosophic problems of the universe?"

"But David—"

"No buts—just don't think about it."

"But I can't help thinking about it!"

David was beginning to use the same tone he took with a very little child, almost crooning. "I'm sorry about Fairlight, Christy. Really sorry. I know what she meant to you. But you will get over this, you know."

"You still don't understand. I have to know that Fairlight isn't just gone, vanished forever—or I'll go crazy. I need to know that she's close to us somehow. Maybe that she can hear us talking right now, that she's trying to tell us that everything is all right. Can't you understand the need to be sure, David?"

"Of course, I'd like to be sure too. But death is a very great mystery. Maybe it's always supposed to be."

"What are you sure of, David?"

He looked at me oddly. There was a spot of pink in each cheek. He shifted the weight on his feet. "Christy, it's a lot easier to ask these questions than to answer them. I can give you good theological answers to your questions, but knowing you, that won't be enough."

Suddenly, Aunt Polly's face rose before me, the old lady's hurt and disbelieving eyes as she was being offered schoolboy answers instead of the reality she needed. I did not want to be back there in Aunt Polly's cabin, but I was there. And David was holding words like a screen in front of human nakedness and need.

All at once I had a yearning I had not known for a long time—to cry, with my head in mother's lap. I wanted to feel her patting my head.

I looked at David again and saw him as I had first seen him: handsome, clean-cut, likable, and anxious to do the right thing. He was more uneasy now than I had ever seen him. Even in my own torment, compassion for him stirred within me.

"I'm sorry, David. You're right. Of course, I'll get over it. It's just that I hurt now and I want something to stop the pain."

David's expression cleared. Once again he drew me to him. He stroked my hair and said softly, his lips brushing my cheek, "Christy, there isn't anything I wouldn't do for you. You know that."

"Yes, David. I know that."

After a restless night, I got up shortly before dawn one Saturday morning, dressed hastily, and tiptoed out of the house. As I reached my woodland retreat on Coldsprings Mountain, the sun was just rimming the top of the far ranges. The sky was rosy, with streaks of golden light filtering through the trees. Dewdrops still glistened on the leaves. The woods were quiet, so quiet, save for my own footfall and an occasional bird call.

It was a beautiful morning. My eyes saw the beauty, but I could not respond to it. The anger against God that I had felt at Tom's funeral, for which I had gotten no satisfactory answers, was compounded now. God? Where was God? Far away? Indifferent? Never there at all? A figment of man's wishful imagining?

Or if there, then why had He not done something to prevent Fairlight's death? What were a few typhoid germs in a human body as against the power of God unless— unless belief in a God of love and caring was just a hoax, a gigantic hoax. Unless Dr. MacNeill was right, and there was nothing but a machine-like universe that ran by "natural" law. And when the natural law went against you, it cut down the good and the beautiful along with the wicked and the profane. All alike, no difference. Just cosmic machinery. In that case it would not matter how we lived our lives—whether selfishly or unselfishly, whether good or evil. Willy-nilly, the steam roller flattened everyone in its path. Those who were not standing in its way were lucky, that was all. It was all a matter of how the wheel turned, how the dice fell.

So the bitter thoughts rolled and seethed inside me—too much inside me. Suddenly, sitting there on the hillside, I remembered the presentiment that had come to me on a higher hill that day when Fairlight and I had climbed the mountain. Then, with an intuitive knowing, I had been sure that indeed it does matter how we live our lives, that there is One who cares. Thinking of that, I knew that it was wrong not to speak out my rebellion to the One at whom it was directed. I could at least give Him a chance to defend Himself.

Speak it out! Yes, and act it out. It must have been my isolation that gave me the courage to let all constraint go.

I heard myself saying aloud, "Why? Why? I've got to know *why*." Then on my knees in a bed of dry leaves, I was flailing my fists on the earth as I saw in memory Fairlight's lovely face. Never again on this earth would I see those perfect features. What my friend had feared most had come about. That gentle form, those pleading eyes were even now in a box covered with clay on the brow of the hill.

"Christy," I could hear her voice again, "I git the trembles when I think of being put in a box and a-lyin' out thar somewheres covered with dirt" ... Dirt ... Dirt. I scooped up a handful of the rich woodland loam and crushed it hard and tight in my fingers. Only dirt now for this one for whom doors to life had just begun to open, this one whose children needed her so; she who could have been the catalyst for so much that we wanted to do for the mountain women. The good and the beautiful cut down. Oh God! Oh, *God—*

I don't understand, God! I don't understand. I don't understand Tom's death and Fairlight's death, and I don't understand You. Why are You so inscrutable? Why are You so hard to find when the need is greatest? All that time when I was holding Fairlight in my arms, I could not get through to You. The ceiling of that room was like galvanized iron. I asked You for help. Did I plead with a void, God? Did I?

Gradually I quieted down. The rain of my words ceased. There was no answer immediately. I had not expected there would be. Yet the leafy quietness enfolded me, soothed me. I was aware of a thirst to drink deeply of the silence, the soothing silence. It was deep within me, yet also behind the façade of nature around me. The flesh of my body, sometimes sitting quietly, sometimes moving restlessly, was the exterior shell for the inner stillness; the scudding clouds and the tossing trees and the flying birds were the covering for that other stillness without.

I wanted to stay there a long time. But Miss Ida would be holding breakfast for me with that tight-lipped smile she reserved for latecomers, even those of us who had won our way into the small circle of people she approved. But I decided that I would return again and again to my mountain sanctuary until some response, some insights were given me. Or else, or else—there was always the stark alternative that there would never be any response because I was indeed speaking into nothingness.

I began setting my alarm clock for a quarter of six each morning. Then on the hillside propped against the trunk of my favorite locust tree, I would watch the sun rise. By the second morning, I stopped hurling invectives verbally and began writing my questions in a notebook. Some of what I wrote bordered on blasphemy. Yet there was a feeling of hard soundness about being honest. If there was a God, He would have to be truth. And in that case, candor—however impertinent—would be more pleasing to Him than posturing. Gradually the torment of my grief fell away. In its place was left a great wistfulness and a terrible aloneness.

I knew that Miss Alice sensed my isolation, yet she did not intrude. Then one morning on my way to my woodland room, as I reached the edge of her yard, I saw that she was up and saddling Goldie.

"You're out early, Christy." It was a half-question.

"Good morning, Miss Alice," I parried, my eyes taking in the picture she made in her smart navy blue serge riding habit and soft leather boots. "Is it Big Lick or Cataleechie?"

"Big Lick this week." She put out a hand to stroke the sorrel's neck and Goldie responded by laying his head on her shoulder. I started to wish her a good week and walk on, but her intent look held me. "Christy, child, I've been noticing something."

"Yes, Miss Alice?"

"Thee is in agony."

"Yes."

She was silent for what seemed like a long time. Still, her eyes held mine. "As some of the dear old Friends used to say, 'I have a word of edification to build thee up.'" Her voice grew warm with feeling. "Christy, those who've never rebelled against God or at some point in their lives shaken their fists in the face of heaven, have never encountered God at all."

"You mean it's good to rebel?"

She smiled at me and then turned to adjust the girth and close the flaps of her saddlebags. "I mean that rebellion against our human lot and admitting that we don't understand are clear steps on the way to finding reality."

"But I don't seem to be able to find anything."

"Christy, did you ever read Job?"

"No."

"Job rebelled too. Read him. And King David had his troubles too. He poured his misery out in poetry—the Psalms. It's reading that I recommend for you right now." She mounted and sat holding a loose rein, looking down at me, her eyes luminous and full of feeling. "How can I say it to thee? If I care about thee so much, He does too. And more, so much more."

And she blew me a kiss and cantered off.

I felt better, not quite so lonely and lost. During the week that Miss Alice was away, I did open my Bible and there I found astonishing companionship. Other men and women long ago had asked the identical questions that I was asking. Miss Alice was right, that was what the book of Job in the Old Testament was all about. Job too had shaken his fist in the face of heaven as I had there on my hillside. It gave me a strange feeling to find that his words were my words too:

> I will not refrain my mouth;
> I will complain in the bitterness of my soul. . . .

And I found that Psalm after Psalm had been poured out in the same agony of spirit that I was feeling and set down by King David in naked, unashamed emotion:

> All the night long. . . . I water my couch with my
> tears. . . .
> Why standest thou afar off, O Lord?
> Why hidest thou thyself in times of trouble?

Even my feeling that perhaps I wanted no part of this heaven, others had felt too and had written down:

> Therefore they say unto God, Depart from us; for we
> desire not the knowledge of thy ways.

The words were like understanding hands reaching out for me across the centuries. Their cry and mine, those others whom I had never known in the flesh, was the cry of the vulnerable human heart. There was comfort in the knowledge of our common humanity.

Morning after morning I returned to my hillside room to reach out for the stillness as a thirsty man reaches for a cup of cold water. I had never experienced anything like this before: a silence so complete that it seemed palpable, sensate, an entity in itself.

Yet the quietness was no sterile emptiness. Those who craved oblivion could not have tolerated this. Or those who wanted to escape themselves would flee this. Perhaps if I could stretch out my hand and stop the clock of time or listen deeply enough, I would not then miss the gifts the silence held out. For now I knew that at the heart of the stillness there was food to feed upon, wisdom to accept humbly, satisfaction to be quaffed. Irresistibly the silence drew me because it promised that where there was hunger there would also be bread.

And slowly, almost imperceptibly, out of the stillness during that second week my answer started coming—only not in any way I had expected. No effort was made to answer my "why?". Instead, I began to know, incredibly, unmistakably, beyond reason and beyond doubting that I, Christy Huddleston, was loved—tenderly, totally. Love filled me, washed over me, flowed around me. I did not know what to do with love as strong as this. Back off from its intensity? Embrace it?

My tears flowed. I could not stop them.

Then the thought came: wasn't this the confirmation for which I had asked? This love disclosing itself was no cosmic Creator of a mechanistic universe, for the revelation was intimate, personal. Perhaps the assurance always has to be personal, revealed to the inner person alone, since only man sees other men en masse, whereas God insists on seeing us one by one, each a special case, each inestimably beloved for himself.

The world around me was still full of riddles for which my little mind had not been given answers; David had been right about that. Nor could I know what the future held. But the fundamental doubt was for me silenced. I knew now: God *is*. I had found my center, my point of reference. Everything else I needed to know would follow.

That morning the sun came up in a blaze of glory.

Forty

UNTIL TYPHOID FEVER came to Cutter Gap I had known little about the disease, only that it had a connection with polluted water and that sometimes the patient's hair fell out. Now circumstances were forcing knowledge upon me. Ten days after Fairlight's death, eight more persons had the fever: Rebecca Holt, a nephew of Uncle Bogg's, and one of the children from our school, thirteen-year-old Bessie Coburn, with five additional cases reported across Raven Mountain.

The mountain people called typhoid "the summer scourge" because many a year as soon as warm weather brought thawing ground and flies, the fever would begin. But typhoid could just as truly have been tagged "the autumn scourge," for it was the fall rains washing human and animal waste down the steep slopes into creeks and springs that, as often as not, started the epidemics.

People remembered those bad years: "That September Arlie took sick and died" ... "And Verta and her baby—the babe was buried in her arms" ... "Recollect ye that one day when six folks was lowered into their bury-holes?"

There was scarcely a family in the Cove that had not lost at least one child to the plague some year or other. The fever would leap from house to house. A case here, a case there. Terror in the hearts of the mothers, not knowing where the fever would strike next. Hardest to bear was not understanding what caused the sickness or how it spread. There were autumns when it seemed that no amount of effort on the part of doctors or those who nursed so patiently could stop the onward march of the virulent monster, nothing that is, except November's sharply dropping temperatures that killed off the flies and froze the suppurating ground.

Only recently was the country at large beginning to accept the fact that typhoid was a disease of filth, though often not of the person affected. I had seen state health bulletins in Asheville and posters on courthouse walls heralding the news that the scourge could be prevented:

A LITTLE MESSAGE TO POST
on the Wall and to Remember:

TYPHOID FEVER
is a Wasteful, Dangerous Disease
That can be Prevented
By Care and Cleanliness
DO YOUR PART!

The notice went on to explain that the fever was spread by a well person taking into his mouth human filth from a typhoid patient, the germs carried by something like fingers, flies, food, cooking utensils, bed linens or towels.

Miss Alice told me that in the summer of 1910, Lyleton had had an epidemic that had started in a family who lived at the head of a creek. Miles downstream, children playing in the same creek had come down with the disease. Sometimes the carrier turned out to be a person nursing a typhoid case who went directly from the sickroom to milk a cow or to pay a call.

Although Dr. MacNeill was hopeful that this year's cases would not turn into an epidemic, already he was so rushed in trying to visit all the sick that it was no longer feasible for him to spend time going back and forth to his cabin. So we set up a cot for him in David's quarters where he could stay whenever he liked.

Of an evening more and more frequently he would stop by the parlor, weary from his rounds, eager to relax and talk. To us he could speak with a frankness not possible elsewhere and thus unload some of the matters troubling him. I sensed an emotional base to his anxiety about this particular disease unusual in a physician and thought for the hundredth time about his young wife Margaret—Miss Alice's daughter. As I had heard the story, some three months before their first baby had been due, Margaret had fallen ill with the fever. After battling for her life for three weeks, labor had started and the baby had been born prematurely. The baby son had lived only a few hours. The mother had died the next day.

Fingers now moving restlessly through his hair, the Doctor told us, "What *looks* like beautiful, sparkling drinking water may contain billions of typhoid bacilli. That is, if the spring or creek from which the water is taken is at the bottom of a hill—as most of them are—with anything and everything washing into it.

"Yet here in the mountains, people are proud of their water. Crazy contradiction! Every family thinks their water is best—whether it's limestone, freestone, sulphur, iron or just achingly cold."

Talking seemed to release the tension pent inside him. He stretched his long legs out full length, took his pipe out of his mouth and waved it in the air. "I can hear them now: 'Why, Doc, you're plumb crazy. Ain't no better water anywhars than the spring on our place. Hits bound to be pure. Bubbles right up out'n the ground.' Or else when I question them, they'll protest, 'Why, Doc, I raised twelve young-uns on branch water. Hardly sick a day in their lives.'

"There are two keys to the situation: the ordinary housefly and the wrong kind of privies—or none at all. As you know, most families around here haven't made any effort to deal with either problem.

"As for nursing the cases of typhoid we have already—trouble is, to pull most patients through, I'd have to own an Aladdin's lamp to get the right conditions: a room to themselves, no visitors, continuous nursing, every mouthful of food controlled by the doctor.

"You've all seen it," he went on. "Every last relative and friend has to visit the sick and the dying. The sicker the patient is, the more folks gather round. Nobody wants to miss a deathbed scene. There's always the outside chance that the dying might make a startling confession. And while they wait, the audience chats, sings, prays aloud, and moans."

When he talked like that, I was reminded of my reaction to him that first afternoon in his cabin: the Doctor seemed from the mountains, but not of them.

"Why, I've had patients who so enjoyed being the star of the performance that they proceeded to surprise everybody and get well." He laughed at his own recollections. "Naturally, I always took full credit for the patient's recovery.

"Well, anyway, enough of that. Many more cases and I'm going to have to yell for help. Guess I can send an

437

SOS to Knoxville for some young medical student who wants to get experience. But I hope that won't be necessary.

"It's a good sign that the rest of the Spencer family have stayed healthy. By the way, Christy, when is school supposed to open?"

"October twenty-eighth—if you think it's safe."

"No use postponing school that I can see. I guess you understand that typhoid isn't considered contagious in the sense of being airborne?"

I nodded.

"Your children will be as safe at school as they would be at home. Safer in fact, because the school's cleaner."

When Miss Alice agreed with the idea of going ahead with school, I was relieved. Now that we had such an assortment of boarders in the mission house, we needed the school routine to keep them busy and happy. Little Guy was staying on for a while longer to give Clara a better chance to adjust to her difficult new role as mistress of the Spencer household; Dr. MacNeill wanted Wanda Ann Beck with us so that he could watch and treat her eyes. He had written out a page of complicated instructions for us: cold compresses; the application of both nitrate of silver and copper sulphate once a day to the inside of her eyelids; Argyrol drops; scrupulous care to protect the other children. As soon as Wanda's inflamed eyes were better, the Doctor planned to operate to remove the worst of the granulations on her lids.

Then there was the problem of Lundy Taylor. Since Bird's-Eye was still at large, Miss Alice felt that Lundy should stay at the mission house rather than live alone. And Isaak McHone simply wanted to be with us. So great was the need of a supervised program that of a morning I had taken to gathering all the boarders into the schoolroom for informal work and play, calling it "vacation school."

It was two days later, in the schoolroom, as I was reading a story to Little Guy and Wanda Ann, that I was interrupted by a cry from Isaak.

"Teacher, teacher, he's a-bleedin'!"

I jerked my head up to see Lundy Taylor slumped over a desk. Blood was pouring from his nose.

Snatching up a pile of the handkerchief rags from my desk, I dashed down the aisle and pressed them to the

438

boy's face. "Lean your head back, Lundy. Not forward, back."

He complied instantly, but my order was a mistake because he was soon choking on blood in his throat.

"Lundy, stretch out on the floor, In the aisle—"

"Can't hear ye. Ears a-roarin'—"

I raised my voice. "On the floor, Lundy. Lie down. Here, straight out. Full length. Yes, that's it."

As I knelt down to hold more rags to his nose, I saw Wanda Ann standing rigid with fright, one fist in her mouth, her bloodshot eyes wide and staring.

Since coming to Cutter Gap, how often I had wished that I knew more about first aid. But now I did remember something . . . "Lundy, lift your hands and arms up above your head." I took one arm to show him what I meant and held it in the air. It took a long time for the bleeding to stop.

As soon as the immediate crisis was over, I could see that the big boy, always starved for attention, was enjoying his prominence. "Lundy, better lie there another minute or so." He grinned up at me. I noticed that his always-pimply skin was mottled pink and white. "I'm going to send you over to the big house to rest awhile," I told him.

I took Isaak aside. "Will you go with him, Isaak? Explain to Miss Grantland about the nosebleed and ask her to put Lundy to bed. Tell her that Dr. MacNeill should see him."

That afternoon on his way to two other urgent requests for help the Doctor stopped by. David and Miss Alice were off somewhere, so after examining Lundy, the Doctor sought me out. "Not much question, Christy. It's typhoid all right—early stage. Now we do have a situation on our hands."

Immediately I was concerned for the other children in the house. "Isn't it dangerous for the other boarders?"

"Dangerous for everybody."

"What about Little Guy? Shouldn't we send him home?"

"Probably. We'll talk about that later. But first, Christy, we need supplies—medicines and disinfectants, more than I have in my saddlebags. There's plenty over at my place but I have two other calls to make this afternoon. Could you—would you ride over and get some stuff?"

I glanced out the window. The clouds which had been

439

building up all day were towering storm heads now, dark and threatening. "Of course I'll go," I said.

"Then I'll write you out a list so you'll know what to bring." He pulled out a piece of paper and began to scribble.

I threw my body against the door, the driving rain that had been pursuing me to the Doctor's cabin pelting at my back. The door flew open and the wind almost blew me inside. With my back I slammed the door against the weight of the gale and stood leaning against the hard wood to catch my breath. The mustiness of the house not lived in for days closed about me: stale tobacco, the smell of leather, burnt bacon grease. There was a ghostly appearance to the room in the afternoon light, waning now, and all but extinguished by the thunderstorm.

I knew that the locked room, where the Doctor had said I would find the medicines, was somewhere to my right. A flash of lightning momentarily illuminated the interior of the cabin and gave me an idea what pieces of furniture stood between me and the locked door. After a few steps I walked into some cobwebs and had to fight with the gossamer tangles in my face and hair. Then my right leg banged into something and I almost fell over it. Groping fingers told me that it was a chest of some sort and I stood still, rubbing my leg, awaiting another flare of lightning. Perhaps I should use the next brief light to search for a lamp, but unless there were matches beside it, I knew that I would never find them in these murky shadows.

Outside, the thunder rolled and rumbled and crackled like a violent artillery bombardment. I thought of Buttons out in the storm and hoped that she was all right.

There was another growl of thunder and lightning zigzagged across the sky, flaming at the windowpanes. I found no lamp close by, but I did see that the floor area was clear between where I was standing now and the locked door. My fingers felt for the key in the pocket of my jacket—an old-fashioned brass key, much larger than the ones made nowadays. The hard cold metal was reassuring and excitement rose in me. The Doctor had entrusted the key to me. Whatever the secret of the locked room was, I should soon know.

I walked with one hand stretched out to keep from colliding with the door, then slid my fingers over the panels to locate the keyhole. There was a moment's difficulty fitting the key into the lock in the darkness, then I turned the key to the right—but it would not move. I took both hands and tried it. No good. But I thought all keys turned clockwise. Fighting off a feeling of panic, I tried twisting it to the left. The key now turned easily and the door swung open.

There was an odor of chemicals, but I could see nothing at all. This room was even darker than the outer one. Since this was a smaller place and might contain all manner of breakable objects, I dared not move a step. *Actually,* I thought, *the lightning is a boon.* The next flash came—but, disappointingly, did not light the room at all. Then I understood. The windows were covered.

Now I had to find a lamp. Cautiously I stretched out one hand and moved it in an arc around my body. To my right there was a shelf, and oh, great relief, an oil lamp waiting, as if necessary for anyone entering this room. In that case there must be matches close by. Steadying the lamp with my left hand so that I would not knock it off the shelf, I groped with my right. A canister with a top. Yes, inside were matches. I struck one match with such haste that I broke off its head and had to reach for another. Then I held it with shaking hand while I removed the glass chimney and lighted the wick.

Lifting the lamp aloft, I scanned the room eagerly, trying to take in everything at once. A laboratory! I was in a laboratory. It had been a bedroom once, for a bed was pushed sideways against one wall, and there was a mirror and an old wooden trunk. In the middle of the floor stood a stool and table with a microscope, an alcohol lamp, beakers, and a lot of other equipment on it. Against the wall to my right just beyond the lampshelf were standing cabinets with shallow drawers, not of the kind that even a fine mountain craftsman could possibly have made. Doctor MacNeill must have sent to a city to buy these. I moved across the floor and with great curiosity—feeling as if the Doctor were looking over my shoulder—pulled open a drawer. Slides, many of them, meticulously arranged and numbered. I pulled out one drawer after another, all full of slides, hundreds, thousands of little glass squares, each one labeled, each one representing—what? And all together, how many years of work were contained in these endless files!

Another wall was covered with charts, several of them

large pictures of the human eye. Some were of a normal eye and others were dreadful pictures of raspberry-colored eyelids or heavy upper lids drooping half-shut. I did not want to look, so I turned to the other charts. They were big squares of paper covered with notations in Dr. MacNeill's handwriting. I held the lamp closer but could make nothing of the memoranda, a combination of figures and abbreviated medical terms—many of them in Latin. This was not the usual physician's illegible writing; rather, the neat scrupulously ordered notes of the scientist.

At the far end of the room, shelves had been built floor to ceiling, one section for books, the rest for bottles of medicine and pills. This must be the Doctor's private pharmacy where I would find the drugs for which he had sent me, actually the only part of the room that should concern me.

Yet I stood for a long while letting the yellow light from the lamp flicker over the walls and ceiling, trying to understand. A covering of dark cloth had been carefully placed over the two windows so that no passer-by could look in. This was not the sanctum of an ordinary backwoods doctor. Some type of research, important to Dr. MacNeil at least, had been going on here for a long time. Standing there, new admiration and respect for the owner of this room rose in me. It had not been easy to find all the necessary hours for the work accomplished here while being the only practicing physician in this entire region.

And David had been right: I had misinterpreted Dr. MacNeill's carelessness about personal appearance to mean sloppiness in general. Yet there was no untidiness in this room; quite the opposite—an extreme of precision.

So now I knew the truth about the locked room, and it was more logical and more significant than all the rumors I had heard. The Doctor had known that the mountain folk would not understand the type of research he was doing. He had not felt that he could explain. Nor could he run the risk of the woman who came at intervals to clean his cabin, moving this equipment to dust it, or tampering with the slides—or having access to the drugs, either, for the mountain people liked to sample any and all medicines.

But more important to me was what this room divulged about the Doctor. Depths in him which I had glimpsed briefly, at odd moments, and tried to discount ... Then I wondered about something. With the storm coming on,

442

couldn't Dr. MacNeill have left the list of drugs for David, asked him to go when he got back? Or had he wanted me to see this room, me in particular, wanted me to read some message written here?

That unusual looking trunk, what was in it? Cautiously I made my way toward it. The floorboards creaked under my feet, and jumping guiltily, I looked over my shoulder almost expecting to see someone behind me. I set the lamp on the floor by the trunk and the yellow light illuminated the initials MHM just under the bass lock. I should not be snooping; this was really none of my business. But experimentally, I touched the lock and found it open. Then impelled by a curiosity I could not put down, I lifted the lid.

It was a deep trunk—not filled to the top. I held the lamp to peer in. A woman's clothes—dresses, a bonnet with fur on it. So this was where Dr. MacNeill had gotten the dress for me that day old Theo dropped me in the creek. And there was a pair of knitting needles stuck in some yarn. The yarn looked yellow in the lamplight. Perhaps it had once been white. Shyly I picked it up. It was a half-finished baby's jacket. Mute evidence of a life interrupted, a mother's and a baby's. Gently, I put the tiny jacket back where I had found it and hastily shut the lid of the trunk. I must get the drugs and start home.

I carried the lamp to the shelves of bottles, each jar and bottle carefully labeled: *Chloroform, C.P.* . . . *Nux Vomica, NSP* . . . *Ext. Gelsium, LY* . . . *Iron Quin & Strych* . . . *Wampoles Formolid* . . . One jar contained nothing but empty capsules to be filled; another, corks. On a nail stuck in the wall was a sheaf of invoices from Masengill Brothers, Pharmaceutical Jobbers in Bristol, Tennessee—Virginia. There were rows of empty medicine bottles, one row marked "Sterile," the others, "To Be Sterilized." Like all country doctors, Dr. MacNeill had to be his own pharmacist.

I took the list of wanted drugs out of my pocket and laid it on the shelf close to the lamp. Such odd names. To me, hieroglyphics! It took me a long time to search over the labels on the tall bottles and find each medicine: *Bismuth* . . . *Sulphate Quinine* . . . *Morphia sulphate 6-⅛* . . . *Glycerine* . . . *Carbolic-acid* . . . *Dover's powder* . . . *Stractine* . . . *Calomel and Sodium Tablets, 1 gr* . . . *Rubbing alcohol.* Then having located what was needed and set the bottles aside in one place, next I had to pour a specified amount of each into sterile containers since my instructions had been, "In no case, bring it all, Christy. I can't have my private supply stripped of any one drug."

At last it was done and I looked around for some box or basket in which to carry the assortment of bottles and pill boxes out to my saddlebags. There was nothing—except a mortar and pestle. Finally, in desperation, I removed the pestle and stuck the bottles in the mortar, cramming my pockets with the rest.

There was a sense of urgency now. I had no idea how long I had already tarried in this room. Quickly I returned the lamp to its shelf, turned down the wick, blew out the flame, shut the door and locked it.

Outside I was relieved to find that the fury of the storm had abated. It was still raining, but softly now with only an occasional clap of thunder reverberating in the distance. Buttons, delighted to see me, nuzzled my hand as if eager to be off and back to her warm stall. After carefully arranging the medicines in the saddlebags, then carrying the mortar back inside and pulling the front door shut after me, I mounted and rode off as fast as I dared toward the mission. There was so much to ponder.

Forty-one

NOW THAT LUNDY was ill in the mission house, as a precaution we did send Little Guy back home. Soon we saw that Lundy was going to be an ill-tempered, demanding patient, though his case did not seem serious; even the evening rises in temperature were only moderately severe.

"Maybe I was wrong," Dr. MacNeill admitted to us one evening after taking Lundy's temperature. "Typhoid's fooled me before. It can wear more guises and present more variables than almost any disease I know."

"What guises?" Miss Alice questioned.

"Well—let's see." He looked toward the ceiling and thought. "It can look like colitis, meningitis, malaria, nephritis, influenza, pneumonia, endocarditis—"

"Enough—enough! Now thee is over my head."

"But Dr. MacNeill," I said, "I thought Fairlight had both typhoid and pneumonia."

"That's right. She did. Pneumonia can be a typhoid complication. And speaking of complicated cases, I've some rough ones across Raven. Too many. I'm riding over tomorrow. I may have to stay overnight."

We hoped fervently that no emergency would arise in the Doctor's absence. But he had scarcely disappeared down the road in the direction of Fairview Flats flagstop when Rob Allen was at our front door with the urgent message that Ruby Mae Beck was "took bad." Her husband Will had brought word of the emergency to the mill and asked that it be relayed; he could not leave his young wife longer than that.

"Didn't Will give any details?" I asked Rob.

"No'm."

"Does he think it's typhoid?"

"Said he couldn't rightly tell. Jest that she be awful sick."

The primitive cabin which Will Beck was building himself on the back side of English Mountain was in the opposite direction from Raven Gap where Dr. MacNeill had gone. This meant that someone from the mission house would have to go.

Rob went with me for a hasty consultation with Miss Alice. Once she had heard the situation she did not hesitate. "Of course I'll go as soon as I get some supplies together."

"I'm coming with you," I told her.

She looked at me thoughtfully. "No, Christy, that's not best. No telling how long this will take. With Lundy and Wanda Ann thy hands are full already."

I hesitated. I had never before questioned Miss Alice's word. But into my mind came the picture of Ruby Mae standing behind David in the kitchen doorway staring over his shoulder at me on my first morning at the mission. I thought of how she had trailed me around the house and grounds, all but driving me out of my mind. And suddenly I knew what I had to do. "Right from the start Ruby Mae's been part of my special bundle," I told her. "It's one of your favorite sayings and I'm quoting it back at you—so I have to go."

I did not think Miss Alice would dispute this. Nor did she, but she surprised me by asking, "Does thee really want to go?"

"Yes, I do. It isn't just duty. I care about Ruby Mae and I want to help."

Still she looked at me searchingly. "All right then," she said quietly, "but will Ida take on Lundy's nursing?"

I smiled at her. "I think so. Miss Ida's been a real friend since that night we were besieged. I'll talk to her before we leave."

By "getting a few things together" Miss Alice meant some professional medical supplies. Since coming to the mountains, circumstances had often forced her into the roles of practical nurse and midwife. On occasions when no doctor was available, faced with emergencies like the top of a foot hacked by the mis-stroke of an axe or a mother suddenly in labor, she had learned to take over quite adequately. Often she had borrowed Dr. MacNeill's medical books and questioned him until sometimes, in amused exasperation, he would light his pipe, settle comfortably into a chair and give her the equivalent of a medical-school lecture on how to handle lacerations or broken bones or the more common complications of childbirth.

Since Miss Alice had a retentive memory and a high degree of ability to bridge the gap between theoretical knowledge and applied skill, she had learned a great deal. Years before, she had sent to Philadelphia for an obstetrical kit and a doctor's bag which she carried in her saddlebags. I watched her check the contents now: a thermometer that looked like a pen with a cover; the usual stethoscope; small wire objects that she told me were splints for setting bones; a tiny alcohol lamp; assorted syringes and probes; and an odd-looking little object Miss Alice called a "speculum," assorted vials, ointment cans, and medicine bottles.

Inside the Beck cabin, we found Ruby Mae flushed pink with high fever. Her features were drawn, her eyes too bright and staring. "Oh, I'm sick, so sick," she moaned over and over. She was finding it hard to get her breath so that her words came out in tight gasps. "Water, Will. More water. Please—so thirsty."

Miss Alice took her temperature, looked at her tongue and felt her pulse. After a while she left the bedside and motioned Will and me outside the cabin.

"Some questions, Will. When did this start?"

"She was feelin' on the go-down since yesterday. Said her side hurt when she took her breath."

"Just since yesterday?"

"Yes'm. Seemed to be 'bout like always before that."

"Will, she's a mighty sick girl. Temperature's 104. This may be typhoid—or it may not. I can't tell yet. If it is, it isn't following the usual pattern."

"Say ye?"

"I mean it isn't starting off as most cases do. I'm almost sure of one thing though. Ruby Mae has pneumonia. Double pneumonia, I'm afraid."

"She *does!* What are we going to do?"

"She hasn't coughed at all, has she?"

"No, Ma'am."

"It would be better if she were coughing."

"Better to cough?" Will asked incredulously.

"Yes, because her lungs are— Dr. MacNeill would say

447

'consolidated.' Poultices . . . Wish I had some veratrum."

"Say ye?"

"Just thinking out loud. Will, how are you fixed for onions?"

"Onions! What in tarnation! Law, ye mean for supper?"

"No, no—not to eat."

Will looked as puzzled as I felt. "Well—considerable onions," he answered.

"As many as a bushel?"

"Reckon. They're in the loft with the pumpkins and the leather britches and apples."

"Then we'll try onion poultices," Miss Alice announced crisply. "They'll do. They work fine—sometimes. You get the onions for us, Will, lots of them, and your skinning knife or any other knives you have and we'll start peeling. This night, my boy, you're going to work harder than you've ever worked."

The young husband grinned at her. He was a young giant, muscular and broad-shouldered, but still a boy in so many ways. Relieved to be told something that he could do, he leaped into action, chinning himself up through the hole into the loft. Soon he was back with Ruby Mae's washtub and a piggin heaped with the onions and he and I began slicing them as Miss Alice had told us to do. She was tearing unbleached domestic and folding it into large squares for the poultices.

Almost immediately our tear ducts were raining water. "Strong onions these. Have a right smart effect on me," Will observed.

I smiled at him. " 'Smart' is the word. And look at the pile left to peel. We're crying like babies already."

"Everwho heerd of doctorin' with onions!" Will exclaimed, wiping his face with his sleeve.

"Guess Miss Alice has to make do with what she has. She's a good one for that."

There was nothing for it but to go on peeling, let the tears roll and smile at one another's ludicrous look while we marveled that our eyes could rain such a never-ending supply. In a way the tears and the sting were a relief; they kept our minds off our fear for Ruby Mae.

As soon as we had a skilletful, Miss Alice cooked the cut-up onions until they were heated all through. Then she put the hot onions into the muslin squares and gently placed the poultice on Ruby Mae's chest. I watched her hands. There was something loving even about the way

448

they moved. She made no effort to shield herself as she bent closely over the sick girl, almost—it seemed to me—blessing her with her hands. The cabin seemed filled with an atmosphere of benediction.

As fast as the frying pan was emptied, Will and I would fill it again. For the next poultice, Will helped Miss Alice turn his wife on her side so that the hot onions could be applied to her back. "We'll have to keep turning her," Miss Alice explained.

Though the chimney was only half-completed with that end of the cabin open to the outside, the room was soon damp with the odor of steamy onions. We lost all sense of time, knowing only that it was dark now. It must be well into the night, I guessed.

My knife bit into the tissue-like covering of yet another onion. Marvelously constructed, the onion, I thought as I tried to get my mind off the smell. Would I ever again want to see an onion, much less eat one? Layer after layer. Slice it through. I had thought that I was coming to help nurse, had pictured myself being a sort of ministering angel, and here I was spending the night peeling onions.

Miss Alice stood at the stove stirring yet another pan of simmering onions. Her hair clung dankly around her flushed face and beads of moisture stood out on her temples and her upper lip. Carefully she took a big spoon and raked the cooked onions between layers of the domestic. "Better put this one on her chest again," she said, and I leaped up to help her, eager for the chance to stretch my legs and move around.

Ruby Mae no longer seemed to know what was going on around her. She was perspiring profusely now, the sweat running in rivulets down her temples. The bed was wet, and in between changing the poultices, Miss Alice kept several heavy quilts tucked in around her. Often she sat on the edge of the bed, tilting the sick girl's head and getting her to swallow as much water as possible. This time as she removed the cooled poultice and applied the hot one, I saw that the inside of Miss Alice's hands had blistered.

"Let me handle the poultices for a while," I told her. "Give your hands a rest. I've been watching you so I can do it."

She nodded absently, all her attention centered on Ruby Mae with no concern for herself or her hands at all. *She's learned the secret all the way, hasn't she? How to love other people. She really does care about these folks. Nothing held back. This is what I've been learning with Little Burl and Mountie and Opal and Fairlight. Fairlight most of all. Fairlight ... Fairlight ... Could I see in Ruby Mae something of what had meant so much to me in Fairlight? Yes, yes I could—a little. It's love like Miss Alice's that heals.* And suddenly I was sure that we would win. Ruby Mae was going to make it.

A little later I slipped out the cabin door for a minute, grateful for a few deep breaths of the pure mountain air. The morning stars were out. Dawn must not be far off. I picked out the Big Dipper and the Little Dipper and Mars and Venus. Somewhere a hoot owl gave his eerie signal. Then at my back I heard feet scrambling across the floor. I got to the door to see both Will and Miss Alice rushing toward the bed. With no warning, Ruby Mae had sat up in bed and was coughing violently. Will stood by, moving his big hands in futile gestures. The cough was loose and deep and shook the bed. All at once from Ruby Mae's mouth poured a stream of dark red mucous and pus. Miss Alice grabbed a pan and held it under the girl's mouth while I ran to support her head and her back. No wonder she'd been sick with all that stuff in her lungs. I had to look away to keep from gagging.

"Get it all up, child. That's it. Just what we've been working for. Good!"

Then another paroxysm and ropes of the highly colored phlegm emptied into the pan. "Enough for now," Miss Alice said. "Lie back and rest now. You're going to be fine." Tenderly she eased the exhausted girl's head back on the pillow and moved immediately to get the soiled top quilt off the bed and to clean up the mess.

"We need some more water here, Will." Jubilation was written on Miss Alice's face. "You have succeeded," she said to Will and me, as if her part in it had been negligible. "I've never seen onion poultices do a finer job. She must have had a lung abscess, a bad one. But I do believe she's going to be all right."

About an hour after dawn, Will came in to report that he had seen Dr. MacNeill riding up the trail. Without thinking, I rushed out to meet him as he came jogging into the yard and slowed his sorrel to a walk. His face broke into a grin as he saw me and, ridiculously, I blushed. Why did I always act silly when he was around?

"You should have been here last night," I said, laughing to hide my self-consciousness. "You missed a crying party."

"A *what?*" he asked as he dismounted.

"We've had Ruby Mae all wrapped up in cooked onions. Will and I spent most of the night peeling them."

He inspected me with his eyes and chuckled. "You look it. And how's Ruby Mae?"

"Better, I think."

Then Miss Alice appeared, obviously relieved to see him, and between the two of us, we described the all-night vigil. The Doctor listened in surprise at first, then began nodding his head. "Under the circumstances, I think you did just right. There may not be a thing for me to do."

Quickly he moved into the cabin, sat down by Ruby Mae and proceeded to a systematic examination. Even then she only half awoke to acknowledge him groggily. Finally, he looked towards Miss Alice in approval. "I wouldn't dare make a final diagnosis quite yet. Looks like typhoid—and pneumonia both. The onions did their work. Of course," he bantered, "There are those who think the odor of the cure is worse than the disease!" Then he was serious again. "No medicine at the moment, I say. Total rest. Lots of liquids." Here he addressed himself to Will. "You do understand, don't you, Will, nothing but liquids?"

Then as an afterthought, he turned to me, "Were you up the entire night?"

I nodded. "But I'm all right," I said lightly.

The Doctor turned again to Miss Alice. "And you were up too. You both need rest. I'll stay with Ruby Mae for a while. You and Christy go back to the mission and get some sleep."

Miss Alice shook her head. "I'd like to stay on. You need sleep more than I do, Neil. Why don't you drop Christy off at the mission house?"

The Doctor did not protest. His eyes were bloodshot with deep hollows beneath them. Yet there was a lilt to his voice and a spring to his step that surprised and fascinated me. Clearly, the increasing crisis was demanding every resource he possessed. Yet instead of being overwhelmed Dr. MacNeill seemed in some way fulfilled by these demands.

Not until I started to mount Buttons did I realize how tired I was. There was a ringing in my head and a queer numbness to my arms and legs. Instantly, the Doctor recognized the situation. "You're going to ride with me," he ordered.

I started to argue, but he paid no attention to me. He obtained a piece of heavy sacking from Will and threw it over Charlie's croup behind the saddle. Then he mounted and reached down a hand for me. "Hand up—"

I obeyed him instinctively and felt myself lifted up. "Comfortable? Hang onto me." To Miss Alice standing in the doorway, he said, "I'll look in on Ruby Mae again tomorrow. Get some sleep. Will can keep watch. I'll send someone to pick up Buttons." Then we were off.

As Charlie moved into a free-swinging easy gait and the cool morning air flowed past my face, I began to feel better, no longer exhausted, just comfortably drowsy, as though I could sleep forever ... One part of me wanted to relax against the Doctor; another part of me resisted vigorously. Why was I always so divided about this man? Why did he annoy me so often? Yet this morning I had been so glad to see him. For a while we rode in silence as I tried to puzzle out this paradox.

One thing I did not like about Dr. MacNeill was his conceit. He was always so sure of himself! He was the one who really knew these mountain people; he knew best how to handle the still business; he was so quick to criticize David; he rarely consulted Miss Alice; he always had the right answers for everything.

The Doctor's voice broke into my thoughts. "Christy, I'm worried about you."

I was startled by the strong note of concern in his voice. "You have enough people to worry about without adding me to your list."

"Every instinct inside me says that I should keep riding on down to the El Pano railroad station and put you on a train to Asheville."

"You're not serious."

"I'm dead serious."

"Well, you'd better not try it unless you think you can tie and gag me."

The Doctor threw back his head and laughed. It was so irrepressible that I laughed too in spite of myself.

"I've known a few girls in my life, Christy, but I don't believe I've ever met one as stubborn and as know-it-all as you are."

"Thank you. I was just thinking the same nice thoughts about you."

The Doctor chuckled. "Well then, if I can't persuade you to go home, can I persuade you to take special precautions?"

"Anything you say, Doctor— Sir."

"That's better." He reached back and took one of my hands as though to indicate we were in agreement, but he did not let go. I pulled it away. He said nothing more and after a while I relaxed, leaning lightly against him. We were back at the mission sooner than I would have believed possible.

I started to dismount, but Dr. MacNeill would not let me. "You promised to follow my instructions, so hold on a moment while I assume my best medical stance."

"You're not standing. You're sitting on a horse."

"So I am. And so we'll both remain until I finish. First, take off every garment you're wearing and don't put a piece of it on again until everything's been washed in lye soap and sunned. Wash your hands in 70% alcohol or bichloride solution. Wash your hair right away. And I want you to get lots of sleep." All the levity was gone from his voice; he was deadly serious, all doctor.

Then a strange thing happened. I was not tired any more and I didn't care if I ever got off that horse. Something inside me loosened, unknotted. Compassion and warmth welled up in me. I knew that I belonged here, helping these mountain people. There was nothing I wanted for myself, I just wanted to give. All these new feelings washed over me in a matter of seconds.

Impetuously, I leaned forward and kissed Neil MacNeill gently on the cheek. Before he could say anything, I had vaulted off Charlie's back and dashed into the mission house.

Forty-two

WHEN SOME of the neighbor-women came in to help nurse Ruby Mae (who did have typhoid) Miss Alice returned from the Becks'. Then since she was so needed in Cutter Gap, she canceled her regular week at the Big Lick Spring school. And as Lundy's illness dragged on, she insisted on assuming much of the burden of his care though his case still seemed a mild one.

That Thursday afternoon I was at work in the empty schoolroom getting our supplies in final order for the opening of school on Monday, when I heard someone coming up the steps. The door opened and Miss Alice stuck her head in. "Ida said I'd find you here. Am I interrupting something important?"

"No, not at all. Please come in."

As I stood watching Miss Alice move easily down the length of the aisle toward me, I was fascinated all over again with what a striking figure she was. Even though she was tired, she held herself so erect. She had what my mother would call "presence." I pulled out my desk chair for her and I slid into the seat of the nearest pupil's desk, delighted always for a chance to be with Miss Alice.

Her level eyes searched mine. Then she said abruptly, "You've been wondering about Margaret, haven't you? About Margaret and her marriage to Neil."

"Yes, but—" I didn't go on.

"But how did I know? Christy! How much do you think stays out of those big eyes of yours? Ever since you were in Neil's laboratory—where Margaret's things are—you've been aching to ask questions. Would you like to hear it from me?"

This was an unexpected boon. I tried not to sound as eager as I felt. "Yes. Yes, please."

Miss Alice seemed to be looking over my shoulder at

some distant horizon. The room was so quiet that I became aware of a single angry fly buzzing against a windowpane. When she spoke, her voice was soft.

"She was tall. Hair like mine, only even more abundant and more copper than blonde. Shining bronze hair, it was. She had a slight lisp that only added to her charm. Full of energy, laughed a lot. A merry laugh. When she was younger, often my mother would chide her for laughing at inopportune times. She didn't feel that Margaret was sensitive enough to sacred occasions or to people's feelings. I can recall Margaret answering her, 'But Gee-Marm, the laugh's in me and has to come out.'

"She was a headstrong child, willful. Early she learned to get her way with my father, partly because she was surprisingly articulate for a little girl, partly because from the beginning she'd had an instinctive knowledge of men.

"I was an easy mark too. This part of the story, Christy, you can hear as a sort of confession, further proof that I'm no tin-plated saint. I had accepted fully father's philosophy that parents can do nothing greater for their children than giving them a joyous childhood, so I set out to create what I called 'the habit of happiness' in my daughter.

"Since my decision had been for honesty, early I had told Margaret about the circumstances of her birth. Not the biological details, of course. Just: 'Our family is different. I never knew the care and protection of a husband. I've loved you all the more because I haven't had a complete family to love.' She seemed to accept that with no difficulty.

"I was so young myself when she was little. We were like two children. Together we slid down haystacks and went to every circus that came to town. We read a great deal; she acquired a rare knowledge of literature. There was one period when we had three cats, two monkeys, a parrot, a pair of doves and a dog as members of our household. There were silly indulgences like buying her a small parlor organ. Unheard of, for a Friend!

"Perhaps too, I overprotected her from our Quakerisms bcause some of them had always seemed silly to me. When she was fourteen, someone gave her a beautiful silk shawl with fringe a foot wide. Margaret was ecstatic and my mother was horrified. She insisted that no proper Quaker girl would ever don such gay apparel and, therefore, we were going to have to shorten the fringe. Margaret cried and stormed. Mother actually had the shawl spread out on the table, a ruler out, about to cut, with Margaret standing there entreatingly, certain that when the scissors cut that fringe they would also cut into her heart. I couldn't bear her agony and intervened because, in fact, the length of the fringe didn't seem important. This sort of thing was like that Friend who longed for scarlet geraniums in her window boxes, but didn't dare to grow them. Like my own grandmother who considered men's suspenders and that new invention—the sewing machine—contraptions of the devil. And believe it or not, one old lady I knew had false teeth made and then felt 'scruples' about using them. So she deposited the precious teeth in her top bureau drawer and painfully gummed her way through the rest of her days."

I laughed aloud. "I know I shouldn't," I said. "It's funny, but it's sad too."

"Yes, it *is* sad. But don't misunderstand me, Christy. Those Friends were God's savory salt. They were erring on the side of goodness. If that's erring, it produced great people.

"What I didn't understand then was that they were training their wills in the only way a will can be trained—by practicing giving up what we happen to want at the moment. Also while it was probably healthy for *our* relationship to have it out with my mother on cutting the fringe, it also reinforced my daughter in her selfish, determined ways.

"So Margaret grew up—vital, full of 'frivol.' The cry of her spirit was for freedom and more freedom. I could sympathize. I've always been something of a rebel too.

"But in her teens Margaret fell in with a group of people—young intellectuals, writers and artists—to whom freedom was a way of life. Not freedom *for* anything, just freedom from restrictions or irritations or responsibilities of any kind. They talked a lot about women's 'rights' and feminism; about the 'new' intellectualism; the revolution in child labor and sweat-shop laws and trade-unionism in general; and the 'cult' of art and the new poetry. To Margaret, all of this was intoxicating.

"Then came the moment in her teens when she insisted on knowing more details about her birth. The scene is etched in me: I, sitting on the bed beside her, answering all her questions as quietly and gently as I could; she, listening carefully, scarcely saying a word. I remember

456

how I sought to draw her to me. How I needed some sort of response from her! There was none. On her spirit there seemed to be a kind of high gloss that reflected back only coldness, like the glaze of ice.

"Soon after that she discovered that the manner of her birth made a great impression on her new friends. In our Quaker circle, where the facts had always been known, of course, it had made no difference. Oddly, with the young intellectuals, her illegitimacy gave her added acceptance, even glamor. So suddenly she swung into full rebellion. Everything that I or my parents or our community of Friends were for, she was against.

"It was about that time that she met Neil MacNeill, in his first year of postgraduate bedside training at Jefferson Hospital. Neil liked Margaret's independent spirit. In her rebellion she had a kind of fiery beauty. Her personality reminded me of one of those Fourth of July sparklers, twinkling off in all directions. Her eyes would glow, her wit flash, though there was sometimes a cutting edge to it.

"On Margaret's side, young Dr. MacNeill seemed perfect, especially since her family's fond wish was that she would find a husband within her own Quaker circle. He was not from a proper background at all, she thought, but from some wild place down south, she didn't know or care where. Then the Doctor boasted that he had taken science as his god and that he needed no other. That too suited Margaret's mutinous spirit. She told him too about her birth. 'A bastard child,' she called herself—and he liked her blunt honesty.

"So they ran off and got married. But I fear there was a flaw at the heart of the marriage—a certain feeling of unworthiness in Margaret. I was never sure of this, but at least once I heard her refer to herself as an 'accident conceived in man's lust.' And since she was discounting God, naturally she had no understanding of some of His greatest miracles: bringing good out of man's treachery and baseness.

"Poor Neil! Margaret's devaluating of herself had been so cloaked behind her happy-go-lucky personality that he never saw it until after their marriage. Even worse, I think, was his inevitable discovery that Margaret had picked him as a husband because she thought of him as also inferior and therefore, a proper mate for such as she."

She paused. "Am I going into too much detail, Christy? Do you really want to hear all this?"

"Oh, yes—yes, I do. Please go on, Miss Alice."

"Well then—in the first six months of their marriage, Margaret wrote one short note to me. After a while, when all my letters went unacknowledged, it became apparent that she and Neil meant to sever every tie with home.

"I'd long since learned that no difference in viewpoint should ever be allowed to cause the least break in love. Indeed, it cannot, if it's real love. True, Margaret and Neil had wandered far afield from my faith. But relationships can be kept intact without compromising one's own beliefs. And if we do not keep them intact, but give up and allow the chasm, we're breaking the second greatest commandment. I couldn't do that. So—uninvited and unheralded—I traveled down to Cutter Gap.

"As I anticipated, Margaret resented my coming, interpreted it that I was unwilling to cut the apron strings—so naturally, I didn't stay in Cutter Gap. By then I was a bit wiser and had learned that there's only one way to give advice to the young: give it, and then be perfectly unconcerned as to whether they take it or not. God alone is capable of managing other people—even our own children. So I explored other sections, and that was when I started the Big Lick Spring school. Still, the necessary contact with Margaret and Neil had been re-established, and this was right.

"In time I think all these relationships would have been made right. As the quiet months went by and Margaret watched her husband's work in Cutter Gap and saw his need of her, she began to see rebellion in its true light: as the easy way, so much easier and safer than commitment to positive values. She and Neil seemed slowly to be finding their way to a love based on something more enduring than partnership in flight. I believe that sooner or later love—Neil's and mine—would have dissolved Margaret's feelings of unworthiness.

"And then—that summer the scourge came early. All during her pregnancy Margaret felt depressed. Openly, she voiced the thought that perhaps it was wrong to perpetuate 'her kind.' And suddenly, she missed her own group of friends from Philadelphia; life in Cutter Gap seemed dull, devoid of intellectual stimulus. Once again, she withdrew into herself and the hard gloss reappeared.

458

And so with this attitude of depression, along with the typhoid, she had little will to fight for her life.

"With his young wife's death, Dr. MacNeill's rejection of religion was complete. In his eyes, what the Society of Friends had tried to do for me and my daughter in giving us love, had failed. Perhaps in his eyes, I too, had failed. Therefore, Christianity just didn't work! Let others get whatever they could from it; it was not for him. For a long time after Margaret's death his attitude toward me was nothing more than a polite, cool aloofness.

"Lately our relationship has improved, especially after I built my cabin in Cutter Gap following Margaret's death, and we got to know one another better. Neil has strengths and depths in him that not many of the mountain people understand."

I nodded. "All those hundreds of slides there in the room where she died. I saw them too when he sent me for supplies. What are they?"

"Neil's the only one who understands enough about them to tell you. It's research on trachoma. For years he's been using every spare moment trying to track down the cause and to find a cure. No cure yet, of course. Just new techniques of treatment. He's written a paper on his findings, published in the *Southern Medical Journal*. It was very well received, I understand.

"You mightn't guess it, but Neil is a man who carries dreams in his heart. One of them is to turn his practice in Cutter Gap over to someone else for a year or so and concentrate on research on eye disease. He has a medical hero—a Doctor Ernst Fuchs in Austria. Neil dreams of being associated with him in Vienna for a time." She arose. "I must go. I've been away from Lundy too long."

"Miss Alice, how can I thank you? You didn't have to tell me any of this."

Her eyes were warm as she looked at me. "I see her in you, the same vital force. So much ardor; the eagerness to grasp life—all of it; impetuosity; that spice of old Adam in thee that will not quite be put down. Anyhow," she twinkled at me, "I told thee, I always toady to the young too much."

The next morning Dr. MacNeill arrived early at the mission house and insisted on gathering us three women and David into the parlor for more detailed instructions on sanitation. His clothes were disheveled, his face deeply etched with fatigue and worry lines. He looked as if he had not slept properly for many nights.

As the Doctor held the parlor door open for me, he gave me such an intent look that it flustered me, and I walked by him hastily. My thoughts swung back to my impulsive kiss that morning we had ridden back together from Ruby Mae's. It had been a gesture of gratitude, nothing more. It meant only a change from suspicion— and, yes, hostility at times—to acceptance of Dr. MacNeill as a friend. There was admiration and respect in my feelings toward him now. But his scrutiny was so speculative that it made me uneasy. Surely the Doctor could not misinterpret my light heedless gesture. After all, I was in love with David. The Doctor must see this!

"Situation doesn't look good," he began. "Two new cases again yesterday. They're so scattered that it gives me no clue as to the source." Absently he ran his fingers through the back of his hair, his forehead creased in thought.

"But I called you in here to try to help you protect yourselves." Here he looked directly at me. "Christy, you've had no experience nursing typhoid. I'll write all this down, but I want to explain it too. First off, all water drunk in this house from now on has to be boiled—"

We groaned, thinking of the extra work. Miss Ida's face was a study.

"We'll use formalin for disinfecting Lundy's room. I'll show you how. After handling anything from the sick-room, hands have to be washed with 70% alcohol or bichloride solution. I'll make up some solution for you. All linens used for Lundy to be soaked two hours in carbolic acid solution, then boiled, then washed in lye soap." He went on and on, with each sentence sounding more like a sergeant-major snapping out orders.

This professional side of Neil MacNeill always seemed so inconsistent with his tousled sandy-red hair and his careless clothes. "You've got to think of all urine or stools as pure culture of typhoid bacilli," he persisted. "It all must be taken out to the woods and buried in a deep trench. Your job, David, I'm afraid. Sorry, Christy, no use to turn up that nose of yours. Disease isn't pleasant. No way to make it genteel for you. Let's strip off the party gloves and talk straight about it."

That night Lundy complained of a raging headache over his eyes. For the past two days his temperature had

460

risen steadily. He kept trying to sit up, but then would fall back giddily. I was frightened to see him picking and fumbling at the bedclothes exactly as Fairlight had done. His temperature continued to rise, and the next morning Miss Alice told us how his mind had wandered in and out of nightmare and delirium all night.

I was beginning to understand what devoted nursing typhoid required around the clock. There was the endless carrying in and out of pails and water basins and chamber pots. We must bathe and sponge the boy two, three, four times a day to try to bring down the fever; regularly rinse out the mouth and apply glycerine to tongue and lips to keep the brown fur and the typhoid sores from forming. But most continuous and time-consuming of all was the liquid nourishment which Miss Alice spoon-fed to Lundy every half hour.

"Everybody says, 'Feed a cold and starve a fever,'" Miss Alice commented, "but since typhoid can last five to six weeks, they've starved many a patient to death. So Doctor MacNeill claims it's best to keep pouring the soup and the eggnogs in. Nothing solid, though."

So Miss Alice raced up and down stairs, back and forth between the kitchen and the sickroom for beef bouillon, milk with sugar of milk added, peppenoid, gruels, buttermilk, whey, oatmeal, cream soups, soft custard . . . Lundy was in too much of a stupor to be hungry; he pushed away the food, and she had to force it between his lips.

I helped some, and so did Miss Ida. But Miss Ida was still resentful that our patient had to be Lundy Taylor. She would stand in the kitchen and rail, her thin lips drawn even tighter than usual, "A fine thing! Our fingers worked to the bone as it was for that young ape! He would be the one to get sick."

But when Miss Alice came to breakfast on Saturday morning with red-rimmed eyes, Miss Ida took pity on her. "Don't care a picayune about that boy," she said tartly, "but I do care about *you*. Alice Henderson, you get away from here. Go on over to your place and sleep. *I'll* nurse."

Miss Alice nodded gratefully. She was almost dozing at the table.

"And I'll take the night shift tonight," I told her. So it was arranged.

At ten o'clock that night, Miss Ida had finished giving Lundy some bouillon and was getting him ready for the night when Miss Alice came into the room. "How is he, Ida?"

"Last temperature reading's 103. This one's no rose-Matilda to take care of, I can tell you. I hope he'll sleep," she added as she went out the door.

"Christy, I came over to see that the cot was set up for you for the night watch," Miss Alice said, gesturing toward a camp bed sitting against the wall. "Also I've had my comfortable chair carried over. Try to snatch some rest, Christy, between jumps."

"I'll manage fine," I assured her more confidently than I felt.

She stood there a moment looking at me with such a warm smile flickering across her features that it was almost a caress. Then she left.

When I turned to my patient, I saw that he was wearing an old patched nightshirt which Miss Ida had found somewhere. His eyes were open but I was not sure that he recognized me. His arms and legs were thrashing at the sheet and one quilt over him. "Hot kivers ... Toes be tetchious," he complained in a whiney voice. "Untellin' misery in toes ... Take beddin' off'n me."

Since Miss Ida had said that the last temperature reading was 103 degrees, I did not think it a good idea to remove any covers. But as he continued to kick about and complain, sticking his big feet out from under the covers over the side of the bed, I looked gingerly at the toes. At least, I thought, for once he's clean. But I could see nothing wrong with the toes.

"A-hurtin' in my feet. Git that thar counterpin off'n me," he ordered whimperingly over and over. Finally I concluded that his toes must be sensitive for some reason I did not understand, so I placed a straight chair with its back against the foot of the cot and pulling the covers out at the foot, draped them over the chair to lift the weight of the bedclothes from Lundy's feet. In a little while, after a drink of water, he dozed off.

I blew out the lamp, keeping it by me, then sank into the easy chair and fell asleep almost at once. I was awakened by a terrible stench along with groanings and mutterings from the cot.

Lighting the lamp again, I took it to the bedside, and steeling myself, lifted the quilt and sheet off the hot body. The diarrhea which I had seen noted on a tablet lying on the table was still unchecked. Fortunately, Miss Ida had put several thicknesses of what amounted to a huge diaper on the big boy. Above the diaper his stomach was bloated, with rosy spots on it.

Now began as repugnant a task as I had ever faced. I covered Lundy up again, and went running downstairs for buckets of water. Using the pump at the sink, I filled two pails and one additional pan of water for scrubbing myself afterward.

But the water was icy; too cold to touch that feverish body. Since Miss Ida had banked the fire in the range, there were some coals left. I found small sticks of kindling, opened the damper on the stove and got the fire blazing, put some lumps of coal on to hold it, and started the water heating.

Then in Miss Ida's clothespin basket hanging on a hook on the back porch, I hunted for that new kind of clothespin with a spring on it, found one and put it in my pocket. I waited until the water was warm enough, then leaving the one pan on the stove, carried the pails upstairs along with a pack of old newspapers.

The foul odor met me at the top of the stairs. I set the buckets down and carefully pinched the clothespin onto my nose. It might look funny, but there was nobody to know or to see.

In the next few minutes my thoughts moved as fast as my hands. *No need to feel sorry for yourself. Lots and lots of people have to endure worse than this. Student nurses have unpleasant duties all the time, more disagreeable than this. Put your mind on things like—like what? Well, Grandmother Rudd's rose garden. Remember the old-fashioned white roses with the light yellow centers and the delicate fragrance. Or that cerise rose, one of Grandmother's favorite bushes. Beautiful only in bud though. The mature blossoms always droop.*

How I wished for rubber gloves! I wondered if Dr. MacNeill had any. I would ask him tomorrow. The clothespin was pinching my nose, but I welcomed the nips of pain. Now it was hurting badly so that my attention was focused on the pinching rather than on the smell and the odious task under my hands.

Finally it was finished and I stuffed the soiled diaper and the wet rags into the chamber pot, put the lid on tightly, and set it in the hall. In the corner of the sickroom on a pile of clean rags I found some of the outsize diapers neatly folded—and blessed Miss Ida for that. As I put the diaper under Lundy and brought up the corners to fasten them with safety pins, I thought, "Giant baby boy." He was so huge.

I found myself thinking what a ludicrous contrast this situation was to my sheltered girlhood. And Dr. MacNeill had laughed at me during Ruby Mae's wedding infare. He had thought I didn't know enough about life. Well, I was learning. Now there should be few embarrassments left. I pulled the covers over Lundy again.

Downstairs I dumped some water and chloride of lime into the pot and set it outside the back door. In the morning the contents would have to be buried in the earth with lye.

Then I began scrubbing myself, grateful for the scalding hot water and the carbolic acid solution. By Miss Ida's battered alarm clock ticking so loudly on the shelf behind the range, I saw that it was only ten minutes past twelve. I couldn't believe it! My vigil had scarely begun.

When I returned to the bedroom, Lundy was as feverish as ever, tossing from side to side, thirsty again. I offered water, but he would not take much, so I went back to the kitchen thinking I would try lemonade. But I had forgotten for a moment that I was not at home. Of course there were no lemons here; exotic fruit like that was a luxury item in the mountains. I settled for some cold buttermilk, and sitting by Lundy's bed, fed it to him spoonful by spoonful.

The boy's beard was growing out black. I must ask David to shave him. The slits of eyes looked at me unblinkingly. Once recognition flared in them. "Teacher," he whimpered like a hurt animal, "Teacher, I be a-hurtin' ... Sick ... Sick ... Paw, where's Paw ...? Teacher ..." Each word trailed off. He pawed the air with his hands, and I saw that the palms were yellow and perspiring.

He fell asleep then, though his legs still moved restlessly. Grateful for a respite, I lay down on the cot and pulled a quilt over me. But a peculiar dead-mouse odor was in the room. Now I knew! It was the odor of typhoid. Having once smelled it, how could anyone ever forget it! I turned on my side and burrowed my face in the quilt, trying to shut it out.

The night seemed interminable. After a while, I lost track of how many times I was up and down, numbed into moving mechanically, doing whatever had to be done. Miss Ida's clock in the kitchen ticked away, yet somehow the hands scarcely moved, creeping so slowly that half the time they appeared to be standing still.

Sometime toward dawn it began to drizzle, the rain beating a gentle tattoo on the tin roof. The rhythm of it lulled both Lundy and me to sleep.

I was awakened by the sound of a knocking—different from the patter of the rain. I sat up, listening, at first unable to locate the sound. Then I realized that it was coming from the back door. I lay there drowsily, hoping that since it was near her getting-up time anyway, Miss Ida would hear it. But she did not because her bedroom was at the front of the house. The tapping came again and again. Whoever it was, was knocking so softly—so hesitantly, and yet would not give up.

At last I dragged my sluggish body off the cot and down the stairs once more. At the back door I turned the key, slid the bolt, and cautiously opened the door partway to have a look. In my groggy state it took me a moment to comprehend what I was seeing.

I drew back, startled. It was Bird's-Eye Taylor standing there in the rain.

Forty-three

"I COME BACK," Bird's-Eye told us when the household
had assembled for breakfast, "because I heered 'bout
Lundy. Plumb tuckered out heelin' it too. Ain't got no
stummick left for hidin' out or being spied on. If'n we
could make fair weather betwixt us——"

Miss Ida's response to this overture was closer to foul
weather than to fair. "Mercy sakes alive," she grumbled
behind the closed door of her kitchen, "that Bird's-Eye—
creeping back here, pestering us, acting like butter would
melt in his mouth. Why, if that man kissed the Bible right
in front of my face, I still wouldn't trust him. And as for
dishing up any cooking of mine for that one, I'll be
blessed if I'm going to. There now! I've said it." And she
pursed her lips and stalked out the back door to hang up
some clothes.

David was only slightly less suspicious. "I don't know
what he's up to," he confided to me, "but I know Bird's-
Eye. He's got a heart as tough as seasoned hickory. The
contrite act doesn't fool me: these mountain men just
don't eat humble pie like that."

Miss Alice stayed around the mission house almost
continuously the first day Bird's-Eye was back, and I
noticed that she was studying him closely. She made no
comments on Miss Ida's or David's reactions; she was also
there to see the reunion between Lundy and his father. It
was pathetically typical.

"Is he took bad?" Bird's-Eye asked at the door of the
sickroom. We did not need to reply; his first look at
Lundy told him. Yet he had no idea how to express his
concern for his son except with the usual gruff insult:
"Are ye bein' as leather-headed as ever with these folks?"

With heavy lids drooping over the slits of his eyes,
Lundy blinked at his father in surprise and delight.

466

"Why, ye're a-grinnin' like a possum! Made tracks to git here, son. Ought to box yer jaws jest so ye'll know hit's me." Then, ill-at-ease, he backed out of the room, twisting his grimy black felt hat between his hands.

In the hallway he appealed, "With Lundy fast to his bed like that, I'd like to stay and help for a span."

It was Miss Alice who answered. "Bird's-Eye, we appreciate your offer. We could use some help. But I must tell you this. We can't harbor you here to hide you from the law."

"I knowed that when I snuck back."

She looked at him closely. "You're willing to have us contact the officers? They still want you for Tom's murder, you know. You would stand trial?"

He looked at the floor, then into her eyes. "I've mommicked things up good. Ain't no use a-runnin'."

To our surprise, Bird's-Eye followed his words with deeds. Without complaint, he helped with the menial chores: taking the ashes out of the kitchen range; chopping and carrying in firewood; emptying chamber pots; bringing water from the spring to boil for drinking water and to Lundy's room for bathing; boiling the boy's bed linens in a black pot in the yard and then scrubbing them in lye soap; and that task that David found most repugnant of all, burying the patient's body wastes with lye in a trench four feet deep.

Although David was glad for the help, he appeared to find this new Bird's-Eye harder to bear than the old one. At least he had understood the old Bird's-Eye and had felt justified in a kind of righteous indignation against him and all he represented.

One morning as I was sitting on the front steps to rest my feet and enjoy the mountain air, I heard David remonstrating with Dr. MacNeill. "Who does he think he is, putting on this big act? Why should we be taken in by a murderer? Or his no-good son! It kills me to see all the women nursing Lundy. Even Opal McHone's been coming to help." The voice coming through the open window from the parlor was rising with emotion. "You'd think he was the Prince of Wales! Lots of other people are down with typhoid in this Cove and none of them are getting bathed three times a day and fed every thirty minutes. And Lundy Taylor of all people!"

There was a long silence. Then the Doctor's voice: "I understand how you feel, David. But when I was about to

467

begin practicing medicine, I took an oath. The Hippocratic oath. I can't forget it. Therefore I have to do my utmost to save lives, any life, all lives. So—" There was a pause, then the voice went on "—we do the best we can for Lundy. Unfortunately, we can't nurse them all. Three more deaths this week."

David must have swallowed his protest. The voices ceased.

Indeed, before the weekend was over there were so many new cases of typhoid that we had no choice but to cancel the opening of school and hope that it was merely a postponement. Every one of us was needed now for nursing or to prepare food or carry it to the sick. By the end of that week a total of fifty-four cases had been reported.

I would not have believed that the base of our lives could change so quickly, but then neither had I known before what the dread word "epidemic" stood for: scarcely a family left untouched by the disease, sometimes with no one left to cook or care for them; a soup kitchen set up at Miss Alice's with every man who owned a horse or mule pressed into service to carry pails of soup to this cabin and that; the bone weariness of never getting a full night's sleep and the raw nerves and the snappish tempers that followed; the interminability of the nursing with the soles of one's feet sore from standing and walking and running; above all, living with so many unknowns in connection with the disease: What caused it? ... What was spreading it? ... How to protect ourselves? ... Always with the specter of fear hovering over us, forever wondering where the pestilence would strike next.

In one week Dr. MacNeill brought in on his saddle hump the pathetic surviving children of a mother who had died two days after her husband in a cabin in Raven Gap: first little Eli McDade and his older brother, Holland, and then three days later ten-year-old Nora.

In the midst of circumstances like these, viewpoints and values were shifting too. For example, one of the peculiar by-products of the epidemic was that every blockading still began producing to full capacity and many new ones were set up. The mountain people had the fixed idea that home-brewed liquor killed the germs, that to drink some liquor each day kept up strength, and that no herbs or medicine could be taken without it. We all realized what was going on, and to David it was one more frustration to bear.

Perhaps the most amazing shift of all was that everywhere in the Cove, folks who had seemed lackadaisical and without incentive rose under the crisis to almost unbelievable heights of performance. Whenever I could pause long enough to think about it, I found myself wondering wistfully what had been the missing factor in the mission's presentation of religion in ordinary times that the motivation of disaster now provided. Was not our faith meant to build a fire under people, to provide an equal incentive for the rooting out of apathy and evil and unforgiveness, and to help us get on with the job of becoming the kind of people and the kind of community Cutter Gap was surely meant to be? Did people always have to wait for pestilence or war or tragedy to be shocked into forgetting about themselves?

Of course, chief among those for whom the typhoid plague called out epics of selflessness were Miss Alice and Dr. MacNeill. They seemed to be everywhere—doctoring, nursing, comforting, cheering, ministering. But I saw surprising tensile strength in Miss Ida too. The more pressured things became, the more the complaints and dark looks fell away and in their place stood a determined, cheerful presence.

David too was doggedly giving his all, only not—I noticed when I began to watch for it—with the invalids themselves. It became apparent that he disliked being with anyone infirm or crippled or sickly. Bedside scenes made him so uneasy that he would go to almost any length to avoid them. Perhaps, I thought, it was because David had always been such a vigorous and robust man that he had no basis at all on which to understand the plight of the sick. So he stayed on the road almost ceaselessly, carrying soup or fetching medicines and food back from El Pano or off the train at the Fairview Flats flagstop, usually accompanied by Isaak McHone, who reveled in being David's chief helper. The new telephone saved many a mile's travel since we could ring up El Pano and have necessary supplies brought in by train.

As the situation worsened, it got so that I hated to see David and Isaak come in the front door since then we would hear about the latest case or yet another death. It was a black day when they reported that Zady Spencer had a fever and rose spots on her body.

"David," I asked, "don't you think you should go up the mountain and bring her here before she's too sick to be moved?"

"No, I don't think so. Christy, you can't take on any more."

"But Clara won't know how to take care of Zady. She's just a child herself. You know how important good nursing is in typhoid. Life or death—that's all."

David did not seem to be listening to me. He had a letter in his hand which he was folding and unfolding.

"Christy, I've been bothered by something for days now. You need to get out of here, to get back home. This is no place for you now."

"David, I'm talking about Zady Spencer!"

"But I want to talk about you. You're in danger."

"No more danger than you or anybody else."

"Yes, you are. You're pushing yourself too hard. Besides, young females your age are more susceptible than anybody."

"Who says so?"

"Neil."

"Do you mean to stand there and tell me that I should run away? That I shouldn't think about anything or anybody but my own skin?"

"I wouldn't put it like that."

"Well, I would, and I just can't do it."

David suddenly looked so frustrated and tired that I felt a pang of guilt. "You see, David, it's just that when I volunteered to come to the mountains, I thought it was from really lofty motives—because I loved people and wanted to help them. But now I know that wasn't the reason at all. I came for *me*. So—well, I can't turn around and leave now for the same reason."

A long silence fell between us. Finally, David said carefully, "There's another reason why I had to bring this up."

I waited.

"Your parents are frantic with worry about you. I had a letter from them."

"So that's it! What did the letter say, for you to 'use your influence'?"

"Something like that."

"That's like Dad . . . 'My girlie—take care of my girlie.' I guess if I were in their place, I'd be worried too. I love them and I understand how they feel, but David, there comes a time when you have to do what you feel is right. And right now I owe it to Fairlight to take care of her child."

We stared at each other. *We're too tired to be arguing like this. When we're this exhausted, quarreling is so easy . . .* So I said nothing more.

"Do what you want to do then," he shrugged—and left.

At first Dr. MacNeill gave us a ringing "No," saying that whenever possible it was preferable not to move a typhoid patient. Then he weighed the danger of this against the superior nursing Zady would get at the mission house, and finally decided to wrap her up and bring her himself. I knew that he and David had agreed between themselves that I would expend more energy riding back and forth to the Spencer cabin than in nursing Zady close by.

With her coming, our big back room began to look like a small hospital ward. Sheets were hung to divide one patient's bed from another's. And everywhere in the house there were the strong odors of carbolic acid and alcohol and the semi-cadaverous taint of typhoid.

BY THE THIRD WEEK, Lundy's temperature was dropping toward normal and his appetite had returned. In fact, he was ravenous all the time.

Once again, Dr. MacNeill gathered all of us into the parlor—including Isaak and Bird's-Eye—this time to talk about how to handle typhoid convalescents. "Lundy's lost sixteen pounds," he began, "so naturally his body craves food. But this is the trickiest stage of all. Typhoid's one disease you can never relax over. Even when the fever's gone and the patient's up and about, there's still grave danger." He lit his pipe, then hunched forward.

"Let me explain it this way," he continued. "The walls of the intestinal tract of a typhoid patient are thin, with sloughs or what you would call ulcers. If the patient eats bulky or solid foods too soon, they can perforate the intestinal wall, sometimes with hemorrhaging—depending on how deep the ulcers are and whether or not they involve blood vessels."

He glanced at Bird's-Eye who was looking puzzled. "In other words, Bird's-Eye, if Lundy eats any solid food too soon, holes can be torn inside him, perhaps with bleeding."

Bird's-Eye wagged his head, clearly pleased at being singled out from the rest of us.

"Perforation is always serious, in most cases fatal. That means death, Bird's-Eye. So the only safe rule is to stick with soft foods until a full ten days after temperature drops to normal. Women, give Lundy thick soups with lots of nourishment—like potato, pea. Milk-toast, mashed potatoes, a boiled or poached egg—but very soft. You're to stick to this soft diet no matter how much Lundy clamors for solid food. Got that, Bird's-Eye?"

"Doc, I'll lay it by in my mind. But that young'un's always been a rapscallion. He can carry on like a wildcat to git what he craves."

"Sure, he can—and will. But I called you in here with the rest to enlist your help in keeping your son in line. As he begins to get up, he's going to want to eat everything in sight. If we let him eat what he wants to, he may die. Think you can handle him, Bird's-Eye?"

"Shore, Doc. If'n he gits rippin' around, I'll smack the fire out'n him."

Dr. MacNeill had spoken none too soon. Two mornings after that I was in Lundy's cubicle of a room tidying up. Now that he was feeling better, he acted as if I were a combination mother and best girl. He was always reaching out to touch my hand or trying to detain me under any pretext. "I ain't restin' easy," he complained.

"You look fine to me, Lundy."

"You don't pay me no mind. Always a-pullin' out'n here."

"I have things to do. Zady and Nora and Eli have to be nursed too. And Zady's the sickest now."

"Girls shore take on a sight."

"She doesn't complain half as much as you do, Lundy."

"Why don't you rest yerself on that settin' chair thar and talk to me? You ain't bashful, are you?"

"No, Lundy, I'm not bashful."

"Wal, it's not like I was gonna ask you to shoot yer granny."

"Naturally not. Tell you what—you sit in the chair and we'll talk while I put fresh sheets on your bed."

He snickered and climbed out of bed. "When's me and Paw a-goin back home?"

"I don't know. Not until you're well, anyway. Hey, what's this!" In tucking in the bottom sheet, my hand had bumped into something under the mattress. I pulled out a sack of hard candy.

"Where did you get this, Lundy?"

"Ain't a-tellin'."

"You know you're not supposed to have it. Dr. MacNeill told you why."

He ignored that. "Vittles here don't suit me. Lady-cookin', that's what it is. Onyway," the whine crept into the voice, "jest look how I've fallen off."

I set the candy outside the door in the hall and went on making the bed.

The plaintive voice went on, "Bin a-lyin' thar smacking my mouth thinkin' of hot corn pone and a thick piece of ham-meat. Crave licorice sticks too."

I looked at him in alarm and pity. "You'll get all that soon enough. But what Dr. MacNeill told you is important. He's thinking about you, Lundy. You'd better heed it."

"Doc don't scare me none. Candy never hurt nobody."

Supper that night was hectic, with each of us eating at different times in order to feed our bed patients and get on with our own work. Gone now were the leisurely times of banter and lively discussions around the table. Though Miss Ida had relented after her initial refusal to cook for Bird's-Eye, I noticed that she managed never to be at the table with him. David had eaten early and had gone on down to his bunkhouse. Miss Alice was at the Coburns' to see about Bessie. Bessie—so full of promise; I had high hopes for her this next term in school.

I had little interest in my food. I sipped half a bowl of soup, picked at the meat loaf and potato, refused the bread pudding. Under normal circumstances, this would have brought a contemptuous grunt from Miss Ida, but now she picked up the untouched dish without a word.

The epidemic had changed everything. I thought of my schoolchildren and of the special plans I had prepared for this term, using so many of Grundtvig's ideas out of that book *Among the Danes*. Now our boarding-school had been turned into an infirmary; there was no time to teach the other women who hoped to learn to read; no chance to develop the idea of making and selling native products conceived that day at Miss Alice's Sewing Circle.

Thoughts tumbled over themselves in my tired mind: that matter of Miss Alice telling me about the Doctor's marriage.... Why? Did she think I was falling in love

473

with him? No, that could not be; Miss Alice knew that I loved David. There was something else though. She said I looked like his Margaret. I didn't care for that. Even if I were interested in the Doctor, who wants to be a replacement for some other woman?

What about the Doctor? Stubborn, a bit of a show-off ... Opinionated, contemptuous of Christian faith ... It was no wonder we clashed so. Yet he was all man. He cared about the mountain people. He had compassion.

Then that laboratory of his ... It was typical of the Doctor's reserved and stubborn nature that he would do all that research for years and keep it a secret from most of the Cove. Yet he had wanted me to know. Why?

I shook my head to try to clear away the mists of confusion in my mind. My thoughts went to David. Poor David. He had been so miserable since the outbreak of the typhoid. His plans for finishing the church and organizing his work had been set aside to handle the epidemic. The important jobs now were checking water supplies, trying to get the people to clean up barnyards and to build privies, burning clothes and the effects of victims. It was dirty work. David hated it, all of it—I could tell. Since Lundy's illness had begun, he had scarcely spent an extra minute in the mission house if he could avoid it.

My heart suddenly went out to David. He was having it harder than the Doctor really. Neil MacNeill was doing what he had been trained to do: David could do scarcely anything for which he had been trained.

Sitting there alone at the table, a great warmth grew inside me. *I love David ... Yes, I really do. And I haven't been much comfort or help to him recently.* Then the thought pierced me, *Why, David asked me to marry him—a long time ago. I never have given him a clear "Yes" or "No."* For a moment I was numb with guilt. *Has David been waiting all this time for me to make up my mind? Sometimes I wonder about myself. Are all girls my age often confused about love? Am I in love with David or just in love with love?*

There had been a feeling of pressure on my temples the last few days. I pressed the palms of my hands against my eyes. *And he needs me. He said so, and it's true. I can give him strength.*

Moved by a sudden compulsion, I slipped away from the table and walked out into the starry night in the direction of David's bunkhouse. A momentary feeling of doubt was dissolved by sudden resolution.

When, at my tap, David opened the door, he was obviously surprised. "Why, Christy! Anything wrong?"

"No, nothing. I need to talk to you, that's all."

He seemed uncertain. "Well, we could take a walk or go up and sit on the porch."

I was surprised at my own calm boldness. "We can talk right here. May I come in?"

He stepped aside for me to enter. Then, obviously embarrassed at the messy room, he hastily closed the door and began trying to straighten things up. I pushed aside some books to make a place for myself on his couch.

"David, please don't look so startled. If we love each other there's no reason why we have to be so stilted and formal. I think I've been a little childish in my attitude toward you and I came down here to tell you so."

"Why do you say that, Christy?"

"Because I think it's true. I was hurt by Fairlight's death and somehow expected you to make the hurt well. That was asking too much. I know that now."

"I knew you felt let down. But I don't think there are any really satisfactory answers for a situation like that."

For a quick moment I wanted to argue the point, but I pushed that aside. "Anyway, David, I realize there has to be both give and take in real love. I guess I've been mostly a taker."

A light came into the brown eyes. He relaxed and moved closer to me. "Christy, I never know what to expect from you." He kissed me softly on each eyelid and then drew me to him with sudden intensity. There was such urgency in his lips now that I drew away.

David looked at me in surprise. "You're not sure what it is you want to give, are you, Christy?"

"Yes, David, I do know. That's what I came to tell you—what I want to give. But you never want to talk. I need to know what you're thinking."

"Well, if you really want to know what I'm thinking," he said lightly, "it's how soft your hair is against my cheek."

The boyish look in his eyes and the banter silenced me for a moment. In an instant he had me in his arms again. Yet all my questions were still there between us. "David, please . . . can't we talk for just a minute?"

"All right. What about?"

I drew a deep breath. "Do you remember the night you asked me to marry you?"

"Sure, I remember."

"It was so sudden, the last thing I expected to hear from you right then. So I told you I needed time to think it over."

"I was impulsive, I suppose."

"It didn't seem that way to me. I was—well, flattered. Any girl would be."

David did not respond to that. After a pause he said, "Well, maybe. But there've been times in the past few weeks when I wasn't sure how you felt about me."

"But, David, you've never asked me how I felt. You've never tried to find out."

There was an awkward silence. David seemed to be struggling within himself. All at once I was aware again of the half-made couch-bed, the litter of books and clothes scattered around the shabby little bunkhouse. "David, do you think it's all right for me to be here?"

"But why not? You certainly didn't hesitate to go by yourself to Dr. MacNeill's cabin."

The words had come out abruptly. For a moment they hung there in the room as if suspended. I tried to understand this new thought, but my temples were throbbing again. There was an air of unreality. Was this really me sitting here in David's bunkhouse? It did not feel like me.

Perhaps I had not heard correctly. Was David accusing me of something involving the Doctor? Surely he knew that my visit to Dr. MacNeill's cabin had been to get medicine.

I started to say these things, but no words came. I got up from his couch and walked out the door.

Forty-four

DAVID APOLOGIZED the next morning. "Christy, I'm sorry about last night. I don't know why I acted the way I did. Will you forgive me?"

"Of course, I forgive you." But on the inside something was crying out, *Oh, David, what's wrong? Why can't you receive love? I'm afraid to admit it even to myself, but you don't love me. You don't really want me to marry you or you would have said so last night. I gave you every chance. You only want me in your arms, with my body against yours. Oh, David ... David, somehow you can't give love, you only want to make love.* But it was no use. How could I say such things to David? So aloud I only added lamely, "It's all right. We're all worn out, not like ourselves at all."

It was true. Total weariness had caught up with us. It was into the bloodstream and the bone marrow, behind the eyes, befogging the brain. Nor was there any respite. East Tennessee was having a mild late autumn. Here it was into November, and still no freezing ground. The plague spread and spread.

What do you do when strength is called for and you have no strength? You evoke a power beyond your own and use stamina you did not know you had. You open your eyes in the morning grateful that you can see the sunlight of yet another day. You draw yourself to the edge of the bed and then put one foot in front of the other—and keep going. You weep with those who gently close the eyes of the dead, and somehow, from the salt of your tears, comes endurance for them and for you. You pour out that resurgence to minister to the living.

At night in my room, I would look into the darkness and see all around me faces with eyes glazed with fever and unrecognition, and hands picking, picking at bedclothes. I would turn over and bury my face in the pillow to shut out the phantasm of the freshly dug graves on the hillsides and that vacant desolation on the faces of the children left, and the look of the women with empty arms.

ZADY'S FEVER was going down; the crisis was over. We permitted Clara into the sickroom briefly to see her sister, and I used the opportunity to inquire about Bessie Coburn. Clara and Bessie had been inseparable at school last term.

"She's up and around," Clara answered, "but even more puny than Zady here. Most too drug out for onything. Worst is, her mama's took with the miseries now."

"Miseries? You mean typhoid, Clara?"

"Reckon so. Mistress Coburn's ailin' right bad."

"Is she in bed?"

"Yes'm. Bessie's jest one big bundle of worry for her mama. Says she has fearful dread in her heart."

"Aren't the neighbors helping?"

"No'm—only one neighbor's in hollerin' distance. They can't pitch in and help do because some has had to drap into bed themselves and the rest are plumb give out."

"If things are that bad, I'd better go up there tomorrow."

"Bessie'd be obleeged to ye for that. Says sometimes she's a-feelin' like to die and no one to holp a-tall."

That decided it. The next morning early I started for the Coburn cabin on the back side of Coldsprings Mountain, taking with me some eggs, a bottle of tonic for Bessie, and a jar of broth. As I climbed the hill I saw a tall thin figure in the distance toiling up the slope carrying a bucket. It was Bessie, coming back from the spring at the bottom of the hill. Every few steps she would shift the pail from one hand to the other, then straighten up to catch her breath.

I wondered if, all unknowing, Bessie was carrying more typhoid germs up the hill in that pail. Dr. MacNeill never had ceased talking about the necessity of cleaning out all springs, of being sure that no human waste washed into them, of being certain that no pig pens or barnyards were adjacent to a source of water. Yet even with so much dramatic evidence spread before the eyes of the highland- little that the Doctor said about sanitation had any Few people had changed their ways.

I made my way across the brown stubble field at the top of the knoll and reached the weathered fence surrounding the Turner yard. No picket fence this, just unpainted pieces of board and some split logs nailed together hit-and-miss. Bessie had reached the porch but had still not seen me.

I paused for an instant at the gate and let my eyes take in the scene: a hog pen on one side with pigs confined to be fattened for butchering; the yard so hard-packed that even in the summertime no grass could grow, "swept clean" except for some islands of butterfly bushes and pretty-by-nights—scraggly now, bent over by frost; the iron wash pot swung under a tripod with the battling block and soap trough nearby—all mute evidence of Lety Coburn's work-worn hands.

This one-room cabin was smaller than most because there were only three Coburns. A fieldstone chimney poked into the sky. There was a tiny porch across the front of the cabin, its ugliness softened by a dried gourd vine trailing across it. Close by the porch was a single ancient apple tree, partly dead now, broken limbs silhouetted against the soft blue of the November morning. Kyle Coburn's two limp-eared hound-dogs saw me and ambled over to investigate, though they looked almost too lazy to make that effort, much less bark.

At the two puncheon steps up to the rickety porch, as Bessie tried to step up, her right leg collapsed under her. She put the bucket on the ground and, taking both hands, was resolutely lifting the leg onto the step—her face set in grimly determined lines—when I called out to her and started running. "Hi, Bessie. It's Teacher. Let me help." I grabbed the pail. "You're too weak to be carrying water."

"Howdy, Teacher." It was a wisp of a voice. "Plumb tuckered out, I reckon. The water's for mama. She's bad off." Her voice broke. The blue eyes looking at me were pools of misery.

This was my first glimpse of Bessie since she had recovered, and I was shocked to see how emaciated and hollow-eyed the girl was. In the aftermath of the disease she was losing most of her blonde hair. It gave her a picked-chicken look.

A man's voice, high-pitched and almost shrieking, came through the open door, though the words were garbled. "That's Paw," Bessie explained, nodding toward the door, "a-tryin' to git some toddick down Mama."

I picked up the bucket, crossed the porch and stood in the doorway, only to be met by the odor of typhoid. *I can't abide any more of it. So long as I live, I'll remember this peculiar smell.* At least the pungency of the carbolic acid dumped into tubs of water standing in the sickroom helped a little. The carbolic acid was supposed to cleanse the air and eliminate the smells or "funks," as the people expressed it.

Ordinarily Mrs. Coburn was a heavy woman, which had always made her seem older than she was. But looking at her lying motionless in bed, I could see that she had lost many pounds. Not even the soiled chenille robe she was wearing fastened across her ample bosom with a huge safety pin could hide the wasted flesh. On her the weight loss looked worse than on Bessie, who had always been thin.

Mr. Coburn was standing by his wife's bed shouting into her face, but the sick woman neither moved nor opened her eyes. Kyle had a jelly glass in one hand, a spoon in the other. I knew that the "toddick" would be whiskey in water with a little sugar—if any was available—or else honey mixed in.

"Good morning, Mr. Coburn. How is she?"

He looked at me briefly, his forehead creased with worry, fear in his eyes too. "Howdy do, Ma'am. Lety's taken a turn. Every bit and grain of her be on the go-down." He paused for no sympathy from me, but returned to the task at hand. "Lety, do you hear me? Open yer mouth, Lety. This'll pearten you up. Lety ..." His voice was like a trumpet blast in the patient's ear.

"Paw, don't beller so. You're jest a-plaguin' mama that-away."

"Hunh! Lety, I'm a-talkin' to you. Can you hear me, Lety? Confound it all, woman."

Finally Mrs. Coburn stirred slightly. Her husband took quick advantage of this to force the spoon between her lips. "Right betwixt yer lips spang in yer mouth, Lety. Thar now."

Miraculously, the muscles of the sick woman's throat contracted and she swallowed involuntarily. I hoped that the liquor was diluted enough so that she would not cough and choke.

The patient had no sooner swallowed that spoonful than her husband, encouraged, began shouting at her to "peart up" and take some more. But not even the few drops of whiskey had revived Lety Coburn. She looked to be in a deeper stupor than when I had entered the room, her features pinched and drawn, her lips so parched that patches of dry skin stood up like blisters.

"Lety, one more swig," the raucous voice boomed out. "Open up, Lety. Lety, you hear me? Le-*ty!*" But the sick woman did not stir.

I sank down on a homemade bench pushed back against the wall.

"Paw sounds like a pond full of screechin' geese." Hearing the apologetic note in Bessie's voice, I deliberately withdrew my attention from the scene at the bed. But when the girl saw me looking at the room, she was even more embarrassed. With Bessie and her mother ill one after the other, it was scarcely surprising that dirt and disorder were everywhere, "slut's wool" under the bed and in the corners, unwashed dishes on the single table, flies over everything. Even with the door open, the ventilation was not good either. The cabin had only one small window, propped up now with a stick.

Indicating the room with a sweep of her hand, my young pupil tried to sound gay. "Ain't it a sight in the world! House all gaumed up— I'm still so weak I can't do much more'n piddle at housekeepin'. Aimin' to git the dishes washed up today—"

"Don't apologize, Bessie. But what about food?"

"Well'm—" she hesitated. "Rations air runnin' low."

"Then I can do something about that. I'll find somebody to carry some food up from the mission house."

"We'd like that the best in the world," she said gratefully.

I glanced back at the bed. Suddenly the sick woman's jaw sagged open and she began breathing through her mouth. It showed her teeth and the tip of her tongue covered with brown fur. Immediately, Mr. Coburn thrust in the waiting spoon. But this time the liquid trickled across her tongue and splashed out the side of her mouth and down her cheek.

"Blame! Made a bobble of that 'un." Kyle wiped his wife's face with a far from clean rag and set the glass down.

"Mr. Coburn, has Dr. MacNeill seen your wife?"

"No'm. Put hit off. Bessie gott along without. Figured Lety would too."

I knew that I had to be cautious. "Mr. Coburn, I think

481

your wife is really sick. When he gets back to the mission, could I ask the Doctor to come up here?"

Rather than resisting the suggestion, the man nodded, relief in his eyes. "Hit'd be an accommodation. I'm plumb give out, a-tryin' to holp Lety."

I rose to go, but as I got to the middle of the room, I knew that I could not leave Bessie in such a plight. I thought of all the pails of water it would take to scrub this cabin properly. And each one would have to be fetched from a spring a quarter of a mile away! Sanitation? In a situation like this with flies crawling over those unwashed dishes, it became a farce. Yet here was thirteen-year-old Bessie, so weak that she could not lift her legs up two steps.

"Look, Bessie, I've got to help you a little before I leave. What do you wash the dishes in?"

My pupil looked startled. "Teacher, hit's not fitten . . ."

"I wash dishes at home in Asheville. I've washed dishes all my life. Come on, show me the pan. Some of your mother's homemade lye soap too."

Kyle Coburn's face was a study in amazement. I decided to strike immediately. "Mr. Coburn, Bessie and I are going to need more water here. Would you be so kind? As a matter of fact, if you have another bucket—as soon as I empty this one, would you bring me two at once?"

I knew perfectly well that Kyle considered carrying water women's work but that he dared not refuse me. So as soon as I had poured the contents of the one bucket into the wash-up pan, he strode out the door with a pail in each hand.

Knowing that Bessie needed to rest, I suggested, "Why don't you take over with your mother now? You sit in this chair by her bed and wipe her forehead, give her water if she wants it, and talk to me while I work."

She looked at me gratefully and sank into the chair.

By the time I left two hours later, the cabin was considerably cleaner. We had made Lety Coburn as comfortable as we could, though there were no sheets in the cabin, clean or otherwise. We had gotten her to swallow two more tablespoons of liquid, had sponged her face and hands, tried to wash out her mouth, and put sheep's tallow on her parched lips. I would send glycerine to put on her tongue and more carbolic acid for disinfectant, along with some food—and Dr. MacNeill.

On the way home I was aware of aching legs, a throbbing head, an odd twitch—like a tic—in the muscles of my face and a bitter taste in my mouth. Tiredness, I supposed.

THE FEEL OF CRISIS met me at the front door of the mission house. I could hear footsteps running up the stairs. At the sound of the door opening, the figure on the stairs turned to look. It was Opal McHone carrying a pail of water.

"Opal! Anything wrong?"

"It's Lundy. Awful sick." She rushed on.

Several people were running around upstairs and I could hear gagging. I didn't even wait to take off my coat, but with dread in my heart, climbed the stairs to Lundy's room. Miss Ida was standing to one side of the open door, looking in, disgust on her face.

"Hurts! Ow-whee-ee!" Lundy groaned. "Got a-hurtin' to my stummick."

Miss Alice had been holding his head over a basin. "There now, lie back." Her voice was gentle. "I want to see where your stomach hurts and take your temperature." She looked up at me briefly. "Christy, would you shake down the thermometer and put it in Lundy's mouth?" Then to her patient, "Straighten your legs out, Lundy. I have to see where the pain is."

"Can't! Ain't a-gonna do it!"

His legs were drawn up rigidly. "Under your tongue, Lundy," I ordered, and Miss Alice used the moment of distraction to grip his big legs with firm hands and unbend them. Her hands moved over the left side of his abdomen, pressing lightly. "Does it hurt there"?

"Um-m-muh." He shook his head.

But as her hand reached the right lower side, he bellowed, "Oh, A-oo-oo!" and I had to snatch at the thermometer to keep him from swallowing it.

"I'm sorry it hurts, Lundy."

I took the thermometer out of his mouth, looked at it, and handed it to Miss Alice. It stood at 103.6 degrees. Yet I knew that Lundy's temperature had been normal for eight consecutive days.

"All right, Lundy." Miss Alice pulled the covers back up. "Just lie quietly now."

"Can't ye give me no easin' powder?"

"We'll see." She motioned us into the hall.

"Ida," Miss Alice asked in a low voice, "has Lundy been sneaking food yesterday or today?"

"Not that I know of. Of course, with that young hellion you never can tell what he's up to."

"Would you have a careful look around your kitchen? See if you miss anything?"

Miss Ida went off looking as if she relished the assignment.

I asked, "The pain's only on the right side. Couldn't it be appendicitis?"

"Perhaps," Miss Alice answered thoughtfully. "Always possible, but not likely." She sighed. "We need Neil."

"Where is he?"

"All the way across the river in the direction of Lyleton. I don't think we can expect him back under three hours."

"And Bird's-Eye?"

"Took some soup to the Allens. He didn't want to go there, of course." Her eyes twinkled. "I have my reasons." She walked back into the bedroom. "Lundy, have you eaten anything you shouldn't?"

"Naw."

"You're certain?"

"Ain't et nothin' but mincy lady-vittles."

Opal came out into the hall carrying the pail and urinal. "He's a lyin' puppy," she whispered to me.

"How do you know?"

"By the vomit."

Miss Ida came back up the stairs and Miss Alice stepped into the hall to hear her report. "I think I've found what you want to know," Miss Ida told her. "I'd hard-boiled a dozen eggs—getting ready to devil them—and left them in a pan on the table. Two are gone."

Miss Alice looked frightened. "You're sure about the number?"

Miss Ida smacked her lips. "Absolutely sure. I knew that boy couldn't be trusted."

Miss Alice's eyes were wide with apprehension. "If he's eaten hard-boiled eggs, they could cause either hemorrhage or perforation. If Neil were here and diagnosed it perforation, he'd want to operate immediately."

With a look of desperation on her face, she went back to the bedside. "Lundy, Miss Ida says that some hard-boiled eggs are missing from her kitchen. Did you eat them?"

He turned his head away from her and muttered, "Naw—"

"Two eggs are gone. We're trying to help you, Lundy. You'd best tell us the truth."

"Waal, what did you expect," he lashed out, "givin' me smidgens on my plates, a-starvin' me most to death. You needn't hack at *me*." Then he grabbed his stomach as a new paroxysm of cramps gripped him. "OO-oo-law! Can't you *do* nothin' for me?"

For the next two hours Lundy's temperature mounted steadily. Bird's-Eye got back and took over the unpleasant part of the work, for there were two more attacks of nausea, and Lundy had to use the urinal every few minutes. I had never seen Miss Alice's usual calm so nearly shattered. She went to her cabin to study what her medical books had to say on typhoid perforation and came back looking more troubled than ever. "Osler even specifies that in perforation the pain is likely to be on the right side. The only suggestion is to turn the patient on the left side. Then if that doesn't relieve the pain—operate. If only Neil would come!"

Soon after we got Lundy onto his left side, hiccoughs set in. The look on his face was changing, so I decided to take his temperature again. When I found that it had dropped a degree, I went to Miss Alice, elated. But she only shook her head and looked more distressed than ever.

The hiccoughs went on and on. Miss Ida made Lundy sit up and try to hold his breath and drink from the far rim of a cup. It did not help.

Then Bird's-Eye suggested his pet remedy: to scare the hiccoughs away. He got his hog-rifle and, without warning, fired a blast out the window two feet from Lundy's bed. The boy was startled all right, then grinned. "What you a-tryin' to do, Paw, hawk hell out'n me?" But then the hiccoughs began again.

The next hour saw his temperature dropping even more. Oddly, the pallor of his face was being suffused by a pink, almost dusky color and his forehead was beaded with perspiration. He was breathing rapidly and shallowly, not protesting so much now. Miss Alice kept feeling his pulse. Opal, great compassion in her eyes, stayed close to the head of the bed, wiping the big boy's forehead. I saw Bird's-Eye watching her. His eyes were as soft as I had ever seen them.

Hearing someone at the front door, I ran to the top of the stairs. If only it would be Dr. MacNeill ... It was! And David and Isaak. "Are we glad to see you!"

One look at my face and Dr. MacNeill came bounding up the stairs; David and Isaak followed more slowly. I stayed in the hall with David and explained to him what had happened.

Our momentary relief at seeing the Doctor soon faded. He had gotten back too late to operate. Lundy had sunk into deep shock. His temperature had dropped a total of seven degrees and his heart action was erratic and feeble. The big boy lay unconscious with half-open eyes, his breathing shallow, his body turning blue and bathed in a cold sweat.

Surely we haven't put in all these weeks of effort to have it end like this, I thought. David's face was stony. Bird's-Eye stood to one side, almost against the wall, watching his son's face on which there was now no flicker of consciousness. Once I thought I saw a tremor around Bird's-Eye's mouth.

Dr. MacNeill, having done everything he knew to bring Lundy out of shock, now sat by the bed with his hand on the boy's pulse. His face was set in grim lines. Alice Henderson was standing at his elbow, ready to help in any way she could. Without turning his head, I heard him speak almost in a whisper to her, "Saying a prayer, Alice?"

"Yes, Neil, I was."

"Prayer, Alice, isn't going to change the course of typhoid."

Finally, he put Lundy's hand down, felt his chest and listened to it, examined the eyes, straightened up. "It's all over." He turned to speak to Bird's-Eye.

But Bird's-Eye had slipped from the room.

Forty-five

AROUND THE SUPPER TABLE that evening we were a restrained group. Miss Alice did her best to pull our thoughts off Lundy's body lying in the bedroom over our heads by telling us story after story about Dr. Ferrand and his genial eccentricities. I could not keep my mind on what she was saying.

As I toyed with the food on my plate, I was wondering how much Bird's-Eye really understood about the cause of his son's death, whether he would blame us. If only the boy's death would not dishearten Bird's-Eye to the point of snapping that fragile life line of his new resolutions. He had made a promise to Miss Alice. What if he had now decided to flee the law after all?

The questions were answered when Bird's-Eye showed up again after supper. All of us except Dr. MacNeill were sitting in the parlor too weary to start the next round of chores, reluctant to leave the comfort of one another's company, when he appeared suddenly in the doorway. "Bin a-trompin' and a-trompin'," he began, speaking directly to Miss Alice. "I'm needin' to talk to you. To Opal too."

Miss Alice drew him into the room and, with a gesture, indicated that she spoke for us all. "We're glad you decided to come back, Bird's-Eye. Dr. MacNeill is out searching for you. We haven't even had the chance to tell you how sorry we are. We're grieving along with you. You know that."

"Oh, I ain't faultin' none of ye, Ma'am. Doc nuther. Couldn't nobody do nothin' for that Lundy. Never could learn him nothing, so stiff-necked he was, and raspy."

"There are a lot of details to be attended to," Miss Alice went on hastily, as if eager to turn off that line of talk. "Opal and Ida have volunteered to take care of the laying-out, but we need a coffin. Will you build it, Bird's-Eye?"

The pale blue eyes in the weathered face looked at her unblinkingly. If there was emotion, I could see none. "Aye. Tomorry." He ran one hand over the stubble of several days' growth of beard on his chin. "Reckon, Preacher, when we lay Lundy by, you could make one of them long speeches over him?"

David's face was a study. All he said was, "Sure, Bird's-Eye, I'll make a speech."

But the mountain man had something else on his mind. He came a few steps farther into the parlor but was too self-conscious to sit down even after Miss Alice indicated a chair. Although the bravado of the old days was gone, the bloodshot eyes with the deep vertical lines between them held no cravenness—only a determination to say what had to be said. "No need to let no grass grow under my feet, guess." He looked directly at Opal who was sitting opposite me on the other side of the lamp table. "My give-out is about Tom. Like I writ ye, Opal, it wasn't me kilt Tom. Bin a-wantin to tell you, but with Lundy sick to his bed 'n' all—" His voice trailed off.

David was looking at him narrowly. Isaak was standing beside his mother. She reached for his hand as to hang on to him.

"That day you fed me, Opal, you said how I couldn't eat gredges and how hate wouldn't fill my stummick. Said most ony addlepated fool could pull the trigger of a rifle-gun, but that it took a *man* to fix things. Wal, got to thinkin' on that considerable. Left yer place, shoved fer Bob Allen's mill, but he warn't thar. Studied on hit some more. Knowed you was right—I couldn't do no good a-killin'. Had my craw full of hit onyway. Took my three men, cloomb back up the moun-tain to my place.

"Nobody was thar. Lundy had gone traipsin'. Didn't know whar. He come in at rooster-crow, a-packin' my old hog-rifle, braggin' that he'd done hisself proud—squawkin' that he'd kilt Tom. Said now he'd holped me, so he was a man-person."

I heard Opal suck in her breath. Isaak stood there clenching and unclenching his free hand. The bitter taste was in my mouth again. *Most any addlepated fool can pull the trigger of a gun.* The small pig-eyes in Lundy's unintelligent face floated before me. *A fool . . . An addlepated fool.*

David's voice boomed out, "Just a minute, Bird's-Eye. Seems to me this is mighty convenient timing. If this story's true, why did you let so many weeks go by without telling us? You wait until the night your son dies to blame Tom's murder on him—a dead boy who can't defend himself."

"You ain't believin' me?"

"What I believe isn't the point. Any court of law is going to ask for more proof than your word." David's lips curled in scorn. "Your word hasn't exactly been noted around here for its sterling quality. What proof can you show that Lundy shot Tom"?

For a moment Bird's-Eye looked nonplused. Uneasily, he shifted the weight of his body from one foot to the other. "Don't reckon," he said slowly, "I've got no ev-i-dence to show. Onct my passel of cronies heerd 'bout Tom bein' shot, said they warn't takin' no chances of ruination with the Big Law. They was that oneasy 'bout hair-cuttin' Prince and a-firin' yer pul-pit. So they lit out back home acrost the ridge-line into North Carolina—and they warn't mosyin' nuther. So they ain't here to back me up."

He shrugged. "Onyway druther be clomped in jail myself than Lundy. Couldn't turn in my own flesh'n'blood. That boy was high-stocked in honery-fixin' and low-stocked in brains—and that's the dyin' truth."

Miss Alice leaned forward in her chair. There was a light in her eyes. "But there is proof, David. I've known for a month now that Lundy shot Tom."

Silent amazement gripped us all. Every eye in the room was turned to Alice Henderson.

"After Lundy got sick Bob Allen came to see me. He said he was concerned about our nursing Lundy here. Said he knew something that was weighing on him—"

She paused to regard the group, her gaze coming to rest on Bird's-Eye.

I glanced at him. The mountain man was staring back at her with a look of total absorption. Opal was still clinging to Isaak's hand, waiting almost breathlessly for the next sentence.

"Bird's-Eye, that night you left the McHones and went to Bob's mill, Bob Allen was on his way to David's bunkhouse. At the edge of the mission woods, he heard the shot that killed Tom and saw Lundy fleeing. Nobody else was around."

Excitement crackled from the man standing in our midst. "Saw him for shore?"

"Yes. For sure."

But then the excitement died. "But he wouldn't holp me. He be an Allen."

"If Bob didn't mean to help, he would have kept quiet. Bob and I have had many talks. He hasn't found hatred very good food either."

This was too much for Bird's-Eye. Conflicting reactions struggled with the flint-like quality of his features, like a sledge hammer smashing a mighty boulder to bits. And in the breakup, for the first time, real emotion showed through. *This is one of those moments, one of those great moments.* I looked at Opal, the lamplight falling across her face. Though obviously she had found it agony to go back and relive any part of that night of her Tom's murder, there was a kind of triumph on her face. *Something important is vindicated for her. When she fed Tom's enemies that day, she stepped out in faith—her own kind of faith. And she was obedient to speak the words rising within her. Homely words ... But they had life in them. Like an arrow to its mark.*

And Miss Alice, whose love endured all things, faltered at nothing ... All that time she was nursing Lundy, she knew. She knew!

There was that swimming feeling in my head again. My feet were leaden. I did not feel like making the effort to move out of my chair. The others were leaving. I heard Opal's soft voice speaking to Bird's-Eye on the porch. Then closer by, Miss Alice's voice saying, "David, would thee come on down to my cabin? I have a story to tell thee—"

I opened my eyes. Only Miss Alice and David and I were left in the parlor. David was sitting in a chair, hunched over, his head bowed in his hands.

"Tell me right here," he said. "Whatever it is, I'd like Christy to hear it too. I have something I want to tell both of you."

Miss Alice looked uncertain. For a moment there was that look on her face that I had come to recognize, almost as if she were listening for an inner signal. Then she relaxed and sat down again. "All right—Christy, I was going to tell David about a man to whom God gave an assignment." Her eyes smiled at him. "God told this man to travel to a far country where there was much wickedness. He was told to warn the citizens that if they did not change their evil ways, their country would be destroyed. And the man obeyed and delivered the message.

"But to his surprise the citizens listened. In fact, even the king took the warning seriously and issued an official edict, decreeing a time of national fasting and prayer. And in the face of this repentance, God decided to call off the punishment.

"Now ordinarily we would expect the messenger to be delighted that his words had resulted in the community's revival. Not a bit of it! Instead he lashed out at God, 'You told me to warn these people what would happen to them, and now nothing's going to happen at all! So where does that leave me—looking like a liar and a fool!'

"Whereupon, angrily, he stomped off to the outskirts of the city where he sulked under a gourd vine and pleaded with God to let him die."

Her gray eyes looked unblinkingly at David. "Thee is not unlike that old prophet, Jonah."

David gazed back at her, stark misery on his face. "I sure agree with you on one point: I look like a fool. Everybody lately seems to come off better than I do. Even Bird's-Eye Taylor." The voice was tinged with bitterness. "I can't do anything right. I even snarled things up between Christy and me the other night."

. I couldn't bear it. "Oh David, no! Stop it—that isn't true."

He ignored my protest. "There's something else I want to tell you both. I've made a decision. As soon as the epidemic is under control, I'm resigning here. I'm going to head back north, make my report to the seminary, and then clear out of there too. There's only one good thing about this experience in the mountains. At least it's showed me what I needed to know: wherever else I belong, it's not in the ministry."

I felt sick for him. "David, you're beside yourself tonight. All this will pass. David, please—"

"Nothing stings like hurt pride, David," Miss Alice said calmly. "Take a look at why thee hurts. The man who challenged thee before everyone has listened and turned—"

"That's right, heap it on. I've read Jonah too. Right now I feel like that worm chomping down Jonah's gourd vine."

Miss Alice laughed. "You're no worm, David, and you still have a sense of humor. As for not belonging in the ministry, the Friends say something that speaks to that point: every one of us belongs in some kind of ministry. 'Ministry' isn't just a profession of the church, David. Give thyself a largesse of credit. Thee has been ministering in a hundred ways, day after day, before the epidemic and through it."

"Sure, I've been busy. I suppose you could say a lot of it has been God's work. But there's such a thing as doing His work and yet not feeling a part of His work. You know God in a way that I don't, Miss Alice. You have an inner sureness that I envy."

"Could it be, David, that deep down thee has never really wanted it—or Him?"

"Yes—you could be right. I think I've been running away from a lot of things in my life."

"Not things. A Person and persons. And now you feel like running again?"

David did not answer immediately. His face was flushed and he was sliding his finger up and down that bent part of his nose. "I don't want to stay where I'm doing more harm than good."

"Your work here is much on the plus side, David. But that's beside the point. All your life you've had people at home telling you what to do. You've resisted and resented that—often quite rightly—because it was a threat to your manhood. I've heard you lay at your mother's door your decision to enter the ministry. But perhaps there was another reason. I wonder, David, if thee didn't see in the ministry the chance to tell others what to do—for a change. But it doesn't quite work out that way, does it?"

Her voice had become so low and gentle that it was like listening to the patter of soft rain. "Could it be, David," she went on, "that your deepest fear is calling anyone Master and Lord?"

David looked at her, obviously struggling with the questions she had flung at him, but he did not reply.

Then as often happened when I was with Miss Alice, a new idea fell into my mind. By now I could recognize these special thoughts by a certain luminous quality—like those thunderheads during a storm piling up over the mountains, outlined in light: *Is Miss Alice really saying that David can't love me—or anyone—until he has given himself and his love away to God?*

Miss Alice rose, smoothed her skirts, and stood looking down at David a moment longer. "Whether or not thee belongs in the church professionally isn't for me to know.

If not, thee will find another avenue of service, equally fine. But David," here her voice grew warm with feeling, "there's just the chance that this wormlike moment of facing thyself, this knowledge and admission of thy own need, is the needle's eye to a new life for thee. It could be the sign that thee does belong."

David glanced up and there was pain in his eyes. I was agonizing for him. "You've both made me look at myself and see things I haven't wanted to see." Slowly, he unbent his long frame and stood up. "I have some tough thinking to do. I'd better get on with it."

I got to my feet too, only to find the room whirling around me. I reached out for the table to steady myself. Dizzy! So dizzy! I swayed. The table was tipping. *The oil lamp is on that table. I must— How can I—?*

As I pitched forward, there was the crash of shattering glass and—as from a great distance—David's voice.

THE BLANKETS WERE heavy, so heavy— They were crushing me. I had to get them off me, had to escape. Why were they keeping me here, pinned down with all this weight? If only someone would come to help me.

My tongue felt dry and swollen, too large for my mouth. Water would taste good. Pick a sprig of the mint first. There it is, growing moist beside the cool, dripping water. Chew the mint. Ah, where is the water? Sweet water! I should get some for myself.

But first I must open my eyes. I was in my room, but it looked different. Bare. Denuded. Some pieces of furniture had been moved out. There were not even any curtains at the windows. A lot of bottles were on the table. There was a smell like creosol.

It was Miss Alice bending over me. I liked the feel of her cool hands on my forehead. I looked up into her face. "Am I sick?"

"I've been waiting for you to wake up to give you a drink. You've a little fever, that's all. You're going to be fine, Christy. You just got too tired."

My eyelids were so weighted that they shut themselves. Dutifully, I opened my mouth when I felt the spoon touch my lips. The cool liquid trickled across my tongue and down my throat. But my throat was sore like my tongue—

something was wrong. I was sick. I must find out what had happened. I could not think.

Day melted into night.... Night into day.... People came and went. Why would they not leave me alone? I wanted solitude so that I could feel the strength of the mountains enfold me. I would lie here for a long time and let the bed support me, and never move for a long time.

So many people. They kept opening my mouth and pouring drinks down my throat. Someone was always fussing with my covers, washing my body. Why did they wash me so much? They should know that it did not matter. Nothing mattered, nothing at all. Peace, just to be left in peace, that was what I wanted.

Dr. MacNeill's face was over me. He must be talking to me, but I was not sure what he was saying. I would ask him to repeat that. No, I could not; it was too hard.

His hands were on my body. He had gentle hands. Now he was pressing my side. That hurt. Why was he poking my stomach?

Light ... darkness. Hours ... days. Time? What was time? Springtime ... autumn. Months ... eons. I could not tell. Nothing mattered. Starlight ... moonrise ... dawning ... melded into one. All the same.

The voices of those men were angry. I recognized one voice. It was Bird's-Eye Taylor shouting at—oh, no! At David!

"Preacher, I'm a-warnin' ye. Keep yer religion inside the church-house, lessun you want to see yer great-great-greats real soon."

I could see him because the wall of my room was glass. He was raising his shotgun to his shoulder. I called frantically to David, but he could not hear me through the glass. I must warn him!

Out through the upstairs hall I sped, down the stairs, almost to the front door now. But my feet were so leaden. Jerk the door open. Across the porch. David had a gun in his hands too. And those awful black ravens were swooping round and round his head. "David, watch *out!* The birds! Duck, David—fight them off."

But he was staring at Bird's-Eye, paying no attention to the ravens. His gun was cocked. *They're going to shoot it out! Maybe if I stand between them ...*

"David, how can you? That's not the way, David. Put the gun down!"

I put my fingers in my ears to shut out the sound of the

494

explosion. A wreath of gunsmoke hung in the air. There was the groan of a wounded man. Which one? I could not bear to look. I had to look. It was Bird's-Eye, staring up at me—but not seeing. He was dead. David had killed Bird's-Eye.

What do we do now? I was in David's arms, sobbing on his shoulder. He was crushing me in his arms. "Why did you do that? David, you shouldn't have done that. You killed a man—"

Miss Alice kept telling me that it was not so, that of course David had not killed anyone. But she did not know; she did not understand. Miss Alice was so good and kind. She could help us. If only I could get her to believe me, that it had really happened.

"Miss Alice, please don't leave. Stay with me. Why do I ache so? Am I on fire? I never felt so hot before. Miss Alice, what will you do with my dresses . . . ?

Days and nights . . . No difference. That deep, booming voice. That could only be David. He sounded teasing. "I hear you're worried about me. On my honor, Christy, I haven't been shooting it out with anyone. Bird's-Eye's very much alive. He and I are friends. Opal and I have him firmly in tow."

I heard his words, piled-up words. Perhaps later on I would understand what the words meant . . . "Want you to know something else too. I'm not going to quit. I've gotten a letter from my seminary—they've asked me to come for a talk. May be a new opportunity. I sure was tempted to go. Then I remembered Jonah. I just can't run like Jonah. Now I know—I have to stand my ground and find myself right here. Not sure what I'm supposed to do in the future, but I *will* know. Christy! Understand me, Christy? You do understand what I'm saying, don't you?"

His voice had that old jocular ring. That was good, that David was himself again. He sounded happy. I was glad that David was happy. The deep voice retreated.

But there was something strange about it all. I was letting something go. What was it that I was letting go? Perhaps I had not understood all of it. Whatever it was, it was all right. David was happy. Wearily, I turned over.

Miss Alice was back. I wanted to talk to her. It was always fun to talk with Miss Alice . . . "Remember that mountain that Fairlight and I climbed? The high one? I want to lie there in the fairy meadow. I want to lie on the very summit. I want to be a perch for the red-tailed hawk, his wide wings soaring on an updraft across the valley, sailing into the vault of the sky. I'd like to be free to soar like the hawk ..."

Bend with the wind. Don't let the wind suck your breath away. The gusts were stronger and wilder. They were going to blow Mr. Pentland and me right off that cliff. I tried to feel my face with my mittened hands, but there was no feeling in my fingers. My eyelashes were rimed with powdery snow. Mr. Pentland seemed to know where he was going. He was a nice man, a friendly man. I was safe with him ...

Sights and sounds ... I could hear the sound of an axe ringing out in the crystal air; the tattoo of hoofbeats on the frozen road. Footsteps running. Why it was Little Burl! "Teacher, Teacher, I come to swap howdys with you."

I took him in my arms and hugged him. "You're cold, Little Burl." I was dancing up and down the hillside to warm him up. We were both laughing hilariously as we danced.

"Teacher, tell me the story of the Little Yellow Dragon. Never did hear the finish of hit."

Silly little boy! Dear little boy! I plopped him on the ground and stooped to his level and gently pushed that shock of red hair out of his eyes. I touched his freckly pug nose with my fingertip. "I have a secret, Little Burl! Can you guess? ... I love you!"

Forty-six

MY BODY FELT LIGHT, almost weightless, as when I
was a child and could run and skip and jump with abandon, skimming over the earth, covering great distances
through meadows and fields unaware of time or of anything except glorious freedom. There was joy in me,
flowing through me, dancing in me, aching for expression,
demanding release. Why—the thought came fleetingly—
had I been so serious so much of the time? What had so
many people been so bothered about? But then the joy
rushed in to overflow the question.

Light was drawing me irresistibly, dazzling light, reful-
gent light of a quality I had had but hints of before. The
light was up ahead, still in the distance. But even here it
bathed the glen through which I was running in shimmer-
ing splendor. The grass was dotted with flowers—I spotted
buttercups and the orchid of fairy fringe and the vermilion
of fire pinks, and mountain bluets like patches of sky
fallen into the grass—all of such intense coloration that
they were not like flowers at all: they were explosions of
color. I did not understand and longed to pause to exam-
ine the flowers more closely. But I could not stop for that
now. The light . . . I must get to the light!

Then I came to some sort of barrier. Not a wall
because I could see through it. Not glass because when I
put out my hand I felt—nothing. But I was stopped there
nonetheless. Some sort of decision seemed to be required
of me. I could go on—or I could stay on this side of the
barrier: the alternative was mine. I had been stopped in
my joyous dash to make certain that I would pause to
consider my choice.

Over there was the light . . . green wood, green wood,
flower-starred grass. The air was crystal. It was as if some
sun of suns was glinting off numberless prisms, shattering

497

the light rays, deflecting them, reflecting them so dazzlingly that I had to put my hand up to shield my eyes. Once before I had seen something like this. Oh yes, now I remembered: that ice world reflecting back the colors of the setting sun at which I had gazed from the train windows. Only this sun was not sinking like that other one, it was at its zenith.

Bathed in its luster, the leaves on the trees, the blossoms on the boughs, the blades of grass did not seem to be lighted from the outside. Rather the light appeared to come from the inside of each object, from its heart, from its very nature, so that each leaf, each petal stood apart from all others, living dynamic forces somehow poised in motion, energy in balance.

Something had been stripped from my eyes. I was *seeing* in a manner I had never seen before. Unbelievingly, my eyes fastened on the colors, the vivid pulsating colors, the riotous intensified colors, drinking them in, feasting on them. All of my life I had cherished color and light, but never had there been such colors or such light, never in all the world. *In all the world . . .* I remembered something I had known long ago: *For now we see through a glass, darkly; but then face to face . . .*

Now into the scene trouped a group of children and they were playing with the same abandon that I had felt as I was skimming over the fields and the glens to get here. They were beautiful children, but not with the ethereal beauty of fairies or angels because there were chubby little bodies and skinny ones, pigtails and dimples, freckles and snaggleteeth. One rangy-legged boy was whistling. A fat-cheeked little girl, blonde and dimpled, laughter burbling from her, poked the whistler and then dodged and ran. An older girl with nut brown skin was carrying a baby. One tiny boy stood on tiptoe trying to catch sunbeams in his fists. "Jeter cotch it, Jeter cotch it," he exulted over and over.

I did not recognize any of the children—and yet I did. "Jeter." Where had I heard that name? The scene floated back . . . The Spencer's front porch, Fairlight's voice, "Jeb and I . . . lost a newborned gal-baby. Front name was Ceclie. Then Jeter. He was three when he was took bad with the croup and left us."

Just children. Still there was something different . . . I could feel the love that surrounded them, and out of the love flowed harmony. No discordant note. No dissonance.

So the joy of the dimples and the pigtails galloped and cavorted. They were like spirited colts out for a frolic.

And there among the children, right there, was the happiness that all men seek and so few find. *The joy of the children . . . I want the joy of those children.* Yes, I will go on. Yes, I want to go. I must . . .

At that instant I saw her walking along the bank of the stream that flowed under the trees and through the meadow. It could not be! But it was. Fairlight! It was Fairlight. . . . She was barefoot, wearing a gingham dress I knew well—a blue plaid one with a wide white collar—only the gingham had a new texture and the white was as glistening as new-fallen snow. On her arm she was carrying one of those homemade honeysuckle baskets, swinging along with that erect carriage of hers, with the easy grace of a highland princess. Why, she looked *happy*. Every worry line was gone; no hint of any shadow across her face now. The texture of her skin, like the gingham cloth, was different too—smooth as silk, glowing with vitality. I could not take my eyes off the beauty of her features—so serene, so confident.

She had not seen me. I wanted her to see me. Fairlight . . . Beloved Fairlight! I started to call out to her—but something held me back.

Now she was running lightly toward the children in the meadow, toward the brown-skinned girl. The baby held out her arms to Fairlight. She took the baby and cuddled her. And then with the baby still in her arms, she sought out Jeter and took him by the hand. The three of them went back to the stream where she put the baby down on the thick carpet of moss.

She was kneeling now, planting on the bank of the stream—of all things—lady's-slippers, gorgeous snow-white ones with lips of brilliant pinkish-purple. As she worked, she was singing softly "The Green Bed"—that haunting ballad of rare loveliness that I had so often heard in the Spencer cabin:

> O come you home, dear Johnny,
> O come you home from sea?
> Last night my daughter Polly
> Was dreaming of thee . . .

Her hands, those red and work-worn hands, were beautiful now. Soft and white they were. As she burrowed in the dirt and tenderly mounded the earth around each plant, tamping it in firmly, the light danced on her moving fingertips, splintering into diamonds reflected in the water, tossed back into the air, caught in her hair.

"Fairlight! Oh, Fairlight—I'm almost there. I'm coming. We'll plant them together. We'll . . ."

From a great distance someone was calling my name. The voice was familiar. Whose? . . . I did not want to hear it. The voice was weight pulling me backward, drawing me away from the light. I would ignore it. I had to go on. The decision was made.

But over and over the voice called my name. No matter how I tried to stop my ears, I could not ignore it. Why? Why could I not go on? There was something in the voice that pulled me back. Now I recognized it—in the voice there was love too, like the love I had seen among the playing children. There was pulling power in that love. But the weight, the awful weight. I did not want that earth-bound weight along with it.

Fairlight still had not seen me. She had finished the planting. The lady's-slippers stood up straight with heads erect, as if they had always grown happily in that spot. And then Fairlight and Jeter waded into the stream, splashing, skipping from rock to rock—as she and I had so often rollicked together. The more the baby splashed, the more the baby lying on her mossy bed kicked her feet and moved her tiny hands and gurgled. I stared longingly, wanting to be there beside them.

Then I knew. *Suddenly I knew* and bowed my head with the knowledge. I *had* to go back. Someone (who was it?) who loved me, still needed me. The light was not for me yet. Not yet. But sometime. Oh, *sometime!* Fairlight, you will wait for me, won't you? *Won't* you? Fairlight. The weight, the weight. The fading light . . .

I WAS HEAVY, so heavy. My eyelids were leaden. They would not open. The familiar voice, a man's voice, very soft. He was talking to me, calling me. "Christy, Christy, you've got to come back to me. Christy, wherever you are, listen to me . . . Christy, I love you, love you, *love you.* Christy, can you hear me? Down in your spirit, at the depth of you, do you hear what I'm saying to you? *I love you!* You cannot leave me without knowing this. Christy—"

And then the tone of the words changed. "God, I have fought against You because I have not understood. Not only fought, God, but cursed You. I did not understand why You let Margaret die—and our son. I did not understand anything about You. I still don't understand anything—except that somehow I know *You are love*. And that in my heart has been born so great a love for Christy as I did not know could exist on this earth. You, God, must be responsible. You must have put it there. So what do I do with it now?" The voice broke. The bedclothes muffled a man's sobs. I wanted to comfort the man in some way. I tried to lift my hand, but it was too heavy. Still my eyelids would not open.

The voice was hoarse with emotion. "Lord God Almighty, Lord God of heaven and of earth, I have been stiff-necked and proud, arrogant and stupid. I am not worthy of—of anything, least of all to ask any favors of You." The voice paused. The room was very quiet. I could hear the sharp intake of the man's breath. "Lord God, You are the Creator, I am the created. I am helpless, as helpless as all other men. As a doctor, I thought I knew something. Now there is nothing more that I can do for Christy. Nothing at all.

"So I offer back to you this love you gave. It's all I have to give You, God. Here are our lives—hers and mine—I hold them out to you. Do—with us—as You please." The voice fell silent.

So his was the voice that had called me back. Dr. MacNeill's. He needed me. He *loved* me. He loved me like *that*.

There was a warm glow in the room. Warmth came into me, starting at the top of my head and flowing steadily downward, into my brain, into my face—my eyelids fluttered open. Familiar objects in the room came into focus. He was still there beside my bed, his head sunk on the covers, one hand stretched out with the bowl of that old pipe of his clutched in it, but the stem of the pipe was broken. It had fallen from his hand and lay on the rumpled covers of the bed.

And still the strength and the warmth flowed—into my chest, along my arms. I could move my fingers now.

I felt across the counterpane until my hand reached his, the big hand with the blond-red hairs on top. My fingers closed over his hand and gripped it. His head came up.

"Christy!"

The joy of the children was in his voice.